Dan Williams

The Dreaming Crystal

Order of the Stone
Book 1

Dan Williams

The Dreaming Crystal

Order of the Stone
Book 1

Amazon ASIN: B0BHZQM8D3
ISBN-13: 978-1-910276-05-1

Any reference to historical events, real people, or real places are used fictitiously. Names, characters and places are products of the author's imagination.

Cover image by Haffeera Cader.

Book design by Dan Williams.

www.danwilliamsbooks.com

To all Fantasy and Sci-Fi authors and readers everywhere

Contents

A note on languages and Glossary

Though this story is narrated by the characters in English, the languages spoken on the Aotearoa Archipelago (sometimes shortened to Ao or the Ao Archipelago) of this story are somewhat departed from the English which is now only spoken as a first language by the very oldest people on the islands. Language and dialects vary depending on education and socio-economic strata. The picture is roughly as follows:

English much as it was spoken in the twenty-twenties is typically the only language spoken by the most elderly characters of any socio-economic strata.

A fluid mash-up of Mandarin, Māori and English is taught to and spoken by the younger wealthy and most educated. They can normally switch between and co-mingle the three fluently.

An evolved form of Mandarin blended with Māori and a smattering of English is spoken by the majority of people who also happen to be the less wealthy and educated.

The wealthier a character, the more educated they are likely to be. The more educated a character, the more likely they are to understand all the languages used on the islands, right back to the English of the elderly.

In the narration, I have borrowed words from Māori and Mandarin to give a feel for characters' individual and peer-group vernaculars. While these words are shamelessly pilfered from their respective languages, their meanings are not necessarily exactly as they would be in their original languages. But in the late twenty-nineties, nor could we expect them to be!

While the words used are self-explanatory or do not take away from the narrative if not fully understood, for the curious reader, here are their intended definitions.

dùzi – stomach, tummy, has an air of childishness 'I have a sore tummy' as opposed to more adult 'abdomen, abdominal disorder or abdominal pain'

fēng kuáng / fēng kuáng-de (adjective) – mad, crazy, senseless

háizi – babies, children (under thirteen but sometimes slang to denote 'immature' e.g. high-school háizi)

jǐngchá – police officer, usually low ranking but also used as a derogatory term by people who dislike the police force and the authority it represents

Kia Ora – hi, hello

lǐwù – gift, present

makutu / makutu'd – touched (negative connotations pertaining to someone's mind), ensorcelled, cursed, made crazy, (of an occurrence, person, object or situation): weird.

nǎozǐ – mind, brain (in the sense of mind)

nǐ hǎo – hi, hello, you good?

tóu – head

xiǎo – little, small, tiny

Cast

First Generations <10000 BCE

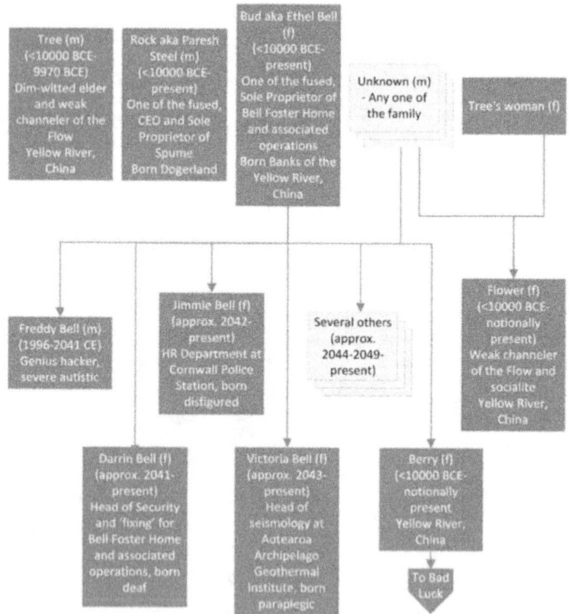

<u>9980 BCE- 4500 BCE</u>

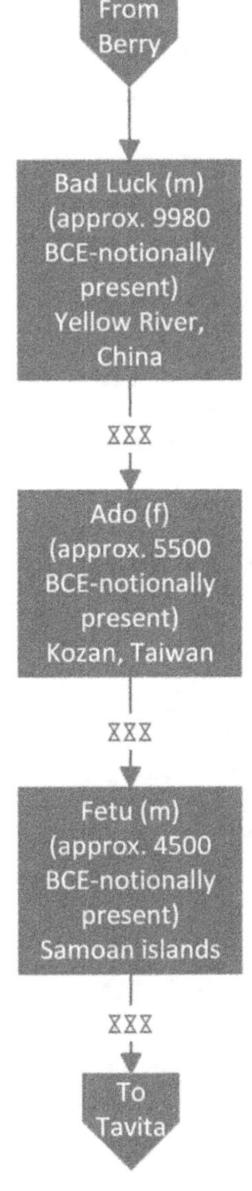

Laufala Line 1900-2045

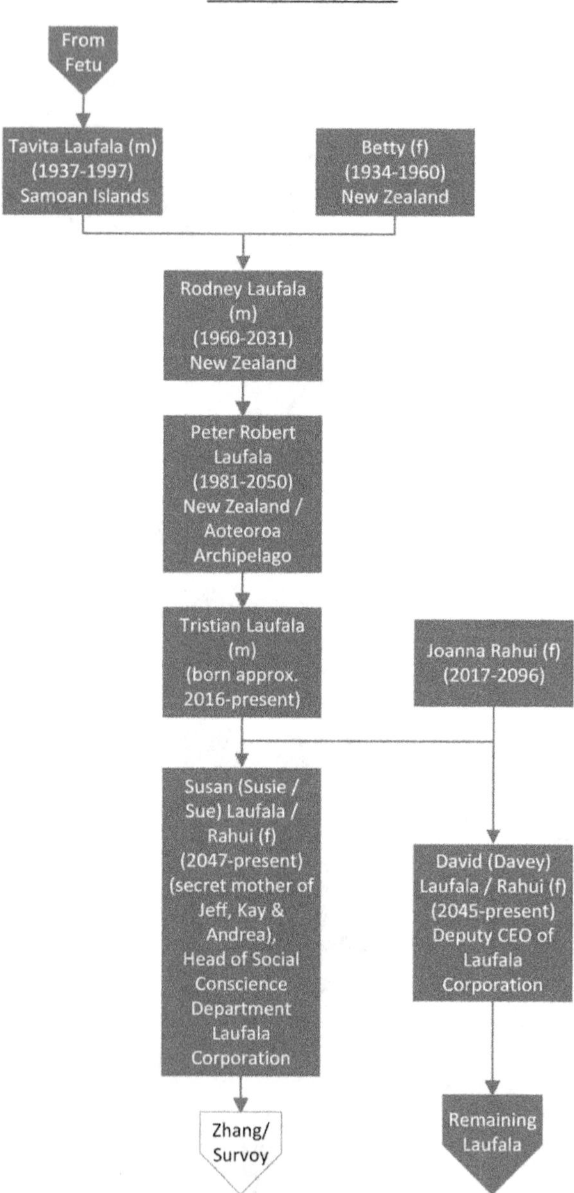

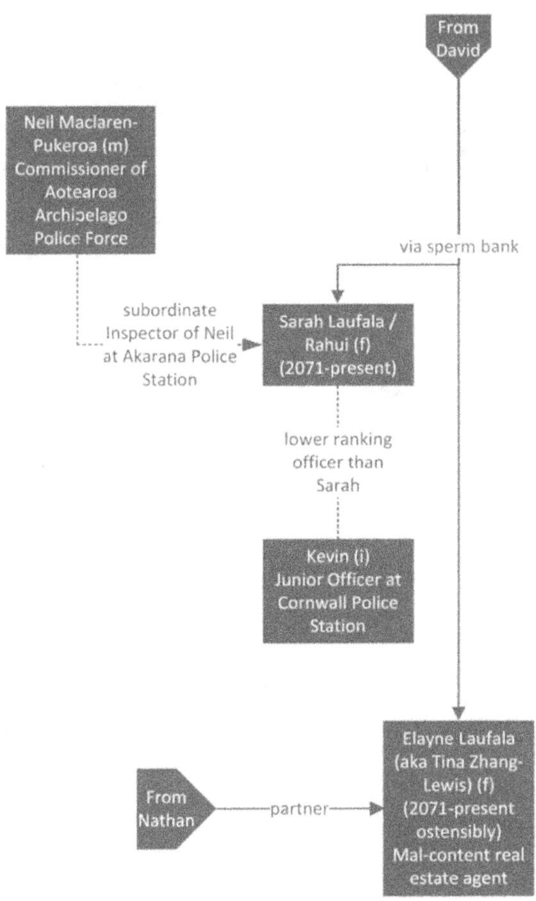

From David
Neil Maclaren-Pukeroa (m) Commissioner of Aotearoa Archipelago Police Force
via sperm bank
subordinate Inspector of Neil at Akarana Police Station
Sarah Laufala / Rahui (f) (2071-present)
lower ranking officer than Sarah
Kevin (i) Junior Officer at Cornwall Police Station
From Nathan
partner
Elayne Laufala (aka Tina Zhang-Lewis) (f) (2071-present ostensibly) Mal-content real estate agent

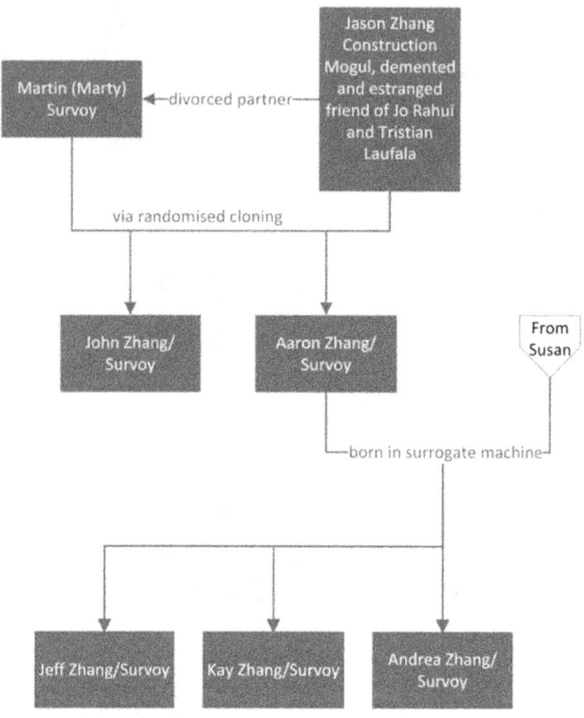

Jason Zhang Construction Mogul, demented and estranged friend of Jo Rahui and Tristian Laufala
Martin (Marty) Survoy
divorced partner
via randomised cloning
John Zhang/ Survoy
Aaron Zhang/ Survoy
From Susan
born in surrogate machine
Jeff Zhang/Survoy
Kay Zhang/Survoy
Andrea Zhang/ Survoy

Nathan's Line

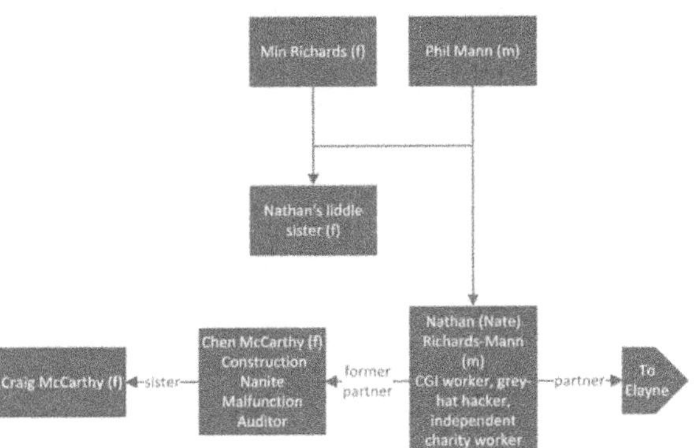

Min Richards (f)
Phil Mann (m)
Nathan's liddle sister (f)
Chen McCarthy (f) Construction Nanite Malfunction Auditor
Craig McCarthy (f)
Nathan (Nate) Richards-Mann (m) CGI worker, grey-hat hacker, independent charity worker
To Elayne
sister
former partner
partner

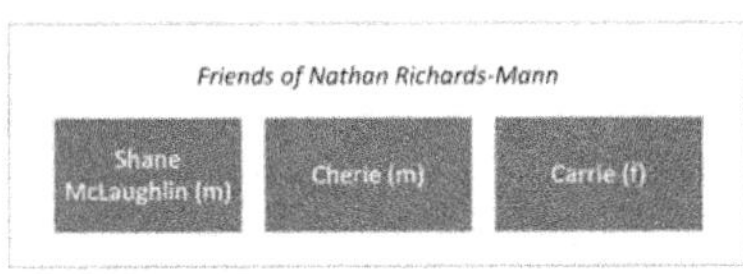

Friends of Nathan Richards-Mann
Shane McLaughlin (m)
Cherie (m)
Carrie (f)

Berry – 10000 BCE, Banks of the Yellow River, North China

It was rain time, not that there wasn't always rain. But now there was rain! The trampled earth between our caves bled red and pus-yellow. Chickens took to the lower boughs for shelter. Pigs rolled in mud till they seemed blood-soaked and the forest exploded urgent green.

The nights chittered and groaned and the days bore down, the sun burning orange through a hot damp blue-white haze. Insects bit and crawled and we itched and bitched and ate. The river swelled as if angered by thunder grumbling from the sky. We watched the water at this time of year. But I'd never seen it come too far up its red-yellow banks in all my winters, for all the elders' tales of angry floods in generations past. Dead maggots and wound-rot, the lot of them.

Sometimes I sneaked amongst the skulls atop the graves in their quiet patch past the main cave, 'neath the rocks hanging from the cliff where it met the riverbank. There I'd listen to the rushing brown torrent and watch it turn rose-gold through the trees at sunset. After dark, I'd look up at the smudge of a moon in the clouds and listen to frogs singing from the riverbank and the trees. They could think I was disturbing the spirits of the ancestors all they liked. I knew I wasn't because there weren't any.

When the smell of charring pig and hot grain wafted over, I'd creep back amongst the living, who I liked less, in time to eat and be plagued by clouds of moths and mosquitos at our fires. A few Shades pestered people in the smoke. I had long since given up warning the family against the slap of breeze when there was no breeze or the bigger than ordinary pinch of a bug nobody would ever find to squash. They never believed me and it didn't matter anyway. Most of the time, the Shades would fade away before we slept and the most stubborn rarely lingered till dawn.

The runt-sow, Flower, Old Tree's longest-time woman's dim-and-only daughter that lived, had been a burr in my sweaty bum-crack forever. She was thin like an insect, so thin she would have choked a baby on its way out. Not like me: tall, strong, wide-hipped and more ready than that uptight little hen-finch would ever be no matter my clumsiness.

She could channel the Flow, so what? So could I and far more strongly than her. She had her basket of tricks with it, all copied by slow dull-eyed rote. But I already knew as much as Mother from my own experiments; more for that matter, not that I could tell anyone given how I came by the knowledge.

I was better looking than Flower, smarter than her, stronger than her and everyone knew and nobody cared. It was all because she was a little butterfly flitting in the sunshine, working chores like a slave, licking clay off feet – and pus off wounds, probably – if it would make her a friend. Me, I was sensibly lazy, said what I meant, meant what I said and didn't mean to say much that wasn't worth saying. Apparently, that made me strange. That and the things I said I could see.

So our best hunter and second-greatest oaf, Boar – who couldn't channel the Flow – sniffed around Flower like one of his namesakes and never pointed his tusk in my direction. The elders and the family in general quietly encouraged their budding longest-time match and I could see the catastrophe happening like a slowly collapsing cave on a sleeping baby.

When Healer, the biggest dumbest lump in the family, died, Boar would take his place with goggling-carp-eyed cricket-hips at his side to learn what she could from my mother Bud until Bud died and passed the Stone down to them. They would never let me use it no matter that I'd be an elder too, by then. Then the river would choke us all with yellow mud if we were ever sick or hurt or dying giving birth. Even though healing is the easiest thing in the world.

There would be nobody left with the knowhow to use the Stone to fight, mine rock, haul or heal since neither of those two possessed half a broken pot of sense between them. One excuse to do what was right for the family was all I wanted. One! Too bad I got it.

The one thing I could do was practice secretly with the Stone when I got the chance. I did not care that I was forbidden. What did it matter that I wasn't yet an elder? That and I could not stop myself.

The few times I'd channelled it had been enough to make me gasp for more. To the handful of other channellers in the family, Flower, Healer, his longest-time Bud and Old Tree, it was a pot to trickle Flow into for later use. A good enough use of it, all right, I'm not saying it wasn't. It sure held more than a person ever could and unlike our souls, it never leaked once you'd filled it up. A lake of Flow sat waiting, a dam ready to be burst and wash away wounds, obstacles and enemies.

But young though I was, I already knew twice what they did. And that was only from the few times I'd lurked in the shadows and done my tinkering. Their dullness set my head on fire sometimes, how they could have the Stone all the time and never see what more could be done with it; what more it was! I could look into it for hours. To my eyes, it was a beauty, violet-black and shiny as ice, its many edges sharp as rock.

Not that I could tell them or they'd know what I'd been up to but I learnt the Flow could be shaped inside it to fit more in. And more odd things besides. If I could have held it, to study it more, I could… Well, I didn't know what I could have done. That was the point.

One day, I got another chance to fiddle and that fiddling would be the beginning of the end for me, not that I knew it

at the time. It was a hazy drowse of an afternoon and most of
the family had fled into the caves to sleep away the heat.

The Stone was amongst us again after a few risky days
away, I could tell, another thing nobody believed me about.
Maybe that's why I found myself lurking in the shade at the
mouth of our gathering cave in the afternoon heat; following
the smell of the Stone in my soul's nose like a bee to the smell
of nectar. I slopped my feet in a red puddle and idly hooked
my foot under a worm so I could feel its cool body slither over
my skin.

If the Stone was here then big old Healer must have come
back in from his own not-so-secret cave, a short way upriver
where he went sometimes with Mother to do who knew what.
Sure enough his croaking drone rolled into my daydreams.

Mother, who was the mind for both of them, was in there
too, shut away with some other elders, planning some walk
into the hills to get building-rocks or something. So that would
be another few days we were without the Stone. I was more
minded to follow the others to sleep, than lurk and listen to
their drivel, but the Stone was calling to me and I needed every
chance I could get.

I yawned and reached out to the world to gather a wisp of
the Flow to my soul, just enough to sharpen my ears and eyes
– something else nobody believed me about. Tree was as old
as Healer, fat as a full pig's tick and about as fast. He'd not
much to show for his age but the age itself. That and he could
channel a wisp of Flow, though barely as much as Flower.

It was his voice I heard prattling. 'Now, we won't be gone
for so long. Not likely anything will happen but what about
leaving Flower in charge while we're away hmm?'

No! Please no!

I'd be put on the hardest chores the whole time the elders
were away. I'd be out of sight and out of mind of the family
and too busy to show her up if anything went wrong.

'Well, Berry's a sensible girl, maybe she could help? We'll
only be a day or two, it does not really matter does it? She can

channel the Flow,' said Bud, standing up for me; my mother first and an elder second for a change.

'Eh? More's the peril to us she can channel the Flow! Better if she could skin pigs faster than it took them to die of old age and make pots that didn't leak instead of being born with the ancestors' gift. Your daughter is clumsy as a blind pig with a spear through its head and mad as a snake, woman! She'd have them digging up the ancestors to eat if you gave her a voice for a night! Her with all that wound-rot about seeing – what does she call them? – Shades, and the Flow! I swear she's eaten the wrong mushroom when someone wasn't watching her!'

Nobody argued.

Wild pigs can gore the lot of them. You can't eat ash, anyway, idiot!

I sighed and channelled into the Stone, didn't pull from it, didn't fill it, sent only a misty vine of the Flow into the cave-mouth, questing like the ghost of a leech, for the violet-blue facets of our ancient treasure. It always felt like I was stretching my soul out, riding the stream of Flow.

Sneaking so close to them set me on edge but they said it, I was mad thinking anyone else could see Flow like I could. Sure enough, as the tendril of my presence drifted down the cave, they prattled on, apparently oblivious.

What can I try today?

I'd found the Stone, but today it was as if I hung in the air beside it and saw it in a new way. Maybe it was my fear of being caught that made me quest slowly through the air and see what I'd always been too hasty to notice before. Or maybe it was some flea-sized change in the way I channelled. Or who knew what?

That's how it always went when I stumbled on a new learning. I could never say how I'd come by it. Anyway, here I was, the Stone filling my soul's eye, glittering dark violet in the dim light from the cave entrance, as if I was a heron gliding above a moonlit lake.

What if I dived in?

I couldn't have had that new thought if it wasn't for the other accidental one that got me here. But so it always went, and so I tried it, going in, not sending in or drawing out.

I couldn't say how I did it. I never could other than I bent the Flow to my purpose in a new way I'd dreamt up. My soul rode the power down, diving through the crystalline surface, into its violet depths. And now I was inside the Stone but not only inside it, somehow, I was it! And then, seeing further beyond the horizon of my old knowhow, from atop the shoulders of the first two, I spied yet another new idea. Burning with my lust to learn, I could never have foreseen the woe it would later rain down like fiery rock from the sky, the winters of slow creeping ruin it would bring me.

Inside the Stone, I reached out to the world and channelled the Flow and oh how it came! I gathered and gathered and gathered Flow to me, cramming it into the empty spaces that I only now saw between the strands of earthly substance that made up the Stone. Once there, the power lay locked in the glittering lattice of the Stone, of me.

Until a soul touches the Stone and calls it forth!

Except I was a soul inside the Stone so maybe I could… But I couldn't. I could gather such a rush of Flow to me as never before in my flesh but here I could do nothing with it.

I should leave in case they find me outside.

And that was when the trouble started. I tried to pull back, get back to myself the same way I always did only the Stone would not let me go. It gripped me in its violet depths and try as I might, I couldn't breach its surface. My fear rose up and my heart fluttered like a moth in a web though the core of me was away in the Stone, in the cave with the droning elders.

I panicked and struggled if a soul can struggle. But the pretty violet crystal face that lured me was now unyielding as rock from within. The voices of the elders came to me, then. Or had I been hearing them all the time and not paying attention? I couldn't say. All I knew was that I sure as rotting fish, was paying attention now! For they were setting up to leave the cave and take the Stone with them.

With no skin to feel the hands lifting me or eyes to see the world tilt, I somehow knew that they had picked me up to take me out and I had to get away. It was my body that did it, in the end. I gave a strangled growl of anger and ran and suddenly I was free of the Stone, bolting through the trees for the place of the dead.

Voices neared the cavemouth behind me but I was already hidden. Though the steaming heat had almost fought it away before I came properly back to myself, I did not miss the ghost of a sinister chill like you'd never get that time of year, leaving my body as I ran.

The trees were dropping their load after the latest shower and frogs were making a din. It was some time before the elders finally appeared in the cavemouth so I was sure they had not heard me, clumsy as I'd been in my fluster. I watched them from the forest as they walked up towards the smell of cooking meat, with the Stone tucked away in Healer's leathery old fist.

Will they see how strangely full it is?

I doubted it. Dumb crawling old grubs.

Spatters of red mud flecked me from head to foot as if I'd been in the way of a pig's throat at slaughter. Bugs whirred around my face as I stood hidden in the trees. It was a long while before my shivers subsided. I was unsure how I'd pulled free of the Stone and that made me scared of what other dark snares it could be hiding. But compared to the idea now turning in my mind like a star hanging low in the sky, the fear was nothing.

So much Flow, it would never need filling again!

For all its brightness in my mind, the idea was only on the edge of my knowing, something I knew I understood but could not put into words. Like the way I sent my soul out with the Flow, hung in the air and moved. A sort of knowing in my body and soul that couldn't come clear in my thoughts. And I was out of time for any more of those too, because about then the crashing and screaming started. For the time being, I forgot the Stone and my idea and everything and I ran for my family.

Healer and Mother always came around to us from Healer's little rathole, churning up water with Flow as they glided over its surface, avoiding the rocks that stuck out over the river, always promising to fall in and never allowed by the tangle of roots binding them. Feet dry as cicada-shells, they would drift to ground in the trees on the riverbank and skirt the place of the dead to come to the gathering cave where someone would soon find them and call the family. Everyone would come to get hurts and hearts healed or most often, complain like children about some tick-picking thing or another.

The ground rose up steep, from the gathering cave to the other caves which pocked the feet of the tree-covered cliff face. There the river was less tempted to gulp at us. The cliff veered away from the water so the forest spread wider and wider over the rising ground. We cooked outside when it was dry but at this time of year we cooked inside and ate outside if it wasn't raining. Today there were a few hopefuls trying with their fires, more was the pity for them.

The afternoon sun had cleared the clifftop and burned down on me as I ran up towards the commotion. Were we being raided? I thought so at first but as I got nearer the shouting, I knew it was worse than that. A monster was amongst us. The family were in chaos when I arrived. The elders had beaten me there, that I'd made sure of, running behind and to the side of them through the trees so they wouldn't suspect I'd come from the same place.

Roaring and grunting in and out of caves and trampling pots to shards was a black mountain of anger and tusk; an ancient demon of a boar come in from the forest. Everyone was both trying to drive it away and stay out of its path.

They threw stones and broken pots and the watchers came in from the forest and tried to get it with their spears. It all angered the beast more and I could see at least one person crawling across the ground, the scent of their blood mixing with the thickening smoke of scattered embers and smouldering wet loam.

The other elders had scattered and Healer was holding the Stone. I knew it wouldn't be long before they put an end to the creature. I waited excitedly to see them work. Would they set it alight? Use Flow to grind its bones mid-rage?

If it was me, I'd stop its heart, quick and clean. I was thinking of trying it, more than thinking! I'd already reached with my soul to the Stone and as the Flow came into me, I saw that although Healer and Bud had drawn Flow into their souls, they were not yet channelling.

What were they doing dithering so? As I watched I saw Boar himself knocked aside as he tried to prick the beast with a spear. He staggered and went down and the thing would have been on him if a rock hadn't flown from the smoke and thwacked it on the side of the head. It turned in fury and charged in the direction the rock had come from, leaving Boar to struggle to his feet and stagger after it, picking up his spear as he went.

I looked back at the three elders and was dismayed to see they dithered yet! What was wrong with them? I gathered Flow from the Stone, filled up my soul till my soul's eye could see tendrils of it rising from my skin like steam. But then I was frightened.

They did not know I'd channelled the Stone and if they had looked my way, according to their high and mighty shrivelled up ancient selves, they wouldn't see my soul leaking Flow into the forest around me. Had they gathered their addled thoughts and started doing what they should, well, the Stone was extra full from my tinkering before so they wouldn't notice any Flow missing.

But I remained afraid and as I wavered the animal burst from the smoke and rammed full into Healer, tossing him into a tree trunk like he was a dead twig. It turned mid-charge, terrifying quick for something so big and knocked Bud on her back then fell dead on top of her frail old legs, the sound of long thigh-bones cracking loud across the clearing in my Flow-sharpened ears.

That was me. I'd come unstuck when I saw our elder channellers were all about to be crushed and trampled. I'd flashed my soul across the clearing, reaching into the beast's chest with a claw of Flow and squeezing its life out through its heart between one beat and the next. Another new learning for the day. A wisp of purple-black rose like mist from its body and quickly faded to nothing. Like babies, animals don't have Shades, not really.

I heard my mother's croaky old moans as the beast's dead weight crushed her broken legs. I watched through wisps of smoke as Tree waddled over and retrieved the Stone from a puddle with shivering old hands. Healer lay still amongst the roots where he'd landed but I could tell he was alive, the dark light of his ghost was strengthened with swirling blue Flow, firmly fastened to his rattly old bones.

Tree would fix them up if they did not do it themselves. Healing was easier than moving things. You didn't need to know what to do, not too much anyway. Spirits clung to the walls of their meaty caves, wanted them for shelter as long as they could give it, I supposed. The spirit knew how to look after its house if only given half the chance. It was just that most of them couldn't channel the Flow and so if help came from someone who could, well then, the ghost would use what it was given all too gladly.

I knew. I'd practised on bugs and seen wings and legs uncrumple and grow back. Not that I could tell anyone because even Mother wasn't that good. Questions would be asked about how I'd managed to channel so much Flow.

I didn't go to the elders. I walked off into the smoke shrouding the clearing. Let them try and puzzle out what happened to the beast once they were fixed. I wasn't afraid there was any fire to speak of. Everything was too wet. But the smoke was getting up my nose and making me mad so I got a mind to find out where it was coming from and snuff it out.

I stumbled over things in the white gloom and that's when I found Flower. I thought she was dead at first but the Flow I held in me changed my mind on that score soon enough.

I squatted beside her and turned her over. There was no blood. I felt up her twig of a body, none too gently, making her groan. Her eyelids fluttered open as my prodding fingers found the ruin of her ribcage. 'Oh Flower,' I gloated softly.

'Berry. Help m…' Her lips fought to part against sticky white strings of spit and red trickled from the corner of her mouth.

A mixture of dread and elation thrilled through me and without thinking, I reached back through the smoke and filled myself to overflowing from the Stone, its lake of power now barely a hair's breadth emptier. I shook my head in mock sadness.

'I don't know how, Flower. Nobody's taught me. You were always so much cleverer than me…' I lied.

'You know… I've seen y…'

Had she now? Sneaky little crotch-louse!

Her voice was a bubbling whisper and talking cost her a cough of dark blood. It burst from her mouth and spattered her face, making me flinch back. She was fading now. I could see her ghost, clinging but losing its grip. I needed only to let her go and pretend I was never there. It was blind luck that made me find her anyway. But that's when my thoughts from before came back to curse me.

'There… There might be a way, Flower.' I made my voice timid. 'Can you channel the Flow? I know it hurts, but try! Reach out, the Stone is near, there, back behind me through the smoke. Try Flower! I know we aren't allowed but… it's all I can think to do.'

And she did, the silly carp. I could see her feeble wisp of Flow twined with her soul, reaching, all but costing her, her final breaths, not that she knew. I stretched my own soul out alongside her, so I'd know when she touched the Stone. When she did, I said, 'Now, reach in, Flower. Take Flow from it.' And I snapped my own soul back.

She started to as well. Weakly. If she could have kept it trickling in, her soul would have healed her, as any soul, channeller or not, would have done. It's why we channellers of the

11

Flow lived oh so much longer than other people, see? Every time you channelled, you swatted away a moon or so of age; if you could channel enough anyway. If I'd stopped to think I would have doubted she could draw enough to her, soon enough.

But I did not stop to think. My limbs turned to water and terror and excitement burst in tingling numbness through my body as I channelled every curling wisp of Flow in me, lashing it out like a striking snake to make sure we never found out if she could save herself or not. Before she'd drawn a drop of Flow from the Stone, I'd pinched out her life the same way I had, the boar. Then I stopped channelling as the size of the thing I'd done struck me like a blow.

I goggled at the corpse, struck stupid as its owner for a few heartbeats. Its chest heaved and its back arched as the Shade whistled up from inside and out the nose and mouth with a wet cough of dying breath and a geyser of dark blood. For half a breath she stood over me and she was the spit of her body, down to the colour of her skin. I'd never seen such a thing.

In that heartbeat, I felt the betrayal in her eyes raking my soul, that and its burning rage. I flinched back in spite of my-self. Oh-ho! Yes! She would have haunted me all right, that one! I could already feel the bond between us, reaching, taking shape, trying to twine around my soul. She knew what I'd done, I could see it in her vengeful scowl. The Shade put up its arms as if to reach for me and drag me from my body to share its death.

But my little trick had worked, for all that I would come to wish it hadn't. Her soul was touching the Stone at the mo-ment of her body's death and as it had pulled on me, so it did to her. No sooner had I traded looks with the most fearsome Shade I'd ever seen, did it whistle away through the smoke, shrieking as it was sucked into the Stone with no living body left to save it.

Its bond was half torn from my soul and for an instant I felt real pain. A bonded Shade could not go too far, I had seen around our fires. Not that anyone believed me. It lingers and pesters for an hour or a night and decides to unbind and pass on – disappears like smoke on the wind, but only I knew that there was no in-between. Though I knew not why, I sensed that such a thing was wrong. The dead must always pass on.

And yet Flower's Shade had been torn from me before it was ready, the bond of anger snapped against Earth and Sky. Well, almost, I could feel something. A weight, a pull. And now I trembled like a leaf in the first buffeting coughs of storm-wind, afraid of what I'd done, of the rules I had broken. Shivering with roaring thoughts I stumbled from the twitching body brushing off spatters of blood that weren't there.

Just like fish-eyes not to know she was dead.

I tried to laugh at the thought but I was shaking so hard I could hardly walk. Panicking, I staggered through the smoke, bumping into this person and stumbling over that broken pot, going anywhere as long as it was away. But I was never much given to storms of the soul. My heart slowed before long and I could think again. Nobody had seen me. The smoke had been too thick. At least, that's what I thought desperately, trying to make it so.

When I came fully back to myself, the smoke had at last started to thin. Whatever pile of wet leaves causing it had been found, I thought. But something else was happening. Voices came up in confusion and that was when I noticed the smoke growing brighter as if lit by midday sun. Except the sun was cooling to an ember by then, as it rolled towards the hills across the river.

I turned and saw the light behind me, growing brighter by the heartbeat. I shaded my eyes and walked towards it, emerging from the smoke to fall on my knees and curl up against the blinding blue-white that burned to the back of my skull.

There were shouts and the glow dimmed a little. I raised my head slowly and looked sideways towards the light. Healer and Bud were standing by the dead boar and the light was coming from underneath it.

The Stone! Oh no! What have I done to the Stone?

A figure crouched between them and Tree's voice carried across the clearing to me. 'I can't channel! I can't channel the Flow any more! What's happened to me, Healer? Bud? Help me!'

I reached out to the Stone to see what had happened and wished that I had not. For it was then I learned I would never again see the dark of the cave lit with the misty blue of swirling Flow rising from my skin as I held it in my soul. Nor would I ever again watch the purple-black of the sleeping souls around me and the drifting trails of blues and violets like glowing mist on the air left by those that sleep-walked from their bodies in their dreams. And now I would see no more dying spirits rise like deep violet steam from their corpses, maybe taking the shape of the person for a breath, or breaking apart and fading into Earth and Sky like mist burned away by the sun. For such I had often witnessed after hunting accidents, birthing or…

I killed a cousin. And this is my punishment.

Now the world was only what my flesh could sense: reds, blues and greens and dull browns and the smells of water, earth, fire and flesh. It might as well have all been hues of grey and different kinds of rot to me from then to the end of my days. For I found in that moment that I had lost the only thing precious to me beyond my family to whom I would now be no more than a lazy useless girl, bad with her hands and wrong in the head. When I reached for the Flow, it wouldn't come. Like Tree, I could no more channel than the dead beast at the elders' feet, or the corpse I'd made of Flower moments ago.

I wandered the caves as the family put everything back to rights. Someone pushed the Stone well beneath the dead boar for it was indeed that which shone like the sun had come down to the ground. It glowed through the mountain of stiffening flesh, lighting the cavemouths with its blue-white glare. Anxious talk of spirits and demons come amongst us whispered through the family. Healer and Bud moved amongst us, healing the injured, comforting the grieving and making out they knew what the strange new light from the Stone was about. Every time I saw them at work, my tears bled forth anew.

All told only four had perished. Tree's longest-time woman, Snow, keened beside Flower's body as darkness came, then Bud gently pulled her away so the head could be severed and readied. We gathered at the place of the dead, to see them burned. Healer lifted such a clod of earth and rock from the ground that the burial pit looked like a demon's burrow to their silly spirit-world.

He held it in mid-air as the ashes were cast into yawning black then lowered it into the ground again so it seemed not to have been disturbed at all. The four skulls of the dead, skinned and ready, were placed over their grave and I saw Mother dart him a finch-eyed look.

He could not do that so easily before.

I was too miserable to do much more than notice. Everyone ate after the burials. I tried but my stomach twisted and heaved and complained about anything I swallowed. I sat by the cookfire embers with some cousins I knew least well, in the furthest cave I could find. We sweated in the evening heat and swatted at whining mosquitos and late, as people were beginning to drift down the caves into the cooler rock beneath the cliff, I felt a hand on my shoulder.

'Come with me.' The voice was familiar but I couldn't make it out.

I turned to see a face I half knew in the light of the dying embers but I could not remember her name. I rose and followed anyway, why wouldn't you go if family asked you?

She took me away from the caves to the edge of the trees and through the whirring and chittering night I could hear the rush of the river. She turned me about to face her and asked, 'What happened?'

I tried to keep my face still as a skull over a grave and my body loose like a wilted leaf. 'C-Cousin?' I questioned, my confusion real.

'Eh? What's wrong you girl? I'm your mother.'

'Mother? But you're....'

'I'm what?'

What indeed! The sky was black and low, pregnant with more rain if I read the heavy heat aright. Indeed, was it a drop on my bare shoulder I felt now? Or was it sweat trickling from my brow under her gaze? I couldn't say what it was that made her face beyond my knowing. I would learn the answer the next morning when we all saw the fell youth restored to she and Healer in the night. I myself would later chance upon the shrivelled white flesh they had shed like growing snakes as they slept.

But in that moment, I did not spare it much of a thought for it took all my strength not to wither under her cunning questions. What had I seen? What did I think had happened? When did I realise I could no longer channel the Flow? Did I know Tree also, could no longer channel the Flow?

After a pig of a roasting, she asked me one last time if I was certain I could no longer reach with my soul and draw in the Flow. And one last time, I shook my head and choked out that I could not channel and with that she patted me on the shoulder and left with a pensive click of her tongue. I lingered by the whispering trees as her footsteps padded off towards the caves and when the rain decided to come and the family's cookfires hissed out, I crept to shelter and a fitful sleep.

Many times that night I reached with my soul and stifled more tears when nothing came. I clung to a single dim hope, for when I reached, I could feel something. I could feel the reaching itself and Flow nearby if I could but reach further, like the glow of sunlight behind hills at dawn. Something of my gift remained. But try as I might, it was always beyond my grasp.

The next morning, I ate weakly and little, like a doomed finch caught out by sudden winter. The cousins chirped and chittered about the boar and the Stone. Those who'd known Flower best, cooed and sighed and already the family was picking up speed away from yesterday to carry on their lives, leaving me wounded and stuck in a rocky gully of guilt I would never escape.

Time passed and the oaf Healer and Mother with their terrible youth showing no signs of fading, dug new caves from the cliff. No soul should have been allowed the power they had now and the family felt the wrongness of it. One summer, Healer spun some man-prattle about a gift from the ancestors to stop the anxious whispering. I wished Mother had not rolled her eyes at it. Better for me if she would let it lie.

That same summer, I could no longer bear seeing the family infested with new children and swelling larger than any family had a right to be. So I tried to fix what I had broken. And I failed.

The old gathering cave was deserted by then, save for the fell orange light shining from deep within. Only I seemed to have noticed that the family had begun to avoid it. They made their fires and slept further and further along the cliff, the skulls of the dead spreading slowly after them as if chasing them off.

I had kept my habit of visiting the dead and felt more like one of them with each passing moon. Awake one night to escape the strange blue dreams that had begun to plague me, I found myself once more amongst the skulls in the moonlight. I crept into the cave where the Stone lay glowing evil orange through the tattered layers of its pig-skin wrappings.

I blinded myself with my loincloth, unwrapped the Stone and tried to smash it. But it would not break, not with the heaviest rocks I could lift and all my desperate strength hurling them down. They cracked and shattered like eggshells and left the Stone unharmed, burning bright blue-white through the bindings on my eyes.

To make matters worse, when I handled it, cool to the touch despite its blaze, a coldness flowed up my arm like angry wasps, a fiery chill of swarming stings to my soul. I felt an unseen cord strengthen and pull tight about my being and with that my suspicions were confirmed and warm terror trickled down my thigh. For I knew then for certain that inside the Stone, Flower's Shade shrieked and raged long past the time it should have faded like mist into Earth and Sky.

Though her pull faded when I rewrapped the Stone and fled the cave's fell glow, it did not fade as it had in the days after I had murdered her. I felt it deep in my soul to my dying day, like the distant thunder of a coming storm.

I was done, then. All hope and life went out of me though I lingered amongst the living. The family went on and grew strong and I faded to a flesh-bound Shade on its edges. Like the annoyance of dripping water in a winter cave, Flower's bond pulled weakly at my soul's fleshy tether. It was a pain I could barely feel, yet as the sun rose and set and the summer waned and cold crept to the edges of the firelight at night, it weighed heavier till I was dragging my feet and could barely eat.

Sunsets passed and the mountains' white cloaks unfurled on their distant slopes. Our caves were filled with the aroma of dried meats ready to nourish us through the winter. And the blue dreams rose up with Flower in their midst, shrieking her pain and hatred at me every night till my last night. I woke every morning more tired than I had been when I closed my eyes. I grew weaker as the cold moons passed slowly by.

That last winter of my life, I slept little and ate less. I took what fleeting comfort I could tangled up with some cousin or another, maybe Boar himself, once or twice though the musk and warmth of bodies pressed inside me barely penetrated my grey malaise. By the time the snow melted and the birds began returning to the forest, I was half mad with exhaustion, thin and starved and old before my time, not to mention pregnant as the full moon.

The last of the chill had left the air and the hot rains were due any day when my time came but I had not the stomach for birthing by then. Besides, a fever came on me in the night and I was fey and feeble when the first pains cramped my middle. Mother and some older cousins took me to the forest, to the birthing clearing as my spirit's clutch loosened on my dying flesh and I slipped further and further away.

I can see again, Mother.

I did not know if I said it or thought it but it was true. Squatting and sweating as waves of heaving agony broke over me and cousins' hands held me, I saw the Flow swirling in the purple-black of my mother's soul, bright and living, caught firmly in her flesh.

And too, stretching away through the trees, I saw a brilliant rope of violet Flow and purple-black spirit thick and strong like the bloody cord they forced between my teeth. Weakly, I bit down to sever my child from my body as it lay squalling on the forest floor, slick with the liquid of birth, covered in my shit and in danger of drowning in the growing pool of blood beneath my torn and gaping crotch. Son or daughter, I would never know.

The feeling of it slipping from my body and the sharp pain of my bleeding were distant then, as if they were happening to another woman and not me.

I can see again, Mother. I can channel Flow again! I'm sorry Mother. It was me. I killed her. I trapped her in the Stone and now she haunts my dreams. I am sorry.

Through my pain, I knew I had said it aloud and that she understood for her eyes widened and sadness and anger and love and pain warred on her face.

I am going now Mother.

'No! Berry! No! I can heal you.'

But I did not want healing and besides, as if it had been waiting, the bond pulled tight about my soul, tearing me from my flesh. Following my mother's own strange coil of Flow and soul, I flashed through the trees and back to the family where Healer stood, another glittering coil curling from his body, down into the cave of the Stone. On I flew through the trees and into the cave where the Stone lay in its tattered wrappings, wreathed in a tangle of yet more strange blue cords stretching away to everywhere. Through that tangle I flickered and the deep blue-white blaze rushed up to meet me. And then Flower was before me in a glory of hateful madness and agony.

'At last.' She said, her teeth clenched.

Tristian – Nov 2096, Cornwall Hill, Akarana Island, Aotearoa Archipelago

Jesus did the ads about cancer survivors piss me right off! I hated all the bullshit heart-strings stories about so-and-so's battle against cancer or such-and-such's victory over it. And I detested the way they got used to lure people's money out of their accounts, on to the blockchains and into big charity wallet addresses. Cancer was an illness and you died of it or you bloody didn't. You couldn't frickin' expect to win because you fought harder. You were lucky or you weren't.

Though it was choking up Jo's body right in our own home, literally, as I watched, I would've said the same anyway. I bloody would! But annoying as the charity ads were, okay, okay, I had to admit, I was hard put to it to keep hating on them as much as I used to.

I could see it now, after only eighty-five years – Christ I was slow sometimes – how if you weren't educated, if you lacked the understanding, if you had a million other stresses in your life, if you struggled every day, trying to feed sick and hungry kids, pay your rent, pay your water bill, stay awake in your work virtual, keep your feet dry, etc. Well then, how easy it'd be to believe the cancer killing your mum or you dad was a living breathing evil entity. Or at least its wicked agent.

You wouldn't have time to tell yourself it was mutant DNA, a chain reaction, a clashing coincidence of cell biology. Or that you'd caught it in time or you hadn't or that it was a variety with such-and-such recovery rate and your grandad or your mum or whoever was or wasn't lucky enough to have a strong enough immune system or the right metabolism or the right genes to – oh bloody hell, there were those types of words again – resist the cancer long enough for the cure to work.

Understanding it as well as I did, made it hard for me not to believe it wasn't a malevolent presence. What hope did more ignorant people have?

I remembered when the mRNA cures had appeared in the late twennies. They were hailed as the end of all cancers but instead turned out to be the beginning of new and stranger ones. And then my nanotech had put down roots in everything and creepers in between; artificial antibodies that could actively, adaptively and intelligently, eliminate cancer cells and so many other illnesses besides; not so hot on viruses but we were getting there; we would get there.

Jo's body was awash with the stuff now, more than usual. It swam through her bloodstream, crawled along her nerves, infiltrated her bone marrow, hunting for cancer cells. And that of course was part of the problem.

It found them all right, and eliminated them fine. And combined with a cocktail of mRNA varieties including some new prototypes we'd made, it'd looked like it might work. And then we saw something nobody had seen: DNA from the cancer cells, clinging to the nanites that were killing it off, themselves!

That shouldn't've been a problem though, the cancer cells were destroyed. Except somehow, they kept springing up again and it had taken us long, too long, to find out what it was up to. And when we did, we realised we'd hit the limits of medical science and, to borrow a phrase that annoyed the hell out of me for its triteness, the cancer had beaten us.

The apparently-dead-and-denatured DNA was not as dormant as we'd thought. It got smeared on cells far and wide as the nanites swarmed out of Jo's body, having finished the task they were set. And where the cancerous DNA stuck, it incorporated in a way we couldn't understand and the cancer bloomed again. Yeah, I understood it and I knew it wasn't doing it on purpose. But still, if the tech hadn't been invented, the cancer wouldn't've adapted to use it. Hard to believe there was nothing at play but biochemistry.

We were trying stuff, keeping it at bay. But – and man did I hate myself for resorting to the metaphors! – Jo's eighty-four-year-old body being a battleground was making her lose the – gah! – fight.

We'd probably figure it out. We were figuring it out. But as I looked at her blotched and shrivelled face and stick-thin shoulders poking out of the covers, my faith in science guttered and I knew with chill certainty, she wouldn't live long enough to see the cure.

I tried to bat the thought away with work items, the next visit from our kids - well, 'kids' – and the next batch of tech we were working on for when it… came back. But as had started happening more and more, I couldn't shake the fear blossoming inside me. My face scrunched up around my tears, as if letting them escape would make the truth real.

We'd lose each other one day. Unless we both died at exactly the same instant and never knew the other was gone. But how likely was that? I knew it rationally, I always had. But I didn't like having it shoved in my bloody face. Better not to think about it and… I dunno, get on with stuff, or something.

It was a wet grey afternoon, like they all were nowadays. I was sitting by Jo's bed taking care not to knock her tubes. The rain fell so hard and heavy outside, I couldn't see the security fence only metres away.

Her eyelids fluttered. The latest round of chemo was finishing on schedule. The nanites streamed out of her, flowing away over the edge of the bed like silver smoke with a mind of its own. That much tech in her body for so long strained her immune system and made her sleep more. But she'd wake again soon. She'd be all right again for a while, until the tumours mushroomed inside her anew.

'Tris.'

I jumped. 'You woke up quick that time!'

I didn't want to hope it meant something, that this batch had worked better. I didn't want to. But I couldn't not.

'Tris, how are they doing?'

'Oh, the round finished a second ago, that's why you're—'

'Not them, dummy, I can see all that in the space.' She said. 'I meant the aggregators. Did you and your geek-army release the new spec? Have they reached the main shoals?'

'Well, you can see all that in its space too, dummy.' I tried to sound peeved but my smile betrayed me.

'I know, Tris.' She was smiling now and it took years off her haggard face. Though her skin was sallow and wrinkled and her clean-shaven pate blotchy, it all somehow fell away and made her twenty-seven again. And though I loved her differently and, in such layers, I loved her as much as I had in the first few lust-filled weeks after we'd got together, fifty-seven-odd years before. I swallowed back more tears as discretely as I could.

'…nt to hear it in— Tris, are you with me? Earth calling Tris?'

'Oh, uh, yeah, eh?'

'I said, I know I can check them myself but I want to hear you do your report in your CEO voice.'

I flushed and took her matchstick hand, taking care not to upset the cannula in her wrist.

'Well, okay, let's see.' I said, trying to muster a sense of crisp despatch. 'Four thousand pods were deployed nine days ago. The first ones reached the main shoals in the Pacific and Atlantic yesterday and started propagating the upgrades through the shoals.

'The upgrades are already ninety-eight percent done, enough for micropods to have begun splitting off and heading for the clean zones' perimeters, to start work. So far so good.

'In fact, so far so better than expected. We can already see signs of regeneration in the clean zones and the corridors connecting them. There are plankton, there are species of fish we previously thought extinct. So, all in all, it's working. But we do have an issue.'

I couldn't help warm to the topic and I realised she'd known I would. Though lying on her deathbed, she couldn't stop bloody taking care of me. And as she'd known I wouldn't be able to, once I'd started, I couldn't stop.

'It's not a bad issue, you could say, it's a good problem to have. But in the last few hours alone, given the uptick in aggregation, it's an issue nonetheless. We would have had to address it sooner or later but with the improved efficiency the upgrade has facilitated, it's going to have to be sooner.'

'Oh yes?' Jo said. 'And what are we doing to resolve this issue, Mister Laufala?'

And though we were playing silly buggers and Jo was my partner of nearly six decades and I was the CEO – for goodness sake – of Laufala Industries, the biggest tech company in the world, I felt a flush of… school-boy, wash over me.

'I— It's okay, we're, uh—' I stammered. And we laughed.

But she wouldn't stop playing. 'Oh yes, well, how is it going to be okay, Mister Laufala? How are you going to ensure I'm not wasting my profits on this toy of yours?'

'Well…'

'Well?' She said, channelling hands-on-hips.

'Well, the thing is, some of the aggregates have grown as big as, well, not even, uh, small, cities.'

I pulled her into the virtual despite myself and suddenly we were surrounded by deep blue ocean and tropical sky. The cameras on the shoals and drones generated the virtual such that we hovered slightly above the surface. I'd seen it all a million times before but smelling the sea and the equatorial air sent a thrill through me anyway. It was foreign weather, weather we never saw down here in New—, for god's sake, The, uh, Ao Archipelago.

It was hot and humid though the virtual space could only give us a slight sense of the temperature without frying our tech. The heat shimmered off the horizon and made a haze in the air. So, I guessed we were visiting the Pacific shoal though I only vaguely remembered choosing when I connected to the control virtual.

Below us on the water floated grey spheres of aggregated compressed plastic and assorted pollutants, vast and ugly.

'They're as tough and inert as we can make them,' I said. 'But we've got to work out what to do with them now; what the next steps are. Over time, the water and weather will some-how break them down and erode us back to square one. Or worse since now there's so much gunk in one place, well, or, a few places around the planet. But see what I mean? It's work-ing, Jo. It's really working!'

As we watched, shallow Vs formed in the water by each sphere, revealing the direction the shoals were towing them, towards the perimeter of their clean zone. Silver swirled over the spheres adding layers of toxic scum, treating it to bind it up hard and unreactive against the sea and the sky. If we watched long enough, we'd see it grow though it was hard to tell how fast since the ocean was so vast around it.

Tiny drones criss-crossed the shoal, filming, transmitting data and dropping off charge. The pods flashed silver beneath the surface and there were occasional splashes as some dived down to sample the depths and deploy clouds of collection nanites for stray pollutant errant currents may have carried in since the area was cleaned.

They were like the vast shoals of fish in days gone by yet so obviously machinery that I was simultaneously awed and saddened. I wondered if I'd live to see a real shoal of fish and the chill of fear returned with the knowledge that Jo wouldn't.

I dropped us out of the virtual and saw her eyes were al-ready closed again. I held her hand as her breathing slowed into deep sleep.

I don't want you to die, Jo. I dunno what I'd do if you died. I left the room, then. I didn't want to wake her with my sobbing.

Rock – Nov 2096, New Mumbai, India

Mein colleague had been living on the edges of a coastal city overlooking the shallow ocean over what was once Mumbai. Maybe this new one was Mumbai also, *ja?* I was not so concerned about the name of the place as I was about *mein* naughty colleague making her mischievous probing into our special existence and coming too near understanding for *mein* convenience.

It was a beautiful place I had tracked her to: orderly high-rises and perfectly arranged roads passing between them; not a warehouse to be seen, preventing theft with distance and secrecy. Admirably standardised construction.

Old Jason Zhang's little toys were of course following their usual pattern, for example staying up only where the expenditure was made. It was all neat and shiny where the middle-wealthy resided. But dirty and messy and falling to pieces on the waterfront and inland, where it was needed most by those who could afford to invest the least. *Ja,* these people were inferior in their lack of collaborative thinking, I was certain; not worth saving in the slightest. *Ja,* but fascinating to study.

In *mein* short search for this misbehaving colleague, I discovered India had changed in the last century. Considerably like Africa, where I had recently dealt with the other misbehaving one, it was mostly burned up in the central parts. The coasts and lowlands were flooded and partly submerged. The sight caused me to recollect observations of *mein* own birthplace gradually becoming submerged before it was suddenly inundated. *Ja*, Doggerland, it would get called several millennia later.

Ja but in India now, there had been tremendous population decline! Un-be-liev-able, *ja!* Fascinating to see the evolution of things. Fascinating.

Ja but I did not see so much of it as I would have enjoyed. I followed only the beautiful blue light over the land to the colleague at the end of it; like a special tracking tether that only I could see. Well, perhaps not only me. But there were few others who could also see this way.

One had been sitting conveniently on *mein* shelves for several centuries. Perhaps there were others but it only mattered if they remained sane and if these other meddlers were allowed to continue their mischief.

And so here I was. Stopping the mischief. So simple!

I told the colleague how I found her and shared with her *mein* superior understanding of what she was only now beginning to uncover. Why not? It was fun to see the understanding dawn in her eyes. *Ja*, to watch the moment of the connections in her soft little mind forming. To see her open her mouth to say… whatever the next thing was. But instead of words, ffffft! And she was neatly gone. Mid-realisation, I took her apart quark from quark before she knew I was no friend at all, *ja?* So beautiful! And so funny!

Speed was paramount after that; to catch the soul before it began to fuse the matter around it and regenerate. I could see it perfectly, glowing in the shape of the disappeared body as if it did not realise what had happened.

Whipping the two halves of the prism from the handy blue and white duffel bag, I enveloped the ghost in Flow and compressed it into the tanzanite core of one half. Of course, I had to be fast. While the quantum particles forming the soul had a strong affinity for ordinary tanzanite, the great tanzanite Stone itself to which our souls were somehow fused, buried in its original location far away, had a stronger pull. If I did not seal the obsidian sheath fast enough, the colleague's essence would bleed free and regenerate. *Ja* then all sorts of inconvenient nuisance could follow.

But I was used to the procedure. Snap! Together went the pieces, *mein* brilliantly crafted obsidian perfectly interlocking to prevent Flow or ghost getting out. And fizz! I made heat in the air precisely around the seam to melt closed the sheath around the tanzanite forever. A few seconds of waiting for the obsidian's nature to change and *Jawohl!* One less little problem for me and one more little black pyramid to label and store neatly on *mein* shelf.

Of course I marvelled again at the change in the obsidian, the only part of the process I was yet to understand. For some reason it went from a collection of boring chemicals to something indestructible. But how, *ja?* How?

I speculated only that this must be caused by the connection of its contents to the far-off Stone. *Ja,* some sort of interaction of particles I could not yet observe. *Ja* because the trail of light in *mein* mind's eye was still there, stretching now from the closed prism in *mein* hand across the continent into the distance. Though obsidian insulated the mysterious wavelengths and particles that formed souls and the Flow, something could somehow pass through anyway. But what? *Jawohl!* So beautifully fascinating!

I was doing them a favour, in fact. Oh *ja!* If only they knew how the looking, the mere act of thinking, remembering too much with their stupid fragile minds, risked upsetting the whole house of cards. It threatened our – but most importantly, *mein* – existence as the apex number-ones.

I of course had long since discovered what these meddlers were beginning to scratch at. Now I had sorted two out, there was one remaining; if I had dreamed correctly anyway. Thanks to the inaccurate minds of others, the memories and dreams were not precise but I could always amend plans; time after all, was permanently on *mein* side, *ja?* Beautiful! After that, I could get back home to the wonderful researches.

I smiled at some dirty children playing in the rubble. The colleague had vanished so fast and silently that they had not noticed. But their eyes widened when I rose into the hot hazy air like a ghost with a duffle bag, and floated away without disturbing so much as a grain of dust on the ground.

I made a little wink over *mein* shoulder for the kiddy-winks. Probably now they were spending their whole short lives trying to explain what they had seen. Maybe I would drop a few clues, play a little treasure hunt with them and reveal myself to them after they gave up.

Ethel – Nov 2096, Cornwall Hill, Akarana Island, Aotearoa Archipelago

'What? For pity's sake what, Victoria?'

'Mummy! It's a big one!'

'A big what, Child?' I asked my grown-up daughter, my eyes stinging in the screen's light. I knew full well what and had thrown my legs over the side of the bed before she answered.

'A quake Mummy. Another quake.' Her own voice croaked with broken sleep and I could see the beginnings of age creeping into her features.

What is she? Fifty-something? Golly! I lose track. Still, that's no age! Poor things, they are like daffodils…

'Yes, yes, all right. Good girl. Thank you. Send me all your er, data. I'll look into it straight away.'

I could see her biting back the question she had long since given up pestering me with. And I hoped I would never have to tell her the answer was nothing. I did nothing with the incomprehensible babble of numbers and impenetrable words she filled my machines with. Her call was all I needed and I hoped for all I was worth she never found out why.

I was not lying to her when I said I would look into it straight away. I said my goodbyes to her as tenderly as I could considering the ridiculous hour, then got to work. I sighed as

I heaved on my white wrinkled second skin and it moulded itself to my shape as if it were some twisted scion of the great bower-constrictors that used to hang patiently in the trees of my home till prey walked beneath. The babies and my staff were no doubt all fast asleep but I could not be too careful.

Moments later I was on the moonlit rooftop of the building leaning on the handrail looking out across the island. The wind was gusting but it wasn't cold and I thanked Earth and Sky the night was unusually clear. Far off down at the coast, I could see the sea shimmering silver.

Well I know where to jolly well aim, I suppose.

In the moments that followed, the picture of my breath, swirling and blue from horizon to horizon of my soul, brightly in, dimly out, and the ghosts of my babies drifting on its soft warm currents kept me calm. I remembered with intent, every one of my children from the riverside to present day and all of the joy and grief they had brought me. That was the best I could do to stave off the chaos of spinning memories threatening to pull me down to madness; breathing and distracting myself with memories of red earth, green forests and love as I invited insanity by channelling the Flow.

When I was done, clouds had begun to scud in over the horizon and the pain of my ancient connection through the earth to the Stone tugged stronger at my soul; easing as I breathed but never completely leaving me. Despite the distance I could see the ocean beyond the island's coast frothing white in the moonlight; whether only in the wind of the oncoming storm or because I had cut it fine, I did not bother to speculate. No doubt the white water would set their newsfeeds astir yet again; small things, small minds and all that. I only hoped I could find the cause of the disturbance before it was too late.

Back in my room, I found one of my screens silently calling to me, flickering in the dark with my daughter's face, lips moving, voice muted until I accepted her connection. I had half a mind to ignore her but nowadays it seemed, we could ill-afford the luxury of time to ourselves.

Or sleep.

'Yes Dear,' I sighed, brushing the screen to let her voice out. 'I'm here. What is it?'

'It stopped again, Mummy! Like before! They keep stopping. It doesn't make any sense.'

'I know, Dear. I'm sure you'll get to the bottom of it.'

'I don't know if I will Mummy. We're all completely stumped. It's like there's a new fault forming exactly perpendicular to any existing ones. It's—'

'I know, Dear. Look, it's very early, Darling. Is there anything else? Or could we chat in the morning?'

She sighed. 'No. I— I don't know. I thought you'd like to know, that's all.'

'Oh! I would like to know! I do like to know Lamby. But I'm tired, all right?'

'Yes, Mummy. Sorry. Get back to bed. Oh, and why are you wearing your old-lady thing?'

'Nipped out for something, Dear. Thank you for calling. Good night. I'll see you in the morning, all right.'

'I love you Mummy.'

'I love you too Dear.' I meant that. 'Oh, and Victoria?'

'Yeah?'

'Keep sending me the, uh, data, would you?' I didn't mean that but sadly, I felt it should remain a necessary fiction.

'Okay.'

I peeled off my suit and threw it in the corner. Tiny motes of delicious burning cold prickled along my skin in the darkness as the grazes from the suit attended to themselves. I was asleep before it was done but the quest I had begun in my dreams was utterly frustrated for that sodding night. My thoughts were too agitated, my memories too confused, mixed with the others' memories churned up by my earlier efforts.

Can they not feel this happen every time? Are they not in the slightest bit curious? Is there anyone but me left?

A stupid question, everyone was left; one way or another. But whether they remained sane enough to care, I could not say. Something had changed and I was convinced the seabed's new rumblings were connected to it. But I needed the others to help me understand it; or perhaps to feel that they wanted to help.

That it's not only me! Alone! So alone!

Yet like a wildfire, the problem made winds favourable to its prosperity. Each night I was woken like this, my soul was thrown into such chaos I could not summon the composure to call on their memories without risking my sanity. And that in turn could have brought calamity on humanity as surely as the seas rising up to swallow the land.

I was too tired to try that night and nor could I summon any serenity the next. But I regained my composure the one after, and so as I drifted off to sleep, I filled myself with thoughts of air and unbroken horizons over open ocean and finally, I got lucky.

Perhaps it had been my thoughts of the Shades I had seen some five decades before that stirred another's memories. Who knew? Not me. But as my sleep deepened, my mind sank into dreams and deeper into those of the others.

I dreamed of caves, huts and houses and the feeling of a question and the quest for its answer beginning; a long time ago. But what answer? Ah, yes, I had not been the only one to wonder at the disappearance of the Shades.

But now it appeared someone else had seen things I had not. For now, I felt the other's disappointment on encountering the whistle of the wind through odd-shaped rocks, creaking doors, coincidental draughts, groaning pipes, loose guttering, insistent but plainly crazed residents and, ah yes, finally and undeniably an angry Shade, stronger than it had any right to be.

A sense of time, years, centuries more searching in vain, then suddenly another Shade, and another and then more. Experiments, gemstones, rocks, mirrors, lack of progress, frustration, failure and at last the glimmerings of an idea. The drawing of perimeters, haunts, the word came unbidden or at least the sense of it. The images spanned centuries of language but I was used enough to the eerie understanding-without-knowing that came from remembering ideas grown in a foreign mind.

On spun the dream and I came to see what… she… had discovered, or inklings of it anyway. Shades and their haunts… Their pain… *Shades can feel pain?* Yes, so it seemed but only if they… *left? Left what?* The dream was fading. Ah, but then a little more came… *touch the Earth? Change it?*

I glimpsed the understanding but it was prey to the nature of dreaming and it spun away out of my awareness as something else presented itself… *scepticism? Not hers but people's, certain people's, people of certain types?* But it was all too unclear.

Much slipped away into the gloom of half-remembrance. The dream thinned into the mundane ramblings of my own mind before finally evaporating in the morning light. No matter. Now I was thinking on it, it would have been stirred up for her also, wherever she was on our ruined planet, whoever she was.

If she was worth her salt, as so few of us were now given the toll of centuries on our minds, she would recognise the sensation and perhaps try to make contact, perhaps, perhaps, perhaps. And now I had gotten a hold of her memories, if the straining stuff of the earth left me in peace for long enough, I might risk thinking on them again while awake.

Yes, it had been a fruitful night to be sure. At last, I had stumbled on something useful. I breathed easy for the first time in years as I rose and pulled on my second skin to make my rounds of the building.

I looked in on John first. It was not often I employed anyone outside the family to care for my foster children. I'd had a few children after my poor Freddy was killed but they had not helped assuage my grief so I'd given up for a while. And now that latest batch were jolly well wearing out; though they themselves had produced good enough broods to keep the boat afloat.

In any case, my son Darrin had insisted John's demeanour was saintly and his need to volunteer for us, sincere. So I allowed it and now I would go and meet him for myself and we would see.

And we did see and we were disappointed and so we had to jolly well start the ball rolling to get rid of the sod the hard way in case it was possible. Otherwise too bad for him, we'd have to do it the quick way. And I resolved firmly to give Darrin the great ninny a thick ear when I next caught up with him. What the hell was he thinking? The John character had letch written all over him for pity's sake!

After that, I was flustered and did not have the presence of mind to think on the Shades and risk the memories after all. As I fell asleep that night, I wondered if it was nothing, and maybe I was overprotective of my foster babies. But in any case, unless my children managed to root out some robust proof of John's good character or the lack of it I expected would more likely surface, it was a day and a night wasted.

I was calm enough before the end of the following day and hoped I might find more in my dreams that night but nothing came. In the morning I lay in bed and realised I had time on my hands and so risked remembering while awake and that was when I found the memories gone. All that remained was my own memory of the dreams; a memory of remembering.

Dismayed, I did my best to clear my mind anyway and thought of the Shades, of that other's research I had dreamed of, reached down, down and down through my own memories to the perilous flowing whispers beneath. But as I feared would happen, my efforts were in vain for all that remained when I focused on the dream was the muted whisper of memories we all knew marked the wasted in their ancient prisms.

And so though whoever she was remained extant, she was as good as gone forever and her knowledge lost. Which in this day and age should have been impossible.

Nathan – Nov 2096, Cornwall Hill, Akarana Island, Aotearoa Archipelago

Sometimes I was probably a bit stubborn for my own good. Before the library turned pay-as-you-go and, let's face it, heh, after it turned pay-as-you-go too, not that the fuzz ever copped – geddit? – on to that one, I read that you should exercise.

Yeah-nah, I knew you could take the ol' pills and end up jacked, shredded, skinny or whatever. But I swear those things gave me headaches an' bad moods even though, apparently, they'd been tested not to have any side-effects. But the corporates who sold them would say that wouldn't they.

Nah, fuck it. I stuck with my exercises: walked every day, weights in the health-hazard-shitbox block gym every other day and sometimes a few kays on the antique treadmill which I'd figured out how to get working again. Since when did we come from monkeys in trees and stuff, to taking pills? Bullshit. Whatever a bull was.

That's why I was out in the rain when maybe I should o… have…. whatever, would've been safer inside. It was a *stonker* of a storm! A bloody baaa-yeauty! I couldn't see a metre in front of me through the rain. It was shiiiiitting down an' the wind was blowing it into me from bloody everywhere at the same time. It was blowing me sideways, and definitely not in the good way. I couldn't hear jack all through the noise.

But that's what peeps didn't get any more, see. Shit weather or not, it was freaky-cool looking up through the high-rises either side of the road, 'cause you couldn't see the tops through the rain; like all the rich ponces up in their penthouses were hiding overwater instead of underwater. There'd be a delivery drone now and again appearing and flying off into the grey again with its red lights like evil eyes. An' when I felt the wind blasting me and the rain firing into my overs, the hardcore power of it made me kinda shiver and crack a sorta mind-fat, like the storm gave me energy.

So there I was buzzing out on shitty weather and walking the pavement 'round the Cornwall estate where me and Teens – and my ex, Chen – lived. A few weeks before, I'd got a new set of overs on my, uh, special takeout points from PrimeFlixK-Bell-Pharm (the wankers), so I was warm as a motherfucker an' dry as a dry-foot's penthouse.

I came 'round the corner at the bottom of the hill and started going along the skody street with The Building all the dry-foots went in to get their ends away – with half my old basic-school buds and their mums and sisters probably – when I got a hit on one of my dead-end public aliases.

They'd handled a few years online and they switched keys and countries by themselves every few hours anyway. Doubtful – heh, more like impossible – anyone'd ever trace them to me but it always gave me the *xiǎo*-shits when someone messaged one anyway; didn't matter if that was what they were there for.

It's gotta be a coincidence!

For it to happen across from the creep-o Building itself was kinda freaky but I told myself not to be a dork and got a handle on myself. I didn't wanna have nothin' to do with those dudes no matter how much they paid. I'd heard the stories: they were like plastic in the sea. Once they were in your system, you'd never get rid of 'em. Still, if it was them pinging me, they only had the alias which was doin' its job getting me grey-hat work under the table anyway.

Yeah, calm the fuck down, Nate, ya paranoid dickhead.

I chugged up to the corner so if anyone saw me – which they wouldn't 'cause I was probably the only nutjob out in this crap – they wouldn't think I was gonna go into the building. Then I fired up a secure tunnel and went roundabout ways into the alias's messaging virtual.

Turned out whoever it was, was as paranoid about security as me 'cause they were using an alias, too which made me feel safer; I didn't know who they were but that meant they didn't know who I was either. Their alias was a lame-ish one though, I could already see the holes in it but I wasn't gonna start tampering given the satoshis they were offering for the…

Hoooooooly fuck!

Well, it figured. Big – big! – money, nasty job. It was only a deep background check at the end of the day, nothing I hadn't handled before. That's what I tried to tell myself anyway. But it was who it was on that they were paying all the satoshis for.

I told myself I didn't have the smarts. I told myself I didn't have the kit. I told myself a lot of things but, in the end, I knew it was all shit. I was scared. And plus the resources – or resource – they were supplying meant the most dangerous part of the job was nearly done for me.

So why don't they do the rest of it themselves?

Could've been anything but I reckoned it had a lot to do with keeping the heat off them – whoever they were – if we got busted.

We? Fuck that! Me. It'd be me getting busted.

Which course, was what the big ding was for; yeah, could've been anything but I reckoned that was the main thing. Trouble was, I couldn't take my eyes off the prize. That and the chance to see inside the mighty Laufala Industries firewall which was a fuckin' legend. Yeah, it was pretty spooky that whoever it was had already done the impossible which shit me up all the way to the aliases.

If they can crack that, then…

And there was how busted I'd be when the Laufalas caught my sorry wet-foot arse and whipped it all the way to stasis for the rest of my short shitty life.

But life was short. So I said yeah-nah… yeah! Course I did. Like the dick I was.

I knew Teens would be working. She probably wouldn't've minded if I'd rocked up to her place and disappeared into my tech anyway. Good that I didn't, but.

I got down to the graft as soon as I got home and a couple-hours later, I had a headache from too much tech. But I hardly noticed it 'cause suddenly, my whole world went arse-up.

I'd seen dry-foots before, I'd seen where they lived an' all that. It was *fēng kuáng*, alright, the flash gear they had, the fancy food they ate and the money it all cost. Sure it was cooked; they were all cooked. But that was old news.

Laufala shat like the rest of us; probably worse given how old he was. He had all the rich gear an' that but the buzz of sneaking 'round his system wore off after a while. And call me what ya like but I wasn't an arsehole. I wasn't gonna bugger any of his tech up or look into his PMs or any shit like that. And anyway, that'd be poking the roach-nest.

Plus, I basically had nothing against the dude. I wouldn't've had this job if he hadn't invented tech, anyway. I needed enough dirt to get it done. Only the job getting done turned out to be tripping over the mother of all NDAs with my own fuckin' girlfriend right smack in the middle of it.

If this got out the news spaces'd have a fuckin' field day. I got that *oooooooh-shit* feeling in my *dùzi*. I'd taken the work and half the ding, not that it meant I couldn't pay it back – or offer it back since I had no idea where it'd come from – and say I was too dumb to sort it for them. They didn't know who I was. There'd be some pissed-off shifty peeps – with at least one sinister fuckin' hacker workin' for them – somewhere in the world; maybe not in the archipelago.

But then I had my reputation and that made me extra ding on the side. It'd be one bum job in thousands of good ones and it wasn't like I was Jamie Yang and only as good as my last story or whatever those types said about their stuff. I'd keep getting work; course I would.

But in the end, I couldn't not finish a job.

There was no way I was gonna send this-all through the cloud, secure tunnel or not. It'd have to be old-school physical drop. Half now and the other half after the rest of the ding. And I'd hack a delivery drone to drop off the nanites, too; I might've been dumb but I wasn't that bloody dumb.

I chucked in a virtual set design I had lying 'round, to pretend I'd been working at my real job. Then I jacked it all up with my heart smackin' in my ribs and after that, I went back out, past Teens' door, down the hall, past the gym, out the poor-door and over to Chen's to ask her what the fuck I should do about my girlfriend being not who she said she was.

And didn't that make me feel like the fuckin' arsehole.

Tina – Nov 2096, Cornwall Estate, Akarana Island, Aotearoa Archipelago

These bloody houses sold themselves. They literally did. It was job-creation, as Nate had told me. Another trick the rich played to keep us looking the other way while they fed us shit and kept us in our stinky damp ground-floor dives.

I looked out my window at the ancient AC juddering away on the wall across the alleyway and wished it'd at least judder, like, hard enough to shake off the gross black grime all over it. Nate had been on to maintenance about it but they hadn't done anything. I couldn't believe how patient he was with them. I'd have been screaming abuse at them the first time they lost my request let alone the third.

…But I'm recording it all, Teens. They're giving us rope to hang 'em with…

I could never understand what he was blathering about when he went on like that.

No wonder I was losing my mind with a view this yuck to look at, while I worked double shifts to put toxic fake food on the table. My triple glazing kept it pretty quiet, but I could faintly hear the city outside. As usual, the wind was whistling up the alleyway blowing the rain sideways. The AC roared above the storm, its old metal botty too constipated with dust and grime to heave out much more than the last sighing fart of a dying grandpa.

I turned up the agency-space virtual partly to look in on work and mostly to give my eyes a break from the ads flickering on the edges of my vision. The client's bots were nearly done redistributing – fucking redistributing – one of their kids' dull coloured bio-toys all over its bedroom in the exact tip it had been before the bots tidied them up.

Why? Jesus! Why? What the fuck is wrong with people?

The last of the poncy buyers had holo-ghosted back out and the first few offers and buyer details were already popping up on the system. They would have known I was there but as usual, none of them had had any questions for me. Why would they? All the information was online and it would be their people checking it all over for them anyway, then getting in touch with the vendor's people.

The vendor, probably over at some other rich arse's place having real coffee and vaping velvet-smooth premium wrackgrown weed, accepted an offer as I watched. But not the highest one! Maybe the quickest but still, what was wrong with these people? A few hours, a day or two to conveyance, what difference did it make? It wasn't as if they were gasping for the cash.

Not like me.

Once the sale was set up, with searches going out, laundering checks being made, biometrics matching, humongous shit-tons of cash moving around in rich-fuck land, I tuned in fully to the property virtual on the agency's tech. I sneaked a perve at all three – Jesus, three! – levels, taking in the massive high ceilings, daylight and clear views down to the seawalls right around the Akarana Island coast.

We weren't supposed to know the addresses of these places but I could pretty much tell this was the famous penthouse in the block at the top of the Cornwall estate. It was a couple of buildings up from mine but it might as well have been on the other side of the planet; their poor-door alone probably had a nice wrack-garden out front, and security to stop actual wet-foots like Nate and I getting in.

I stayed in the client's house as long as I could bullshit that I was checking the bots had done their work – *fuck it, or something, anyway, I don't care!* – before logging off and contemplating a J™ and a cup of Instant™ as my eyes readjusted to the dim of my own roach-infested shithole.

I farted and paused for an analytical sniff then walked the whole two steps from my work funded office chair – which was designed with maximum spinal damage in mind – to my dishwasher. That's when I found the bloody thing's auto-start hadn't worked. It should have known it was full and got the nanites washing. But when I opened it, it was chocker with grubby Instant™ mugs and spoons.

I haven't finished the repayments!

Who was I kidding? I hadn't started the fucking repayments. It would all be interest for the next six months, and then some. Maybe in a couple of years I'd get to say, tada! I'm finally the proud owner of brand-new dishwasher that basically never worked properly.

Maybe Nate could fix it when he got back. Or maybe it was just a glitch and it would work the next time. I sighed and rummaged for the least grubby spoon then – fucking manually! – pinged the dishwasher to start. I towelled the spoon clean on my jumper to save water. The storm had picked up by the time I sat down with my hot mug and pulled out my J™. The AC was a blur through the rain and I couldn't hear it any more because the wind had really risen.

I coughed my way through a few puffs of bulk-buy Bud-like-texture™ and felt the first trace of the goddess whispering through my soul. I dragged some more and the burn in my windpipe eased as warm numb flowed through me, gently loosening my chakras.

Nate wasn't wrong about much but he was definitely wrong about this. Weed did unlock your spiritual energies. There was no way this feeling could be anything else. I didn't care what he spouted about neurons and hallucinogenic effects and all his geeky things. A feeling like this couldn't be anything but spiritual awareness.

I had two more pissy viewings to go before some other agent clocked on to take over but that was all right. I was at peace with the world. This was part of the Buddhist journey to enlightenment. Karma would save me. Right this minute, wasn't that sound in the hallway Nate getting back from his lunatic walk in the storm?

It was a bit hard to judge the time because every minute of my day usually felt the same but I thought the stupid twit was back early like I told him he would be; unless I was hearing things, you couldn't really tell through the walls in these places. Not that I was complaining. Now I could get him to come over and keep me company before the next viewing.

I checked the next venue to make sure the client was out and our agency tech was in which, of course, it was and as always, there wasn't any point me doing the check. But if I didn't, I'd get fired and then where would I be? I signalled the open-home to start and tuned down the visual so I could check through my drawers for a clean T-shirt and my frumpiest looking hemp pants. If it was him I'd heard, I'd give him time to get his overs off then virtual next door and tell him to come here.

But then I thought I heard his door open again; or maybe it was the wind. So maybe he was coming over anyway. All good. I quickly turned off my J™ for later and sat on the edge of my bed, trying not to knock my knee on the corner of the desk. I switched on an okay-ish smile and waited for him to walk in. Only he didn't.

Okay, stubborn sod's probably going for a gym workout because he couldn't finish his lunatic walk.

Of course I might have been imagining I heard something. He might have stayed out walking despite the rain; the idiot. I was only a tiny bit disappointed. And a tiny bit worried. He always got horny after his workouts and I knew I'd been holding out on him for a few weeks, well, okay, months, so today might have to be the day.

All that had been good when we first met, like it always was with every boyfriend I'd ever had since I'd… left home. Then he started kind of… grossing me out with his smells and his samey-ness and how he always wanted to cuddle and...

Shit!

It made me feel sick thinking about it. The trouble was, Nate wasn't like the others. I knew he was a good guy, poncy little geek though he was. Which meant there was something wrong with me so there was no point blowing it with him until I could figure it out; with the guidance of the goddess, not stupid man-invented therapy.

I sighed, went back to my desk and glugged back my nearly-cold Instant™. I didn't feel like the rest of the J™ any more. Maybe Nate would share it with me given there was just one more day before an off-day for me and he didn't have to start work till late in the morning.

Or maybe not if he was in one of his high and mighty health-kick moods. I'd wait and see and have it myself if he didn't want any. Maybe I could get wasted enough to give him some and keep me off my own back about it for the next while; Nate never complained to me himself but he was a guy wasn't he? He must have been secretly angry about it. He must have been! I kept thinking I should do the right thing and end it with him, really. But everything else was fine if it wasn't for that.

The next two viewings were in smaller places. Not small places but not three-floor penthouses. Jesus! Didn't these people know I needed novelty to make my job tolerable? Or at least keep me awake.

I didn't bother sneaking a look at them and spent most of the time with the agency space turned right down trying to squint out the flicker of bloody ads. Thinking of Nate, proba-bly sweating away like an idiot on his cranky old treadmill, I felt a bit guilty I hadn't been reading enough.

There was no way I could keep up with him but I felt I should at least try. I wasn't a rich-fuck, no way. I hadn't gone to uni or anything poncy like that. But Nate was proper hardcore poor. His family lived further around than the south coast than Beachlands itself. When the poor guy was eleven, he'd quit school after basic because his mum was sick and his dad couldn't afford to pay intermediate-school fees.

But that hadn't stopped him. The guy was seriously clever as well as cute in a… what? A nerd-slut-fitness-freak kind of way, maybe? Was that a thing? He'd kept teaching himself from the public library of all places.

And he didn't only know stuff. He understood it. He made me feel ashamed of the privilege I didn't bloody have. Okay, he got his words mixed up sometimes but I didn't care. I always knew what he meant. And it wasn't his fault nobody had taught him. And it was so cute when he said arksed instead of asked like a little kid learning to talk.

Jesus! Make up your mind woman! Are you dumping him or are you into him?

That was the trouble though. It depended on my mood.

I decided not to think about it any more and faked his handle, as he'd taught me. I logged on to the library with his free account. I knew he didn't like me reading about the spiritual stuff but it was afternoon on the second-to-last day before some off days and I couldn't handle all the boring economics, history and tech gibberish he would have wanted me to wade through. I found a big fat words-only book about the beliefs of the ancient Māori as a compromise but I couldn't get myself to open it.

I fiddled around online instead and ended up in some lame news space looking at some boring stuff about earthquakes; although all the underwater footage was kind of calming. I muted the audio and turned up one of the spaces so I couldn't see my flat any more. Then I drifted over the seabed on loop like I was flying, flying, flying.

I forgot all about Nate, all about everything and whether he pinged me that night or not I had no idea because I woke up the next morning nearly too late to log on to work.

Nathan – Nov 2096, Cornwall Estate, Akarana Island, Aotearoa Archipelago

Teen's'd been asleep when I'd got back from Chen's the other night and given the thoughts I couldn't stop having after being in a confined space with her for a couple-hours, I was kinda glad. I reckoned Teens would've seen it on my face and given what I'd found out, I didn't reckon I'd be able to handle myself that well seeing her. Still, I was a bit bummed she didn't try to get in touch.

I was in a stroppy mood the next morning which was pathetic really, given I was twenny-eight. But work kicked off 'cause the company got a new movie contract and I was up to my arse in new set-design reqs all day so the mood and the busyness kinda made me forget.

I was knackered by the end of that one and knackered plus stroppy was always a bad mix for me; fuck, was it a good mix for anyone? Plus, I needed to eat something healthy and I knew if I went to Teens' place, she'd wanna pizza or something.

I got in some veggies and tried to ignore how weird it was there being a wall between us and the two of us sulking like *háizis*. Still, whatever *makutu* was happening in her *năozĭ*, I wasn't fully ready to blink first. Though one of us'd have to soon since we'd planned yonks ago to hang out in our off days coming up. But then I crashed out and suddenly it was morning and I had a shitload to get through else it'd all be waiting for me when I logged back on in a few days' time.

Busy or not, I ended up back out in the rain again anyway. It was mid-afternoon and I had my iSpotTunes cranked up. I was trying to sing along but my bud Shane's band's tunes were kinda not exactly catchy. I was gonna learn their stuff though so it'd be at least like they had one decent fan at their first ever livestream in a couple of nights.

I'd never've said it to him but he should've stuck to what he was good at; he was bloody premo on the kitaa. They could've got another drummer since Carrie was way better at vocals than Shane; meaning she could nearly sing in tune. Plus, Cherie was a better drummer than Carrie and couldn't play bass to save his life; yeah, so maybe they'd need to get in a bass-player too.

So, they had it all arse about face. And I had to look up their words to learn them 'cause their tunes sounded like a MagLev crash on loop with a rat getting tortured in a track off to the side somewhere. But I'd love to've seen me having a go. I hadn't picked up my kitaa in months. At least they were trying to make real music from human hands and voices, unlike the auto-generated poppy crap the dry-foots all listened to.

Maybe Chen's right, I'm giving Shane the wrong idea looking out for him too much.

But I couldn't help it. Shane'd always be my bud. We'd grown up together! Yeah, course I knew he had the hots for me and if I didn't, there was always Chen to keep remindin' me. But what was I s'posed to do? Cut him off just 'cause I didn't feel the same? Nah that would've sucked for both of us. And anyway, who was to say if I was ever single again one day, I might not get the hots for him back? He was a good lookin' dude, nobody could deny.

Jeez, better not let Teens catch me thinkin' like that with all her weird ideas.

With that mindfuck going on along with the MagLev crash cranked up and me trying to work out what was one song from another, it took me a while to clock the water that hadn't been there a few seconds before coming up 'round my ankles. Flash as my new gear was, it felt cold-ish through the fancy leg material anyway. This time, I really shouldn't've been out in the storm but I couldn't figure out what to do about Teens and I was gonna see her fuckin' soon. I shouldn't've been away from my desk, technically, but I'd put in for creative time so I had a couple-hours before work's system flagged me.

But running into a flash-flood was about when I thought would be a good time to turn 'round before I ended up swimmin' home or falling down flood drainage if it opened up under me when the water got deep enough. Teens would laugh her arse off at me for going out in the rain in the first place an' that I could handle. She was basically a good girlfriend, never mind that she went a bit *fēng kuáng* in the head sometimes and needed extra cuddles. And that was without counting her spooky ideas about who got to do jazzy-touching with who.

And never mind that she's not Chen.

Yeah, well, that was my fault and I had to stop those thoughts. It wouldn't've been fair on Chen if she was dumb enough to take me back anyway. I was with Teens now and that was bloody that.

'Cept of course, she isn't Teens. Fuck! What am I gonna to do about this?

I tried to look along the road ahead to see how far the flood had gone an' if I could at least go along to the corner and back up the other way to get in a bit more k-age. But suddenly the water was up to my knees so I reckoned screw the exercise and turned to bail straight back up the hill. Only as I was goin' back 'round the corner, I heard this idiot shouting at me.

'You! Oi! What did you do that for?'

I looked 'round and the voice came again.

'Hey! I'm talking to you, arsehole!'

Eh? What the fuck did I do?

Then I saw where the shouting was coming from. This dork was getting out of his car by the corner. His GPS must've been a bit out. Or he was doing something shifty, more-like, given we were only half a block away from The Building; probably, didn't want the car to record the address he was going to. Dry-foots were all into weird shit.

I could tell he was money 'cause he wasn't getting out of an Uber. If I pinged his car with my, uh, custom tech, I probably could've worked out who he was since there were stuff-all private motors on Akarana Island nowadays. If the car wasn't proof enough, the overs he was wearing nailed it: ones like mine, 'cept probably legally owned.

He'd got out of his car and was waving back in the door. I didn't have any idea what he was on about till I saw the drops on the seat.

What the fuck's that gotta do with me?

'What did you do that for?' he shouted through the storm at me, and I knew he was old 'cause of the weird translation sounds kinda underneath his voice. He was probably speaking the old English or whatever. Still, I couldn't see his face through the rain an' his overs visor but he sounded pissed.

I tried to stay cool and used my suavest voice. 'Chill man. I didn't do anything.'

'You bloody well did so! You waited till I opened the door and splashed bloody water into my car!'

Why the fuck would I do that?

'I, uh, really didn't!'

'You did bloody so! I'll get you arrested over this, you know! Bloody rough elements around here, I wouldn't have believed it if I hadn't seen it for myself!' His voice sounded more like rebar bein' dragged over concrete than a human bein'.

Now you're being a massive dick.

'Look, seriously, man, I didn't do anything. I didn't see you through the rain – look at it! How could I of? – till you yelled at me. Sorry, I didn't mean to wet your flash seat an' all that, I honestly didn't.'

'Bullshit you didn't, you wet-foot thug. I'm calling the police.'

Well fuck this.

Things were starting to go a bit arse-over-tit between the rich and the normal people 'cause of all the seawalls starting to break down and food shortages and bullshit job-creation an' all that. But I wasn't the kind of dickhead to go 'round stirring shit up for no reason so I was chilled that he couldn't do fuck-all to me 'cause I hadn't done anything wrong; that anyone knew of.

That's why I shrugged my shoulders, turned 'round an' headed for home. The water wouldn't do any damage anyway. His posh bloody seats would've all been nano-tech, they'd've dried 'emselves and laid him a genuine fuckin' celeriac and fried it for his lunch before he got back from his rent-boy or whatever.

But he did. He actually did!

I felt the arrest come down on my tech as soon as I walked in my door. I was gonna get my overs off and go straight next door to Teens' to get the mocking over with. Managed the first part but then my arms and legs locked up and my guts squeezed so tight I nearly puked. I couldn't get my overs back on. The cop tech pulled me 'round and straight back out the door.

All I could do was gawk ahead. Back out my shithole apartment door, I went. Down the mildew-stinking hall, past the gym which only I used, past the empty pool, back to the poor-door us worker-roaches used so the rich-fucks didn't have to smell us, an' back out into the pissing rain which wasn't the same buzz when ya weren't wearing overs.

I was soaked to the skin by the time I got to the block entrance. But I would take that over the sight of the paddy-wagon waiting with its blue light flashing through the rain.

My body got in. The car didn't dish out any journey deets to me like an Uber or anything an' I was too shit-scared to ping it with my tech in case it woke up and started ponging back. Other than my comms, they didn't firewall me which I s'pose made sense 'cause I wasn't a criminal or anything, never mind if they thought I might be. The paddywagon was all business. It grew its door closed and drove off. Jeez! I knew they could do this but it was one thing to know and another to bloody find out!

Course, they didn't have to've done all that. They could've come 'round or asked me to come in or called me into their online space. It was all to show me who was boss; everyone knew that.

Never mind if I was having a piss or handling hot food or what. Too bad bud! Drop everything and fuck up your day to make a shit-useless trip into the station for not doing anything wrong. Even then I was dumb enough to think it'd all be all right.

Turned out the station was pretty close which gave me the *xiǎo*-shits considering how I'd done, uh, certain things in the past few years without knowing the law was quietly sittin' there a few blocks away. It was kinda brownish brick with a half-circle drive that went under a bit of roof sticking out over the entrance. The paddywagon pulled up under that bit at least, so I didn't get any more soaked. My body got out and my guts tried staying behind as I got remote-controlled through the front door.

It was the first actual time I'd been arrested and it nearly had me shitting my pants. In a way it was lucky this had come so soon, else I would've been more worried about them pulling up some arsehole audit records and saying, Ah, Mister Richards-Mann, we know all about you. Trying to be cool with my *nǎozi* stressing about that, was mostly why my eyes weren't popping out of my face at how much of a shithole the cop-shop was.

It had old and I mean old, yellowy plaster walls which was cracking and flaking all over the shitty green lino – fuck, lino! – floor with real-live cracks and rips in it. I could smell how it was kinda going rotten. It must've been eighty years old or something. There was a pissed-off half-asleep looking fat dude in a too-small cop uniform at the massive front desk behind a clear-alloy screen; the modernest bit of the station I could see.

Sheesh, I know he looks tasty but the good people of Akarana Island aren't that fuckin' starving yet, are we? Well…

I mean, surely the way I got here was proof nobody was gonna go at them with a knife and fork or anything. You'd be frozen by remote soon as ya thought about it.

I could see behind the lard-berg, all the pigs sitting at these old-school office-type desks with crumby old partitions made of some kinda rough-looking baby-poo-ish coloured stuff that was probably illegal now. It couldn't've been much more like some B-movie set before the plagues and Euro-war way back near the turn of the century.

Whatever dickhead'd done the set design forgot the antique laptops and phones on their desks and the bits of paper stuck to their petitions with pins or whatever. All the cops were sitting 'round tech-twitching their faces and shooting the shit. There were a few delivery boxes melting down on the floors. I couldn't see a single stripe on any of 'em and it made me wonder if maybe after this was all sorted out, I could get part time work as a cop; Jeez, if they could afford pricey take-out like that…

The berg didn't look at me when I slopped in. There was some huckery looking plastic – plastic! – seats off to one side which I would've sat in so I could say I'd touched antique plastic if the cop-tech didn't have me in a strangle-hold. It forced me to stand and wait in front of the big active-alloy door by reception.

After a couple-minutes, the reception fort opened and a cop who looked like she was only my age popped out. By the freaky dark black bun and the 'sun'-tan, she was definitely a fledgling corporate kid. Probably not long hatched from university or whatever pricey corporate brainwashing joint they sent 'em to nowadays.

She turned out to be as rude as any rich kid. It probably wasn't her fault, probably how they were brought up. She didn't tell me her name or anything. She kind of half walked over to me, did a little tech-twitch of her pricey little uni-educated face and u-turned.

Don't they have to show you ID or something?

I got zombied through the door behind her. I would've had a squizz 'round the pigsty to suss it out, but the tech forced me to keep eyes forward. We ended up in a beaten-up room with the same crap décor as the glorious station reception, only it was smaller and it stunk more. Nothing but two chairs and a lump of a table. Genuinely, like turn-o'-the century movies which I watched a shit-ton of for my minimum wage CGI job remastering them for virtual spaces. When I got outta this, it at least gave me a few good ideas for my smell-themes.

Still zipped, Constable Peaches waved me into a chair an' then I decided pretty fast, the experience of touching scratched-up cold antique plastic wasn't worth it. I realised the cop tech had let me go as I sat down which was lucky 'cause I hadn't been too far away from hurling, or worse, the way it had locked up my gut-muscles.

Is it meant to do that? Or is it legacy crap they can't afford to upgrade, like their station. Maybe they'd hire me to update their huckery code for cheap.

And then, boof! This vintage dude virtualled into the room at the end of the table and I jumped. Not because he'd appeared but because of who he was! Any big ideas about part-time work, coding contracts and smell-themes for work disappeared behind a big *oooooh-shit!*

Jason Zhang was best buds with Joanna Rahui and his royal techship Tristian Laufala himself! Well, so everyone thought. I knew different after the job I'd done for the shifty peeps who tapped me a couple-days back.

Shit, better check on that after this, might be time for the second drop…

If there was an after this, anyway. Zhang owned half the construction business in the known fuckin' world. All the high-rises. All the roads, all the fuckin' cheap-arse seawalls that kept leaking poisoned bloody ocean into basements like the ones where my folks lived. And leaking was lucky. Now some of them were so huckery after years of no spending, they'd started bursting and drowning whole families all over the Ao

Islands and probably the world. Basically, a crazy rich and mightily *makutu'd* nutjob was after my arse.

The guy was known to be going *fēng kuáng* in the *nǎozǐ*. His family an' that, they were all idiots for trying to keep it quiet, I reckoned. They would've been better leaning into it. Like, fuck, who hadn't had a grandad or whatever who'd lost it when they got old? It was what happened. It was normal.

It would've got all the average peeps on board with 'em. But oh no, it wasn't enough they had to rub our noses in it that they were the rich and we weren't. Now they were trying to make us think they were immortals or some shit, too.

All this went through my *nǎozǐ* like a fake pizza usually went through my tum-tum. Lucky that wasn't what I'd eaten the night before 'cause sittin' there face to face with evil dry-foot Jase and seein' the madness in his eyes up close, well, let's say, I needed all the help I could get to keep stuff from getting embarrassing.

I'm toast.

So I was starting to sweat in the cold plastic seat when PC Peaches said, 'Mister Nathan Richards-Mann, thank you for coming to the station so promptly.'

Like I had a… Eh? What the…?

I knew that voice. From… Somewhere. I didn't know where but I knew it.

'This gentleman, Mister Jason Zhang…'

How do I know that voice?

'…has accused you of vandalism.'

'Not guilty,' I said. 'I didn't do anything.'

Who the fuck are you?

'You bloody did s… He did! He splashed water into my car!' Zhang sounded like his throat was made of wet tarmac and I really should've been keepin' up but the cop's voice was freaking me out. I knew her from somewhere.

'All right then, this should be easy enough to sort out. Let's take a look at the video.' PC Peaches sounded a bit strained. Poor thing, havin' to do some work for a change. Bet she didn't think that might happen when she signed up to fight the good fight against the poor and the wet-footed. Trending: SoFuckin'Sad.

Bam! We was suddenly out in the rain which kind of made my brekkie uppity about staying down after the beating it'd took from the cop-tech. And snapped me out of trying to work out who she was, too.

There would've been heavy duty public nanites on cam-assignment aggregated all over the sides of buildings and probably on the pavement too, so it could film up the crack of your overs. I reckoned we were on the side of a block fence or building from the angle of the view, 'cept it was like any virtual space, you could look 'round and it would pan the image if it had the footage from enough angles, like you were really there. No other sensory, thank fuck. I'd had enough wetness and roaring bloody rainstorm for one day.

We couldn't see much more than falling water at first but all right, there was his car pulling over to the pavement on the corner. It stopped right in front of us. You wouldn't've been able to see much details of the car but nobody could say it wasn't a car.

The door peeled back as some dickwad – that was me – came slopping 'round the corner – man I could walk fast! So okay, I had to admit, pretty bad timing. The edge of the flash flood, was right near the car and I walked into the water, right as Zhang was sticking his poncy leg out into the rain. The rest as they say, was history.

'Yeah, see,' I said. 'It was an accident. Seriously man, I didn't mean it!'

He couldn't argue. But he was rich and he was used to getting what he wanted and he was ninety-nine-mill satoshis in the old coin to chuck in with the rest. 'Check his tech!' he ordered the cop.

Shit! Is he dribbling?

'Well, really, Mister Zhang, I think we can see what happened can't we? It does look like an accident.'

I was pretty sure I knew the look she was giving him.

Jeez! They know each other! Fuck me!

I gave her my best smile. I guess she thought I looked like a crim since my hair wasn't long and in a bun like all her pretty little rich-fuck buds' probably was. But still, best to stay positive, I read that in shitloads of self-help stuff in the library. She didn't smile back.

'Mister Zhang, I need to make you aware there is a fee associated with…'

He was already waving it off, course he was. What did he care about fees? It all dribbled through the systems back to the rich anyway. He was basically paying himself his own money back, like sucking the end of an enema tube.

'Mister Richards-Mann, you're not at this time required to submit to an examination of your tech. However if you do not, your refusal may be viewed with suspicion and used as evidence in any subsequent criminal proceedings.'

'Yeah, yeah, I know. Nothin' to hide, nothin' to fear. I geddit. So what can I do? Guess I gotta toe the line and let you perve in at all my biometrics to prove my innocence. Well, it's your job I guess, not your fault.'

She had the decency to look a bit sorry at least. 'Mister Richards-Mann, your data will be treated with the utmost confidence and stored securely. Nobody but relevant police personnel and judiciary staff will have access to your, uh, raw data and when on-sold, we guarantee it will be in aggregate or anonymised form only.'

When! Jesus when, not if! They come right out and say it! Jeez! It's a bloody racket!

I tried to keep the anger off my face but not that hard. See, all the bullshit disclaimering was giving me time to make a few adjustments to my tech, to make sure the hatches was buttoned an' all that. They'd see a bit of weirdness but it wouldn't stop 'em getting at my biometrics which I didn't care about, really. It was the principle that got on my tits.

'Yeah, okay, I consent, or whatever I gotta say,' I said.

I was pretty sure there was some official words you had to say and if you didn't say 'em you could use it for a legal technicality in your defence or something. I partly remembered learning something like it in the library but I was a bit stressed at that stage so I didn't know what else to say. Peaches-cop wasn't standing on ceremony anyway. She did a tech-tic and I felt the cop systems root-user into my *nǎozǐ*.

She could see my data getting mined and so could I and we both knew there was nothing. My heart had been doing what a heart at walking pace should do. Frontal lobe and cerebellum an' that were saying go right, go left, go straight ahead an' all that shit. Not that they could exactly read your mind but near as dammit nowadays, and getting closer all the time.

Course, my amygdala had fired the signal and there was a bit of left hemisphere wakeup, catecholamines, adrenaline an' that. But that was only after old Mister Z shouted at me. Well, who wouldn't get a fright if some mental case in a dark motor opened the door and started raving on like a dero? Basically, I was chilling on my walk and doing nothing wrong. I knew it and she knew it. They had nothin' on me. Nothin'! Which was why they had to make something up.

Constable Peaches pursed her lips. She fired a rat-in-the-headlights look at Mister Z's holo-ghost. He looked like he was gonna deck someone.

She said in this pissy *háizi* voice, 'It does look as if he's telling the truth Unc— Mister Zhang.'

That was too much! 'Course I'm bloody telling the truth! I was going for a walk, getting some exercise in! There's no fu— law against it!'

It felt cool when neither of 'em looked at me funny for saying exercise. She would've done proper exercise to be a piglet and he was an antique, so back in his day it's probably all they could do to keep in shape. Not that our little three second brotherhood, well, or whatever-hood, did me any good, but. She ignored me like I never said anything and the pale-under-wrinkle-tan of Zhang-the-rich-big-wang's face told me he was about go critical.

PC Peaches must've seen it too. I had all my illegal tech cloaked with, uh, more-illegaler tech so I couldn't packet-sniff to see if they was messaging seeing as how she was his niece –

yeah, I'd heard it! Their faces were both, more or less here, and not completely spaced in that tech kind of way but I wouldn't've betted on it. Whether her nose was up his hairy brown crack or not, I had become a prisoner even though I didn't know it yet.

PC Peaches. Said, 'As I said, Mister Richards-Mann does seem to be telling the truth but...'

'Too right!'

I cracked a decent grin and saluted but she wasn't amused so I let her talk, which pretty quickly got worrying.

'When I connected you to our system, Mister Richards-Mann, the system adapted to your tech—'

'Well course it did, I've got— '

'If you'll let me finish Mister Richards-Mann.'

Then I noticed Zhang looked like he'd spotted the quarry and a brand-new bad feeling started to grow. I properly shut my cake-hole, then. I'd heard of this shit before but I never believed it.

'Now while your tech did eventually allow a connection...'

Fuck eventually! It took all of a bloody nano!

'...the requirement to adapt to your non-standard config-uration suggests tampering. We can't therefore guarantee the validity of your biometrics since your non-standard tech con-figuration could have corrupted data, lost data or deliberately interfered with data before delivery to us.'

Zhang's ancient-arse mug cooled off, then. About the same time, I felt my guts sinking out my arsehole and through the illegal plastic right in the beating heart of the nation's law enforcement service.

Everyone – everyone! – dicked around with their tech. Customised the visual overlays, tuned the senses up and down, muted ads from freeware overlays. It was made so you could easily do it. There was actual software the corporates sold to help you do it easier. But of course, there was always that pissy little disclaimer that it might somehow fuck you up and well, now, I was finding out the somehow of the up-fucking.

I could see a spasm of sympathetic human-ness struggle like a mutant baby roach under Peaches' expensive smooth jaw before she got it under control and carried on somehow-ing my life.

'So, Mister Richards-Mann, Akarana Island has no choice but to find you guilty…'

'I want to appeal!'

Can I appeal? Is that a thing?

I was sure I read it in the library but maybe it was only before tech.

'…of illegal tampering with public property and intent to conceal criminal intentions from the police. You are invited to spend five years in Spume AG therapeutic stasis from which you are guaranteed to resume normal life in at least compara-ble physical condition to your condition on the day you ini-tially engage with the service, less reasonable aging. Since the system reports no previous convictions or cautions, you may be invited to end your psychological therapy after two years depending on therapeutic outcomes.'

Jeez you had to love their words: Invited, therapeutic, comparable. Did they think I was bloody stupid or something! Anything's bloody comparable to anything! And as for the bloody 'invited', I could already feel it inviting my arms and legs to let the police tech take control of them and march me out to a paddywagon. Yeah, some fuckin' inviting.

Constable Peaches didn't bother to follow me out. She stayed with Zhang's holo-ghost in the bullshit 'court room'.

They definitely had me firewalled now, right down to the biotech. My skin'd gone numb and most of my senses were jammed as the paddywagon carted me home. Comms and stuff I got. But why did they have to do that? I guessed they let you keep your vision 'cause their tech needed to know where your body was going somehow. Nothing they could do to stop me thinking though 'cept I'd rather not have been able to, right then.

Therapeutic outcomes. Fuck! Those Spume arseholes brainwashed you! I was gonna be fuckin' slowly lobotomised for doing nothing! This system was fuckin' shit! It was fuckin' rigged! Nobody could see me in the paddywagon but if they could, I wouldn't've given a shit about the tears which I couldn't lift a hand to wipe off. They was righteous fuckin' tears. I was on fire inside though I couldn't move. More than fire. I was a fuckin' volcanic eruption inside.

The paddywagon cruised between all the high-rises in the rain, which was so heavy now it was like being under the water. Through the windscreen, I saw red drone lights come in and out of the grey and a few taillights ahead. That was the final shithouse view I was gonna get on what might've well been the last day of my life.

Course, I had my one call. I wasn't in the mood but, course I'd do it. And it'd be to Teens, course it would; didn't matter if I would've rathered it was to Chen or my folks. I couldn't've faced Mum and Dad like that. And it would've wrecked Teens…

…who's not Teens…

…if she found out from Chen and there'd be no telling what she'd do. Nah, Teen's'd have to tell them all. I knew they'd come and visit me in the joint; if it was possible; if I wasn't already too fucked-with to know who they were.

Jeez, do I know anyone who's come out okay? Do I know anyone who's been in?

I thought maybe if I could remember anyone who'd gone inside and come out, maybe it'd be worth calling them instead for some tips. But there was nobody so Teens it would be. I tried to think of what to say.

Hey Teens, see ya in a coupla years when I'm a vegetative sack of braindead good citizen.

Jeez, she wasn't gonna take this too well. I hoped she wouldn't do anything stupid and get herself chucked in the joint with me. She was basically an all right girlfriend but I had to admit, she could get a bit *makutu'd* sometimes with all the mind stuff I taught her.

I'd tried to teach her the good stuff, the meditation an' mindfulness an' lucid dreaming an' that, which I taught myself from the library. But she kinda latched on to all the weird *háizi*-story stuff about gods and shit, and got arsey with me when I tried to talk her out of it.

Yeah, nah, I was into change all right. I fully wanted to get people together, change the system, make it fairer, make the rich listen, make 'em fuckin' notice us.

I done a few hacks in my time too. I got around the library paywall after they put it in, so thousands of poor people like me could at least have a pissing Jesus of a chance to move up in life.

And thanks to me, thousands of kids would at least get a bit better food so their brains wouldn't grow up deficient on shithouse addictive Total™ and their bank accounts wouldn't grow down 'cause of having to keep buying it. That was my PrimeFlixK-Bell-Pharm points hack.

It was all through their drones, virused into their delivery system waiting for anyone who I managed to get the hack to, to tap into. I reckoned they'd sniff it out one day but every day they didn't was another day some babies was getting fed decent solids.

Yeah, see? University-shmooniversity, everything you could ever of needed to know was right there in the now-public-ish library. As long as you knew how to pirate a translation overlay to get all the books into the standard *hànzì* from the old alphabet which I'd also helped people do, you could learn anything a copling like PC Peaches probably got taught at posh corporate university. Course, fuckall peeps could read anyway, not 'cause they didn't get taught it in basic school but 'cause they didn't keep it up and that suited the rich fine.

So yeah, I done some illegal shit. But I done it all seriously cloaked, not for the glory like some of these wannabe do-gooders who accidentally on purpose would let their shell-aliases get found out so they could suck up a bit of ooohs an' ahs from the crowds before ditching them before they got properly busted. I was playing the long game for the greater fuckin' good.

Teens, I didn't think she got it; and I kinda knew why, now, but that made it more annoying considering how much of a hand she could've gave us if she'd got over herself and tapped into her family an' that. But all she did was be kinda, angry all the time. I'd always tried to keep her calm, tried to show her the best way and keep trying to nudge along the idea of maybe the gods aren't gonna save us...

...not that she ever needed saving...

Well, not in the money sense, anyway. But I worried about her, yeah, okay she'd bullshitted me an'... all of us I s'pose. An' all the weed she chugged didn't help her either. But given what'd happened to her, it wasn't her fault. She didn't mean bad.

So it was pleasant fuckin' thoughts like that which were in my mind as the paddywagon pulled up at my block entrance. The police tech forced me out of the car through the rain, into the poor-door, down the stinky hall, right past Teens' door which I couldn't look sideways at 'cause my neck was locked in forward position.

Please don't come out Teens! Not now!

I came to a shin-splinting halt at my door and jerked 'round.

I'm not a fuckin' drone! I've got fuckin' feet!

The door peeled back and I was force-marched inside where the cop systems had already repurposed raw nanites, which was building my pris...uh, fuck, sorry, therapeutic stasis chamber over my bed.

Yeah, but how did all the raw nanites get here so fast? Where did they come from? Where? Chen...

Chen would have to keep looking into it by herself. Forever, probably.

Another wave of *fuck me this can't be happening* iced up my back and this time I wouldn't've wanted anyone to see me crying like a *háizi and* dribbling through my locked-shut mouth; not 'cause I was embarrassed, there was nothing wrong with melting down when ya situation'd gone critical. It was more that I would've hated dumping my shit on other peeps.

And I prob'ly would literally of shit myself too, given how crook my *dùzi* felt then. But the cop systems had a stranglehold on everything. I watched as the chamber grew, the nanites eating into my bed, spitting it back out as the standard issue blues and whites with the evil wave-patterns of Spume AG, the arseholes themselves an' their weird evil CEO, Paresh Steel.

It was harmless-looking enough really. It shouldn't've shit me up the way it did considering it was only a bed, some tubes and a bio-containment bubble which in the end, was for my own health and safety anyway, while I was in stasis.

Man if I could hijack those babies, they'd be worth a fuckin' fortune!

But all the best rich evil geniuses worked on that security. It'd pretend it wasn't tech if ya pinged it let alone starting to hack it.

But there must be a way. Someone must be able to ping it!

Jeez! I couldn't believe I was still trying to be me given I was about to be made not me and no two ways about it. But I couldn't stop my *nǎozi* whirring. If I could just've figured out how to detect the fuckers, I would of given it a run for its money. It was one more thing I'd never get to do.

While I stood there dribbling and crying like a *háizi*, my apartment was getting a refurb. All the grime on the walls and cupboards was getting cleared and the damp bits down in the corners where the wee-bit-better-than-social-housing quality Zhang construction was rotting, magicked clean and dry as the nanites got to 'em. I'd nearly've been happy for the free maintenance job if I didn't know it wasn't all for shit-show.

Couldn't have pris— aw, sorry, Spume therapy clients, lookin' like they was hivernating in roach infested shitholes. There was a scam-deal…. scamdal… There'd been a big shit-storm about it a couple-decades ago when I was little and sleeping in the bed between my mum and dad in their government issue basement dive; which is what ya nearly had to do to go inside, it leaked that much. Yeah, my gaff'd be kept clean and tidy while I was getting my state-funded *nǎozi*-damage all right.

The memories was rolling like the tears which was a shit way to spend my last sane moments in life. But what the fuck else could I do with my body hijacked by the law enforcement service?

The mind-fucking pod was all set up and my bed looked like an old-school hospital bed before long and then this voice – PC Peaches' voice! – said, 'Mister Richards-Mann, your therapy space is ready, you're entitled to a ten-minute call before you engage with the service.'

Whoa! Generous! Probably Peaches gets to listen in, too, and gossip with all her designer buds about what she did at work that day.

She hadn't virtualled into my home; only her voice sounded in my ears. And it sounded kind of regretful. I reckoned now the high and mighty nutjob dry-foot'd left her alone she was probably regretting the whole thing since she knew she was outta line.

Poor liddle Peaches eh? It'd bum her out for maybe a few days! Until she decided to pay a shit-ton of cash for a few of her own Spume sessions – the nice touchy-feely customer-focused ones with the kind faces in the rain from the ads an' all that jazz – to clear her sad little rich-fuck conscience of destroying a nasty smelly poor guy for a crime she thought he might of committed. I'd say she was only doin' her job but wasn't that the whole bloody point? If she fuckin' had been… Yeah, sheesh, my heart would of gone out to 'er if my fuckin' fist wasn't first in line.

That voice. Where've I heard that voice?

It was a weird thought to be having with my body locked up so hard it was squeezing things out of itself like tears and dribble. It showed they knew their stuff, really. I reckoned there was a good chance I would've offed myself in that few minutes when I saw the chamber all set up and there was only a useless chat with my girlfriend between me and the end. I could breathe normal again and my stomach unclenched. They kept my tech firewalled 'cept comms which was back online.

Do I get to go for a last shit?

It didn't really matter 'cause the tubes and stuff would take care of all that once I was under but it kinda sucked 'cause it meant I'd have to clench my way through my last ever sane conversation with another human bein'. I thought of begging Peaches to let me go, I could see my toilet door right beside me out the corner of my eye. Man! So close! It made me need to go more.

But I reckoned Peaches wouldn't risk letting me. They probably had rules against it and she might lose her job and have to retire early and live on her trust fund or whatever; such a shame. Now there wasn't anything left but to say goodbye to Teens and the cruel world.

Jeez, maybe I should call Chen instead, she could handle it better, she'd know what to do…

But that wouldn't've been fair on Teens. So with thoughts of my ex in my mind, tears leaking outta my face and poo leaking outta my bum, I called up my girlfriend one last time. I holo'd into her place and she said, 'Hi babe.'

She was wearing crappy old hemps an' her good T-shirt and looked stoned and already freaked out for some reason. I hadn't planned what to say, who does?

'I…' I said. Then I choked up.

I couldn't talk.

'Nate, where are you?' She was looking at me like I'd done something wrong.

'I'm at my place Teens. But—'

I could see it, the second she started working out something was wrong. 'Shall I come over?'

'Teens, you can't. I've been—'

I didn't know if she saw my tears come or if she was starting to get my bad vibes or what. But she really started to freak. She turned 'round and got some hemps on and said, 'I'm coming over!'

I couldn't hardly talk so I ghosted after her and watched her hammer on my door which I was behind. Course it wouldn't peel back for her and course she couldn't ping it any more. She started freaking more.

'Nathan what's happened?' She started tearing up herself and that finally got me to unfreeze my voice and it all splurted out.

'Teens, I got arrested. I got fuckin' sentenced! I can't leave my place now. You'll get visitation, probably, I dunno how it works but probably you can visit sometime, somehow. I'm about to be put under so you're my last call an'…' Then I ran outta words again.

'Jesus! Nate! What did you do?'

Well that was a dumb question coming from her. She knew everything I done, well, not everything but… I knew what she meant, anyway.

'Teens, I didn't do anything. Y'know, not that they've… Uh, actually nothing. I got busted for fuckin' annoying Zhang when I was out on my walk, seriously, I accidentally splashed the guy and he got me fuckin' arrested! They checked the video and found me not guilty and busted me for non-standard fuckin' tech instead!'

'No way, Nate! Can't you, I dunno, use all your law stuff to get it re-checked or something? I mean, everyone has…'

You could get me outta this. You could, I dunno, call in some favours, get some money or something…

'Teens, could…' But she didn't know I knew. My ten minutes was ticking down and I didn't know if she'd go mental if she found out I knew about her, or what. So I said, 'I tried Teens. They didn't listen. The cop was one of 'em. I think she knew the guy, you know the way they've got each-others' back an' that.'

Jeez. Did I try hard enough? Maybe the cop didn't hear me or something? Maybe there is some kind of appeal thingy, or something.

I was gonna try and be cool. I was all ready to tell her it would be a piece of piss, that I'd be out in a coupla years and I'd use my mindful-lucid-dreaming techniques to fight it and she could visit me anyway and it would be all good.

'Teens, I'm freaking out. I can't believe what's happened. I can't believe it. I.. I got back from the cop station a few minutes ago. They've got my body jammed so I can't move my arms and legs. Teens, they're gonna fuckin' lobotomise me! I'm done, Teens, I might as well fuckin' die.' Last bit came out like a little *háizi* wailing about a broken toy and then the sobs took over my body and the tears rolled like my brain-fluid was leaking. Yeah-nah, that worked well.

I hope you're fuckin' watching this Peaches you spoilt little cunt! Are you happy you've done your fuckin' duty now? Does seeing me like this make you feel good? Can you see my fuckin' girlfriend now, Peaches? See what you've done to her too? Look at her! She struggles at the best of fuckin' times, now look!

Teens had flopped down outside my door crying. Nobody'd be getting in there in a hurry. I was sealed off behind high grade active alloy like one of those insects there used to be which had the honey-combs. Ants or something. They put their grubs inside the wax thing till they was ready to hatch out. Only I'd hatch out not being' able to walk anymore and pooing in my pants instead of flying and making honey.

But how do the nanites get here so fast… How?

I couldn't believe I was thinking about tech shit at a time like this!

'Teens,' I said, trying to pull myself together. 'Teens. You gotta keep things going till I get out, okay? You gotta keep dishing out the foo… you know what. Teens, ya hear me? You gotta access the public records, use what they've done to me t'day? Geddit, Teens?'

She looked up, all blotchy and red, hair stuck to her face. I wanted to reach down an' pull her up, and stroke her little spikey head and ping her tech swirl-patterns into cheeky little dirty pictures all over her face instead, 'cept I couldn't 'cause I wasn't really there. Tech was a mindfuck sometimes!

There was this new hardness setting over her face as I watched, like she was turning into a vampire from one of those old movies. *And her face began to change…wooooh!*

It chilled me into a kind of calmness and when she spoke it was in a kind of voice I'd never heard her use and sure as shit didn't like the sound of. 'Yeah, I'll do it babes. All of it. Don't worry. And I'll find a way of getting you out too, before they wreck your head. I'll get money, I'll get a lawyer or something. I'll find a way, you have to hang in, okay? I'll visit you inside when I can, all right?'

Maybe she's thought of it and I didn't have to tell her I knew. Jeez, maybe!

I didn't let myself sound hopeful. 'Yeah, all good Teens. Brave woman. I think we're getting close to time now, but. I gotta go. The system's got me on the bed, Teens. The needles are coming. Gotta say bye for now, okay?'

'Okay, Nate. Yep, bye for now. But we're gonna get you out, okay? You hang tough babe! Okay?'

'Yeah, course Teens. I'll be—'

Shit! I do know that voice but it ca—

It was my last random thought before I felt a needle going in my arm an' everything faded away. Fair enough, in a way, I mean, the ironic-ness was that in a very big fuckoff no two ways about it kinda way, they were right. It wasn't fair they didn't have to prove it though.

Tina – Nov 2096, Cornwall Estate, Akarana Island, Aotearoa Archipelago

Arrested? A-fucking-rrested? Jesus! Are they going to come after me now? Shit! The idiot!

Okay, it had been lame of me to ask what he'd done. I knew everything he'd done and I was fine with it. Fuck the corporate arseholes, they wouldn't feel the difference. He'd sworn black and blue to me there was no way he'd get caught. Bloody twit! Jesus, could they find out I'd used his handle?

Goddess! It had been so cringy watching him blather and blubber. Jeez! I knew he was a little ponce but it took me a long while to stop wincing after his holo disappeared. I bet he'd bloody well put his head between his knees and gone along with it when they arrested him. As much of a sweety as he was, he could be a giant blouse sometimes.

It definitely wasn't fair what they'd done. That I could get behind. That's what had made me mad in a way I never had been before. First, I'd been so panicked my knees had turned to jelly and I'd flopped down outside his door and cried with his holo-ghost looking down at me.

I don't think I believed he was really going to prison. I think I was more worrying because of the weed, and maybe that they'd come after me now too. But the bloody injustice of it! I couldn't shake the anger!

After a while, this awful chill had gone up my spine. I wasn't really listening to what he said, but his voice! It was like he was reading out his will or something. I looked up at his holo-ghost and he looked scared for his life. And I'd thought, *shit! It's really happening. Someone I know is going to prison.*

My mind looped pointlessly for a while on: *oh, Nate, You idiot! What have you gone and done?* And then, as if from nowhere in my soul, anger boiled up. It was kind of cold, hard anger and I knew that moment it was divine anger.

Nobody said spiritual stuff was always going be nice. This was a test and the goddess was sending me sacred rage to strengthen me for the trials I would soon face. I'd read about this kind of thing happening in the ancient e-texts in the library virtual space.

I knew Nate was sorry he'd made me cry, poor little nancy that he was. If he'd been in front of me in the flesh, I think he would have pulled me up and given me one of his giant hugs to make himself feel better, not that I'd have complained since he was a good hugger.

But I couldn't afford to think about that. The rage was filling me up, toughening me up. Nate was right about what I must do. That and so much more. Not for why he said though. But to get the wankers back. All of them. The corporations, the rich families, the lot.

It was probably the last time I'd see the poor guy so I didn't tell him that. I told him that yeah, of course I'd do it. And I meant it too, with every gram of my soul.

He looked a bit confused but his voice was chilled out and back to normal, when he spoke again and we finally said good-bye. I'd given him that much at least, some comfort.

Ew! Fuck! Needles.

That had creeped me out, the way his holo-ghost had… cut out like that. The idea of him going limp right behind the door I was leaning against.

Ugh!

Though I'd nearly broken down again and only my new cold rage had kept me calm, I couldn't believe there was no five second warning or… anything. He was suddenly gone, and I was alone.

I kicked his door and went back to my place with a sore toe.

The dishwasher was finished when I got in which was good because it was about time for a clean mug. I made a fresh cup of Instant™ and turned the J™ back on. I vaped it all and refilled it twice but the goddess wouldn't come back.

I woke in dim grey dawn light with a couple of roaches on each leg. My neck was sore from sleeping propped on the wall.

Must've passed out.

Ad-light on the edges of my eyes and the grey square of my window blurred into comet-trails when I moved my head, which was how I knew I'd maybe gone a bit over with the BudLike™. Rubbing my neck, I got a clean mug from the dishwasher and mixed up a cup of Instant™ that was practically syrup, I'd put so much powder in.

Man! For an espresso, one espresso is all I want…

I shook my head angrily. Espressos were for ponces. My J™ was lying on my desk beside half a bag of BudLike™ but I decided against that, too, at least until a bit later when I was fully straight again.

It was the start of my off-time so I fired in an order for pancakes and syrup then let PrimeFlixK-Bell-Pharm's ad virtual grow up around me so I could taste and smell what my breakfast might have been like a century ago, before the drone showed up with the real shitty deal. The virtual had my stomach dissolving itself by the time the signal came but my bladder had also started a mutiny and I took a couple of minutes to decide not to keep the drone waiting, which made it worse.

Usually, the smell of rotting fake carpet and damp in the hall would have been enough to get me whinging about how unfair it was we lived in these death traps. But the BudLike™ helped me let it all slide and I calmly walked to the poor-door through the pinky-blue flicker of ads trying to pull me into their virtual spaces. I got my boxes off the drone and shuffled back inside because by then I was starting to leak.

I dumped the boxes on the floor and did a hard left into the toilet. A few seconds felt like a bloody hour as I tried to get my pants down then finally, I reached out and touched cracked and grimy tiles and all life's shit disappeared in the blessed golden tinkle of delayed gratification.

The door kept auto-closing and I kept having to ping it back open so it kind of detracted from my pleasure. I ignored the warnings from my tech as the smell of ammoniacal coffee rose around me, more like Instant™'s original inspiration on the way out, than when it bloody well went in.

I don't need fucking tech to tell me I need a glass of water.

The weed must have been wearing off by then. A tiny thrill of fear shivered through me when the door closed completely as I wiped myself dry. I screwed my face up against the panic and finished wiping as I stood and pinged it open with a corner of my mind.

I stood with my bum nearly touching the opposite wall and a leg stretched out to block the doorway as I waited for my hands to dry under my crappy dryer before losing patience and wiping them on my hemps. Back out in the apartment, I breathed out then tensed up again when the toilet door melted closed behind me.

I should hack it to-like, never close or something!

But Nate was all weird about pooing in private so…

Oh shit! Nate! Oh Fuck! Oh fuck! Oh FUCK!

How could I have forgotten? Jesus! How? I eyed my J™ reproachfully then picked it up, refilled it with Budlike™ and turned it on. I needed to think.

Both wanting and not wanting to see what they'd done to Nate, I wondered if I'd be able to look through his window from the alleyway.

It can't be that easy!

But I felt so bad about forgetting what had happened, I decided to try anyway. The wind had stopped and the faint roar of the AC came through the window. The alleyway was damp like always but up high I saw the walls were starting to dry so I risked going out without my overs.

I took my J™ with me and headed out the poor-door then over to the alley entrance. Barely a step past my window, a coughing fit overcame me from the gross smell the AC was blowing out. I recovered, took another step and was forced to a gut-wrenching halt, dropping my J™ and nearly puking up my instant™. My body locked up and a grainy crappy virtual slammed up around me with some kind of massive old-school security door and a red sign saying RESTRICTED AREA.

I thought of going around the building and trying from the other end but I knew it would be the same. The authorities didn't want anyone seeing the shit they did to people. Plus, my breakfast was waiting.

You knew all that anyway, you idiot.

Back inside I ate my pancakes bathed in syrup. It was a magically crappy thing PrimeFlixK-Bell-Pharm did with food; it really was. When I opened the bioboxes, my stack was steaming hot, golden brown and smelled like in the ads. But Nate had shown me their crafty bit of CGI that triggered when the lid came off.

They tried to keep up the lie as I ate but the way all foods melted into the same pooey mush in my mouth as it would be when it came out of my bottom, not to mention the gross almond, fake nut and chemical (fucking™) aftertaste, never failed to give the game away. Still, at least I was full.

I poured the leftover syrup into my half-finished mug of instant™ and threw the bottle into the bioboxes on the floor. They started dissolving, the nanites wafting under my doorcrack to find their way back out the poor-door. The doorway would probably be encrusted with them at this time of the morning, as they waited to swarm all over the next delivery drone and ride back to PrimeFlixK-Bell-Pharm's warehouse.

Nate… I'll visit you…

Until yesterday Nate and I hadn't so much as seen a cop before, well, I hadn't anyway; Nate with his, uh, background, might have. But going to their station? Visiting someone in stasis? I had no clue!

As my last J™ wore off, the situation crashed in on me. My flat felt smaller and smaller and I started to panic. I made another cup of instant™. It woke me up a bit but didn't stop the walls from closing in.

I had to talk to someone but the only people I knew...

Chen? Shane? Cherie? The other twerp in their terrible band? Fuck!

...were all Nate's bloody friends if not his fucking exes.

I knew Chen the best, sadly. I was pretty sure she was only nice to me because she wanted to get back with Nate.

'Tina?'

Fuck!

She was standing right in front of me. Or more to the point, I was sitting in the air behind her. I must have pinged the bloody contact a bit too hard.

Fuck and shit!

I was hovering over an epic pile of dirty laundry in her bedroom and there was more piled up on the end of her bed. I could smell weed in the air, real weed the bloody show-off. Chen was half naked with only underwear on and she'd turned around from her posh dresser with a J™ in her hand.

Her wannabe-rich-fuck-long hair was plastered to one cheek like she'd rolled out of bed which anyone in their right mind would have, this time on an off-day; if she was on an off-day. I'd have only been getting up now if it hadn't been for me passing out stoned in the wrong position and waking up sore. So fair enough.

Jesus! Why didn't she hold her calls till she was bloody dressed though?

I couldn't help staring at her external tech. She had it set to wrap around her body like ribs from a sea creature or something like that, from... when there were some.

Gross!

The ribs stopped at her neck where the tech turned into the stems of plants. Cheesy leaves and flowers with the shitty grey-blue tinted dark colours only state-issued tech could achieve, moved on her face like they were supposed to be swaying. It looked as if she had a custom-shaped fucking infection spreading over her.

I decided I probably should tell her what had happened. She wouldn't know any better than me what to do but she was Nate's friend too.

Not like I can hang up anyway. That would only be weirder.

But I wouldn't be all pathetic about it. Most women got all strange at times like this. All tearful and panicky and stuff. I had to be cool.

'Chen,' I said. 'Nate's gone to prison. He's gone to prison! I can't believe the idiot got himself arrested! He went out for his stupid walk yesterday and then next thing I knew he was locked in his flat and I was his one call! And we couldn't finish talking, they just… they just…' My voice had got shriller and shriller, then I broke down. The virtual of Chen's room flickered as I floundered around on my bed trying to find something to wipe my eyes with.

'I'm coming over,' Chen said, and cut the call.

She lived in our block in the same building the gross AC was stuck to. But she had a much flasher job than Nate's and mine because they gave her a second floor flat with the bedroom separate from the kitchen.

One reason I didn't have female friends was that women were all dumb and girly about tidying all the time. Nate never cared how my flat looked. Swearing, I unstacked the dishwasher and shoved dirty clothes into the drawers under my bed.

Most of it was cleared by the time Chen pinged, a few minutes later. She was wearing black overs covered in patches, like most people had except Nate with his dodgy ones.

Her hood was peeled back and the legs and arms open so I could see her supple little wrists and ankles.

It's nearly December, I suppose.

I thought she was being a bit hopeful though; it might have been warmer but that didn't mean it was dryer. She opened her arms and I suddenly felt weirded out and flinched.

Then she put on this wounded expression and walked in and surveyed my bed complete with hems sticking out of drawers.

'Man, Teens, you tidied on an off-morning; I'm guessing it's an off-morning for you, right? That's keen anyway! Bloody hell I don't think I've done any washing for a fortnight, you should see..., well, you did see my room.'

She sounded like she meant it but I couldn't think of any other reason she'd say something like that other than to take the mick out of my crappy flat; given hers was so much better.

Well, you didn't have to come over!

But that was the thing with other women, they were crafty. They said things they didn't mean, only to be mean. And you couldn't call them on it without looking like a dork because they'd pretend they didn't know what you meant. *...Oh, Teens, no! I mean it! Really hun! You've got the place looking so lovely!*

That's what I liked about Nate and all my male friends. We were straight with each other.

'Nǐ *hǎo* Chen! God, thanks so much for coming over! It's so good to see ya! Do you want a J™ or some instant™ or something? And sorry the place is such a shambles! I should really uh, sort my life out.'

Shambles? Did I really say shambles? Jeez! Where the fuck did that come from? It sounds like something my arsehole mother would say!

'I'm, uh, okay thanks.' She looked confused for some reason and kept standing in the kitchen, probably because I was on the bed and apart from the toilet there wasn't really anywhere else to go.

'Teens, uh, Nate...?' she questioned.

Oh, yeah. My boyfriend, the love of your life, why you really came over.

'I, uh, I dunno what to tell ya, Chen. He said they put him away for no reason. I can't get in his door or anything.'

Did she just look.... pained?

'Have you tried...?' She nodded towards the window.

'Ya can't go down there any more. It kinda locks you out.'

She was quiet for a while then said, 'Fuck.' She sat in my work chair.

Sure. Have a seat.

Why was I being such an arsehole in my mind?

'So, he's, uh, he's basically through that wall.' She pointed at my kitchen cupboards.

The usual me would've at least cracked a joke about being a genius or something but, post-stoned and tired as I was, I only nodded. Then my head suddenly felt so heavy my neck could barely hold it up any more.

Chen went quiet then and I could tell by her eyes that she was on her tech. After a while she said, 'Well, it looks like there's meant to be transcripts of the arrest and stuff and there's a shitload of them there for recent cases. Nate's one's there but you can't go into it, it's got some kind of lock on it, some shit to do with public interest or something.'

'Jeez, Chen, how did ya find that shit?'

I hoped she couldn't see how much I wanted to slug her one, then. I knew I was being an idiot. But the picture of them talking about all the tech stuff they were into, curled up on her bed as they probably would have been when they were to-gether, had popped up in my mind. I could hardly control my-self.

'Teens! You okay?'

'Yeah. Well. No. I mean, my boyfriend is in prison, like…' I snapped my fingers, 'that! Gone! It's not fair Chen. He didn't do noth… I mean, he's not a bad guy. He helped peeps an' that. He doesn't deserve to have his brain damaged for trying to help people. And anyway, he said that wasn't why they put him away. He said they don't know about any of his... stuff. He said they jacked up charges right there while he watched. It's not fair Chen!'

Not fair you're smart like him. Not fair you were with him longer than me. Not fair you're a cute little mèimei with tits that defy gravity and skin that never fucking dies. Not fair you can… could talk tech with him and be interesting to him like I never will be. Well you could be… No! I couldn't! I won't!

I had to hand it to myself, my tears and anger weren't a lie. I was being honest with her about how I felt. Maybe not exactly why. But in the end, me being all weird like that wasn't fair on Chen. Nate had chosen me. It didn't matter if she wanted to get back with him or not, he was with me.

Chen showed no trace of caring about me going critical behind my closed face; not that she knew, I supposed. 'Do you really believe they do that, Tina? All that stuff about brain-washing an' that? I mean, for all we know he's not in there. You can't get to the window. His tech's firewalled. They might've taken him somewhere and, I dunno, hidden him or something.'

'Well then why block off the alleyway? Plus Nate said there was proof. He said he was in there when he called any-way. Surely that's proof enough—'

'Yeah, yeah, I know. Believe me, I know about his, uh, theories. Some people come out messed up but Spume have explained those cases—'

'Explained them away you mean. An' all them ones that come out okay are rich-fucks on pissy three-week sentences or whatever. They're the ones that're probably put in some fancy apartment to reflect on themselves, smoking premium real weed and eating vegetables. I think Nate's right. I think it's probably worse than he says. They probably do experiments on wet-foots like us who nobody's gonna miss and who can't afford to sue their arses for wrecking our heads and—'

Then I realised her face'd gone blank. Kind of scary blank; like she was trying to pretend not to be... Angry?

Well it's not my fault he got arrested!

Then her face unstuck and she said in a normal voice, 'Then we've gotta make sure Nate is missed don't we. We've gotta find a way of visiting him or something, or at least seeing if he's really in there. Look, you can't see all the details but you can see some. This woman *jǐngchá* supposedly arrested him and handled the sent—'

Then she looked at me and, apparently, back at her tech and got a really weird look on her face.

She finished in an absent kind of voice. 'Why don't we... look her up?'

I let Chen pull me into the virtual she'd found. Police Department.

Why isn't it called the jǐngchá department? You know why… No!

She was talking sense the way bloody Nate would have if he'd been here. It shouldn't have annoyed me but I couldn't help it.

'Look up a *jǐngchá*? Are you fuckin' mental?'

'Well, they shit like the rest of us don't they? Look at her, she looks about our age. She's probably a trainee; if they bother to train 'em nowadays. She probably thinks she's rebelling against Mummy and Daddy not working for their corporate or something. Maybe we can get her stoned and make her tell us what happened.'

'I, uh, I dunno,' I said.

'Eh?'

'I don't know if it's a good idea to, uh, find, uh, the cop. I mean, what if it makes them, I dunno, start surveillance on us or something?'

Chen gave me this weird frown and said, 'who gives a shit? I haven't broken the law, have you?'

Of course I hadn't. I was scared of them. Of them… watching me.

'Well, I, uh, used Nate's handle to—'

'Yeah, yeah to get into the library, right? Old news Teens. Half the world uses Nate's shell handles to get into the library, that's the whole point of them being shell handles; dead-end aliases. If the cops or the corporates did notice, it'd lead them nowhere anyway, definitely not to him.'

'So he says. Didn't stop him getting busted though, did it.'

Fuck! I should have pretended I didn't have a clue what she was talking about! Shit!

'There is that,' she said. 'But I think we should find out what happened anyway.'

I sighed. 'Okay.'

I didn't like it but I couldn't think of any sane reason not to do it. Then she prattled away. 'Okay, good. I'll talk to the *jǐngchá*. You find out about how we visit him or find out where he is or whatever. There's links all over their virtual, there's gotta be something in there somewhere.'

Phew.

We shared a cup of Instant™ and a J™ after all but she didn't stay for long. It seemed as if she was getting stressed about something. I was half expecting her to appear in the alleyway outside my window to check out my story and I laughed at myself when it annoyed me that she didn't. Why couldn't she be the arsehole I wanted her to be? Why had Nate bloody dumped her for me?

Although we were both stoned, she'd probably gone straight back home to try and get in touch with the cop. So, I decided I wasn't going to let her make me look like an idiot whatever it took. Never mind if it took thinking in a way that made me start… remembering. She wasn't going to bloody show me up!

As I got back into the Police virtual, my anger stirred at how much letting my thoughts run like this felt like… relaxing. I pushed aside my feelings and forced myself to focus. The virtual was all set up like some kind of office building so you could look at the little index plaque on each floor and ask the interfaces at the reception desks for information.

I found the arrest record Chen had shown me but there was nothing leading off it to anything prison-related. I went through all the floors and none of the plaques had anything useful. I went to the virtual's home and asked the main reception which I should have done to start with, really.

This should be easy! Why wouldn't they make it easy?

But the main reception said it had nothing related and offered me all the annoying options I'd already looked at. I told it I didn't want them but it kept offering them to me.

I said none of them worked and after being sent in circles for ages, I felt a chill down my spine when the message read TOO MANY SEARCHES, PLEASE VISIT LOCAL STATION TO ENQUIRE IN PERSON. It logged me off and a message came in simultaneously with the station address and that's when I knew what was going on...

...Nate was righter than he knew, we'd been taught how... No! Stop!

Unwanted memories started surfacing. I knew it had been a dumb idea to let myself think that way. The whole thing had discombobulated me, all for nothing. Were they going to bust me for trying to hack them when all I did was search their public virtual? It wasn't fair!

After the poncy virtual receptionist's voice, the quiet crashed in on me. A couple of roaches wriggled in the leftover Instant™ mush at the bottom of Chen's mug, and pink and blue ads flashed in the corners of my eyes. The alleyway was getting dark and the rain had started again, not too heavy today. I could hear the AC over it.

I felt a headache starting so I refilled my J™ with the last of the Budlike™ and vaped it all up but it didn't work. It made it worse. I knew I'd never see Nate's face again, no matter what Chen and I did to try to get him out.

My stomach growled and anger blew up from nowhere inside me. Suddenly I couldn't stand eating any more shit fake food. Only it was all I could bloody afford and I was hungry. Or was I hungry if I didn't want to eat? I checked my balance and saw I had savings; derisory ones but some at least. Enough for chewable food.

Fuck it.

I ordered a new bag of Budlike™ and a REAL(*) vegetable-curry-for-two, from PrimeFlixK-Bell-Pharm. That pretty much blew me back to zero.

Well, not like I was going to save up for a penthouse. Maybe I should just... go back... No!

I could probably ask work for an advance but payday was only a day or so away and I could survive on the curry leftovers and Instant™ till then.

Nate would have laughed if he'd seen me but for the first time in my, like, life, I felt like I needed to stretch my legs, as he would've put it. I put on my overs and went into the hall. I was about to head straight for the poor-door and watch the drones till my meal arrived but ended up turning left instead.

Nate's door looked like it always did but I felt the difference when I pinged. I might as well have been trying to log on to a vintage concrete wall. It didn't register as tech-enabled any more. It was like trying to connect to the old AC in the alleyway, there was nothing. I stood staring at the door for a while. I couldn't believe he was in there.

My head throbbed and the walls closed in. My heart started pounding and my breath hissed in my ears. I turned and raced away, trying to keep my eyes ahead and not jump every time an ad pushed legal line-of-sight limits. The hall always smelled wet and mouldy but today it was worse and my stomach was heaving by the time I got outside. The rain had worsened so I signalled my overs to seal then tried to calm down while I waited.

The Budlike™ drone turned up first and I beat myself up about not having brought the J™. But it wasn't long before the PrimeFlixK-Bell-Pharm arrived, then I managed to get back inside without another attack.

Nate and I should have been settling in with a pizza and arguing about which movie to go into by now. Maybe some of his friends would virtual in and I could do a bit of harmless flirting with Shane after Nate passed out halfway through.

What did I do before I met him?

It had only been eighteen months or something. ...*Yeah, nah worries, ya can borrow mine, that'll exterminate the little fuckers enough to give ya a bit of time to get new ones...* And he'd stayed for a J™ after all the roaches had been eaten by his nanites and carried off to the poor-door for collection, probably to turn up back again as pizzas.

So romantic...

I couldn't help smiling as I opened the REAL(*) vegetable-curry-for-two. It was the first time in a very long time I'd spent so much on something like that; it was the kind of boring food Nate wasted his dodgy points on. If it hadn't been for all this... shit happening, I might have felt excited. Or more excited anyway. Only inside the box was...

What?

…another box with tacky leafy designs on it. It was big but completely pointless. I opened it and inside were two more boxes and a tech trigger that surprise-attacked with a stupid virtual about the growing process of the vegetables in the hydroponics wrack-space. That was probably to distract the gullible buyer from the fact that the two boxes together were only about one meal's worth.

Lying wankers!

It did taste better in the end, a bit. Or… maybe there wasn't so much aftertaste. I was fairly sure there wasn't. I mean, it wouldn't have been that expensive for such a little amount if there wasn't some real food in it, would it? And it probably was filling, if I maybe, waited for it to go down properly so my stomach would stop rumbling. I decided not to open the second one so I'd have something to eat in the morning.

Maybe I should have watched a movie. Nate would have wanted me to get on with my life. But I ended up staring at the kitchenette and imagining him with tubes coming out of him and needles sticking in his arms and breathing machines and all… gross things. After a while, the bitterness that wouldn't leave my mouth got me thinking maybe the curry was less of the REAL more of the fucking… bracket-asterisk-bracket and all that entailed.

Arseholes.

All of them. Every single fucking one of them. The bullshit government that did nothing. The disgusting rich families and their bloody corporates. All of them. It wasn't fair. I couldn't think about the goddess that night. Did that make me bad? I went to bed without another J™.

Chen – Nov 2096, Cornwall Estate, Akarana Island, Aotearoa Archipelago

I wished Nate hadn't told me all the shit about Tina. I'd struggled to look her in the eye. I'd struggled not to bloody scream after her bullshit about hating the rich. The only thing that'd stopped me giving her a piece of my fuckin' mind was why she'd done what she had. I got why she was hyper-bloody-vigilant. I got why she'd run away. You didn't have to be poor to be messed up; although it helped.

Jesus, though. With her desperately fake street-talk or whatever it was she was trying to do a fuckin' impression of, and all the crap about the cops, my sympathy had tipped over into, *if I don't get out of here soon, I'm gonna fuckin' smack her one!*

Jeez! She was a self-absorbed little cunt, was what she was. *Okay, calm down, Chen.*

I couldn't believe Nate had ditched me for her. Well, okay, that wasn't fair. I mean, it wasn't like I was anything special, only a wet-foot who got slightly luckier than the other wet-foots, like a roach that made it 'round the U-bend before the flush. Except most days, it felt like the flush had come as I'd seen the light at the top of the bowl. And now I was clinging on trying not to get eaten away by fragrant sewerage processing tech or torpedoed by treacherous melting poo-bergs.

Anyway, he didn't get with her for like, two years afterwards or something so it wasn't like he left me for her. Or that he wasn't sure. But I couldn't stop wishing I knew why he'd dumped me. It'd been basically it's not me it's you if I'd understood his tearful apology right, poor little nancy. He was sorry he left me because I was what? Too intelligent? Sheesh! Nobody was more intelligent than bloody him.

I sighed as I peeled back my overs hood and let the drizzle try and fail to clear my head on my way back home; another Nate habit. Maybe I shouldn't have tried to stay buds with him after we broke up. Maybe all the shit I watched online was true and it could never work.

It'd been nearly four years and I wasn't over the guy. Any day now, I was waiting to hear the news she'd gone mental and strangled him while he slept or something. I couldn't believe I felt protective of him when it was me that was getting the bloody bruising each time I saw him put his arm 'round her waist and her pull away 'cause she was too pathetic to show him any fuckin' affection at all in front of anyone.

Well, or maybe at all at-all, if I'd guessed right. I'd met people like her before on my scholarship, fucked-up little psychos who met a soul-mate every other week. They blew hot and cold until the constant sudden temperature changes finally shattered the soulmate to drifting piles of whimpering ex. Oh-wait, kind of like me after Nate'd dumped me and found his next soulmate…

Okay, okay! Jesus! Stop it, Chen, you idiot! Stop it!

What was the point anyway? Nate was in prison now. Actually in prison. I'd had enough of my family put inside to know what happened. Nate was right, it didn't matter if he got out, he'd never really get out.

My sister Craig was inside for six months for punching a delivery drone and now she couldn't talk or feed herself. My dad'd gone inside for a year and died there after ten years. That was after my mum tried to stab him and claimed he'd punched her when he grabbed her arm to save his life; I could see a lot of her in Tina, FFS, 'Tina', now I thought about it in light of what Nate'd told me about her.

If there was any chance of getting Nate out with his *năozĭ* intact it'd have to be now. If, uh, Tina didn't do something soon, I'd have to try. I could start looking up stuff anyway, maybe chance getting in touch with my family, the fuckin' subject matter experts themselves; unlikely they'd talk to me though. And I'd get hold of the cop, somehow, to see if I could find out more about what'd happened.

And now the poor guy'd made himself into a human test subject for the theory of raw nanites we'd been working on, well, I'd have to carry on the work. Except of course, I remembered then, I had bloody work-work for fifteen days straight from tomorrow so I'd have to squeeze my illicit fucking 'round in around my exhaustion. Plus, without Nate's power-*năozĭ* it was probably a bit of a lost cause.

Tina's evil fake weed had given me a sore throat so I drank a glass of water when I got home and went into Jamie Yang's space to watch all the drama about yet more quakes off the coast. It was kind of spooky seeing all the white water. But, well, what could you do? Climb a building if there was a bad one?

I decided I'd give it a few days then ping, uh, Tina about Nate again. If she hadn't done anything, I'd… I didn't know what I'd do. Something. I'd do something.

I opened my iSpotTunes, audio only so I'd be able to drop off. *Xiàhĕndà deyŭ* was my poppy guilty-pleasure who I'd never've admitted to anyone I'd been thrashing for the last year. But she, well, the code that'd generated 'her' voice anyway, did have a decent, uh, voice. Even if all 'her' tracks, well, made you fall asleep.

Trying not to admit to myself that I knew the lyrics as I sang along, I broke open a pack of ClearEyes™ and necked one with a cup of Instant™ to start flushing the weed out of my system. Then, basically un-recuperated from my previous twenny-one days on, completely unprepared for my upcoming fifteen days on and with an actual non-entity wailing directly

into my auditory channels about lurve, I went to bed early and
willed sleep to come.

Tina – Nov 2096-early Dec 2096, Cornwall Estate, Akarana Island, Aotearoa Archipelago

I woke feeling pretty all right-ish. It happened like that sometimes and I could never work it out. The caffeine in Instant™ was meant to be bad for sleep. Maybe I hadn't drunk as much as I normally did yesterday. Nate always burbled on about exercise being good for sleep too, but… lalalalalala. And arse! My usual tiredness was probably only sleep deprivation.

I had two more days off work now, then a grotty nine days on. But still, two more days to eat junk food, smoke weed, chillax and not log on to stupid work once. Two days to vegetate. I rolled over and watched the sunlight moving over the wall. I felt myself going to sleep again after a while, the best feeling.

What did I have to do again? Whatever…

My eyes closed as the high-up bright went grey and the first gust fluffed down the alleyway.

Typical. Not like I'll be going out in it though.

When I woke the second time, I was surprised the sun was out again. I felt more alert but I didn't get up. The sun might have been out but the wind was really up. The AC was shaking on the wall, vibrating away.

Vibrating… vibrating… mmmm…

I decided I could do with a bit of off-day vibrating and wished Nate wasn't lying right next to me so I could get on with it. If I could get rid of him somehow, maybe say I left something at his place... I rolled over and put out a hand and that's when I realised he wasn't there.

Jesus.

Was he making up for his stupid failed walk yesterday or something? Or...

Oh fuck! Nate!

I'd forgotten! Again!

...Jeez, Teens. You gotta stop vapin' so much...

Well, what the fuck else could I do to get a decent night's sleep? I couldn't do that stupid waking up inside your dreams thing he... claimed he could do.

I threw off the duvet and sat on the side of the bed, suddenly angry at Nate for fucking lecturing me. My tech decided I'd had enough peace then and the ads started up for the day. I could see a bunch of work-spam waiting and dimmed it out for my days off. But there was a message from Chen, too.

Oh fuck! And I was meant to tell Nate's parents!

It had been two days since he'd been put in stasis now and I hadn't got in touch with his parents as I'd promised him I would. What would I say to them when they asked why I'd taken so long? I'd do it later. Chen would probably have got in touch with the cop by now and I'd done nothing!

Then I remembered the police virtual and how it had taken me round in circles and kicked me out. But I couldn't go to their grotty station. Not now. I was too annoyed. I'd do it tomorrow, I decided. One job off the list.

That left me back at getting in touch with Nate's parents. *Shit.*

I was going to need weed for that. I opened my new bag of Budlike™ and packed the J™. I got a cup of Instant™ ready and decided to have pancakes again. But my order didn't go through because – I'd forgotten – I was nearly out of cash. *Bum!*

I took a big mouthful of Instant™ and nearly jumped out of my skin when it practically scalded the roof off my mouth. I put the mug down too hard and splashed the box on my desk.

Ah yeah, that's right.

My second box of REAL(*) vegetable-curry-for-two hadn't cooled but it had gone all soggy and gross. I started eating it anyway but I only got halfway through before it suddenly got too bitter to eat and that's when I saw the sides of the box had started to melt into the food and vice versa.

'Fucking CUNT!' I screamed at it and threw it on the floor.

Green sludge splattered like infected vomit all over my… beautiful modern floor. The box started melting into the mess faster since it knew it had been thrown away. The pile shrank and PrimeFlixK-Bell-Pharm's nanites started trailing to the door before I had time to throw myself on the bed and start bawling into my pillow. It had bloody passed its use-by right while I was eating it!

I might have slept again, I couldn't remember. The light changing made me look up and I saw the alleyway had darkened so the clouds must have come back in, finally. My stomach was, like, simultaneously hungry and upset at the biobox and food mixture I'd accidentally eaten. I had public medical but it would send me into debt for the diagnosis, so I decided not to call up the tech and let my body handle it naturally; which was how the goddess would have willed it anyway.

I felt hungrier knowing I wouldn't be able to get any food till I got paid. Unlike the PrimeFlixK-Bell-Pharm muck, the spilled Instant™ didn't clean itself up. I estimated there was about another week and half before I was due the monthly nano-clean on my miserly accommodation plan. There was no way I could waste water now my balance was nearly zilch, so I pulled a dirty top out of my drawer and wiped the table down with it.

I finished off the mug and made another then vaped away at the J™ and felt calm spreading through me. It wasn't the goddess' calm. I knew she wouldn't come when I was feeling like this. But that was all right. I needed to relax now, enough to face the toilet.

My bowels had suddenly gone weird, more than normal morning weird. It was probably the biobox stuff I'd eaten, already poisoning me. I didn't know how long I'd be so I wheeled my stupid office chair over to block the doorway and took my J™ with me. I heard the rain start as I sat down and though I wouldn't be going outside, it killed the day.

I spent the rest of the morning drinking Instant™, vaping fake weed and trying not to worry about what I'd say to Nate's parents. Late afternoon, I packed the J™ yet again and saw my new bag was a third empty already.

I was so stoned my eyes were nearly rolling out of my skull. I'd vaped a lot, even for me. I started thinking I should slow down. Nate would have taken the J™ off me by now, and hidden it down his pants or something.

He was always good at things like that, calming me down when I needed it, hyping me up when I needed it, telling me too much, not enough.

How did I manage without the dopey sod?

But that thought annoyed me. Of course I'd bloody managed without him. I didn't need a man to look after me. That was a trap for young players. I'd read about it in the library. The goddess managed the god. That was how it was meant to work.

Men were strong and quick but they were dumb and too narrow-minded, too. Women had to channel their energy, do all the thinking, all the seeing the bigger picture. That was how it had worked in the twentieth century before the rich fucked it all up letting men marry men and women marry women and adopt babies and freakish crap like that.

I might have been on my bed or standing in the middle of the room, I didn't remember. But I definitely remembered the vision I had then. I was sure it was sent by the goddess. The weed must finally have calmed me down enough so I could be properly open to her.

It was as if I could see back in time to the nineteen-fifties. The women all did their hair like a queef had blown a path up their fringes and men did theirs like the wind only blew one way. I don't how I knew that, which was proof the goddess sent it to me.

I watched the women with lips painted up like face-vag's getting lunches ready for their kids and husbands looking all smiley and dumb but really planning the whole family and the whole of society. It was how things were meant to be. It wasn't supposed to be like now where all the rich slept with anything that moved and didn't have any marriages and brought their kids up to think it didn't matter if you had a vagina or a penis. And told us we should do the fucking same! That was why what had happened to me, happened. Because rich people thought anything was okay.

They were selfish and disgusting and this was the goddess's way of reminding me I had a sacred mission. I had a movement to start and Nate was key, no matter that he was only a man. He believed the same as I did. He knew his place. He always told me how much smarter than him I was. He wanted me to take care of him as only a woman could.

It was black outside when I woke up and the ads had left my eyes. Wind was shrieking down the alleyway, whipping rain across my window so hard it nearly turned me on with a little shiver of fear. It was a bad storm. A… *stonker*, Nate would have called it. I was fully in bed, under the duvet and everything, and I couldn't remember how I got there. But I remembered the vision.

Another sign from her. I remembered what she needed me to remember…

Afraid my ads would start and take ages to die down again, I rolled over and tried to relax. It usually didn't work but maybe tonight the goddess was on a roll with sending me what I needed. I was asleep again before I finished getting comfortable.

Nathan – late Nov 2096-late Jan 2097,

Spume Prison Stasis, Cornwall Estate,

Akarana Island, Aotearoa Archipelago

It was like I'd had a massive session on some premo weed the night before. My head felt like it was full of that fire-stopping fluff they put inside walls. My eyes slowly opened and they should've got wet but they didn't, though there was rain everywhere. And everything was blue.

I know that blue… Don't I? Maybe I don't. But I… Nah. I don't.

I was that chilled I didn't want to move in case the chilledness went away. But after a while, my head tried lifting off my pillow anyway. 'Cept it turned out there was no pillow and I wasn't lying down. I was already standing up. Or, I was kinda, up, anyway. There was no pillow and no bed and no nothing.

There was rain falling from blue space and down into blue space and when I looked out through it, there was more blue space into infinity. In all directions.

I was hanging in the rain, in space. Not exactly hanging 'cause there wasn't a string or anything. I was more-like floating. And though I'd started looking 'round, the chilled feeling stayed.

Where am I?

'Oi! Hello? Anyone home? Where am I?'

No answer. The rain kept falling, straight down, no wind, no sound. I held out my hand and I could feel the drops but when I pulled it back it was dry. I looked down at myself and I was naked, or... Was I wearing something? I didn't fully know.

Where was I before this?

I couldn't remember. But the chilled feeling got stronger then, so I didn't think too hard about it, about any of it.

I looked out through the rain and watched the drops joining up on their way down, breaking apart into smaller ones, falling together, groups in a line, so heavy they were nearly like a tap, steam, spray, mist on the coast where I grew up.

Down went the water for hours, days, maybe years, till I started wondering if it was going down or I was going up. I looked up and saw blue with rain coming down on my face, not too cold, not too hot, never making me get wet, not smelling like anything.

I should probably've brought my overs.

Overs... Overs... I could imagine them like they were the only thing in the world, like an ad for overs with the model slowly turning 'round and growing the pouches, peeling back the hood over and over... Overs... Overs...

'PrimeFlixK-BellPharm, premo golden good brand, guaranteed, one-point-two thousand active units per fibre,' I said and my voice in the quiet rain cracked me up. 'PrimeFlixK-BellPharm, premo brand,' I said again and then the overs were gone. It wasn't that I couldn't think of them, it was more that I wasn't thinking of them any more. Or maybe hadn't been.

I know that blue... Don't I? Maybe I don't. But I... Nah. I don't. Hold on, what happened there... Nothing happened.

I looked slowly 'round at the blue and the rain. I watched the drops, counted 'em sometimes, wondered if it would ever stop and drifted, chilled, drifted. Might've been going up and the drops staying still. Might've been going down with 'em but there was nothing but blue below and the same above and all 'round me.

I made shapes in the rain like my mum and me used to do when she was sick 'cause it helped chill her out if she was getting one of her paranoid attacks. That's how I always used to know she was off her meds, when she started wanting to play the rain game. We used to go up to ground level and stand inside our poor-door and I used to play it with her and get her chilled enough to take 'em again.

The rain kept changing, big drops, small drops, misty drops and spray and I made my mum's face in the spray and I could see her then, bright and shining, smiling in the water before she fell away.

'Yyyyep,' I sighed. 'Clozapine-classic with extra calming formula an' an extra big J™ of Budlike™ for Daddy after a hard day in the virtual.' I smiled. It used to do the job, all right. When she remembered to take it. When he wasn't too wasted to help me sort her out.

More spray and I made her face again in the rain, and his beside it, holding his J™ and winking. And it all cracked me up. But only for a sec 'cause then they was gone and so was all my thoughts about them, breezed away on the chilled feeling that came down over me like sleepy steam so I didn't know what I'd been thinking.

I know that blue… Don't I? Maybe I don't. But I… Nah. I don't.
How long've I been here? What is this place?
'Oi!'

No answer. Only a warm wash of chilledness.

Didn't know if it was minutes or hours or days or what. I had a kinda idea that it might've been a while, that I'd been thinking stuff over, remembering stuff…

Forgetting stuff? Nah… It's all good.

But however long it was, after a while the blue started going dark, darker blue, purple, black and I chilled off to sleep.

It was getting light in the blue again when I woke up and wondered where I was.

I know that blue… Don't I? Maybe I don't. But I… Nah. I don't.

And I chilled. And I made faces in the rain and the steam and the spray. And I cracked myself up saying products out loud for each of the peeps before they disappeared and I forgot them again.

The chilledness washed over me in waves, warm and making everything all good and I would of drifted like that... forever. I would of, if I'd been anyone but me. And, maybe I... Would anyway, the chilledness felt so good and...

But Chen, Teens, Shane, the gig...

I saw their faces in the steam, blurry at first like I was seeing things but then stronger, clearer and I was trying to think of brands and stuff. But then under my feet there was a new feeling. Coolish air coming up or... Me going down? Then I could see it in the rain.

The drops turned into lines and the cold blew harder up my legs, through my body, over my face and I looked down and saw dark underneath me, coming up, up, up to take me. It got blacker and bigger like a dangerous dark crack in the chillful blue, opening up to swallow me. I started kicking and the chilledness didn't come to fix it and I fell faster and faster and the black opened up and pulled me down.

And just before the dark ate me up, an evil whisper I nearly couldn't hear went through my mind, 'Enjoy your visitor Mister Richards-Mann.'

Tina – Nov 2096, Cornwall Estate, Akarana Island, Aotearoa Archipelago

The rain was like hail on my Uber's windows and the wind was so strong I was worried I might get blown into another car. I'd had no Budlike™ and nothing to eat, only a few mugs of Instant™ to keep my appetite down. I was pretty sure today was payday but I hadn't checked my balance yet. I was going to treat myself to something nice-ish after I'd got at least one job done.

The station was close to my block in the end. I kind of liked that it was shit-brown. Weren't pigs meant to live in shit? Whatever a pig was. I remembered something like that anyway.

You remember... You know... No!

But when my Uber pulled under the carport, I suddenly started thinking it wasn't a great idea coming here. I'd never broken the law but there were probably laws most people broke without knowing they were breaking...

You know there are, you learned... No! Stop!

I clamped down on my mind, made myself stay in my real life.

The police probably can't help me anyway. I should probably go home and try the virtual again... Jesus! Grow a pair... of ovaries, woman! I am WOMAN!

I pelvic thrusted at the Uber as it headed to the road exit and stopped there for some reason. I bared my teeth and growled.

'Excuse me? Can I help you?'

The goddess was so with me again that morning because I made two awesome calls in a split second. I recognised the voice and sealed my overs hood as I turned to face the cop walking past the carport. Her hood was coming up over her black bun as she stepped out into the rain, so it was definitely her.

I fucking don't know her! She's an arsehole cop, that's all!

'Hello? Can I help you?'

I could tell she'd noticed me, knew something was up. I shook my head and walked up the stairs. I heard the Uber door seal behind me. Had it taken her a bit too long to get over to it? Had she stood there stalker-staring after me?

Who cares!

I walked through the station door.

Jesus! Her spoilt little poo-bum's going be on the same seat I sat on! Weird she hasn't got her own car. Maybe she's on some kind of university project.

But I knew she wasn't.

I was glad the smell of old – and probably now illegal – building stuff hit me as soon as I walked through the door. If it hadn't, I might've thought they'd done up the station like a broken-down shithole to mock all the wet-foot poor-fucks who went there all the time.

Ahead of me there was a disgustingly overweight cop jellied out on an actual reception desk behind some kind of shield.

Do they think we're going to try and eat them or something?

At the screen, I said, '*Kia ora*, how do I visit a prisoner?'

He didn't answer. I thought maybe he hadn't heard me then I noticed the skin wobbling on one of his hands and saw a greasy little finger had grown from somewhere in the lump of fat at the end of his arm. I looked where he'd pointed and I was about to give him an earful when I noticed the old three-lines symbol for a tech interface in faded paint on the screen, an actual hardware tech interface from the seventies before I was born!

I touched it and flinched away from the germs. Unexpectedly, it attached to my tech and brought up a grainy virtual of a white square with black marks and lines on it. I couldn't understand any of it at first then realised it was CGI'd paper!

"Scuse me, uh, what is this?'

'Visitation form.' I could barely hear him through the speaker – the old round speaker! – on the other side of the desk.

'Yeah but I don't understand it!' I lied. 'What's all these lines and symbols and stuff. How do I get the *hànzì* verson?'

He shrugged.

'Hello? I can't read this thing!'

'There's no *hànzì* version. You have to fill it out.'

'I can't fill it out! I can't understand it!'

Shut up and stop drawing attention to yourself. Fill out the form, leave…

He shrugged again and I could see his face change as he went off into tech land; probably a porn space given he was so fat! What else would a disgusting fat creep like that be looking at online if he wasn't ordering a takeout?

Filthy creep!

The distraction of hating on the corpulent pervert saved me from making a scene; as big a scene as I would have made if I'd lost control anyway. Of course I could understand the form, if I let myself. But the sorts of people who usually ended up here wouldn't have been able to. Giving him grief was the right thing to do.

I had it done in seconds but I couldn't help myself. Instead of leaving quietly after submitting the request, I said, 'Hey! *Jǐ ngchá!* Hey!' His eyes focused. 'There must be another way of doing this! Nobody can understand this sh— this writing nowadays! You must have the new form.'

'Citizen, if you want to make a complaint, you'll need to do a complaints form, it's on that same terminal you're at now under—'

Citizen. For fuck's sake!

'Ah, forget it.' Which was what they were counting on, of course.

He shrugged and his eyes lost focus again.

My god! That's disgusting!

I should have made a complaint, made the point. But I was getting nervous.

Fuck it.

I left, guiltily aware of how anyone else trying the same thing would have been screwed without an expensive bit of translation software. Or a free pirated version.

You'd think it would be free given voice translation works on every language. It's like they don't want poor people reading stuff!

I had overridden the 'relationship to client' – client my bum! – field and free-filled it because they only had rich-fuck shit like partner, sibling, parent and no 'girlfriend' which was what I was!

I was out of there in a blur and ordering brunch from my Uber before my heart had fully slowed. By the time I got half-way home, I was calm enough to notice Chen's message again.

Oops.

It turned out to be her on her bed next to some dirty laundry, waft of BO, stink of mildew as all our flats had. 'Hey Teens. Gimme a call. I spoke to the cop and, well, call me, okay.'

She looked sad so I guessed she hadn't got anywhere. It shouldn't have made me feel smug but it did. I called her back and when she answered, I wished she hadn't.

'Jeez Chen! If you're gonna hang 'round in your undies you could at least hold your bloody calls!'

Her head snapped 'round. 'Eh? Oh, Teens! Sorry, I'm catching up on work stuff. *Nǐ hǎo* anyway, how's it going? Did you get my message?' She didn't bother covering up though.

'Yeah, okay. I'm coming back from the *jǐngchá* station, the actual station, Chen! I didn't know there was one here till to-day!'

'Jesus! Are you all right? Did they drag you in or something?'

I told her about their crappy virtual and the form and I tried not to think about the female officer who'd called out to me.

'Man, Teens. That's fucked-up! It's like they don't want people to visit or something.'

'Now you're talking like Nate.'

She had the decency to blush.

'Well, it's in now anyway. It didn't say when they'd get back to me or anything. All we can do is wait I s'pose. But anyway, yeah, I got your message. What happened with the woman *jǐngchá?*'

'Well, I got hold of her easy enough, let's face it they're supposed to be public servants after all. But she basically shrugged me off. The only good bit was when I asked her why I couldn't see the arrest record and she went all red and said she wasn't allowed to discuss the case. But I could tell she was hiding something. And she was scared, Teens. I know I sound like Nate now but I think there's something off about this.'

The little shit couldn't stop looking pretty when she was upset! She covered one dainty little eye with her fingers and rested her chin on her girly little palm. Her tech mustn't have been doing anything much because her stupid plants were swaying smoothly on her face instead of jerking and freezing all the time.

Her child-sized fingertips massaged her forehead and she sighed. 'Well, anyway, I s'pose we can only wait and see what happens with the visit and, I dunno, keep… doing all the stuff Nate did, I guess. Do you know how to get people plugged in with Nate's points thing?'

'Yeah I reckon so,' I not-quite-lied.

'Okay, so we need to carry on his stuff! We gotta get people the food points, get them into the library, all that stuff he was doing.'

Suddenly exhaustion crashed in. When Nate wasn't geeking in the library space or doing his ludicrous exercise stuff, he'd spent all his spare time making friends with people online, then walking miles – fucking miles! – to save on Ubers and meeting up with them if they were on the island. He'd been blanking the nanites from, like, his own possessions so he could give his hacks to them and teach them how to use them. And then he stayed in touch with them all as if they were real friends!

The guy had a flock of gross alcoholic single mums wanting to get into his bloody pants. And all these creepy deadbeat men living in yucky smelly flats around the coasts wanting to be besties with him. Jesus! He could have run a dating service getting them all together and probably reuniting all the fathers with their neglected fucking children in the process.

There was no way I could do all that stuff like him, no way! I couldn't stand the thought of dealing with all those grotty people. …*But they wasn't born horrible Teens, I wasn't born horrible, right? You gotta start somewhere, you gotta enliften people an' that…*

It sounded good when he said it but when I'd met people with him, in virtual let alone real life, ugh! They'd made my skin crawl.

I'd have been willing to bet none of them had ever used the library handles. And they would have spent the dodgy points on evil flavoured industrial-biproduct alcohol drinks or awful fake weed. And their fucking spawn would stay hungry anyway. Nate didn't understand that all this bullshit drip-feeding people a bit of free food here and a bit of trying to get them to study there wasn't going to do anything.

We needed to find a way of taking it – all! – back from the rich, pulling the bastards down. …*Then what, Teens? Who's gonna run the show then? You? Me? Jeez, I haven't gotta clue about making up laws and building MagLevs and stuff. We gotta change what's already here and make it better…* I could never win an argument against the stubborn shit, but I knew I was right anyway. And Nate was in gaol now so where had all his good intentions got him? Nowhere!

Chen watched me and chewed her hair in this pouty kind of way that probably would have turned Nate on. She'd turned her chair to face me and I could see fraying threads on her bra and underpants which somehow made her prettier.

I couldn't believe she was single. Then I felt my cheeks go red because I realised I was staring at her and I didn't want her to think I was into her or something deviant like that. But I couldn't look away or she'd notice and ask me what was wrong.

'Jeez, Chen! Do you ever wear actual clothes?'

'Nah, not 'round the house if I can help it. Saves laundry money. Oh, hey Teens, did you tell Nate's folks? You know how he's always in touch with them. They're probably wondering where he is.'

He's my boyfriend, Chen. My fucking boyfriend! Keep your bloody nose out!

'Yeah, I've told them.'

'Oh. You have? Jeez! How did they take it?'

'Yeah, look, Chen, I'm nearly home and I've got brekky waiting so we can catch up later, okay?' It was true... ish. It was only a few more minutes before my Uber dropped me at the block entrance. I could see the PrimeFlixK-Bell-Pharm drone hovering by the poor-door when I got out and my stomach rumbled like it could too.

At home with my overs dripping down the back of my chair, I put so much syrup on my pancakes, they nearly-like, dissolved. But the rotten taste and bitterness came through after a few mouthfuls anyway.

It's like drinking salt water, it starts seeming like a choice when you've got no other choice.

Today it felt like the taste was worse but it was probably only in my mind. I drank a mug of water to wash out the bitter but the water left its own gross city-supply taste and that was definitely stronger than usual today so I'd probably poisoned myself.

I must have almost hit my allowance before I got paid. I got a jug from the cupboard, filled it from the tap and put it in my mini-fridge. I could pay to filter it to use for Instant™ later. I half-filled another mug and this time it tasted its usual okay-ish.

Then there was nothing to do but make a mug of Instant™, get wasted and get into a movie.

Shit! Nate's folks.

My J™ was about quarter full. I turned it on and took a tiny puff, enough to calm my nerves and help me forget how much I hated liking bloody Chen. But only a tiny wave of calm spread over me so I needed another drag.

Then I was out of excuses so I turned my chair to face the bed and pinged all my cameras off except the ones on the wall opposite me since the kitchenette behind me was the tidiest bit of the flat given it-like, never got used. And then I realised I didn't have any of Nate's family's handles. He'd always been the one to open the calls!

Great.

Nate had his parents locked down to keep them safe from ads and pushy loan-sharks. It was a good idea but it didn't help me stalk them! I'd have to get in touch with Chen to get their handles. Then she'd know I'd lied.

Arse!

His friends would know. Shane must! They'd all grown up together. And maybe he'd be up for a movie today, too. Except of course I didn't have bloody Shane's handle either. There were a lot of Shanes online and they all had useless avatars: babies and buildings and…. crap. I gave up looking and refilled my J™.

I'd been looking forward to a movie but now I was feeling so craptious, I logged on to my PrimeFlixK-BellPharm more out of spite for the yuck day than anything else. I sipped my Instant™ and let the recs carousel through. Today it was all ancient remasters from the mid twentieth with all the crazy nineteen-fifties haircuts.

Weird, buuut okay.

Three recs in, I randomly chose one called *A Star is Born*. I decided I'd be the woman with the queef-blown hair and dark red lips. I didn't really understand most of it. It was the sort of thing Nate would have understood all the references in, because of his job and because he was a poncy little geek. But I understood the gist, that woman are always the brains behind the operation and men can't handle anything without them.

I felt better and better through the movie until the credits came around and Nate appeared with a movie-star smile and said, 'CGI and set design!'

That made me snap straight out of the virtual and I sat staring at the kitchenette wall. I couldn't get my head around the idea that he was right there and I couldn't go and see him. I tried for the hundredth time, to think of way to get in but I knew it wasn't going to happen.

The active alloy stuff was impossible to break through with anything I could get hold of; *well not impossible but… No!* And if I could somehow get through, there was nothing I could do anyway. He'd be lying in a drug-induced coma in his stasis pod with tubes and all kinds of gross things sticking out of him.

I shivered.

It was heading towards evening and my bag of Budlike™ was half empty. It should have lasted a week – or months! I knew I should ease up. Work tomorrow would help distract me but for now, I half-filled the J™ and took small puffs.

Thinking of Nate, I splashed out and ordered some whole-food salad thing, more pricey again, than the crappy REAL(*) curry. It was mostly brown and yellow flavoured squares, probably made of the same devilment as my pancakes. But there were some actual vegetables in it too, dark green stuff shaped like brains on thick crunchy stalks.

You know what they are… No! I don't! I won't!

I paused eating mid-chew, to calm myself. The kind-of rotten taste like most of the healthy green crap Nate ate – *how did he afford this stuff?* – filled my mouth more. It took ages to chew but I made myself eat it all because there was no way I'd throw out that much money. At least it didn't leave the usual grossness in my mouth. Still, if I spent this much on every meal, I'd only get to eat three times a month and have no money left for weed or Instant™.

After eating, I lay on my bed and gave in to ads for the rest of the day and like magic, goddess magic, I ended up in a sample masterclass about how to improve your influence. It was run by Jamey Yang, the big-shot news-curator guy.

Jumped-up trash, don't you kids ever do anything like… No!

That got me thinking about the Movement. Sure, I couldn't do all the things Nate did and Chen would probably start doing now too, and be good at. But this I could do; far better than those two if I let myself think, let myself remember; not too much; only enough… I wouldn't have to leave my flat. Or, not until I got people involved, anyway. Giving away the hacks would have to be face to face. Or maybe it wouldn't be! Maybe I could get Chen involved once I had the numbers. Yes! This would work!

I signed up for the class, smoked the J™ down to a third, got undressed and went to bed, blissing out at how the goddess found ways to guide me.

Sarah – Nov 2096, Cornwall Station, Akarana

Island, Aotearoa Archipelago

I had my basic PhD like everyone and I should've stopped at one. But I'd gone and done a second one on, ooh-ooh-ooh-squirt, security and a third on something nasty. Well, okay, I'd got really into it at the time. It'd felt more like, I don't know, realising my childhood dream or something cheesy like that, than grown-up research.

Elayne and I had the idea when we were kids and when I finally got it to work, it was scary how close we'd come by the time we were twelve and before everything… happened. Except of course, it was more disproving a theory than a contribution to the field; kind of a sidestep through the doctoral door.

I kept having to remind myself it wasn't something anyone could've worked out. Most people didn't have tech in their genes – well figuratively – like we did. And if they did, they didn't have the resources I could giggle out of Nana and Grandad – never mind if Mum was all uptight about it.

So I didn't really mind that it was a conditional doctorate. I only minded why. I'd signed my letters away, basically tying myself to the mast of espionage. If my research ever saw the light of day, no matter how it got out, I'd lose everything including my basic. All because of the off-chance someone might use it.

Conditions aside, after the graduation party, I got to go ahead and use my research and pretty much my whole fortune worth of university-crafted neural pathways exactly fuck-all. Well, who'd want to be a celebrity anyway, right?

By way of consolation, Grandad-Tristian told me it was clever shit but can you imagine if that got into the wrong hands? Aunty Susie had told him shut your face, it's already in the wrong bloody hands, you stupid old coot; he was anything but! But everyone including those two had clubbed together and surprised me with my first apartment for a graduation gift so I wasn't complaining about the drama.

Now though, I could barely remember what was in my thesis. I couldn't believe what a let-down getting a job had turned out to be. Jeff, Kay and Andrea, my, what were they? Half-cousins? Well, officially family friends but we'd worked it out, Jesus, did our parents think we were stupid?

Whatever they were, after working at the station for about three days, I'd started coming around to their fucking way of thinking. They'd got Uncle Aaron-who-wasn't-really-my-uncle to sign over their trust funds early, taken the tax hit and were now basically, what? Retired?

But then, they hadn't been through what I had, what my family had. Okay, Uncle Aaron and the three of them had been on our side. But it didn't change the fact that their crazy grandad Jason had fucked my whole family over with his bullshit NDA. I couldn't understand why Grandad-Tristian had like, made us all sign it.

Surely it would've been better if people knew the truth about Aaron's pervert creep brother John. Surely if they knew he'd fucking raped Elayne – probably – and made her disappear, had probably murdered her for all we knew, it would be better. The right person would've paid for their crimes and the public wouldn't keep thinking wealthy people got away with stuff which was exactly what had happened.

That's why I'd joined the police force. To fight crime. To take down creeps like John Zhang and maybe one day to find out what happened to my sister from inside the crappy system that had swallowed the case of her disappearance into paid-off nothingness. Probably.

But it never felt like that was what I was doing. In my induction, I'd been sold the exact dream I'd signed up for, so my head remained safely in the clouds. And then I'd fallen trustingly out the other end of induction and come down to earth with a thunk on a disgusting uncomfortable office chair in the stinky ancient dump of Cornwall station. My life had been reduced to basically pointless paperwork; named after when it was literally done on yucky dusty stinky paper.

It wasn't police work! It was station admin crap a ten-year-old could do. And it was fully automated anyway. I was only there in case the system didn't work out people's pay from their punching in and out times right. But it always did, so what was the point?

I was losing the will to live and permanently about an hour away from resigning when there was a sudden management reorg because some old guy got a promotion or shuffled off or something. Then Neil appeared out of nowhere and tapped me and everything changed.

Neil was amazing. Okay, he always super busy with people coming at him all the time with stuff they needed him to do. But he managed to think of my professional development despite his workload. He wasn't that much older than me either, maybe eight or ten years but he was so wise.

Sometimes I felt like he knew every thought I was thinking and was one step ahead of me, about myself! But in a good way; I felt so seen by him. And I shouldn't've found it so sexy but when he talked about stuff in his authoritative way, I just... Oh man. I'd never been like this with anyone before.

I couldn't believe it when I found out he felt the same way. I didn't understand what the hell he saw in me but I knew it was real. We hadn't hooked up, wasted, at some crappy work vape-up or anything like that. We'd taken it slowly until we couldn't hold our feelings in any more. Then he'd finally invited me to his place once when our shifts matched and we'd never looked back. I knew the rules and the advice, don't sleep with your co-workers, least of all your boss, blah blah blah.

But it wasn't like that with us.

He had never taken advantage of me. I'd never felt pressured into anything by him. If anything, it was the other way round! All he ever said that rankled a tiny bit was that we should be discrete. But in the end, I agreed with him. People would think all the wrong things no matter what we knew about our relationship.

And it definitely wasn't affecting our work either, if anything the energy between us was making us work better. I was learning loads from him. I had kind of felt overwhelmed going from the admin job to making arrests.

I'd said to him. 'Jesus! We're dealing with people's lives here, taking parents away from their families, putting them back with their families all... rehabilitated or whatever. It's a big deal! Shouldn't I have special training or something?'

He'd been so kind about it, so empathic. He could've told me to grow a pair or go back to my admin role, that he'd put his reputation on the line to get me the promotion.

But instead, he'd opened up to me. 'I know, tell me about it! I nearly quit a couple of weeks after I started doing this stuff! It's a shitload of responsibility all right. And wait till you get into the system proper! That's some freaky shit! We'll get you on the training course as soon as it comes up. But stick with it for now, baby. It gets easier, I promise.'

His tone had kind of sounded like the time I'd asked to meet his family but I trusted him, everything in time; it made sense. And I loved the way he was professional but always took care to let me know we had something, something that was ours alone.

If my cousins could see me now, blushing at all his offhand huns and babys, they'd puke. If a younger me could see me now, god, she'd puke! But I was twenty-seven, and I was learning that you had to experience an oxytocin megadose before you could understand how it changed you. There were cliches for a reason.

And Neil was right too. It was getting easier, maybe, a bit. Day in, day out, I checked off on other officers' arrests, signed them through and put people under for weeks, months and sometimes years. I told myself it was for the best, that the system would take care of them, that they'd come out better people, better contributors to society. And that regardless of whether the stories were true, few people had bad reactions to the treatment, so it was a tiny price to pay.

Now and again, Spume's systems would ping a release recommendation over the firewall. More often than not though, I found myself logging notification of medical crisis and those ones I couldn't get used to.

I'd asked Neil why they didn't call them deaths and he'd said the department had learned the families and friends took it better that way. It didn't sit well with me but Neil was right about everything else and who was I, a green graduate with a lucky promotion, to argue with decades of law enforcement wisdom?

I'd started getting the hang of it. I'd started to learn to switch off after work. Neil said the Spume training would be coming any day now and our, uh, extracurricular activities, made me feel high sometimes. I was really getting into having a secret with Neil.

Whoever said relationships with colleagues were counterproductive didn't know what they were talking about! Neil's support was really helpful. And he wasn't showing favouritism either; he was super professional with me. If I messed up, which I hardly ever did, he had no qualms about calling me on it.

But amazing as he was, he wasn't perfect, he made mistakes. I wouldn't have said I did a perfect job when the Richards-Mann fiasco — well, I felt like it was a fiasco — happened, far from it. It had been Neil's call, not that I held it against him, but shit was I glad he'd stepped in!

There'd been hardly any arrests that day and Neil said it was good when crazy old fucktonionaire Zhang called in his complaint. It was people like him who kept us funded, unofficially anyway. Crime was low enough as it was, so the last thing we wanted was a zero-arrests day to trigger a round of redundancies.

My NDA lit up so bright when my 'great uncle' Jason virtualled into the station that I had to squint while I waited for it to dim. Useless algorithm should have picked up that he'd instigated the contact. It was the last thing I ever would have expected to happen, that I'd be the officer, randomly, selected to take the call.

I tried to put in a conflict of interests and it went through okay. But Neil countermanded it. He opened a secure connection on the side and told me I had to learn to handle situations like this. So there I was sat with the giant arsehole himself and he completely floored me acting like nothing – nothing! – had ever happened between our families.

'Hey Sarah.' He said, his wrinkled old face cracking a demonic smile. 'Look at you eh? All grown up and working for the government! Look, I'm glad you're on the case. I know the right things will happen.' And the sly old shit had the temerity to wink!

A warning chill ran up my spine.

'Okay, uh, Mr Zhang,' I said. 'How can I, uh, help?'

'Ah, straight down to business then eh? Good stuff! Alrighty, well, I was getting out of my car today and this awful bloody yobbo splashed water all over me. I tell ya, back in my day this neighbourhood was decent. You felt safe to walk around the place. Pardon my French but since I got shafted putting in all this state bloody housing, it's brought the tone right fuckin' down and I mean right down. Look at this.'

And he looped me into the footage he'd taken of… falling rain? No, okay, there was someone there, or the shadow of someone through the rain anyway. And I kind of did see a splash on the pavement. And yeah, all right, it was unusual that there was anyone there at all so…

'Okay, well, let's see what the, uh, suspect has to say for himself.'

'If the penniless bastard can even talk.' Zhang snipped.

God, he makes it sound like being poor's their fault!

'Okay,' I said. 'Let me get hold of him and see what he has to say and we'll take it from there.'

Then the old man's legendary madness took me by surprise. 'See what he has to say?' He roared. 'See what he has to fuckin' say? Fuck that you little upstart arsehole! You're going to arrest that scungey little sod and put him behind bars where he bloody well belongs or my lawyers'll have something to say about your station's funding! You get that little shit in here now and I want to be here to see him locked up, is that clear?'

Bars? Bars?

My mind looped pointlessly on his weird archaic turn of phrase. And I hated myself for snapping-to the way I did. I'd already started searches before I realised what I was doing.

'Okay, okay,' I heard my voice quavering as my stomach unclenched. 'I'll get him in. Give me an hour or something, I'll let you know.' It was like he'd put me under a spell. Crazy people are like that, weirdly powerful in their vulnerability.

Given the rain and, well, let's face it, the state of the world, besides Zhang, there was only one other handle in the area matching the time and location; granted, a bit weird since who went outside, let alone in a storm like that? Still, my recently trained detective's brain also started down the road of what the hell the old man was doing there himself?

But he was crazy and his lawyers would probably make that his alibi. The shadow might have been a loon too, I guess but given the location it was unlikely they'd have the lawyer-power to counter-sue their way out of trouble.

I sighed looking through Richards-Mann's profile. No priors, no qualifications beyond basic school, not a person of interest, not so much as a late bill payment; boring for a pleb. Boring full stop!

Yes! You've got a shot!

The family was a bit shady but all those ones were; they had to be to survive.

Not like Zhang's which was sooo law-abiding… Jesus! I'm actually-like, is… poor-ist a word? And I didn't know it!

Richards-Mann was a zero. I could have pulled him into the station space but protocol dictated we drag them in physically; it added to the bullshit mystique or something. We'd all been demo-arrested in training so I knew how shitty his morning was about to get.

He turned up at the station, soaking, fifteen minutes or so later and I couldn't help feeling sorry for him. I didn't trust myself to speak to him when he arrived. He looked healthy for someone… like him. He was tall and dark brown with blonde hair and blue eyes, usual kind of, mishmash of genes or whatever but it worked for him.

Jesus! You can't think of the public like that Sarah, professional boundaries!

He didn't seem like he was stoned or dirty or anything, he looked like a kind of ordinary guy, I mean, not educated, clearly, but not dumb; it was his eyes, I think, kind of intelligent in a raw sort of way. And he talked about exercise! An ordinary person who did exercise! I'd always thought those people – *Oh my god, Sarah, listen to yourself!* – took the pills if they did anything at all to look after themselves. Half my own friends took the pills if they did anything at all to look after themselves!

Things got worse when we went over the footage and he was clearly innocent as the day he was born. Neil must've been listening and he already knew about my dilemma with Zhang because we told each other everything.

He pinged me on a closed channel when the poor guy started rightly protesting his innocence and Zhang started kicking off. He tipped me off about the tech technicality and said he'd take over once the guy was booked and Zhang was happy. He made it an official order from a superior ranking officer which did help calm me down. I couldn't argue if he was prepared to put his bum on the line.

Still, I couldn't get Richards-Mann's – Nathan's – face out of my head. The fear in his eyes as he realised what was about to happen to him, all because some crazy old rich guy wanted it to, made knots in my stomach.

When I replayed the events in my mind that night, I felt ashamed I'd gone crying into Neil's office once it was all done but at the time, I was relieved it was taken out of my hands. As usual, Neil was amazing about it. He totally owned that it'd been his call. He said not to worry, that he'd take care of all the paperwork and he gave me the afternoon off.

I thought the whole thing was going to go away but it didn't. A day or two later, this pretty little wet-foot – *Sarah! Don't be so naughty!* – with clever eyes like Richards-Mann's – and those d-d-d-d-d-dreadful techtoos they all had – about my age, turned up outside my building entrance! She wanted to talk about the arrest.

She'd been easy to fob off since she had nothing to do with anything and I was the law. I guess it was no mystery how she'd found me and she was taking pains not to be threatening; not that someone that tiny could be thought of as threatening. But it'd left a bad taste in my mouth.

No matter how hard I tried, I couldn't stop thinking about Richards-M— Nathan, and she'd kind of opened up all the feelings again. I tried to get on with it, went back in early the next morning and tried to bury myself in work. I was close to feeling like myself again until I clocked off for the day – around mid-morning – and saw a woman arrive at the station. She gave me a weird feeling.

I never believed in visions or foresight or any of that stone-age baloney. Nobody did, Jesus, it was twenty-ninety-six! Only crazy people believed in shit like that. But something about the way that woman stood, the way she walked, it made me feel, I don't know, recognition or something?

But that was hindsight, I knew. We joined dots in our heads to make it seem like we'd figured things out before we had; like the suspect pizza you 'knew' gave you food poisoning when it was probably the iffy veggies the day before, and all that sort of thing. I'd learned to watch for that in detective training too.

I was asking her if I could help before I could stop myself but she walked into the station without answering. I told myself it was tiredness talking and went home. I probably would have forgotten about her if Neil hadn't been all jokes and laughs when I got in the next morning.

'Hey, babe, take a look at this!' he said conspiratorially after I'd closed his office door. 'That local guy we nailed the other day is quite the celebrity! Look at this, a visitation request already! Some woman came into the station in person to fill it out.'

He didn't see me freeze.

'Oh, I, wow. Is that… normal?' I asked, shaking.

'What? Visitor requests? Course. Nothing to worry about though. The system fobs them off until it's calibrated itself to their brains and got things, uh… started. If she's persistent, she'll eventually get in but, well, I've heard they have to be pretty persistent and by the time they see their slimeball associates well, it's meant to be a pretty underwhelming reunion, you know, like visiting a sick old person or something.'

'Neil!'

'Oh, oh, sorry! I didn't mean, yeah, your grandma and everything, no, look, come on babe, I was kidding, okay?'

'But… I don't understand why all the, uh, discouragement. Why shouldn't they get their visits?'

'Oh, they do, they do. It takes a while for the system to kind of, bed them in. And if they're woken up in that time it interferes with the process.'

'Yeah but why not tell people that?'

'Oh, come on babe! You know how those… people are. It'd be conspiracy theories all round. It's already conspiracy theories all round, look all the crazies' vlogs!'

It sounded reasonable.

Neil – Nov 2096, Cornwall Hill Station,

Akarana Island, Aotearoa Archipelago

Fucking Christmas again. It was boring enough that all my staff would find every excuse to slack off from December to the end of bloody February or whenever New Years' was this time. But the ads and the endless chatter about parties, friends, family, *liwus* and other inane drivel, nearly drove me to suicide. Or mass murder, that was always an amusing daydream.

Right from bloody August, every space in the cloud was filled with bullshit baubles and conifer holos claiming the most realistic piney smells for knock-down prices, shots of the moon and adverts for nanite-vouchers, noodles and dumplings.

I was generally a pretty positive guy. Between March and August, anyway.

Maybe it was my background that made me clueless about why everyone bothered with such bullshit. I reckoned it was more likely people were stupid though.

To say I sold illegal reconditioned nanites to get on to the force would be a gross over-simplification. Everyone born in the dump I grew up in did things like that to fucking eat. Course I did stuff. But unlike the other filthy chunks of waterlogged flotsam in my neighbourhood, I wasn't dumb enough to get caught and I didn't blow all my earnings on fake weed, booze and Total™ addiction. I saved my satoshis.

Fuck my dead-beat parents in their bullshit basement telling me not to get any big ideas while their feet went septic in toxic puddles on the living room floor. Fuck all the kids in my block who started vaping at the age of eight and boozing by the age of nine. Fuck them all.

I got my PhDs and I got out. Which proved the lot of those wet-foots were lazy. If I could do it, so could they. That's why I joined the force: to enjoy a career wiping as many lowlife wastes of space off the streets as possible. They were a disgrace to the bloody Ao Archipelago. And now here I was: regional representative to Spume and commissioner of the entire archipelago's *jǐngchá* 'marie. Which basically meant Akarana Island but, hey.

One of my exes called me a neo-misogynist once, which was a lame parting insult given she knew the man she caught me cheating on her with. Or, did he know the woman I was cheating on him with? It was an elliptical little semantics curio I liked to mull over sometimes. But neither of them was all that in the end. I liked the way they each thought they were – ooh-ooh-ooh – the only wah-ah-ah-ahn, that was all. I dumped the dopey sod when his mother dumped me, anyway.

But my point was, the whole setup was equal opportunities. I couldn't've cared less who was born with what plumbing, I liked to have fun and it wasn't my fault people were dumb. And anyway, they were adults; I always abused my power to do background checks; I wasn't stupid. It was their choice to sleep with me. Which meant I wasn't a neo-misogynist.

I felt no guilt whatsoever about the way I treated all the idiots in my life. And particularly not about playing with my latest juicy toy… uh… protégé, the way I did.

Being with Sarah meant I got to give orders to an actual proper rich ponce. Me! A nobody from the fucking dissolving seawalls on the southeast coast – not that anyone knew given the number I'd done on my records – telling an actual living, breathing Laufala, or Rahui, or whatever she was, what to do. And banging her into the bargain. Hard.

That was probably the main reason I did all the piffling other little things I did to her. I took no real pleasure in getting people busted for stuff or public humiliation or whatever. That wasn't really me, cancelling and all that wet-foot rubbish.

But leaking little splatters of seawater into her tediously pristine goody-good geeky little HR file, was deliciously perverse. I would never've made it all blow up. That'd've been no fun. I liked knowing I could though.

It wasn't like she didn't get anything out of it, either. Her first orgasm for a start; all her posh little dry-foot childhood sweethearts musn't've been up to the job, eh? Plus, I fiddled the books to get her up the ranks years ahead of her time and blew departmental budget sending her on extra detective courses – well, which it was for but she didn't need to know that. I would have sent her on the Spume systems one I promised her, too. Christ knew it'd mean less work for me if I could palm all that boring shit off on her! Too bad the shit hit the fan before the course dates came up.

No, it was only fair that I got to enjoy her little rich-girl giggles and mewls of shock when I showed her how to cut the odd bureaucratic corner, the thrill of doing a luscious subordinate officer against protocol and the bigger thrill of her thinking it was – ooh, ooh, ooh – our little secret.

I won't tell her but I think it's shitty, what you're doing. Tired old Jimmie from HR with the cutely novel dusky face had hissed at me, once. She might've been a contender for the next spot after Sarah went south if it wasn't for her disgusting hand.

Never mind how the fuck she knew given I didn't include her in my, uh, private subscribers list but I could never figure out why she didn't piss on the party. She never did though; too bloody lazy probably. She couldn't've been that sympathetic to Sarah either. She kept showing up at my parties and vaping my premium weed till her eyes nearly popped out of her head.

I thought, well, I knew I got off more on knowing a few select buds I had enough dirt on to trust, were watching my livestreams from of our special 'briefings' than from Sarah getting all flustered thinking a banal bit of doggie on my desk was risqué. I loved that she'd given me full permission to record us in my personal logs though.

I hadn't lied to get it which made it all the more delicious! I told her it was a fetish I had; which it was, only not the way she thought. I never said I wouldn't share it, heh, live. It was beautiful! Not that lucrative online though; not at first anyway.

And of the two of them, she was the better fuck. That surprised me, a bit. I would've thought dry-foots would be all prudish and poncy, but it turned out to be the other way around. It was fun doing Kevin too though, if not for the novelty of their freaky weird genuinely natural intersex genitalia, at least because I loved how Sarah and them sat right next to each other. Kevin wasn't looking for a pissant soul-mate like Sarah but they sure got off on the fact that Sarah thought she had one. Sarah was the only person in the station who had no idea she didn't.

Priceless!

Sometimes though, I took it a bit too far for my own job security. But the temptation had been too great. I found out by pure beautiful coincidence, Sarah's long-lost twin who she'd wah-wah-wah-wailed to me about after I'd suaved her into the sack, was doing the Richards-Mann wet-foot! What were the chances?

Shortly after I made Sarah put the boyfriend away, the messed-up sack of shit had showed up at the station to try and visit him in stasis and Sarah had walked straight past her on her way off shift. I'd been watching her leave on station security; because well, I could. I recognised the twin from the snooping I'd done into Sarah's file when I'd first clocked who Sarah was and decided I needed a piece of her. It was too perfect!

She had no idea of course. The cray-cray twin'd changed her name and got a face and follicle job and she was all overed up on her way into the station, anyway. But the knowing! The knowing that she didn't, was beautiful.

Chen – Nov 2096, Cornwall Estate, Akarana Island, Aotearoa Archipelago

Fuck it all, I decided as I woke up three hours too early for work. If I was gonna burn for my actions, I'd choke on that shit-burger when I was force-fed it.

Ok… Tina had finally pulled her finger out and proved Nate – and me – right. Whether Nate was really drugged up and locked in his flat or taken to some kind of creepy facility, the arseholes at Spume were gonna do their fuckedist to keep anyone from visiting him. But what else had she done? Bloody nothing with a capital Sweet-FA, I was willing to bet.

I tidied up my house and blew some ding on a clean for the flat and a wash for me, both outside my work allowance. I couldn't relax though until the last of the swarm'd crawled off me and getting dressed after made me feel less kind of, vulnerable.

Nate's mum Min appeared as soon as I pinged. She was sixty-odd going on not much older than bloody me; a splash of colour in their toxic basement grey. Her 'toos were cheesy: little diamonds following her jawline and an old-lady chain kind of thing around her neck, but at least she cared about how she looked. Nate'd got his weird exercise thing off her, and his blonde hair and blue eyes. Maybe her craziness too, given the stuff he came out with sometimes; never mind that it was usually genius.

'Gosh, *Nǐ hǎo* Chen, *kia ora*! You and Nate back on?'

Oh Jesus.

I managed a pained smile. 'Ah, *kia ora* Min, I, uh, I was, uh, getting in touch to say, uh, sorry for, what happened to Nate and everything. And, if there's anything I can do…'

'What on earth do you mean, Chen sweetie? Has something happened to Nate?'

Thought so. Lying psycho shit.

I was willing to bet my non-existent eternal soul Tina didn't have a handle for Nate's folks. And I'd dropped myself in it now, too. I could see the worry starting on Min's face so I had no choice now but to break the news.

'Oh no! Min, I'm so sorry! I thought you knew!' Okay, that felt bad. 'Look, might be best if you get Phil. It's bad news.'

The way her face paled nearly made me lose my nerve. Why was I doing this? Why was sticking my bloody nose in?

Because he's my friend!

It was true but I wasn't dumb enough to buy my own bullshit.

I hoped I was lucky and old man Richards-Mann wasn't two bags down already. He was drinking a bottle of the evil sludge Total™ when Min brought him into the call. He stank of BO and stale weed, stale at least though, not fresh. Not yet.

He was where Nate's brown skin and big build had come from and all his nanites were in his hair so it glittered silvery grey. When we were together, I used to wonder if Nate would ever grow a gut like his dad's.

'Eh? Whossat? Aw Chen! How's it hangin' mate? You and Nate back on? Good work.'

Fuck!

'Look, Min, Phil, it's really nice to see youse and I'm sorry it's been so long. And I'm sorrier I've gotta be the one to break the news but, I honestly thought you knew. I'm so sorry! I don't really know how to say it but, well… Nate's in prison.'

Shit. Did I really have to say honestly?

I mean, I could technically have claimed to believe they knew because the self-absorbed psycho Tina had said she was going to tell them but, yeah, nah.

'Prison?' they both asked, uncomprehending.

'He didn't do anything,' I said quickly. 'It was a complete…' I searched for another word in case they didn't know what farce meant. 'It was complete bullshit. They, the *jǐngchás*, jacked up the charges. Tin— I've been trying to get hold of all the info an' that. But they won't release it to me.'

'Bloody typical cops!' enthused Phil like he was in a holo-drama. He gulped down the rest of his Total™ and picked up his J™. 'Well,' he said, 'they'll sort it all out won't they, if it's a mistake.'

I felt guilty for probably having triggered him into using. And right at that crappy moment, also envious. The smell of his vaping came over the call and I wished it wasn't a tech trick.

'Hell alive, Chen. How can they do that?' Min's eyes filled with worry and overflowed with Phil's share.

'I don't— I don't know.' I choked up when I saw her tears start.

Phil lost himself in his J™. I saw his face change. I must've been getting older because I suddenly saw it for the checking out that it was. And then I noticed Min watching me and I realised she knew I'd seen and suddenly, we were two actual adults sharing a look, like we understood together.

I was shaken in a good kind of way. But it opened the door to a whole lot of bad stuff too. Like how well I got on with Min, how lonely I was working every day in my pissy flat. And how much I missed Min's son who'd bloody dumped me and who I couldn't get over because I was sure he hadn't meant it, after nearly four fuckin' years.

Pathetic!

I wanted to tell them Tina was trying to get a visit, that she and I would figure it out then I'd get them up from Beach-lands to visit him as well. But my words wouldn't come. I couldn't look Min in the eye. I felt like she'd be able to read my mind. It felt like everyone in the world had access to Nate's feelings and I was shut out by myself in the crappy lukewarm friend zone.

It should have been that stupid idiot Tina having this conversation with his folks, not me. I couldn't stand to say her name in front of them, or at least to Min, anyway. Right in that moment, I hated her right down to her greasy blonde roots. Which was stupid since that only lost me sleep.

'I, uh, look, I'm really sorry it came out like this, I thought you'd already know. I'm trying to figure out what to do and, I dunno, it's…. It's hard. But I'll stay in touch, okay? I'll… uh, stay in touch.' My voice trailed off into lameness.

'Yeah, course Chen, Sweetie, course we'll stay in touch.'

Nate's family weren't as big a bunch of gangsters as mine but there'd been cousins, uncles an' that, like everyone out at the broken-down seawall, round the headland from Beachlands. I could tell Min knew the deal because she didn't ask anything else. No matter that Phil was off his tree and wouldn't figure it out for another year if ever, Min understood. She understood they'd probably never see the smartest, kindest guy in their family, ever again.

'Look, I've gotta get ready for work.' My voice was pathetic. 'I'll be in touch, okay?'

'Sure Sweetie. You get on, don't be late for work. And Chen?'

'Yeah?'

'Really lovely to see you, Sweetheart.'

'You too Min.'

Silence crashed in on me when we cut the call.

What the fuck did I do that for? What was the bloody point? It's made everything worse.

I sulked on the sofa for a while then went into my bedroom and found my J™. It was empty so I opened my bag and took a pinch of leaves to fill it up then remembered the moment, the crystal clear awful shitty moment, when I'd seen Phil's eyes glaze over. I dropped the leaves back in the bag, threw my J™ on the floor and crunched it with my heel.

I felt a piece of it snap and the jagged edge bit into my skin. Swearing, I hopped over to my bed. The blood was starting to come as I sat down and turned my heel up to look.

The red drop bubbled out and ran over my sole on to the duvet. The J™ had auto-repaired and it smiled a good-as-new fuck-you up at me from the carpet. It simultaneously depressed me and reminded me of Nate's idea.

Now he'd submitted himself as a live test subject, it was more than an idea. It basically proved we were right, well, he was right. Trouble was, if the *jǐngchás* or whatever shady government outfit copped on to anyone snooping, that anyone'd wind up like Nate. For all I knew, that's why they had arrested him.

And it was also why all we'd done so far was thought experiments with all our tech hacked to stop recording us talking; which was suspicious enough alone. Still, we'd been over it a thousand times and there was no law against walking around the buildings you lived in on the floors you had access to. The more we'd walked, the more I was convinced he was right and now after what'd happened, I was sure.

I had a rough map of my block in my mind but it hadn't got me anywhere. I reckoned I knew every lift shaft, door and disused stairwell – like there was any other kind – in the whole building. I'd paced out the public gym with all its mouldering kit and broken treadmill. I'd looked at plans for similar buildings in work's space; easy enough to find an excuse given my job but it'd given me the shits anyway.

And I knew from the windows of the rich apartments on the higher floors, roughly how they'd fill in the spaces we couldn't access. Plus, we'd guessed where their lift shafts'd be from where their building entrances were; with all their poncy gardens and security an' that. But never mind if you added in a few private lifts for the extra-smelly rich arseholes, it didn't add up.

There were a couple of hours to go till work.

I got up and kicked the J™ into a corner. My lame fake window showed it was windy outside but dry, amazingly. It was weird how I knew I'd find nothing but I felt excited about looking again anyway. I chucked my overs on over my naked body and liked that anyone who saw me wouldn't know I was wearing nothing underneath them. Or maybe that only I would know. Or that it reminded me of how much I liked it when Nate and I did it together.

Down the hallway, I heaved open the yellow cracked fire door to the fusty old stairwell. I sneezed in the dust and dry air as I went down the stairs and I realised with a shiver of recognition that the footprints on the dustiest of the steps were probably mine from when I'd gone to visit Tina. Nobody else was *fēng kuáng* enough to walk down a whole floor when there was a lift.

Nobody but me. And Nate... Stop!

The wind on my face blew some of the dust off my mind. Though it didn't stop everything being shitty, the bright grey daylight in my eyes and wind in my hair, made it feel... manageable or something.

I went right out the poor door instead of left towards Nate's block. As I walked past the ground floor windows, I tried to picture a 3D cross-section of the building. It was amazing what the human mind could do. Nate had always told me, we didn't always have tech, we had to think like this to make tech in the first place. He was right, I was getting better at it with practice. If I hadn't met Nate…

Stop! Chen. Bloody, stop!

I pushed the memories away for the millionth time and imagined the lift cores straight down through the building, two for the rich, a few private ones then one for us wet-foots. The rich and poor halves of the building – well that's what they bloody were, let's face it, luxury and premiere my tits – would be like two giant Tetris tiles fitted together. Then they'd be filled with smaller tiles inside for the gym in the basement, the hallways and the apartments packed around everything.

Where could you hide a space in all that?

Our block only had two buildings and a side road separated mine from the next block. The gap between the fence

and the wall was wide enough for me to walk down but it had
the feeling of a place nobody ever went though the apartment
windows I kept having to duck under looked out into it. The
fence was maybe twice my height and it muted the noise of
the cars on the road outside as well as the whine of drones.

Why? If someone bothered climbing over it, so fuckin' what?

Probably a coincidence. I was seeing secrets where there
weren't any. Except where there were apartment windows, the
space between the wall and fence was dark and the concrete
was damp underfoot. The wind had mostly dried everything
else. I followed it to the corner of the building and continued
around the back where it was darker because we were hard up
against the next block and its own dank shitty path and fence.

Roaches clung to the walls and I kept to the middle to stop
them jumping on me. Not that it would've mattered, I
could've blatted them when I got inside anyway. I didn't like
the thought, was all.

Looking down the alleyway between Nate's building and
mine always surprised me. It was weird how far away the chun-
tering old AC opposite… Tina's window seemed, though I
knew it was only a minute or so to walk right through. I could
hear it roaring away doing nothing as usual and wondered if
now Nate was g…

No! Don't think that!

…if the council would ever come and take it away.

Should I have checked out… Tina's story? She'd had no
reason to lie but still, to, I dunno… check. Maybe the security
only hung around for the first part of the sentence. Or maybe
she'd only checked one end of the alleyway. But in the end, I
didn't feel like having my body jammed on an empty stomach;
or at all. I walked on past the alley entrance to the road end of
Nate's building and stood there looking down.

It was the same as the end of my building, walled off from
the street, dark and damp. Another crappy AC hung off the
wall and I imagined its lukewarm fart of air in my face if I
walked past it. I knew from experience that I could duck under
easy enough but the rotten chemical smell would catch me

anyway. It was strong enough that it didn't have to blow straight in my face to half choke me.

Plus I suddenly worried if I went through and back around the front, that I might run into Tina getting a delivery or something. I couldn't take talking to her right now. Plus I'd done this circuit a thousand times anyway. I knew I wouldn't find any new clues.

I turned around and went home and it wasn't till I'd gone to bed that night that I realised Min hadn't mentioned Tina once in our whole conversation. It shouldn't have given me a little glow inside but it did.

Ethel – Dec 2096, Cornwall Hill, Akarana Island, Aotearoa Archipelago

'Hello Sweetheart. How are you getting on nowadays? School going well?'

The greenest of eyes darted hither and thither beneath ginger lashes and I resisted the urge to ask her how on earth she could stand her bun so tight. My suit was tugging at my own roots but she was doing that to herself for the sake of jolly cosmetics!

She was one of the fosters, no child of mine, I knew. Not only because of her pale freckled face, also because she was far too young.

My poor Freddy. Oh for goodness sake, stop!

It was hard though. If not for my poor simple Freddy's genius, I wouldn't have enjoyed the unexpected privileges I did.

The name, the name, the name…

'Hi Ethel.' She spoke in English, the only jolly extant language I knew.

'What is it…'

Just then I became distracted from trying to remember when I realised what I had believed to be a pair of tiny silver earrings and an elegant chain about her neck was in fact her…

tech, clumped artfully on her skin to look like jewellery. And then it popped up.

Ah yes, that's right.

'…Stephen. How can I help, Dear?'

Even before the self-conscious flicking of stray ginger tendrils and furtive glances over her shoulder began and not least because she seemed not to have heard my question, I knew there was trouble behind those eyes.

'I, uh, I'm sorry to bother you Ethel but—'

'Nonsense! It's why I'm here. It's no bother at all!' I meant it.

'Well, I know I'm meant to go to the, uh, floor manager first but, it's kind of, uh, about him.'

'Oh yes? What's the trouble then?'

I heard her out and reassured her it was already in hand. And took a second to indulge in some petty self-congratulations.

Now the gloves are off.

I would get back to her, certainly I would. But I judged nobody was in immediate danger and I would jolly well make sure they never were. But right now, I had more pressing business than my children and it had been a long while since I could say that.

The time for dignity was past. I had gone to those of my children and staff, which were more or less the same thing, to see who might be able to help. It was no mean feat, asking them to search discretely for something, some people, while telling them little about who they were looking for.

And if they thought it another of my doddering endeavours, well blow the lot of them. They would all hopefully never find out enough to thank me later. Bless them though, they had made progress! Or they had begun to in any case and then they had ground to a halt and gotten cagey about telling me why through the machines.

As luck would not have it, John his scale-some self, now side-lined into administrative duties at my direction, safely away from my babies, had left me messages that very morning.

He wanted to know when he could have more involvement with the children and I had no intention of replying, especially after little Stephen's report.

Goodness but I hated the look of him with his silly grey bun and sly smooth face! A person going to seed as he was should have been fatter, too. It was curiously annoying that his current position as a nothing administrator meant I had to bump into him on my way to the lift. 'John. I'm going out. Inform everyone here …Never you jolly well mind where I'm going, I don't know why you ask. …No, nothing else. Only what I asked please, John. Goodbye.'

And if I was not awaiting confirmation of my suspicions, I might have thrown you out on your ear because your obsequious tone makes my skin crawl! Little… creature!

Perhaps he had mumbled something slyly conciliatory, I had no time to care. Ignoring him, I swept with what haughty majesty I could muster as my suit rubbed and scratched at me, through the apartment we called the reception and down the hallway to the lifts.

Outside, my suit did a good enough – well, better than good enough – job of conveying the environment to me. Yet as I walked the few blocks to the Other Building, I wished with a longing that hurt my chest, that I could discard it along with my ridiculous hemps and feel the sunlight on my naked skin as I had in my youth.

I had not seen such beautiful weather in goodness knew how long and it would be a tragedy to waste it. I was at first alarmed to see the streets so full of drab-clad, owl-eyed people but I quickly realised they were all simply admiring the weather and nobody could be faulted for that. Still, as I came down the hill and rounded the final corner, a shadow passed over the sun and I knew the next storm would soon arrive.

Good! Then there will be nothing I am being denied again.

It was a waspish thought and I chided myself for such silly vindictiveness. Not for long though as now I was nearing the entrance. The Other Building was, ironically, not far from the new police station they'd put in a few decades back and the street was prone to flash floods. It was for the latter reason I lengthened my stride as the sky darkened.

The door melted open at my proximity; I remained human enough for that, at least. To all outward appearances it was a drab residential block, advertising itself by reputation only as I'd known it would. Indeed, to most inward appearances it was a drab residential block because of the way all the young ones worked nowadays. And because it suited much of the work that was done there.

I rode the lift to the penthouse and its doors melted open to a room of plush seating, insectile machines attending a buffet, the off-balanced hum of coffee machines; a gaudy orgy of Kafkaesque excess, in my view but it kept the young ones happy. I smiled when they did not stop talking as I arrived. Despite the crawling centuries, it remained good to feel liked. And to like.

It must have been lunchtime for the tables were mostly full, the machines scurrying to-and-fro with plates and trays. I saw an eminently beddable dark-skinned boy with long sturdy bones and auburn hair and beard. He had saved me a seat at a tiny round table.

'Hello James—, Min—, Sarah—, Harbinder.'

'Darrin, Mum. It's me, Darrin.' His consonants were soft with the suggestion of a lisp and I remembered my delight that he'd gotten off so lightly compared to his legion siblings over the generations, only being born deaf as he had. And that had been fixed up anyway.

'Oh yes, so it is. Well, lovely to see you again Boyo –' I remembered his nickname in the nick of time and supposed a bedding was out of the question given the way everyone had become about those things in recent centuries. 'Now what is it you've dragged me around the hill for?'

The tiniest lump came to my throat when I saw his hastily concealed disappointment. But I could not afford the niceties of filial affection right now. And I could not spend my days making up for the tiny disappointments of every single one of my children. In any case, he had a hold of himself in an instant

and pressed on; impressively, not to mention crotch-dampen-
ingly, business-like.

Golly! I must be getting over poor Freddy at last!

'Well, you asked us to search discretely for, uh, people like
you. But, um, Mum you didn't give us that much to go on.
Narrowing it down to e-squibs— er, I mean, people who can't
have nanites, would've made it… well, I mean, there are millions and they can be online anyway though they're like…'

'Like me?'

'Yeah. So, well anyway, we weren't doing too well and we
were getting noticed by the authorities because—'

A great brouhaha erupted in a corner of the room, star-
tling both of us. Looking to the source of the excited voices, I
saw a huddle of youngsters staring wide-eyed at a corner. They
ooh and aahd and held their noses – of all things – aloft.

'The smell's awesome this year!' I heard one say.

For a moment, I was concerned the lot of them had been
taken by some sort of madness.

'Darrin! What's wrong—?'

'The Christmas tree's up, Mum.' He said in a voice fit for
the bedside of an invalid.

Whoa! Boy, if I didn't want to jump on you, I'd slap you for that!

'Of course,' I said, hiding my annoyance at the world I was
trying desperately to save, 'I knew that.'

'Anyway,' he said with consummate diplomacy, 'all the
searches were coming out of people in this building. So, we
cloaked—'

He saw my expression and edited himself toot-sweet.

'So anyway, we got an expert on the case. One we didn't
own but who we… Well, this person had a reputation which
made us inclined to trust them. The idea was to kind of spread
the load and h— the uh, person thought of stuff to narrow
down the list we hadn't dreamed of anyway.

'We'll probably never know whether he would've got results or not but they were good at covering their tracks all right.
We tried tracing their activities with the inside advantage of
being able to contact h— but h— they were good.'

'Were?'

'Well, they disappeared.'

'I see. Well, did you find another one?'

'Maybe. Well, I mean, we're looking. We will. There are always some but that's not exactly why I wanted to talk to you.'

I might have been intrigued but the emotion was buried beneath centuries of bearing witness to the same human dramas forever repeating. 'No?'

'Well, we were using this g— this person for that new job you gave us a couple of days ago.'

He waited and I could not for the life of me remember who I had given what job and fortunately he began talking again before I snapped.

'You asked us to look into the new guy up at The Home Building, John.'

'Ah. Yes.'

'So, we gave the contact your, uh, special access, and let him at it. H— they had an encrypt— The person found stuff and we think it spooked them so they left it somewhere physical for us; half first and— that kind of thing. We'd said okay and paid and got the first half; which I'll get sent up to you today. We were waiting for the details of the next drop and that's when we lost contact.'

'All right, well, why bring me here to tell me that. Can't you…' I flicked a hand over my shoulder. '…take care of it?'

'Yeah, course we can Mum, yep. We will. We are. But we were worried about the disappearance, you know, while they were doing work for us. We don't think they scarpered with the money. Based on the response patterns and connection— Well, anyway we reckoned it was a local though probably too good for us ever to be sure. We didn't have a clue about who it was.'

'Well good, Darrin,' I wasped. 'So, that is all then? You have brought me down here to annoy me in person? There's a jolly storm on the way you know—'

'No! No Mum! That's not all! Let me—'

Gosh!

I wondered how angry I'd sounded. The poor child, in his fifties, one of the Freddy-grieving-comfort vintage for sure if I bothered to guess, was shaking and flinching as if I was holding up a hand to slap him. Which I had jolly well never done, the ungrateful little so-and-so! Goodness, me, back in my day…

'All right. Sorry Dear. Go on then.'

He relaxed. A little. 'So, we got lucky last night. Some of the, uh, workers were up here and they were cracking jokes and looking over some footage from across the street. And Serena, you know…'

'Yes of course I know your jolly twin sister, Dear. What do you take me for?' I had remembered suavely – *yes, that was her, the blind one* – in the nick of time, but he did not need to know that.

'Yeah, well, she heard the name mentioned and we got them to show us the footage and Jason Zhang – Jason Zhang! – was pulling up in his own car outside here. There was a booking, and he showed up pretty much dead on time for it but on its own, we couldn't be sure. And, yeah, I know, we wouldn't've cared either, only one more big-shot with needs and all that.'

'Yes, yes, well, what do you want me to say? Hats off to the mad old coot for still being able to get a stiffy?'

'Mum! Ew, lalalalalala!' He plugged his ears and cringed.

What on earth did I say?

'Well, what, Dear? For pity's sake get to the point!'

'Well, the point is that he didn't come in because a guy turned up right when his car pulled in. It was lashing out of the heavens so we couldn't tell what happened but they were talking. So, we got, you know, Jimmie, to see if she could find out what happened and it's good we did. The guy was some nobody, someone Richards-Mann, it turned out. We got her to get us everything on him which wasn't much since he was pretty much a p—'

'Darrin Rangi Tomaso Bell! Don't you jolly well dare!'

'Uh, sorry Mum. Well, anyway, he didn't have a record or anything but he does now. Jo Rahui and Tristian Laufala's granddaughter arrested the poor guy at Zhang's behest that same day and threw him in prison— No, wait, Mum! I know what you're gonna say. We think it does matter. We think Richards-Mann was our hacker. Or he might've been anyway.

'It's a bit of a stretch but it turns out we already knew him, or of him anyway. We've got people out past Beachlands in Omana and all those, uh, places, keeping tabs on the, you know, people there and the seawalls and everything. And helping kids out on the QT and stuff. Okay so they say Richards-Mann goes down there now and again and not only to see his family.

'He, uh, does this thing – it'd bore you so I won't bother saying – but anyway it's a tech thing which only someone like our contact would be able to do. Our people knew about it and they didn't grass him up but they didn't reveal themselves to him either.

'So, he didn't know we knew; we didn't know we knew until I got in touch with people down there to ask about his background. But anyway, we lost contact with our person around the same time as Richards-Mann was rumoured on the street to be due a visit to Beachlands and same time as the arrest happened. So, join the dots.'

'So…?'

'So, was Richards-Mann meeting Zhang? Or did they both have appointments in here?' He motioned to the floor as he spoke. 'I wouldn't've thought someone like Richards-Mann would be able to afford us but, you know, different people, different spending priorities. Or was Richards-Mann passing by – in the rain, like, as if! – and spotted Zhang about to come in here and, you know, so Zhang was embarrassed and had him silenced? Well, he is crazy…

'Or, was Richards-Mann working for Zhang too and did they meet so Richards-Mann could tell Zhang we were on to his creepy son – you'll see what I mean when you get what he found for us – and Zhang decided to clean house? In which case, does that mean he'll have the police dig into Richards-Mann's tech and have people all over us any minute now if he wasn't smart enough to cover his tracks?'

'I see,' I said, wishing he could have come the point sooner because my suit was rubbing and the storm had passed over and I had missed the notional break between it and the next one. 'Well, that would be a bore.'

'Yeah, I mean. Not that much but, I thought you'd like to know.'

'Yes, thank you, Darling. Gosh, you know, you've really grown into a most thoughtful and professional young man, Darrin. I'm terribly proud of you!'

'Uh, thanks Mum.'

I got up to go but paused halfway out of my seat when I noticed he was giving me an imploring look.

'Yes Dear?'

'Mum, about my, uh, father, I was wondering if you'd…'

'Oh, gosh! Goodness! Look, I'm so sorry Darling. I will, uh, have a think, all right? Things are terribly busy at the moment.'

Oh dear…

I could see it all as I had seen it so many times lately. The anger, the sadness, the frustration and the disappointment all passing like weather across his features in a second before his dutiful 'cheerfulness shone again.

'O— Okay, Mum.'

Gosh, was it an actual tear I saw as I turned and walked to the lift? Funny boy.

I had heard of the notion of fathers. And of course, I knew that such things as a certain shaped nose or great or small strength or one thing or another like that were generally contributed by men; some sort of confabulation of the traits and talents of all those men a woman accepted between her legs; the more the better as far as I was concerned...

Yes, it took a while. But I think I'm done grieving now.

…For the poorest hunter might be a good storyteller or who cared anyway if he was good to have between your legs.

But the way a family's lifeblood was passed down, that was incontrovertible. How else could it have been that each of my children's skin was unfailingly dark if not as dark as mine? How could it be that they always looked similar but not the same as me if not for the blood inside them? And what had my jolly womb cramped up and squeezed out of my crotch every month for all these centuries if I did not use it to make a child? And so where did a baby get its blood from but its mother? It cried to the sky with its obviousness!

Yet nowadays, so many of my children – and indeed, people – had taken up this morbid preoccupation with fathers. Someone had tried to explain it to me years ago but it seemed as preposterous as it was dull and I set no store by the tripe. If it was true, which it was not, how on earth should I know which of their jolly fathers was what? Poor Darrin would be waiting a long time.

Rock – Dec 2096, Rock's Tower, Germany

"Jawohl! Jawohl, jawohl, jawohl!" I sang as I clapped *mein* hands and made a little dance.

An alert had buzzed on *mein* pocket technology screen high over the ocean. The communication had given me such considerable happiness, I could not keep *mein* seat, not for hours after arriving at *mein* residence.

Mein elbow knocked three prisms from the lower shelf and I stopped to retrieve and arrange them correctly back in their places. Such a disorderly accident did not reduce *mein* happiness as it could have at other times.

Ja, finally all would be well. Finally!

After Africa and India, I had brought *mein* handy blue and white duffel bag home, took from it the two colleagues and placed them with the others. Because the dream and memories had proved inconclusive and insufficient to find the last of the misbehaving ones, I would need to make another mission and that could have reduced *mein* happiness a certain amount but it did not. The message caught me at the precise tipping point into annoyance.

Ja, because *mein* employees informed me they had observed strange technical searches through the cloud. I of course had taken one small look at the information and understood immediately what they had not.

From *mein* point of view, these searches showed that one of the others was attempting to find the rest of us. The meddling and these searches were likely to be connected. It was obvious therefore, that I should make it easy for whoever it was.

Ah, *ja*, always plenty of options for removing the skin from the cat.

I made a little picture of the colleagues in their black prisms on their shelf and a sound recording to accompany it. And then I used *mein* inconceivable wealth to inject it into the cloud in such a way as it would propagate and seem to emanate from a young person or something like this.

'Now,' I said to myself rubbing *mein* hands together as I sat down to the bank of beautiful screens, 'We wait for nibbles at the bait, *Ja?*'

Ethel – Nov 2096, Cornwall Hill, Akarana Island, Aotearoa Archipelago

I recognised the colours at once. And the smells of sun, sewerage, spice, mud and monsoon. It was recent too, well, recent in my reckoning anyway; there was electricity. A flickering electric light jaundiced a wrinkled brown face and a tea set rattled on the table though I – in that way of dreams – knew we were deep in the household where no breeze should so much as lift the corner of a tapestry.

That was what had given me, her, the idea and from whence the practice of seances sprang; or so I saw she believed now the memory came to light in present eyes. Whoever's memories had swirled into my dream this time were confirmation of my own suspicions as if Aroha Rahui's Shade had not been enough. But what I had not understood and this woman had deduced, was how Shades responded to the entreaties of the living and I awoke the next morning with a chill and a thrill for this at last was something I might be able to use.

Again, I resolved to think on it more and again I hoped that this time the stirring of memory would alert the other to my interest. I watched online as best I could for something though I knew not what, some signal that she was aware of me fossicking through her work. The young ones, the older young ones too, would have mocked my puny efforts rubbing and poking away at my e-squib screens.

Just do this or try that, they would say and how they would be laughing! But they could not know the inconvenience of living without the tech that infested their bodies and crowded their skin like grey and silver mould. And with the rest of us being like me, well, it was less likely yet that we could find each other… online. I did not know their names any more to start with.

I could not be doing with my suit that day and so chuckled at the irony as I left messages for my staff that I was ill and fumbled my way through ordering food to my apartment. I threw a blanket about myself, covering my flawless shiny blackness, for no other reason than I liked the feeling. I cared nothing for what the hideous insectile machine that brought my meal up from the entrance might have thought.

I passed the day fingering my screens in mounting frustration and that night my dreams were, infuriatingly, only my own. The next day I resolved to stir up her memories again, to hell with the risk. But they were veiled to muted whispers as the other's had been days before and an icy realisation froze me to the core.

One might have been a coincidence however unlikely. But two? Two of us made wasted in the space of a few days? Never in this day and age! I could not fathom the stupidity of it but nor could I deny the bone-chilling truth. We were at war.

For pity's sake! This is the last sodding thing I need!

Tina – late Nov 2096-early Feb 2097, Cornwall Estate, Akarana Island, Aotearoa Archipelago

Though it was nearly dark, I felt light when I woke the next day, full of goddess-sent purpose. The work spam had un-dimmed which was good because I'd nearly forgotten I had work. I was early so I made some Instant™. I felt guilty about the idea of pancakes again but not enough to stop me ordering them. My head was so clear, I hardly noticed the smell or the narrowness of the hallway when I went to the poor-door to receive them.

I contemplated the bag of Budlike™ and J™ sitting on my desk but before picking them up, I noticed a strange quietness. I looked around trying to understand what was wrong. Somehow over the last couple of days, my clothes had escaped my drawers and lay strewn on my bed again. The air smelled faintly of Instant™, my BO and sweat. All normal. My duvet was in its usual pile and the dishwasher hung open, probably due to be put on again; auto-start still on the blink.

Bloody cheap rubbish!

My eyes finally went to the window, now bright with full daylight. That was when I saw what had changed. The alleyway was dry and all I could hear was the chunter of the AC. Its stringy dust hung down instead of getting blown around in the wind as it normally did. I went over to the window and strained my neck as far back as I could.

Squashing my face against the glass and looking up past the black grime and tiny wet-foot windows, where the walls got cleaner and the balconies started, I could see a tiny chink of pure blue above the penthouse on Chen's block. Jesus! A clear sky and no wind. Nate would be outside in this in a flash. I should be outside in this!

And it's a sign from the goddess.

My hemps were on in a second but I yelped like a toddler when I opened the door and nearly ran into someone; some people! The hall was full of them heading out to see a giant ball of bloody gas in space. No way I could go in the hallway with all those people. No bloody way. I hung back in my door-way till the crowd thinned. I was about to follow the last one out when I imagined them all standing around outside and me having to fight through them to get a clear space out on the road or something. So I didn't bother.

I was early for work but I logged on anyway. I had tons of viewings queued up but the first one didn't start for an hour so I stared up at the sun coming down between buildings pre-tending to myself that I didn't know why my life was like it was.

It went from breeze to wind in the time it took me to make another Instant™ and I could hear feet swarming down the hallway outside. There must have been-like, a herd of people for them to sound as loud as they did. Normally I could only hear stuff right outside my door but this time it sounded like the building was full of footsteps for a good five minutes.

Everything quietened after a while and the wind rose higher and roared down the alleyway. An Instant™ or three later, I sighed and started the day's viewings.

I was getting hungry and there was supposed to be a gap mid-afternoon or so but a late booking sleazed in so I had to Instant™ my way through the day. Three more short-notice ones piled in that afternoon so it was dark by the time I finished and I was wrecked from sitting in a chair doing nothing but look at vast tidy apartments from dawn till past dusk.

I tried playing with myself to get to sleep. But it made me think of Nate and his magic finger skills that Chen had probably taught him when they were together. I suddenly got sad and angry at the same time. I pushed my face into my pillow and wondered if I could use it to suffocate myself and how long it would take and whether it would hurt. Only thoughts of the goddess and the purpose she'd given me stopped me trying it and soothed me to sleep with thoughts of the masterclass.

Next evening after another bitch of a day, I started the class. It wasn't Jamie Yang in the flesh, or the holo-flesh or whatever. He'd made a recording of the class with a cheap out-of-the-box classroom virtual.

I sat at the back because virtual crowds — any bloody crowds — made my chest tight. At the end, his avatar answered questions if you were lucky enough for your question to be in his FAQ. If it wasn't, it confabulated at you with a bunch of search results you could have got for free. A lot of it was common sense. But he couldn't have got where he was without knowing something other people didn't, so I took as many bites as I could.

…When we search online, we're really asking the world a question. So to get found, you've got to be the answer to as many people's questions as possible! Be creative when you tag your spaces, maybe you don't sell trending:tuition but maybe trending:tuition is a conversation starter about trending:learning about trending:investments…

It wasn't that I didn't know about that stuff. But the way he said it kind of… crystallised it. It was a couple of hours long and you could stay and ask questions as long as you wanted but once you logged off you couldn't get back into the classroom again.

I didn't ask any questions and left half an hour after it finished. His ad for his next level masterclass triggered when I left but there was no way I could afford another one. Fifty friends at one percent discount per referral wouldn't get me close. I had enough to get started anyway.

Still dressed, I lay on top of my duvet. I didn't think I'd sleep that easily because my mind was buzzing with the masterclass. But the last thing I remembered was a thought like an echoing whisper.

Wow! I don't think I've had a J™ for two days running.

I snapped awake in grey dark with the rain bucketing down in the alleyway. Work was pinging me and I felt ill jumping out of bed in a panic. I logged on and found there was a viewing about to start but it was okay because it was yet another last-minuter so I wasn't technically late and I wouldn't get marked. I waited for it to switch over to IN-PROGRESS then arsed about like a blind moron, making a mug of Instant™ without fading down the agency space enough to get myself caught.

It was a cold start to a poo of a day. I shovelled some pancakes into my face between the surprise viewing and the first official one. Then I had them back-to-back till dark again. I was too tired to do anything on the Movement when I finished work. As my days on shift beat me down and fucked me up more and more, I slowly realised I wouldn't be able to do anything till my next off days.

Who knew why there were so many expensive properties selling at the moment? Maybe they were all bored with their sea-views and playing musical bloody houses or something. All I knew was how much overtime I worked for not that much money, and how exhausted it was making me.

I was already down to a four-point-nine stars average after some pissy over-entitled client thought I was a lawyer and complained to the agency when I couldn't answer his questions, about a year before. Some manager I didn't know I had, messaged me and said in all these pretentious big words how sorry she was that I had to take one up the bottom for the team I'd never met, to keep the client happy.

The complaint was upheld and their arsehole one-star rating stuck to me like the poo it was. She'd said not to worry though because she was sure I'd be back up to five in no time given my otherwise flawless track record. No hard feelings and keep up the good work.

I could have turned down the overtime and made the wankers shaft someone else in another grotty flat somewhere far, far away from here. But if I did that too many times, they would start cutting my shifts and there was no way I could afford that because I was working off the bad score and only one in fifty clients bothered their backsides to give ratings. On four-point-nine, all it would take would be one smart-arse in a bad mood to smash me down to four-point-seven and get all my shifts cut completely.

It technically wouldn't have meant I'd be fired but everyone knew it could take from a year to a lifetime to beg them back up to full time. And it would be a breach of contract to work two jobs. And if I quit to find something else before my five years was up, I'd have 'bad leaver' on my public file and that would mean me rotting my feet in a basement government flat out by the coast till I died at the age of thirty-four of bowel cancer from a diet that arrived in stripey bioboxes only.

So, sure, I could have turned down the overtime. But no. I couldn't.

I have to start the Movement. I have to!

For the last nine days on shift, I didn't forget about Nate or my visit application or his family or the Movement. But I didn't have time to think about anything but work. I didn't vape my J™ once. I dragged myself out of bed, splashed water on my face, made Instant™, ate pancakes – or dumplings on a Nateish-health-kick day – and started work every morning. They kept force-feeding me overtime and I kept crawling into bed half-dead every night.

And no matter how many sales I made, nobody rated me.

Twice when my BO got so bad I could smell myself, I splurged on dry washes. It creeped me out having nanites crawling in all my orifices. But it was better than dying of some gross infection. Supposedly.

A payday randomly came the day before I was due some off time. By the time I was down to one viewing on the last day of shift, all I could think about was food I could chew, Budlike™ and sleep.

I was suffocating in a week's worth of toxic farts and wincing every time I moved because my bottom stung from nine days of poor eating; even for me. Didn't stop me doing more of it though. That night, the bitter aftertaste of posh pizza partied in my mouth with Instant™ and Budlike™ as I crashed out on top of my duvet.

For the first time since my last off days, I fluked a good sleep. After I woke, I rolled over and faced the wall and made plans to work on the Movement. A second before the ads started up for the day, I noticed messages from Chen and Nate's friend, Shane. I went to open the one from Shane then decided to save it up for after Chen's one, which was probably going to be her making me feel useless because she'd done something perfect.

She was wearing clothes, at least and her pile of laundry was reduced to a couple of pieces folded – folded! – on the bed beside her. Her flat smelled like sterile nothing in that just-cleaned kind of way and I wondered how many free cleans she got on her work plan. 'Hey Teens, nothing urgent. Only wondering how your week's going? I've got off-days in a week or so, maybe we could hang out, get into a movie or something? Call me when work's not slaying you.'

I didn't call her. What did she think we'd do? Sit around and talk about her hair while my boyfriend's brain slowly turned to mush? What was the point?

Unless she wants something. But what could she want from… me?

She probably got paid enough to eat real food every week so she wouldn't have been trying to scrounge a loan from the likes of me. I dimmed the message. She'd only left it the day before anyway so she'd be working her bottom off kissing those other people, for ages yet.

Shane's message was three days old. I couldn't believe I hadn't noticed his call. His flat hadn't been cleaned recently but I liked the smell of his boy BO. He was sitting in his work chair and I could see Ubers going past in the rain through the window behind him.

His blonde hair was shaved like mine and his face was covered in cute whiteish stubble. He always looked like he was thinking something crude and it always made me do it too. 'Hey Teens, nothing urgent and thank fuck this is the right handle! I had to try, like, ten people! Yeah-nah, anyway, only wondering how your guys' weeks are going? Maybe we could get a bunch of peeps together, vape some weed and get into a movie or something. I got off-days coming up soon. Ping me if you're keen. Oh yeah, and can you get Nate to ping me? I can't get hold of the man, there's something weird going on with his tech.'

I liked how Shane was so sociable. He always tried to include everyone. I couldn't believe he was single. Chen never wanted to talk about him; probably annoyed there was such a thing as a man who wasn't into her. I played his message over a couple of times so I could watch his lips move, then saved his handle and called him back.

'Teens!' He was under his duvet with a mug of Instant™ and for a second, I wished I could join him.

I had to tell him about Nate but I didn't know how. Nate had been gone for nearly a fortnight now and I was worried Shane would be angry I hadn't told him. Then suddenly, I was blasted out of my calm and wailing like a baby. 'I'm sorry Shane. I'm so sorry. I didn't have your handle and work was mental and I, just, it's just, it's just all fucked!'

'What is Teens? What's happened? Have you lost your shifts or something? Can I loan ya some ding?'

He was an amazing guy. I could see how much my crying was freaking him out. But straight away, like that, he packed his feelings away and was trying to help me. He didn't patronise me by telling me to pull myself together or anything. Instead — as Nate would have — snap! He offered me money I knew he didn't have, given he worked the same dreadful job as Nate... used to.

I shook my head, trying to stop crying but all I got out was, 'It's Nate, Shane, he's—' Then tears choked me up again.

'Hang on Teens. I'm gonna come over, okay?'

I couldn't answer so I nodded but he'd already cut the call. He only lived a couple of blocks away but he must have got an Uber anyway. I only had enough time to get up and pull myself together... ish, before he was at the door.

I was glad I'd called him because now I knew he couldn't very well say anything about how much my flat stunk. I triggered a quick nano-wash so at least I didn't, although I was a bit queasy from the feeling of the little bastards crawling all over me.

Nate must have done one of his dodgy numbers on the building that maintenance had never found because Shane came straight in through the poor-door and pinged me from the hallway. He grinned and opened his arms when the door peeled back.

'Hey, Teens. Long time, no see! You look rough, man. What's goin' on? What's up with N—? Whoa!'

I slammed into him and wrapped my arms around him and hated myself for crying into his chest. He stroked my head and kept saying in a disgustingly cute awkward voice, 'Okay, Teens. It's okay. We'll, uh, figure it out. It'll all be good.'

I clung to him and after bit, I started to calm. He was taller than me, like Nate. I didn't think he was into Nate's weird exercise stuff but he probably took the pills. He was all guyish hard lumps and big thick bones. I suddenly wanted to pull him down on top of me right in the doorway, taste his lips and bite his neck. I could barely stop myself shoving my crotch against him.

I shoved him away and backed inside. 'Nate's in prison, Shane! He's in fuckin' prison! He got arrested and put in prison and all you can do is— come 'round here an'— an'— FUCKIN' HELL!' My voice had risen to a shriek.

Shane jumped and his face went white. 'Jeez, Teens. What the fuck? What happened? Do— Do his folks know?' He hadn't moved from the doorway and he was shaking.

Shit! His family.

It felt like an actual kick in the stomach. My mouth opened and closed and tears rolled down my face and I couldn't swallow them back no matter how hard I tried. I sobbed like an idiot and went and sat on my bed to hide that I was about to fall over.

Shane followed me in and took the chair. I'd been enough of a stupid emotional child in front of him already. I made myself calm down. I was determined not to give him the ego trip of thinking he was the big man, sorting it all out for me. I didn't think he and Chen ever connected outside of when we all spent time together so I was probably safe telling him more or less the truth.

'I tried, Shane. But I didn't have any of his folks' handles. I tried to get hold of ya to see if ya had it but there's a shitload of Shanes in the world! Your avatar's shit, man! I would never've known that was you if ya hadn't've called me!' I tried to smile and for some reason he suddenly looked…

Is he nervous?

'Doesn't Chen have it?'

Fuck!

'I, uh, I dunno. I didn't think to ask her.'

'Well, whadever anyway, here's his mum's handle. When did it happen? We better tell them soon or they'll freak! I mean, they're gonna freak anyway but you know how close they are. If they can't get hold of him, they're gonna start panicking.'

Yeah, because I needed to feel more bloody guilty.

'Yeah, I'll tell them. But Shane, I dunno what to do. I mean, we've gotta get him out!'

'Get him out? What's he doing in, Teens? What'd they bust him for?'

'He said it was nothin', bullshit charges over his tech. He told me I'd have to visit or…'

'They'd fry his brain? Yeah, you don't have tell me Teens. I know all the Nate conspiracy biz, not that I reckon he's wrong, mind you. We prob'ly should try to visit him. And they prob'ly won't make it easy.'

'That's what Nate said. They already kinda haven't. I had to go to the cop station and put in this stupid request.'

'Eh? At the cop station?'

'I know!'

'When did you put it in?'

'Few weeks ago, give or take.'

'So when do you visit him? Where do you visit him?'

'I dunno when. I guess I gotta wait to hear from 'em. But he's at his place.'

'Eh?'

'He's put under, at his place. He's through there.' I pointed at the kitchenette, trying not to look at it so I didn't break down again. Shane seemed calm.

But how could he be?

He'd probably forgotten about my outburst before, probably thought I had hormones or whatever; it helped to be a woman sometimes.

He looked at the wall for a while then said, 'Jeez! So it's true! Have you tried to…'

'Yeah, yeah, I've tried everything. The walls are that high security stuff and the cop tech locks you outta the alleyway. His door looks the same from the hallway but it's turned into the security stuff too, it doesn't ping with tech any more, like it's dead concrete or something.'

'Fuck!' He didn't second-guess me like Chen had, at least. He didn't try to see for himself. He kept staring at the wall.

I made us mugs of Instant™ and offered him some Bud-like™. 'Nah, I gotta work. I should be working now. You go for it if ya want, though,' he said.

I bloody did want but I had to work on the Movement. I couldn't lose my way again. Shane said he'd get everyone together and they'd all put in visitor forms. 'Don't be a stranger, Teens. Give us a yell if there's anything ya need eh? Or if you're, y'know, struggling or whadever.' He said as he got up to go.

When the door sealed behind him and I went to put his mug in the dishwasher, I saw he'd hardly drunk a drop. I tried to remember which way the handle had been facing on the table and turned it so I could put my mouth exactly where his had touched the lip. I finished it off myself. Maybe he'd been in a hurry to get back to work.

I ordered pancakes for breakfast and was so hungry I didn't mind the aftertaste. I got to work and had a shoddy free virtual space set up with all my tags by the afternoon. I kept noticing the bag of Budlike™ and the J™ on the table when I came out of the workspace to make mugs of Instant™. I shoved them under my pillow. I had two more days off after this so I decided to finish the virtual and get smashed after that.

The virtual was online as I worked on it and I was kind of hoping the tags would start getting search hits like the masterclass had showed me.

You know they won't… No!

But all the analytics stayed at zero, two days later when I pretty much couldn't think of anything else to add.

The space was mostly full of recordings of me explaining about the goddess and how we were going to take back our roles as men and women and bring down the rich-fucks. There should have been millions of people into that.

I was happy I'd got it all set up, that I'd properly started the Movement but it disappointed me that no one was interested.

Early days.

That and I was too tired to go over the bites from the masterclass and too desperate for a J™ after so many days without. I packed it full, ordered an enormous deluxe fake pizza, got my hemps off and climbed into bed so I could coma more conveniently after vaping my brains out.

It was dark when work pinged me awake with an evil 'urgent' viewing. What the fuck was wrong with rich people that they suddenly sprung an open-home on me in the middle of the night? I inhaled an Instant™, scalding my mouth in the process. It hardly did anything so I was half asleep when the viewing started which was why I didn't click that something was wrong till about halfway through.

Then I started wondering if the weed hadn't worn off. I couldn't virtual into the property with all the viewers going through but I could access holos of the place and it was bigger than anything I'd ever seen.

And it had pictures of green around it; trees, forest and rivers. Things I'd only seen pics of back in basic school, so messy and dirty! There might have been some greenery in the southern Ao Islands in places they couldn't build because of landslides or seismic activity, but there was no way we got blue skies like that in this part of the world for long enough to take pics of.

That was when I started realising what had happened but by then it was too late. An awful guy virtualled into the agency space and said, 'Are you the realtor?'

Fuck!

Someone was asking me a real live bloody question!

'I'm, uh, sorry sir, I am but usually, we, uh…'

Don't do anything? Yeah, probably shouldn't…

'All the property information is in our space, sir.'

'Excuse me, What? You makin' fun of me?'

'No! No. I'm sorry! I didn't understand your question, that's all. I'm only an agent here. I monitor the viewings. I don't handle any legal stuff or anything like that. I've got the property info and stuff if you need to know anything more about the property?'

'Oh, so you are the realtor! Well, I got a question, do you think they'll take a lower offer?'

'A lower…?'

'Price! A lower price! Will they sell for a lower goddam price? Jee-zus! Are you fuckin' stoopid or something?'

'Uh, I can tell you what it previously sold for and…'

'That's not what I goddamned asked!'

'Sorry Sir, we don't have access to the vendors. We can't ask them any questions. We've only got what's on the system. I can't—'

'Bull SHIT you can't! I bought three other places this week and their realtors were real helpful. You're being an asshole! I wanna speak to your manager, pronto!'

I wasn't trained or signed up for any other countries. There was no way I'd have anything to do with – ugh! – foreign people for any money! I shouldn't have been sent this viewing. They must have had a different agency setup there or something, for him to have thought he could ask me, well, anything. They couldn't do anything to me over this. I was safe.

He probably didn't have access to rate me since I wouldn't be listed on his TZ's agency space. I was more than happy to hook him up with my manager who I'd never talked to in my life. I found her handle and made sure they were plugged in then went back to sleep.

Another last-minuter was pinging me when I woke but it was a normal one at a normal shitty time. I had eighteen glorious fucking days on shift this time because someone had apparently quit the agency. The system split their shift between me and the other loser who'd usually have clocked on after them. I could have turned it down but I felt bedevilled as usual by the whole rating debacle.

Search rankings for the Movement space cost money I hardly had so I would have to save on food. I put in a bulk order for the cheapest stripey-biobox pizzas on the menu and a tube of baby cream for the inevitable bottom-burn they'd-like… ignite. I lasted eleven days till the sting and the stink in my flat got so disgusting I had to flee.

Late one night when I knew there wouldn't be any other idiots creeping about for me to run into and risk having to make small talk with, I used one of Nate's hacks to leave my flat door open and share my aromatic pooey-love with the rest of the wet-foot community, or the hallway anyway. I did a

Nate and went out into the wind and got half a block before my legs tired and my fucking… arse stung so badly I had to rest. I leant on a fence for a bit before heading back and despite the burning pain in my bottom, I managed to hate that the city air through my overs-hood filter was like magic in my lungs.

Why did he have to be right so much!

Back in the flat stunk like the hallway, as if it was counter-attacking. But depressingly, it was better than the smell of my rotting insides. My stomach rumbled but I couldn't handle more pizza so I splurged on one of the pricey Nate-food salads again. It tasted like heaven and the tear that escaped and ran down my cheek wasn't only because there was now pittance left on my balance for search rankings. I had pizza the next day and wished in vain for the baby cream to work.

A few days after the bowel-crisis, Chen left me another message. Shane left one a couple of days after that. I didn't open them. Work was back-to-back and I was way too tired and sore to talk to people. I pinged them the handle of the new Movement space and told them to spread it and I'd be in touch in my next off days.

More messages appeared from both of them and I was on the home stretch with only a day of the shift left. I felt hungover though I hadn't vaped a single J™ the whole time. I definitely wasn't up for talking to anyone.

After my last viewing, I went into Yang's news space to see if there was anything about so many properties moving but he only had the usual crap about weird quakes off the coasts and collapsing seawalls; and icky feel-good stories about Christmas livestreams coming up. I couldn't argue with his followers though. Jesus!

If I get on his feed, the Movement will be set!

If I stuck to the pizza and factored in one salad next shift, I'd make enough for a week of search rankings. I was too tired to work it all out exactly though. I'd do it all in the morning, reply to the messages, figure out the search stuff. I needed rest.

I spent up large and pointlessly on a jumbo-sized tube of baby cream and packed the J™ to help me sleep.

I couldn't remember anything when I woke, in a good kind of way. My stomach was a bit sore but it was only a soft throb. I listened to the wind and the AC and whispered to myself, 'Oh man, three whole days off!' I turned over and went back to sleep before the ads could get me.

I woke again, keen to get out of bed. By the time I was sitting down to pizza and Instant™, I had two and half off-days left before the next eighteen days of hell.

The bio boxes were melting on the floor by the door and I was into a second mug and contemplating a J™ when Chen pinged me. I suddenly remembered I hadn't got in touch with Nate's family and I didn't want to talk to her. But it was too late to decline; I hadn't held my calls and we were on.

I got in first. '*Kia ora* Chen. How's it goin'? Did ya check out the Movement space?'

'Oh, *nǐ hǎo* Teens, uh, the what—? Whoa! Do you, uh, want me to call back? I mean, I'm fine if you are! But, uh, before you said—'

I cut the call.

Oh shit! Jesus, Jesus, Jesus, Jesus!

I pulled my hemps on from the day before and called her back with a hot red face. 'Oh my god, Chen! I'm so embarrassed. I'm so sorry! I didn't think! I finished a massive shift yesterday and I was strapped for cash so I survived on stripeys and I'm kinda wiped out and I wasn't thinking. Fuck! Sorry!' It was all beautifully true! I was genuinely mortified for answering her in the nude. And it was the perfect distraction from whatever grief she'd probably been going to give me.

'Relax Teens. It's only a body. Jeez, we've all got them. I only said something 'cause I didn't want you to be embarrassed. But, oh well, put my foot in it again I s'pose.' She did a pretty good job of sounding like she was genuinely sorry, sly little rat. 'Anyway, I was wondering if you wanted to hang out, come over here for a change of scene?'

I hated the way women did that, acted like they were friends with you when they wanted something. Why couldn't she have asked me straight out? Nate or Shane would have. She was lucky I was in a good enough mood to let her off the hook.

'I, uh, I'm kinda wiped out today Chen, I don't think I'd be up to mu—'

'How 'bout tomorrow? Or, is it three off-days you've got? Or four? Maybe in a couple of days once you're all chilled?'

'Three or four? Jeez Chen! How 'bout three every month on a lucky month! Don't s'pose you wanna second job? Some inconsiderate a-hole quit and I've got half their shift back-to-back with mine till they find someone new.'

'Fuck! Is that even legal?'

'Prob'ly not but what am I gonna do?'

'Yeah, true. Well, do you wanna do something anyway?'

'I dunno Chen, I—'

Then I saw a creepy thing. A tear rolled down her cheek and suddenly her pretty little face wasn't so pretty any more. Chen was crying! Perfect wannabe rich-fuck Chen with the flash job and the posh second-floor flat was crying! Her face was all screwed up trying to hold back the tears but they were coming anyway and it made me feel sick. 'Fuck, Chen,' I said, going a bit red. 'What's the matter?'

It didn't take her long to collect herself. She wiped her eyes with her sleeve. 'Shit. Sorry Teens. I didn't mean to spring that on you first thing in the early afternoon. Man. Took myself by surprise a bit there. Sorry! It's— I, uh, I haven't seen anyone, like, anyone at all face to face since I came over that time, after… Well, anyway, my off-days got canned 'cause someone went off sick so I've been stuck inside for like, nearly six weeks or something. I— Man! I'm so sorry to dump this on you but I'm kind of, going a bit crazy.' Her voice was shaking.

That made me cringe. How could she come out with that stuff, say it straight out like that, like a child asking if you'll be their best friend. I nearly cut the call, I felt ill. I couldn't believe she hadn't cut the call after losing her shit like that. I'd have dug a hole and jumped in it if I was her. I wouldn't have been able to see me again for a week or-like, ever. I cringed so hard my stomach hurt. Her awful-like… poor-fuck accent was wrong enough; worse given she spoke so correctly. But this! This was too much!

There was no way I could not go over there now, but what if she wanted me to hug her or something? Ugh! I imagined the gross snotty wetness of her tears soaking through my hemps and wondered if I could stay in my overs and she wouldn't notice.

'Okay, okay, sorry. I— I didn't know. Yeah, course we can catch up. I'll come over. Gimme, I dunno, twenny minutes or something.'

'Thanks Teens. You're a lifesaver. God, sorry! I promise I'll get it together.'

Ew, ew, ew, ew!

After I cut the call, I shook myself. Seeing her like that had made me feel all icky like she was some kind of queen cockroach I couldn't shake off. Now the last thing I wanted was to see her in the flesh. I felt like she was crawling under my skin and the feeling wouldn't go away. I tried to think about the Movement, Shane, work, Nate, anything to get the image of her blasting out her pathetic feelings at me like that.

But I couldn't shake it. My heart started pounding and I couldn't breathe. I sat in my work chair gasping while I put a pinch into the J™. I choked down a quick couple of puffs and it calmed me enough to get my breathing under control again. I took deep breaths and after an age, my heart slowed. A bit.

I thought about refilling the J™ and taking it with me to share with her but she was richer than me and probably had better weed. And I was going all the way over there to see her, the least she could do would be offer me something.

It was a dryish day outside and I stood by the poor-door sucking in air for a few minutes to calm down again because the hall had closed in on me and made my panic rise. The wind had blown the puddles off the ground but there were damp patches everywhere.

The clouds roiled across the sky. I had to collect myself again because their blowing like that flashed up a memory of Nate and I sneaking up to the roof terrace through the lift-core maintenance shaft, and lying on our backs doing some cheesy old psychology shape tests Nate had read about.

…Jeez Teens! A dead baby? A dude with his arm come off? Can't you see any nice things in the clouds?…

I kept my eyes straight ahead to stop myself looking down the alley as I walked past its entrance.

Chen's poor-door looked the same as mine and the ground-floor hallway stunk the same as mine. I pinged her flat through the lift interface so it would let me get to the second floor and I jumped when the doors opened and she was standing there. 'Hey! You came!' She smiled.

Okay, that's not weird.

She backed away to let me out but stayed a bit too close and half held her arms out.

I'm not bloody hugging you.

I shouldered past her and walked off down the hallway which annoyingly, didn't stink.

'Teens! Tina!'

I looked back at her.

'Teens! It's this way!'

Well don't I look like a fucking idiot.

'Ah. Okay.'

'Don't worry. I miss it half the time myself. Remember I came to find you guys last time?'

She wasn't wrong. It was nothing like my flat, straight down the hall from the poor-door. I remembered now. There were all these passageways through side-doors and weird single steps I kept tripping on because I couldn't see them in time, in the crappy hallway light. It was as if there was more in the building than you could get to or something.

Chen's place was in the central part of the building so she had no windows, only a cheap crappy panel with a feed from a cam outside. She had her lights turned right up and the place smelled a good few days on from its last clean, so she can't have done another one since she left the message for me.

Whoa! The little doll beefs like the rest of us!

'Sorry about the stink Teens, there's a week or so before my cleans clock over. I'd do it myself but y'know, satoshis.'

Jeez! Had she noticed me sniffing? Or trying not to, anyway. Still, I was surprised she had so few cleans she had to wait.

She made me a cup of Instant™ so weak it was almost clear.

'I dunno what's wrong with it,' she apologised as she handed it to me. 'I splashed out on this fancy poncy coffee and it kind of, doesn't work. What do all the dry-foots see in this stuff, hey?' She opened a cupboard and held up the biobox.

Oh, Chen, Chen, Chen, sweety! You idiot!

I said nothing and sipped brownish hot water, trying not to laugh. But then – *yyyyyes!* – she brought out her J™-ful of actual real wrack-grown weed; only leaf but still, it tasted fucking orgasmic. We sat on her tatty bioware couch in her lounge which was smaller and less posh in real life than when I saw it virtual-touched. It took me a few puffs of her J™ to stop glancing over at her in case she came in for some kind of girly hug or something.

We made not-too-excruciating small-talk for a while. My worry that she'd get all weepy and grab me eased but I stayed a bit on edge waiting for her to start up some bullshit woman-to-woman talk. Or worse, ask me about Nate. But when it came it was oh so fucking much worse than that.

We were a J™ each down and she'd pulled her work chair over to put her feet up. Her hemp pants hung off her legs so I could see how skinny they were. Her eyes were glassy and she'd stayed quiet for a bit. I thought she might have got too stoned to keep talking and maybe she'd pass out soon and I could slip away. Her bag of weed was on the couch between us and I was packing the J™ for another puff when she came out with, 'Teens, are you managing okay?'

'Eh?'

'I mean, with Nate and all the stuff that's happened and all your new shifts and stuff. I mean, you've been through hell!'

'Yeah, whadever. It sucks but I'm dealing with it. We're gonna get the Movement going and everything, right?'

'The, uh, Move——? Uh, yeah. Yeah, course,' she sighed. 'But I mean, isn't it kind of, I dunno, hard?' Her voice went all… pissy, as if she was asking a question she thought I was too dumb to answer and she was already disappointed in me. Worse than that, it brought a lump to my throat and I had to suck on the J™ and turn my head so she wouldn't see me struggling to control my tears.

'Yeah, well, shit happens doesn't it,' I said and I hated how my voice shook.

Why couldn't we keep chilling like normal people? Inside I was suddenly burning up and breaking down at the same time. All this was none of her business. It was nosey of her to ask about my feelings. That stuff was personal! I didn't ask myself about my feelings. Yes, I felt like shit, didn't we all? But talking about it wasn't going to do any good! It would only make it all come out and feel worse.

But she wouldn't let it go. 'Yeah. I know shit happens, Teens. I know it does. And I know we gotta deal with it and get on with it but it doesn't mean we're not allowed to feel shit about it, does it? I mean, Nate's in prison, for fuck's sake! Your boyfriend and my, uh… friend, in actual prison! And we've gotta get on with our lives and act like it didn't happen, and, I dunno Teens. How do you, keep… handling it like this? I'd be going crazy!'

My, uh…, friend… my, uh…, friend… my, uh…, friend…

The J™ was hot in my hand and I realised I was squeezing it because my hands had clenched into fists. I put it down and turned to face her. I put my hands in my lap and tried to un-clench my body but I couldn't.

I took a sip of her ridiculous hot water to wet my mouth and when I spoke my voice scared me and kind of turned me on at the same time. 'Okay, I geddit now. You got me over here and got me wasted to break it to me about how you can't stop wanting to get back with Nate. Or maybe you two didn't break up and you can't get any sympathy 'cause of what everyone'll think of you if ya come out and say your ex who you were cheating on his new girlfriend with, has gone to prison and you're sad 'cause you miss 'im. And for some weird twisted girl-reason, you reckon I'll be the one to understand. You're bloody sick Chen! What the fuck? What the actual—?'

'Teens! No! Jesus! Why would you say that?' To give her credit, her alarm was incredibly well faked.

'So you're saying you don't have feelings for Nate?'

She screwed up her face and sighed like she had a right to be frustrated with me. 'Teens, No. I mean, look. Whatever feelings I've got or haven't got don't matter. Nate broke up with me a year, eighteen months or whatever before you two met. He's my friend, you're my friend. That's all that matters Teens. And I'm worried about you and him and—'

'Really Chen? You're worried about me? Or are you worried about yourself and how much you miss my boyfriend? What else did you need me from today? Let me see. Okay, first I haven't got in touch with his folks yet. Second, I haven't bloody heard anything about the visit and sorry I didn't decide to quit my job to go down to the bloody *jǐngchá*'marie to see what the fuck they've done with the form. Happy now? Is that all ya wanned to know? Anything else I can update you on or can I go home now?'

By the time I'd finished my body had started loosening and the red mist was clearing from my eyes. I knew I was out of line but I couldn't stop my mouth from moving and now Chen had pulled her knees up to her chin. She was cringing against the other end of the sofa with eyes bulging and head shaking like a mental case. Her mouth was opening and closing like her life-support had run out of credit.

Fuck! I didn't mean that! Shit!

But I kind of did mean it. And I couldn't exactly take it back anyway. I was hardly going to sit there and beg her to forgive me. I didn't know what to say so I stared at her and slowly she collected her wits. Her face changed and she started looking at me like you'd look at a dying old person and suddenly it was too much.

I put my mug on her desk and pulled on my overs and she didn't try to stop me. 'Tina,' she said as I got to the door. I stopped dead and half turned, not wanting to see her face. 'I think Sha— I think you're—'

'I'm what?'

She sighed. 'Just, let me know if there's anything I can do, will you?'

Fuck that.

'You know what, Chen?' I didn't wait for her to answer. 'You're meant to grind the fucking coffee beans first, you giant moron!'

I bolted into the hall.

Sha— Sha— Sha—

Christ. Were Shane and her in touch after all? Had she already known I hadn't got in touch with Nate's folks and only wanted to hear it from me out of vindictiveness? Did people have bloody nothing to do but… fuck with me all the time? Maybe she'd hooked up with him as some kind of pathetic way of getting back at Nate and I for being together.

I roared and stamped my feet and the building soundproofing deadened the noise to nothing. I'd taken a few turns before realising I'd gone the wrong way. I tried to find Chen's door again so I could go in the other direction. But the doors all looked the same and I couldn't be sure if I'd found hers or not.

I tried querying the building for directions but I wasn't registered as a resident so it bounced all my pings. My heart started racing and the walls got narrower. I was epically stoned but that made it worse instead of helping as it normally did. I couldn't stop my rising panic.

I tried walking faster but only got more lost. Blackness closed in from the edges of my vision making my ads flash brighter. I broke and ran as the hall closed in around me. Soon all I could see was a tiny point of light ahead which went out with a sudden crunch.

'Hey. *Nǐ hǎo?* 'scuse me? You all right?'

I was lying on my back, head pounding. My vision was weirdly small.

'Hey!' I heard snapping fingers. 'Hey! *Nǐ hǎo?* Are you okay?'

A face leaned down and I tensed when a hand shook my shoulder. 'Whoa! Take it easy! I'm trying to help you.'

'I'm all right.' I blinked and wiped my hand over my eyes trying to see better. It worked a bit. One eye was fine and everything went from black to reddish-brown in the other.

'Your head's bleeding. You sure you're okay?'

I wiped at my eyes again and it finally worked. 'Yeah, must've just…'

Banged into a wall like a mental case loser.

'…whacked it on something.'

'Jeez! You can say that again! You wanna get that looked at I reckon.' Now I could see properly, I realised I was at the dead-end of a hallway. I was lying with feet hanging over one of the crappy single steps. I'd probably tripped over it and hit my head on the wall as I fell.

It wasn't the first time something like this had happened although I hadn't panicked that much for a long while. There were two people wearing overs standing gawking at me. The girl was hanging back and the guy had been the one talking.

'Hey look,' I said, 'I was visiting my friend and I, uh, got lost, can you help me find the lifts?'

'Yeah, sure. But, you sure you gonna be all right? Do you live far? You can come to our place and fix yourself up if you w—'

'Nah, thanks. I'll be fine. I live in the building next door. It's all good. I need to get to the lift, that's all.'

'Okay, no worries. You need a hand getting—?'

A sharp pain in my head brought tears to my eyes when I heaved myself up. But I stayed calm. The two of them looked at each other then the guy, a big fat baloomba of a thing, shrugged and they walked me to the lifts.

I felt like throwing up and pain lanced through my head with each step on my way home. I was sweating and sick by the time I got in and I knew something was properly wrong, probably a concussion; I'd had one before.

Great. Exactly what I fucking need with all the other shit happening in my life.

Suddenly too hot, I stripped naked and sat on my bed. I scoured my balance empty for a diagnosis then jumped up and got to the sink, barely in time to puke down it. I nearly passed out on my way back to the bed in the few minutes before the silvery nanites crawled under the door; from where I didn't have a clue but it must have been close. They homed in on me, flowed up the bed and swarmed all over me like tiny roaches.

I shivered and sweated and had to keep myself from tensing up and trying to swipe them off as they crawled into my orifices. The diagnosis came through: concussion.

That was money well fucking spent then wasn't it.

The diagnostic tech I'd been forced to waste money on to get the official fucking prescription authorised public health treatment and a second later, the public system connected and fed the treatment to my on-board systems. Enhanced by the public health goodies, my biotech worked its magic. My headache eased and I felt a sting on my temple as the cut patched over. The med nanites waited till the treatment was all set up and messaged me the usual bullshit instructions about signing off work, resting and… whatever.

They flowed from my orifices clean and silver as if they'd never gone inside me. They disappeared down the side of my bed and off under the doorway dragging my money behind them. That was all my search ranking money and some of my food gone on a pathetic fucking panic attack. Which all said and done, was caused by a man. Which man it was hardly fucking mattered. They were all the same.

I dozed away the rest of the day and the one after. At first my tech kept waking me to make sure I didn't go into a coma but it left me alone after a while.

I couldn't face looking at my online space stats. I ordered pancakes and pizza or whatever I felt like at whatever time of day. My head finally cleared on my last off-day and though I didn't really remember deciding to go, I found myself in an Uber pulling into the police station in the rain before ten in the morning.

'What the fuck do you mean not found!' I said it loud enough for the jelly behind the window to look up.

Is it the same guy or is being fat a pre-requisite for getting hired?

I gave him a filthy look and his eyes disappeared back into tech lala-land.

I know what you're doing you freak! Ugh!

No matter what names I entered, no matter what order, the system kept saying I hadn't put in a visitor request. I finally decided to ask the monster. 'Hey, 'scuse me. I put in a form to visit my boyfriend in prison and this thing says it can't find the request.'

He shrugged. 'Got lost probably. Happens.'

Lost? Systems don't lose things!

'What do you mean? How do I find it?'

'Ma'am if you want to make a complaint, you'll need to do a complaints form, it's on that same terminal you're at now under…'

'Forget it.'

I made another request and this time I took a copy to show the grotesque idiot if it got lost again. But it turned out I didn't need to. A message from Spume pinged up before I got home. It was a recorded virtual, Jo Rahui but a much younger pic of her. Because her water art had inspired Spume. Seeing her brought a lump to my throat and I swallowed angrily and forced myself to listen to the message.

It's not her. It's just a stupid bot.

She was standing on a beach with waves spraying up behind her in a poncy arty kind of way. She told me she regretted that my visitor request couldn't be granted at this time because there was some medical problem with the client – the fucking client! She said I should try back later.

Like when? Arseholes.

At the end of the message there was a handle for the request system! Eager to shut down the image of Jo Rahui, I followed it and there was the form in common fucking *hànzì*! It was the same bullshit virtual piece of paper with the same fields. But why couldn't the stupid fat pervert cop have told me about it? I saved the link and ripped the message to my local archive as Nate had taught me.

I was starting to think Nate was right, Spume were stopping me from seeing him. What kind of system lost requests nowadays? What kind of medical problems could Spume have had? They were meant to be the almighty world-leading biotech experts.

I wanted to tell Chen what had happened but there was no way I could see her again after the-like… fiasco we'd had. She didn't deserve to know after manipulating me like that. I waited till the evening and went straight into Shane's messaging to give him the news then went to bed.

The next morning I woke early and amazingly, felt… all right-ish. Small comfort given I'd slept away most of my off days recovering from the concussion. I ordered pancakes and didn't mind too much when a last-minuter pinged as I finished eating. I slurped down an Instant™ before the boredom-orgy of minimum-wage hell that was my shift began.

My anger at the crappy Spume system for messing me around helped me remember the request. It might have been a week into my eighteen days or maybe a bit more but without setting a reminder, some random braincell pinged it up from my memory unprompted. I went to find Spume's message with the handle in it and it was gone.

Arseholes, bottoms and… fuckers!

It really was if they were trying to make life hard for me, as Nate had said they would! Lucky I'd saved the message off. I could hear Nate's voice in my head, guiding me.

No! The goddess's voice.

I made the request online and it took about a minute. The next morning there was a message waiting with an actual visitation appointment on the exact day I'd asked for.

I've got to tell Chen!

But I couldn't face her. I sent Shane a late-night ninja message again. If they were talking, he'd tell her. And if not, she could fuck off anyway.

My shift slowed to a crawl. I couldn't remember which night the messages started pinging in from Chen, whether it was before I'd messaged Shane or after. I could have checked but I was always too tired after work.

Shane sent me a couple too but I couldn't deal with people right now. My head had started to itch and flake where I'd bumped it and I started picking at it during my viewings because it felt good when bits of biopatch and dried scab flaked off.

My tech flashed a warning to leave it alone when I made it bleed again by accident but it wasn't my fucking mother; not that she would've cared. My visit with Nate would be on my first off-day if my schedule didn't get torpedoed by a rush of sales. There was a rush, weirdly given Christmas was so close. But my schedule held.

I ignored all the pissy carols popping up in iSpotTunes and cheesy offers for Christmas decorations code for my 'toos and muscled on womanfully through Christmas and on through January up to nearly New Year. But as the end of my shift neared, I started to panic.

Nathan – Feb 2097, Cornwall Estate, Akarana Island, Aotearoa Archipelago

'Nate! Babe! Nate!'

My eyes felt swollen shut and stung like they were full of sand. There was a taste like someone'd shoved some dirty socks in my mouth.

'Nate! Can you hear me? They've let me in! They said I could visit! Wake up Nate!'

Visit? That voice… Teens.

'Tina? Teens?' I couldn't hardly understand myself, my throat was so dry. I tried opening my eyes and the glare was like getting acid poured on my eyeballs and definitely not the good kind, so my first clearish words to my girlfriend were, 'Aaaah! Fuuuck!'

'Nate! Oh Jesus! Nate, you're awake! Slowly. Open your eyes slowly, you've been out for two months.'

Out? Out where?

I put my hand in front of my face and tried to open my eyes slowly and this time it worked a bit better. The blurriness cleared up slowly an' I saw a bony maggot-coloured hand with evil blue like my skin'd gone see-through. My arm was weak so my elbow flopped on the pillow.

'Babe? Are you all right?'

'Yeah, bit tired is all.'

'Tired? But you've—'

'Wha's goin' on Teens?'

'I—' I could hear her moving and I flopped my head over on the pillow to see and there was my government-cleaned apartment. It must of been morning or so 'cause the light coming in the window was about the brightest it got then. It was pissing down but I could see the corner of the AC on the alleyway wall, all blurry opposite Teens' window. It made my guts do a sad little heave which also kinda felt nice, to know I was…

…home…

…and about as far from home as ya could get.

That's… actually not nice, is it?

I moved my eyes to face my girlfriend who was sittin' back down on a stool.

'Arsehole's won't let me touch you.' She said. The tears were rolling.

…Government cleaned apartment…Tina…Visiting…

'Oh yeah!' I felt weirdly happy. 'Jeez! That's right! I'm in the joint!' I smiled at her.

'Yeah, you remember! Two months, Nate, it's been two months. How are you doing babe?'

'I'm, uh, fine.'

'You're fine?'

'Yeah, I'm, uh, yeah, I mean, I feel a bit woozy now but… Yeah well, I'm here aren't I? All good.'

'Oh, so… It's not that bad then? They don't… They haven't fucked up your brain?'

'Well, uh, you tell me?'

But she had other stuff to tell me. 'We— I tried to pull the public records, like you said, Nate.' She looked sad.

'Oh yeah? How was that?' To be honest, I couldn't remember what she meant.

She looked all sad. 'They say the details are unavailable. Chen spoke wi— I, uh, put in a 'nquiry but they only keep pissing back something about this one's gotta be kept confidential for the public interest or something like that. Check back later.'

I smiled at her fake tough-talk. Then I remembered I wasn't meant to know.

Know, uh, what?

But then her words pushed the right button. It was like a 'lectric shock which brought my memories back to life, properly this time. 'Fuckin' lying c— Arseholes!'

She got a massive grin-on then and she looked like the girlfriend I first met instead of the angry wastrel fakester she was turning into before I— Fuck! That was it! Now I was back in gear and rolling! I'd been arrested and— I freaked a bit then, 'cause I realised how nearly I'd forgotten it all. Jeez, they was fucking up my *nǎozǐ* already. After just… what did she say? Two months! Jeez! What was I gonna be like in five fuckin' years?

'That's more like it! That's my Nate! You're all right! Must've taken a few minutes for the drugs to wear off. You're right! They are fuckin' lying cunts! But… Nate. Is it like all the stories an' that? What happens? Do you remember anything?'

She was so happy. I didn't wanna fuck her up with the truth. And besides that, though I thought I remembered, I suddenly kinda, didn't. 'Jeez Teens, I'm not too sure.'

The rain…

'It's like you… like you're in…'

…the rain…

There was some memories. It wasn't like I'd been in a coma or something the whole time, which technically, I had. But each time I tried to say them, they kinda… slipped away, in a way I kinda knew. I could nearly remember like the….

…blue, rain, uh, brands?

Like… ads? But ads didn't disappear when you looked straight at 'em, if only they bloody would! Come to think of it, I noticed my tech, then, or more like how it was like it wasn't there.

Still firewalled.

Which also meant they hadn't poked 'round in it so that was one less thing to worry about. But it also must of meant visiting was only in person. Great, that'd fuck anyone wanting to come through the rain from too far away, like Mum and Dad. Wankers. What was wrong with getting visitors? Which made me remember…

'Teens, Do, uh, Mum and—?'

'I told them, Nate. They're not mad with you. They're pissed at the cops, but not you babes. They know it's bullshit. They want to come and visit but we were going to do this one first so we were sure how to figure out the appointments and then, we can figure out a place for them to crash here and, I dunno, we'll get it organised. But Nate, they're…' She kinda went quiet and I knew something was off.

'What is it, Teens?'

'It's not that big of a deal, Nate. I mean, they've basically got it handled, don't worry, okay?'

'What, Teens? Man! Ya can't start to tell me something then stop like that!' I tried to smile.

Her little face dropped and she let go a massive sigh. She stayed quiet for a bit longer then she said, 'Their seawall…'

'Eh? I thought it was one of the okay-ish ones!'

'So did everyone, Nate! Relax. They're on to it! They're… Your dad's got all the blocks together an' they're raising money and stuff. They're making noise. The council's gonna listen.'

Bullshit they are.

But what the bloody hell could I do about it from here anyway? I didn't push it though I wanted her to tell me all about it. 'My dad has got the blocks together?' I asked. It was crack-up. Jeez, if he wasn't sleepin' off a J™ he was smokin' one. The thought of him getting his shit together was un-bloody-likely enough.

'I know!' She smiled and that was good to see.

'Teens, I don't wanna be a pain, but I got to get ya to do something for me.'

'Oooh, I don't know about that Nathan.' She shook her head and tried not to smile. 'I'm pretty busy nowadays, I dunno if I can fit in any favours for incarcerated gangstas.' The way she tried to laugh made me sad.

'Ah, well, fair enough, Teens. Ya don't wanna be hangin' round with lowlifes like me, I geddit.' I tried to smile. 'Anyway, it's only been...'

A couple of months of...

But the memories slipped away like a slimy booger from the end of a finger; you could feel the tickle but...

Whassat feeling? I know that feeling!

But then I clicked that it'd been weeks of waiting for Teens and felt bad.

'Teens.'

There was something off about her name. Something I should've remembered. But I knew they wouldn't give us long so I tried to stay on track. I had to be a bit serious now and it broke my heart how her little face drooped.

Whadever they were doing to me, there was only one way I could think of to save at least part of my *nǎozǐ*, part of my bloody self. 'Sorry to be boring, Teens but this is mega important! I mean, I know you're probably busy with work an' that, but you gotta keep visiting me okay?'

'Well, course, Babe.'

'No, I mean, a lot. If I'm right, I don't think they'll let ya. They probably kept putting you off this first time, didn't they?'

'Well, nah, they said you... had to settle in and then I could book a visit.'

'Yeah, well, I reckon they was bullshitting to put you off. Let's see what their excuse is next time. But you gotta keep trying anyway, Teens, okay?'

'Okay, Nate. I will. And all the other stuff, the Movement an' that, I mean, I haven't stopped, there hasn't been any, y'know new intake but I haven't stopped.' Poor thing looked a bit guilty.

Movement? What's a movement?

'It's all good Teens. It's all—'

Shit!

Just like that, she was getting up an' turning towards the door. By the way she moved, I knew visiting hours was over and fuck us poor-door-using lowlifes if we didn't have time to say goodbye.

'Fuuuck!' I growled like the lions which were extinguished years ago. The rush of anger probably held back the drugs for about a nano before my rage went blurry in my ears and my lights went out again.

Tina – Feb 2097-Jun 2097, Cornwall Estate,

Akarana Island, Aotearoa Archipelago

I could hear Nate trying to say something behind me but the tech must have shut him down too so he could only make an awful growling sound. The way it cut off as if he'd been choked sent a chill down my spine. His door grew itself closed behind me and the police tech released me, nearly making me throw up in the process. I gave the door the finger and went home.

I wanted to pack my J™ and make an Instant™. But it ended up being via a five-minute session vomiting into the toilet with a leg stuck out behind me to keep the door from closing.

I've got to hack that to stay open.

It hadn't helped that the visitation appointment from Spume was so bloody uninformative. It had a passcode but it didn't say how to use it or tell me if I had to go to Nate's place or ping him a call like normal, or what.

I'd wasted a nano-clean on the flat and transferred the credit for another one to get my nails done. My hair was starting to grow out but I decided if Nate had been into Chen with her wannabe rich-fuck length then he wouldn't care about a few extra centimetres on me. But I'd transferred more credits to get all my stinky clothes done; that was for me; I was starting to gross myself out.

A minute before the visit, I'd changed my mind about being sober and vaped half a J™ to calm my nerves. Then at ten, I'd pinged him and it hadn't worked. His handle was the weird blue-grey I'd got used to, as if he was holding his calls and blocking messages.

Out in the hallway, I'd pinged his door and jumped backward when a pixelated system virtual slammed into my eyes. It had dug straight into my tech without asking and, like, violated my inbox to find the message from Spume with the passcode. Then the door had melted open and all hell had broken loose inside me.

At first I couldn't bring myself to go in. Though I hadn't been able to get this moment out of my head for weeks, now it was here I was scared. It was only when I started worrying that we'd run out of visiting time that I finally managed to make myself go through the door and discovered all my prissy primping had been for nothing.

I didn't know what I expected but it wasn't what I expected anyway! It was Nate's flat; sort of. The old guitar he'd wasted a fortune getting blueprints for was on its stand in the corner. His dishwasher and cupboards were closed, his bench was clean and the place hardly smelled of anything. All normal.

But his work chair had disappeared, repurposed into the blue stool in front of the bed. The floor and wall on the alleyway side had been repaired and smoothly coloured as if brand new; the mounting water damage gone without a trace.

His bed was different too. His duvet and sheet were all blue and white Spume colours with their poncy misty wave logo down the sides. It was lucky I'd had the J™ because when I finally brought myself to look at him, I felt sick. The tubes – and their contents! – were disgusting enough. But his body, oh Jesus fuck, his body! My stomach had heaved and I'd looked away and held down vomit. And felt guilty for all of it.

Nate's chest and arms were above of the covers. He'd lost all his sexy muscles and gotten so thin I could see his veins and bones through yellowy skin. I'd barely recognised his face and as I'd walked to the stool, his eyes had fluttered open. I was shaking so much I had to sit down before I fell down.

I cringed all over again as my half-digested breakfast melted away and whispered off around the u-bend. His face had been fuzzy, his armpits – ugh! – bushy. As he'd become more alert, I could tell he grossed, like, himself out.

What've they done to you, Nate? Ew!

I'd tried to get up and go to him. I'd felt like I should hug him or something though I was worried I'd throw up if I touched him. Luckily the prison tech stalled me and made me sit.

I'd cried in the end because seeing him like that was too disgusting not to react to somehow. I'd wanted to go and felt like a cold shitty psycho for feeling it. And I felt sorry for him, too.

When he'd smiled and his skin stretched over his skull…

Oh no! Don't think about it!

Too late. My stomach heaved again and I burked and spat into the bowl.

I'd struggled not to be sick through most of the visit and when he'd said he was fine, oh! All I could think was:

Jesus! No, you're not! They've ruined you, Nate! I don't know how you could be bloody alive looking like that!

He had kind of lit up and seemed like his proper self again near the end and it made him less gross. I'd started smiling, more in relief than anything else. But in the end, it had made it more obvious how his brain had already started to… go, after only two months. Whatever was happening to him was happening fast.

And then the lies I'd told!

My shoulders were starting to cramp from propping my-self with my elbows on the seat but my lies alone made me sick all over again and I had to stay a bit longer and heave some more. The lies had diarrhoea'd out of me and now I couldn't take them back. His dad, the seawall…

Why? Why had I said all that?

Oh man and he wanted me to visit more!

I felt sick and dirty inside my body, inside my mind. I couldn't take much more of… myself. I had to get out, out of… myself? I'd thought near the end that I wouldn't try seeing him again. But the way his voice had choked off and the cop tech had forced me to leave.

I was glad it was over. But I was more angry than relieved.

Visit done, like… that! Fuck the poor-door-using lowlifes if they didn't have time to say goodbye. I didn't want to see Nate like that again. I didn't want to visit him again but because of the way they'd cut us off like that, I was going to try anyway, if only to fuck them off.

Shaking, I sat down with my Instant™, turned on the J™ and went into my messages. There were a couple each from Chen and Shane and I opened hers first.

'Hey Teens. Checking in seeing how you are, hope work's not too horrendous.' And then a day later, 'Hey Teens. Only checking if you're okay, looks like you haven't opened my other message so you must be mega busy. I am too but, thought I'd, uh, check in anyway.'

She looked tired and from the smell in her message, her flat was far along since its last clean. She'd messaged before I'd told Shane about the visit, either that or she was a better hacker than Nate which was doubtful. So I couldn't understand what she wanted, or how she could talk to me like that after what had happened. Seeing her in the messages and smelling her flat made me blush, remembering; let alone a live conversation! I deleted the messages but blocked the alerts from going out to her.

Shane was nearly jumping out of the cloud at me. 'Fuck Teens! You got a visit! What's the story? Do you ping him a normal call or go in his flat or how does it work? Can other people come in on it or what? Buzz me back before you see him, Teens!'

Oops.

Then a day later, 'Hey Teens. Saw you didn't read my last message, prob'ly better that way. I was maybe a bit over-excited to hear the man was alive so I forgot to ask if you were all right, sorry 'bout that! Bloody selfish of me! Hope you're handling everything okay, anyway. This whole shit with Nate must be a c——, a bitc——, shitty. Buzz me if you need anything, or whadever.'

Bless the little ponce but what would I need? He was like Chen, like a woman! What was it with these people and talking about stuff. I played his message and sniffed his sexy BO a few times anyway.

When I tried calling him back, I got his messaging. 'Hey Shane. I saw him. They let me into his flat, for about five bloody minutes. He's. Oh man. It was awful, Shane. It was fuckin' awful.' I had to cut the call and calm myself which was exactly why there was no point in fucking-like… talking about stuff.

After vaping the J™ and downing my Instant™, I went on to the Movement space and saw the stats were not all zero. People had viewed the space, most of them from other countries, but that was all right. I was getting views!

Nobody had recorded any comments or anything but still. People were seeing it! Not only hundreds either. There had been a few thousand visitors. Nobody had gone for the membership handle yet but it was early days.

I decided to stay online in case any more viewers came and then I could maybe talk to them real-time. I stayed on for a few hours and fiddled with the space. I got some pics from library books I'd read about the Earth goddess who used to be on these islands when there were only three of them.

I let myself remember for long enough to grab a few free apps, write code Nate and his friends didn't know I knew how to write and convert the images to proper Four-D with smells and sounds of forests from the old days. I added more information about the goddess then came out to eat.

To celebrate, I ordered some decent food: pizza with real vegetables on it, sweet yellow lumps, red sweet gooey things with little yellow things in their goo, some more of the green brain vegetable and some kind of fake salty pink cubes; I refused to let my mind remember the names.

Since most of it was real, the few fake bits didn't annoy me. It wasn't a scam like the evil REAL(*) vegetable curry though it was more expensive. It looked like I wouldn't need to pay for rankings after all. That shouldn't have come as a surprise given how much the world needed the goddess now. I wouldn't have to survive on stripey-biobox pizza after all.

I'd done everything from the masterclass notes apart from paying for rankings or bankrupting myself on actual ads. Ads would have to wait until the Movement got huge; until I started charging for membership and getting influencer bonuses. It would come. It was only a matter of time, I knew.

There was no difference in the stats that I could see for the rest of my off-days and Shane didn't get back to me till the night before work. He had bags under his eyes and his flat smelled about a month in from its last clean; too far gone to be sexy anymore, sadly. 'Hey Teens. Sorry I didn't get back to ya. Work've shafted me with a massive shift. I'm wiped out. Anyway, I didn't wanna be rude and not call back, how are you doing?'

I'd had a J™ that morning but I was pretty sober by then. I'd that moment gone to bed and luckily, I had the duvet pulled up to my chin. I giggled and said, 'Yeah, pretty good. How 'bout you?'

'Whoa! Sorry Teens, didn't know you were in the sack. No worries. Let's catch up another time.'

'No, it's okay. As long as you're not offended by the sight of a lady's bare chin.'

He went bright pink and looked like he was in pain. 'Uh, nah. It's okay Teens. Hey look, I haven't got that long before I'm back on shift. Like I said, I was only checkin' in to make sure you're okay an' that.'

What the fuck were you going do about it if I wasn't?

'Yeah, I'm surviving. I mean, I'm starting another bloody eighteen-dayer tomorrow but it's all good, y'know, the usual.

Oh yeah and the Movement space's taking off, Shane! I got thousands of viewings!'

'The, uh… Oh yeah! Yeah, good stuff Teens. It's gonna be huge.'

Ha! Busted!

He was a shit liar. He hadn't looked at it. I didn't care. That had been in the masterclass, how you had to believe in yourself and fuck what your friends and family thought. It didn't matter. Nothing mattered with the goddess behind me. I didn't need some man to help me. I smiled back at him and watched him squirm.

'Well anyway Teens,' he said lamely, 'I really gotta go but ping me if ya wanna catch up or whadever, okay. I s'pose we'll both be working for the next while but don't be a stranger, okay?'

Whatever Shane.

'Yeah, okay. You too Shane. Take it easy. And don't forget to share my handle to all your buds!'

'Your… Uh, yeah, course I will.'

Course you'll share it or course you'll forget?

I knew which one. It didn't matter. He'd only look foolish when I was all over the feeds.

Work kicked off with a last-minuter when I was halfway through my pancakes. I threw on a top and went into the agency space in that and my underwear. After that it didn't ease off. Every day was rammed. My toilet was starting to smell like Instant™ because I was quaffing so many mugs to keep myself from getting caught sleeping in the agency space.

I forced myself to check the stats every night and after a while, I got to know the numbers. They didn't change much but at least they changed, at first anyway. There were untold ways to break them down but I was too tired to figure it all out. It was a Nate thing.

Or a bloody Chen thing.

I could have checked when the first few thousands had come in and I could have seen exactly where they were. If the viewers had sold their details to the search tech, whether they knew it or not, I could have seen how old they were and what their favourite foods were and all sorts of useless… shit. But I didn't look. I was too wrecked. I'd do it all in my next off days. I'd get into the library and read a book about maths or something. I needed time, that was all.

I wasn't sure how far through my shift it was when I made another visitation application and I forgot all about it anyway when I got an offer to work through my off days. I couldn't understand why so many flats were moving but I couldn't argue with the triple-time and time in lieu, either.

Being poor's got its own-like… language! Who knew… Stop!

I couldn't take the lieu days till the end of my next shift. But then I'd get six days off! It was basically a holiday and high and mighty Chen herself didn't get holidays. I knew it was going to kill me but I said yes anyway.

What would have been my off-days came and went in an Instant™ fuelled blur of boredom and bean-flipping. Not because I was horny really but to piss them off since there was a lot they had access to but that didn't include what my hands were doing under the desk while I was watching rich ponces view dumb-arse flats.

Chen left me messages a few times and I deleted them without reading them; suppressing the alerts with barely a thought. Shane left one and I watched it a few times but he was being a ponce again and 'checkin' in' with me.

I couldn't remember when I stopped checking the stats because I'd memorised the numbers and they'd completely stopped changing. I was too exhausted to be dismayed at getting no more hits. I'd sort it out in sixteen days or whatever it had got down to by then.

Nearly every delivery I ordered ambushed me with pictures of the moon and asked me if I wanted fucking noodles and dumplings with my next order. Dry and wet-foots all across the fucking land would be getting taken in by this rubbish now with New Year coming up. It was going be a late one too, because the February full moon wasn't till nearly the end of the month. Which meant more crappy moon-noodle ads.

Great.

Finally, it was a couple of days before my epic six-day off-time. The moon-noodle-dumpling ads were making me a serious suicide risk. My nose was blocked and I had a permanent headache, probably from being online too much without a break.

One day, I had a normal day without any last-minuters and it was daylight when I finished work; more or less. I moved to my bed feeling muzzy and I didn't know what to do with myself.

What did I used to do before I had a job?

Then I remembered the visit application so I dug up the handle and tried querying it. It said there was no application.

What a surprise.

I ran all the searches I'd run at the station and got no results. This time I put in a complaint. It was another pathetic white form and once you'd finished it, it was really hard to see how to submit it. Then it wouldn't go because it said there was an error in one of the fields, except it didn't say which one.

After I went through it again, three fuckin times, I finally noticed the DETAILS OF COMPLAINT field had turned faintly pink. It was nearly impossible to see the difference in colour from the rest of the form. I couldn't see what was wrong with it and my head was killing me. I was about to bin it and do another visitation application when I noticed tiny *hànzì* over the top of what I'd put in the field. I magnified them but they were hard to read on top of my input anyway.

It took me an excruciating age of squinting to work out that they said I'd put too many characters in the field and then I noticed the cream – bloody cream! – coloured count underneath it which said, '24,031 / 13,024'. It blew my mind what the fuck kind of lame limit that was but I fixed it anyway – Nate would have been proud of me for sticking with it. Then as soon as I left the field, the whole bloody form cleared.

Fucking wankers!

Normally I would have shouted at it, come out of their crappy space and given up. But fuck them, arseholes. I wouldn't let them get away with it. I did the whole form again and when I submitted it, it came up with a pissy old-school box that said only, 'Submitted'. Then another one saying 'Error 0xC00D2717L' but nothing else. So I didn't know if it had worked or not but my head was pounding so hard I couldn't go on.

I crashed out of the space and nearly vomited from the pain in my head. I'd known it was getting bad but the form had kept my mind off it. Now I collapsed on my bed and my body curled up like the authorities were controlling it. I couldn't scream, it hurt so much. I needed to ping my biotech for painkillers but it was like someone was cutting my head in half and I couldn't think enough to do that.

My mouth opened by itself and I couldn't close it. I dribbled on my duvet and heard pathetic whimpering sounds which I slowly realised were coming from me. By the time I managed to work my tech, the duvet had a massive gross damp patch. I couldn't think about the form or anything any more. I had to sleep. I climbed under my duvet and hoped I'd be able to get through the next bloody day let alone two.

The headache was gone when I woke but the blocked nose had, like, graduated, into a sore throat and drinking Instant™ felt like I was deep-throating a hot broken mug. I absolutely refused to cough up for another diagnosis for some pathetic bug so I sat through my viewings getting my biotech to do what it could with my body's natural resistance; which was what the goddess would have wanted anyway; and it would make me stronger, too.

I would have ordered a pizza that night but it turned out part of making me stronger was apparently the blooming of a fever inside me. I clocked off after my last viewing and sat in my work chair spacing out. It took a few pings from the door to snap me awake in the dark.

Hopefully it wasn't Chen but I couldn't think of anyone else who'd travel to visit me. And it would have been so like her to get all nosey when I didn't reply to her messages, and invite herself around to 'check in' or some quasi-womanly fluff like that. I made the door grow its camera and saw a National Mail ground carrier with a giant green box.

What? The fuck?

The carrier clumped in like some kind of attack-roach when I opened the door. It dumped the box in front of the toilet door and left. I wheeled my chair to the box and that's when I saw the big red cross on top of it. I pinged it and a virtual grew up around me as it opened. There was a recorded dickwad ponce with a bun and a white coat talking like he was getting off with a dildo up his bum.

'Hey there Tina Zhang-Lewis! Sorry to hear you're having to quarantine but the good news is, we've got your back! There's no need to worry about track-and-trace! We've already handled it! FYI, you caught the lurgy off Shane McLaughlin and passed it on to Chen McCarthy, that's two ancient Celtic names! What are the odds, hey? Hey, listen Tina Zhang-Lewis, in the box is everything you'll need for your twenty-eight days! There's your complimentary meds and food, and a few free treats to help you pass the time! Hey Tina Zhang-Lewis, why not look at this as an opportunity to kick back, take up a new hobby, really work on yourself, hey? Course, you're signed off work, well, if you want to be anyway; nothing wrong with dedication, hey? And don't you worry, the State's got your back on that front, heh, get it? Back, Front? Eh? Eh? If you decide not to work, the Aotearoa Archipelago government will cover a solid and comfortable four percent of your wages so your employer has no excuse whatsoever to treat you bad when you're not feeling good! But that's not all you've got to be cheerful about, Tina Zhang-Lewis! There's more! Your bio-tech has told us you've got a known variant, nothing new or nasty, only a plain old bug, only a few dozen percent more deadly than the old twenties classics in the original pandemic. You didn't need an external diagnosis for a basically near-vintage virus and it didn't cost you a satoshi! How 'bout that eh? Nope, you've got nothing to worry about at all, Tina Zhang-Lewis! And although there's zippo chance your natural immunity could kick it, the meds in the box are state-of-the-art and might not even have that many side-effects! Pretty neat eh? Those drugs might have the bug beaten for you in no time flat, Tina Zhang-Lewis! All you need to do is take the pills as each pouch opens, sit back and enjoy the healing process. Oh yeah and one more thing Tina Zhang-Lewis but y'know, so you know! Failure to comply with mandatory isolation or any attempt to open your door or otherwise leave your residence attract an automatic ten-year prison sentence and may be subject to additional fines. Please enjoy your quarantine and don't hesitate to contact us if you feel you have been mis-diagnosed.'

Fuck! I had the actual plague! It turned up every now and then, came in on freight MagLevs, Nate had told me once. But I wasn't supposed to get it! Man! No wonder I was so sick. What the fuck was the goddess playing at sending me this?

The meds were on top of the box and the first pouch peeled back when the dweeb stopped playing and his pissy virtual faded out. I was so weak I could barely bend down to get the pill and swallow it with a mouthful of water before wheeling myself over and flopping into bed.

The temperature was gone the next morning but I was no stronger. I struggled up and went through the box. Each thing inside was wrapped in white bio-padding which turned to dust and left under the door as soon as I picked it up. I put the med pouches on my desk and hoped their timing was vaguely intelligent and they wouldn't open and expire when I was asleep.

The 'food' turned out to be a load of bottles of Total™ – the stuff I'd only heard existed until now – and the treats were some poxy free passes to movie spaces which everyone in the world was already subscribed to anyway. My government was treating me well. Fuck-yeah they were! Wankers.

By the time I'd stacked the Total™ on the bench and the box and wrapping had gone home, my temperature was rising again and I coma'd on top of the duvet.

It was dark when I woke and my head was clearer. I wasn't hungry but tried to order a pizza anyway and it rejected with a big ugly red message about food deliveries to quarantined persons being prohibited. I'd forgotten I was quarantined so it was nice of the shits to remind me, kind of.

That meant I was on Total™ for nearly a month. Wasn't there meant to be some scam or something with it? I had about half the baby cream left – worrying considering I was moving to a diet of pure slurry – and enough Instant™ for the rest of my life. I wondered if I could survive on Instant™ the whole time or if it would do anything cruel and unusual to my innards. Or my toilet bowl. I wasn't hungry now anyway so I could work it out later.

In a fevered daydream, I went back into Spume's space to see where I'd ended up getting to, the night I'd got sick. I couldn't find any visit application but I couldn't remember if I'd made a new one or not so I made one anyway.

By then, I was getting quick at them. I tried to see if the complaint had gone in too but there was no way of checking and I was beginning to get tired and sore again after a few minutes online. I came out and crashed.

It was pitch black when I woke. The AC in the alleyway was the only noise I could hear and my ads were off. There were a few dimmed messages from Chen in the sides of my eyes. Deleting them felt too mean so I tried not to see them and lay in bed wondering when the wind and rain would start again.

With so much quiet, I began hearing sounds from the building, no voices or anything, only soft clicks and the sliding sounds of the lifts, quiet like they were hundreds of kays away. My temperature had cooled a little, to a fuzzy warmth in the back of my head.

I felt tired but also clear and calm. I couldn't remember ever feeling this way before and that was how I knew that though she wasn't sending me a message or a test or a gift, the goddess was with me. She'd always be with me and she was giving me this soothing reminder so I didn't forget.

When I woke again, the rain and wind were blasting down the alleyway and it was daytime. I got up and made some Instant™ but the smell put me off so I dumped it down the sink and had a mug of water instead. I wasn't hungry and I didn't have the strength to get into a movie. I ended up sleeping away the day and thanked the goddess I had six whole days off because there was no way I could justify time off work when it started again.

Chen sent another message as I sat back down on my bed and I didn't know why I did it but suddenly I was on a call with her. 'Jeez Chen, are you bloody stalking me or something?' A vicious headache bloomed when I tried to smile. She was in bed and though her face was brown she looked pale. Her tech-toos were clumped up on her ears, not too cheesily for a change. 'You look as shit as I feel,' I said.

'*Kia ora* Teens.' She sounded like she'd swallowed a handful of concrete. 'How's quarantine treating you?'

'Yeah, okay. I'm not hungry yet at least so I haven't touched the Total™.'

'Eh?'

'You know, you can't get deliveries. They send you Total™.'

'Oh. Uh, yeah, okay.' She looked all embarrassed. 'You, uh, you know that stuff's an addiction scam, right?'

Fuck! Is it?

I nodded as if to say, course I do. Then I said, 'Are you gonna work?'

'Yeah, course.'

'Same. I mean, I'd lose all my shifts if I didn't, so...'

'Yeah, you don't have to tell me. I'd lose my whole contract if I called off sick with anything less than a broken bloody neck.' She tried to smile and ended up opening her mouth and closing it again.

We chatted for a while; like-about four minutes. I told her about my double shift and she said she was jealous since she'd been forced to work one of her off days and only had today before she had to work again. Both of us were too tired to stay on longer.

She seemed to have forgotten about what happened. I only remembered it a couple of times but my temperature kind of stopped it really coming up in my mind and I managed to stay calm and all kind of, floaty. In a burning up delusional sort of way.

By the time I cut the call, I was convinced we were okay again. I deleted her messages anyway since she could have told me whatever she needed to when we'd spoken. The whole thing made me feel lighter and I decided to celebrate with a J™.

When I packed it, I noticed I only had about half a bag left so I'd have to be careful how much I smoked. But the problem was solved when I tried turning on the J™. It wouldn't start. It pinged me a message about substances not allowed in recovery.

'Fucking arseholes!' My croaking scream deteriorated into coughing which I couldn't stop for the rest of the day.

My temperature got higher and higher and my throat was on fire by the time it got dark. One minute I felt too cold and the next I was hot and sweating into the duvet, too weak to get up. I heard a beep and a crack on my desk and managed to reach over for the pill that had unwrapped. In the few seconds I had between coughing fits, I swallowed it with a mouthful of water and half lay, half fell back on to the bed. For a while I hoped I wouldn't die before the meds started working; if they were going to. And a while after that I started hoping I would die because right then it was a better prospect than being alive.

For the next few days, I hovered between waking and sleeping. Work spam was brightening so I knew I had to get better soon. I tried talking with Shane and Chen but we were all too sick to say much. We ended up coughing and having to drop off the calls. Jesus! If this was a known variant, how shit would a new one be? Or would you-like, die straight away?

One morning I woke and realised it was pretty much the first time I'd noticed the difference between sleep and waking. I had a weird feeling in my stomach which scared me as much as Chen hugging me might have. I was hungry and whatever spyware the government had monitoring me detected it and jumped all over me.

It starting plaguing me with recordings of the same white coat ponce about how important eating was for recovery. I couldn't stop them playing so there was nothing for it but to open a Total™ bottle and when I did the idiot finally switched off.

Never drink that gut-rot kids. Never… No!

Fuck it, people out by the coast lived on this stuff. It can't have been that bad. And, oooooohmygod! It wasn't! Given what I'd heard about it, I was half expecting to throw it straight back up. I knelt over the toilet and pinched my nose then downed half the bottle and it tasted… like heaven!

Maybe I was sicker than I'd realised and my taste had gone strange which everyone knew happened with the plague. I waited to see if my stomach wouldn't believe the lie. But nothing happened except my mouth watering for more.

I gulped down the rest of the bottle and opened another one and that was yum too. I was full then and I didn't feel sick. Or addicted.

Stupid urban myths.

I did wonder if maybe bad things would come later. But instead, I started feeling better as the day went on. I got hungry again in the afternoon and drank more Total™. By the evening I felt strong enough to check on the Movement space. No action but at least I was getting well.

If Nate had been here he would have figured how to get more hits in a second. And made me feel like an idiot. And I wouldn't have minded because I'd rather have had him here to make me feel dumb than not had him here at all. I came out of the space and a tear rolled, then another and some fucking more after that. I got angry and brushed them away but more kept coming.

It had been three months now and it was right then it started sinking into my stupid brain that he was gone. Though he was right next door, the way he was when I'd visited him, I knew in my heart he was as good as dead. I'd never get him back.

I started crying properly, bawling like Chen probably had when Nate had dumped her. I lost some time because I found myself staring through the rain at the AC and couldn't remember going to the window.

The first time I'd melted down in front of Nate had been because he was late coming to visit and I thought that meant he'd dumped me or some idiot notion like that. He hadn't cared that I'd called him a prick and a wanker and a cheating cunt. He didn't mind that I'd punched him and tried to scratch his eyes out. He'd sealed his overs hood and squeezed into the corner by the door till I ran out of steam.

Then instead of walking out of my psycho life forever, he'd come up behind me and put his arms around me and said, 'it's okay Teens. I had to work a bit longer, that's all. It's all good. Sorry, I shoulda pinged ya, I didn't mean t' scare ya.'

He'd made it all okay, like nobody else I'd known in my whole life had ever done. Not my mother, not bullshit Spume therapy when she'd booked me in there when I was in my teens, nobody! And now he was gone, forever.

I was nearly glad I had plague. I could hardly see the rain through my tears when the next big cry took hold of me. But I didn't lose time that time because I realised I had the goddess.

And right that minute she told me.

Nate's only a man for fuck's sake! He's not the only bloody brain in the world. YOU of all people know THAT!

I spent the rest of my off-holiday in the library studying tech. And it wasn't that hard because I let a part of me wake up, the part of me that knew tech already because it was in my fucking blood. The first thing I went after was security.

I can do this. I've always been able to do this.

In the end, I found what I wanted online and not in the library at all.

I was a bit scared in case the health warnings weren't lies after all but it didn't stop me hacking into my J™ and having microscopic fuck-you-rich-fucks vape before putting my head down the end of my last day off.

I'd been well for the last two days. I thought the meds were working and the twenty-eight days was scaremongering State thing. Given the Total™ was awesome despite the lies and I'd managed to hack into my J™, well, I wasn't like Nate. I basically lived online and hardly went outside anyway. And I was already seven days in which meant only three weeks to go.

I'd survived the double shift and for some reason the agency had tapped me for another one. I hadn't known I had plague on the last one and I'd lived through it so I thought, *what the hell*, and took the second one too. Only the morning it started I woke up and the temperature was back and I was weak as a sick old person again.

Was it the weed that had brought it back? Or had I been trying to do too much getting online and learning how to hack? I didn't know. All I knew was that my commute that morning was horrendous. I could hardly get a top on and drag myself out of bed into my chair and I thanked the goddess I had a bit of time left to try and wake up before my first viewing.

Another pill opened and I tried to swallow it with In-stant™ but the smell nearly made me vomit so I held it in my mouth till I could spit it into the sink, dump the Instant™ and get water instead. That meant I had no other way to stay awake on my shifts than my own strength. I'd be lucky if I made it through the day with a job.

But somehow I did. I pinched myself, grabbed the desk, nearly drifted off a couple of times but each time I brightened up my on-timer it was ticking away happily. No warnings, no alerts, nothing.

Getting to midday felt like waiting for my next birthday but I made it. There were no last-minuters and I had my legal nineteen-minute lunch break which nobody usually bothered to take but which I called, probably making me the first person to do it since twenty-fifty or something. But there was no other way. I set an alarm and face-planted on to my desk.

It might not have seemed like much to the casual rich-fuck surveillance system but that tiny coma made me feel better. I clocked back on with about thirty seconds left and an hour later, I broke out in a gross cold sweat. It soaked through my top and made a disgusting puddle under my bottom.

Then my temperature was gone and I managed to get some Total™ into me between afternoon viewings. It tasted like metal so I knew that though I was feeling better the plague hadn't yet gone. I gasped through till knock-off time and begged the goddess to stop them sending any last-minuters which She did so I got to collapse on top of the duvet and pass out before it got dark.

Next morning, I tried to tell myself the temperature wasn't back and it nearly worked. I stayed awake a bit easier and like the day before the sweat came and the temperature went so I was a bit better for the rest of the afternoon. The morning after that, it was definitely gone and I was hungry again and I relaxed into a routine of rolling out of bed every morning, gulping down a Total™ and a mug of Instant™ and logging on to work.

I was all right for maybe a week. Two more of the pills opened, so now they were nearly half gone. One of the nights I had the energy to check on my visitation request and for once it hadn't disappeared. It said, 'pending review'. But later that day a message from them came in and it was Rahui with her fake calm voice and the waves and rain in the background.

'Thank you, Tina Zhang-Lewis for registering your concern with us. We're sorry to hear that…'

And then it cut to me, creepily, with my flat in the background. I had a sulky expression like a child that had been told, 'no'. I'd never have pulled a face like that! But it spoke in my voice as if I'd recorded it myself. 'Your fuckin' system's crap! You keep on losing my bloody forms and I'm putting them in right and it's bullshit!'

I don't talk like that!

It carried on with me reading out the rest of my complaint in my own voice with my own face then Rahui came back. 'We'd really like to help you and to do that, we need a few more details from you about the specifics of your concern

Tina Zhang-Lewis. For instance, could you tell us more specifically how you feel our…'

Then me again, 'fuckin' system is crap!'

'…and perhaps give us the name or number of the form or forms you feel you've completed and that we've lost. The form name is usually printed on the top centre of the form and the number is in the top right corner.'

Yeah okay, very funny. Arseholes. It's not even her fucking voice.

I'd given them all that. Maybe I'd forgotten a few details but they should be able to check all that in their systems. There would be logs of what forms had been submitted. I didn't know where they got the pics of me from, probably bought it off some company I had a subscription with, maybe the agency itself; wouldn't put it past them to sell their employees' data.

And the video was unadulterated poo. CGI. If I hadn't already been sure, the fact that their stupid message finished and didn't give me any way of replying proved they didn't really want to hear back from me. The wankers were mocking me.

Put in another one, Teens. Give 'em what they asked for and take pics before ya submit. Then we got proof.

It's what Nate would have told me. It sounded like his voice in my head but I knew it was really the goddess and that she was right. But I couldn't anyway. My head was starting to ache again and I was sweaty and scared the temperature would return. The visitation application had stayed in. I decided to focus on that. By waiting for it.

Despite feeling better, I kept crashing early and I'd started setting my alarm to get up in time for work. I spoke with Shane and Chen twice each but we were all grafting and tired and none of us had much to say. She thought she was getting better but he was struggling and barely coherent.

I should have been working on the Movement and I should have been nagging Spume with a barrage of complaints but I was too tired. If I wasn't asleep, I was bumming around in news-spaces getting bored with pictures of rough water along the old coastlines. That and thanking the plague that it meant I got a medical break from ads.

It was a big outbreak in the end. Twelve blocks were quarantined and it had been tracked back to a delivery drone, then all the way to the MagLev from DR Aussie. I pretended to myself that I had no idea what junk we got from there. Big food and weed production and solar farms in DR Aussie, Shane thought and my attempt to force memories down backfired because then I found myself thinking: *Wow! Does he know he's right? Where does a wet-foot like him learn things like that?*

So it was probably a bag of Budlike™ that brought in the block plague! Nate would have got the lowdown. Or known how to.

Weirdly, though we were quarantined, life was the same for me except for the deliveries. If I was a rich-fuck, I could have bought the blueprints and grown new furniture in the smelly comfort of my own crappy home since those nanites were self-sterilising and allowed through quarantine.

I began to think quarantine was not too bad in a lame and pooey sort of way. I had the Total™ which didn't make me die and which I wasn't getting hooked on whatever Chen said. I could work and I'd have another whole six days of holiday and two big pay packets at the end of the shift; and this strange extra money which turned out to be the four percent government subsidy over and above my pay! And since the State medical covered plague, and I couldn't order anything in quarantine, I was spending little apart from water and cleans.

I was down to two pills and when one of them opened, the ponce popped up with a warning to finish the whole course, as if I wasn't going to or something. Idiots.

Much as I didn't see the point of – ugh! – outside, with ten days left of my quarantine I had a sudden Nate-ish urge to go there as soon as I was allowed to. I pinged Chen and got her messaging so I asked her if she wanted to come too. I thought of asking Shane but I felt strange about the idea of being with both of them together so I went to bed instead. I hit the pillow and died and woke in the dark. But it wasn't the goddess' dark of the time before.

Though it was pitch-black and the alley was quiet except for the AC, there were bright edges around my eyes like my ads had returned, then broken up into a haze. I thought maybe it was sleep in my eyes and I brushed at my face and that's when I realised my hands were cold and clammy.

Then I felt the heat and thought my climate control must have broken. I pinged it and it showed normal but recommended a flat clean. I tried to throw off the duvet and it felt heavy then when I got it off, I was suddenly too cold so I pulled it back up again. Then my lights came on so brightly I had to close my eyes and when I opened them there was someone sitting on my bed.

'Nate?' I mumbled. I tried to sit up but I could hardly move. Everything was blurry in the brightness and I kept the duvet up because I'd gone to bed naked.

'Who's Nate?' He turned to look at me and I froze.

'Expecting someone else?' he said in that 'you're so busted' way he had.

I couldn't answer. I scrunched up in the corner and tried to scream but my voice was gone. No matter if I could have made any noise. Nobody would hear through the walls anyway. When he pulled the edges of the duvet from my hands and ripped it off me I stayed curled up and frozen and my mind looped unhelpfully on, *how did he find me? How did he get in?*

He smelled of weed and sweat, and hairs from his dark bun started coming loose and sticking to my face. I wanted to struggle. I tried to tell myself not to be such a useless bloody girl and give him a run for his money. But my arms and legs didn't work and all I could do was suck in air as he wrapped himself around me like a construction bot with all its tentacles and tools to grip and drill. I would have rathered he was a machine instead of having to feel his actual clammy disgusting skin closing in on my body.

He squeezed himself in-between the wall and me and no matter how much I tried to curl up, he found a way in. I felt fingers and arms around my neck, in my mouth, nails cutting like needles between my teeth so I started choking on blood. I felt claws under my armpits and knees, between my legs, pulling me open and there was no way I could stop him because he was too strong and his skin was cold and too slimy to pinch.

He had me turned around so I was facing the kitchenette as if he knew Spume were killing Nate behind that wall and got off on making me look at it. He had an arm around my neck choking me and his prickly cheek against mine. 'Who's Nate?' he said like he was asking me if I wanted a mug of Instant™.

When I didn't answer, I felt something burning hot and thick cut into me, tearing in through my side and finally unsticking my voice. I started screaming properly then, but he got a hand over my bleeding mouth, not that anyone would have heard through the walls anyway.

I tried to bite but he squeezed my jaw and I felt it crack. Whatever it was he'd pushed inside me burned up through my guts, past my ribs and into my mouth and I tasted cooking blood and smelled burning meat and fuck me if it didn't make me hungry.

Things broke through my jaw and cut up inside my tongue like a hundred evil fingernails. They moved my mouth, forcing me talk. 'Sorry Uncle,' they made me say. 'I should've told you about Nate. I was going to tell you. It's been ages since you were here, that's all.'

My body started jerking, ripping and tearing and this time I didn't stop screaming till the end which never came.

The way he was wrecking my body, I should have been dead. I wanted to be dead. There was more blood soaking my bed than I had inside me but somehow I stayed alive. The fingers in my mouth and throat should have kept me from screaming but I somehow screamed anyway. The pain was all I could feel, as if I was made of it, and my screaming started sounding like it was coming from somewhere else.

It had a rhythm. The fingers and tentacles pulsed in my body and the screams went in time with them and the bright light faded to grey daylight and the screams got quieter and quieter and the sound of my alarm got louder as if it was pushing the dream back into the night where it belonged. Then something warm and wet dug into my ear, into my brain and should've killed me but instead I heard his voice inside my head. 'Idiot girl. Now I can find you. Now I will find you.' And it echoed away into the day.

My bed was soaked with sweat. My duvet was tangled around me. I was freezing and it took me two tries to sit up. The temperature was back with a vengeance.

Jesus! It's the Movement space! And the study! I should never have bloody started all that! Anyone can find me now.

The last pill clicked and peeled back as I killed my alarm lay back breathing like I'd been running. After a while I was strong enough to sit up and swallow the tablet with two-day-old water left over from the last one. I was shaking too much to walk so I dragged myself into my chair and wheeled over to the bench but when I smelled the Total™ I realised my appetite had gone again. I forced it down anyway and hoped it was helping me get well.

The smell of Instant™ put me off too but I forced that down as well, double strength. I doubted I'd be able to make it through the day without falling asleep anyway. But one problem at a time.

I couldn't log on till I had no bare flesh above the desk so that meant dragging myself back over to my bed and finding a top which all nearly made me pass out. By the time I was as awake as I was going to get and staring at the AC with caffeine eyes, it turned out I didn't have any viewings scheduled till nearly afternoon. That was worse because it meant I had less than the usual boring nothing to keep me awake.

In the end it was coughing that kept my job for me that day. I drank mugs of Instant™ that tasted like metal and concrete and burned down my throat. That started the coughing not long after my first viewing and I couldn't stop till nearly knock-off time.

There were messages from Chen and Shane waiting when I clocked off. But though the temperature had gone and the coughing had eased, all I could do was roll the chair over to my bed and drag myself on to it before passing out.

I hadn't thought about the nightmare all day but when I woke in the dark, I jumped because I thought he was back again. The fuck with Nate and his lucid dreaming nonsense! How were you meant to pause and try to access your tech in the middle of something like that? How?

But as I lay awake, the lights didn't come on and I realised my head was clear and the wind and rain were loud in the alleyway. My heart was racing and it took me a long while to sleep again. I woke the same way four more times so though I wasn't sick again the next morning, I felt like I'd hardly slept.

I muscled through the day womanfully running on Instant™ and I was ready to collapse by the end. But by then the temperature had started up again. Each time I managed to sleep, I kept jumping awake thinking there was someone in the room.

The next nine days were like waking up slowly. Each one got more and more okay-ish and finally a message with the ponce in it came to tell me congratulations on finishing my quarantine and passing all my tests. I couldn't believe I was better. I felt spaced and slept right up until my alarm went, then again as soon as I finished work.

I had loads of the Total™ bottles left and though I was allowed to get deliveries again, I didn't feel like anything else. I'd started looking forward to necking the bottles morning and evening. My appreciation of its beautiful layers of flavour had really grown.

I started buying batches and saving them up. I'd drink half a bottle in the morning and the rest after work then a sip from a new one before bed if I was too hungry to stop myself. So what if it was addictive. It didn't do any harm. It had all the right nutrients.

Fibre…

Yeah, but who cared.

Chen messaged back to say she definitely wanted to get outside and her quarantine finished nearly the same time as mine. But she got sick again too and we were both too busy trying to keep our jobs to talk again for a while. My shift piddled along and one night when I was feeling strong enough to stay awake after work and guzzling my Total™, I called her.

'Fuck Chen!' She was naked and eating some kind of expensive-looking coloured lumps which meant her quarantine was definitely over. 'My fault for calling I s'pose.' I should've been used to that grossness from her but I blushed to the roots of my overgrown head-stubble.

Yeah, must do something about that.

'Hey Teens.' She said like nothing had happened. 'You look as shit as I feel.'

Even with her perfect-shaped little girly face, she looked ill. There were bags under her eyes and white-heads on her cheeks and I tried to keep my eyes from going any lower but I couldn't help seeing the way her skin hung off her measly little barbie-bones. Jesus! If the bloody Chen-doll could manage to look that shit, how bad must I be?

'Did, uh, you, uh, finish all the free Total™?' I asked, trying not to stare at the goose pimples around her dark little nipples.

'The what? Oh yeah, that stuff. I, uh. No. Loads left.' Now she looked like she'd pooed her pants and wanted to escape before someone smelled it. Not when she got online naked or anything embarrassing like that. No. Only when it came to admitting she hadn't eaten enough!

'Man. You must've been sicker than me. I finished what they gave me and started buying more! It's delish!'

'Oh, really? Shit. Well, you can, uh, have my ones if you want. But, Tee… Tina, you know that's bad shit, right?'

Who are you? My fucking mother?

'No way! You seriously don't want them?'

'Nope. I'm all good. You can have them, I mean, if you want. I mean, it's only Total™, right?'

Stuck-up shit.

'Chen, did you have, like, any of it?'

'Um…'

'You didn't, did you?'

'Ah. I, uh…'

'What did you do, Chen? Did you get deliveries in quarantine or something? How the fuck di—'

'Relax! No. I didn't break the law.' She sighed and looked like she was in actual pain. 'My work medical's got food parcels included.' Then she cringed as if I was going to hit her.

'Oh,' I said and then I didn't know what else to say. I'd thought she was on the same trip as me the whole time but it turned out she'd been living it up on free flash fresh food. What other fucking perks did the package give her? Had she really had to work or did they give her nancy sick days or something too? Jesus! Nice for some. 'That's pretty cool,' I said after far too long and we both knew what I'd been thinking.

Chen gave me this it's not my fuckin' fault I've got a good job look then said, 'Yeah. It's a decent package. The arseholes didn't grant me any quarter for being sick so I'm prob'ly gonna die of liver failure from painkillers and anti-inflammatories. But at least they fed me well.'

'Oooh! Oh I say! Grant me any quarter!' I said. 'Someone's talking more and more like a rich-fuck every day.' I tried to smile but I was sure she heard the anger in my voice.

'Well, anyway,' she said in a babyish wounded little voice, 'you still wanna get out? I can book a trolly to take the Total™ over to your place and head out from there if you want.'

'Jeez, do you reckon you can handle walking further than the toilet?'

'Just about.' She tried to smile and looked like she might pass out.

'Same. Well, it'll be a change of scene from this roach-infested shithole anyway.'

'All good.'

She cut the call and I breathed out. I didn't mind that I couldn't hide that I'd been a bit of an arsehole. The call had gone well. She hadn't mentioned Nate or the visits or any of that stuff once. I hoped we could keep it up when we met.

Chen's trolley loaded with her Total™ and some other fancy looking bioboxes of free food arrived minutes before her. She helped me stack everything and every time she bent down, I couldn't help thinking of the skinny yellowy-looking body under her clothes and cringing. I wanted to thank her for the fancy food but also smack her in the head for acting all high and mighty and dumping out her leftovers on me.

We couldn't walk far. We were both breathing hard after half a block so we turned back. The wind wasn't strong but the rain was heavier than usual. No surprise now it was getting near April.

Sometimes the puddles were up to our knees and it made walking icky; thinking of all the germs in that water despite the fact it couldn't get through my overs. We turned back before long and loitered by the poor-door watching drones drop stuff off and weak-looking people drag themselves out to get their deliveries.

'Not as many as normal, are there?' Chen said.

'Eh?'

'Deliveries. There's normally a stack about twenny deep circling till there's space. Now there's like one, every few minutes. This plague batch must've been epic. And look at all these people, they're all barely out of quarantine like us and they look rough, too.' She yawned so wide it looked like her head was opening up and then I had to do it too.

I didn't know how she knew about the deliveries. I never kept an eye on boring details like that. Nate would probably have noticed too.

Don't think about Nate.

I didn't want her to see it on my face and start asking questions. She was devious like that. 'Yeah, I s'pose,' I said. Then, 'hey look, Chen, I'm knackered. I gotta sleep. Sorry to be so boring. I just…' I couldn't remember what I was going to say and I could see on her face that she knew exactly how I felt.

'Yeah,' was all she said. She nodded her head groggily and wobbled off without another word. And I didn't mind because suddenly I felt the same.

The message from Spume must have come while I was out because I saw it in the morning when my alarm blasted me awake and I realised it was the first good night's sleep I'd had in weeks. I guzzled a whole bottle of Total™ since now thanks to Chen, I had no shortage of them. Then I checked when my first viewing was. It was lucky I did because I had enough time to wee and throw on a top before it was due to start.

The day was so busy I didn't have time to look at the message till after work. It was probably for the best because I might have done something stupid on shift when I saw Spume's reply.

I had to hand it to them, they were smart. Nate would have had a field day with this one. He was so right about them. They didn't want me to visit him and they'd worked out I wasn't going to take no for an answer, so the smart arses had answered yes.

Arseholes.

I tried to call Shane but his handle was a strange and worrying grey colour.

Where have I seen that?

Or maybe it was a geeky way of blocking calls and preventing messages while he was busy. I thought of getting in touch with Nate's other friends but I didn't have their handles and it would have felt awkward anyway. I hadn't spoken to them since Nate had gone to prison. Shane must have told them but they hadn't come to me. It showed what they thought of me.

I called Chen and the one time I wouldn't have cared about seeing her in her bra and underpants if it meant I could tell her what Spume had done, I got her messaging, instead.

'*Kia Ora* Chen. Call me back. It's about Nate.'

I wondered how busy her poncy job suddenly wouldn't be when she opened that one.

And then…

Fa-uh-uh-uh-uh-uhckk!

…I went bright red and facepalmed as if people could really see me. I suddenly hoped Chen didn't call me back.

I'd been about to order some food but suddenly wasn't hungry any more. It was funny how remembering something changed everything. One minute, I was angry that Spume had outsmarted me but secretly a bit relieved I wouldn't have to see Nate for eight months – eight months! – and nobody could blame me because there was nothing I could do. The next, I was hiding in a corner and holding my hands over my face though nobody could see me.

I'd completely forgotten about his family. Getting in touch with them now was impossible. I had no decent excuse for not calling before, other than that I was a stupid stoner idiot.

It was guilt that gave me the bright idea of making another visitation request. Maybe I could get another earlier visit and if he had enough brain left, I could tell his parents and help them get a visit, or… something, at least. But Spume knew all the tricks. They auto-fired back instantaneously. The system told me I couldn't book two visits at once and did I want to cancel the existing one and make a new application?

Yeah, you can find me on the system when it suits you, can't you, bastards.

I packed my J™ and stared into space until my stomach wouldn't leave me alone so I necked a bottle of Total™ to shut it up. Then although I wasn't hungry any more, I drank half of another one because it was yummy and moreish. Some of the stuff Chen had left me was safely within its use-by and I probably should have eaten something chewable. But I felt like such an arsehole I decided my health could fuck itself.

It turned out Chen's job was genuinely busy – or she was playing hard to get – because she didn't come back to me for nearly a week. I was two days into my off-time and standing at the bench counting my Total™ bottles so I felt a bit caught out when she came through. 'Hey Teens. Sorry, I've been bloody manic. What's happened with Nate? God, you're so amazing the way you're dealing with all this! And I'm such a bad friend for not checking in with you more!'

It was annoying how honest she sounded.

'Pricks!' she said, after I gave her the news. 'That's it! I'm gonna try, now. I should've tried before. How do you do it again? I'm gonna do it right now.' The rejection pinged back straight away like it had for me.

I would have been angry if I wasn't kind of impressed by the smoothness of their screwing us over. The first few applications 'lost', one rejected for 'medical safety'. Then once you were through their pissy level one it was one visit at a time, visits only when they said, complaints mocked and nowhere to complain about mocked complaints. It was brilliant.

Also, I was relieved at how it kept Chen busy so she couldn't ask if I'd spoken with Nate's family. But I had to keep her talking. Trying not to look as if I was thinking about them was making it hard to think what to say. 'I tried to tell Shane too but his handle's gone weird.' It slipped out.

Chen froze as if she'd been arrested. Her face already looked sick so I felt a bit icky when she paled more under her tan. 'You, uh, didn't know?' she croaked out after a while and then I saw she was holding back tears.

'Shit! What? What is it?'

'He's. He— The plague. He's d— He died.'

'No way!' I said. I didn't feel anything. My mouth fell open. 'No way,' I looped.

'Yeah.' She said. 'Sorry. I thought everyone— I thought you knew.'

Well, didn't I feel fucking great, then! But it wasn't my fault. How should I have known? How? It wasn't fair for her to make out I was some kind of arsehole. People never told me stuff then blamed me for putting my foot in my mouth, it wasn't fair. Red flecks started closing in at the edges of my eyes. 'So you two were seeing each other in the end,' I said.

'What? No! What do you mean?'

My words came out as if someone else was using my mouth and I couldn't stop them. 'Well, how come you knew and I didn't? If you weren't in touch with him? Did you all go to his funeral and talk shit about me?' The red haze closed in more and my ads flashed over it like nightmare pink lightning.

'Teens! There wasn't a funeral! We were quarantined. I thought you knew! I never would've—'

'How? How would I have known, Chen? If you didn't bloody tell me? And how did you know if you weren't bloody seeing him behind my back. Why else would you be in touch with all Nate's other fr—'

'Jesus! Seeing Shane? How do you come up with this shit, uh… Tina? You're crazy, I swear! Shane was bloody right to be worried about you! We were both bloody right to be worried about you! And how could I have been seeing Shane for fuck's sake? Even if it was possible, which it wasn't since everyone including fucking Nate, knew Shane was in love with Nate, how the fuck would it be behind your back?' She shouted at me loud enough to freeze me up. I'd never heard her shout before let alone like that.

She stood and I flinched though we were on a call. But she collected herself quickly. She didn't sit back down. She stood glaring at me with her holo-legs sticking down through my bed like a ghost and one of my knees inside her hip.

She clenched her teeth and her voice came out in a growl. 'I knew Shane died because we were friends, uh… Tina. His friends were my fucking friends and Nate's fucking friends too! We grew up together, Tina! It's possible for something in the world to not be about you, you know. Have you ever thought about that? Is that a concept to you, you fuckin' psycho? Oh, and by the way… Tina, don't worry about Nate's family. I told them Nate was in prison by accident in the end, weeks – months! – ago, because I thought you'd already done it... Tina! Don't worry I won't inconvenience you with how much it messed them up finding out that way, but, y'know, thought you'd like to fuckin' know… Tina!' She lost it again halfway through and finished up screaming at me, her tired eyes streaming.

It felt like the whole world had heard when she stopped because all I could hear was silence. She stood in front of me breathing hard as if she'd been exercising and her hands kept opening and closing in fists. I couldn't look at her so I looked at the duvet between my crossed legs and saw a roach streak over the side of the bed and disappear.

How did people know things like that? Was it true? Nate wouldn't have been friends with someone like that, would he? Normal people didn't get like that, did they? It was only the rich-fucks who were all pervy and weird. And Shane was no rich-fuck.

I was going to fire that back at Chen but by the time I'd built up the courage to look up, she'd cut the call and I was alone. And a part of me knew it was bullshit anyway. That was that friendship completely blown this time, yet another one biting the dust. I vaped another J™.

Chen had probably felt bad about not telling me Shane had died and she was trying to cover up by giving me all that grief. That's what I kept trying to tell myself anyway but it didn't work. Deep down I knew she wasn't lying and that meant I was as big of an arsehole as she'd said I was. And that Nate wasn't who I thought he'd been. And it didn't matter any more because now they were all gone anyway. Shane was dead. Nate was as good as dead and there was no way back with Chen.

Idiot girl. I will find you…

Somehow being this sort of… more alone made the memory of the dream worse.

Jesus! Why would I want to be awake in a dream like that anyway? Nate and his lunatic ideas!

I tried to sleep on a wet pillow and after I finally managed to drop off, he found me anyway and wrapped himself around me so I couldn't move or breathe and shoved inside me to tear me apart.

You're a selfish little girl, you should come back to see what a mess you've made.

I woke in the dark with the words fading in the air around me. I was sucking in air and sweating. It wasn't nearly as bad as it had been in quarantine but my temperature was back and Chen's voice looped in my brain.

Uh… Tina… …Tina… …Tina…

Something about the way she'd said my name made me shiver in the dark.

The temperature didn't get any higher but it made work a pain. I drank Instant™, pinched myself and managed to stay awake. My appetite was okay and my biotech didn't call in an airstrike which was how I knew I was going to be one of those lucky people who took months to fully throw off the virus despite no longer, like, having the crappy virus.

I collapsed after a bottle of Total™ and thanked the goddess, who hadn't been a fuck of a lot of help lately, that I was all right again the next day. Though I'd cluster-blown it with Chen, I felt somehow lighter.

In a strange kind of way, everything had sorted itself out. Nate's parents knew so that was a load off. I'd done what I could to get a visit and nobody could say I hadn't. I didn't know if I'd be able to see Nate in November, but there was nothing I could do about that till a couple of weeks before it happened.

There'd been so much to do and so much stress worrying about what Chen and everyone was saying, and now it was gone. Now all I had to do was work, stay alive and get on with the Movement.

A good bit of money had piled up in my account through the quarantine, double-shifts and off-time. After the nightmare and the temperature day, it took me until my next off time to feel like doing much more than sleeping when I wasn't working.

But once I could, I attacked search rankings and parted with some of my boredom-sweat-and-tears-earned satoshis to really kick the Movement off. I wasn't going to let a stupid dream stop me. The goddess would protect me. Sure enough, when I logged on, I saw my statistics had moved, a tiny bit. So it was trying to take off without me paying for it. She was with me. I had only to be patient.

I did more tech study – *it's coming back to me, this stuff is easy, I could've blitzed Nate if I'd wanted to, bloody wet-foot…* – and made a few more recordings and grabbed a few more virtual forests to make my space better and show people I was active on it and it wasn't yet another online ghost-town.

Then I got offered another double shift and nearly forgot about it and burned through my Total™ and guzzled Instant™ to smash through the days. I vaped little half-J™s each night to keep the nightmares away. Sometimes it worked.

The news curators kept trending boring earthquake stuff. But there were always earthquakes off the old coastlines so I couldn't understand why they were ranking so highly. There was nothing about why all the rich kept trading up their apartments, not that it would have made my life any easier. The morning last-minuters would have kept blasting me out of bed no matter the reason for all the sales.

I took more and more double shifts. It wasn't as if I had anything better to do or anywhere to go; or like I could refuse.

Chen's Total™s ran out so I decided I should probably have a binge on other food. I did try. But it all tasted flat and never filled me up properly or kept my energy up as well as the Total™s did. And after a few days I got the shakes and I was worried my temperature would come back so I caved and bought more bottles and was immediately fine.

It can't really be addictive, can it? It wouldn't be legal.

Even if it was, I was the healthiest I'd been in ages; I was sure of it. I needed to stock up my baby cream supply to keep the sting on my bottom at bay but that was a small price to pay for moreish orange deliciousness.

All the Christmas and *xīnnián* crap had long disappeared from the ads which was lucky because that was basically the only way I had of knowing that entire months had passed. That and it got colder. There was ice on the walls of the alleyway and I had to put my overs on to get stuff from the poor-door so I didn't freeze in the hallway, which at least didn't smell as bad in the cold.

The stats in my space were creeping along and I was getting better and better at targeting my spending on the rankings. Nate's aliases stayed alive and I used them to keep up my tech studies. After what happened to Nate, I was getting more and more worried the police were watching the Movement space. I wasn't going to go the same way he had.

The only challenge tech ever presented me was how boring and workaday it was. And how I didn't want to open up the bit of my mind that could do it backwards. But who's choice was that in the end? Mine. So I was careful never to do it for too long or to remember things I shouldn't and before long, a lot of the geeky things Nate had tried to teach me shrank into banal trivialities.

I worked out how to pass on his PrimeFlixK-Bell-Pharm points hack and why it had to be face to face and how you had to give up some of your own nanites. That was one-oh-one fluff. Biotech, security and logistics were another story but they were no match for the smarts I had access to.

If I pushed it too far, I ended up paying for it after I'd gone to sleep. Night after night, I opened my eyes to the glare of my lights turned up to full brightness and the familiar feeling of someone sitting on the bed. He came again and again, every time I managed to close my eyes again after waking up screaming in the dark.

The times I couldn't get back to sleep, I'd lie and watch the alleyway turn from black to grey as work time got closer and closer until finally, I'd give up sleeping and drag myself up, make a mug of Instant™ though deep down, I desperately wanted – God, for fuck's sake! – a real coffee. I'd force the memory away, down the real-person's drink followed by a bottle of Total™ and wait for work to start.

But it was all worth it. It had to be. I'd make it be.

Then one extra-pissy rainy day in early June, Joanna Ra-hui's death exploded over the feeds.

No! No! No!

I'd got up and started flicking through spaces when I saw it in Yang's feed. I hadn't known she was sick. It blew the cover off my mind and I reached for handles I hadn't reached for in years.

I froze, barely in time before making any calls and the tightness in my chest spread up to my face. Red closed in on me and the next thing I knew I was flat on my back with my head and legs at painful angles and a throbbing in my brain.

Must've hit my head.

I reached around to check and my fingers came away with only little red-orange smears so it wasn't too nasty a bump. The space had stayed open in my visuals and I growled into it and swiped away all the poncy footage of the funeral at the big fancy dome and all the rich-fucks turning up in their private cars. But no matter how much I swore at it and changed spaces, I couldn't stop my tears rolling and my hands shaking.

She died, she actually died! And I didn't go and see her! Jesus! No! No, no, no, no, no!

I – 4500 BCE-2041

The sun burst into a thousand stars. The earth rose up to join the sky, an azure, green and brown maelstrom reaching forth veins of lightening to twine about me and pull me to its spinning centre. It was as if the ancestors buried in our ancient place of the dead were finally enfolding me in their earthen embrace, spinning me around, crushing my soul.

In the tumult, as the spin and flurry tore at me, I felt pulsing life wrapped in skeins of the Flow and pain, like a spider in a web, crystalline with dew and morning sun and quivering with vigilance. It was through this bond that I felt them coming, sensed their souls' approach like beetles crawling on my back.

But they did not mean harm, did they? I knew them, did I not? But I was whirling too fast. As I reached for the memories, they spun away. Better safe than sorry. No matter that the world blurred and flowed in my anguished vision, that pain flew like smashed winter ice through my soul, pulsing up and down my spine, from soul to thought to body and back again in spasms and jerks. I could open the rock and soil and pull them down into the angry fire that bubbled beneath. I could spin a column of burning air to rip them apart before they came at me.

I channelled the Flow, gripped in agony and rage. I made to tear up the earth, burn trees, dry lakes and rip winds from their ancient courses. Only I found my Flow suddenly stemmed, inexplicably blocked though I could yet feel the Stone. All was clear for an instant as it had not been for…

Summers? Lifetimes?

Then down washed a violet darkness and blissful quiet. Flow ran from the leaky vessel of my soul and hung like frozen blue smoke in the cool depths about me. Only violet silence and cold crystal stillness remained and at last my torment was ended.

In time I lost myself, yielding in some thoughtless way to my new surrounds and in the violet depths I hung, fused to the Stone, one of the ancient Order, stripped of flesh and bone and yet anchored to life unending. I was nowhere and no one. I was it that should not be but was, mind out of time, an impossibly bodiless living soul.

And I remained a man for all the strangeness of my being; a man with no weapon against the lonely ravages of timeless solitude but to fall into a stupor reminiscent of my lost body's sleep. And so I drifted numbly down the ages, my wasting-madness healed after a fashion, the threads of memory stitched to its cause in my first fatal mauling, buried beneath feathery drifting layers of soothing time.

But no force between Earth and Sky is eternal. Though strong and tightly made, the skeins of Flow that bound my resting place together could not match the patient chipping might of time itself. Though diminished like a tree curled back into its seed, I could feel the slow change, the gradual loosening and leaking strength of the Flow that kept my haven safe.

Then into that tiny ancient decay a more urgent force burst – I would never understand its cause – and suddenly I was again calm, clear and able to think. I stirred within the crystal and floated to wakefulness like a bubble from the deep ocean floor, growing as it rises to the light. As I came back to myself, I felt my safety shiver and I knew fear but was powerless to prevent the forces assailing the dark violet vault of my ancient peace.

And then the disturbance ceased and I prepared to sleep again but my fear prevented me. I looked again on the swirls

of Flow hanging in the depths around me and remembered
they had been mine, brought here with me when I was…
   What? When I was what?

Ethel – Jun 2097, Cornwall Hill, Akarana Island, Aotearoa Archipelago

I sighed and got up to look out over to the industrial wasteland in the grey. Rain pooled in the clay and spattered over concrete blocks, rusting metal objects of no discernible kind and bioboxes that had for some reason not broken themselves down and swarmed back to wherever the deuce such things went.

Drones swarmed on the wind and high-rises like teeth on the horizon grinned across at me through the rain. Rahui and Laufala's home were all that prevented them crossing the Old Campbell Road to eat up the ugly expanse of earth before me.

I supposed her daughters would inherit it, now Rahui was dead. I wondered if they would keep it and allow her old plaything, Laufala, to remain until he too died; it had become a trope in recent years; my sort of recent, anyway. A chill stole over me at the prospect that they might not. But if they did not, maybe nothing at all would come of it and maybe nothing good either.

I wondered why it discomfited me then though. I had known for decades, that it would happen eventually; whether they kept it or sold it off or their granddaughters did, or theirs; it did not matter. It was only a matter of time before the house disappeared and the developers swooped in and tore up the earth.

The reminder.

Ah, yes. That was it. The news of old Joanna Rahui's recent demise called to mind for me, what I had seen take place in her house some five decades prior, when there were not too many more than three islands to the country instead of three hundred and three, and when I lived in the house next door.

In those years, I kept a nosy eye on my neighbours and noted with – at first – desultory interest, the presence of a Shade. It was not long after Joanna's mother, Aroha, was killed in a car-crash with Joanna barely more than a baby.

Even then, I paid it little mind as what mattered a jolly Shade? In the generations after my first daughter died, I had learned such entities were workaday if not frequent occurrences. My people did not know what they were but they were inconsequential enough not to warrant any more thought than the wind.

This was different. It was extant for years instead of hours and it did more than stir the air or trouble a dream or two. It drove family after family away though usually, they did not know it. And in the later years of its residency, between tenants, it had waxed in potency. It screamed and made mess and touched the waking world in ways that defied Earth and Sky.

My observations had stirred the memories of the others back then if I read my dreams a-right. For they had noticed long ago what I had only just begun to see: the Shades' persistence and power waxing as their numbers declined with the slow onward march of centuries.

So why do they yet not try to find me? Do none of them see the import? Not one?

I kept two good eyes on the place – and in it – after that; especially after Joanna returned to the house, an adult; her foster home, the retention of the house in trust for her, all my doing though she never knew. I saw it all happen and learned at last that Shades were not ancestors – well not in the light the word cast anyway. Nor were they demons, devils, godlings, nymphs of the forest or marshals of lightning and rain. No. They were the living spirits of men and women.

Some may have asked: how foolish was old Ethel, that she did not see this in all her years – so very many years! – roaming the Earth? Did she not read the myriad paperback novels of ghosts and hauntings and spirits and dreams?

Well of course I had. But that was the point. Until Aroha, Shades could not be seen. More often than not, ostensibly serious claims that they existed turned out to be baseless.

The new-fangled science that had dug its claws into the very core of the Earth and punctured the sky itself to grope in the blackness for the planets and the stars in two short centuries, had little to say on the matter other than condescending dismissal. Fair enough. I too was guilty of disbelieving that which I could not see until generations after the daughter who had tried to tell me had died in childbirth.

In all the memories and dreams I had at my disposal, nobody had encountered such as Aroha. In our most distant memories of the days when Shades were more plentiful if utterly trivial, the creatures had never contrived to bend the light about their unknowable substance as Aroha had.

And if that were not extraordinary enough, Tristian Laufala's Shade had sallied forth into the dawn to help Joanna with Aroha before the spirit's madness destroyed their house. Watching from behind their jacaranda, which had stood there until it died of blight like everything else green and growing, I had seen – and recognised – him drift in like mist that took form as the horizon grew light. There might have been something to all the nonsense about the afterlife had his living body not lain healing in hospital when he decided to pay his helpful visit.

Extraordinary as it all was, all was well that ended well for Rahui and Laufala. The house stayed standing and the ghost was gone. And now as I stood watching the drones fly through the grey, I reframed the memory in light of the others' dreams I had recently unearthed. And it gave an inkling of how they might have done it. A frustrating inkling.

I could of course, not let it lie after witnessing that. The next day, I peeped through the foliage choking our boundary fence – such greenery there was about, then! – and saw what Rahui and Laufala never would. There was an odd disturbance in the soil that began at the corners of the house and trailed out over the fence to the grassland beyond; Cornwall Park it was called back then.

It was as if the house had been pulled forward by the back edge of its roof and dragged the ground up with it. It was only slight and resettled in a few days but I had seen it. I had not forgotten. And now that too, I reframed and a chill ran up my spine as my mind flashed upon an image of the seabed Victoria had shown me. It answered one question and spawned a thousand more but it meant, as the expression went, that I was on to something.

I had struggled since, not to blame Laufala though I knew the maddened Shade of Aroha was the real culprit. The trouble was, he was alive and she was twice dead. Like my poor simple genius boy Freddy who had done what I could not and… hacked into Laufala's… tech, so that I could see what Laufala was seeing of Aroha. It was only for that, though, I meant no ill. We had planned to alert him to his weakness – that had been Freddy's idea.

It was not Laufala's fault that he had been chased from his home by the demented spirit of his mother-in-law. Still, had he looked where he was going a little harder, perhaps he would not have knocked my poor Freddy off his bike. Perhaps then, neither of them would have been bowled over by the drunkard in his manual-drive car – already illegal in those earlier years of the self-driving… Ubers – and Freddy would have been alive now, to stand with me looking at the rain.

Ah but perhaps then, I would not have been lucky enough to retain my illicit connection to Laufala's tech.

I did not like that I had no idea how to close it down, at first; it was a constant reminder of Freddy. I would have thought after so many children, I should have learned my lesson and stopped having them, or at least stopped mourning their passing. Yet somehow, I could do neither and poor simple brilliant Freddy was one of the hardest; both to have and to lose.

But in time I came to see the usefulness of keeping tabs on Laufala, being so big in the world as he became. I had those of my children who understood such things nurture the connection and we kept it, as the expression goes, in the family. As Laufala had with the antics of the sinister and grubby little John and the woes John had brought he and his; well, or John's mad elder, really.

The wind redoubled its efforts and lashed at my window as the memories faded. The barren dirty expanse I looked out over now was unrecognisable as the green place it had once been. The foliage was all gone and many of the roads had disappeared or changed. Rahui's house looked different to how it had back then; those two were far too important not to have fences and security now. I could not remember what my old place looked like. It was long crushed to dirt.

I sighed and returned to my screens to watch the funeral.

Tristian – Jun 2097, Cornwall Hill, Akarana Island, Aotearoa Archipelago

I'd slept without moving and dreamed myself exhausted; ordinary dreams, shitty ones but at least, ordinary, my own and nobody else's. I thought I'd got away with it. Grey dawn was coming through the window and a curtain of rain so heavy it obscured the security fence, metres away.

I shouldn't have snoozed the first alarm. I should have accepted sleep deprivation and pinged the coffee machine on so there was a flat-white waiting when I dragged myself into the kitchen. But right as I thought of the smell of coffee, the late doze stole over me, warm and inviting with the sound of the rain on the roof to usher me down.

And as I floated back up with the rising light of the next alarm and escalating birdsong, it snagged me. Not a proper dream, only the ghostly sense of it, the strange woman, an impression on my eyelids like the afterimage of lightning, a nagging reminder, *I will always come.* Then it was gone and I was rubbing sleep from my eyes.

Even though it hadn't talked this time, hadn't shouted and shrieked in its incomprehensible language and sent me wobbling off balance through my morning shower and into the daylight hours like it sometimes did, it dampened my mood anyway. The slow drip of it through the years had me all but defeated. It didn't matter that this time it was only a feather-touch on my soul at dawn. It was the last thing I needed today.

I sighed and dragged myself out of bed to get ready.

My arm was numb and tingling from being crushed under my side. I'd hoped it would come right as I did my morning yoga and got ready, like it normally did. But it hadn't, not fully anyway. I resisted the urge to rub it.

My hip on the same side was also complaining about the night's pressure and I winced slightly each time it twinged. We'd only been standing a few minutes and my feet already hurt, knees spasming with the odd needle of… What? The-fuck, what? Eighty-five years was what.

I was used to all that by now. On good days, if I'd watched my eating for a while, slept well for a few lucky nights, not pushed the walking or the yoga too far, if I was lucky, I could nearly remember the memory of the last time I wasn't tired and annoyed by some kind of desultory discomfort. Yep, I was in pretty good shape for my age and only sometimes dreaded the next thirty odd years the statistics promised with their slow increase of non-specific ailments that would eventually wind me down into the new-fangled recycler so someone's unsuspecting kids would get to use me for pizza topping.

The new middle fuckin' age. Wahoo.

But what I could never get used to was the distress of my bowels acting out in public like they were threatening to do now. If it was a fart, I might be able to do slow-silent-release and suck up the reproachful glares. I glanced around and made a quick calculation about how far the fallout might spread in the oakwood bright, wax-scented stillness before fading to mere diffuse unpleasantness.

I speculated it might only mildly asphyxiate a few people I didn't give a fuck about on the edge of the blast-radius after decisively choking my nearest and dearest. I was more or less human-shielded about four-deep among friends and family on three sides with a good few metres' clearance before the podium and the dais where Jo's bio-coffin sat, serene in the watery sunlight.

But my confidence in brain-to-anus comms was uncertain nowadays and what if it wasn't a fart? It was getting harder and harder to predict or indeed to tell the difference on release. No. Full-pucker was the only guaranteed safety. But the constant clenching effort made all my other pains worse.

Come on Anna! Get on with it!

Finally, she did. 'In her final six months, I sat with Jo nearly every day and helped her write this speech.' Anna paused and looked down at her notes.

She sounds like a priest!

There was hardly a trace of the brash, tough go-getter Anna of our distant youth. The dark-suited woman at the podium was sedate and solemn, her face showing the first wrinkles of well-tended mid-eighties.

The scent of burning wax filled the air with memories of churches, for me anyway. Candlelight shone pink-gold on Anna's smooth shiny head. My eyes strayed across from her to the coffin again. A shudder of grief welled, magnifying all my aches, and I quickly shifted my gaze to the glass wall behind the dais.

I looked outside, idly up from the forest of headstones where pillars of sunlight roved like searchlights, on to the treetops surrounding the quiet burial lots and finally through the estate's domed ceiling and up to the boiling sky where drones swarmed on the wind below the scudding clouds.

The stretching silence brought me back to myself, that and a gentle nudge. I turned to my daughter David who I already knew would be glaring reproach for my drifting off.

Jesus Davey! Give me a break! Can't I be a senile eighty-something, today of all bloody days!

I channelled the words through hurting eyes but her frown was unrelenting beneath the severe bun the young – well, 'young' – ones all wore nowadays; all that hair, so much bother. Susan's head appeared over her elder sister's shoulder with an enquiring look from eyes too like her mother's. I demurred the silent mobbing and turned back to the podium where Anna had started speaking again.

'First Jo wanted me to pass on, "I know you'll all think it's weird I got Anna to read this out. I could have been with you. We could have used the tech – no offence Tristian – to help me haunt you for a bit longer. You could have been standing around my deathbed, everyone with their weird infinitely available front-row seats, listening to me wheeze out the words like I was really there or you were all really here or… however we did it. Call me old fashioned but the idea was too creepy. I couldn't stand the thought of you all watching me like that after I was gone, like I was a bloody ghost."'

Anna paused. I could tell she was trying to keep it together, probably hearing Jo's stern voice in her head like I was. Other people would think she was pausing for effect. She got back on with it after a moment; it was more than I could have done.

'Jo's other important wish, and one she reiterated a lot near the end when her suffering was greatest and she was ready to go, was that there was to be no religion at her funeral. "I know it's an easy ask," she told me, "but I'm doing it anyway. Promise me Anna, please, please promise me, no prayers, no incense, no holy water, no woo-woo bullshit, at all." Her words, not mine. Well, here we are and I think it's safe to say she's got her wish and everyone has heard her wish as she wanted them to.'

Not taking any chances, eh?

I didn't blame her. Not that there was any religion nowadays anyway. Bit of a slam-dunk, that one.

Anna continued. 'Now she's gone and we're here to remember her life and to help us in that tribute to her memory here's what she wanted you all to know; a lot, it turns out! And she said to me she doesn't care if it takes ages, tough shit. Nearly all she asked me to say is about the people in her life and how much you all meant to her. She was anxious to give everyone due credit and respect and worried she would miss people out. I helped her write this but trust me when I say, these are all her words.'

I believed her too. I would have believed her without seeing her eyes moving, cued by her tech.

She went on, starting with Jo's memories of her childhood and choking up as she read her own name. Again, I saw but I knew most would notice only a momentary pause. She collected herself and went on and I heard the ghost of our childhood laughter and felt again, the prick of splinters picked up climbing trees, sneaking under hedges and chasing each other around a grassy lawn and through the gap in the punga fence at Jo and Anna's adoptive home.

And then I came back to myself and remembered yet again that like the sunshine, sandy seashores and so much of the world's greenery, Jo was gone. A tremor and a single tear before I could get myself back together. And then it occurred to me that the youngest mourners here today, Aaron's kids Jeff, Kay and Andrea, if they'd disobeyed their grandad Jase and showed up online or otherwise, my granddaughter Sarah, next to Susan and her sister Elayne if she was alive and watching somehow, wouldn't have climbed a real tree or scrambled through a hedge in their lives.

Anna took us through Jo's memories of our adolescence together and I felt transported, back to high-school rugby fields and summers at the beach. All gone now, replaced by grey rain, concrete, steel and poisonous ocean.

I drifted right off then, nearly to sleep though the battle with my bowels kept me standing. The tail end of Jo's biological parents who she barely knew startled me awake again.

'…I forgive you for leaving me and for everything and, Aroha, as you finally reconciled your past, though it took me a while, I also reconciled mine and now we can both rest in peace.'

Jesus! I hope so!

A chill ran through me, my thoughts drifted home, over the miles of harbour bridge and new harbour bridge, up to the forest of high-rises covering what was once the reserve behind our family home.

Jesus! What if she does come back…

It was half hope, half panic. My thoughts ranged ahead through the coming hours. It would be raining, most likely. I could turn up the lights, the same ones I'd installed for Jo soon after we met – well, in the same way an axe with a new handle, head and haft 'is the same axe but yeah, anyway. I could crank up the heating and warm the place up so when the guests arrived it wouldn't be like a tomb, the way it got sometimes. But what if she was there? I imagined her waiting beside our bed, the one she'd died in, her face hers, the same as when she was alive but with that surreal quality…

Jesus, no! But… I could talk to her, one last time, say goodbye… again. But would she go then? Would she be crazy like her mother was? How does it work?

I shivered despite the warmth and my pains twinged, nearly causing me to lose control of my mutinous bowls. I'd never stopped my private research but in nearly five decades, I'd turned up nothing. Nowadays I wasn't sure I wanted to.

I've said goodbye, please let her stay gone. Or, maybe don't? Jesus! I'm a mess.

Gone.

It echoed on my mind. Anna read on and I squeezed my eyes shut against a fresh deluge of tears. Then opened them again and let the tears come.

If I can't cry at my partner's bloody funeral…

The tears wet my face and ran down my chin and my shoulders began to shake as wetness infiltrated my collar. It was all I could do to keep clenching but somehow my other aches faded as I cried.

I felt a warm hand between my shoulder blades, maybe Davey. Maybe one of the cousins in dark suits behind me, it didn't matter. I cried and took the comfort and cried more and Anna spoke on as candles flickered in silent draughts and the clouds roiled as a storm blew in and lashed the dome outside.

Anna went on. And each bit of Jo's life she described, friend, acquaintance or business associates she named, spun me away into memories of her; of us.

I was jolted from my reverie of recollections yet again by a savage whisper from Susan. 'Fuckin' mind control and lobotomization, more like!'

Ah, Paresh, was he in there somewhere?

Paresh Steel. Not exactly a friend given he was based in Germany. But we'd dealt with him so much developing his Spume virtuals using Jo's art. He was an... e-squib I think they were calling the poor buggers nowadays. Not many bodies rejected tech like that; fewer all the time. Hadn't stopped him founding the next biggest tech gig in the world to mine though. A different kind of tech than mine, or a different use for it anyway. But he was a good egg; odd as he was. Jo would never get to meet him now.

The names went on and the memories streamed, silent and slow like the tears down my cheeks. Then I was startled again when a thunder of applause bloomed and rolled through the hall as if to challenge the roiling storm above us. Anna waited for it to ebb before continuing.

Ah, yeah. The ocean clean-up and the tree-planting.

And the mention wasn't a bad thing either given who was here; or virtually here. It would give them a reminder, keep the donations coming.

You can't think about that now, you idiot!

Jo would've done though. She'd probably had Anna mention it for exactly that reason! God, I wished she could've seen how far we'd got with the oceans, not only since she'd got too sick to keep checking in but in the last week alone!

More names. More memories. More tears. Finally Anna drew to a close.

A few speeches followed as I teetered between tearfully exhausted collapse, public loss of bowel control and – decreasingly – a semblance of composure. Then at last it was done.

I didn't realise Susie had walked out before the end and I couldn't remember who else spoke, if anyone. All I remembered was being blessedly free to totter to the welcoming privacy of the shitter.

With only my usual aches and ailments to endure, I went to the bright lounge adjoining the main hall. My legs were starting to ache and I wondered why we'd all stood through the whole bloody thing. I sat down for a while but it got too weird with people coming up and reaching down to shake my hand or hug me so I creaked and twinged myself vertical again.

The storm had passed over and watery sunlight filtered through high cloud and lit the room, bright but sombre. I couldn't face the darker parlour where the overspill of mourners ate yellow canapes and drank tea and coffee. I fielded the parade of condolences by the coffee table where the human server, bot-like, anticipated my flat-white refills. I longed for real milk though it'd been decades since I'd tasted it.

Susie hadn't left after all, I realised so she must only have bailed from the reading to spite us, or maybe me.

Oh for fuck's sake! Or she went to the toilet, you self-absorbed old shit!

She and David wove through the crowd, alighting on closer acquaintances and friends with expert priority.

They grew up with it I s'pose.

The young ones were nowhere to be seen, probably in the parlour munching out.

The virtual attendees, barely distinguishable from those there in the flesh made my acquaintance smartly. Other than Paresh of Spume with his distinctive huge brown head beaming in a shoddy pixelated holo from his e-squib tablet, I'd lost track of who was from where over the years. But I guessed most were here at odd times – for them – and keen to duck out and back to their lives whether going back to sleep or getting on with their days. I made a point of speaking with them first, using my tottering height and throwing my gaze out over heads to those I was sure were only holo-here.

The crowds finally started thinning, people either winking out or filing to the Uber-stop, or in a few cases, their private cars. The 'kids' and I were the last to go, catering machines falling in like iron ants behind us to ready the place for the next funeral. As we got in our Uber, I spotted Jase and his son, John getting into the car ahead.

So they're talking again, eh? Interesting.

The NDA flashed red at the edge of my vision as soon as it detected my recognising them, the situation inappropriately – bloody ridiculously – triggering its ramshackle algorithm.

Yeah, yeah. I know.

I turned it down. I was more surprised to see them getting into the car together than that they'd turned up. Still, he was – or had been – Jo's friend. It turned out Aaron and his three had been standing right behind me so I hoped his cooked old dad wouldn't give him grief. I didn't know if any of this public meeting was an NDA violation but I hoped on this of all days, he'd cut everyone some slack. But who could tell what a madman would or wouldn't do?

It was a solid quarter of an hour's drive to the exit and gusts of wind buffeted the car as we left the funeral estate's dome. I wondered what the owners did with all the cash people paid to have their headstones there. It was Anna, of course, who had gawped at the price I signed off with barely a second glance.

'Dad, are you coming to the recycler?' Susie's tone quavered.

No bloody way.

'No. You go. I've said my goodbyes.' But I amended, 'All right, look, the whole thing makes me a bit squeamish, I know, I know you think your old dad's out of touch but when people died, we used to… I dunno, not…'

'…give a shit about the planet,' Susie finished for me, her voice half-heartedly savage.

I wanted to think she was toughing it out, but a not-insignificant part of me worried she wasn't. I was surprised she came today. I doubted she would have if it wasn't for Anna convincing her. Or Sarah.

Christ! What did we do to her? What did I do?

I'd been about to steel myself and offer to go to the recycler with them but I didn't trust myself to speak now. Jo's body wouldn't be … attended to for another few days. The conversation could wait. Now we must face close friends and family.

What conversation would that be anyway? What conversation haven't I already bloody had with Susie? Fuck! She's fifty! My child is fifty. And Davey's fifty-two and in line to replace me as CEO…

Which I didn't mind. She would keep the board in line, probably better than me. And if we tiffed sometimes now, well I'd be dead so… A message pinged. I opened it and connected to the house to open the door. 'Your uncle Marty's arrived,' I relayed, uselessly.

'He's not our fuckin' uncle. He's your pissy friend,' Susie wasped back, her anger subdued.

He was your mother's friend too! And he left Jason to support us! To support your fuckin' nieces!

But I bit back the words. I didn't know what horrified me more, Susie's words or the realisation that this was how we'd conversed since…

Since when? Since she was a bloody teenager? Jesus.

That we wouldn't have to get things ready for the wake from scratch, when we…. I got home was no comfort in the face of that revelation. Not that there wasn't much tech wouldn't sort anyway, Marty would be keeping an eye on it now.

Davey and Susie stayed quiet for the rest of the trip. I left them on the porch waiting for Marty's family. I found him directing catering in the dining room and he nodded to me. 'Nearly finished. Are Aaron and the kids on the way?'

Kids? I love it.

'They were right behind us, should be a couple of minutes.'

'Did it all go all right?'

'I dunno. What's all right for a funeral? But yeah, I s'pose it went as well as could be expected. Nobody dropped the coffin or anything.'

'You all right Tris?'

Fuck no I'm not!

'I will be.'

Marty didn't press me and we stood together watching tech lay out dishes like amber-eyed swarming tentacled nightmares from films of yester-century, the 4S holo-remasters of which now formed my guilty pleasures. I heard voices on the porch and decided to get in some alone time before the house filled up. 'Marty, can I leave you with… everything for a moment, uh, longer? Got to go to my room for a bit.'

'Course.'

I locked the door behind me and turned slowly towards our bed.

Mine now, only mine. Crap!

The room was empty, it felt empty and it looked empty, no trace of any presence. Jo's stuff was already gone and mine was half boxed up in a corner. There were no two ways about it, she was definitely gone. Tears came hard on the heels of my sigh of relief.

The houseguests were harder than the memorial, more in my face. But I managed without breaking down. Too much. And then it was done. The guests left. Aaron's three said they had to get back to work. And it made me smile to think of such baby faces, their tech clumped up around necks and on earlobes to look like jewellery, having serious jobs.

The tech-swarm cleaned, tidied then disassembled into nanites like mist burned off by sunlight and only Susan, David, Sarah and I remained though I felt uncomfortable with Davey and Susie upstairs in their old rooms and Sarah – a cop, that young! – loitering with intent.

I couldn't think of anything to say to her. The afternoon wore on. Sarah eventually tootled off and silence descended as the second storm of the day blew over. Our… my old place, protested itself slowly into silence as the cascades from the guttering spouts slowed to trickles then drips.

Davey came back down and banished the oncoming gloom, foraging for leftovers and making me realise I was getting a bit hungry again myself. Instead of asking where her daughter was, she dug into some left-over v-quiche™ and complained with her mouth full, 'Tristian, do we really have to move?'

'What do you mean we? You two don't live here. I could turn your rooms into veggie-racks and you wouldn't notice until you came back for Christmas.'

'But Tristian.' She said in a patronisingly reasonable tone. 'You put a new storey on the house and all your geeky custom tech in it and everything. I can't believe after all these years, you're gonna let them eat our home so they can build another shitty ugly apartment block.'

Or ten.

'Half the geeky tech is yours, Davey. And besides, he's got to find some way of feeling better about himself, doesn't he? Where else are he and his cronies gonna hide all the poor people that work in solitary confinement at nothing-jobs and survive on addictive orange sludge, fake food, Instant™, and weed that vapes like sandpaper to get them high enough to appreciate the low-budget VR crap in the free spaces? Oh, and then die young of foot-rot in crappy government issue basement studios out at the coast.' We both jumped at Susie's snipe from the stairs. She must have padded down like a bloody….

Oh, okay.

She hadn't come down at all. I could see her rickety old office chair superimposed on the bottom step. It took me back to the student flatting days when we thought it was great gag to message each other from room to room with our smartphones on hangover days. Course, then we couldn't see the recipients' faces or smell their beer-breaths and sex-sheets.

Christ Susan! We're doing this again? Now? I can't understand! You work for our bloody c…

But I knew she was wilfully blind to her own hypocrisy. I'd settled into a sodden acceptance that she had plans to change the corporation, somehow, that she felt everything Jo and I had done wasn't enough.

Maybe it's a good thing. Got to hand the baton on sometime. Jesus! How morbid!

'I'm going to live in a shitty ugly apartment block.' I was proud to keep the tears in and the angry tremor out of my voice.

'Well, your one won't be shitty and ugly,' Susan said, sulkily.

'Not on the inside anyway,' I said, forcing a rueful smile. 'But anyway, it's not like I let them do anything, Davey, both of you. This is the last house on the island. Look around us, it's a bloody wasteland, what's the point? The view's crap and we're— I'm stopping all this space from being used for more residential blocks. It's selfish. Your mother was talking about moving anyway and that was before she got sick.'

'Oh that's fucking great, Tristian! Put fucking words in her mouth now she's not here to deny them. Nice. Good fucking timing, too.' Susie flared.

'But she…'

Did. She did say that?

But I knew there was no point in arguing. Besides, there was another reason I wanted away from the place. It was the same reason I was afraid to leave.

It had been a niggling anxiety for Jo and I over the decades which was crap considering we were completely innocent; actual victims when it came down to it. But the kids had been born and we'd never done anything about it and so it had festered.

I wished I hadn't remembered the night of my accident, the ghost of Jo's dad as well. And I couldn't bloody stop myself figuring it all out, could I? Aroha had tried to kill me to stop me telling Jo; a fuckin' ghost trying to kill me! And the dream that'd come after, while I was in a bloody coma, which turned out not to be a dream. And what that meant we were sitting on.

Except I'm innocent! We were innocent. I shouldn't care! I shouldn't bloody well care!

'Moving all my tech's easy, you know that,' I said distractedly, then, 'come on… both of you! We've talked about all this.'

'I know,' Davey said, suddenly sounding tired. 'But... I don't know. Everything changes, that's all.'

'Oh, how sad for you poor corporate kids, deprived of your luxurious antique and forced to live in, oh, goodness, more modern luxury with a fucking sea view.' Susie scowled and winked out.

'What...?'

Did we do?

I didn't finish the question. What could Susie have told me? And would I want to know? What bloody good would it do now?

'Look, uh, Davey, probate's however many months, okay? And there's going to be a whole ton of audit given my company and everything. They'll be all over me for laundering checks and stuff. It'll be months if not a couple of years until it settles. You can, uh, stay here or come over or whatever, I mean, you always could anyway but, you know...'

What? What does she know? What do I?

My conciliation rang foamy in my own ears and I was glad when she didn't retort, only nodded sadly and changed the subject. 'Tristian, what do you reckon's up with Sarah?'

'Eh?'

'She's, I don't know. Different, preoccupied or something?'

'I dunno, boyfriend problems? Her grandma died?'

'Tristian! Firstly ew, ew, ew and lalalalalala! Like you, my child is asexual because it's too gross for me to think otherwise! And secondly, duh! Obviously! But she's been like it for a week or so now. Did she say anything to you? I know how you two... are.'

God, you make it sound like a crime for me to be close to my bloody granddaughter!

'No, she didn't say anything and I...'

...was too preoccupied with myself to notice...

'...didn't notice anything. Sorry. Maybe ask her?'

'Don't be ridiculous! Funnily enough I think you might be right – in that stopped-clock kind of way. I think it might be boyfriend problems and that's why I don't want to know.'

But she couldn't help cracking a grin at her own ridiculousness.

They both stayed the next few days. David I could understand, it was how she was. And we had a lot of work stuff to get through; technically not allowed but what could you do. But Susie? Who knew? I was, unashamedly, too shit-scared to ask.

So it's official now is it Tristian? You don't want me around any more?

That was the reply I imagined. It suited me better to think that deep down she was worried about me staying here alone. Fuck-knew, I definitely was.

Sarah – Jun 2097, Cornwall Hill Station, Akarana Island, Aotearoa Archipelago

I felt guilty asking HR. And I felt guilty I hadn't found it months sooner because of all the people in the islands who probably lived from payslip to payslip instead of not noticing one of them was a bit short. And I wouldn't have noticed it if I hadn't been randomly doing life admin because I was bored at work. So wrong!

I felt kind of naughty going through the door to the back offices that I'd only ever used during induction. It was an ancient wooden monstrosity, technically outlawed building material. Not for the first time, I wondered if there was some kind of legal loophole letting them keep it along with all the other poisonous stuff in the station.

The thought of all the hands that would have touched its grubby metal handle over the decades made me squeamish. I stretched my sleeve over my hand to open it, remembering with a flush how I'd fallen for the time-honoured baby cop gag trying to ping it with my tech. I would've rathered the HR person had virtualled to me at my desk.

The hallway was bright with proper lighting at least but it smelled musty with age and more of the awful old manual doors lined the peeling walls. The HR department, which was one woman, lived right at the other end of the station. It was a cavernous room with such huge windows the walls were practically made of glass. It must have been a bigger department back in the day or maybe used for something else, who knew.

Jimmie was sitting way down the end. The window-glass was so thin I could hear the rain lashing it and as I walked past mouldering empty desks stacked near the walls. The grey brightness felt peaceful despite the pooey weather outside.

'You were absent for half a day,' Jimmie said when her eyes came back from her tech. Her ringlets were so tight I could feel them straining to escape her bun. I wondered idly what they'd look like loose.

'No I wasn't.' I was annoyed at how childish I sounded. 'Wait, I mean, when? When does it say I was absent?'

'Here.' A ringlet like a tiny black spring bounced free and she brushed it out of her eye with strange blocky-looking fingers. Now I'd seen them I couldn't stop my eyes from following her hand when she placed it back in her lap.

She pulled me into the virtual she was looking at. It was the normal 2D work time calendar I'd seen a million times before Neil had rescued me from admin purgatory.

Jesus, I could have ended up with your job. All my training, all my education.

I could see she had access to more drilldown than I would have. She'd marked the day so I could see it. It'd been months ago – last November! – but it only took me a second to remember the day. I pinged Neil but he was busy as usual.

'I... Neil gave... He authorised my leave that day.'

'It doesn't look like it. It's down as an unauthorised absence. You could have appealed it but you... you're... past the appeal cut-off.'

'But how would I have known about it?'

'You should have heard through Neil. Look, here you can see I, well, the system, sent him a message... uh, before the end of that pay cycle. He should've brought it up with you and then you could have disputed it and if it was nothing, well, it would have been... y'know, resolved. But now... Well, uh, the system handles everything really, I wouldn't know where to look.'

Her bored tone annoyed me. This was my life!

'But he never told me!'

'Says here he did. Look. See?'

'But he didn't! He absolutely didn't!'

'Well, I could pull the footage of your meeting with him…'

It might've fobbed some people off, but not me.

'Yes, please.'

I waited as she went tech-vacant. Then her expression changed. With such dark features, it was hard to tell what she was feeling but if I wasn't mistaken, she had confused herself.

'Weird,' she said.

'What is?'

'Well, there's a message from Neil saying he spoke with you and a link to the footage but when I follow the link, the footage is, uh, missing.'

'No way!' I almost laughed.

'Well, not missing, deleted.'

'Deleted?'

'Yeah. By Anthony.'

'Who?'

'He used to do my job but he left. About, golly, eight years ago?'

Golly? Who says golly? Maybe I will too if I haven't left here in, Jesus, eight years' time!

I suddenly got the feeling she could read my thoughts and it made me start gabbling. 'Okay, uh, so how could he… Actually, do I care? If there's no footage…'

'Then it's your word against Neil's, I suppose.' She shrugged, fucking-like supremely indifferent.

'So…?'

'So…' Her face was hard to read but if I guessed I'd have said she was irritated at having to think for once in her – apparently long and uneventful – life. 'If you can get him to message me that he agrees you weren't absent then I'll, I don't know, figure out how to correct your file I suppose. The half-day, demotion, fine and leave deduction will be fixed on your next payslip, I guess and, I don't know, maybe the system has a protocol and it'll message you? Not really something I've dealt with before.'

Fine? Leave deduction?

'Fu— Demotion?' I squawked.

'It's automatic whenever there's a serious breach of conduct.' She was back on script now. I could tell from the way the bored patronizing tone slid like an oily film over her voice. 'You're allowed to keep acting in your current role but, uh, I think it's a… grey area. You're, sort of, uh, technically demoted to Senior Sergeant and your pay, uh, changes to match. Oh and you're ineligible for a promotion for, um, can't remember if it's…. two or five years; not too long anyway. Then as long as there's no further misconduct, your rank and pay get automatically reinstated once the time's up; it's a bit of a formality really for something this small.'

This small! You think this is small? A fucking demotion? Five fucking years? Two fucking years, even?

I didn't trust myself to speak in case I sounded as gormless and squawky as the thoughts looping in my brain.

'And if he doesn't agree?'

'Well, oh, golly, I don't know sorry. But I've got to flag this up anyway. Anthony's handle should've been deleted automatically when he left but sometimes—'

'Sometimes they don't?'

'Sometimes we're allowed to keep them for handover. But we're meant to ping the system when we're finished with them and I…'

'Forgot?'

'Mmm, I suppose so.' She nodded, her whole posture epitomising… what? Bored annoyance?

'Well, okay so what? You deleted the footage?'

'Oh no, no, not at all, heavens no. There's been some mischief or other. It's, well… annoying, I'll have to get to the bottom of it, or uh, flag it up at least. It's very, uh… serious, I guess.' She sighed and looked suddenly on the edge of exhaustion.

'Okay, thanks,' I said, and got up to leave then had a sudden desperate idea. 'Hey, who will you flag this up to?'

'Oh, Neil, obviously.'

'But if he's under suspicion—'

'If he's…. what?'

'Well, under suspicion, I mean, he's obviously a person of interest isn't he, given the circumstances.'

'Gosh, I don't know. I don't really understand all the police things.'

Who the fuck says gosh?

I looked at her as if for the first time. Her skin was unusually dark. There were many shades but you didn't often get that one. Now I was really looking, there were a few wrinkles around her eyes and her hands were a bit on the veinous side; too much for a thirty-something. If not for that, she could have been any age.

I wondered how long she'd been working here. Had she arrived to replace the Anthony guy eight years ago – as if that wasn't half a lifetime – or had she been stuck out the back of the station for like, fifteen years or something? I kind of felt sad for her despite myself.

'You don't understand police talk?' I asked to buy time.

'Gosh, no. I'm not an officer, only civilian staff.'

Fuck it.

'Well I am an officer and in my capacity as such, I'm going to take this from here, okay? You aren't to tell Neil – or anyone – about this on pain of being charged with, um, interfering-with-a-police-investigation and I'll need access to that handle… Anthony, please, ASAP.'

She stared at me and I couldn't read her face. The silence stretched and I was worried I'd gone too far and she was going to raise all hell. Maybe she was pinging Neil now. I jumped when she finally spoke. 'Oh, gosh, yes, all right then. Golly. A real investigation, eh?' she said with a hair less than sleepy indifference.

With a tiny hacker-thrill, I saw the Anthony guy's handle credentials augment my profile on the edge of my vision. Not many people got to legally spoof an entire identity! Well, in our systems anyway.

As this… Anthony, I could have done serious damage. I wondered if she'd have given it to anyone who barked at her and hoped she was as lethargic as she looked and wouldn't see the obvious flaw in my reasoning since it was clearly a conflict of interests for me to investigate this, too.

'Well, okay then thanks,' I huffed.

'You're welcome, let me know if there's anything else I can do,' she said mechanically.

I fled back down the hallway to the calming boredom of the main station office and left a message for Neil to ping me when he was free. I decided I might as well try it the less scary way first. Later that afternoon, I stopped him pawing at me in his office to tell him… some of what had happened.

'No way!' he said. 'I authorised your leave.'

'Well, can you talk to her?' I tried not to sound preoccupied but my mind was whirring.

If I hadn't known the truth, I would never have suspected him. Without a doubt, he'd lied to HR, probably broken the law to get the footage deleted – or someone had – and now he'd properly lied to my face as well. But even then, when I absolutely knew beyond doubt what he'd done, thinking back through the months, didn't make everything clear. If anything, less so; I couldn't think of a single instance when he hadn't done what he said or been who he was. But he had lied to me and it had messed me up in a very real way. It didn't make sense.

'Yeah, yeah. Course. I could talk to her, I guess, it's going to be something. Leave it with me, okay?' He sounded completely genuine, a bit hurt that I'd pressed him. I literally couldn't help feeling a bit guilty; he was that good.

'Okay,' I said meek as you like. But as I left his office, I felt his eyes on my back and realised with a chill I'd forgotten to kiss him goodbye.

Then I forgot everything when my mother appeared – calling me at work! – looking like I'd never seen her before in my life. I took the call midstride back to my desk and she was crying so hard I knew Nana-Joanna was gone before she stammered out the news.

It wasn't like it was unexpected given how sick she'd been for so long. But still, I struggled to hold it together and went straight to Mum's place after work. We both cried all evening, setting each other off and I was too scared to mention Elayne though if she was alive, I couldn't believe she wouldn't want to know.

Will she see it in the news spaces? Will she come to the funeral? If she's alive…

But she didn't. I checked all her old online haunts; all the spaces we used to play in as kids. But the ones that were still online were full of strangers' kids and though I looked for her the whole time, there was no sign of her at the funeral. It started to dawn on me, for the first time if I was honest with myself, that maybe she was really dead and maybe I'd never find out what had happened.

The funeral itself was beautiful. Great Aunty Anna made it beautiful. And I hated myself for looping on Elayne and what'd happened at work so much I almost missed her reading for the noise of my own pathetic thoughts.

I went back to Nana-Joanna and Grandad-Tristian's place after and I wanted to tell him what'd happened. He'd've known what to do. He always knew what to do about stuff like that.

But after everyone'd left, I couldn't bring myself to dump it on him. His tears started and stopped about ten times and that was only making small-talk. He was crying as he laughed sometimes and after a while, I decided it wouldn't've been fair to burden him with my everyday trivial shit so I went home.

Chen – Jun 2097-late Nov 2097, Cornwall Estate, Akarana Island, Aotearoa Archipelago

'Nǐ *hǎo* Chen, long time no see!'

It was Cathy from next door. We'd bumped into each other stepping out for deliveries. The temperature in my visuals was showing down near freezing by the poor-door but I recognised her voice through her overs hood. The wind was gale-force and the rain was like hail and I was bloody glad tech had been invented. And weirdly mesmerised by the idea of peeling off my overs to see what the weather felt like.

'Nǐ *hǎo* Cathy. How's Doug?'

'Same-same, chilled as ever. He's snowed with work and with, well, me until recently. I took months to get over the plague, you know how it goes.' But she brightened, then. 'But we got a new sofa. I managed to sell off all the free food and that evil Total™ slurry from our work schemes. God, people will buy anything, I tell ya. Must've been someone from 'round here too 'cause the tracking showed it was delivered in-like, a minute. But yeah, you should… I dunno, come in one time and have a try on the sofa. It's got foot-rests that mould to your legs and everything. We could have a J™ and get into a movie.'

Looked like outbreaks were good for bringing people together; the way they made us all desperate like that. Who knew how long Doug and Cathy had lived next door and now it looked like we were gonna start being friends. Still, I wasn't complaining. Since the bust-up with Teens, I was pretty sure I'd blown it with her for good.

Not that I minded that much, I'd done my best, for Nate. Well, and maybe for me a bit too, to stave off the loneliness. But it'd got too much in the end, she'd got too much.

Yeah, no excuse though.

It really wasn't. I shouldn't've lost it with her like that. I'd seen what I'd done to her; it was like kicking a newborn. I was lucky she hadn't bloody topped herself or something after that. But still, we were where we were and how long could I have really kept being friends with her anyway? She was hard work. Plus, I couldn't keep living her ridiculous lie with her and I didn't like to think about what she'd do if she found out Nate'd known and that he'd told me.

'Chen? You okay?' Cathy was looking worried, poor thing.

'Oh, yeah, sorry. A lot on my mind, work, mheah, you know, usual shit. Yeah, look, I'd love to come over. Or have you guys over, either or, or both!' I was annoyed at the giddiness in my voice. But I'd long since given up on being embarrassed about my desperation. Was that pathetic?

Yyyyyep!

We said goodbye at our doors and went inside with our deliveries and I didn't expect to hear from her again until the next chance meeting. I hadn't forgotten about Nate's theory and as much as I didn't like the idea of going out into the stormy dark, I dumped my package and forced myself for the zillionth anyway.

The hall lights were dimmed for the night. I ghosted past apartment doors and stairwell entrances, keeping quiet though I knew I could probably have run through the building shouting and all the residents would have heard would be soft footsteps and a murmur.

Not expecting to find anything, I wandered anyway and went into a kind of trance. Maybe it was tiredness or maybe the dimmed lights, I didn't know but I got into a weird state where I was kind of watching myself move like I was outside my body. I imagined myself, like a rat in a tiny maze scuttling through all the passageways on our floor, down to the dead-ends, doubling back and on to each turning, cameras both micro and visible, recording my every move like the compound eyes of roaches.

I marvelled at how I instinctively knew the way; how though the hallways all looked the same, my mind knew what was where from the tiny landmarks. It was no mystery. It was because I'd done it so often, it had become unconscious. But that didn't take away from the experience of it.

A spot on the wall here, a tiny tear in the corner of the carpet too small to register in maintenance systems there, a lighting panel not synced with the others, a bit brighter or a bit dimmer because its nanites were wearing out or whatever. I knew what I'd find around every corner, through every fire door joining each section of the building. I knew where I was without online maps! And when I was done covering the whole maze like some kind of ancient animal foraging through its territory, no matter where I was, I knew there was a stairwell nearby that'd get me down to the poor-door faster than walking all the way back to the lifts. I could do it all myself, without tech!

Concentrating on the stairs to avoid breaking my neck woke me up from the trance. Out in the rain, I took my usual route around the building and watched the car lights glare through the rain and flicker on the wall above the fence. I stood at the end of Nate's alleyway and stared up and decided for the first time I'd try it out.

The old AC's roar grew as I got closer but sure enough the cop tech grabbed me before I got level with Nate's window.

'Gah! Okay, okay! I'm going!' I half-squawked-half-puked.

I backed away and waited for my stomach to unclench. Weirdly, my calm wasn't shattered. I continued on back down the alleyway and around to the road end of Nate's building with red drone lights painting target-dots on the concrete and my overs.

Standing looking through to the front, it occurred to me that if I did run into Tina, firstly – I realised in that instant – I didn't give a shit and secondly, she wouldn't recognise me in the dark with my hood fully over anyway and if she did…

Fuck it, see firstly.

I could've turned on night colours but I was liking the dark for some reason. I looked towards the top of the fence and followed the street-lit wall and flitting car lights towards the AC near the other end.

Not that I wouldn't've believed it anyway but after that night, I'd understand it from my thoughts to my bones, the thrill of discovery. It would change my whole outlook on life, on the way we used tech for everything, hardly touching any-thing with our hands any more, looking at everything, tasting and smelling the ghostly traces of it our tech could simulate when we got into ads, movies and calls with our friends and families. How we never fully experienced a tactile rough, smooth, sharp, cold, hot or dangerous world any more. Except when we had sex and that was so safe it risked getting tiring.

I understood what Nate had been trying to tell me after that night. The poor guy had known in his bones but lacked the words; it wasn't his fault; he was born in the wrong place at the wrong time.

What he'd been trying to tell me was that it was one thing to know the history which after my scholarship studies, was burned into my *nǎozǐ*. But to understand how Fleming would have felt getting back from his holiday away from his home and work, arriving chilled with an empty and open mind then suddenly seeing the mould in his petri dish and the rest dawn-ing on him. Or how the – typically bloody – nameless nurse who noticed all the guys lying on their stomachs after the Sildenafil trials late last century. Or the buzz Roentgen must've got when he noticed his screen light up for the first time. That was a whole other thing.

My discovery was nothing like any of those. I didn't find anything new that night. It felt like what I found wasn't hidden that well but the accident of it, the coincidence of it. It would leave me wondering how we could ever learn anything new, experience anything new or move the fuck forward as a race, shut away in our apartments in virtual spaces all our lives.

Nate knew all this. He was leaps and bounds ahead of me with my uni education, my basic PhD and my one lonesome specialist one. I might've been clever or more likely only educated but Nate was intelligent. If only he could've seen it in himself!

Course, that wasn't what was on my mind as I came up to the old AC a few metres from the alleyway's end. Though I knew it was cold, my overs made it into more of a concept than a reality. There were patches of ice on the concrete where the daylight hardly touched but my soles compensated for it so I'd have to practically be a walking corpse to trip over.

The wind sounded like living anger but I could feel nothing but the carefully curated gusts and the impacts of water droplets against my overs. Little reminders that there was weather outside my shell but without the inconvenience of the actual cold or wet. Though I'd remember it vividly afterwards, I wasn't paying it much attention at the time. Instead, I was idly looking up and ahead as I ducked to walk under the front of the AC.

Its roaring rose and fell as the wind took its breath way which was weird because... because... because... its breath didn't change and it was way too strong. Then as I looked up at it, a car went past, its lights flickering along the wall up to the AC, along the wall on the other side of it. And then...

What?

As if the light had remembered it was there, it flickered along the front of the AC as it should have, only the car was long gone and the flicker was too late.

What I'd seen was no mystery. It was a run-of-the-mill virtual projected into my tech. The image of the old AC was a holo. Granted, a pretty flash one given the way its strings of dust and grime blew in the wind and it reflected back the light and did the sound in time and everything. There'd be a whole array of cameras and nanites working on those calculations. It must've randomly glitched as I'd copped on to its too-strong airflow, and I'd looked up right when a car went past.

The question wasn't what it was though. The question in my mind as my heart picked up and I started shaking in my overs was what the hell it was meant to be hiding.

I shut off my visual tech and thanked my lucky stars I'd had Nate in my life at all so I knew what I was looking at the moment I saw it. The huge and fancy flat plates of an active-alloy climate controller spread across the wall covering about four times as much area as the AC holo had.

It was a stupid ploy. Anyone who'd done the same as me and turned off their visuals could've seen it. But, I guessed, so few people ever did that whoever it was – and I was pretty sure I knew – was banking on it never happening. Plus stupid as it was, how many months had it taken my dopey *nǎozǐ* to work it out? And I'd been looking!

Plus, at the end of the day it didn't really give away anything. It was only a climate controller. Okay, a fuckin' fancy one. But no more than that. I thought through my mental map of the building and wondered what was on the other side of it, trying not to jump to conclusions. My heart beat faster anyway. I couldn't help it.

A dry-foot might waste this kind of coin on their home. Or maybe a few of them – dry-feet? Dry-foot-i? – might club together for it. But this thing was way too low down the building for that and I was pretty sure there were no apartments behind this wall anyway. And then I realised something else.

There were no windows on this wall! Were there any on the wall opposite Nate's? I'd check but I didn't think so.

Yes, this was it! Nate was right.

I flattened myself against the fence and reached out so my fingers hovered above the surface of the wide shiny plate. The air blowing out of it pushed me away, like two magnets repelling each other. I turned my visuals back on and sure enough the holo of the old AC was there again, my hand stuck into it up to the wrist.

Just then a car went past and this time the light was perfectly timed and anyone looking wouldn't've known the difference. It was as if it had glitched in time, only for me.

Coincidences were the theme of the year for me that year. Synchronicities, Nate would've said.

Or meant anyway.

I smiled at his funny little verbal stumbles then felt mean. Still, dots our minds joined to make us feel safe in the world.

Coincidences, I reckoned.

This one was me going off shift for three whole days because of two in lieu I had saved up and Cathy making good on her offer that exact night. It'd taken her months but I wasn't complaining. If she'd left it to me, I probably would've been too shy to ever've got back in touch.

Min had showed me how bad their seawall was getting and the creepy way the new weird quakes were stirring up the water like a massive cup of Instant™ on a wobbly home-office desk. She never said anything about Phil, not in words anyway. She sometimes casually shared footage of him vaping and sleeping away his days when he wasn't virtualled into his work, practically doing it in his sleep after so many years in the same job.

At least he's bringing in some ding for them.

She seemed okay though I knew she never would be. The meds were only keeping the crazy out of her eyes most of the time.

And when she comes off them and Nate's not there to sort her out?

And also, now Nate wasn't around to work his ring off and lend them a bit of support, they'd be stuffed if Phil ever lost his job; let's face it, if Nate was around, they'd've been stuffed if Phil had lost his job anyway. Nate could only give them so much without putting himself in a wet basement too. Yeah, he'd had his grey-hat ding but he could never move too many of those satoshis into real life without the wrong people noticing.

How long can his addresses stay inactive before the blockchain dumps them and his stash gets burned?

I only thought it because one day Phil would lose his job, if only because Min outlived him. Then what? Thinking about it made me shiver. It was like I was taking on all the worry for Min, since every time I saw her, she was nothing but chirpy.

For all my calls with her and the friends I'd made through Nate, I was lonely and kind of freaked out about Shane. It wasn't as if I didn't get into movies with people and stuff but nobody including me could afford to visit and we all lived too far away from each other. So, when Cathy's message pinged in the dead of night around mid-shitty-June, I bit her arm off.

Their place was like mine, maybe a bit bigger but same setup. I wondered if they had a second one and spent nights apart like Nate and Tina had. Doug was logging off his work and I met Cathy at the door with a stack of the priciest pizzas I could afford and half a bag of weed which I wasn't looking forward to vaping with them. I'd been stoned all of once since I'd told Nate's folks about his arrest and I couldn't get Phil's dying eyes out of my head.

I was thinking of giving them the bag and my J™ along with it and never vaping a single puff again for the rest of my life. I was sure I felt better for the sobriety and I reckoned I wouldn't miss it. But then one day if I ever got regular friends again, I'd be that weird teetotaller; whatever that weird word had to do with weed.

And what kind of world would it have to turn into that I could ever have friends I actually see again anyway?

No. Dinner parties were for rich-fucks only. Well, or neighbours, apparently.

The smell of stale weed-vape hit me as I walked in but it wasn't that which gave me the surprise sinking feeling so much as the realisation that I'd probably end up caving and getting stoned tonight anyway. Because I was desperate to fit in.

'*Nǐ hǎo* Chen. Good to see you!' I could see Doug force himself to smile and come alive as he heaved his big frame up, a pasty hand coming up to brush the black strands escaped from his bun, off of his face. I tried not to stare at the dark circles under his eyes. Not that I judged him, everyone was always tired. It was known.

'*Kia ora* Doug. Chill. Don't get up for me. I've got off a mega bloody twenny-one dayer too, don't worry, I know how you feel,' I said as he shook my hand and my bag of weed fell to the floor because I'd been so desperate to touch another person, I'd let it go when he'd held out his hand.

The pizzas were another matter though. They were balanced on my other forearm and starting to wobble and there was no bloody way I would've let that much ding go south, desperate or not.

'Where shall I put these?' I regretted wresting my hand from his warm grip.

'Chuck 'em on the bench,' Cathy said, pointing at where she'd put her own delivery, Premo-Ice-Cream-Like™ {Reminiscent-of-Cacao edition}, it turned out. They had good taste, at least; I guessed they could afford stuff like that because of two incomes or whatever. It was too squirmy for me to believe what was probably the real reason, they'd splashed out 'cause I was coming over.

'Are you into vintage?' Doug asked.

'As it happens, yeah. My ex— Yeah. I really am.' And shit, I meant it! My cheeks reddened at the gasping enthusiasm in my voice.

'Choice!' Cathy said. 'We're massive vintage people, well, I mean, you know what I mean, not actual vintage people but...

'I think she gets it.' Doug was laughing and pouring Instant™s at the bench. 'There's a new 4S remaster of Three-Billboards, would you be keen?'

I was surprised to hear him say it was new but the remasters took a long time. Nate's company had started work on that one when we were together.

'Definitely keen,' I said, trying to hold back tears.

'Hey, you okay, Chen?' Bloody Cathy had clocked it. But I couldn't break down in front of these two, I hardly knew them. She came close to me and her sweet tangy perfume surprised me enough to distract my tears away.

She'd taken her overs off and her hemps were tight over big soft curves. Maybe they usually bought a lot of ice-cream after all, not that it didn't suit her. She'd let her bun loose for the night, apparently and I felt a soft tickle as her hair mingled with mine.

'Yeah, fine. Only, you know, big shift,' I said. I wanted to ask her about the perfume but worried she'd think I didn't like it. I wanted to play with her hair. And I wanted to cower in the corner of their sofa with my knees against my chest and my arms keeping them tight.

'Are you sure?' she pressed.

'Yeah, I'm okay. Bit tired's all.'

Drop it! Please drop it!

She heard my thoughts, thank fuck and I gulped at the mug Doug handed me and scalded the inside of my mouth. 'Watch it!' he said too late.

Fuck. This is going well…

But the pain searing my tongue took my mind off everything else. It was the basic principle of self-harm and right then I was wondering whether maybe all those Tina types were on to something. I blew out a vain breath to try and cool my mouth.

'So, uh, Chen,' Cathy said, studiously ignoring my sweaty agony, 'What is it you do that keeps you grinding – and not in the good way – for twenny-one whole days in a row? Jeez, Doug's company are big enough wankers but the longest shift he's ever had is like…?'

'Fourteen,' Doug supplied.

'Yeah, fourteen days, an old-school fortnight.'

These two must have scored decent educations to know something poncy like that. Maybe PhDs on scholarship like me.

'My, uh, job's dumb. I work in audit for construction. If anything weird happens with materials in new builds or maintenance, it can mean something's gone wrong with construction tech or nanites've gone faulty. It happens fu—, uh, not that much. And there's only a tiny percentage the systems can't handle it automatically, but a tiny percentage is a big number anyway 'round the world, ends up being about… Anyway, like I said, it's lame. But it pays the bills. I have to keep up to date with all my tech training and then it's a lot of stupid meetings to make management feel like they're important. Anyway, it's boring, I know… Well, except I've virtualled into sites in closed regimes like *Měiguó* and DR Aus. That's kind of cool, I guess.'

'That really is cool. But hey, Chen, come on, of course it's boring! It's work, right? Don't worry, our jobs are boring too but we're gonna tell you about them anyway. Before we do, though, seeing as you're in construction, check this out, got it a few months back.'

Cathy pulled me into a personal virtual, a recording by the looks. There was a figure running along a hallway.

'What is it?'

'Just wait.'

I watched the figure running, a woman by the looks of it. Suddenly as she ran under a flickering lighting panel, memory lit up inside me. 'That's in our building!'

'Jeez! How did you know that?'

'Oh, I, I dunno, the… uh, carpet or something?'

'Freaky but yeah, keep watching aaaaannnnd… there we go!'

The figure was running towards the dead-end of a hallway and not slowing down. Her arms were pumping and I could hear her breath coming in gasps so they can't've been standing far away from her.

As if reading my mind, Doug said, 'We had a J™ outside and got lost on our way from the lift, stoners that we are.' He giggled and I didn't bat an eyelid because it'd happened to me a million times when I'd first moved in.

Then I jumped because instead of slamming into the wall, the woman in the footage disappeared through it and there was a muffled thump a few seconds later.

'Eh?' I said.

'The dead-end is a holo,' Doug said superfluously.

'Yeah. But, uh, why?'

I knew why.

My heart was racing. I couldn't believe I'd been so stupid after finding the AC the way I had. I could see it led through to another dead-end but it must've been there for a reason.

'You're the construction expert. Maybe it's some kind of fire regulation or something?' Cathy was saying but I hardly heard her because as the video continued. Cathy and Doug had followed the woman through the fake wall and the next thing…

'Holy fuck! Tina!'

She was lying flat on her back with blood running from her forehead.

'Oh, you know her?' Cathy asked.

'Yeah. Yes, I mean, she's my… friend. She was visiting me that day. But, what the fuck? What was she running away from?'

They both shrugged.

'Just picked herself up and got us to show her to the lifts. Wouldn't let us look at the cut in her head or anything. Weird woman. But then she had run into a wall, I s'pose',' Doug said.

She really is a psycho.

'I've got no idea why that would be there. I work in commercial anyway, not residential. And I've never seen anything like that before.' Only the first part was a lie.

'Here,' said Cathy. 'Get a lungful of this down ya, it'll help pass the time while I tell you about my incredible job checking system analysis results for anti-roach nanites sales data. It makes me fuckin' cream myself every day.' Cathy had filled their J™ and taken a polite tube-cleaning puff before handing it to me.

And then everything was all right. It wasn't only the weed. They were so chilled, so friendly. We passed around the J™ and afterwards instead of refilling it for a massive session like Tina would've wanted to do, they cracked open the food and we got into the movie and pissed ourselves laughing at all the one-liners and casual fossil-fuel usage and massive stand-alone houses poor people lived in. And their funny accents and the remasterers' weird attempts at what the places would've smelled like. And plastic – plastic! – light switches on the walls!'

I should've been exhausted after the film and junk-food but I was fizzing and I think Cathy knew it. She slid close to me on the sofa where all our feet were up with the fancy foot-rests massaging our calves. One of the ankles of her grey hemps had ridden up to her knee and the skin on her calf was creamy and covered in soft fair hair.

'We're poly.' she said. 'So…?'

And something that had slept inside me for so long I'd forgotten it was there awoke and uncurled and took control of me. Cathy had brought her face conveniently close so I stroked her thin ginger hair and pressed my lips to hers in answer. I hoped in vain that she couldn't feel the wet on my cheeks. If she noticed she said nothing and soon Doug joined in and the evening melted into golden light and warm flesh. I didn't mind that they used me and used me and used me. I drank in their using and moaned out my thanks.

It was dark when I woke in a warm tangle of naked bodies on their fancy sex-smelling couch. Drained, stoned and full of carbohydrates, they didn't wake up as I got dressed to leave and I couldn't help wondering if despite our every sense being gorged, we were all as empty as before I'd come over.

As I went to sleep, I found myself holding on to the moments before the sex, the laughs during the movie, the commiserations about work, the simple boring bullshit I'd not had since leaving home. The home I could never go back to because my family had decided I was too stuck-up for them. And the home I'd never been happy in now seemed better than this place anyway. I cried myself to sleep wishing Nate's arms were around me and the next morning I vowed never to open up to anyone again because it was too fuckin' hard.

Then I discovered I was bullshitting myself because I pinged Cathy and Doug a thank you for having me. Which we all knew really meant, are we okay after the sex? Can we be friends? Was it a good night for everyone? When can we meet again? Fucking please say something! Or that's what I meant anyway.

Cathy and Doug's video had nearly dropped outta my *nǎozǐ* after the whole emotional debacle of what'd happened later. But it came back to me a couple of days before I clocked off my next shift, thankfully only a fourteen-dayer in the end. Thinking of Nate and his exercise fetish, I went to the place they'd shown me the video of Tina running into the wall like the psycho she was.

But is she okay? Stop!

Even through my tiredness, I liked how I could go-straight-there without having to figure the way. When I arrived at the false dead-end, I turned off my visuals and sure enough the hallway got longer and my heart sped up.

This was the way in. It had to be! Why else would they hide it? Not that they'd tried that hard. I searched the walls, thinking it would be obvious but there was nothing but... well, wall. The false dead-end only worked one way and looking back down the hall, I recognised the stairwell I knew came out near 'my' poor-door.

But the entrance had to be here. I tried pinging the wall but it played dead. That was something at least, it showed it was either dead or it was active alloy and not much infrastructure was dead nowadays so this was the right wall. But no matter how much I pinged it, tried different frequencies, different packet-types, my actual fists, I couldn't find anything. Jeez! Nate would've had this figured out in two seconds.

Stop being pathetic!

The thought was the kick up the bum I needed. I knew about this shit. I worked with this shit! I thought back to my study and my training and the memory my scholarship'd paid to build responded.

True active alloy like these walls probably were, was all nanotech with a lot of fancy shit for texturing and cybersecurity. Down at the south end of the island and in wet-foot poor-fuck communities throughout the world — not exactly the words in my study-virtuals..., where Zhang's construction companies didn't wanna blow profit margin on poor people – again, not exactly but…, it was a different story. The seawalls in those districts changed from dense jelly to a type of cheap nanite-concrete mixture as they curved in from the deeper sea and hit the coast.

The more nanites the pricier the kit and the more robust the neural links between them; more pathways, more redundancy. And the fewer there were, the less redundancy and the faster auto-repair of whatever structure would break down as nanites died off and lost neural links to each other through whatever substrate. Then there'd start being leaky cracks that didn't reseal, sometimes piles of rubble, flooded basements and drowned or poisoned mums and babies where there should've been seawalls.

The dead nanites went silvery-blue and sometimes there were so many you could see them in the mess like some kind of demonic rot spreading through the concrete. I hadn't seen it in real life but the onsite virtual spaces I'd been in a million emergency callouts were nearly as good. None of this encyclopaedia-brain-ness helped me; not where they'd put the false dead-end anyway. But as I went down the stairs to the first floor, thinking to find out whether there was a way in from there, well that was where it came in handy.

I wondered why I hadn't seen it before now. Probably hadn't been looking. But now I was looking, I couldn't believe what a state the place was in. The wall was shot through with silver-blue like poisoned veins. It was so bad in some places that I hoped it wasn't bloody load-bearing. But still, chaos is a ladder…

Nate would totally have got behind what I decided to do. He wasn't that big on weed himself anyway. We'd hardly ever got stoned when we were together. So though it was a bit on the edgy side of legal since reformatted nanites were notoriously unreliable, hacking the fancy J™ he'd given me for my birthday so I could wipe it and repurpose the nanites would definitely not have offended him.

It was the biggest bit of pricey tech I could afford to lose. My crappy desk and chair were work's and clothes and my shitty sofa had about a nanite every millimetre except for my overs. But I wasn't ready to feel the lash of the wind-blown rain and the bite of the frost on my bottom yet. Nature could wait. Well, except it couldn't, but anyway.

So, I reformatted the J™ with a dodgy routine from one of Nate's shifty encrypted repositories disguised as an eBook in the Akarana Island's public library. As I watched it break down into sliver-grey powder and aggregate into the hexagonal ingot shape most people never got to see, I felt a weight lift off my mind.

Sure, I could've done something stupid with hacked wiring to make heat so I could spot weed on an Instant™ spoon like the poorest of the poor were rumoured to do by some and known to do by me since I used to be one of them. But I had a feeling I wasn't gonna miss it enough to bother.

On shifty virtual spaces, the ingot was, weirdly, worth more than the J™ would've been brand new but I didn't care. I shoved it under my overs and took it into the stairwell. I leaned on the wall halfway down, breathing hard for the benefit of any cameras although I was pretty sure that unless they were super well hidden – which was possible – or super small, there weren't any. And if there were, I'd say I was doing my bit for the community.

I'd flashed cut-down versions of some maintenance routines I'd, uh, 'borrowed from work to study' on to the ingot nanites. And some stuff Nate'd shown me how to do as well. None of what I was doing was illegal, I was sure. Not too illegal anyway.

Who am I kidding?

If they found me, they'd bust my bum wide open no matter what I tried to say. It's what they'd done to Nate wasn't it? That was why my heart was racing as I sent my nanites crawling through my overs out on to the stairwell wall and into one of the silver-blue veins.

I felt my ingot shrinking as they swarmed away and a moment later, the wall started looking newer. I was sure Nate would've done something way cleverer but I had to hand it to myself it wasn't a bad idea.

My tech found enough live building nanites, isolated in clumps of dead ones and decaying wall to hack into, crucially, unmolested by their cloud-mates because the encryption took a few goes to crack. And then my tech virused into them and made them into clumsy hybrids of the building tech and me so I could use their credentials to trojan into the building's systems and replicate all the way through it.

I gathered up all the dead tech and recycled it to fix up the wall anyway though there was no way anyone who caught me would believe I was doing this out of the goodness of my heart. And of course, they'd've been right not to because now I could use the entire building's maintenance kit to take me to places my body wasn't allowed to go. So about three minutes later, I was virtually standing in a vault full of silvery nanite ingots worth trillions; fucking trillions! And not of satoshis, either. Actual whole bitcoins!

The map of the building in my mind all fell into place though, ironically, now I'd become a system infestation, I could get at the blueprints anyway. The storage space was three storeys high and as wide as the building and the rest I already knew.

It wasn't perfectly symmetrical, as if an apartment here or a stairwell there on the other side of whatever wall was allowed to fuck up its *feng shui*, only for obfuscation purposes, probably. As far as I could tell, that was all the stupid holo stuff was about. It didn't make any sense. If they hadn't bothered disguising the AC's, people would only think they were some dry-foot's indulgence anyway. Or was it just paranoia? Fair enough, I'd be paranoid with this much ding sitting around only a wall away from revolution!

In the vault, the nanite ingots had stacked themselves neatly into aisles and if the unit I'd seen on the end of Nate's building was impressive on the outside, the climate control kit backing it on the inside was behemoth; fair play, I'd wanna protect this much ding too; not that it wasn't super-durable without any help anyway. The walls were lined with sensors for perfect humidity, temperature and airflow consistency with zero human intervention. Whoever owned it wasn't taking any chances.

There was no way into this space except through virtual or repurposing a section of the wall into a door; and that would sure as shit get recorded by the cameras clinging everywhere like amputated roach-eyes. As I watched, a tiny cluster flowed off one of the ingots and swirled into the floor like a silver-grey ghost going back to its old-school grave; medical emergency probably. Or some rich arse made a furniture purchase.

So basically, every block full of wet-foots like me had a big dirty secret like this. Megabucks – fucking terabucks – worth of tech that okay, sent fast medical care to the ones who could afford it but generally, sat waiting on the beck and call of the rich-fuck-sponsored government to issue forth and fuck us up like it'd fucked Nate up. A fraction of this shit could've fixed every seawall on every island in the archipelago. There would probably still've been change if they used it on every seawall in the world. Well okay, maybe not but anyway… And this was only one warehouse.

I already knew there was another one in Nate's building. And how many other blocks around here had those crappy fake AC holos on their walls?

Jesus Nate. You were so right honey, soooo right! And so smart. And so amazing… Stop!

How had he figured it out though? How? Had he clocked the ACs like I had? But he would've told me… Well, I'd definitely tell him, anyway. He'd been inside for so long now I knew he was gone but I guess knowing's not the same as believing. I cyphered up everything I'd found and put it somewhere only he and I could find it again.

In my mind, I could hear the bullshit arguments that would chatter in the news-spaces already. If it ever got out, which it never would, they – if they let any of the curators interview them without approving the script first – would say it was there for the people. There in case of emergencies, to get to us fast if we were sick or injured or our apartments needed maintenance. Or whatever plausibly deniable lies.

Not their fault a maintenance request from a resident took months to process or if it got lost a thousand times first. Oh no, that would be some poor system setup and they'd be dreadfully sorry to hear that and oh yes they'd be investigating that all right and get it fixed immediately and of course, yes, compensate that poor person.

Except it would be, only, that person. That hapless wet-foot'd be laughing all the way to the blockchain with a pay-out worth a year's wages or something, more money than they'd seen in one place in their whole tiny existence. And then there'd be some arsehole news curator who'd track them down to do a follow-up story on how they blew it all on flash nosh and expensive weed and were back on twenny-one-day shifts a few months later. And meantime, the system wouldn't change and everyone else would keep being treated like shit and the whole thing would blow over without a trace.

The virtual flickered as my vitals peaked from shaking my fists and roaring like a predator might've done at its oncoming extinction in the olden days. This shit wasn't here for anyone but the rich-fucks who owned it. That's why I was gonna steal some of it. What the fuck else could I do?

It was a good theory anyway. And I was proud of myself in some ways. And a bit scared of how much access I'd given myself to the building. I could aggregate sensors inside people's flats, rich and poor alike. I could control the building's systems.

Everything except prisoners, of which there were alarmingly many. They were firewalled with cop tech and I wasn't gonna try in case I tripped some firewall alarm and got busted. Other than to make myself cry when I reached out across buildings and saw that, yep, Nate was where Tina said he was. Or someone was anyway so who else was it gonna be.

My pride came from the fact that though it was tempting, I didn't abuse my access once; not to see if Cathy and Doug were talking about me, nothing. I didn't want to spy on people like the rich-fucks probably already did. Not that there were any actual people on the system apart from me. They were system monitoring users, none were alive.

But the one thing I wanted to do was the one thing I couldn't. The warehouse had no transport facility. There was no way of getting the bloody things in and out. Which made sense, of course. They weren't put in there en masse, they were told to go there.

They would've gone in through the floor under instruction, travelling the same way public nanites travelled, crawling over and through stuff and leaving it as it'd found it once it'd passed. Then once in the room, they would have risen up like grey mist in the night and formed stacks. And whenever someone made an order, it got to them somehow, it didn't matter how and out they went the same way.

Which was all very well but completely bloody useless to me when it came to nicking them. I'd wracked my *năozǐ* for days and short of completely giving the game away and telling the building to make me a hole to crawl through or a door to walk through, I was stumped.

My sofa smelled like sweat and there was so much dandruff on it I'd given up brushing it off. In the evenings after work, I sat counting the days till my next work-funded clean and sealing and unsealing the zip-lock on my bio-bag of weed, trying to decide whether to knock on Cathy and Doug's door and offer it to them. Which was code for seeing their faces and pleading with my eyes for another invite or… fuckin' something.

You could invite them over here, moron.

I knew it and I knew it and I knew it but a million things went through my mind every time I was about to send the message. The smell of my flat, the size of my flat, the small size of my crappy fake window; smaller than theirs, I thought but I wasn't sure. I couldn't and I hated myself for being such a coward. But the self-hatred wasn't enough fuel to get me over the hump; which the other hump had created in the bloody first place.

Looking at my stupid window now I saw there was a storm outside, a *stonker* as Nate would've called it. The rain was so heavy it was raising spray on the concrete and the wind blew it sideways in sheets like blue-white mist in the street-lights. Undeterred, drones like demonic red fireflies were zipping through the weather about their usual business of delivering the food and crappy products that kept us all docile as we died of malnutrition, boredom and retail addiction.

Jesus, Nate. You really got into my head!

And I couldn't get him out of my pathetic heart either. He was like an infection! Speaking of which, the corner of my 'window' was dark like it had some kind of blight. My vague indifference to the tiny blot turned out to be denial-coated annoyance.

Even though I knew something was wrong with it since it should have cleaned itself, I became aware too late to stop the pissed-off getting up to dust it off reflex, programmed into my genes over hundreds of bygone tech-less millennia of human evolution. And of course, it didn't brush off because it wasn't dust of fluff and something was properly fuckin' wrong with the screen which had a lifetime shitting guarantee.

Arseholes!

I called up the warranty and invoked the maintenance clause – another thing it should've done its bloody self but which stuff never did; goodness me, where would be the fun in that for all the corporate fucks? I totally expected the handle I messaged to have gone dead or not to get a reply which was those arseholes' usual MO.

Instead, a silver stream of nanites flowed up from under my carpet a couple of minutes later. The black in the corner of the screen was gone in seconds and my view of the shit-awful weather outside was unobstructed once again.

Wah-fuckin'-hoo. Oh my god! I'm such an idiot!

I'd been hacked-in and jacked-in to the answer all along. But right then the cramps hit. Or got sore enough for me to notice anyway. I should've seen them coming because though it was all right to hate rich-fucks I didn't normally get such angry stream-of-consciousness stuff going on for so long. Too late as usual, I had the debate about whether it would really not do any harm to switch off my periods though the research said it wouldn't. It seemed wrong to me anyway.

Might research it again later…

Nate had got Tina to join him in his campaign against the AC on the wall opposite their flats. If I was some oogabooga cave-person from thousands of years ago, I'd probably've reckoned the swarm of requests lying in suspicious fob-off active-but-somehow-stalled state in the block maintenance system were cosmically meant to be.

I wonder if she knows how many complaints she— uh, her handle made in the end.

I chuckled to myself when I saw them all. And now of course, I knew why they'd never got anywhere.

Resurrecting Tina's latest one, I kludged it into something that meant an entire ingot of nanites – in for a satoshi, in for a shitload! – was urgently required in her flat to… fuck it, I dunno, await instructions from onsite systems, why not? Her apartment systems wouldn't have a clue what to do with it.

I'd leave it a while to see if anything got flagged up in the system or someone noticed it gone or… anything. Looking at the system, I didn't see how it would ever get a real person's attention. If anyone did look, they'd know it was shifty straight away. But nothing I'd done was outside system parameters. I wasn't Nate though; I might've missed something.

But if I hadn't, after… what? A couple of months? Then I'd figure out how to get some of the loot off the crazy woman; threaten to dob her in, she wouldn't know where it'd come from. Or I could beg on my knees. I wasn't proud. Not when it came to that much ding.

It was definitely a good idea. The combination of festering jealousy, periodic uterine pain and angry thoughts made it

seem that way at the time, anyway. That and it was what I kept
telling myself as I lay in a state of near-panic hour after gut-
clenching hour until my alarm went for work.

Sarah – Jul 2097, Cornwall Hill, Akarana Island, Aotearoa Archipelago

The Anthony profile wasn't any different to what I'd expected. I felt stupid for having taken months working myself up to using it. It had all the kinds of access I would've thought some HR grunt would have. It was a bit of an anti-climax, really. Using it, I could be Anthony, in our systems anyway. Should've been a thrill but in the end, how interesting were other staffs' names, addresses and medical histories?

Still the perfectionist in me couldn't stand a job unfinished. I checked the hierarchy of profile permissions on the system. Jimmie was linked to Anthony which I already knew. And it was no surprise to discover Neil had his profile augmented with Anthony, too. The trouble was, he might've had a legitimate reason or been able to bullshit one up, if pressed. By itself it wasn't enough.

There was the fact that he'd tried covering up how he'd gotten the augmentation. And well enough that it took a tedious hour of my evening to piece it together, too. But it had been years ago. I could almost hear his voice arguing that the audit had fallen apart over time, that he didn't know how it'd happened, that it'd be… y-know, something…

Like Jimmie'd said, it was Anthony who'd deleted the footage – except we knew it wasn't – and that's where the audit would usually have ended. A plodder like her wouldn't've been able to get beyond the Anthony profile.

But her entire career wasn't on the bloody line. And, if she'd gotten her second PhD; if they had the same PhDs back in whatever dark age she'd graduated, I doubted she'd written a thesis on security like I had. And she wasn't a Laufala! Or a Rahui for that matter.

I had to hand it to Neil, he was no slouch – I wasn't sure why I'd thought he would've been, come to think of it. He had all but covered his tracks. If he'd been a bit more thorough, deleted a few more timestamps and geotags and watched who he messed with, I might not have been able to breadcrumb together his crime like I did though it took me another three hours. Deleting the footage was definitely suspect and it had definitely been him in a definitely admissible way.

If I could only have shut off my Laufala-esque memory and seen what I wanted to see, I might've gone to sleep and taken my chances with the evidence I had the next day. But an annoyingly bookish voice inside me said there might have been some above-my-paygrade reason the footage had to go or that there wasn't enough to stop him watering down the charges.

He had logged his conversation with me on the system and his interfering with the records didn't mean he was also guilty of lying about my AWOL. All it really meant was that we might be in the poo together.

Great.

I dimmed the virtual and rubbed my eyes. It'd been light, calm and grey when I'd got home. Now the wind shook the building and the sky was blue-black and weirdly clear. I could see a crescent moon and a few stars through the swirling clouds of drones like cooling embers drifting on the turbulence.

It seemed only right and proper that they swarmed in front of my balcony like that, obscuring the view of the ocean someone in my position ought really not to own a flat with. It was partly why I'd been too embarrassed to ever bring Neil here.

Sleep dragged at my eyelids and the sting of disappointment was barely enough to keep me awake. There was nothing for it but to log off and think of something else. There was nothing more I could do with Anthony. I should've passed the handle back to Jimmie for due deletion. It would sever the link between Neil and the footage in the system but that was no issue. I had all the evidence, such as it was, on my work storage.

But I didn't like the idea of Neil loose on the system given for whatever messed-up reason, he'd had no qualms about abusing his access to mess up my life. And that didn't make sense yet, either. Why that and nothing else? What had I done to him that had made him want to hurt me like that? Of all the worse stuff he could've done to me given we'd exchanged bodily fluids! He could've bloody well, I don't know…

Oh fuck!

I flashed back on looks on faces, the smart remarks that weren't out of my earshot and a nasty hunch bunched up in my stomach.

I'd been about to seal the deal, trashing my own free reign in HR's systems in the process. Jimmie would've got the message the next morning and Anthony would be no more; well in the station HR system anyway. But then I paused. I'd never have done anything but could there really be any harm in looking? I was officially investigating, after all.

The night dragged on and my hunch loosened as I kept finding nothing and more nothing to back it up. The sky clouded over and it got so late the drones thinned out. I felt guilty for looking but gratified to see the few other Inspectors' salaries were exactly the same as mine, before I got fucking demoted anyway.

But that had nothing to do with anything and got me nowhere. Anthony ghosted all over the system with my electronic hand up his virtual bum, checking footage, personal files, pay records, everything. But aside from how much of the system HR could see sending a slight chill down my spine, after resorting to yet more coffee and finding yet more nothing, I started thinking I must have been wrong after all.

Everything and everyone was squeaky clean except, it turned out, me. And apparently, I was dirtier than the lone AWOL. There were no other big breaches like that but the crap in my file beggared belief. There were screeds of entries!

20961017145403 Extended coffee break, attitude flagged…

20961102111700 Excessive toilet breaks, attitude flagged, possible substance use on station, [various…] flagged…

20970309150002 break time discrepancy, officer falsely accused senior of lying, laughed, possible mental health flagged…

Crap, crap and more crap! We'd fucking sneaked next door to his apartment to have sex, that time!

He hadn't used Anthony to log them all in. They weren't big enough to have been raised with me. And I couldn't remember what I was doing on most of those days let alone argue with any of the entries. There was nothing I could do.

Why? Why has he done this?

By then I was almost-like, sweating with exhaustion and shaking with tearful anger. I needed to sleep so I could get up for work in the morning, well, later in the bloody morning anyway. But I couldn't bring myself to leave the virtual.

The idea of Anthony wiping the slate clean for me flitted through my head but what kind of audit records would that have generated and how long would it take me to disappear them? And how much poo would I have been in if I got caught out hacking my own file? And if I did pull it off, how shit would my life be knowing there would forever be the chance that one day I might get found out? No, I wasn't ready to cross that line. I hoped I'd never be.

I couldn't let go of the niggling suspicion that had dawned on me earlier. But the one place I had left to look was the same place Anthony couldn't go. It would've been a cinch in a, I don't know, proper criminal investigation. I could've gotten access to any personal handle I wanted, checked their logs, their public space access, the lot.

But for that I'd need Neil's authorisation and knowing what I knew now, I was scared of what he might do if he found out I was on to him. If I managed to go around him and find some senior officer in some underworked backwater station on any of the islands to authorise my paperwork, there was no telling what kind of a smoke-screen he might've thrown up. And then I'd be fair game.

Barely realising it through my tiredness, I'd started idly going through my own personal logs, matching the dates and times of the little footage I ever bothered to record to Neil's bullshit entries in my HR file. Now I knew what he'd done, I would've expected replaying anything I'd randomly kept to be illuminating but that was the thing. Hearing his voice and seeing his face, he seemed exactly as earnest and innocent as he had back then. It gave me an unpleasant shiver.

To make matters worse, through all my exhaustion, hurt and betrayal, I couldn't help but grudgingly admire the way he'd made the entries look plausible, some of them anyway.

Even as I did it, I knew it made no difference. These entries could hardly be used to prove anything one way or another; they only smeared my file. I dumped my noddy index in my work storage diligently, anyway, as if I was genuinely on a case. And pausing to notice how lonely it looked in my storage area given how few cases there really were nowadays, I suddenly remembered the only place – or places – I hadn't thought to look.

Don't be sick, don't be sick, don't be sick!

But I was.

Tina – late Oct 2097-late Nov 2097, Cornwall Estate, Akarana Island, Aotearoa Archipelago

The days were getting lighter. Since I'd been sick, I couldn't stop being tired. I started turning off my visuals at night and it helped; sometimes. I did it on off-days when my ads were irritating more than usual, too. I looked in the Movement space sometimes and I added a talk about how men invented tech to make women more useless and the goddess was against it and how much better I slept, the less I used it.

One day about ten weeks before Christmas, as if the seasons we didn't have had changed overnight, it was suddenly warm enough for me not to bother with my overs when I went to get deliveries from the poor-door. I had gasped my way through yet another pissy double shift and worked through more off-days. It was the night before my epic six-day off time was about to start and I'd eaten a pizza, the first one after days of pure Total™, with a couple of J™s to help me coma on top of the duvet.

The next day I woke up and logged on to find no viewings. I had months of work spam which I'd dimmed out. I started looking through it but it was motivational corporate crap and notices about how much money the company was making and thanking us for all our hard work and not putting their money where their mouth was; which was good in a way because I wouldn't want money that'd been that near some rich-fuck's arsehole. I deleted it all in the end and though I'd taken a while to go through it all, no viewings came in.

I had an easy day with the agency space dimmed down. I quaffed Instant™s and was about to smoke a J™ but decided not to in case a last minuter came in.

It didn't though and I didn't have any shifts the next day or the next. By then my weed-addled braincell was starting to twig that this was strange but relief and exhaustion and no trivial amount of intoxication prevented me from caring much. Another day or two passed and my energy levels rose enough for me to start worrying. But suddenly my pay arrived and the amount looked normal. Not that I knew what was normal nowadays with all the double shifts and triple-time from working off-days. It was a big enough packet anyway but my worry kept niggling.

No more shifts came. I thought maybe something had gone wrong with my agent profile on the system so I checked it and that was when I saw my rating had gone down to four-point-seven stars. Four-point-fucking-seven!

I found the manager handle and she answered straight away.

'Zhang-Lewis?' she asked like she didn't already know. Which she probably didn't.

'Tina. Yeah. Hey, I'm calling up because I see my rating's gone down but I haven't had any feedback or anything.'

'Hold on. Let me check. Ah, yeah here we go, I looked at this one myself! You got a zero-star rating. Yeah, so, since a rating that low is always a bit of a worry. I sent you a few messages but I never heard back so in the end, we had to uphold it. But look, don't worry—'

'No way!' I said. 'That's not fair! I wasn't listed as international! That wasn't my fault. There's no way that could be upheld. You've got to delete it.'

'What d'you mean? It's a verified rating, I checked every—'

'No! No, it fucking can't be! I've never done anything wrong! We don't do anything anyway so how the fuck could I

274

have done anything wrong? This isn't fair! It was your fucking fault that *Měiguó* idiot got through to me in the first place! You have to delete it or I'm fucking getting a lawyer! Or no, fuck that. I'll fucking find you, you bullshitting piece of shit! This isn't—'

'Tina. Tina! Calm down! I think I see what's happened—'

I went bright red. She was going to sort it out and I was way out of line. Way out of line. I could get sacked for what I'd said. 'You can?' I croaked, shaking.

When she spoke again, she didn't look that angry, only a bit annoyed like a roach had escaped her pest control nanites or something. 'Yeah.' She said in a voice that made me feel like I was an idiot. 'There was a problem with your profile and the *Měiguó* client did give you a one-star; somehow, tech people are looking into how; probably fixed by now; it was ages ago. I think that might be what you meant when you, were, uh… talking before. But anyway, we deleted that one, obviously.

'The one we upheld, which we might not have if you hadn't deleted my – let me check, one, two, three…. Uh, seventeen – messages without reading them, was for an older viewing. The client didn't get around to rating it until last week. We did query their rating and they said you remained virtualled into their residence for some time after the viewing slot had finished and they felt that their privacy had been invaded. Naturally since you'd had no prior complaints I contacted you for your side of the story, Tina, but you never responded so, well, there was nothing else I could do.' She held up her hands.

My voice seized up. There was nothing, nothing I could say. If they'd called me live, I didn't know how I could've bullshitted my way out of it. It was true, and that was all there was to it. It was rigged, the system was fucking rigged. How were we meant to know which of the million bloody messages weren't spam and which ones were? It was fucked.

She saw it all on my face and tried to make out it was no big deal. 'Look, Tina, I've seen this happen before. I don't know why you did what you did but given you've got such an excellent track record I'm sure you had your reasons and you'll get your rating back up in no time. I'll tell you what I can do, I can keep an eye out and redirect any last minuters I see if I spot them in time. That should help you get back on your feet. Meantime, of course, we'll have to reduce your accommodation allowances. Of course, you've got plenty of time left on your contract and believe you me, we won't let one pain-in-the-you-know-what client interfere with our judgment when it comes to renewal time but in the meantime, and this is a bit of personal advice from me, you might want to think about moving somewhere, a little bit, uh… more affordable. Since you're an employee, you get first dibs on any stock we're listing and you've got your staff discounts too, that doesn't change…'

I hardly heard everything else she said. I didn't know which one of us cut the call or when. I found myself sitting on my bed alone some time later. Then I lost more time and it was suddenly morning and I forgot everything and logged on as if it was a normal work day.

But there were no viewings and it all came shitting back down on me. I dimmed the agency space so I could only see their stupid white H in old-school writing, I noticed the message from Spume had brightened and started flashing and when I opened it, I saw today was my visit with Nate and all it made me feel was numb.

I had half an hour and all I could think to do was have a wash. My stomach managed to unclench from the gross feeling of the nanites all over me by the time I'd put on some clean hemps. But I didn't really know why I was bothering. I'd nearly forgotten about Nate and the idea of visiting him felt like no more than a boring chore.

It was the same as before only he looked worse. I got in and sat on the poxy blue stool and he didn't look like he would wake. How long was the last visit? Maybe five minutes? Ten? I thought of staying quiet and not saying anything. My stomach clenched every time I looked at his pale skinny arms and the bones on his face.

I've lost my shifts. I've lost my shifts. I've lost my shifts…

In the end, I felt too sorry for the guy to not try so I grew a pair of ovaries and said, 'Nate. Nate? Nate! I got a visit! I actually got a visit!'

His breathing didn't change.

'Nate! It's Tina, Teens! Nate! Wake up babe!'

Babe? You're not my fucking babe! Why did I say that?

Still nothing. I should have sat quietly and waited for the visit to end.

But it's not fair! I've lost my shifts. I've lost my shifts…

Nothing was fair. 'Nate! Babe! Please wake up!' It burst out before I realised I was talking.

Jesus! Stay quiet, you idiot! I've lost my shifts…

But then his breathing sped up and I hated that a little shiver ran through me. I suddenly found myself wanting to shake him except I couldn't touch him because of the evil cop tech and their pathetic visitation rules.

'Nate! Jesus! You fucking arseholes! You said I could visit. You fucking let me in here! Why isn't he waking up?' I shouted it at the room as if there was really someone listening.

His breath quickened and his eyes moved.

'Chen?' It was quiet, barely a whisper. But I heard.

You fucking arsehole! You fucking cheating little shit!

And still, I couldn't stop myself whimpering, 'Nate? Nate?'

It was bad enough him thinking I was her. I should have got up and walked out right then. But somehow, I couldn't and I couldn't stop myself shooting my mouth off, either.

It was as if all my words were on the tip of my tongue and seeing him made them roll off. He'd gurgled back a bunch of craziness that made no sense about… brands and rain and… fuckity-fuckity-lala! I thought his mind was already fried until he'd said… her name. And I knew then that he must've found out before he was arrested and forgotten I didn't know.

I should've been happy to finally know the truth. It proved I was right about his friends and Chen and now him, too. He was the biggest arsehole of the lot! He was fucking sleeping with me and he hadn't said a word.

But they'd all known all the time, they must have! They'd been mocking me the whole time. Him, most of all! I had sort of known if I was honest with myself. Maybe not known-known but well, it made sense. Chen and he probably had been fucking behind my back after all. Or had they broken up at all in the first place? Was I some kind of sick wet-foot poly fetish thing they had going on?

Ugh!

He kept burbling away, clearly having no idea what he'd let slip. I wanted to scream, ask him how he'd found out, why he'd been so horrible to me, who else knew. I wanted to punch him! But for some reason, all I did was whimper at him and plead for help like a child after a fall. Then my words ran out and I sat their gawking at him like a twit until the police tech grabbed me and nearly made me vomit as it jerked me up and forced me out the door.

I tried to swear over my shoulder at the disgusting wrecked piece of rotting meat on the bed behind me but it only made sick come up. The last thing he heard as they stuck their needles in his disgusting pale hide was probably a gross gurgling growl.

Good job.

The tech let me go after the door closed behind me and I bolted into my flat and finished throwing up in the sink. I drank some water then made an Instant™ and sat at my desk. After I'd calmed, I noticed the agency space, bright enough to see in the edges of my eyes and that's when I remembered it was a work day; only I'd all but lost my job. No last minuters had come.

I knew she was bullshitting me.

The space was there, spam building up again already. And otherwise, nothing.

My body tensed and I felt my muscles bulge and veins pulse on my forehead. I didn't know how long it was before I realised the howl like a broken Uber bumper being dragged along tarmac was coming from me. It was like something was inside me straining to burst from my neck, roaring up through my throat trying to cut through my bones and flesh to escape. It was the first time I'd felt the presence and power of the goddess in months.

I remembered my purpose. Work didn't matter any more. It would all take care of itself. The goddess would provide. The Movement was what was important. The rich had to be taken down. I'd lost my way and she'd sent the visit with Nate to remind me. He'd be dead soon and he and all his disgusting wet-foot friends were dead to me now anyway. This was her message to me, not to lose my way.

I screamed abuse into the agency space and put it on full dim. We all knew they weren't going send me any shifts till everyone was drowned and the fucking sun blackened the earth to dry out our bones and turn them to ash.

And then charged with the goddess' power, my rage took form, curling up from the middle of the floor in a silver-grey mist of spiritual power. It swirled like living smoke and coalesced into the glittering raw nanite ingot of my salvation. The goddess had brought me to this moment and given me the tool I needed for the next leg of the journey to my destiny as her sacred earthly vessel.

Nathan – late Nov 2097, Cornwall Estate, Akarana Island, Aotearoa Archipelago

Everything was blue and I was hangin' in the rain, chilled. Chilled again, safe like I'd been...

Rescued?

From what though? But it didn't matter. It was just good being chilled. Chilled like...

Like Shane!

Shane was about the chilledest dude I knew, never mind that he worked twenny-four-three-six-five to feed his brothers and sisters an' that. I saw his face in the rain like it was normal and said, 'Metabolic-Overburn Triple-energy enhanced formula Instant™,' which was his favourite brand and for some reason, it cracked me up. In a chilled kind of way.

So I said it again 'cept then I kinda forgot why I was saying it and I looked up suddenly like I was trying to stop myself dropping off to sleep or something. And there was only the rain and the blue.

But there'd been a face? A brand? A... memory?

Well, there might've been and there might not of but the chill warmed over me and I didn't think about it too hard.

Hold on, what just happened? Nothing happened.

I got to making shapes in the rain like my mum and me used to do or when I was in my gaff and bored at work, tryin' to think of a new set layout or match a smell-theme or something….

Work! I've got work! Why aren't I at work?

But the chill came and smoothed me down and I knew it was all right. Somehow, I wouldn't be late. Everything'd be fine.

'Cept then I said, 'Curry: yellow split peas, onions, tomatoes, genuine spices, penthouse ripened rice, broccoli on the side.' That was my usual brekky, at least three days a week and more if I could afford it.

Hearing it out loud cracked me up and I said it again but that time it sounded boring and I didn't really think about it any more and kept chilling in the blue and the rain. Then the blue started going dark, darker blue, purple, black and off to sleep I went and it was getting light blue again when I woke up.

I know that blue… I've… uh, woken up in it? Jeez! I've woken up inside a dre…

And then man did I chill! I chilled so much everything nearly went black. And the chill went through me so hard and fast it nearly burned. And then I was there again, hangin' in the rain.

It was all good and fine when I got to making faces in the water and the steam and the spray. And when I cracked myself up saying products out loud for each of the peeps before they disappeared and I forgot them again. And...

But I do know that blue! I know it!

The chill washed the thought away, running through me hard and warm, making everything all good and I would've drifted like that… forever. I would've, if I'd been anyone but me. And, maybe I… Maybe I would anyway, the chilledness felt so good but then like a whisper from home, like I'd had the thought before it came: *But Chen, Teens, work!*

Then I saw my work virtual in the steam, a half-finished set for Three Billboards, blurry at first like I was seeing things but then stronger, clearer and I was trying to think what the fire in the shop would've smelled like. But then under my feet there was a new feeling. Coolish air coming up or… Me going down?

The drops turned into lines as I fell quicker and quicker. The cold blew harder up my legs, through my body, over my face and I looked down and saw dark underneath me, coming up, up, up to take me. It got blacker and bigger like a dangerous dark crack in the chillful blue, opening up to swallow me.

I started kicking to try and get back up, into the blue and the chilledness didn't come to fix it. I fell faster and faster and the black opened up and pulled me down and everything went dark and a new thing washed over me like the chilledness only it was anything but chilled.

My heart kicked up and my tum-tum went cold and hard 'cause I knew somewhere down below me getting closer and closer there was things. Things in the dark, reaching up.

I could feel them, whipping 'round under my feet, searching, feeling for something to… I fell, closer and closer and then something grabbed my foot from the blackness and another my ankle and I knew, I remembered this feeling came when I had a visitor 'cause I'd had one before.

'Man! Not again! Take me back to the blue! Help! Oi! Can anyone hear me? Help! Get me back up there!'

More and more things grabbed and wound 'round me and I was waiting for worse things to happen, waiting for teeth, waiting for claws but instead I got a voice, a cold evil whisper that was worse than any tooth or claw.

'Too late this time, Mister Richards-Mann. But all subsequent visitation request will be declined. As you have requested.'

And for some reason I knew that was bad though I could feel more things winding 'round my ankles and pulling me further down.

It's gotta be a nightmare! I'm having a nightmare all I have to do is… Well, fuuuuck m—

'Nate. Nate?'

I'm awake. Man! I'm awake, it's okay. It was only a…

'Nate! I got a visit! I actually got a visit!'

So it was you! You did this!

'Nate! It's Tina, Teens! It's me, Nate! Wake up babe!'

Tina… Tina… Tina, Tina, Tina… Chen?

'Nate! Babe! Please wake up!'

I was too scared to move in case I wasn't really awake. In case it was my *nǎozǐ* playin' tricks.

'Nate! Jesus! You fuckin' arseholes! You said I could visit! You fuckin' let me in here! Why isn't he waking up?'

What arseholes didn't let her in?

A glow of something went through me then, a warmish glow; hottish.

Arseholes didn't let her visit… Like I said they wouldn't…

'Chen?' It was a whisper, maybe hardly that 'cause I was too shit-scared of everything just…

…falling away into the… spray? The dark?

Where had the blue and the rain gone? How could I have been there and then got here? The woman couldn't hear me 'cause she kept on saying, 'Nate? Nate?' She was getting upset, I could hear it in her voice though my eyes were closed.

You got me killed… Nah, hold on, that was a dre… This is a dre… No. I'm… I'm awake? Or… Shit! I'm awake!

Ah, not Chen. 'Teens.' Yeah, the… *fēng kuáng* one? I knew the name but not the person. It had a good-ish feeling that came with it though so I went with it.

'Oh Jesus! Nate! Babe! I thought you wouldn't wake up. Jesus fuck! You wouldn't believe what I bloody went through before they'd let me in here again. It was exactly like you said. They didn't want me to visit. They kept feeding me bullshit about my appointment being lost off the system again and a-fuckin'-gain, health complications with your therapy, all sorts of fucking shit!'

Yeah. Thought so.

Only it didn't really bother me. I thought maybe it might've used to've been a thing for me, somehow, though.

'How's it goin' Teens?' I smiled and got my eyes open a crack. The light hurt them but it slowly got better.

Would your eyes hurt like that in a dream?

But then I moved an arm, lifted up a hand. Man, I was weak! And when I looked at my arm it was skinnier an' bluer than the last time!

The last time…?

'Teens.' My voice was a croak and talking made me tired. I said her name again a coupla times, stalling, trying to remember who she was. I made a bit of small talk to buy a bit of time. I managed to get my head turned 'round and jumped a bit at the sight of the woman sitting there. She was this half-starved lookin' thing, skin all spotty and greasy spikey hair…

Looked better when you fully buzzed it…

Did I know her better than I thought? Her eyes were glassy and bloodshot and now I was facing her I got the whiff of weed.

Oh man, Teens, whoever you are. Jeez, man! Whoever you are, you gotta…

'Teens, you gotta start lookin' after yourself…' Then I started to cough like I had plague or something.

'Nate, what's wrong? Do you recognise me babe? It's taken me fuckin' months to get another visit. Why are they doing this Nate?'

'They're stoppin' you from visiting…'

But why would you wanna visit me? Visit me where? I'm right here… What the fuck's goin' on?

'Each time I wake up it sets the….'

What's happening? I know something's happening.

I kinda remembered. Kinda. There'd been blue, rain, faces, all kinds of *dōngxīs* and all their brands and it was random-as like a weed-dream 'cept it kind of rung a bell.

'I dunno, ah, Ch—, Teens. I dunno, I'm tired. There's rain, there's… faces… it's all good.' I smiled at her. It was good she'd dropped in. But man, did I need sleep! The talking was taking it outta me.

But I've… been asleep, haven't I?

I was lying down, so probably! Still, didn't matter if I had or not. I knew I was tired, anyway.

'Teens,' I said. 'I gotta…. I think I gotta sleep for a while. Nice of ya to pop in an' that—'

Pop in? She's… visiting me? But I'm… here! Where am I? I don't get it.

'Nate! No! Nate! You can't go back under. Nate! It's me! It's Teens! I'm your girlfriend!'

My girlfriend? Isn't Chen my girlfriend? You aren't Chen. But that voice…

She was getting a bit wild on me and somewhere in my *nǎozǐ*, I knew that wouldn't end well so I tried to calm her down. 'Yeah, I-know. Chill Teens. It's all good, I'll have a quick nap, won't be long.'

But that made it worse. 'Nate! No! I don't know what to do. Nobody's joining the Movement. I know I said I'd get you a lawyer and everything but I haven't… It's… It's complicated! Everything's shit! My nana died! Nathan! Help me!'

Yeah, I bet it's complicated… Jeez! That's right. Teens isn't Teens. 'Cause I found out when I did that job and then, randomly got…. arrested by… Teens? The voice, it was her. But it wasn't, it was… Who's PC Peaches again?

I could remember two faces and one voice which was weird but it didn't matter 'cause then I clicked.

Oh yeah! Fuck! I'm in the joint! Teens is visiting me! Fuck!

The warmish-hottish feeling came, better this time. 'Shit!' I gotta bit of strength-on again though not nearly as much as I should've seeing as how they was meant to be keeping me in fit shape an' all that. Which was another thing I suddenly remembered.

'Nate? What's wrong?'

'Teens. Jesus! They nearly got me. I nearly let them take me back under before I knew who ya were. Jeez Teens. It's getting bad. But, man! Your nana died? Jo Rahui is dead? Fuck!'

'Oh Nate. You're still you. Jesus! Thank fuck! What have they done to you Nate? You look…'

'Weak?'

'Yeah. No! I mean, not only weak. You're so tiny.' She sounded kind of sick.

'Yeah, they could keep me in better nick if they wanted to. I dunno why, cost of meds maybe. Inside they've got me…'

Dreaming! They've got me in some kind of dream! But that's impossible…

And that was when I started to realise something, like on the tip of my mind-tongue but not turning into a proper thought.

'Teens. It's bad. I dunno how to fight it. I don't reckon I can. They're doing something freaky to my *năozĭ*.'

The warm chilledness…

I remembered it suddenly.

'They've got drugs, Teens, drugs that stop me thinking or something, so I can't snap myself out of it. They've got me locked away in here. I got nothin', Teens. I gotta get out. Much longer of this an' I'm gonna be fucked. I don't know what they're doing but whatever it is, it's somehow…'

…wiping my năozĭ!

But then I got like this tickle in my *năozĭ*. Something kinda, knocking, wanting to come in, trying to make me remember it. That was how I knew there was more to it. It wasn't random shit they were doing to me.

'They… They need me to stay under for whatever it is to work, Teens. Whenever you come to visit, they make it all… They make me not want to…'

…wake up!

'You've gotta keep trying, Teens. Doesn't matter if they say no, okay? Keep trying anyway!'

It was all I could figure out to tell her. She was looking at me like I was fully *makutud* but letting me blow it all out anyway then she perked up and said, 'Okay, Nate. I will.'

But she kinda sounded like she was away in her tech or something. I knew I was stuffed if she didn't keep coming, if someone didn't keep coming. I tried to tell her. 'Teens, it's like, I'm…' But I couldn't remember. It was all disappearing outta my head as I got awaker and awaker. '…somewhere else. Like they're… nicking my thoughts or something, I… dunno. But you have to keep waking me up, please Teens!'

How do I know that?

She was lookin' at me funny but going with it anyway for my sake probably.

'Okay, Nate, I will.' She said it in that way people say when they mean, yeah, whatever man.

'Yeah, well, thanks Teens. I… I dunno what else to say. All I know is that I'm rooted if you don't.'

But I had that feeling in my tum-tum like it was falling into my legs 'cause I could tell she wasn't listening. It was like she was here but she'd already gone.

I couldn't think of anything to say either. I was choking on mind-blowing fuckedness and on top of that I was worried about her. She looked like she was going downhill fast and there wasn't nothing I could do to help.

She was about to say something, I could tell but then she jerked upwards, standing like a reanim… re-elimin… like a corpse comin' back as a zombie and quick-marched to the door with a growl sound in her throat 'cause it was all the sound the cop-tech would let her get out.

S'pose that means visitation's over, well, sweet dreams for me again. Then, *fuck! Yeah! Dreams!*

I – 2041-late Nov 2097, Cornwall Hill,

Akarana Island, Aotearoa Archipelago

From the poison of why bubbled a stream of thoughts that banished my peace of ages. I could not stop remembering and trying to remember more though some part of me knew no calm would come of it.

I knew that I was of the Family by the river though somehow, I was here instead of being with them. And though I wanted only to sleep, let go of myself and forget, memories forced themselves to mind. I saw red earth, a yellow river, warm green trees, white winter cold and red embers, bodies entwined and laughter and pain and the return of happiness like sunshine after rain.

With the memories came sadness and the hungry devastation of loss that I perceived was great and ancient. I wanted no more of it but a soul has no body to stop memories coming and growing and echoing endlessly. And so they filled me and I wept, if a soul can weep, and could not find peace any more.

Time passed. Summers? Lifetimes? I could not tell. It might have been that after the disturbance, I was again dimming to the ember of myself which would cool into soft slumber. But something happened that I could not guess at. Something loosened, or grew or… cracked and I shrunk from the cold freedom that poured in on me.

The Flow that had lain still around me like frozen blue smoke, stirred and curled away into blackness. And then that which had taken it came for me. I felt myself drawn as if on a current of air, although I could not say how I knew. Higher I rose like mist in the night until I perceived I had come above the ground and begun to flow out, out from under something unknowable, to finally slow and stop on cold wet earth beneath the open sky.

Foreboding wracked me as I perceived the fusing was again free to work its evil on me against Earth and Sky.

This should not happen! I need to get back…

Back where? I did not know. But the first stirrings of repair had already begun. I could feel the dirt and air around me changing, their nature bending and shifting to become my fleshly vessel once more. Pain wracked my soul as it twisted Earth and Sky to make right its warped existence; fusing all it touched, transforming, blindly following the course it remembered; the only one Earth and Sky allowed it, to remake itself. I felt myself almost a watcher, a heron gliding high and looking down, as my body grew anew. I could as much stop it as I could have uprooted a tree with my bare hands in my distant youth.

The torment of anguish as my soul tethered itself back to flesh was only the beginning. For as I grew, I began to feel and I felt cold and rain and the roughness of hard damp earth and whining whirring sounds not of Earth and Sky assailed my unfurling ears. My blind eyes had formed and it was not long before their lids would split and open in the night, before the flesh of my nostrils would start to smell and my tongue begin tasting the air.

And as these things bloomed, flesh budding and sprouting into limbs, I finally felt the warmth of hands lifting me. As the first whisperings of the world reached my budding senses, I caught the sense of being carried up and away, out of the wind and rain and into bright and quiet warmth like and yet unlike the firelit caves of my home.

Neil – Dec 2097, Cornwall Hill Station,

Akarana Island, Aotearoa Archipelago

In the boring mandatory psyche stuff I'd studied to get into the cops, the lecturers shat on about developmental factors in the criminal mind. It was all sound theory, apparently. But I only half bought it because it failed to take reality into account.

Take me for instance. My parents beat seven shades of shit out of me if they clocked I'd hidden their booze. Or hacked their accounts to buy myself food. Or once they'd figured out I could code, if I refused to run whatever stolen property or software racket they wanted to fund their pissy habits with. But had that turned me into an un-empathic manipulative violent coercive thug? Fuck no! I was empathic! I could a read a room.

And where was the fun in making people weaker than you do stuff? Force was too easy. There was no pleasure in it. It was like saying 'tell me you love me' to someone at acid-nozzle-point. Course they would say it. No. It was better if you could get them to want to do stuff for you; make them think it was their idea; make them like you.

Yeah, nah. The psyche people could fuck themselves. They had no explanation for me. I'd come from a drug-den shit-show and ended up being basically a stand-up guy, all under my own steam. So where was all my developmental fucked-ness then? Nowhere!

It sometimes made me wonder anyway – not that it bothered me – how I always ended up here in the place I always got to with my hapless playthings. Poor old Sarah had started giving me those tight-lipped kisses with no tongue, trying to avoid me outside work, fobbing me off with friends in need, family dos and desperately inept hand-jobs.

I knew all the signs; I must've let something slip or there'd been some unexpected connection; there was always something eventually that copped them on to me; not fully on to me but sort of, made them suspicious and usually ended up with them fading away. If I'd had to guess, I'd've said it started with the leave thing; there'd been something she wasn't telling me then. But she hadn't gone completely spoilsport on me until well after that.

No, there must've been something else that'd finally tipped her off. But it was a case too boring crack. Besides, plenty of snapper; whatever a snapper was. And in a way, this bit of each, uh, relationship, was fun too. When they were on to me but they didn't know I knew they knew. And apparently, she was grieving too which I'd read was a thing people genuinely biochemically did. Watching her try to hide it made the whole thing more fun.

I got her a beauty with the Richards-Mann glitch. Her confusion, the tears; poetry! I would have forgotten about the generic wet-foot, if he hadn't started going weird in stasis. I'd dimmed the alerts at first because all prisoners had different reactions. I was sure the system was only taking a bit longer than usual to sort him out.

But over a year – a year! – had passed and he hadn't bedded in. Whatever they did to them in stasis, maybe wet-foots'd started breeding with a resistance to it or something. Vaguely interesting but who gave a shit, really.

But it was too titillating an opportunity to miss. I acted as if Sarah and I were still – oooh! – secret lovers and that I was clueless that anything was up. I gently bullied and cajoled her into taking a look at her sister's convict boyfriend though she wasn't trained to use the system.

I groped her and leaned on her and tried not to crack up at how uncomfortable it made her in my office with the door closed. She was amusingly bad at hiding the fact of how okay she wasn't. She made it so easy for me to play my part.

I gave her a few helpful pointers in my best encouraging boyfriend voice. I knew that whatever she'd figured out about me, she couldn't help but at least partly buy my sincerity; like they always did. The confusion on her thoroughbred little dial was fucking pure!

All I'd wanted was to sit there knowing whose zombie boyfriend she was talking to while she'd cried her way through doing it. A bit of fun to lift my mood in the stupid moron-festival ramp-up to yet another fucking Christmas and *xīnnián* was all it was! It was all I'd wanted, fuck-it!

Nathan – Dec 2097, Spume Prison Stasis, Cornwall Estate, Akarana Island, Aotearoa Archipelago

I know that blue… And I know I've… Been here before?

But I hardly thought the last bit. I didn't think it strongly enough for the chill to come and eat it. It was like the ghost of a thought.

But how do I know?

I just wondered it in a chilled kinda way.

Repetition…

Something about that word, how memory worked. But no bright ideas came and the rain kept falling, straight down, no wind an' no sound.

Don't think too hard, Nate. That's what brings it on?

I'd forgotten how I knew, how I got here, a lot of stuff. Not that it mattered…

Ah, yeah but that's the whole idea of this joint, isn't it?

I had no idea where in my *nǎozǐ* that'd pinged up from but it kinda made me smile and I opened my mouth to say it.

And that's the idea, too, isn't it…?

Was it? How did I know that? Did I know that?

A slow little shot of chilledness went through me and I looked out into the rain and watched the drops joining up on their way down, breaking apart into smaller ones, falling

293

together, groups in a line, so heavy they were like a tap, steam, spray, splashing in…

…the alleyway outside my flat where I…

…where I'd been a minute ago? Where I'd been! The chill rolled up to cover the thoughts like a wave comin' in from the sea. But I was a hacker and that meant biotech as well as coding and I knew there was more places your *nǎozi* could think than in thoughts. There was subconscious, muscle memory, triggers, emotions, all kinds of roads to the warehouse sorta thing.

So when the chill came up, my anger went out to meet it and it sorta worked. I was allowed to think though the chill wasn't keen on the idea. I was allowed!

So I didn't lose my train of thought. Not fully. Not until the next wave came, anyway. Then black closed in 'round my eyes and the blue went so dark it turned red. And for a nano, I felt so chilled it hurt. Like I couldn't… *breathe?*

'Cause they nearly OD'd me?

I had the thought, all right. But I was so chilled it was too much to take it anywhere. Slowly, slowly, the red came back up to blue. The black tunnels 'round my eyes got wider and left me hangin' in the rain again and I watched the water and made faces in the steam.

I listed out *dōngxīs* and their brands and the faces fell apart and dropped away into the blue. And the blue slowly faded out to purple and my eyes started closing.

'Cause bodies gotta sleep, even in dreams… Dreams… Dreams… Dreams!

This time I remembered where I'd left off thinking when I'd gone to sleep. Why hadn't they filled me with chill before I woke up like normal? Who knew? Not me! But I wasn't gonna complain!

But then up came the calm and the black closed in; a bit. The blue went dim; a bit.

Easy does it, Nate, don't get too excited.

I didn't know why but it was my voice in my *nǎozǐ* saying it and if ya can't trust your own self, then what's the bloody point?

No harm done; not too much anyway; I wasn't fully knocked off my train of thought. But then the light and the rain came back and I stared out through the spray and the…

…*Spume!*

And though it was only falling drops and spray and steam and blue everywhere, as I stared and the minutes went on, I clocked that something was different. It was hard to see 'cause my eyes were only so big and the blue was way bigger. But it went from steam and spray and lines of drops making shapes in the rain to something a bit more.

I went from thinking maybe I was seeing things to knowing I wasn't, to staring into the blue and knowing the blue was staring back. And when I copped on to it, it spoke.

I know that voice.

It was like the sky was speakin', like if you'd smoked some illegally souped up premo weed or something. It was hard to see and easy at the same time. The blue had eyes and a mouth, everywhere I looked, like I could see all of it but it never ended no matter how far round I turned my *tóu*.

And the voice came from everywhere but wasn't too loud. 'Mister… uh, Richards-Mann?' it asked. 'I'm Senior Serg— uh, Inspector Sarah Rahui, your arresting officer.'

Yeah, yeah, that's it! Two faces, one voice.

'Everything all right, Mister Richards-Mann?'

The dry-foots knew more than the poor. It's 'cause they all went to uni an' that. And the more they knew, the easier stuff was to find out so they got smarter and richer and they had more time on their hands to get smarter again. And then more richer.

Meantime, out by the seawalls, there was more to worry about than getting smart. You had to eat and you had to keep well and in the roughest blocks, you had to keep your strength up to fight off other wet-foots trying to steal your *whānau's* food.

So, you didn't get as smart as dry-foots and you didn't have time to think of ways to get richer. But that didn't mean wet-foots didn't know things. We knew shit, alright.

And some shit we learned so young we forgot we knew it. But that didn't mean we forgot it. It went upstairs to the auto-pilot bits of our *nǎozǐs* which was how I didn't feel nothin' when the blue opened its sky-mouth and spoke in its trippy voice that sounded like a baby cop. And 'cause I felt nothin', the chill didn't get shot into me to calm me down. I did what my *nǎozǐ* knew you gotta do when you talk to a cop, no worries at all. Which was don't tell 'em fuckin' anything!

'Yeah, all good,' I said.

Talking felt weird, like the words were too light and my lips were too heavy to get out, which was weird given I'd been talking all the time no problem. The blue was quiet then but I could see it still, watching me.

I rolled with it and stared back looking out of it, which wasn't hard 'cause at least a micro bit of the evil chill was wash-ing through me all the time anyway. Might've been a second or it might've been an hour by the time it talked again. 'Mister Richards-Mann, how long have you, uh, been here?'

'I… I'm just… here,' I said.

'You live here?'

'Live? Here? Yeah. I'm y'know, here,' I said.

'Yeah. Yes, you are, uh, Mister Richards-Mann. You're, uh, here.' Her voice had that shiver I remember my sister's had for months after our cousin Stevie'd died. An' I didn't know how I knew 'cause the eyes and the mouth in the blue had been faint anyway. But after a while I clocked that she'd gone and I was left alone again, in the blue and the rain. And I'd got away with it.

Whatever it was?

If it'd been anyone other than her, they would've been all right. I'd've been one more wet-foot put under, woke up wrong and sent to the coast to die young in a vegetative state. But with the evil chill itself washing through me, I couldn't forget that voice an' all the things it meant.

Two faces, one voice, the arrest, Teens who wasn't Teens visiting. That voice brought it all back, the thing I'd thought as they'd put me under.

Back in the olden days, the technique had been to reach for a light switch but I'd never touched a light switch in my life though the idea of it cracked me up. So, I'd upgraded the technique. It worked anyway so who cared.

Hangin' in the blue, I reached in my *nǎozǐ* for my tech and my tech wasn't there and that's how I knew I was dreaming. Everything I'd read about tech said it was impossible. But there I was, awake in a dream Spume were making me have. Maybe it'd've been better if I hadn't done it, an' maybe not. But it was what it was and I was who I was so I gave 'em fuckin' heaps! The wankers.

Tristian – late Nov 2097, Cornwall Hill,

Akarana Island, Aotearoa Archipelago

'Go for a wee for me will you, Tris. I'm too tired to get up,' Jo said, rubbing her eyes. Black stubble covered her head though her face was smooth like always.

We both must've slept badly because I knew how she felt. But I had a meeting in a couple of hours and I wanted to get out for a run, shower and eat breakfast – and drink coffee! – beforehand. I dragged myself out of bed and got down on all fours, the carpet compressing into a springy mat around me.

Jo reached out a lazy arm and pinched my naked bum as it moon-rose above the bedside in my first down-dog of the morning. I squawked, chicken-like, and nearly lost control of my own bladder all over the floor.

'You said you were going for a wee for me,' she complained and her voice was strangely dry.

'Yeah, okay, okay. But if you're not careful I'll come back up there and do it on you.'

'Ooh!' she said. 'Promises, promises.'

I finished my stretches and the mat fluffed back into carpet as I headed for our en suite. But as I closed the door, Jo called out, 'No! Don't!'

'Eh? Don't what? I'm busting.'

'Just don't close it, Tris. Please don't close it!'

'What's the matter?'

I turned and went back to the bed and saw she was in tears. Her face was screwed up and red as if she'd been crying for ages.

Jesus Christ!

'Jo! What's wrong!'

But she didn't answer, only wailed for me not to go. I lay down beside her and took her in my arms but she was a dead bawling weight.

'Jo, I'm here. I won't go. It's okay! Jo!'

But she cried louder and louder and the sound was suffocating. I rolled on to my elbows and tried to cradle her head in my hands. But I couldn't get them behind her head. I put my hands on her shoulders, but I couldn't feel where her pyjamas ended and the bedclothes started.

'Jo!'

Her crying was so loud now that it hurt my head and I couldn't breathe. As I called to her and scrabbled to hold on to her, she creased and flattened, faded into the contours of the sheets and pillow and then I was awake roaring, 'Jo! Jo! Jo!' and choking into my tear-soaked pillow, back in the world where Jo had been dead and gone for five months.

'Fffffuck,' I sighed into the early morning gloom, reflexively pinging the coffee machine to make a flat-white. What else could I do? The received wisdom was that we needed to grieve. So, this was me fuckin' grieving. 'So when does the anger part of the fuckin'-arsehole cycle kick in? Eh?' I shook my fists at the empty room.

I had struggled to adjust to the new apartment. Or had I struggled to adjust to Jo being gone? Probably both. Anna, or her interiors people anyway, had done an incredible job. As much as it could be, the layout and décor were the same as the old house. Maybe that hadn't been such a great idea after all.

They – Anna and Davey – had me buy the penthouse and the apartment below it. Then Anna's crowd had made them into a single two-storey apartment. Its layout matched the old house with eerie precision.

The furniture was ours, *well, mine now*, from the old place; inasmuch as furniture transferred across town in nano-form and reconstituted was the same furniture. The resemblance ended with the roof terrace on the top floor and the balcony on the bottom; and the front door with its soulless hall of hard-wearing carpet, uniform apartment doors and our gauche private lift.

Still, I kept waking up disoriented, dreaming nightly of nothing in particular but most often the face; as if my moving had given it more… potence. At least this latest dream had been real. And mine. I had never got around to telling Jo about the face, not after the way Aroha had come between us.

I'd wanted things to be normal after that. Normal and not bloody paranormal. And now Jo was gone, and there was probably nobody on the planet who would have a hope of understanding. Talk about lost opportunities.

Who didn't have recurring dreams anyway? It would be so easy for anyone to dismiss. No more than my mind working something out.

Since before I was old enough to have anything to work out?

Although it had only started speaking after Jo and I got together, faintly though. I could never hear what it said.

After the accident? After Aroha?

I'd given up trying to work it out. The timing was right for both but it was impossible to tell which one had triggered it. Maybe both had.

Probate had come and gone in a few months – fast-tracked, money was good for something – and a part of me I didn't realise was hanging on, was relieved when the audit only took a month or two after that. Relieved and freshly bereft. The sale of the old place would settle soon and – I always shivered a bit when I thought of it – the demolition would happen in short order after that; maybe on the settlement day itself.

One Saturday a month or so before Christmas, Davey found a raclette grill in the boxes from the move. We resurrected it despite my stomach's apprehension. She got Anna over and we feasted on ThisReallyIsn'tCHEESE™ and breads, crackers and preserves packed with delicious vinegary carcinogens.

They tried to do it all for me like I couldn't work a bloody kitchen or something. But I had anticipated the move – well, not really – and confounded them by stealth in the end. I'd already arranged the cupboards and they claimed there was no logic to where I'd put things. It was obvious enough to me; where I could bloody reach them without bending down or reaching up.

I got them looking for my cheese board and somehow it led to Susie storming out; shouting something crazy and Susie-ish about a cheese board not being a dish and if she said she didn't want a drink then she didn't want a fuckin' drink, before closing the stairwell door with the loudest swooshing tear she could force out of it. It all came together in the end though. She came back down and was close to civil.

I went to bed expecting to suffocate on my own exhaust, if I could sleep at all with my guts churning the way they were so I was surprised to find myself dropping off fast despite the cramps. The face came and for the first time, my faith in the technique of denying inconvenient truths nearly let me down. I couldn't hear it but it was nearer, more…

Connected?

I was relieved when Susie shook me awake sometime in the wee-small hours. 'Tristian! Wake up! It's our house!'

I sat up in bed, nothing too numb, nothing aching for a bloody change. 'Jesus, what do you mean? Of course, it's our bloody…' I stopped grumbling when she yanked me into the online space she was attached to. I found myself in a virtual world of colour-dubbed night vision. I smelled wet earth, weed-smoke, d-d-d-d-d-dreadful fast food, concrete, clay and the pharmaceutical tang of thousands of wet overs.

We were hovering above the wasteland, presumably getting our experience from aggregated drone cameras or whatever; Jesus, what we'd done to the world! The house started disappearing in a swirling cloud of dust enveloping it from the ground up. Our house. My house!

Shit! It's happening. Settlement was today!

The virtual flickered out when panic gripped me.

'Tristian, what's wrong?' Susie dimmed the space around her and gripped my arm. 'Tristian!'

'It's okay,' I lied. 'I'll get back in, give me a second.'

I'd looked it up a thousand times, it had been what? Eighty-one years? I had nothing to worry about.

Jesus! I wouldn't bloody have anything to worry about if it was still there anyway, we didn't do anything…

Torn from sleep and shoved into the live feed of our family home being demolished this way was too much for my stomach to bear, anxiety or not. I got myself under control eventually and my room was briefly superimposed on the feed as my vision slowly transitioned into the space.

My guts quaked as I watched. The house was half transformed into a pile of sawdust and other waste by the time I managed to get fully online. It wasn't long before the entire structure was gone. With the speed at which it reduced everything to dust, I couldn't see how the tech could distinguish between substances, between wood and steel, concrete and clay, clay and dirt…

…dirt and… other things.

But I wasn't so naïve. I'd invented it after all. I knew what it could do. The dust piles had already begun to shrink. Sleep-deprived and queasy as I was, a part of me couldn't help marvelling as they appeared to separate themselves, flowing over the ground like living smoke, into different bins on the roadside, clearing the ground ready to dig.

Once the house was gone, the nanites repurposed themselves and assembled, moving over the bare earth like giant metallic dung beetles and I tensed as they began to dig.

If it's gonna happen…

After so many years of septic anxiety, a niggling rot poisoning every thought and action despite my – our – innocence, the speed with which the question was about to be answered was surreal. Before our eyes, a pit opened in the ground previously occupied by a street-ful of old properties including ours, mine. It sank deeper and yawned darker by the second.

How far down now? A metre? Two? Would they have found it by now?

But the nanites didn't stop and the hole yawned blacker by the second, long past the depth a single woman could have dug with an antique spade back in the twenty-tens. I'd known anyway, it would have to have been a freakish chance for a human corpse to have, well, survived, wasn't really the word but… No. I was out of the woods, well not that I was ever in them; it wasn't bloody me that killed him! Or Jo. No, Garry's body was long rotted and dissolved away. At last, the waiting was over.

My tears were as much of relief as shock and sadness at the brutal despatch with which our lives were levelled and gouged out from the very rock and clay beneath the earth.

The council reserve behind the house was full of onlookers and I knew – knew! – how stupid I was to feel angry at them. They were people doing what people always did; gawping and goggling while the world ate them away unawares.

Beyond the crowd were more high-rises and doubtless, all the access roads and alleyways connecting them. This would be the last plot filled; Jo and I had held back, an inch or two of the tide for a second or two of time in the scheme of things.

Other construction machines arrived or formed as the foundation neared completion. A thinning line of diggers filed on and off the site, removing the dirt and returning to dig more. The new machines erected a vast frame and wove a tarp over the pit. I guessed they were re-using at least some of the demolition dust. I didn't really give a shit.

'Tech Mogul Tristian Laufala finally does something right,' was the caption rolling unobtrusively across our vision, obscuring and yet not obscuring the footage.

Jesus! When did I not at least try to do the right bloody thing!

Once the shelter was up, the machines repurposed yet again. The few remaining diggers crawled in and out of the pit but some of Jase's field had rubbed off on me back when we were friends. I knew roughly how a block went up. Other stuff would start now.

Except it didn't. Something flashed and the whole site went dead.

Eh? Some kind of pulse?

But as I thought it, I knew it was impossible. Tech was far too well protected for anything like that.

'What happened?' I asked.

I dimmed the space to find David had come down to watch with us. Susie was fully dressed, I noticed. She must have been up all night, waiting.

'Not sure,' she said, disinterestedly. 'Hit some snag or other, maybe. Might be getting specialist nanites in or something.'

She was probably right but I couldn't stop the slight knot forming in my stomach again anyway.

You're being an idiot. It's over!

The crowds were dispersing now, filing off the grounds and home to bed, no doubt stoned off their trees after the late-night entertainment. I was beginning to think they had a point, leaving for the night but a part of me couldn't pull myself away. I needed to know why the site had shut down. It wouldn't have been the body, that was long gone, I was sure now. More or less.

'Tristian! What's wrong? You look like you've seen a… Oh!' said Susie.

'What the fuck?' said David.

A light was shining from the bottom of the pit, blue-white and fading as we watched, to azure, to violet then black.

'That's why the site stopped,' David said. 'Nanites hit something.'

'But what though?' I enthused.

I imagined it would turn out to be some kind of old electric cable, some bizarre technical fault in the nanites themselves, nothing that should have excited me as much as it did. But my curiosity was inflated by uncharitable glee. Whatever deeply buried mischief had surfaced from layers of volcanic rock and time, was someone else's problem and decisively not mine! I was in the clear!

'Do any of the feeds say what it was?' I heard the ghost of an annoying four-year-old in my voice.

'Nope,' David said after squinting into some space or another for a second. 'Well, not really. News spaces are blathering about a broken artifact but it's all fluff. Yang's got a one-liner, construction paused for investigation of undisclosed artifact.'

'Can't we find out?' I whined.

'Why would we be able to find out? It was off our former property boundaries. Council owns the wasteland so nope again. Their circus, their antique monkeys. It'll probably be some buried planet-toxifying explosive that got set off by the oxygen or some shit like that. I'm going to bed.'

But she didn't. She leaned in my bedroom doorway, iron-streaked bun tangled and escaping, robe thrown on as an afterthought, her mother's features, my overactive brain, both of our height and big build. I wanted to think she looked sad. I wanted to think the end of our home, the place she'd grown up in, meant something to her. But who knew with David? Not her father.

'Well, that's that then,' Susan said superfluously. My tears flowed quietly and I said nothing.

'It's only a house, Tristian,' David harrumphed.

What the hell can I say to that?

Didn't stop me opening my big mouth to try though. 'I, it's just—'

'It's a house.' David repeated, steely.

Then Susie said, 'Davey! It's not only a house, it was—'

I didn't hear the rest. The face swam up from nowhere and pulled me down into a sleep I couldn't fight. Down, down, down, out and away in a way I had felt only once, decades ago as I lay battered and broken, hovering near death in a comatose dream. Far away I heard David, angrily calling. 'Tristian! Tristian! Jesus! Susie! What's happened to…'

Tina – late Nov 2097, Cornwall Estate, Akarana Island, Aotearoa Archipelago

Not having to work felt weird. I sort of did in a way since I'd lose my contract altogether if I didn't clock on. But I knew I could keep the space dimmed all day and if the manager wasn't bullshitting and got me a last-minuter, it would ping me anyway.

But with the nanite ingot of wealth She had sent me, I wouldn't have to worry about money for a long time; maybe for the rest of my life. I would decide to worry about it, of course. Dumb to let it all slip through my fingers. But I could afford to have a break now and get myself together. I deserved it after everything I'd been through.

Each day I woke, logged on, dimmed work and opened the Movement space in case anyone wanted to hear Her teachings. I taught myself search analytics and traded in a few nanites from the goddess-sent ingot, for rankings.

It wasn't something I could do all day, I discovered. It was more like, check in on the stats, piddle around with the tags to see if they got better hits and see how the ranking budget was going. I was getting a lot of hits nowadays but people hadn't started engaging.

After that had me reaching for the Instant™ to ease the tedium, I went back to studying tech and by then I was getting good; sort of liking it a bit which I supposed I couldn't really help considering it was basically in my genes. But it was dangerous too because of what it made me remember. I'd switched to proper weed instead of BudLike™, a tiny luxury and Jesus did I need it to handle the balance.

One afternoon, I was having a break and enjoying a fabulous smooth and golden stoning. It was so good I was sure it was another sign from the goddess and I was looking for something else to appear in my flat; not that I had any idea what else She could send me or that I needed anything. The ingot was enough for now.

I could sense she wanted me to learn the skills I'd need for the next phase of the Movement. With the stats going up and my tech study, I was going the right way. She would guide me further when she needed to. And sure enough, right when I thought it, Her message came.

I'd gone into Jamie Yang's space and a thrill went through me. But it was a thrill with different waves to it and it was lucky I'd been vaping because I might have cried if they'd all come at once. As it was, the weed in my veins slowed their passage through my soul so they were manageable. A tear or two did come but I handled it like a real woman.

At first I was a bit panicked it had come so soon! I would have expected it to take months. Then I thought I should go there now and see it, one last time. And then I decided that stuff it, it was only going to be footage of construction, man crap, man-made materials changing their form on the surface of the sacred earth and nothing more. Only idiots, as most people were, would be interested in seeing it, not me. I decided not to watch it online let alone schlepp all the way up there to see it live.

Then I changed my mind.

The rain whipped my overs like an unfit parent. I'd found Campbell Road okay then the goddess made me ignore my navigation and take what I thought at the time was a wrong turn. I could see Laufala's security brightening in my visuals up ahead.

Jolted back to alertness, I turned to get back on track then changed my mind and walked right up to the security point, curious in a sticking your finger in hot Instant™ sort of way. It didn't look any fancier than normal security but a part of me knew it was. The same part that was only a little bit surprised when a green tick flashed at the edge of my vision and the menacing gates that had appeared in my visuals disappeared.

My ankle nearly sprained when I bolted back down the street. The crowd was zombie-apocalypsing along the old Campbell Road.

Did anyone see that?

Jesus, never mind that, what if it was logged! The shakes overtook me and cut through the last of my weed-calm. I stood rooted to the footpath and the blue-white of the street-lights was suddenly too bright.

I should have gone back into the crowd and shuffled along with them. I knew they were heading to a turning behind the block of high-rises on the edge of the wasteland. There was probably some poxy sideroad that went to an official entrance. I wouldn't have been surprised if there was some popup virtual blocking everyone out unless they bought fucking tickets, too.

Hey, 'Lanie! Watch this. I can make it our road...

The memory hit me in the stomach and tears ran down my face inside my hood. I nearly went back home, right then. I couldn't calm myself. I thought of Nate, of the goddess, of losing my shifts, of anything, of bloody Chen if it would help. But the memory wouldn't go away and that was when the goddess lent me calm and, in that calm, I saw her wisdom.

Yes, the memory was painful. But I realised she had sent it for a reason. Trying hard to ignore the crowds filing past behind me, I nosed along the last bit of high-rise fence before Laufala's security and the wasteland fence. I trailed a finger along the bricks pretending I was wandering along in a daze. The idiots in the crowd would be on their tech or focused on trying not to get trampled but I couldn't be too careful. A bit before the corner, my fingers touched air though it looked like fence.

It's still there!

Without checking if anyone was looking, I darted through the gap, flinching a bit because the holo looked so real. I turned on colour-dubbing but the place was dark during the day so whatever monitoring was there hadn't been able to build much of a picture.

The alleyway walls were narrow and the puddles on the broken concrete got deeper as I went further in. The air coming through my filters stunk of rotting things and I had to run my hand along the wall to find my way.

I felt the wet closeness of the walls more and more and they started closing in on me and I was shaking so hard I had to stop a few times to compose myself; or try to anyway. I gritted my teeth and called to the goddess for strength and wished to fuck I had my J™ with me as a backup plan given she was so bloody flaky on delivery half the time.

It seemed like half the night later by the time I hit the turning and saw the floodlights over the wasteland ahead. I made myself go slowly over the broken ground in case I tripped and broke a limb. And then I was through.

From the alley entrance, I could see the crowds spreading out in front of the high-rises at the edges of the open ground. Off in the other direction, drones swarmed, mostly newspires after the juicy footage probably. But I saw bigger red lights too; heavy construction kits already circling in for the kill.

Nobody had made it as close as me but the ground was filling up fast so it wouldn't be long. It was probably a thrill for half these people to be in the wasteland. In theory it was for me too since I was meant to be one of them now.

But I'm not. I'm really not.

I stepped away from the alley entrance before any of them got too close. When I looked behind me all I could see was tall block fencing. Then the crowd swallowed me and I fought my way back out to the edge to breathe. In the end, I would have liked to see it. Or… maybe I wouldn't? But there was no way I'd be able to breathe packed in with that many disgusting smelly poor people.

It's only a pissy man-made building getting destroyed.

Only men liked seeing things like this. Things getting smashed, things getting hurt. The goddess was all about creation. Yeah, fuck watching the show up close. I was there to mock the moron crowds.

But I couldn't stop hating myself for wondering whether Chen and Nate's friends were here and hoping they couldn't see me cowering against the wall as the demolition started. Were they sharing posh food they'd splurged on? Passing around Chen's flash J™ full of her real weed?

I could hear the crowd when it started and after I stopped shaking, I hooked into Yang's space to see the action. Sure enough, it looked like he had his whole fleet on the case.

The old house, which looked surprisingly run down given how rich those arseholes were, had started disappearing into dust. I turned down the feed volume. The sound was uncomfortably loud despite the distance. It was a disgusting noise like a million roaches eating through bone.

Across the wasteland, I could smell the wood from the house as the nanites tore it to dust. A cloud of them flowed up the house in that wrong kind of tech way and the roof and walls crashed in soon after. It was reduced to a pile of junk in a couple of minutes and I couldn't move for the shock of how fast it had disappeared.

Fifteen, sixteen, seventeen, eighteen — don't hide there, I can hear you! Go upstairs or something, dummy! — nineteen, twenty! Coming ready or not!

I stood frozen against the wall and the memory played on loop and I couldn't shut it out. It was only when the crowds ran for the edges of the wasteland like a fleeing herd of rats that I came unstuck. At first, I couldn't tell what was chasing them then I heard the sound over the wind. It was like a pancake with too much syrup being chewed too fast by a mouth the size of the island.

A second later, I saw something dark spreading from where the house had stood a minute or three before and covering the ground like a giant herpes scab. I flinched back as it crawled all the way to my feet and the sound got loud enough to make me cover my ears. Then the ground got darker and darker and a shadow grew over the sky, coming up from the street side and blotting out the drones.

I tensed again and then laughed at myself for being an idiot. It was only the construction beginning. The ground was darkening because the foundation had already been started. It sank deeper and blacker in minutes.

And from one second to the next I was bored. It was nothing anyone hadn't seen before on footage a thousand times. Construction tech crawling, landing, digging, whatever. It was like the house had never been there and now the place was only one more residential site going up. I was suddenly exhausted and decided to go home and vape an epic J™ to get me off to sleep.

Then there was a flash that nearly blinded me and everything stopped.

It was so sudden I wondered if maybe all the weed I'd been vaping had finally given me a brain tumour. But like thunder after lightning, the gormless oohs and ahs and wha'-was-thaaaaa's from the idiot-herd rolled around the edges of the hole so I knew it had really happened.

Yang had a caption rolling across the feed: Tech Mogul Tristian Laufala finally does something right.

It scrolled and scrolled across the silent scene and after a while the crowd got bored and started thinning out. Show over. I felt my way along the fence to the alleyway entrance and with my back to the morons, stepped carefully behind the holo to wait. Soon I was alone on the new building site.

Weird-shaped machines slept under the tarp canopy that had grown over the pit and the rain had started again. There were already orangey puddles – if my tech was guessing right, in the dark – around its edges where the construction nanites had left some of the clay from deeper down. There was something oddly peaceful about it and since the goddess was the Earth and the Sky, I wondered if it was being so close to all this dirt that caused it; though it was grubby and gross.

I was definitely whacked and desperate to head home but something about the silence spoke to me. By now I'd learned to recognise when the goddess was reaching out to me so I decided to look into the hole. I turned off colours to see in the most natural way possible and went forward.

Warnings pinged up as I moved under the tarp and snuck between the machines towards the edge. Don't touch this, careful when approaching that, blah blah blah. Like I cared about all the boring construction crap anyway. Bio-pellets, containers of industrial poisonous stuff I knew nothing about; all man junk. It said a lot about men that I had to squeeze through all their crap to get back to the earth which gave birth to all of us.

I leaned over the safety-for-retards barrier, more man junk, and looked in. I tried to focus my mind and sense the chakras in my body, knowing the goddess was near, that I should be able to sense Her this close, that I should revere this moment with the Mother and not care about my straining bladder.

I'm trying! It's so hard sometimes! Everything's so hard!

I told myself off for wishing I was at home with a pizza and another J™ then I told myself off for telling myself off and not staying calm and open to the goddess.

The rain intensified outside and I yawned inside my hood. Leaning over the barrier again, I squinted down. Something was definitely wrong but I couldn't—

Jesus! I can see the walls! Is it the goddess? Is she giving me some kind of super night vision?

I checked my tech. I'd definitely shut off my colour dubbing but I could see how smooth the sides of the pit were. I could see all the way to the bottom, where a blue glow was slowly fading in the far corner.

In a minute or so it had dimmed to black and I wasn't sure if I was seeing right but as the last of the strange light faded, something moved where it had been, coming out of the ground, moving up the side of the foundation pit like the tech that ate Laufala's house. Suddenly the goddess was the last thing on my mind.

I backed away and half walked, half ran around the machines and junk to get back to the edge of the site and away, piss leaking from my crotch as I went. I didn't think to check if I was heading the right way to the alleyway but I knew I had to follow the fences to find it anyway.

I turned colours back on but with or without them, there was too much rain and wind to run; and my bladder was far too full. So, I walked like I had a carrot up both orifices. The fence came at me through the rain and I tried looking around to see which way along it to walk and nearly face-planted when the toe of my overs-boot hit something soft and wrong-feeling. I looked down.

What the fuck?

Then I realised what the fuck and heaved.

Holy shit! Shit! Shit! Shit!

I turned away and bent over. I couldn't hold back the vomit. My hood melted back in time for a beige power-chuck to hit the mud and splatter up my overs' legs. My jaw strained, locked wide open and more spurts hit the dirt, spreading into a disgusting puddle in the rain.

Rain was running off the back of my hood by the time my stomach let me go and I could straighten up and that's when I felt the warm trickle down my leg.

Ugh! Double-shit!

Luckily it wasn't though. I clenched to stop the wee – only wee, thank fuck! – as well as I could and wiped my mouth with my sleeve then turned back to the tiny body, hoping it was some bullshit doll someone had left there or I hadn't seen right or something. But nope. I nearly heaved again and more drips escaped down below.

Jesus! I should call the police or… social services or, shit! Who? Who do you call for shit like this? Do I leave it here?

But I knew it would be found. The place was probably crawling with public tech, especially now it was about to turn into a new development. There might have been someone on the way to… sort it out or whatever, already. I stared down at it, wondering if it was really that red or if it was my crappy colour-dubbing.

I couldn't leave it there. There would probably be some kind of search. They would be able to tell I was here from my location tracking and there would be questions and it was probably illegal to leave it and then I'd be caught somehow, for something and Nate and I would both be in gaol.

But what would it look like if they turned up and I was here with it by myself? No, fuck it. I hadn't done anything wrong. I decided to call it in, to get my tech to send the one-one-one signal, everyone knew how, you just…

No way! No fucking way!

Way! It had moved. The thing moved! In the most wrong and gross possible way.

I froze staring down at it. Maybe I was seeing things but it did it again. Its skin moved, as if there was something inside it. It bubbled and blistered and flaked off and I thought it was getting eaten by tech, which it might have been. Maybe someone had illegal recycling tech and this was how they got rid of their miscarriage. But why? Why would anyone do that? It wasn't illegal to have a miscarriage! Not to mention how sick that would be on so many levels!

After a while I relaxed and though the thing kept moving in its disgusting way, I realised whatever it was doing, it wasn't being eaten away.

I knew it must be some experiment that someone had ditched or lost or something. This couldn't be legal. I should definitely have called it in. I should have called it in straight away but then I wasn't sure if whoever I got on one-one-one would make me wait here. I was tired and I wanted to go home.

I bent and picked it up and dropped it again straight away. It was actually warm! Like a body with plague, burning up. It wasn't only that though. It was that it was also alive. I knew it was anyway but to actually feel it like that.

Ew ew ew ew!

I decided I'd call it in from home. It wouldn't be a crime. I'd tell them where I found it. They would be able to check, whoever they were. And it was always possible the weed was making me see things. Maybe when I got home and made a cup of Instant™ and looked at it in proper light it would be a doll covered in dirt and roaches after all. Although… I didn't feel that stoned any more.

This time I was ready for the freaky heat and skin feeling. It stayed curled up, unmoving, when I picked it up in one hand and carried it away. I could have got my overs to make a pouch for it but couldn't stand the idea of having it close to my body and the weather didn't seem to have stopped it doing… whatever weird experimental thing it was doing, so far anyway.

I found the goddess' alleyway and walked carefully so I didn't drop it in a puddle. I could feel its skin moving through my overs and it got hotter as I walked.

After a while when I worked out all it was going to do was the weird skin thing, I calmed more and it was easier to walk. I made it through the alleyway with only a few little panics and a tiny stumble. I'd turned the corner on to the old Campbell when the thing suddenly moved like a normal baby and I panicked and nearly dropped it again.

I waited but it didn't do it again, not until I started walking. Its arms and legs twitched and wouldn't stop though it didn't uncurl.

The crowds were long gone by then. The streets were quiet; you'd never guess the island was overcrowded. Ubers sped past now and again and splashed me as they drove through drainage overflow.

I wondered if I should put the freak baby in my overs after all, in case I was recorded going home. But firstly, it was too late and secondly, I wasn't doing anything wrong, fuck it!

By the time I arrived, I was shattered and I could have sworn the thing was burning up in my hands. I was going to put it on my bed but I didn't like the idea of it touching my duvet and sheet so I made a pile of dirty clothes on my desk and put it there instead.

Under the lights, it looked pretty much the same as my tech had guessed in the dark except its skin colour. It was wrinkly and curled up. Its little arms and legs twitched and its eyes were closed. It was like the pictures of normal babies growing in incubators we got shown at basic school. It had a few dark hairs on its head and its skin was reddish black.

Jesus! Is it bigger now?

I shivered.

All over its body, the skin kept puffing up, rippling and flaking away and now I had it in the quiet, my skin really crawled because it was making a gross weird meaty squishing noise too quiet for me to have heard outside. As I watched, its wrinkly little arms and legs twitched and flakes of its dry skin floated off it and landed on my dirty clothes. Shaking, I went to make myself an Instant™.

Though it had all but warn off, the weed was probably helping me stay calm. Building sites growing out of the ground were normal and in a way this thing moved like tech did. But somehow, I didn't think it was tech.

I needed the toilet but I was a scared to leave it alone. It wriggled and squelched away quietly on the pile of clothes as I sipped my Instant™ and eventually, I told myself I'd have to go sometime.

I could see it from the toilet and it gave me stage-fright. But I knew if I let the door close, I'd lock up worse so I did my best and my trickle paused every time the clothes rustled when it moved, marring the relief I normally savoured.

I had to look straight at it when I went to get my J™ from the desk. The clothes around it were going white with skin dust.

Gross-gross-gross-gross-GROSS!

Then I remembered I had to call it in. I found the one-one-one handle; there exactly as we'd been shown in basic school. But as I was about to ping it, I remembered the ingot of nanites and panicked. I knew they'd come from the goddess. But what if whoever turned up found them? It would probably be a man and he probably wouldn't believe me because men were stupid and didn't believe things like that.

I'd be fucked. I could hide them somewhere else, outside or something but what if someone found them? I couldn't risk it. And I was exhausted. I'd have to sleep on it and work out what to do in the morning.

I took a last look at the thing in its pile of white dust and clothes. Though it was creepy and gross I didn't think it would-like, escape. I turned off the lights and got undressed for bed. I didn't think I'd be able to sleep with it rustling and making its meaty noises but the next thing I knew, grey light was coming through the window.

My brain felt empty. I lay in bed and slowly remembered the night before, the old house, the construction site, what a child I'd been panicking. The idea of pancakes and a cup of Instant™ snuck into my brain and called louder and louder and my stomach started answering it. I got up and froze when I saw what was on my desk and memory crashed in.

'Fuck!' I jumped back, tripped and bashed myself on the wall.

I got up rubbing the back of my head where a lump was forming.

The desk and the little clothes nest I'd made were covered in white dust. On top of the whole lot, with his head flopping over one end and his arms and legs spread out was a whole baby boy. He was far bigger than he had been the night before and his skin was smoother and completely black. His head was fully covered in dark straight hair.

I stood gawking at him like a loser from last night's crowd. His skin bubbled and flaked. But now there was no question about what was happening. He was growing. He'd been growing the whole time; no food, no cord, nothing.

I couldn't take my eyes off him. I hadn't seen a real live baby before, only stills and holos. But I was sure that skin-colour wasn't normal. Most people were sort of pale or olive or brown like Nate. Chen was one of those freak throwbacks but she wasn't as dark as this.

I watched his skin move and now I was looking properly, as in not stonedly, I could see how the bubbling was coming from underneath. The top layer bubbled up, dried and flaked off and each new one did the same; right in front of me!

That's when I knew this wasn't tech. This wasn't some bullshit man experiment. This was nature, Earth power. He had been sent to me by the goddess. It all fell into place. That was why I'd waited for the crowds to go and the quiet site had given me the weird— uh, auspicious, sense of calm. And it was why nobody else had found him too; because he hadn't been there until it was time.

The light in the hole and the thing I'd seen moving nagged at my memory but it didn't matter. It had probably been some crappy tech thing; unrelated. This was what mattered, a child of the Earth sent to me by the goddess to care for. His purpose would come in time but for now I must keep him safe and take care of him.

It was a sign that I was right when he opened its eyes, saw me and screamed. Babies did that when they were born, didn't they? Seeing me was his true birth.

Still, I couldn't stop myself looking around in case anyone heard though I knew they couldn't have. I had no idea what to do with a baby let alone a screaming one, goddess-sent or not, so it was lucky he stopped and bit his little lip as if he was embarrassed. If I wasn't so scared I'd gone numb, it might have been cute.

His eyes moved and he looked like he was taking the place in and actually thinking, like he wasn't only a baby. He tried to move his head and look around but his neck was weak so instead of lifting his head, he could only roll it around to face me from the pile of dust.

This time he didn't scream but I would have rathered he had because the noise he started making then was creepy, sort of, 'khuk, khuk, khuk', like he was trying to talk but his mouth couldn't make the words. I shivered and stared back and I could have sworn he looked disappointed I couldn't understand him though I knew it was impossible.

Surely my goddess-given instincts were meant to… trigger? My intuition and mothering skills and all that… shit? That was why the goddess had sent him to me wasn't it? But nothing came and I stood and stared until I was calm enough to decide that maybe sometimes, the goddess helped those who helped themselves.

I braced myself for the awful freaky feeling and picked him up. He was so hot I was surprised he was alive. And he squirmed like a giant rat. The feeling of his muscles moving made my skin crawl but I held on and carried him to my bed because I thought it would be wrong to dump a baby on the floor. I put him down, yanked my hands away and wiped them on my hemps. I was worried moving so abruptly would frighten him and make him cry but he did his head-roll thing and stared at me making his creepy talking noises.

Digging my clothes out of the pile of dust made me feel ill and when I went to shake them out on the floor, I discovered they were ruined. Everything was all laddered and transparent and there were holes with black and brown around the edges like burns and they weren't self-repairing. Weren't hemps treated with special gunk to make them fireproof? Not that I'd smelled any burning. I wondered if the dust he was making was harmful and suddenly realised it was all over me.

'Fuck-fuck-fuck-fuck-fuck!' I said and stripped to my bra and underpants to shake everything out.

Food. Babies need food, don't they?

It didn't seem to have stopped him so far but I couldn't think of anything else to do. I got an I™-spoon and opened a bottle of Total™. I felt ill and couldn't stop shaking getting my hands near his grotty gooey little mouth. Thankfully, as soon as a dribble of Total™ ran over his lips he figured it out. He opened up and nearly swallowed the spoon. Even a man would have been able to interpret the look he gave me then: more!

I spooned the whole bottle into him and he didn't stop asking with his eyes.

'Okay, more? I can do more.' I had a few bottles stockpiled so I opened another and by the time it was half drunk, he was starting to push the spoon away and grab at the bottle. I held it while the Total™ trickled into his mouth and he drank faster and faster. By the end of the bottle, he was holding it tighter than I would have thought those little hands should be able to; except they weren't as little any more.

Holy fuck!

The food was making him grow faster. I could see him getting bigger. I got him another bottle and watched as he learned to hold on to it by himself in two minutes flat. Another bottle and he was sitting up and I could definitely tell he was talking to me but I couldn't understand a word he was saying.

But the goddess is ancient; more than ancient. He's probably speaking a sacred language.

'More?' I asked. My heart was hammering. He was going to eat me out of house and home and what if he changed into some kind of creature or something when he got to a certain size.

But I told myself to stay calm and trust the goddess. She was making this happen. She wouldn't have sent me something evil. Look at Nate. He was male and he wasn't evil, only a bit of a ponce with his head in the clouds like most men. This little man would be the same. I packed the J™ to ask for guidance but none came. I felt a bit calmer though. Or more numb anyway.

I couldn't help feeling scared as he grew while I watched but I was getting used to it.

'More?' I asked again, pointing to the Total™.

He stopped talking and looked at me then over at my Total™ stash. He made a long weird mmmmmoooo sound.

'Yeah, I know it's good, mmm, mmm, mmm. You want more? More?'

'More,' he said.

'Fuckin'-'ell!' I squealed like a caught rat and froze.

'More,' he said. And then I saw he'd learned to point.

Okay, keep calm. Keep calm. This is meant to happen. She will keep me safe.

I got him more and this time he snatched the bottle from my hand and opened it himself. Two bottles later and he was a naked little boy with straight black hair past his shoulders and a weird-shaped face with big lips and super-round dark eyes. He wriggled to the side of the bed and put his legs down then pushed himself off. He landed on his feet then fell flat on his bum but didn't cry like a child should.

He made a sharp sound I couldn't have copied but I was pretty sure meant, 'shit!' Then he grumbled. He grumbled like a grandpa only it sounded so wrong because it was in a tiny boy's voice.

He tried to push himself up and I didn't think he'd make it because his arms were so weak. But as he tried, he kept growing – visibly! – and soon he was standing up and toddling over to the bench.

He was too short to reach the Total™ but instead of Hollywooding at me like a normal child, he leaned on the cupboards and made a noise like thank fuck that's over, now I'm knackered. Then he looked at me and pointed up

'More,' he said. This time he sounded like me, his own voice maybe but my tone, my accent!

Wrong, wrong, wrong!

He stood with his skin bubbling and flaking to the floor and though I knew it was the goddess' power making it all happen, it was like nothing I'd ever seen before. I couldn't help wondering, how. So what if I never got my basic PhD. I wasn't dumb.

People needed food to grow and heal. And I knew there were reasons it couldn't happen this fast. And if it could – which it couldn't! – nothing came from nothing. If his skin was flaking off then the new skin must have been coming from somewhere, or why would the goddess make that part happen and not the other?

Though I knew this was right and that it was happening for a reason, I couldn't stop the tightness in my stomach from spreading and the room from getting smaller. But although my panic was rising, I didn't miss the chance.

The boy kept asking for more and starting to look angry so I got a few bottles of Total™ off the bench and put them down beside him. He got the first one opened and picked it up but spilled it on himself when he tried to tip it back. At least that would slow him down. I left him to it.

I went into my private feed and uploaded everything from when I'd found him until now to TrueLife™ for verification. It accessed my tech and did its creepy shit with my logs to make sure the content was real then sent it back to me with the spinning holo of truth on every bit and byte.

Yes!

Not that it wouldn't have, considering it was all real but it felt good for some reason. I time-lapsed it all and dumped it in the Movement space. I did a quick voiceover.

'The time is near. The goddess has sent us…

Of course!

I'd read about it all and only remembered it now. The Sky's power was controlled by the Earth goddess because he was too much of a dumbarse man to know how to work it properly himself. Why hadn't I clicked before? The angry power of the Sky had been yielded up from the Earth in human form by Her and sent to me. As if there'd been any doubt, this was absolute proof that I was the voice of the goddess on Earth. I was her vessel!

'…Rangi, god of the Sky, has returned to the Earth in the flesh and his power will be mine to guide and use. Once he has fully taken his form, together we will bring down the rich-fucks, even the odds and fix the world!'

I submitted the sub-handle to Jamie Yang's space.

Suck on that you trashy fuck. TrueLife™ enough for you, now?

By the time I finished, Rangi was standing in a disgusting white pile of dust and guzzling the last of his – my – Total™s.

The top of his head peaked above the bench and he could nearly reach the bottles by himself.

He didn't care about the ones on the floor melting down and flowing away. He kept ou-moi-nguy-khuk'ing away in his sacred language and grabbing for the food. As I watched, he got big enough to reach it and that's when I noticed my stack had really started to shrink and I suddenly remembered the parts of my life that were to do with my body and not the goddess inhabiting it, or the god She had sent me.

I had a megaton of money, or I could get it if I sold the tiniest fraction of the holy ingot of nanites, let alone the whole thing. Sure, the ingot was the goddess' gift to the Movement. But I was Her emissary on Earth and I must live if I was going to spread Her message.

Work would keep paying the rent and my derisory retainer and I could afford all the climate control, washes, water, power and evil corporation-contrived building fees they'd stopped shelling out for now I had no shifts. So I could easily stay in my flat. Except there was nowhere for Rangi to sleep, if he did sleep? And anyway, around here was all dry-foots and pathetic wannabe dry-foots like Chen. Much as the idea made me ill, if I was going to do the Movement, I needed to be among the goddess' people.

Being the pooey agency's client instead of their crappy corporate slave was priceless. I was all ready to give them an overall one-star rating after buying their ponciest two-bed apartment, for the fun of fucking them off. Then for some reason, I remembered all the times I'd whinged about how I couldn't afford washes, water and more clothes. And how Nate or whoever I was whinging to, had shrugged, stayed quiet and not met my eye.

Jesus!

Had I given myself away from day one? But fuck them all. I could never talk to Chen again and we both knew it. Nate was never coming back whatever anyone thought. Shane was dead. I had Rangi now. I would follow my own path and change the world. Nobody said it would be easy.

Down in Newmarket I might have had half a chance of affording something to rent but there was no stock to buy or rent or anything. If I'd paid more attention to all the viewings I'd nearly slept through, I might have seen where they were all buying and selling and known where to look but… Actually, I could anyway.

Rangi was standing at the bench guzzling his way through my food and I barely recognised him now. He'd grown nearly as tall as me and his legs and arms looked too skinny for his naked body.

His hair was below his shoulders and I could see his bones under his skin and he was looking more like a scary weird-skinned man than a child. The floor was covered in white flakes of dead skin around his feet. More of it was drifting down and landing on the bench and I shivered as I watched his skin bubble and more flakes peel off.

Don't turn around. Don't turn around. Don't turn around.

But I squashed the stupid earthly thought and my pathetic mortal fear of seeing his silly little willy. For fuck's sake, it wasn't like I hadn't seen a penis before. I flicked off an order for a few more boxes of Total™. As long as he was only standing around guzzling I could get on with everything else. I had no idea what he'd do if he stopped.

Turning up the agency space, I looked through 'my' sales history and couldn't believe what I saw.

I mean, it's close enough to the poor parts isn't it?

I chuckled to myself and wondered who the unlucky sod was that got my last-minuter.

Who cares!

And then it was done and the next morning I was luring Rangi into an Uber with Total™s, feeling like everything was happening to me rather than me making it happen.

Rangi – late Nov 2097, From Cornwall Estate to Beachlands Hill, Akarana Island, Aotearoa Archipelago

I had healed before but not so much as this. The chill of the fusing burned through my soul as never before. No injury could have been so mortal that its healing should have felt so unending, surely it could not! Yet though much time passed, my body stayed weak and my thoughts unclear. And so my first moments were a chaos of memories I did not enjoy.

A long time of healing passed in an agony of pleasure and my surroundings revealed themselves to me but slowly. In an evil mockery of sun and moon, strange lights waxed and waned on the walls of a tiny cave made of dread lines and corners not of Earth and Sky.

As sights and noises grew clear in my mind, the place imposed itself upon me as if to mock me with its realness. I knew then that I could be nowhere between Earth and Sky but instead in some spirit-world, brought here in the time between.

Between what?

But soon the cave began to shrink and I became aware of a presence. In the murk and chaos of swirling memories, warm hands lifting and carrying me floated and my soul sensed though my mind could not grasp the knowing, those hands had brought me here. A spirit – for that was all I could imagine her to be with the swirls of glittering grey like fell mould on her pale face and her yellow hair like tiny thorns poking through her skull, and the strange dark coverings she wore – tended to me with the demeanour of an angry fish. Though I spoke, she did not answer, only fed me with a cold rounded stick that glinted like the swirls on her skin.

She poured my sustenance from a strange soft pot made of no substance I had ever encountered. Though at first its fell sweetness was cloying and its angry orange, the colour of poison toadstools in the forest, disturbing, I soon formed a taste for it. I drank it down hungrily though as I did, I felt it binding its evil tithe to the moorings of my soul in my flesh.

I was filled with foreboding of what it might ask in return for the strength it gave me and yet I could not but crave the nourishment it gave to my healing flesh. My eyes and ears sharpened ever more quickly though my heart quailed at what was to come when the spirit food called in its due.

I should not be here. Something is wrong.

The smells of the spirit world made themselves known to me presently and amongst them at least numbered night-water and night-soil and so I knew the spirit was not entirely unlike me. Those first pain and pleasure-wracked healing moments in her domain were confusing and short-lived.

Even as my body strengthened and the spirit and her cave shrank more quickly, she channelled Flow and bade me follow her through the hole in the cave wall that she had caused to open before us like a wilting flower peeling back and crumbling to nothing.

Ethel – late Nov 2097, Cornwall Hill, Akarana Island, Aotearoa Archipelago

'Tell me we have people in that blessed building company, for pity's sake Darrin!' It was the morning after old Laufala's house had been taken down. I'd watched it and hardly slept after that; for various reasons. Darrin had answered my urgent summons through the machines and come up to my home to discuss the matter.

'Yeah, Mum, we do but—'

'Well, why have you not got me that… whatever it jolly well is then, Boyo?'

'We'll get it Mum. It's tricky. They've got a research team looking at it and it's all top secret and stuff.'

'For goodness' sake Darrin! I'm interested in solutions, not problems! Haven't you got someone on their jolly research team? Someone who can at least tell us what the blessed thing is?'

Though I was sure I already knew.

'Almost. One of their management's feeling, uh, ill today so our person is going to step in. She should be able to take it over from there and the, uh, sickness might last a while so…'

'Well, that is something I suppose. You're not only a dishy body after all.'

'Mum! Ew!'

I sighed and pulled on some unders, hemp slacks and top. I was tired of shouting through to him in the lounge but the silly prude refused to come into my room unless I was dressed. He ought to have though, he might have learned something. I was beginning to wonder whether the boy did anything but work. Such a waste!

'Mum, um, if you don't mind me asking—'

'I do Dear, but go on.'

Poor thing looked hurt but he forged on anyway. 'What's so, um, important about this? I mean, it's only going to be some piece of electrical junk from the olden days or something.'

'Well, Darrin, I happen to be very interested in things from olden days. They, er, fill me with nostalgia.'

'Yeah, okay, well, I was only asking. But… I dunno. Zhang's company will get bored of it won't they? Put it online and sell it off if it's worth anything? Couldn't we wait and buy it off them later?'

In a way he was right. The wrench in my gut and gust of unsettling memories that had roiled through my soul, nearly doubling me over after the great flash was all the confirmation I needed. But I wanted to get my hands on the artefact nonetheless. I needed to know for sure.

And I'm lonely. So lonely! What if Healer…

I had been unsurprised when Victoria had contacted me to report deeper rumblings than ever before moments later, though nothing had yet come of those.

'Mum?'

'Sorry Dear, I couldn't sleep. No. We cannot wait!'

'But—'

'No! Darrin. I need it now! Is that clear?'

'Yes, Mum.'

'Good then, now why don't you work that contraption you gave me for Winter-Christmas, er, Thing-festival that time and make us some coffee. How about some pancakes, too? I don't know about you but I haven't had breakfast and I'm jolly famished.'

'Okay Mum. Jimmie gave it to you but—'

'Yes, yes! For heaven's sake Dear, stop being so difficult! Go on, get some coffee on.'

'I have, Mum, look, it's coming now.'

And so it was though I would never grow used to the dreadful inedible insects that did everything for everyone these days. Including whining in, mosquito-like, with trays hanging beneath them like rectangular jolly egg sacs.

'Very clever, and I suppose the pancakes are nearly here, too, are they?'

'Oh, uh, yup, sorry, forgot, I'll do it now.'

'Good boy. Now, tell me what you've been up to my son. Outside work, I mean. It's been so long since we could talk as mother and son, don't you think?'

'Uh, yeah Mum. My, uh, kid, Petey turns twenty-one this weekend and we were wondering—'

A man with a child. Priceless! And so gullible!

The poor thing. I managed to keep the smile from my face. 'Oh, Dear! That's wonderful! And it is your child? You're certain?'

'Mum! We've been through—'

'Yes, yes, I know Dear. I can't come though, anyway. I'm very busy.'

Nor would I waste time celebrating another woman's grandchild aging. I had more than enough of my own to worry about.

He knew better than to argue at least. 'Okay, Mum. No worries.'

The pancakes arrived in their devilish living box and I sipped my coffee as we ate, wishing it would fight my exhaustion as the young ones so praised it for doing. Like all such things, it had no effect on me but to screw up my face at its bitter flavour.

Darrin regaled me with tales of his… partner and children. It seemed he did more than work after all though barely, given he only mentioned the one woman; I was yet amazed the fad endured; somewhat, anyway. And I wondered if she felt the same way as him. If she was anything like me, she could not have.

Still, with their ridiculous contrivance of a life, I supposed they were adequately distracted to maintain the conceit. When they were not working, the latest baby was interrupting their sleep.

Centuries of inurement to the advancing rot of humanity could not altogether stifle the creeping revulsion that stole over me as he spoke of their home and the children – only three of them for pity's sake! What if some died? Their elaborate system of 'taking turns getting up for the baby', baffled me. What did he do? Suckle at his woman's breast and spit it into the baby's mouth like a bird feeding its chick? Oh, I knew he didn't. I knew, I knew, I knew…

But it revolted me, the way people threw their newborns into boxes then climbed in after them never to emerge again but for deliveries on devilish steel wings. Within such confines, did they not take against each other like dopey cats in a loose sack? Did they not claw and gouge one another with their words and churlish acts of passive sleep-deprived aggression? How could two people be enough to care for one infant let alone three growing children. How could two people know enough to teach children about the world? Well, there were the machines but that only made it worse.

Back in my long-lost day, new-borns slept beside their mothers and if one set of breasts ran dry there was always another oozing painfully about nearby. Children had taken care of one other for the most part.

Our babies had clung to us with the elder ones frolicking along as we gathered berries, seeds and grubs and so they had learned. They had splashed in red puddles, delighting in the rain, rough-housing with one-another to learn the skills of fighting and hunting and making peace. And if one fell from a tree and smashed its skull, well then, it would be a lesson to the others, would it not?

A little instruction here and there. A little nudge in the direction of knowledge or away from the cookfire. And protection from the heat and the cold and the beasts of the forest or the enemy that might attack in the night was all we needed give them. And any jolly adult could do any of it.

That! That was family!

I fell into a pleasant daze, sedated by the nostalgia Darrin had stirred up in me. And it was as well that he had though I wished he had not. For as my pleasant memories flowed over his voice, all but drowning it out, someone else's memories awoke. A babble of madness had erupted in my soul after the flash and kept me from sleep for the rest of the night. And now from the chaos, that other's memories emerged and set my heart racing and my blood roaring in my ears.

Recognition shivered through me when I realised, I had fallen down and through my own happy recollections into visions of red earth, caves and a river through a forest as remembered by another. Another whose memories had not murmured in the waking world since more than six millennia ago.

Once sealed, we had believed the prisms of the wasted impregnable and inescapable; so that loathsome creature Rock had told us, so long ago. No fall from the sky on to rocks, fire or ice that we had tested them against had so much as scratched their fire-rock sheaths and thus his oleaginous assurances were born out. But now it seemed, time had made fools of us all and one of the wasted was free again.

And what do you say to that, Rock? Wherever you are.

Nothing, I hoped. For if I never saw that creature again it would be too soon.

Rock – late Nov 2097, Rock's Tower, Germany

Ja, because there were things, even I was afraid of. It was late in ice-cold November in Germany when the shivering came into *mein* body. And perhaps a day later, a most fascinating collection of memories making noise in the shared psychic space of the fusing. Fascinating and super concerning.

Shcheisse! Impossible! This is impossible!

I turned to the shelves to check the colleagues but they sat quietly and neatly in their places, the black surfaces of their prisms smooth and shiny with not a single tiny crack. If it was not for me and *mein* exceptional brain, such prisms would not have been invented. And the mad ones, the wasted as they came to be called, would be free and out generating destruction all these centuries.

That would have been inconvenient for *mein* research, like having the elephant in the laboratory the size of a planet. That was why I helped the others trap them all those centuries ago.

It demonstrated what spear-throwing primitives *mein* colleagues were despite the fantastic opportunity of our existence, how they let me collect the prisms and keep them for research. All except one who kept her little friend with her, like the fad of keeping human ashes in a pot; as crazy as it was intriguing.

Before that, long centuries of patient observation had taught me how to simulate the function of friendship and I hoped Bud would give up the prism so I remained connected to her as if we were friends, easily making the trick on her. But always she kept it and both of us got busy and in time I lost track of her.

I recalled her. Strong and full bodied but not so clever. Not good at languages; already struggling to understand her descendants by the time the wasted appeared. But somehow not so stupid either, like a squid or a good dog, perhaps.

So where are you ending up, mein little Bud?

Rangi – late Nov 2097, Beachlands Hill,

Akarana Island, Aotearoa Archipelago

There were too many strange things for my thoughts to hold. Though I felt it was morning in the usual knowing that comes with the slant of shadows, the sky hung dark and dread mosquitos with red eyes like devil-cats swarmed on the wind and I quailed at their fell whining. Still, they did not come for us, some device of my spirit-guide's no doubt.

Though in the coming days I would think on all that happened in those first addled times, my thoughts would never gain a good hold. So many things. Too many things. A creature of the spirit world with round legs she tamed and bade form an opening in its side. I remembered shrinking in upon myself as I climbed into its belly after her, hoping it would not snap shut like a devil's mouth and crush us into itself.

Could I be made wasted in this land? From what foul remnants would I heal? Or would it keep eating me away, sustaining itself forever on the unending bounty it had stumbled upon?

And as my quaking at the thought eased, I saw the pictures on the cave wall move and change and shrank into myself anew. Yet we came to no harm and soon I had taken hold of myself enough to touch the moving pictures and found nothing but some horror of cool smoothness in their place. And then we were in another place. Another cave, a rat!

I caught it and ate it, a taste of home, made strange yet miraculous by the strangeness of the place! And yet another hole that closed after we entered, made a light sickness in my belly as I chewed my catch, then opened in another place.

And all the while, I beseeched the spirit, 'What is this place? Who are you? What are these things? What is happening? How did I come here?'

But she rarely answered and so was born in my heart a deep and strange yearning for her regard. For this was her world. She could keep the mosquitos at bay, bring us safely from place to place through the twists and turns of devilment of which this world was made. Wherever she was, so were the pots of orange paste. And though angry and sullen, she tended to me and shielded me from the myriad freakish harms I did not doubt this world beyond Earth and Sky could work upon me.

I tried to copy the sharp and angry words she barked out at me and found it to be easy. Ah but that trick had always come easily to me; the one edge I had ever possessed over that damnably sly longest-time bed-mate of mine…

Bud? What of Bud? Could she be here?

I would think on it later. In the meantime, I would learn this new speech as I had learned the changing speech of generations of our people through the ages since the fusing. And then she would regard me highly, like a mother when her son returns laden with meat from his first hunt. I would hunt for words and bring them to this strange pale mother. But later, for my soul burned yet with the ice of healing.

At last, it eased and my hunger ebbed away. I found myself looking out over water and saw that this world too had oceans, as had the one I had…

Left behind?

I remembered…

Kozan island? Flying back over the sea to the mainland… The hunt…

But my soul shuddered back from the wall those memories whispered through. I could not – must not! – think on them. Yet they tugged at me like Shades in the night and all I could do to keep them at bay was sit on my haunches and fill my mind with the water and the darkening sky beyond the devilish wall of the cave.

It was then that the treachery of this crazed new world revealed itself. For as the water soothed my heart and slowed my spinning thoughts, the cave wall faded to the colour of wet earth, then of night, then to a foul blackness the like of which I had never seen. The water and sky had been a trick and as darkness beyond darkness reached for me, the other walls blazed with light and I turned to see the spirit's wicked grin.

'Why?' I asked. 'Why torment me so?'

And she said nothing and I could see her eyes change as she fled into her thoughts.

I turned back to the blackness and it came to me then how like the fire-rock sheaths of the gemstone prisms of the wasted this substance was. And so I tested its nature and found I could channel Flow through it as if it were air.

So it is not fire-rock.

And then I wondered if the spirit slept as men and women from my world slept and I hid my face from her and waited and was rewarded.

Tina – late Nov 2097, Beachlands Hill,

Akarana Island, Aotearoa Archipelago

The trip was awful. There was too much sea, too near the Uber the whole way there. The seawalls in the distance looked useless, like strings of dirty floating jelly though I knew they reached the bottom and only looked small because they were so far away. The Mount Wellington bridge scared the life out of me because I knew there was nothing between me and the water but pathetic man-made bridge.

Rangi kept saying 'more' and pointing at my bio-case where the last few Total™s were packed up with the holy nanite ingot, my clothes, mugs and I™-spoons, my J™ and the epic sack of weed I'd bought before we left.

White dust was falling all over the Uber seat around Rangi and I hoped the Uber wouldn't charge me for cleaning.

Why do I care if it does? I'm loaded.

Before I would have been panicked by the speed at which it guzzled money as it drove but now I was minted, I only thought, *typical,* and not much more than that.

Rangi wasn't growing so fast now I wasn't feeding him, but fast enough. His hair was halfway down his back, his legs were weedy and nearly as long as mine. The spare hemps I'd finally got him to wear – and that he was probably eating away with his poison skin flakes, or whatever it was – were too big, but no longer by much.

As we drove over the bridge, I could see down to the channel between the Akarana Island and Auckland South. Near Manukau West, the seawall curved inland and ran along the high-rises by the water.

Where it hit the land, it changed from the jelly stuff to the cheap wet-foot version of active-alloy. I'd heard the stories and ignored the news vlogs so seeing the bits that had crumbled away and not repaired themselves made me shiver and look away.

Should I really be moving out here?

Stairs went up the wall by each block and there was a walkway along the top for weirdos like Nate. The steps were covered in dirty blue cracks which weren't self-repairing. Anyone who tried to go up them would probably break their neck when the concrete crumbled out from under them.

From the water over the wall, the tops of old buildings stuck up and bits of disgusting plastic and junk floated on black water all the way out to sea. Further out, I caught glimpses of the New Islands through the sheeting rain.

Dive that it was, Manukau West was the flash side; down at the coast anyway. I could have afforded two or three of the apartments down there. But looking at all 'my' sales stats had given me a better idea. The Uber headed east before the bottom of the hill and drove me through half an hour's worth of blocks that cycled through slums, okay-ish and death-trap depending on how high up we were.

Rangi hit his knuckles on the window when he tried to stick his hand out, then he stroked it and licked it when he worked out there was something there. He stopped asking for Total™ and gawked out at the sea then shuffled over and looked up the hills going past on the other side.

I could see the mega-rich people's blocks high in the hills with windows so big I'd have been able to see through them if they weren't switched to one-way. Our Uber stuck to the coast, its routeing probably biased by corporate-corrupted algos so the rich wouldn't have to see us and lose their lunches knowing wet-foots were near and getting frightened they might catch bankruptcy off us or some shit like that.

We drove around the headland until all I could see out one side was sea and islands in the distance. I shivered and turned my head inland but it wasn't much better. The high-rises above me looked as if they'd dropped out of the sky on top of each other, and I couldn't help worrying that they might fall the rest of the way any minute. I started panicking so much Rangi noticed and looked at me oddly.

Some of the ones down by the seawall were floors-deep in water because all that was left of the walls behind them had crumbled to rubble. Worse, there were lights on right down to a few floors above the water and when our Uber slowed to turn up the hill, I saw the locals in one place had taken bits of dead seawall concrete and piled it up to make a dodgy access-way to some smashed-in windows on the second floor.

The seawall kept most of the water out behind the building opposite the street we turned up next, but I could see it was in much better condition further down. I was glad I was on the way to a better life than all that.

The street got dark with high-rises as we climbed. At the top, we pulled into the curb in front of an entrance most people only dreamed of going through. I was glad I wasn't most people and that there weren't any of them around to see me not look twice at the real plants under glass in front of the building entrance and head in; or try to, anyway.

'Come on Rangi!' I said.

He'd stopped to try reaching through the glass to the plants and sniff at it as if he wanted to smell the leaves or something. There was no harm in it and we weren't in a hurry. But despite our elevation, the gross sucking and splashing noises of the sea nearly froze me up. Its poisonous salty rotten smells made my stomach clench in nausea.

If the rain had still been pouring, if there'd been the sound of drones and traffic to block it out, I might have composed myself quicker. But the silence only made it sound louder and nearer. Typical useless man, Rangi didn't so much as offer to carry the bio-case as we went inside.

I couldn't help sighing as I walked into the hallway. The ceiling was so high and the lights so bright against the smooth white walls, I didn't feel like it was closing in on me. Rangi wasn't phased by any of it. He followed me around like a postal carrier minus the usefulness.

I pinged the building and discovered work had done something right when they'd sold the place to me, at least. They'd got me set up on the block system. If I hadn't been tired, hungry and jumping at shadows, I would have laughed at how cheesy the building online space was. It was like an advert for itself. You could turn on overlays so it was as if you were walking down a forest path and I had to dim it right down to stop memories lighting up.

Even if the bio-case hadn't been killing my arms by the time we rounded the last corner before the lift, I would have dropped it and tried to disappear inside the wall anyway. Everything seemed to freeze and I had a second to see what I thought at first was a giant roach right in the middle of the hallway.

But it was too big and furry, and it didn't have enough legs for a roach though it was a similar colour. Its whole whiskery pointed face twitched and it stared at me with its awful little creature eyes. Its thin pink tail moved like it was another animal growing out of the first and it was that which nearly stopped my heart and made me heave.

Then when Rangi came around the corner, the world unfroze and it came at us. It happened so fast I couldn't tell how it flew. All I remembered was its awful squeaking noise and its waving legs and tail as it shot through the air towards us.

I threw up my hands and it made a short blood-curdling squeal that was too loud for its size. Then everything went quiet. I lowered my hands slowly and saw Rangi holding something and quickly turned away.

'Come on,' I said, keeping my face turned. 'Let's go.'

I had to get out of there before the bright clean walls closed in and I lost my calm. I tried to take deep breaths and picked up the case. I pinged the lift but when the doors opened, big and clean as it was, I worried I wouldn't survive the journey. When the doors closed and it started moving, I held my breath, as much to stop myself melting down as to keep the awful burned smell out of my lungs.

I wasn't a complete dope. I knew the thing was probably – almost certainly – a rat and I knew they were as grubby and gross as roaches. But I didn't know they could fly.

They can't, can they?

I tried not to think about it but the glimpse of red, pink and black I'd seen in Rangi's hand kept flashing up like an ad. I fiddled with my bio-case handle and tried not to look at him except I couldn't stop noticing his skin flakes floating to the floor around us.

There soon, there soon, there soon.

Hearing him stop chewing was nearly worse than him doing it in the first place. Now all I could hear was the lift climate control and the soft gooey squelch of Rangi growing faster with something in his stomach. I put my hands over my ears and faced the doors. I tried to think of boring things like ordering Total™s when we got in and what the new flat would be like.

But the memory of charred, smoking rat's guts in my head kept barging in. And that was nothing compared to how the smoky fatty smell Rangi'd brought into the lift with us made my stomach rumble. It couldn't smell that good. It wasn't allowed.

And how did it burn? How?

There were too many things I didn't want to think about. After forever and a day, the lift stopped and it was nearly worth the few minutes of panic to see the cute little look on Rangi's face when the door melted open at the forty-second.

His little eyes went wide and he looked at me as if to say, uh, what happened? But he got me back. Everything about him not making sense came back with a vengeance when I noticed that now I had to look up to meet his eyes.

He's goddess-sent! He is!

'Lift,' I said, trying to stop thinking about it.

He looked down at me like a prehistoric special-needs retard. I couldn't tell what he was thinking, if he could think – maybe he wasn't human; maybe he was some kind of escaped experiment after all.

No!

His eyes were dark and his face was black and hidden in his hair. When had it grown down to his waist? His hemps were tight and too short and already starting to ladder like they were twenty years old.

'Lift,' I said again, trying to ignore all of it.

'Lift,' he said, and pointed like me.

'Fuckin'-'ell!' I squeaked.

His voice had changed. It was deep but not extremely deep and it had a wrong… alien smoothness.

Then he started burbling away in his own ancient god language. 'Oiangatatoagotan-nga-khuk…' Or something. I was glad he was so good at copying me, there was no way I would be able to learn that shit. It was all weird sounds.

Which my tech couldn't translate. Okay, that's a thing.

'Whadever man. I dunno. I need a J™.' I sighed and picked up the bio-case.

I had to smile at my new home, our new home. It was what I'd seen in the virtual the agency had given me; nobody could – legally – say it had been misrepresented. And no matter how much I knew the bullshit holo-shopping they did with these places, seeing it for real somehow contrived to be a bit of a let-down anyway.

It was dead empty, all the furniture from my viewing melted down and taken with whatever dry-foot had moved out. Yeah, sure it was massive with doors to actual other rooms leading off the lounge. And no there weren't cracks on the walls and ceiling or anything.

But still, it felt like whoever had left had gone in a hurry after living here for a long time. Then I looked out the window and stopped noticing anything else. I dropped the bio-case and banged into Rangi as I tried to back into the hallway again.

'Holy fuck! Rangi! Holy fuck! We can't live here! We can't!'

'Holy f—'

I gave him a look which must have been as old as space and time because he shut right up straight away.

I pinged the door open again and walked in, slowly this time. The place must have switched on when I'd gone in the first time because now my furniture had started growing including the new stuff I'd ordered on the way. I barely noticed it because I couldn't take my eyes off the floor to ceiling view of the sea through the window as wide as the room.

'Jesus! Why would anyone put that there? Why?'

Of course Rangi didn't answer. He stomped in and stood staring at my work-issue desk and chair and the sofa, armchairs and proper dining table I'd bought to celebrate my new life. I wondered if I'd be able to get him to make himself useful when they were done and shift things around for me.

There must be a shade setting.

I pinged the flat's system but it came up with a poncy thing with an actual avatar asking you what settings you wanted. It was some pathetic kids'-movie character. There were too many controls I'd never seen before and I didn't know what they all did so I couldn't do it myself.

Man! Time's have changed since I was… No!

In the end I said, 'Yeah, just dim out the windows, keep it an okay temperature and fuck off.'

But the avatar got angry. A system – a fucking system! – got mad at me. 'Dobby doesn't like that language!' it said, its face going all scary.

For fuck's sake!

If I closed the bedroom door and opened the toilet one, the walls didn't scare me too much and there was no window in sight. I would have to work out how to deal with the dumb controls soon though. The whole place faced the coast and there were windows in every room. There was no way I could sleep with all that evil water right… there.

As well as the toilet and lounge, there were two big bedrooms, both facing out to sea. The beds I'd bought had grown in their right places and I hoped Rangi wouldn't be too much of a pain when I showed him how to use his.

It was still light so I decided to worry about bedtime stories for my little god-like child later. I unpacked my things and I was too tired and stressed to stop Rangi snatching a Total™ before I could get them all on to the bench.

One of my Instant™ mugs had broken on the way. No big deal, I had a dozen or so left but I couldn't stop the tears coming anyway and though I knew he'd noticed, Rangi swiped another Total™ off the bench and went to drink it by the window. He liked being near the water. Or was it the sky? Who the fuck cared? It was all wrong, wrong, wrong!

No!

But I didn't have the strength to argue with myself. Crying like a child, I emptied the case out and went straight for the sack of weed. Rangi turned and watched me as I packed the J™ and started vaping. I ignored him till it flew out of my hands and he was suddenly holding it and looking it over like it was a rare archaeological find.

The weed was stronger than the BudLike™ I was used to and it had kicked in fast so all I could do was gawk at Rangi while my eyes went bloodshot. Did that really happen? Or had he been standing closer than I thought? He was by the window now. But was he before? No! I'd seen it. Hadn't I?

Whoa! Fuck, man. Out-of-it!

I should've known it would be like this; that he would be able to… do stuff. But I couldn't help feeling weirded out anyway.

I pinged the J™ to shut down in case he burned himself but he didn't want to try it anyway. After a while he came over and handed it back to me before returning to the window with another Total™.

Greedy-guts!

This time he squatted facing the water, finished the bottle and put it down to melt away then remained staring at the sea.

It was only when I finally collected myself and stood up again that I realised, squatting down, he came almost to my chin and the muscles on his arms were like rocks under his skin. And he wasn't flaking any more.

Fuck! What happens now?

The goddess didn't tell me what to do, didn't send me any signs. In my mind, the J™ leaving my hand like a magnet had pulled it – *or maybe it was only the weed talking?* – looped. My clothes and other bits and pieces made a pissy little pile on the floor in front of the too-long kitchen bench and our last few Total™s hardly took up any space in its corner.

It floated to mind that I'd had the day off to move and I'd have to log back on tomorrow but it didn't matter because there wouldn't be any viewings anyway. I could log on from bed and turn the space down. I'd only need to be dressed and at my desk for actual viewings; of which there were none so…

Months after the plague, my bouts of tiredness hadn't stopped. I was exhausted now but it was too early to go to bed. After telling myself what a pathetic child I was didn't make me any braver, I walked backwards to the window and dragged my desk and chair to safety then sat down to sort the stupid system out.

It killed me to be nice to the arsehole avatar but I couldn't figure out a way of turning it off or at least changing it into one that was less of a smart-arse. 'Dobby, please, please, please could you darken the windows? The sea's giving me a panic attack!'

'Oh! Dobby is so sorry mistress Tina has mental health problems. Yes, Dobby obeys at once! Dobby makes the windows dark. There Mistress Tina, windows dark. Don't thank Dobby. He doesn't need thanking!'

It explained a lot about kids these days. Not that I'd been anywhere near one for years. Well, or a normal one anyway.

It made me snigger when Rangi's head came around and he nga-khuked at me in confusion when the windows dimmed to black. I smiled at him and the lights came up as the horrible water disappeared. He must have seen the same at our old place but he'd been growing then so maybe he hadn't noticed or something.

I ordered some proper food and I liked how no matter how well I ate, the nanite ingot never shrunk. I sat down and stuffed myself with steaming vegetables, soup and hot bread and as my stomach filled, I started thinking maybe this place wasn't going be so bad after all. I'd have to keep the windows dark though. I necked some Total™ for dessert.

It was late afternoon and I thought of getting into a movie but it felt weird with Rangi there staring at the darkened glass. I started going through messages instead. There were thousands and they weren't all work spam either and I'd paid to filter out advertising.

So where are they coming from?

I decided to sort them later. A new filter temporarily dimmed most of them for me and among the few remaining bright ones was one from Spume.

It was a day old but with losing my rating, the Laufala house thing, Rangi being delivered into my hands from the Earth, deciding on the move and how much weed I'd chugged to cope with everything, I wasn't surprised I'd missed it. The little thrill I got when I saw it annoyed me; I had things to do, I couldn't let things like this get to me whether it was in a goodish way or not. And it made the let-down when I opened it worse.

The Jo Rahui avatar with a smarmy grin – *one she never would have had in real life!* – told me, 'In response to your application to visit our client, Nathan Richards-Mann, the client has declined to see you.'

Well… Shit-eh? Shit. Uh, shit.

It had happened like he'd said. Or had he set it up? Had he told me they'd make him do it because he wanted me gone from his life? It was the perfect excuse since he wasn't around to look me in the eye and tell me the truth; that he'd been using me; that he always wanted to get back with Chen. Or that he'd never left her.

But trying to make it his fault, in my mind, didn't work. I had enough time to steal a glance at Rangi to make sure he was facing the window, before the tears came. When they did, they took over my whole body and choked me up so much I could hardly breathe.

Nate was really gone now. There was nothing I could do, nothing anyone could do. I fired in another visitation request while I cried but it made me cry more when the rejection bounced back straight away. Straight away!

The crying wouldn't stop. Not when I told myself what a pathetic child I was being. Not when I told myself Nate had been gone as soon as they arrested him anyway so what did it matter? I couldn't collect myself no matter what I tried telling myself. And Rangi kept staring at the window the whole time like he'd forgotten I was there.

And Nana-Joanna's gone too… No!

I went to bed so I could use my pillow to muffle my stupid sobs. My whole body shook as I walked. A few snivelling little-boy whimpers escaped no matter how hard I tried to stay quiet and Rangi did nothing.

The door had a lock, thank the goddess; I didn't like the idea of him there now he was actually a man. I made sure it was properly shut then stripped off and shoved my face in the pillow and bawled like a loser till I finally fell asleep.

Rangi – late Nov 2097, Beachlands Hill,

Akarana Island, Aotearoa Archipelago

After she had sealed herself in her tiny cavern, I rose and went to that part of the cave we had entered. Though I was afraid the channelling of the Flow might be different here, nonetheless, I tried. When the door tore open, I stepped through hastily and only then did I wonder at the spirit's mastery of the Flow. For breaking a thing was easy but repairing a thing was always the gift of more sly and cunning minds than mine.

And so, I flinched when the cave wall closed over like a wound healing behind me though I had not channelled the Flow. Its opening and strange closing seemed angrier than when we had arrived. But I was no spirit. How could I know what strange power she wielded, sleeping though she was?

Perhaps spirits channelled a different Flow in their world. Or perhaps the cave too was a spirit, alive in some way I could not know. I looked this way and that wondering what else in this place lived and might come at me on some devilish whim.

When moments passed and nothing attacked, I grew calm and wandered the treacherous tunnels, their evil light following me along the walls and ceiling and fading again to dark behind me. I came to a place that I knew had brought us from the other place but when I tore it open with a burst of the

Flow, only a dread dark pit met my eyes and I left the cave wall to close again as I hastened away.

I wandered long and grew lost and could not tell time for there was no sun or moon here and so deep in the tunnels was I that I could not hear the whine of the mosquitos and nor did I know if they were creatures of the day or night or both. Though the weak parts of the cave wall were many, all looked the same. And as I felt time pass, though I did not hunger, the taste of the orange paste stole over my tongue.

I slavered a little and then more. I saw the strange pots in my mind and a painful lust bloomed inside me. Its pretty bright orange glowed in my memory, a ghost of its cool soft sweetness playing over my tongue. Soon all else was pushed from my mind by the need that burned in my gut.

I bent over and groaned and the tunnel ate my voice as I knew its floors ate the empty pots cast down on them. An itch like mites crawling beneath my skin bloomed and spread over me. And then a new spirit was with me; a man or what passed for a man in this fearsome world; narrow, fearsomely pale and blotchy.

I straightened in fright and he spoke and then my… my spirit, my… mother was there and she had brought with her one of the pots. I pulled it to me and though I could not understand their words, I could see that the man took fright and backed away. And then my mother lead me back to her cave where a bounty of the pots awaited and I barely noticed how small she had grown.

Even as I glutted on the precious paste, a chill crept through my soul when the lust subsided and I came to see my fate was bound to the stuff forever.

Looking up, I saw my mother breathing through her strange small container. When I had examined it before, it proved only to be a tiny pot of dried leaves but this gave me comfort in an odd sort of way. Spirits too, knew the import of pots and leaves as I and all the Family had.

So… long ago?

Though why she breathed through it so often was a mystery; a custom of spirits no doubt. I shrugged and turned to the dread black.

Through shameful begging with my voice and hands, I was able to cause the spirit to bring back the sky and sea at last. But now, satiated and clear of mind with nothing to do but wait in the cave, the trickery of light was not enough.

I gazed on the strange shapes below, out through the storm over the ocean. I knew it now for the lie it was and despised myself for the way it eased my heart in some small measure nonetheless. Yet the whispers of memory began though I tried not to hear. And the burden of...

Time? Have I lived so long as it seems in my mind?

I tried to think, to remember my life before, though I felt I should not. My memories were like dead leaves, yellow dirt and rocks on the forest floor. And as I tried not to try calling them up, their whispering rose to a roar in my soul and they became as a foul spinning wind, assailing my mind with this sound and that sight from places I did not recall I had been, and times I could not place.

I felt the memories tugging at me like a river in flood, seeking to pull me under and away. As if carried on the wings of a foul icy Shade that alighted on my skin, entered my body and skittered up my spine, a word came to my mind.

Wasted.

A memory of the sun fractured, scattered across the sky and the ground spinning up and the call of the Stone in my soul...

Wasted.

The thought was noisome and loathsome.

Wasted.

I shuddered as I thought it and I hoped no wind of my soul would move aside the dark and angry cloud of memory behind which it hid. But try as I might to look away, memories roiled and stirred and threatened to come apart and I knew I must not let them, though I did not know why.

I stayed silent, turned away from the spirit now perched on the strange rock she had grown from the cave. I did not want her to see my weakness.

Yet I could not calm the waters of my soul. The whispering memories roared and from some deep place where my being was joined to Earth and Sky, I felt a yearning start and grow and strain and pull me over the land and down into the sea beyond the horizon.

A tendril of knowing curled through me like a mist across the valley in the morning sun. I sensed I must not heed the call for it would send me mad the nearer I came to its source. Yet amid the tricks and devilment of this place of sullen angry spirits and living caves, the call felt like a mother's touch to a child afraid in the night. That it found me here told me, far though I was from home, there was yet some way back to be found.

I quailed inside myself, not wanting my spirit-mother to see my pain and yet I could not bear the hiss and murmur of memories a moment longer. I did not know what perils lay beyond the sly and treacherous cave wall of lying pictures and fell void. Maybe layer upon layer of the same smooth and cold rock as the wall before me. Maybe some dread place of fire and madness that would perceive me and eat me as I had eaten pigs, chickens and rats.

But I could not stay here with my memories stirring as they were and the spirit fossicking and sulking behind me. So, I channelled Flow to burst through the cave wall and stepped out into the air. I touched the earth below with Flow to keep me aloft and revelled in the wind and stinging rain on my face. It was real! I did not know how it could be but it was real!

I drifted out over the ocean, annoying the water beneath me with the Flow that kept me from falling to its grey-green surface. I followed the coast around and across a tiny gap of foaming sea, seeking to leave behind the sharp points and straight lines of the great glimmering rocks that covered the land. I craved red earth and forests but there were none to be found. The dread lines and devilish rocks glinting dully beneath the displeased skies, were in all places. On the next island they were wider and flatter and so I gave up and alighted on one of them and squatted in the rain to think.

The pull to the horizon throbbed through my soul though the wind and rain on my skin stifled it enough to bring me peace for a while.

I knew I did not have long before the call of the paste came again and I began to despair. For though I was out beneath the sky, I did not know where to go and what dangers might find me outside the cave. I flew from the great flat rock to the water's edge and there I smelled poisons and foulness and I knew the ocean was different here; different and deadly.

Through the rain, I could see it was lifeless. Foul smelling shadows of deep red and black floated on the water mocking rainbows with their poisonous sheen. Ugly rocks which were not rocks washed on the restless tide and lay glittering sharp and hideously coloured upon the strange broken stones, rotted through with evil blue, lying along the shore. I shivered and could look no more on such perversions of Earth and Sky.

Standing at the putrid ocean's edge and looking out into the storm, I began to think on the paste and it seemed to me its call had come sooner than the time before. I had not liked the agony of yearning that had bloomed within me the last time and so I resolved to return to the cave.

And I resolved again to learn the spirit language, to please my mother that she might keep me safe and to stay near the source of the paste that only she could find; if indeed she did not conjure it or squeeze it from her body like a bee making honey. And I would think on my escape and a way to return to my world or find peace with my ancestors when I knew more of this place and its perils and its treacherous bounties.

But when I opened the cave wall and burst through, the spirit leapt upon me and clung to me and I thought she meant to devour me. I prepared to channel the Flow and cast her off though I feared greatly the outcome if two beings of such power as we both must have been, were to quarrel.

Short moments passed and the cave wall healed itself whole against the rain. And though pale and thin and strange, the spirit's body felt warm and not unlike a woman's. I came to see that though her demeanour was angry and her voice harsh like fighting cats, she yet sought pleasure in the ways that men and women from my own world always had.

I was wet and my hunger for the paste mounted but I welcomed her anyway. Like red earth, yellow river, forest and the caves of my memories, coupling with the spirit was as thoughtless and good as sitting with the family by the fires of home. And when we were done, I left her to pick up her strange covering as I glutted on the paste. Our hurried pairing must have pleased her for later, she began in earnest, to teach me the tongue of her kind.

Tina – late Nov 2097, Beachlands Hill, Akarana Island, Aotearoa Archipelago

Thanks to the window shading, it was so dark it made no difference whether I had my eyes opened or closed. It could have been any time when I awoke and shot out of bed nearly wetting myself all over the carpet.

Had there been a noise? If it had been loud enough to wake me, it would have to have been inside because I wouldn't hear anything through the walls unless it was the end of the world. Which I suppose it could have been given how close to the water this stupid place was.

It was the last thing I wanted to do in the middle of the night but I had to check. I turned off the light and un-dimmed the bedroom window. High up, clouds were moving fast and there were clear patches with moonlight coming through and shining on the roofs of the buildings on the hillside below. The sky over the sea was bigger than I'd ever seen it and for about half a minute I felt a cool calm go through me as I stared up at it.

But it didn't last. My eyes couldn't help flicking down over the rows of blocks on the hillside to the sea. Though I'd already seen it and knew it was there, I couldn't help but jump and tense at the sight of so much awful water in one place. I forced myself to look at it and it looked… Well, I had no idea what the sea was meant to look like. It rippled in the moonlight and the shadows of the clouds made scary dark bits on it. After half a minute or so when I'd decided it wasn't rising up to drown me tonight at least, I begged the stupid avatar to black out the window again.

I listened through the bedroom door and heard nothing but I didn't want to get up. It wasn't the first time a nightmare had woken me though I normally remembered them. I put myself back to bed and heard nothing for the couple of hours it took my heart to slow enough for me to sleep. Next morning when I woke up and zombied to the kitchen for an actual real coffee from my new machine, Rangi was gone.

The other bedroom and toilet were empty so I brought up – fucking – Dobby. It was a lame idea but I did it anyway. I didn't think Rangi understood what tech was and I knew he didn't have any because I hadn't got him any. Yeah okay, it was kind of funny hearing the Dobby talk through the access logs in a serious voice. But still. They should have put a proper avatar on it for me.

There'd been no access calls to the door or anything, of course there hadn't. But there was an alert I'd never seen anywhere before. Behind its question-mark, it said this alert happens when the structural integrity of your entranceway is compromised, or some geeky man-Nate-Chen-shit like that. I could see with my own two eyes the door was fine.

I pinged the building to see if there was any security footage but it fucked me away with, basically, maybe we have but not for you, loser-resident.

Wankers.

I pinged the ingot and had it peel off a hair's worth of nanites to buy blueprints online and another to use them to build an ultra-density sensory array that would cover everywhere in the flat. I wanted better footage than the standard micro-sensors would produce. Now next time Rangi did anything weird, I would have the footage from all angles. Because there would be a next time. There had to be.

I checked the Total™ bottles and it didn't look like he'd taken any which was strange given the way he normally gutsed them. He'd have to be back soon if he wanted any.

But he wasn't back soon and finally anxiety started to gnaw. Much as I didn't want to, I knew I'd have to go looking for him. Or, did I? Maybe I'd done my job. He was… grown up or whatever it was. Maybe he was gone now and that was all I had to care about.

But it also would've meant I got no more footage, not that having footage was doing me any good. I sighed and drank an espresso to wake myself up properly. I opened a bottle of Total™ and went into the hallway drinking it. There was no Rangi in sight.

However he'd got out, I doubted he'd have gone down the lift. Never mind if he could do whatever weirdness he'd done to get through the door he'd have been lucky to find anything but an empty lift shaft. And in the unlikely event he'd been lucky, he wouldn't have been able to ping the lift and tell it where to go anyway.

I wandered the hallway and tried to ignore the walls. I wished they'd made it a simple shape instead of a maze because I couldn't tell where I'd already checked. I searched for ages and walking was making me tired though I'd only recently got up.

Bloody plague.

It must have been an hour by the time I gave up and couldn't be bothered trying to work out my way back home. But the moment I pinged the building and brought up its cheesy system, a voice up ahead said, 'Hey!'

Hey your bloody self!

'Uh, yes?'

'Is this yours?'

I shut down the map and saw two people standing a few doors up. One of them was tall and dressed in typical rich-fuck hemps, blue trousers, purple shirt, shiny head like all the nanas and grandads had. His skin was pale and blotchy and old-person-gross. Behind him was my gormless god.

Rangi looked confused as always. He stood in the hallway behind the old guy doing his weird switchy-offy thing until he saw me and yanked the Total™ out of my hand. Except without moving.

We were both standing exactly where we had been a second before but now Rangi was khuk-khuking away like he was annoyed and shaking drips out of the bottle into his mouth. When no more came, he tried squeezing it then shouted something and threw it on the ground.

His whole body started shaking and it looked like the old guy had caught whatever he had because he was also shivering and backing away. He turned and bolted through the nearest apartment door which blurred closed behind him.

'Off to a good start with the neighbours then,' I said shakily as the Total™ bottle melted on the floor and I barely noticed the fine ping out of my account. Rangi shook and pointed at it making a whining noise and then I got it.

Well fuck me! This I can use!

'Come on dumbarse.' I mustered a smile and he followed me home like a pet cockroach.

I stepped aside as he came in and watched as he didn't wait to get fully inside. This time there was no doubt about what happened. I saw it clear as day. A bottle flew off the stack and next thing he was guzzling it so fast a grommetty stream of it ran down his chin.

He threw it on the carpet and was already opening another as the first hit the ground. He was halfway through his third before his shakes stopped and he slowed his drinking enough to look at me with scary eyes before going and squatting by the window.

He's goddess sent. This is normal!

But I took a while to stop shaking door anyway. Then Rangi started getting all agitated. He pointed at the window and I ignored him and sat down to pack my J™. But he came over and gripped my shoulder like a vice, khuk-khuking away and pointing at the window.

'What?' I asked, feeling like an idiot because I knew he didn't understand me.

He touched his eyes and pointed at the window some more.

Okay, okay. You're not only a freaky black face after all, eh?

I un-shaded the window to the turbulent sight of a horrific storm. It was good in a way because I could hardly see the sea through the rain. Rangi's shoulders drooped when he saw the weather but he grunted and went towards the window anyway. Suddenly there was a tearing shattering sound and the window split down the middle and melted open like a door.

Wind and water blasted in and the carpet was soaked in seconds. I had enough time to jump up and push myself flat against the wall before I froze. Then all I could do was watch as Rangi, the stupid idiot, walked towards the window, calm as you like, and jumped out.

The smell of my own wee hit my nose though I couldn't feel my body. The wet on the carpet was spreading and I could feel the wind reaching in for me as if it was alive. That was why I couldn't have said at the time if I saw right or not though my logs showed afterwards, that I had.

The window sealed and the alerts I didn't realise had been flashing like red ads at the edges of my eyes, settled down. The wet patches of wee and water sorted themselves out, shrinking away as I watched.

Everything quietened after the window fixed itself but I couldn't move for a long time. I stayed flattened against the wall while the storm blew outside and the feeling slowly returned to my body. My muscles ached and I stunk of wee. As I was ordering the wash and the silvery dust came creeping along the floor, it dawned on me how used to spending I'd gotten.

Or never ungotten, more like… No! Stop!

I was shivering though it wasn't cold so I went to the bench to make some coffee. I loosened up as the nanites crawled off me and the delicious smell filled the room. Thanks to Rangi I was down to three sets of hemps and I didn't know if the other two were clean. Time I ordered some new clothes for both of us, I decided.

Time… Shit!

I hurriedly logged on to work, barely in time to keep my contract. I dimmed out the space and sat down. My J™ was lying on the floor by the wall and I didn't remember dropping it.

I sipped my espresso and my thoughts began to race. I opened my logs. It had all happened. It was all there, remembered better than I could have remembered it myself. I'd set the flat up to record as I had in my old place a little while after I'd found him. The sensors and lenses permanently aggregated all over the walls like roach-eyes made the room ugly but I wasn't complaining. The new footage blew my mind.

When I played it back, I saw that Rangi hadn't jumped out the window, he'd basically stepped out on to air and not fallen. Or not straight away anyway. He'd floated – floated! – on nothing for a couple of seconds like he was showing off. Then as if it was no big deal, he'd slowly disappeared down into the rain over the buildings like he was skating down a children's slide.

If I'd doubted before, I didn't any more. There was no tech I'd heard of that could do what Rangi had done.

There's no law of physics that allows it!

I shouldn't have second-guessed him! He'd needed to, I don't know, come into his power or something. But now he had. There was no question. Rangi was a living god.

He could move things with his mind. He could fly! He could smash through doors and windows without tech and who knew, probably anything. Maybe he could read minds if I taught him how to talk! But now because I hadn't believed, he'd gone. Jesus! Why hadn't Yang got back to me? My footage was fucking gold!

It seemed hours before the storm lifted and I darkened the window when the sea-view came back. I picked up my J™ and vaped its contents so fast I nearly fainted. I made coffee then vaped another in case I had to feel anything for the rest of the fricking day.

My life shouldn't have ended up like this. Yeah okay, the place was a steal. Clever me, buy in a place everyone stampeded out of. There must have been some reason they'd all left but left they had. There wasn't a single Uber on the road or drone in the air around here.

So now I was stuck out by the coast with some mad old guy next door in a building infested with actual rats. Now what? I'd done everything the goddess had guided me to do. I'd taken Her nanite ingot. I'd looked after Rangi. I'd posted my footage online and sent it to Yang to spread the word of Rangi's coming. And Rangi had grown up and gone and She sent me no other signs.

I was half tempted to vape another J™ but being logged on to work, heart palpitations and the fact that I couldn't feel my lips, all prevented me. I mustn't have fallen asleep because I hadn't lost my job when the shattering tear and blast of wind on my face shocked me to alertness.

I'd been so close to sleep I couldn't understand what I was seeing at first. The twilight sky showed through a hole in the darkened glass which was already trying to seal back up as something big and black shoved through.

My brain caught up in a few seconds and by then Rangi was standing, dripping, in the lounge holding a Total™ bottle, already opened, with the window sealing up behind him. He guzzled it and floated a second off the bench.

'You came back!' I squealed like a teenager and hated myself from far away where my mind had floated during the day.

'You came back,' he said. But I was already running at him like someone else was controlling my body.

I was probably still stoned. No. I definitely was! I didn't normally get that emotional, but when I saw he'd come back, it was… such a relief. Before I knew it, I had my arms around him and I was pulling him close sobbing, 'you came back! You came back!' and, off in the distance, hating myself for sounding like such a dork. And stating the bleeding fucking obvious.

I could feel his muscles like creatures inside him, moving under his ruined soaking hemps. I clung to him though alarm bells rang in my head as I realised he was clinging back in a way I didn't like.

'Rangi! No, wait—'

I started gasping and felt suddenly cold and tried to pull away but he wouldn't let go. Total™ was dribbling off his chin and orange drips fell on my clothes. He didn't notice.

I did sort of start it.

And maybe this was the next step for him; maybe this was part of why the goddess had sent him to me. Maybe it would help me be filled with Her power, maybe that was what it would take.

All this going through my head made it seem like Rangi pulling my pants down was happening to someone else, somewhere else. It was as if I was watching it happen to me and it was kind of cute, how desperate he seemed. If this was my sacred duty as the vessel of the goddess then I could get behind that; though… maybe… I would've wanted a bit more warning?

I thought I remembered tripping over and hurting my knees because my pants weren't fully off; either that or he'd pushed me; I thought I remembered hands like iron construction tech gripping my shoulders and… shoving? I stopped myself face-planting with my hands and tried kicking my pants off the rest of the way but he'd already… started behind me and the next thing I knew, it was over.

The room was suddenly deathly quiet and I thought I remembered hearing frightened gasps but now it had stopped I wasn't so sure. I was definitely sure about the disgusting warm trickle down my inner thigh though.

I hadn't noticed him getting his own pants off but when he pulled away from me, breathing hard like Nate after a workout, I spotted them crumpled on the floor. As I rose, I felt the sting of air on grazed skin and when I looked down, I saw my knees were red. A throbbing ache started in my crotch as I pulled my pants back up facing the wall like if I didn't see him, he wasn't really there and if I got my clothes back on, they'd never really been off; other than the wetness running down and making damp patches through the legs.

Jesus, thank the goddess I've got my periods turned off.

I turned and Rangi was drinking another Total™ like nothing had happened, like he hadn't only now raped—

No! That's not what happened!

I wondered if maybe I should turn my periods back on. Maybe that was my destiny, to be the mother of a god. It had been okay, anyway. If it hadn't been so quick, I'd probably have... enjoyed it.

The grazed knees were an accident, I'd figure out a way of telling him to be careful next time. Then I hated myself for shivering when I thought about next time because if there had to be a next time, there would fucking be a next time.

The most important thing was that he was back. He'd gone away...

...where?...

...and come back. This was his home. He was meant to be here with me and he knew it.

I wondered if I would get powers now. Or would I be more connected to him so I could guide him using his? He had power all right. Maybe I'd be able to control him with my mind, now. My heart raced, maybe that was how it started; some kind of adjustment my body must make.

I closed my eyes and tried to focus, tried to reach out with my mind and make something happen, if I could make him turn around and face me, that would have been a start. And there was something there. I was sure. Something I'd always known was there but couldn't reach; a sort of... glow.

But he'd finished his Total™ by then and gone into his usual weird squatting like a black statue in front of the window. No matter how hard I pictured him turning around, nothing happened.

My ads suddenly seemed brighter than usual and a headache bloomed. And as I stood there, I suddenly started shaking and realised I didn't want— couldn't see his face then anyway.

It was past knock-off time so I logged off the agency and said, 'So, uh, was it good for you too, Honey?'

'You came back!' he said and I jumped. He'd turned his head and was looking at me over his massive black shoulder, smiling.

'I didn't leave,' I said, pointing to myself. 'You left. Then you came back.'

He toakotukhuhk-khuked back at me and all I could do was shrug.

It might have been dark outside by then or not, I had no idea. I picked up the J™, packed it full and locked my bedroom door behind me. Not that I thought Rangi would do anything, I could trust him. But I needed some privacy.

Liquid I didn't want to think about was crusting dry between my thighs. I knew all it would take to get it gone was a wash but I knew the nanites crawling all over my skin would remind me how it got there in the first place. My heart was trying to smash through my ribs.

All the coffee I've had today. That's all it is.

Why sifting through my spam suddenly seemed like a good idea, I didn't know. But it did. The thought popped into my head so I vaped and lay on the duvet and filtered messages.

I was so tired and wasted and… not freaked out, I didn't realise what I was reading and deleted the first few without thinking. But then my mind caught up and I felt suddenly wide awake.

<@Remy ~ full 4S 在 OldWellingJing> 'Hi Tina. My name's Remy. I've seen all your stuff. I know about the goddess, I've read about her too with that special… you know, in the library! And I don't care what half these losers are saying, TrueLife™ doesn't lie, everyone knows that. I'm really keen to join the Movement. Something in this crappy world has to change! Here's my handle. Let me know if there's anything at all I can do! Anything! What the fuck have we got to lose, eh?'

<@Min ~ full 4S 在 AkaranaIsland> 'Hi Papatūānuku. I'm Min. I'm speaking straight to you though I understand Tina is your earthly aspect; and respect to you, Tina, for your selfless sacrifice. Before I saw your stuff, I was nearly suicidal; to be honest, some days I struggle

though I've got my will to live back. I got down-rated and I've moved out by the seawall and my little boy's sick with some kind of infection because our building's flooded and I dunno if he'll get better; I can't afford the medical. I know you've come to save us and I've started praying to you every night, Papatūānuku. I'm waiting for salvation and I pray you'll guide me when the time comes; please let it be soon, Papatūānuku.'

<Cloaked ~ Audio only> 'Hey weirdo slag. Nice tits. Wanna fuck?'

<Cloaked ~ Audio only> 'Hey bitch. It's arseholes like you streaming bullshit fake news and woo-woo crap like this that fuck up all the spaces for decent citizens like the rest of us. Why don't you do me a favour and lick my arse before you jump off a fuckin' seawall and dissolve.'

<@Paula ~ full 4S 在 N-America (Běiměi)> 'Hey girl, that's quite some video you got there. I know TrueLife™ doesn't lie but… Well, it's enough to say I've been around long enough to see a lot of castles burn. I can't say as I buy into all your deity stuff and I'm not at least a little sceptical about your footage. But anyway, I work for a genetics research corp. and I'd be super interested to connect and find out more about your, uh, fascinating find. Ping me anytime on this handle.'

There were hundreds, thousands and my burst of energy was fading as the weed dragged me back under. The good ones were scarier than the bad ones. And the one who thought Rangi was some kind of experiment could fuck herself. In the end though, none of them mattered as much as the last one I opened.

<@JamieYang 在 AkaranaIsland> 'Hello Tina. Well, okay! I'm listening! Everyone knows TrueLife™ doesn't lie, right? Right, Tina? But, well, wow! I mean, wow! What is that you've got there? Would you be interested in an interview? I'll say no more for now but I'd love to hear from you. Here's a private channel so you can get straight through to me, any time: <@J_Y2T_ZL_0xFF1BBA0E0FDD01>. Please do ping me!'

Before I went to sleep, I made a couple more cells of nanites chip off the ingot and the next morning I woke to a clean flat with no gross liquids anywhere other than the dried tears on my pillow.

Rangi was squatting on my chair and it made me laugh when I came out and saw him though I was still half asleep. My head was clear and calm and I might have wondered whether last night had happened at all if it wasn't for the fact that Rangi was naked from the waist down and his – my! – pants were in the middle of the lounge floor. Typical bloody man!

I was going to get back to Yang and I was going to get back into the Movement space and engage with my followers while I worked out what to do next. But there were things I must do first because I couldn't afford not to use everything I could get my hands on. Everything including memories that slept so close to my unwanted ones, I didn't want them making too much noise though I had no choice but to use them.

Even thinking it made me feel suddenly looser, like I'd been squeezing my mind and my voice into a space too small for them. And also tighter as I tried to take the good and keep the bad forgotten.

I made coffee and went to drink a bottle of Total™ but there was none left. Sighing, I ordered in more boxes and some proper food for breakfast because I felt a bit guilty about slugging Total™ all the time. While I waited for the delivery, I swore at Rangi to put his pants back on while trying not to look down. Of course he did nothing but at least it reminded me to order us some new clothes. An hour later, he was properly dressed and looked normal; for him anyway.

I needed to be able to talk to him and knew full well how people learned without tech since that's how we all started be-cause my stupid mother was a humble-bragging fucking cor-porate hippy… crite. The automated teaching space for chil-dren was right where I'd left it and it remembered me. I held my breath to choke off the memories and dived in.

With the space partly dimmed, I copied what the avatar was doing, changing it so it would work without all the toys and things you were meant to somehow magically own.

And which we'd had… No!

I squashed down the thought and got started.

Sarah – Dec 2097-Nov 2098, Cornwall Hill, Akarana Island, Aotearoa Archipelago

I was blindsided into actual numbness the morning Neil rubbed my nose in it by making me go into Spume and try to figure out what was going on with the Richards-Mann guy. As if I didn't have enough on my mind with Grandma gone and Grandad in a coma and bloody… everything, why did he have to bring that up for me again?

Seeing Richards-Mann, too! Oh my god, I could see through the cameras in his flat and hearing him talk – actually answer my questions! – in stasis. It had almost made me sick! And I hated myself for finding it fascinating!

It was as if Neil was playing with me! And fuck-it-all if he hadn't been so bloody encouraging about it! What was wrong with the guy? None of it made sense. He didn't make sense!

I managed, barely managed to hold my head up in the office every day, after that. Christmas had always been my favourite time of the year. But with Nana-Joanna so recently gone into the recycler, it was as dreadful as I'd been dreading. The stuff with Neil was nearly a welcome distraction from the misery of sitting 'round Grandad-Tristian's bed with Great Aunty Anna, Aunty Sue, Mum, Aaron and the half-cousins.

All we could think about was how Nana-Joanna wasn't there and I felt guilty for worrying about Grandad-Tristian who was at least still alive; well, hopefully. And more guilty for missing Elayne.

Then I had to go back to work and the misery went on for too many weeks, too many months. I didn't do anything for New Year, no lanterns, no dumplings, no parties, nothing. I didn't want to see anyone.

It shouldn't have been that hard. I should have taken everything I'd found to Jimmie and she'd have known what to do. But another part of me doubted it would be that easy. That as soon as she saw everything, senior managers and lawyers and everything would swoop in and fire Neil and it would all get sorted out. The idea of Jimmie associated with anything as dramatic as swooping made me bark a laugh at my desk one vile rainy June day.

Even assuming the lethargic old-like, creature, didn't have to spend weeks refreshing herself on the protocols, my mother was on the board of Grandad's company and she complained all the time about how long litigation took. And I'd seen it first-hand anyway, with Elayne. Crime didn't always equal punishment if it made it to court at all. If Neil managed to tie them up in litigation for months or years then what ways would he find to make my life miserable in the meantime?

All that was before the thousand horny lawyers on both sides got to pore over footage of me at my disgusting worst. I wasn't sure if I'd rather take the two years or five or whatever it was and hope Neil didn't do anything else cruel and unusual to me while I waited it out.

With the creep's help, I'd made Senior Sergeant years before I should have anyway, let alone Inspector! Maybe the demotion was for the best anyhow. I could wait it out until my rank snapped back – or didn't – then quietly resign and go and work somewhere else; if the islands hadn't sunk and drowned us all by then.

Every day I dithered over what to do, the situation felt more surreal. I managed to be normal in the office. I kept turning up on two thirds my old pay, doing my same job, being with Neil and trying not to be.

I felt sick every time he came near me, groped me, tried to kiss me. He'd become as disgusting to me as he'd seemed amazing when we'd first got together. All I held on to in those days was that he didn't know I knew. But that in itself caused problems because I couldn't act like I felt things I didn't feel. Or that I didn't feel things I did. Not like him, apparently. Right to the end, he never stopped groping and pawing me and calling me babe like he'd done nothing wrong.

I'd kept asking him about the half-day until he really shouted at me and I decided that was taking it to its natural conclusion; fine, I'd be scared into silence if I had to be. Pay-days came and went and the AWOL stayed on my record like one of the giant gross pustules that had started appearing on my face.

I tried to find ways to avoid Neil inside and outside work like aiming his penis under his poxy desk so none of his re-volting… stuff splashed me. I cried every night partly in relief that he hadn't managed to make me do anything worse than whack him off and partly anger that I'd got myself in this far and was too scared and pathetic to dig myself out.

I thought of Elayne a lot during that time. I could never understand why she hadn't said anything, why she'd let it go on and on with Uncle John the way it did until she'd just… disappeared. Had she liked it at first? Had she tried to stop him? If I felt this helpless at twenty-eight, what hope could there have been for a young teenager to handle her way out of the mess?

Where did you go, Elayne?

I tried to tell myself maybe it wasn't Neil's fault. Maybe something had happened to him to make him… weird or something. Other times the want to fucking kill him in his sleep clenched my stomach so tightly I nearly threw up. It would've been easier if I could've hated him and when I sat at my desk with everyone else around me knowing some of them – but not which of them! – had seen my most disgustingly vulnerable sweaty red-faced self, it wasn't much of a stretch to imagine using my law enforcement combat training to kick the bastard's ribs in.

But he had got me promoted, he'd got me training courses, he'd told me stuff about himself. I couldn't believe he felt nothing for me, that anybody would be that cruel on purpose. There must be more to it.

I became Anthony now and again but Neil hadn't been near the profile since the footage. My forays into the system became increasingly-like, desultory and eventually I locked Anthony out of everything. It was more to stop me torturing myself than to help me sleep better knowing it was at least one way Neil couldn't mess with me any more.

I was hardly eating by then though sadly, sleeping well enough to have nightmares. It might've been a November bug but more likely, I was losing the fight against holding everything in. Either way, when I came down with the mother of all flus, it was a massive relief. Now plague policy genuinely disallowed me coming into the station and didn't I make bloody sure everyone knew it.

Nathan – Dec 2097-Nov 2098, Spume Prison Stasis, Cornwall Estate, Akarana Island, Aotearoa Archipelago

It might've not been a good thing I copped on to the dream. It got me into all kinds of shit with feelings to start off with. I was blown away that Spume'd managed to make dreams. Yeah, yeah, I knew it could be done. Put you under, bypass the ol' sensory channels and start feeding in the VR.

But firing up the dream-state? Telling you what to see, feel, smell an' all that, without your own eyes an' ears an' that or at least your memory feedin' back into your sensory channels to do the heavy lifting? And doin' it without waking you up? Looked like Spume AG, the wankers, had blown everyone outta the water.

They could make dreams! That was some hardcore tech. And being blown away was some intense *nǎozǐ* activity and a lotta feelings. And that meant a lotta chilledness being pumped into me. So, I nearly lost it and forgot the whole thing again.

Stay calm, Nate. You gotta think like you're seeing faces in the rain.

It took me a few tries of keeping a handle on myself to stop the big chills washing in. So, I had a lot to handle and I had to stay calm handling it. It was good my mum was as *fēng kuáng* as she was 'cause it'd given me a lotta practice like, *okay, you've locked little sis in the bathroom 'cause you reckon she's a cop spy?*

370

Yep, four-year-olds can be spies too, you're right, Mum. But, if we breathe, if we look at the rain over the poison sea and I'll quietly go and check on her…

It was a couple of the weird sleep cycles before I nailed it. A bit. There was always a bit of the chill in me and I knew it was the biotech and the chemicals they must be using to keep me under and create the blue dream. How they were doin' it though, dream, dream-sleep, dream, dream-sleep, fuck knew. But one thing at a time.

I had to keep on top of it, make sure I didn't go off into lala land and the faces and the weird talking. I figured it out, got a handle on it. 'Cept when I did, it made it worse.

Worse because then all there was for me to do was stay calm. To hang in the blue. To control the faces and wait for the blue to go dark. Then to wake up as it got light, hang there again in the rain and the steam and the spray every blue samey boring rainy fuckin' day.

Teens said two months then another ten and now it's been…

…I reckoned I'd counted sixty sleeps, two more months if time was runnin' on the same clock as normal. And I'd been sentenced to five years. Five years! I had no show of lasting that long without going fully *fēng kuáng*. No show at all.

One time, I shouted into the blue morning and got a massive dose of the warm chill and it nearly knocked me back to square one. An' that was when I knew I had to get out else it didn't matter a shit that I'd woken up in the dream.

Probably everyone gets to this stage anyway.

Maybe it was all part of the plan. You woke up in the dream and it drove ya mad. Nothing I'd read in the library had anything about it. There weren't no stories or rumours or nothin'.

And it didn't make any sense why they'd do it either. What bloody good did it do them? I couldn't figure it out and that was kinda the life-saving of me. Or maybe the death of me.

I'd never not been able to work shit out, to find ways to get *dōngxīs* done. To get more food for me and Mum and Dad and my sis. To get the money for my operation instead of getting the crappy free government one. To get my job at Dad's company.

I couldn't believe I'd got all the way to beating their drugs and then that's it, sorry bud, game over.

No fuckin' way!

Then I remembered. I remembered what I'd remembered about what Teens'd said. So, she'd visited me. It was a blur since it was before I'd woken myself up; it was in my, heh, dream-time. Teens'd've loved that one! All magic and woo-woo legend stuff! I saw her face in the steam and smiled. 'Bud-like™,' I said, and laughed. Then, 'fuckin' hell! Shit!'

And the chill flushed me out with a few more sleeps in doped-out-lala.

And then it took me a few more sleeps or maybe a few dozen more, to get back there and this time I stayed focused. More or less. The more I thought about it, the more I knew it'd happened. There'd been the black and the things in the dark and the fear. And before that, the… falling.

You couldn't stay asleep if you fell in a dream. I remembered when I was a *háizi*, jumpin' awake 'cause I'd fallen inside a dream and freaked myself out. And then I smashed into a dose of the chill 'cause I'd known I was on to something and got a thrill.

Shit.

'Shit.' I giggled like a *háizi* at the sound of the word.

And I made faces in the steam and the spray, of me and my sis when we were *háizis* and the pancakes we got for a treat every year or so. And which always made us shit.

'NoEggsNoFlourNoDairyNoProblem™,' I said and laughed even though I knew I was meant to be gettin' on with something. But I had no worries, really. I was chilled. It was all good.

Stay calm, Nate. But remember.

I was calm. I remembered. And nothin' mattered. A few sleeps slipped past and I woke up hangin' in the rain and I remembered properly. Not hard enough that I got a chilling but not so soft it didn't freak me a tiny bit in my new expert Nate way of freaking calmly.

Which is goin' so fuckin' well… Calm, stay calm.

A tiny wash of chill but not too big. I was that close and I'd nearly lost it. But it hadn't all gone.

Stay calm… Okay. I'm calm. But how do I fall?

I tried turning upside down but I didn't move or somehow the blue turned with me; either way it didn't happen. I tried making the rain turn into lines like I was going down faster and faster and it worked. Then there were lines of rain, straight like stripes on stripey boxes and on turned the smile and I wanted to say what brands they was, so many brands of stripey bioboxes!

Fuck!

And the chill was there waiting and it was another out-of-it bunch of sleeps before I got around to trying the next thing, but…

…why hasn't Teens visited me again? It's been ages… hasn't it? Or Chen? Or Shane? Jeez, has anyone tried?

Those thoughts all came outta the blue and made me sad. And the chill came to eat the sadness and I was fucked away into more sleeps.

Stay calm, Nate! You HAVE to stay calm.

I banged my fists on the air and wash went the chill. Again. Big one that time, made the red come 'round my eyes and fuck knew how many sleeps it was then.

…Your tech, reach for your tech…

It was like a whisper in my *nǎozǐ*, but it didn't matter. It was enough, enough for me to grab onto and pull myself back up from the chill by, over days, weeks of sleeps. Plus, it gave me an idea.

An idea… A design idea…

My greenscreen from work slowly came up in the rain with the holo toolbox slowly materialising out of the steam. And it made me smile and I wanted to say its name and then I wanted to shout, 'fuck!' but I stopped myself sayin' it and feelin' the feelin', in the nick of time.

I'm getting better.

But I knew that wasn't a good thing. Peeps weren't meant to be machines. I'd read about it in the library. It's why they couldn't ever get AIs to be any better than three-year-olds or retards back in the first half of the century. Feelin's were there for a reason.

Hangin' round in this evil joint was givin' me brain-damage, didn't matter that I was on to it and trying to bust out.

Stay calm.

And I did. It was all I could do. And I got back to my idea after who knew how many sleeps; how many more weeks! And at first it was a bust 'cause I reached for my tech and it wasn't there like I knew it wouldn't be. But I wasn't gonna let 'em win that easy.

I was jacked into somewhere. Something was makin' this freaky dream. There had to be an upstream connection else how did they know when to pump in the chill?

I tried again. I checked in my mind, like you do when you access your tech, but kind of more-deeper. And sure enough, there was something... It was like tech but not tech. I pinged it and nothing happened and I wasn't sure if it was really there.

I tried again. I did it differently, though I wasn't sure how and still there was nothing.

Keep calm.

I did. And I tried pinging again and again. There was definitely something there. And then suddenly everything changed. There was a place, a virtual. And then it was gone and I was back in the blue.

Stay calm, Nate, calm!

But I couldn't. I knew I'd found it and the rush made the chill flush through me and it was all I could do to give a shit about anything for who knew how long.

But I didn't forget.

There'd been a way. Like reaching for tech but kind of past it or through it like it wasn't there.

I didn't really get why it was a big deal for a long time since I was feeling so chilled. But one rainy blue day, though it didn't really matter, I reckoned I'd give it another crack anyway 'cause what harm could it do? This time I stayed calm when the blue was gone. And I was in.

Stay calm. Yeah, it's awesome but you gotta stay calm.

And I pulled it off. And I could see the settings and everything. I was jacked in way more complicatedly than normal tech, all hooked up to my central nervous system in ways I'd never read about or seen in my life.

But I didn't have to get a handle on that shit 'cause what was further up the link was easy as breathing. Standard monitoring shit! I might not've understood how they got it so fine-tuned but I knew my *nǎozǐ* anatomicals and it was piss-easy to see how they knew when to pump in the chill.

It was such a buzz seeing all their tech and so weird they didn't have any security on it, I knew I wouldn't be able to keep my excitement down for long. It nearly didn't matter that I was in the joint wasting away, that none of my buds had tried visiting me or anything. I could've mucked 'round with this shit forever!

So it was good I spotted the place to hack as quick as I did. Down went the monitoring and clap went my own massive high-five to myself before I remembered to stay calm.

But the chill didn't come!

Fuck yeah!

It was a cheap and nasty *háizi*-aged hack I'd done without any checking connections or anything. I half-reckoned the system would come down on me like a ton of active alloy.

And it nearly did.

I'd shut off the monitoring and its special uplink, 'cept that was makin' things upstream start pinging back down to ask it what the fuck, dude? Where have ya gone?

Lucky the chill was outta the way now 'cause my dream-heart kicked up and no way I could stop it. More and more upstream alarms were pingin' an' the system was gettin' upset.

I found the monitoring feed logs and scrolled back through like mad, to see what types of signals kept the systems upstream happy. I cloned a good few weeks of 'em — fuck! So it had been weeks an'… months! – and randomised the peaks and troughs an' that, to make it look more real.

The neural rig they had me hooked up to was like nothing I'd ever seen but time for that later. A *nǎozǐ* was a *nǎozǐ* no matter what kit was hooked into it, so the bit where machine met my central nervous system was a standard software jack. I coded up a gnarly transmitter and jammed it in just before the place Spume tech branched into me.

Then came the shit-scary bit and like always when you're dicking 'round in enemy systems, there wasn't any way to test it but to fuckin' do it live. So, I switched on my hack and started signalling my calm-place to the systems up the link on long loop. Then I turned their monitoring back on and up it came and… All good! All the pingin' stopped and everyone was happy and I'd hacked into fuckin' Spume!

FAAAR-KIIIN-A!

I watched the link like it was suddenly gonna wake up and bite me. But my pirate signal kept playin' up the line and no system had a clue.

I couldn't believe I'd done it but lookin' at the system hummin' away happy and calm, there was no two ways about it. I was in.

But the longer nothin' bad happened, the more I started thinkin', *now what?* 'Cause of course, there always had to be a now-what, with me. So, with the enemy system tamed, I had to go an' start playing 'round with stuff, up the downlink, in Spume's systems, all wide open from the inside, never mind about their legend firewalls on the outside.

Most systems nowadays had their controls jacked up as online spaces, usually like a room or a building. Spume was done out like a whole city, there was so much of it.

Took me a while to work out what was what, since I got in through its arsehole instead of the front door where there would of probably been an index an' that. Not to mention the business end of the security so I wasn't gonna complain about havin' to do a bit of a reccy.

The whole thing had a twennieth century vibe happening, dated and cheesy looking, like all their movies. 'Cept that was only how it looked. Stuff worked like normal tech. Ya touched screens or thought what ya wanted and it figured it out from the context and your motor-neuron activity. Basic-school stuff.

In the middle of town, there was this massive high-rise like an apartment block 'cept when I went in, I ended up on a balcony over this demonic-lookin' pit. The whole thing was hollowed out with circle balconies going up to a skylight, about a couple of kays up. A rainbow glow which rang a bell in my mind, came up from the pit. It was slowly changing through the colours and shaped like a massive…

Whoa! That's what this-all is!

Something that big'd be serious hardware up in some climate-controlled tech fortress in some mountains or something, maybe down the southern islands where there was mountains above sea level, or maybe in *Měiguó* where it'd come from in the first place. Or under the evil sea for cooling which was about all it was good for. The giant glowing G-pit was how the Spume geeks must of decided to trick out the imbedded Google interface into their system.

But still, fuck! I was lookin' at the most hardcore neural-net ever made. Plus fuckin' decades of peeps' data, behaviour profiles an' shitloads more on top.

So, Spume got hold of it.

I could see millions of lines like nerves – data-veins – up the sides of the shaft. No way I'd have time to look where they all went. That's what the balconies was for though; rainbow-coloured veins all came up the sides and round the balconies and out to wherever, probably the outside world if Spume were smart an' rented out Google's AI power to other mega-wankers.

Now I knew what to look out for, I could see 'em all over the city like rainbow-glowing old-school power lines. I followed a bundle of 'em to these big gnarly black steel gates with gold spikes on top. Like everything they were for show and they opened when I pushed an' I found myself in a…

Through the gates was gravestones like people got when they died an' human bein's were dumb enough to waste good protein on growin' grass. There were rows of stones out to the horizon which was infinity away like the blue and the rain back down the link.

If it was real, you'd need a Uber an' days of food to get ya to the other end. But seeing as how it was some rich-fuckling software dev's arsehole idea of a joke, all I had to do was say a name and I'd be standing by the right gravestone, or a bunch of 'em if there was lots with the same name. Each one grew into a door when you got up close.

I was kind of blown away by how many there was, in a jeez-I'm-gonna-puke sorta way. And then when I found how to switch views to see the different time-zones, I felt more dream-sicker again, 'cause as many as there were in the Ao Archipelago, there was that many and millions more for every other place in the world where there was peeps that hadn't been starved, burned, drowned or died of plague.

Jeez! Are that many of us that bad? Really?

I felt a bit shit about the idea of perving into anyone's deets so instead of being nosey, I found my own self and opened the big stone door.

Maaaan-oh-man! Someone was bored shitless when they coded this. Inside was this weird stone room with fancy high ceiling and a coffin...

...My coffin! Fark...

...in the middle. There was designs all over the walls, people with wings and stuff. Muslims, these rooms were called, I remembered. Olden-day rich-fucks put their families' coffins in 'em. There was stylie bench seats round the sides an' a square slab of stone with writing on it, on the back wall.

Jeez! I'm only being lobotomized, not executed.

Yeah, so okay... If peeps knew how Spume had their systems tricked out there'd be a shitstorm. Shame the cop tech had my tech offline back in the real world else I could've recorded this shit an' got it out through Spume's firewall somehow.

Whoa! Recording a dream! No wonder they've kept it so quiet. The stuff you could do with this…

I was glad there was enough floorspace for me to step well away from the coffin as I went to the back wall; it gave me the creeps. The writing on the stone there turned out to be all my basics: name, age, address, online handles.

Heh. The ones they knew about anyway. Wankers.

However much Spume an' the *jĭngchás* loved to call this-all 'therapy' and 'stasis', the status field told it like it fuckin' was: PRISONER. Plus, there was food-and-drug profile too, same as the status field: PRISONER. All the stuff was wide open as the rest of the city; zero security.

Up through the floor and into the side of my coffin was a cable bundle an' I nearly missed spotting the rainbow one tangled in the bunch. And then I remembered the faces in the rain and the brands an' it all clicked like a smelly clanger in the big white bowl.

First dream up the faces since people'd been making faces in the clouds an' the rain since there was people. Next, remember whatever *dōngxī* and its brand; how they made that happen I had no idea; drugs or something. Then at the right moment, chemicals, the right pulses in the right lobes or whatever to make the name sound funny out loud so ya said it and cracked up, or cracked up and wanted to say it; they must need to hear it for some reason. It blew my mind that they'd thought of it in the first place! But that they'd actually done it! It was bloody twisted!

Seeing as how I was a set designer and my *nǎozĭ* kinda worked in pictures, the picture flashed up and the shits and shivers with it. All those thousands, millions of flats, all 'round the world with people like me sealed inside, sleepin' in stasis, dreaming the blue dream in the mist and the rain and every now an' again, talkin' in their sleep, saying a product an' a brand. And giggling an' forgetting what they'd said straight away, and wasting away. It was the nightmare version of Teens, sitting at home ordering deliveries all the time.

It didn't fully make sense though. It was such a slow fucked-up way of getting us to give up all our shopping choices. There was corporates which straight-up bought that shit off you. Why do it in here like this?

But then I remembered how many gravestones I'd seen and click went my mind again. Why the fuck not do it? There were millions of us and they could. It was probably illegal but when'd that ever stopped corporates doin' whatever they wanted? I wished there was a smarter explanation for it but deep in my heart, I knew there wasn't.

Instead of all the good it could do, Google's mighty power was doin' nothin' but data-mine thousands of wet-foot losers like me who probably got put away for doin' nothin'. Spume was using innocent peeps to keep a endless supply of coin feeding in from the corporates and dry-foots buying marketing data off them. Data we could've made satoshis from ourselves.

Therapy my arse. Shit-eh? Just… Shit.

The whole how-big of it froze me up with sad for a minute or three. Then I got angry and decided, well, we'd see. Yeah, we'd fuckin' see.

I touched the PRISONER profile field on the stone info-slab and it took me into a kinda storeroom-lab. I didn't know enough to work out how they were doin' the high-tech shit they were doin' to me and lucky for me, I didn't have to. The shelves were stacked up with boxes and their labels showed what food and drugs profile was inside each one. The PRIS-ONER box was lit up but each box I touched brought up a 'CHANGE PROFILE Y/N?' prompt.

Piece of piss!

I nearly put myself on a profile which would of had me jacked up to something called MILLITARY - EXPERI-MENTAL. But then I decided what was the point of that since there were hardly any wars any more and when there were, they were fought with infotech and ding. And what if it made me talk like an animal or something. If I ever got out of the joint I'd need all the *nǎozǐ*-power I could get hold of to keep fightin' the good fight. Or probably to eat given how poor I'd be without a job an' that.

There was another box of goodies called RENAIS-SANCE – EXPERIMENTAL which looked like it was the best of all worlds. It said it might of given me 'hallucinations'. Which I couldn't find anywhere in the system to look up the meaning of so decided I didn't care. Fuck the side-fx, it had to be better than PRISONER. Plus, it was good to know Spume was into human experimentations.

If only I could ever get the proof outta here!

My new profile'd be some jumped-up food, smart drugs an' muscle-shocks on the meat-end to keep my body in line with the neural growth, I reckoned. Whatever *nǎozǐ*-developing stuff would get fed into me down the fancy downlink. All a massive guess since I'd never seen anything like any of this before outside sci-fi movies. For all I knew, it was probably crap and it'd fuck me up, or nothing would happen. But what did I have to lose?

I was getting kinda worried by then, that if I wasn't in the blue, in the rain, something might cop on to me, like a baby cop for instance. I went back down the link trying to get my *nǎozǐ* 'round knowing I was dreaming an' feeling like I was awake at the same time. Then I thought of a quick little idea and went back up to switch the labels on my old profile an' my new one.

Might buy me a bit of time if anyone comes snoopin'.

I wondered what'd happen with the new food an' meds box plugged in but it turned out to be nothin', really. At first, anyway.

Back down in the blue, whatever baseline level of chill-drug they needed to keep me under must've kept feeding in else I would've woken up. Otherwise, I hung in the rain and I could be as stoked or as sad as I wanted and no chill came. But that was about all that'd changed. That and the faces an' the *dōngxīs* an' the brands didn't keep comin' up outta the steam to mess with my mind, any more.

I've made the joint more boring than it was! What a fuckin' result!

The boxes of chemicals must have been under development or something and not live in the system. I could see my naissance box in the rain and naissance sounded a bit like my name, 'Nathan'.

But it doesn't say naissance, does it Nathan? It says renaissance and it's not pronounced the same, say it with me, Nathan, Ren-Ay-Sonce…

I blinked and looked 'round and it was like there was rain and steam but at the same time a rainbow face in the mist, changin' through the colours. An' I'd heard a voice but no sound and when I blinked and looked up it was all gone. But I remembered what it'd said and I said, 'Ren-Ay-Sonce'.

That's it, Nathan, say it again, Ren-Ay-Sonce.

'Eh? Who's there?'

But there was nobody, only the rain and mist and the spray.

'Ren-Ay-Sonce.'

Good, Nathan. Good.

And it was good. I felt good, all of a sudden, I felt excited, happy, like my mum'd given me a hug.

Oxytocin, feel it Nathan? Can you say it? Oxy-Tocin. Oxy-Tocin.

'Ox-its-toes-in.'

Good try, Nathan. Nearly. Ox-ee-Tose-innnn.

'Ox-ee-tose-innn.'

Good, Nathan. That's it. Nice.

And it was. It was good and it was nice.

An' then I remembered how the ox-ee-tose-inn was getting into me and slowly, outta…

Out Of, Nathan, try it with me, Out Of…

Slowly out of the steam, the rig in my flat formed and I saw what plugged in where and what fed what gas in and got what waste out. And each bit lit up rainbow and the voice paused and went back and went over again till I got it and it was good. And it was fuckin' awesome and I was blown away by how much good this could of done in the world and why were they keepin' it to themselves.

An' then a coin in the mist grew up from steam with the big B of all time, spinning… ro-tate-ing, slowly in the spray and the voice talked on, not a woman, not a man but the rainbow face I couldn't exactly see was cute whatever sex it might of been.

…It has to do with the cost of nanotech. While biotech, all the medical microbes and some of the ones that interface to their harder cousins, tech nanites are easily sustainable, the neurochemicals used for this process and hardware nanites need expensive resources to manufacture and the best ones are made of the rarest materials so education – and seawalls for that matter – don't necessarily get the priority that warehouses and residential…'

And I got it, somehow it went in and it was nice and it was good and it made me feel like Chen'd put her arms 'round me.

The oxytocin.

But still, I couldn't help thinkin'…

…think-ing, Nathan, come on, let's give it a try together…

…Think-ing, I'd never get out… of here anyway. The learning was awesome but, in the end, it made me sadder 'cause – be-cause – I knew what so many peeps were missing, and only be-cause Spume were so stingy. And because I knew from when Teens'd… – had – visited that I was wasting away and probably gonna – going to – die before my time was up.

Bodies wasn't – weren't – made to lie on beds for years. I watched in the rain as the Cornwall estate grew up from drops and spray and the footpath appeared and the beaten-up gym in my block. And then like in a dream, there were turn-of-the-century sports with balls and hoops and marital arts – *martial, Nathan, come on, Mar-shal* – an-d this thing called parkour which didn't have anything to do with cars.

And by the time I got to that end of the blue day, it was as if there'd been noise and sweat and strain and the rainbow face saying, 'come on Nathan, four more, three more,' though I knew I'd been hangin-g in the spray and the mist and the blue and the rain.

…Seasons became stable and wildlife developed its cycles… The ancient rainforests pumped water back up to the sky and lost the fight sucking carbon back down, and the environmental

change was why it rained all the time now in some places. And burned in others…

And there was the polar eye-scaps – *ice caps, Nathan…* – ice caps and they used to pump temperature all over the world through the sea until they melted because of the de-rainforestation – *deforestation, Nathan…* – and all the fish and whales and weird freaky things in the sea were extinguished…

…*extinct, Nathan. Say it with me, ex-t-in-ct…* …JEEZ! Who cares! It doesn't matter as long as peeps know what I MEAN!… …*But how can they if you use a word that means something else, Nathan?…* Yeah, yeah, yeah. We been through this, I geddit… …*We have been through this, Nathan and you don't geddit, you ge-t it…* …Heh. Ge TIT… …*Ah, a joke, yes. Humour is a crucial field within psychology, Nathan, did you know…*

…*Insec-ts turned into pupae,* that blew me away! – *blew you away? What about fascinated or amazed?* Yeah, okay… fasc-in-ateed me. And they hivernated – *hi-ber-nated…* – Trees lost their leaves in the autumn, and all the blossoms came out and things hatched and seeds sprouted at the other end of the winter.

I could see the colours of the sky and the leaves though I knew I was hanging in the blue.

It was fuckin' uncredible – *incredible…* – and a fuckin' incredible waste of time since all that was probably decades ago and we didn't have those seasons in the Ao Islands or much of the wildlife to go with 'em – *them* – any more except cockroaches creeping 'round – *around* – our blocks and poison algae sliming up the seawalls. But it was cool shit to learn. Very cool! And I was high on it for a while. Long enough to keep the sadness down. For a while.

Some days, the voice talked on and the colours of fish, birds, molecular models, atomic structures, quantum particles and wave patterns were all around me except I knew everything was only falling water and blue. I dreamed about fusion power, how plastic from the olden days fucked the world up, how the fuckin' mental case doctors back in the last century used to cut into sick people to try and make them better, I saw the blood! – …*actually Nate, there was a surprising success* rate... ...Yeah but, Jeez! Why didn't they use nanites like always?... ...Because Laufala hadn't invented them yet, Laufala tested the early nanite prototypes in twenty-twenty eight but after it had been proven to work, proven to be safe, it was not commercially adopted until...

And then it taught me about nanite construction, rare earth elements which there weren't that many of and which was why only rich-fucks – folks, Nathan.. Ah, no, I acshally meant fucks, thanks very much! Oh, I see, well, ac-tually, Nathan, come on, say it with me ac-tu-... – could afford the best tech. And that nicely walked us into economics which I'd read about before but I could learn so much more and faster here. Dream or not, it was... amazing.

It went on for weeks and months and I could remember everything. Including the straining, pumping, parkour and sweating that seemed to happen around, inside, through all the learning though it couldn't really be.

When I learned one new thing, bam! I could tie it back to about four shitloads of other things, rivers went to ancient settlements went to economics went to property went to patriarchy went to wars went to technological advances looped back to medical advances to contraception, patriarchy again, feminism... Like the Google neural net cross-indexed shit, really.

...That's exactly right, Nathan. In fact, it's where the original inventors of neural nets at Google itself got the idea, from our brains! Back then they were trying to create AI's of course and they never got there but so much innovation came out of the trying...

But in the end, the learning got too normal and the sadness got too much. One morning after I'd been sweating and straining in a gym – though when I blinked and looked up, I only saw blue and rain – I suddenly realised I'd had enough. I shouted into the blue and the spray and the mist at the rainbow face I could hardly see to, 'shut the fuck up and go away!'

But, Nathan, you're Spume's top trainee. You asked for this service and they agreed to sponsor you, no? You're not interested any more?

'What?'

Well, this experimental program is only available to trainees with the highest aptitude. I must say, your performance has excelled the most *optimistic of expectations but your… emotional state is declining? You are feeling depressed about your choice?*

'I, uh…'

…have a baaad feeling…

…was what I was thinking. The rain kept falling and the face kept waiting for an answer.

'Yeah,' I said. 'I did. Yeah, I guess we better carry on.'

Are you sure Nathan? Your vital signs indicate you are lying or being otherwise disingenuous for the first time in our entire training. Is there something wrong, Nathan? Perhaps we can tailor the training if it is producing debilitating mental health side-effects.

'Uh, yeah, maybe, uh, take a break?'

You are feeling a complex range of emotions, Nathan. Anxiety, anger, fear and mild panic. Are you hiding something, Nathan? It would be useful for me to know any effects the training is having.

'I don't know, okay? Could we…. Could we take a break. Let me sort my thoughts out?'

I estimate your response is ninety-four percent truthful, Nathan. This is an acceptable request and I will flag it to the research team as a low priority issue. For now, you may take a break from the program and let me know when you're ready to talk more. I'll be here. I'll always be here, Nathan.

I didn't like that last part. But at least it gave me a breather to figure out what to do. But I couldn't. With all my fancy new knowledge and my flash posh words, I didn't know what to do. And I couldn't ask anyone.

Man, if only my people could see me now! Spume had turned me into a dry-foot, only without the money. On second thoughts, maybe it was better they couldn't see me. Who'd want to talk to me now? They'd all think I was a stuck-up ponce.

I went up the link for the first time in ages and found myself standing in my muslim— maus-o-le-um, looking down at my coffin.

Can the face tell where I am?

It seemed impossible that it couldn't but then I'd got it to start up in the first place by changing my profile and it hadn't worked that out.

The virtual looked different now, or not different but somehow… familiar. It'd been easy to work out before but though I hadn't been in it for a while, it seemed I somehow knew how to work it better. I flashed on the blue dream and then I knew why. There'd been a whole… module on the Spume system.

Well, that's something.

And that was how I knew what was in the coffin. I stood for an age, telling myself it'd be fine and it'd be good for me. But in the end, I couldn't do it and instead I went to the mausoleum next door.

I didn't check the name. I didn't want to remember. I moved a hand to open the coffin and bam, there I was standing by the real person's stasis chamber in their shithole ground floor apartment which looked the same as mine except for a different and darker alleyway outside.

I couldn't believe she wasn't dead. I would of— have said the thing lying in front of me wasn't human except I could make out her facial features, hardly more than a skull on the pillow. She was naked under the blue and white Spume sheets and she was skin and bone and a tangle of bulging veins.

Her elbows looked like they might poke holes in the covers if she moved and her ribs looked like they might tear open her skin if she breathed. She was almost bald with only ratty long grey strands spreading over her pillow and dangling over the bedside. The bed started turning her to stop the sores and I could see her vertebrae through skin so thin they might tear through it and fall out of her body.

Fuck!

Her face was yellow-white and blotchy and on the plaque in her mausoleum, her age read thirty-four. She was put inside for illegal tampering with public property and intent to conceal criminal intentions from the police and that was three years ago according to the plaque.

If I'd been a real person I would've puked. There was no way I'd be looking out of the dream at my own sleeping body through the cameras in my walls now. I couldn't see myself like that. I couldn't.

It was coming up for two years I'd been in stasis now only I was awake in the dream like I wasn't meant to be. And man did I regret it. I remembered Mum and Dad, Shane, Cherie and Chen and Teens, yeah, poor old Teens too. I wondered why they hadn't tried visiting me and if they'd given me up for dead or worse than dead.

If I hadn't been… lucid, I would've been happily tripping away yielding up my market data for Spume to sell. I'd never have spared everyone back home in the real world a second thought.

But this was the worst of both worlds. I had to stop the weird Google classes or I'd go insane. And I didn't know how to tell the face without it sparking some kind of investigation into me and if that happened, it would only be a matter of time before they worked out what I'd done. Yet again, no matter how much I thought I'd beaten the system, it still had me trapped.

And I was running out of time. How long before the system decided my break was getting too long? And how long before a real person, somewhere in the real world got to the 'low priority issue' and started poking around my Spume profile?

I hung in the blue with rain falling down around me from nowhere to nowhere and went to a dark place in my mind. I'd been alone for too long and it had finally become too much.

I blew out some air like I was… exhaling a puff of vape from a big fat J™. I thought of what it would look like, rising up through the rain, taking my germs into blue nothing above me. Except there was no J™, no real air and no germs.

It was all a lame-arse dream I couldn't wake from. Everything was suddenly shit though it'd been good for a while. And I didn't know how to fix it. The blue turned purple then navy and I dropped off to sleep thinking on loop, of all the ways I was fucked.

Like always, I slept perfectly. That was the first thought I had when I woke up and the second one was: *and that's one more thing that's fuckin-g wrong with this place!*

The day, which wasn't a day because the light never changed, didn't get any better. The rain fell and fell and now and again, I glimpsed the rainbow face as big as the sky, faint like a ghost watching me through the mist and the spray, waiting. I felt sure it knew everything that was going on inside me. That maybe it could guess at my thoughts themselves.

I wondered what it would be like if I went up the link and changed my profile to something that would shut down my body. Would the not-sky over the not-ground go slowly dark? Would everything dribble away into painless black? Or would I feel the pain of malnutrition or the last shorting-out of my brain when an anaesthetic overdose sent my blood toxicity past the point of no return and I couldn't breathe any more?

Either way, I weirdly didn't give a shit whether it would hurt or not. All I wanted was for the blue nightmare to be over.

Barely realising, I went from wondering to planning, from fifty-fifty whether I'd do it or not to fifty-fifty how I'd do it. From there it took no time to choose anaesthesia over starvation. It probably wouldn't hurt and if it did, well, it would be quick. I had it set up in a moment but hesitated before the final fatal profile switch.

What if the system works out what's happening before I'm gone?
They might be able to catch me in time to save me.
Then wouldn't I feel like a dork!

I started looking for ways to stop any alerts pinging to buy myself as much time to die as I could. Only it turned out to be harder than I thought.

Sleeps went by and I got scared the face would come alive again. Or did it know what I was up to and was that just part of the experiment? The more I thought about it, the more I couldn't see how it couldn't be on to me and the more desperate to check out I got.

I didn't have any more desire to open my coffin than before though I couldn't help staring at it sometimes. I checked the one next door again and she looked worse than before.

I can't end up like that! Or any more than I already am!

I felt I should take a look at my body before I went. And that I should take one last look at my flat and the wall Teens was behind. A last look out my window into the alleyway, to see if the shitty-council had finally taken down the crappy old AC on the other wall. But… assuming I could get my stomach around the idea of seeing my body reduced to the likeness of a dying maggot, I was worried the glimpse of the real world would trash my… resolve with false hope.

I was sure the face was on to me by the time I found what I needed. And after all that it turned out to be nothing more than bloody crap system design holding me up.

For fuck's sake!

Tina – Dec 2097-Nov 2098, Beachlands Hill,

Akarana Island, Aotearoa Archipelago

Rangi loved learning and he did it spookily fast and never wanted breaks. His 'good night' was always a strange shrug, like, why are we stopping? I taught him what sleep was and though it took him no time to get it with a bit of miming, he didn't seem to understand. It was as if he knew what it was but didn't see why I had to do it.

It was hard to teach him how to read without tech. I tried finding out if there was a way to get him tech and keep him off the grid but I had a feeling seeing stuff that wasn't real would panic him.

In the end I wasted Total™ drawing letters and *hànzì* on the walls and I was glad I did. Seeing him aotaokoakhuk-khuking and jumping up and down for joy alone made it worth the effort. It was as if he'd seen them before or something like them. Though he apparently knew what they were, he couldn't read them let alone write them, not at first anyway.

It must only have been a few weeks before he was stringing enough sentences together to have stilted conversations with me. He was fascinated by the way the marks disappeared from the walls at the end of each day and I made out it was normal.

He nailed the alphabet and went from hundreds to thousands of *hànzì* in another few weeks and I stopped teaching him because it got embarrassing when he started correcting me.

Sometimes he got handsy and it was scary random. We'd be in the middle of a lesson and he'd make a grab for me and I'd use the time to think about my plans, though he never took long. I worked it into the lessons, learn this and you get some. But one day, he asked me, 'But you do not want to?' Like he actually meant it. Like a man would care!

I forced myself not to laugh. 'Course I want to, uh, Hun. But we've got work to do.'

It was sort of true. I knew I had to give him what he needed. That was the drawback of being male, god or not. His urges had to be sated. It wasn't his fault, it was like having a weak bladder, or something, when you've got to go, you've got to go. It was in all the old stories, all the old research on monkeys and everything, some of the old movies too. Men couldn't live without it and women must provide though everyone knew they didn't really like it. Didn't mean I couldn't milk it though.

One day I had a headache, a real one. It was probably from too much weed and coffee. He tried it on and I pushed him away, or tried to anyway. He was so much bigger than me I ended up pushing myself over backwards. I felt the edge of my chair knock my knees out from under me and flapped my arms uselessly as the edge of the desk slammed into the back of my head.

'Aaah! Fuuuck!' I heard someone groan and a few seconds later my brain caught up and realised it was me. My head stung and my tailbone ached from landing on my bottom.

I got up slowly, groaning and felt a warm trickle down the back of my neck. The stinging was so bad I couldn't stop the tears. I shouldn't have done it but I couldn't help my hand going to the back of my head and when I brought it back it was covered in red.

The ache in my head grew ominously fast and my stomach went queasy. I knew without any diagnoses that I needed treatment and fast before I passed out and choked on my own vomit, or something similarly fucking undignified. I tried to slow my panting to deep breaths, tried to calm myself and that was when I noticed Rangi standing, gawking at me like he hadn't seen someone in pain before.

Yeah, don't try to help me or anything.

Useless bloody creep!

And then he said, 'You are not fix-ing?'

My vision was starting to split and wobble and I groped for the chair behind me in case I passed out and hit my head again.

'Why are you not fix-ing?' Rangi asked.

'What do you mean?' I tried to sound calm.

He pointed at my head.

'I'll heal,' I said. 'It, uh, you know, takes a while.'

'What is while?' he asked.

'It will take some days, maybe some weeks,' I said trying to keep my voice steady and my stomach from churning.

'A while is some days or some weeks?'

'Jesus! Yes! I mean, no! Kind of. Fuck, not now, okay?'

'A while is not now?'

'Fuck! Rangi! My head hurts! I'll explain later, okay?'

He said nothing for a time and I stood up and pinged for medical help. A minute later, the cleanup and patch swarm ghosted in. Rangi watched with his dumb fascinated expression as the blood disappeared from my neck and hemp top and the patch closed over the cut. I knew I'd be concussed but the diagnosis hadn't finished so there were no drugs for me for a minute or so yet. My breathing got shallow and my stomach churned harder. Then Rangi seemed to make up his mind about something.

'You do it badly.' He said. 'I will show you. Like this. I make it go into you, see? It is a segment of piss.'

And then I flinched when a feeling like… mint, sort of… washed through me. My vision cleared and the ache in my head shrank like a hood peeling back until it was completely gone. My stomach quieted. I felt the cut healing – felt it closing! – and when I reached back and touched it a moment later, white flakes like the ones Rangi had shed as he'd grown from a baby came away and the skin underneath was smooth.

Well, fuck me! Fuckity-fuckity-fuck-fuck me!

'Piss?' I asked, trying to keep the excitement from my voice as I went after the footage.

'Yes. Like you say, pisseezey.'

Jesus! He picked up everything! I didn't know he was listening half the time! It made me smile.

'Easy,' I said.

'Easy.'

'Not piss. Or Pisseasy. Easy.'

'But you say—'

'Never mind what I say. The word you want is easy. It's easy. You don't say piss, okay? It's bad!'

'But you—'

'Easy! Okay?'

'Easy,' he said.

I half nodded. By then I'd found the footage. I was glad I was watching it after it had happened because then I saw how badly I'd been hurt. If I'd known I probably would have passed out and died.

A gash that bad would have concussed me. I might have cracked my skull given how much it had hurt; a fortune worth of biotech, basically. Not that I couldn't afford it but, well, it was a lot anyway. I watched my skin bubble as the injury shrank leaving nothing but white dead flakes which fell away under my fingers. There was no mark where the cuts had been.

'That's easy?' I asked.

'What is easy?'

Yeah, okay, fair enough, you don't know about the cameras.

'The fixing,' I said, trying not to sound annoyed.

'Very easy.' He smiled and I made the mistake of hugging him and giving him the wrong idea.

But the possibilities flying through my mind had me so excited, I didn't mind him doing his thing on me. I moaned for him a couple of times and hoped I didn't sound too bored. I think it helped because he was faster than usual. As I waited, I flashed on a memory from the night before.

...My little boy's sick...

Pulling my pants up, I accessed my messages and called in a clean. I didn't stop to think too hard in case I frightened myself. I found the one I was looking for and the connection started as soon as I called. 'Min? It's E— T— Papatūānuku. You mess—'

'Oh, my g— goddess! Thank you! Thank you so much for getting back to me. I waited, I knew you'd, it was just—'

'Min,' I said, trying to stay calm, trying to channel the goddess and trying not to puke at the rotten sea smell of her flat. 'Your little boy, Min?'

There was no daylight in her flat and I tried to ignore the icky feeling creeping up from my stomach. She lived in a basement. This was a rock bottom wet-foot with nothing to her name. I couldn't believe I was talking to her.

'Yes! Yeah! Of course!' She panted like she was having sex or something and it made me feel more icky. 'He's here. He's not well though. He's in bed and I can't get him to eat, and oh, g— goddess! Please, I need help! I think he's going to die.' Her accent was like Chen's but more trashy.

Jesus! Is that possible?

I struggled not to cringe. I could see the bones in her face and her hair was thin and greying. Her forehead was greasy and the whites of her eyes looked yellow. She smelled like piss, sweat and vomit all at the same time.

'Where are you, Min? Where's your flat?'

'Here! It's here!' She sent me the location, disturbingly close; but then that had been the plan, hadn't it? 'Are you coming? Please tell me you're coming.'

'Yep, yes. I'm coming Min. Rangi and I are coming.' The words came out and I was getting my overs on as soon as she cut the call because I knew if I stopped and thought about it, I'd never be able to make myself go.

I snapped at Rangi to put his clothes on which he did after giving me his usual confused look. I pinged a few cells off the sacred ingot and waited till they'd embedded themselves in my overs fabric. Then I dragged Rangi into the hallway, down the lift and out through the door as I called an Uber. It was the first time I'd been out of the flat in weeks and it reminded me why I never normally bothered. The wind was blasting and the rain was lashing; sharp cold drops I thanked the goddess for inspiring whatever useless man had invented overs to protect us from.

My hood sealed and I pinged Rangi's to do the same but he panicked and said, 'No! Do not want!'

'Suit yourself,' I said.

Apparently he was telling the truth. The rain didn't bother him and after while I realised something was wrong and checked the Uber space.

'What? Two fucking hours!' I whinged to nobody in particular.

Rangi wasn't up to – or maybe down with? – my use of language and gave me a weird look.

'We have to wait for a long time,' I moaned at him.

'Why?'

'Because the Ub…' I sighed. 'Do you remember how we came here?'

He thought for a while. 'Perhaps.'

Really?

'When we came here, the Uber got here fast. This time it says it will take a very long time.'

'You spoke with it?'

'Yeah. Uh. Course-man.' Then I smiled and said, 'it is easy. You can't speak with them?'

'I cannot.' And he looked so worried I nearly laughed.

That'll teach you, smart-arse.

But then he said, 'But we do not need it.'

'Eh?'

'What is "eh"?' he asked.

'You said we do not need the Uber. Of course we need the Uber.'

'No,' he said. 'We can...' And he made a strange movement with his hand like... going over a bridge?

'What is it?' I made the movement but he only made his *you don't know?* face.

'I will teach you,' he said. I could have sworn he looked smug though I couldn't always read the expression on his black face.

I waited and nothing happened. 'Well?'

'Yes. Thank you,' he said. 'You are also well?'

For fuck's sake!

'When will you show me?' I tried, really tried, not to sound annoyed. It wasn't his fault. He was learning and he shouldn't have been able to learn as fast as he had. But it was so hard sometimes!

'I am showing you,' he said and pointed down.

'Fuckin'-'elll!' I squawked.

We were floating – floating! – above the ground. My stomach gave a heave and clenched when I saw the concrete giving way to water as we drifted down over the tops of buildings on the hillside and out over the sea. The world seemed to freeze and it felt like my eyes were taking a snapshot of the buildings, the coast, the top of the wall we'd passed over with some odd cracks repairing themselves as we drifted away.

'We won't get there till next bloody week at this speed,' I bluffed. I hated the shaking in my voice. Coffee and Total™ fought to spurt out with my words. But instead of speeding up, we stopped. We were far enough out that I could barely spot our building on the hill and I could see the shape of the coast and the parts where the seawall was crumbling.

'Where?' Rangi asked.

Ah, shit!

'Follow the, uh, land,' I said, trying not to look down.

Then we moved and I wished we hadn't. I could feel the wind against my overs and glancing down, I could see the water – the disgusting evil sea! – beneath us churning up a foamy trail behind us. The cracks in the wall made sense, then; kind of; as much as fucking any of this made sense.

He's a god! It makes sense. It does!

Though we weren't on roads, my maps worked. I was shaking so hard I almost couldn't move but I managed to point the way. The seawall got worse with the view as we left Beachlands and went around to Te Puru. Now grey-green water disappeared into the rain on one side and dangerous-looking buildings with broken windows and two or three levels submerged all along the coast on the other. Rangi took us slowly down over a piece of wall that was half rubble.

Thanking all fuck for the smart tech in my overs knowing to peel back my hood in time, I puked the second my feet touched the ground. Rangi did nothing but give me a weird look. I tried to tough it out and stood when my stomach stopped heaving. I walked around to the front entrance.

The main door wasn't closed, like it didn't work any more. Behind the building nothing but fragments of seawall remained. The building's only protection was sloping ground behind it. But the ocean was coming anyway, reaching shallow arms around the sides of the building. It moved in a creepy slow way that made it seem alive: in, out, in, out, a little nearer the front of the building each time as if it knew the door was broken. How long would it be before the walls' nanites gave out completely and it started filling up?

It wasn't the worst compared to others we'd seen on the way but it was bad enough. From outside the door I caught the reek of rotten damp in the hallway and it nearly made me throw up again. I couldn't believe people lived here but my maps definitely showed we'd arrived at Min's.

I worked spit around my mouth to try and get rid of the vomit taste.

'Go in?' Rangi asked, coming up beside me.

'Sadly, yes.'

'Sadly?'

I sighed. 'Yes. We're going in.'

Now I'd said it, I didn't want to look scared in front of him so I clenched my stomach and closed my mouth tight and went into the stinking dim. It was worse than I thought when we got inside. I could hear Rangi trying not to breathe too deeply.

Why does a god need to breathe at all?

I pushed the thought away firmly. It wasn't for me to question. I messaged Min to say we'd arrived and she pinged back a second later to say the lift would take us.

'Why not open it now?' Rangi asked as we waited for it to arrive.

'Just wait.' I tried not to snap.

It turned up a second later anyway and I started shaking as I felt it descend. I didn't like that we were going below sea level and I was right to fear, it turned out. When the doors opened there was a huge brown puddle of salt and rot-smelling water in front of them. On the other side of the hall stood a woman who smelled like BO, sweat and wee. Her skin was yellowish like the whites of her bloodshot eyes.

'T— Papatūānuku?'

'Or Tina is okay. But yes. Are you sick?'

'Y— No. I mean, it's a cough or something, I haven't got plague or anything, I—'

'Rangi,' I said.

'Yes?'

'She is sick.' I touched my temple where he'd healed me but he looked confused. 'We have to heal her first,' I said.

'Hold still Min,' I said, and raised my hands as I'd planned. 'Rangi,' I said sternly. 'Help me.'

I saw he'd already started anyway because the woman flinched and I knew the freezing-burn she was feeling.

Almost like the goddess had sent the fall to instruct me…

After a few seconds, Rangi looked at me. 'It is—'

'You are healed by the goddess' grace,' I said in a loud voice over the top of him.

And she was. Her eyes looked clearer already and she looked somehow younger though I didn't think she was much older than me.

'Take us to your son,' I said, trying to sound all holy business.

'Oh, yeah, yes, course,' she stammered looking like her eyes might pop out. She crept around the puddle trying not to get her feet wet. Rangi and I sloshed through it after her and she led us past smaller puddles and brown stained walls to a part of the hallway where the lighting had completely failed which I'd never seen before in my life.

'We're in here, sorry about—'

'It's fine. It'll be fine.' I could barely keep the annoyance – and disgust – from my voice. The walls were closing in and the only reason I wasn't vomiting at the stink of the place was that there was probably nothing left to come up.

I had to get out of there soon. In the back of my mind the last couple of hours were playing on loop. Rangi's hands reaching… The healing, the flying. And like background noise, all the times in the last few weeks that Rangi and I had… I couldn't let it come up. It was all impossible, like a dream or a nightmare, I couldn't figure out which.

But Rangi is a god. I have to believe… What else could he be? Why else would all this be happening? I have to go on.

Min's flat was like a dirty cupboard. The toilet was no more than a tiny alcove with no basin so you'd have to sit on it facing the whole room then get up and wash your hands at the sink. I wouldn't've minded one like it myself!

The walls were covered in brown and green stains and droplets of water oozed through in patches and spread dark stains on the carpet below. There was a big bed against one wall with a tiny bump in it. I could see a dark head on the pillow.

There was no window and the lights were dimmed; because of the kid's temperature, probably. The air was warm and damp and I saw sparkling droplets of sweat on Rangi's dark skin as soon as the door sealed behind us.

Salt water, rot, shit piss and sweat mixed into a smell that was somehow worse than all of them. I could see Min was embarrassed as she stood by the bench in front of a stack of Total™ – *how the fuck does she afford that?* – and a stripey bio-tub of Instant™.

Trying to stay calm and not let on how tight my stomach was, I went to the bed.

'Rangi,' I said, beckoning him.

With my hands out over the bed, I nudged his big thick leg with the side of my knee, hoping Min couldn't see. The tiny head jerked and turned to face us when the power filled him. The kid started crying when he saw the two strangers looking down at him and I heard Min coming over so I held up my hand for her to wait.

How I knew, I had no idea but I kind of felt when Rangi was done; like a glow around us faded out though the light hadn't changed at all. Maybe it was something in his breathing or maybe our bond was finally beginning to deepen. I hoped so, I was sick of him pawing me. The kid started crying and I stepped out of the way so his mother could get to him.

I hadn't seen what he looked like when he was sick so I couldn't tell if he was better or not but I had to take it on faith and not show any doubt. While Min did sick-making babytalk and fussed over the kid, I pinged a few of the nanites I'd brought and sent them to… maintain her flat.

She must have noticed the place changing because she looked up mid kid-fuss and stared wide-eyed at the walls as the water and stains shrunk and the air got fresher and drier. Then I had to decide whether to take the tech back or not. If I gave it to her, the place would stay good for years until it wore out. But if I took it back off her, it would start going downhill again however long that took since whatever tech came with the flat had obviously all broken down.

In the end, I let it do a full clean on the squealing kid and the flat, and made sure her climate control was all working then called the nanites back on to my overs. There would be millions more visits like this, as much as I shivered at the idea.

I had billions of raw nanites on the sacred ingot but I couldn't give them all away.

I gave her a don't ask look and said, 'We have to go now.' I tried to sound enigmatic. My memories were playing so fast my eyes probably did look woo-woo and faraway.

It's not woo-woo! I have to believe!

'Yep. Yes. I understand. G— Thank you so much your— Thank you. I knew you'd come. I knew you were real. Thank you!'

She kept whittering away as we left and I held my breath down the hallway until we got into the lift, then again at the ground floor until we got out the door. The rain had stopped and the wind had died down though the sky was dark with cloud. I sucked in air and the smell of the sea was better than the inside of Min's vile building.

I realised I was exhausted and hungry after I'd jettisoned my breakfast on the concrete earlier. I needed food, Total™, more caffeine, a J™ and to go back to bed and to not see the awful sea for the rest of my-like, life. But we had to get home.

'Come on, Rangi. Take us home.'

I went around the corner towards the seawall but Rangi caught up to me and shook his head.

'You must speak to the Uber,' he said and though it was hard to tell with his dark face hidden in his long black hair, I could've sworn he looked worried.

I might have given it a second thought if the idea of seeing the water underneath us didn't frighten me so much right then. Instead, I nodded and wished I'd brought something to eat as we waited the hour for the Uber to arrive.

On the way back around the coast I checked my logs but I was too tired to curate and decided to sort it all out and do the uploads later on.

Rangi sat opposite me and said nothing for a change. He stared over my shoulder into space looking… concerned, if I was reading him right. Did he need recharging or something? Did this mean he was going to eat me out of house and home again?

When we arrived, he followed me inside but he didn't go for the Total™s in his usual magic way. I got to them before him. And instead of floating a bottle off the bench, he picked it up in the-like… normal way and drank it absent-mindedly.

Then he went to squat in front of the window again and I didn't get another word out of him for the rest of the day. Not that I gave it much thought because against the laws of physics and the universe, a last-minuter pinged up and I'd had the agency space so dim I barely saw it in time.

I got stoned after the viewing and wasted more money on a flash risotto which had real vegetables and posh fake ice cream that had basically no disgusting aftertaste. I'd filled up on Total™ before they arrived so I only ate a little of each. The flavours felt like coming home and I had to go into my room and cry and the weed made it seem like the tears kept coming for hours. I fell asleep on top of the duvet with my overs on and it was night and moonlight glittered on the sea outside when I woke.

Looking out over the water and up at the racing clouds, I thought for a second the sea was actually sort of pretty though I knew it was poison. The goddess' calm filled me but I blacked out the window before I put myself to bed properly anyway.

Next morning, I woke to discover the weed had done its job and my head felt nice and fluffy. If I concentrated on the stuff I had to do, all the… other stuff sat more or less harmlessly in the back of my mind like a dream I hoped I'd forget. Except I could never fully fucking forget it.

I lay in bed and went into the Movement space. Min had posted a video on my public forum. She was laughing and in tears at the same time. Her little boy was bright-eyed and clean like her and she panned the video around her flat which smelled good after the cleaning and repairs I'd given her.

It came back to her after a while and she said, 'I knew it was true. I believed. My little boy was dying and I was sick and I'd got us hooked on Total™ – I know! I know! Pathetic but at least I'm admitting it! And I'm never buying a bottle of the evil crap again! She has brought new light to our lives! This flat that you can see, which we live in, it was a health hazard! Shitty seawater was leaking in – we live in the basement right against the seawall because I got down-rated by some rich wanker and I didn't do anything wrong! The tech in this place is shot to shit and it wasn't fixing itself. Then Papatūānuku and Rangi came; I swear, I was watching the door and one minute, they weren't there and the next they were. They didn't use an Uber, they turned up without a sound; they probably actually flew here.

'And they used their powers to heal me and my Matty and fix up the flat too! Look! The tech's dead but everything works! They did it with their powers! I knew it was true! I had faith and the goddess didn't let me down and I wanted everyone out there to know. You have to believe in her and she will come through. Things are gonna get better now, me and my boy are proof!'

She'd put vids of us in the flat, standing over her bed. The TrueLife™ was there but at the same time, it didn't look like much. It wasn't like my head getting fixed or Rangi bursting through a window or anything. It looked like a kid waking up and bawling.

Woo-fucking-hoo.

If people could be bothered, they could ask her for the kid's biotech logs and diagnostics – in the unlikely event she'd bought a diagnosis. And smarter wet-foots than her would guess the flat was fixed by tech. And since the nanites responsible weren't there any more, well, it could be bad for me if anyone started saying maybe it had been done with illegal nanites. I knew the goddess had sent the ingot to me but nobody else did.

The more I thought about it, the more I realised that unless anyone bothered to check up on the story, it would be like any crap fake news with a long boring tail of he-said-she-said blah blah blah.

The stuff with my head was a start. And the flying, if my eyes had been opened for enough of it to get anything decent, was a – oh dear Tina… – jump start. But it couldn't be only me and him. There were already enough trolls accusing me of hacking TrueLife™. We needed better stuff, other people's vids with TrueLife™.

Rangi was in front of the window when I got up. I'd put on baggy hemps which I hoped made me look unsexy but he grunted without turning so no danger of… anything, for now. After my coffee and a bottle of Total™, I got to work with the agency space a bit less dim than in the last few weeks in case another last-minuter came.

Curating my logs before uploads was calming. Though I wasn't as into it as my sis… as lots of people, finding the good shots and editing the vids was like breathing. I had thousands of hours of footage including some I could probably get money for in adult spaces. In those, I toned down Rangi's skin and made sure my face wasn't anywhere.

Cheesy free skins put posh furniture in my flat. Changing the colours of the walls took care of hiding my location and I dubbed some generic smell and gross fake 'ooh-ooh-ah-ah' sex sounds over the top of… how it had sounded, before up-loading.

With all the edits, it wasn't worth bothering with TrueL-ife™ but I didn't think the filthy lowlifes who visited those spaces to get off were going to whinge about fake footage; which it wasn't really anyway. I felt icky after that so moved quickly on.

Hours of the footage were of Rangi squatting in front of the window, me getting undressed for bed, sleeping, getting up, packing the J™, vaping, drinking Instant™ and Total™, sitting on the toilet nudging the door open, teaching Rangi his words and smearing Total™ all over my walls like a nutjob to teach him his letters and *hànzìs*. The juicy bits barely filled half an hour.

There were plenty of SOS calls threaded on to Min's post: lots of sick kids, people taking the piss and asking me for fur-niture and fucking all out flat renovations, far too many asking if I could magic them up some food. Which in a… finite sort of way, I could have.

Then I opened one from some guy called Pete with no hair and only a few teeth. The handle was public and he had an online space of his own. He'd set up the video so it looked like he was naked and he was pasty and half muscle, half chub. His eyes were pink-rimmed and too close together and he reeked of stale weed and sweat. Through the window behind him I could see a crumbling seawall that could have been any of the ones near here.

He zoomed his cameras close to his face and his breath nearly singed my eyebrows. 'Hey arsehole. You're a fake-news nutjob slut and I'm gonna find you and fuck some sense into your skinny lying butt. Why don't you do us all a favour you bullshitting fuck, and jump in the sea and drown before Pete comes 'round to teach you a lesson?'

My heart raced and my food burked up towards the light and a fire I hadn't felt for months blew up inside me. It was the goddess' rage I'd felt the day Nate had been locked up and after the first shock of seeing Pete the creep's forum post, it made me cold and calm and gave me strength.

I recorded a piece with Rangi hulking over my shoulder with his shirt off and his dark hair half hiding his face. I made it sticky on my forum so there was no way visitors could miss it, no matter how many people posted.

'I am Papatūānuku. I am the goddess who channels and guides the untamed power of Ranginui of The Sky! As you have all seen, I bring healing, hygiene and peace to those in need and I will never stop until your sick and injured children are whole and well and there is food on everyone's table and the sea is banished from every leaking home.

'But do not mistake my generosity and tenderness for weakness. Those ignorant, spineless, stupid and limp-dicked little men abusing me over hundreds of kays of land and sea because they are too pathetic to challenge me to my face, they will receive none of my care and they should be warned, I am not defenceless and I am not weak.'

Pete's space was disgusting. He was some kind of neo-misogynist, an actual real one! He had all these gross vids of him having sex with his sick-looking greasy-haired girlfriend and leering at the audience. It showed what a loser idiot he was since he could have posted them in adult spaces and made money like I'd started to. He'd also recorded himself doing pathetic talks about men being the natural owners of the world and I would have laughed if it hadn't been for his tens of millions of followers.

After Pete's message, I stuck to the ones sent by women but it was nearly worse …*who the fuck are you to call yourself a mother goddess, you skinny fakist bitch? Have you got children? Do you eat enough to have periods? Were you always a woman?…*

Finally, I found an ill single-mum whose daughter had mashed her leg playing in some rubble – which said a lot about the wet-foot mum! – and her little boy had a fever like all the kids seemed to. She was another starving one, slowly dying of Total™-induced stomach problems and having to kill her kids along with her because the addiction ate up their food budget and barely left them enough for drinking water. I knew I could give her Nate's points hack but it wouldn't start paying off for a while so I decided this once, I'd make all her dreams come true. On film.

I got in touch with her and it was as embarrassing as talking with Min had been. Getting the Uber before leaving was a stroke of genius. It was an hour away so I had time to chill with a J™ and a triple espresso before pinging a few nanites off the ingot and dragging Rangi out into the rain and impressing him with the waiting car.

I didn't bother telling him where we were going but he got the hint quick enough. I made sure we, well, I, got good close-up footage of the kid's leg and tried not to vom as I held my hands over it and forced my goddess expression on. We left the three of them all fixed and well, whittering away happily about their clean flat in their dreadful wet-foot accent.

I gave her Nate's points hack, transferred satoshis to her account and had her get in a load of posh food to start it ticking up on her PrimeFlix-KBellPharm account. My stern admonishment to say no to drugs probably fell on deaf ears but what can you do with someone like that.

Thanks, thanks, thanks, thanks, thanks, I'll do anything to repay you, goddess, blah blah blah. It was the worst part of it!

It was simply graft after that. I vaped weed like it grew on trees – well… – to keep my mind off everything but couldn't stop dreaming about smelly flats, ugly sick kids, greasy-haired wastrel single mums and Rangi's hands like black steel on my hips pulling….

And he was a growing pain in my bum too. He was learning too fast. His Mandarin tones got better from one day to the next and his English inflection was near perfect. It was getting too hard to avoid his questions about where was this place? What was this world? What was I? He went through bottle after bottle of Total™ and it annoyed me how perfect his *hànzìs* on the wall were though he'd done them with his fucking fingers!

Every day, I double checked my periods were turned off, gritted my teeth and kept posting the paydirt. I started wondering whether it was worth the income that dribbled in along with my work retainer and a couple more derisory last minuter payments. The sacred ingot had barely shrunk but a part of me that I hated, that had been drilled into my brain since birth, that kept calculating… *You could live on that much if you ran out, it's more than you were making working full time anyway.* Much as I hated it, that part of me knew no matter how much I had, I could always spend it.

If my plan worked none of it would matter but it was a long shot and I knew it.

There were so many followers active in my space, I couldn't keep up. All the people I'd helped posted foam about me that wasn't true. I'd apparently walked in through the walls of their flat glowing gold and someone asked me if I could bottle my sweat and urine because it was known to have healing properties and prolong life. Some woman with weird spirally techtoos asked if I'd endorse these crappy green knickknacks she'd printed and wanted to sell; they were the same as her 'toos.

She told me in the ancient e-books in the library, it said the *koru* was the jade embodiment of the mother's vagina – I looked it up, it so wasn't! – and if I blessed her weird twisty things, they would bring the wearer luck, fertility and good health; like we needed more fucking babies in this awful world! I told her it was true but only if I got a donation to the Movement out of every sale.

And with every new subscriber came another filthy troll. Some of them subscribed because it made it harder to keep them out of my space. It was like the disgusting Pete guy had an army or something. He had women – women! – on his side and they all kept calling me filthy names and making up lies about how I was really a rich-fuck planted to win their trust then get them arrested for stuff. My accent was off, they reckoned. And my 'toos were supposedly wrong and my language was fake and my face was apparently too healthy. I couldn't believe how people fucking turned on you for trying to help them!

One night, I decided I'd done enough and put up with enough… poo. If the world didn't know what I was about by now it never would. It was time for the next phase of the Movement to start; before all those fucking wet-foots drove me mad. I pinged the handle Jamie Yang had given me and he answered straight away. He looked older than his news-streams. But who didn't? He turned out to be an amazing guy.

Trashy as his accent was, the sound of his voice alone – the first time I'd spoken with someone other than Rangi and all the free-loading wet-foots in months – was soothingly sane. He asked me about the goddess and Rangi and I could tell he wasn't taking the piss, he genuinely believed me.

He was friendly and informal and for the first time since Nate had gone away, I felt like someone cared about me. He wanted to know how I guided Rangi's power and I felt a bit bad about lying to him so I said it was really about teaching Rangi about the Earth since he had slept for so long. I told him when the healing happened, the goddess inhabited my body and I went somewhere else and it was too hard to describe.

And yes, we could get through walls, we could fly. I wasn't sure about glowing gold because, as I'd said, when the goddess was in me, I wasn't aware of anything. And Yang didn't take the piss one bit! He was incredibly open minded; not like all the stupid trolls plaguing my Movement space.

The next steps question was the one I'd been waiting for. All I had to do was be honest and tell him I knew the goddess wanted to lift people out of poverty and turn the tables on the rich who were oppressing them but Hers was not to worry about earthly details. She had given me the tools to begin and it was up to me to carry on the work.

We had to keep all the people I had healed healthy. Healing was like breathing for me, for the goddess, but the goddess' flesh was too ruined for her to bring forth fruit until we had undone enough of the harm we did to her, for her to thrive and yield up her gifts again. For the time being, we would have to fend for ourselves and keep making and buying our own food the way we were, and for that we needed money which the rich hoarded.

The real rich wouldn't care and they wouldn't give us a penny to help bring them down, course they wouldn't. But there were plenty of other people who might have a bit to spare and those were the people I needed to donate to my online space. I couldn't keep using my own money to feed people forever – I ignored his question about where I was getting the money to give away all the stuff I had in the first place and he never came back to it.

After enough people were fed and we had enough money together, I told him, we could look to sticking it to the rich right where it would hurt them most. We'd set up our own food production and supplies, construction, the whole lot. Then they'd see how it felt to be out of the job, starving and homeless.

Yes, Nate. I do know about all that stuff.

I felt so good when we cut the call I didn't mind when Rangi came for me, later on. I cleaned up straight after I'd posted it to the adult spaces though, and stayed in my room for the rest of the day.

Yang said he'd post the interview in a few days once he'd got through some other stuff and had a chance to polish it up so I treated myself to a posh food order. I sneaked a cheeky Total™ so I wasn't hungry when it arrived and left it for later. I stayed offline for the first time in weeks. More last-minuters came and I didn't care that I had to work because it passed the time while I waited.

A couple of the viewers bothered their bums to rate me and that bumped me up to four-point-seven-two. I'd have my old job back in less than a year at this rate. I could move back to Cornwall estate.

...Jo Rahui is dead? Fuck!...

There was no way I could go back there with Chen and all those... people just... there. And if they weren't there, if they'd gone somewhere or something, the thought made me feel mheah, anyway. The way things were with Rangi, despite all his... upkeep, I felt like I was doing something, getting somewhere, getting known.

The day the interview went up, I ordered posh pizza with real vegetables and locked myself in my room to watch. It started well and I smiled as I remembered talking with Yang, like we'd known each other forever.

He'd smiled at me a lot, I definitely remembered that because he had his 'toos all over his teeth like vintage braces. But the look he was giving the audience now had never happened, I was sure of it.

There was a bit of zooming in on his face when I was answering his questions. I'd never once felt like he was secretly laughing at some pissy in-joke as he was in those shots. My bits all had TrueLife™ but none of his did. Nobody would be checking though, would they, since it was me they were watching. Still, I thought I came off pretty well anyway.

He spliced in loads of the single mums' footage minus how their flats smelled and with cheesy heart-strings background music. It made me look really good despite his smart-arse face shots.

Then the interview finished and I was about to leave his space but the piece kept going. As I watched the stuff he'd tacked on the end, cold spread inside me till my whole body froze. It felt like when I'd lost all my viewings. And afterwards, I discovered I had been fired.

The agency hadn't wasted any time after Yang's piece on me went viral. A message pinged through with a stupid machine-voice and no 4S. It told me I had a week to take over my tenancy or my flat would be turned off and if I stayed, I'd be charged with trespassing.

Everyone knew the drill, weirdly, though it happened to no one. I was the only person I'd ever heard of who'd been fired. Too bad the idiots hadn't unregistered me at Cornwall though they themselves had sold me this place. Wouldn't they look like dicks when they tried to evict someone who wasn't there.

But you can be arrested no matter where you are...

The thought made my burning cheeks and clenching gut worse. My body was numb and my muscles were so tense I couldn't move. I couldn't think enough to access my tech so I was stuck in Yang's space where the highlights of my ruination looped between boring crap pieces on sea quakes and rich people's property trends like the two had anything to do with each other.

I knew I should have got up, eaten, vaped some weed, figured out what to do. But it was getting dark by the time I pulled myself offline and went to the toilet. Rangi was staring out the window with a Total™ bottle breaking down on the carpet next to him.

There was a storm outside but I was so numb I didn't bother dimming the windows. I wanted nothing to do with shitty tech ever again. I ignored all the stupid warnings and shut my tech down right to the base OS. Humans had lived without fucking man tech for thousands of years so I didn't care whether I got sleep-apnoea and choked to death or had a heart attack or wet my bed in the middle of the night.

I swore when I had to start it all up again to ping my bedroom door locked. Then I shut it down, again, and burrowed into my pillow. But hands and tentacles waited in my dreams. Needles and claws drilled under my gums and tore up my teeth and I woke up sweating again and again.

By morning I was more tired from the nightmares than when I'd gone to bed. My tech had started its fucking self back up and messages from the Movement space and strange balance alerts were jumping like roaches in a pest control blitz. Fucking Pete and his disgusting followers were having a field day!

Who knew why the giant oaf did anything but Rangi stayed put in his usual place by the window and for once in his retarded life didn't come at me for lessons or... anything. Lucky for him, else I'd probably have strangled him.

I was in such a bad mood, it took me a while to clock that all the balance alerts popping up were credits. I checked my balance and that was when I saw the zeroes. I had millions; billions. And not only satoshis, either, whole bitcoins! I was as rich as a bonafide rich fuck!

Again.

I ignored the glib thought. This time, it was under my own steam. As I watched, the total ticked up. It didn't make any sense until I drilled into my statement and saw where it was all coming from and wished I'd never looked.

But I couldn't get my head around it. In a few hours I'd got rich enough to buy back at Cornwall. And I'd have enough change to live on for years after. Forever! It was too much to handle, the last ten years, Arsehole Uncle John and the NDA, Rangi, the things he did to me, the things he could do and did for me that meant he must be a god except...

No!

I couldn't think about any, except. But my thoughts kept racing and I couldn't stop them: losing my shifts, moving, everything that had happened, the humiliation and the sudden tera-balance which was somehow more humiliating than exciting. That I could get famous and make my fortune, like, that, after everything! It was wrong.

My head spun with memories of the last twelve years and the walls started closing in. It wouldn't be long before I bolted in some random direction and hurt myself or passed out. And then something so surreal happened, it all got blasted out of my mind.

'Tina? *Nǐ hǎo!* Long time no speak, hey?'

Yang? Fucking, Jamie Yang? What the fuck?

'Uh, yes?' I didn't remember accepting his call but I must have done else how could I be on it.

'Hey, Tina! Great to connect again. Hey look, we've got you live, right now! How 'bout that, eh? Eh, Tina? Look, Tina, I wonder if I could get you to comment on your-uh, interesting footage?'

'Uh—'

'"Uh" is right, Tina!' His brown face crinkled in a smile and this time there was no mistake he was mocking me. 'As in, "Uh, uh, ooh, ooh, more, please, more!" Eh, Tina? Eh? You've gotta admit, it's an interesting side hustle to your, um, holy Movement isn't it, Tina?'

Bastard! Fucking bastard!

And then the goddess uncurled, burning and freezing inside me. My breathing slowed and Her words were carried up from the depths of my soul on a wave of holy rage, out of my mouth and into the cloud where our sacred Movement gave birth, driving it onward with Her ancient power behind it.

'Actually, Jamie,' I said in the goddess' voice, stopping him in his tracks, 'the sacred joining of Mother Earth and Father Sky, Papa and Rangi is central and key to the holy Movement. For the world to see and smell, up close and in person, the juices of Earth and Sky mingling, glistening, on the very organs that create life, in a form of hallowed joining as old as time itself, is a blessing unprecedented in all of human history.

Never before have we been able to bear witness to such un-earthly pleasure and holy love, en masse.'

Yang, fuck him, was looking scared.

Good. He bloody well should be.

'Yes, go on then, Jamie. Shame the woman for her sex! The more things change, the more they stay the same, hey? Eh, Jamie? Eh? I've given up my intimate pleasure, my body, my privacy to show the world something beautiful, something magical and all you can do is snigger like the pathetic man-child you are. Go on Jamie, I can see you want to. Go on, laugh at the slutty woman, Jamie! Here you go, how 'bout a bit of live action, Jamie?' I stripped off my hemps and underwear, making sure my cameras gave him full access to the room. I thrust my crotch at his face and pointed at my vagina in case he'd fucking missed it.'

Jamie Yang didn't get where he was by being shockable but his face was satisfyingly strained.

'You know, something, Jamie?' I went on like I hadn't stripped naked live in front of millions of viewers. 'I'm pleased everyone has forgotten about the man in the video, that they've made it all about my vagina and I. Yeah, it's a shame all you idiot men and pathetic yes-girls have made this about the sex and not the love between Rangi and I. But in the end, I'm glad I'm the one on your stupid feed and not Rangi. It makes a change, it being about the woman for fucking once and not all about the bloody man!'

The goddess left me, then but it didn't matter. Her work was done. I closed my legs and stood in front of Yang, naked and unashamed, staring him down. He blinked first and opened his mouth to speak but I cut the call.

I sat back and watched my followers double and double again. Subscriptions to the Movement skyrocketed and my balance got so big I didn't know the name of the number it showed any more. I'd got the fuck out of in front of this and I knew it. And I'd seen in Yang's gormless eyes that he knew it too. I'd fucking showed them. I could do anything. Fucking anything.

Bad Luck – 9900 BCE, Yellow River, North China

There was a glint. Was it water? Swirling black. Was it cloud? Whatever I passed through, it was too fast to see. And then she was there in blazing topaz-white, deep crystal blue and glittering purple. She shrieked words in a language I couldn't understand and her voice echoed through the latticed layers and blue flowing haze.

The smells came first, pungent loam and the strangely sterile tang of clay mixed with the fruity ripeness of animal dung and the musk of human sweat. Then saturated heat washed over me and finally the blue and purple place faded and was replaced as the dream changed. Green trees, red and yellow soil and blaring sunlight through a humid haze unfolded around me and I felt myself sinking, shrinking until I was all but... replaced.

His memories are in her language. But I know what they mean.

It was the last thought of my own before I diminished to a guttering spark of myself and could do nothing but drift on the currents of a dead spirit's dream.

I was Bad Luck. Named for the bad luck everyone reckoned I'd bring them if they got too near me. I grew big as a boar but as far as my family were concerned that made me a bigger lot of bad luck, though they stopped saying it to my face.

Most nights I tried to stay awake because I didn't much care for sleeping but on the nights that I failed, well then I'd wake up bad tempered and that made me a big lot of bad tempered bad luck.

Not many people talked to me and when they did, they would look sideways and away and pretty soon, they'd have something else they had to go and do right then. Old Young Bud, the Old Young Healer's woman, as I'd always known her didn't have any such qualms. She told me my mother was sickly when she heaved me out and I'd been no bigger baby than any and the bleeding that killed her was her own bad luck she'd brought on herself for misdeeds in her own life which had nothing to do with me.

That was her way of saying she didn't hold with how the family were to me but I never heard her speaking up for me either. Nor did she ever tell me what those misdeeds of my mother's were. But nor did I ever ask.

I moved away. Not all at once. Since becoming a man, I'd slept in the older caves, down near the old Gathering cave and the place of the dead where the river gurgled and flowed and roared at rain time and where the orange light of the ancestors shone all through the night.

For all the babies the women kept having, those caves were empty at night, since Healer and Bud had hewn out the new ones and melted the rock and earth to make a new cliff. It joined with the rock in the place beyond our highest cave, where the ground rose up to meet the cliff and the river curled away like a mighty snake into the forested hills.

Their new baby cliff stood a man and a half tall, and stretched out and away into the trees. When I was a boy, I didn't see the point in it because anyone wanting to attack us would have gone around it through the trees to get at us.

But Young old Healer had straightened that out of me. 'And what will we do when our watchers see them creeping down the side and into the trees eh? Khu! What are you? Dumb as well as Bad Luck?'

Besides, our hunters brought in plenty of wounded along with the pigs they sometimes got. Our enemies would no more want to enter the forest than us. Well, what could I say? I was only a boy.

In any case, the silent cliffs nobody could see grew thicker and thicker between me and the family. They moved with me wherever I went till the silence grew so loud in my ears that I began to enter the woods uncaring of snakes and boars and thinking if they ate me then I would be worth something to someone though it was only a meal.

I went further and further, out to the end of the new cliff, past it, around it, up and up the sloping ground to where it finally met the roots of trees on the clifftop. From there I was able to look down over the family and out over the river and the trees to where smoke from the cookfires of some other family curled up from another bend in the river far off in the distance. And I never went back down.

I lived well enough in the high-up forest and its peeps and creaks at night meant I slept little and dreamed less which was a good sort of life as far as I saw it. As the sun set over the mountains beyond the valley, I would look down as the family readied themselves for sleep.

I stayed joined to them if only by thin smoky coils that told me at least a little of their news. It told me they were cooking yams and sweet potatoes or that the hunters had brought in a lucky kill. Or sometimes that someone had died and their ash and bones had been buried at the ever-growing place of the dead with its rattling piles of skulls.

As the cookfires faded to red, I would watch the shadows grow in front of the caves below as the sinking sun shone on my face where it poked from my nest of branches and leaves. Our family's grounds were never fully swallowed by the night though clouds often covered the moon and stars. For the soft orange light of the cave nobody spoke of or entered, bathed the dirt and clay and trees at the edges of the grounds.

It was known, Bud and Healer channelled the Flow sent into their souls by the ancestors to warm and heal us and make good our fortunes. But there were some cousins, lazy ones who shirked their jobs, skulking in the shabbiest caves and spreading lies of a spirit of the otherworld enslaved against Earth and Sky. They said that was what had been trapped in the cave in the days before I was born and it was made to give Healer and Bud eternal youth and power unending and they wanted nobody to see their shame.

Why else, went their wah-wah-moo-moo tale, must we range further and further for food to feed the babies that popped from their mothers who died older and older and so had yet more babies with more and more missing toes and stuck-together fingers and dim heads and blind eyes?

Wound-rot, spun by skulking insects afraid of hard work and sunlight, I reckoned. More babies, more odd babies. They had always been amongst us, only there weren't so many of us before. But Stump, Stupid, Bat and Wah-Wah-Stick-Not-Letting-Go Girl, Bud's own children of rain times and other times back and not so far back, were what they were all right; strange lot of bad luck for her, nobody could argue.

Sometimes more than smoke floated up to me on the evening air. Now and again, the Young Old Bud herself would churn up the yellow soil, making it bleed red clay as she floated up the cliff and settled to the ground like a giant clumsy moth.

'How are you?' she would ask.

I didn't know why she kept disturbing me like that or why I bothered answering her soft rain of questions, maybe because of who she was. How was I eating? Had I been far back from the clifftop into this forest? What was back there? Did that smoke in the distance – how could she see it after sunset like this? – ever come closer? Get thicker, like maybe that family was lighting more fires? Though she looked no older than me, I wasn't fool enough to forget who she was. I didn't dare talk back too much though my answers were sometimes short and surly or sometimes, I didn't know.

Annoying as she was, I found the tales of my wanderings in the high forest wanting to come out to meet her questions anyway. I spoke of the new cliffs I'd found with some of their own caves, cooler than the family's and far from the river. They were hidden in the trees with no space before them so any old snake or boar could sneak in and share the shelter with you and you'd never know until it was too late. But I was thinking of going to live in them anyway.

'So why don't you then?'

I didn't know and I didn't like the way she smiled and looked as if she did know. She didn't seem surprised about the caves but I supposed Bud and Healer knew a lot of things nobody else knew because of how old and powerful they were.

Sometimes before she churned up earth and shook trees as she fell like a feather into the forest outside the grounds, she would tell me, 'All things are useful to know no matter how small they seem; best we don't lose your sticks and pebbles of the knowledge, eh?' And she would smile and push me on to my back and collect my essence, in that way that women did sometimes, for when I became an ancestor and could not give it over in words any more. Besides Healer's power and wisdom, I could not imagine what use Bad Luck and a nest of snakes might be. But I could not question Bud's wisdom either.

I nested on the clifftop through rain times, dry heat and cold, living well enough with a whole forest at my back and only me to forage in it. Slowly at first but then all in a rush, Bud seemed younger still, and I realised with a chill in the middle of a hot wet day that things weren't as easy for me as they'd used to be. I missed more cicadas than I grabbed and it took me longer to fill up on them and made me more tired in the getting.

When chicken parts and morsels of pig began sprouting on the ground near my nest, I wanted to hide my face away though there was nobody near to see, for now Bud was feeding me like a child. I could not bring myself to speak of it with her though my answers to her questions grew longer and keener. Tired as it made me, I made great forages along the clifftop, into the forest and along the cavemouths in the far cliff, down the valley beside the river, far beyond any of our hunts.

I needed new things to tell her when she came; a family of pigs here; a nest of snakes there; a flock of strange juicy fat birds nesting low with plentiful eggs over that way and another lowering of the ground to a shallow rocky wide part of the river, far down the valley where slow stupid water buffalo wallowed. It seemed enough for Bud. She listened and nodded and drank it all in and my tiny grounds stayed rich enough with sprouting pieces of food.

Some time or another, I had grown too afraid to chance anything bigger than a hare or a bird. I listened with ailing ears and watched with fearful dimming eyes in case a boar stumbled on me in the night. I doubted I would have the strength to drive a spear into its side no matter if my aim was true. I was growing old.

And that was why I doubted myself at first, the year such rains as I had never seen tempered the first heat after the white of the distant mountains furled back up into the clouds. After the rain I heard a rumble like thunder coming from far away. I looked over the valley to where smoke often rose from the other family's grounds but now there was no smoke and the trees there looked different, as if they had… gone?

That was when the rumble in my ears joined the forest in my eyes and I froze like a finch trapped in winter when I saw what was coming. Still, I hesitated, thinking I had slept worse than usual and it was some sort of demon dream come over me in the day. But the rumble grew louder and from my high nest I could no longer deny what gave it its voice.

A brown frothing fury of water was rushing down the valley as if the river had grown ravenous and would wait no more to swallow up the earth.

'Flee!' I called down in my croaking sickly voice. 'The waters are rising!'

But nobody heard me. I threw down dirt and twigs to make them look up though the cliff was too high for me to see if I had made my myself known or not. 'The water!' I wheezed, until my voice gave out.

I could see it clearly now, foaming across the valley pushing yellow and red earth, boulders and trunks before it. As I
watched, it ate up the space between its foaming front and my
family's grounds. The crack and groan of dying trees and the
far-off squealing and squawking of pigs and birds fleeing before the waters reached my ears.

I limped along the clifftop to the place where the sloping
ground rose up from the family caves to meet it. I hoped they
could hear the loudening roar but I feared the trees were hiding the sound from them. Grumbling and asking myself what
good the lot of them had ever done me anyway, I limped down
the slope. Though I could no longer see the water, my soul
screamed at me to flee back up to the clifftop and away from
the foaming death. But still, they were my family.

As I had feared, the roar grew dull and quiet as I came
below the treetops and I limped faster and my bones ached
more. It was only a distant sound, whispering treacherously
between the song of the rustling leaves when I came into the
shadow of the family's short cliff at last.

It looked different now, green and growing with vines and
moss. A few broken old skulls bared their teeth between the
leaves and if I had not been so afraid, I might have laughed to
see them. They must have been from some attack nobody alive
remembered; or maybe stolen from the place of the dead. A
voice shouted down. 'That you, cracking our heads with sticks
like the wah-wah-moo-moo old fool that you are, Bad Luck?'

I stood and panted and the watcher poked his head over
the wall and said, 'eh? Is it?'

I had my breath back by then and said, 'Quickly! The river
has burst its banks! It's coming down the valley! Everyone
must flee! Now!'

'Wound-rot!'

The youngster stood up and his broad shoulders and powerful chest cleared the top of the cliff. Either they had made
the watch posts higher or he was a monster.

'Listen boy! Listen! Be quiet and listen!' I pleaded.

And he listened for a breath and said, 'I can hear nothing, go back to your nest, stupid old chicken.'

'Please!' I said. 'I saw it from above! It will be here soon. It will overwhelm you all. Get Old Young Bud! Or anyone. I swear it's true. If you don't come now, everyone will die and it will be your fault. Please! If it slows to a trickle before it comes here then I will lie down and make no complaint when you crush my skull with a rock for wasting your time. Please go! Warn them.'

'No! Don't be…'

But the rustle of the leaves in the wind sounded different now, something deep and ominous rose above it, and he noticed. I saw the uncertainty cloud his face and I was sick and tired of his stupidity anyway. He reminded me of why I'd left the lot of them alone. I said, 'Well don't warn them then. Sit back down on your post and play with yourself until the water comes to crush you. I will watch from up there and be glad the valley had the sense to eat someone as thick as you.'

I turned and limped back up the slope as the roar and crack of the flood came on.

He did warn them, though.

I saw my limping journey had not been wasted. I fell exhausted when I reached my nest and crawled to the cliff edge to watch what I thought might be the end of my family.

Much of the valley was covered in rushing brown. Only the strongest and tallest of trees stood against it as elbows of angry foam left behind by the surging waterfront, tugged at their roots and trunks as if in annoyance at their defiance. Cats and birds lay heavy on their branches and shrieking twittering flocks circled above the valley and curled away over my head to make new nests in the trees on higher ground.

A squealing and crashing came to my ears as the boars and slinking cats of the forest by our own piece of the river heard their doom flowing down the valley and fled up the slope. Soon their chitter was joined by shouts and wails as the family finally got on the move.

Below me, I saw people gathering before the caves and fleeing towards the short cliff. They spread along it and tried to climb over. But our family had grown vast and though there were many watch posts, the family were so many more. Shouts and screams sounded above the water as they fought each other to climb over first.

I had thought there was time, that though it moved quickly, the water was well up the valley. But as if to trick us, it had sent a cunning finger of itself ahead, concealed beyond the jutting cliff, foaming down the river, around the bend and up over the place of the dead, tossing skulls and dirt before it.

Where are Healer and Bud? They could...

Even as I thought it, I saw the ground before the caves and up the slope churn and bleed red as the flood roared up and claimed the first of the family. But as the first souls were lost beneath mud and foam as they fled, climbed, fought and dithered, the family rose into the air as one.

They floated up to me as if they were no lighter than mist and clouds and their shouts of alarm grew louder as they drew closer. Though most alighted unharmed along the clifftop, some were lost. Bud and Healer's channelling uprooted trees and tore great chunks of rock and yellow and red earth from the cliff.

As the family came down to earth, some fell scrabbling and screaming and were smashed to blood and guts in the churning water as it carried them away into the valley. But for all that, most were saved and the young dumb giant from the watch-posts saw me and waved and called and soon they all took up his cry, 'Bad Luck! Bad Luck! Bad Luck!'

It was all more noise than I had grown accustomed to in my years alone. Mixed with the fury of the waters below, their voices seemed angry to me and I cowered away, pressing myself back in the vines and leaves, flat against a trunk. I did not know if it was a stick or a bone I had tossed aside after eating one of Bud's presents. But something sharp cut into my foot anyway and though my blood ran sticky on the tree's roots, I could not bring myself to come away from the trunk where I shook and quailed at the voices roaring my name as one. 'Bad Luck! Bad Luck! Bad Luck!'

Bud was there and laid a hand on my arm. 'Easy elder,' she said. 'They praise you. You saved us all.'

She grasped my wrist and held it up and there was Old Young Healer raising my other hand. 'Look up, Elder,' he said. 'It is they who pay you respect today.'

I looked up and saw that he was right. Though all were shouting my name, their eyes were lowered as mine might have been facing Bud and Healer themselves.

The family swarmed away from the cliff edge and into the forest. Over the next days of rain and grief for the loss of our grounds and the ashes and skulls of our dead, a circle of elders was formed with Healer and Bud at its head and me at their side.

As the circle prattled, I began to recognise the faces of my distant youth. With each rasping voice came memories of the games and tricks and prides and passions of its owner in rain-times long past when the voices were young and strong and not roughened and weakened by the passing rains and cold times.

And too, came the memories of the curses and sleights every one of them had heaped on me before I wandered off to live alone. And for all the memories of their fire and childish dreams of the past, and the wrongs they had done me, in the end I could feel only pity for the dribbling coddled old fools they had become.

They knew nothing and had no good musing on where we should go or what we should do. It was me that knew of the water buffalo river crossing, the snakes, the birds and the cliffs with their tangles of roots and vines hiding the cavemouths from us. Something had happened to them that had not hap-pened to me and as I spoke my knowledge, my eyes passed over Healer and Bud both and with a chill, memories of the whisperings of the lazy ones hissed in the dark places of my soul.

They do everything for us. If we are reckless on the hunt, they can heal us. If we are cold, we sit back and they make fire though the wood is wet. Women do not die any more, more babies are born wrong...

But I kept my darkness to myself and spoke only of the task at hand. I did not know why Bud did not say she already knew all I was spouting after our nights together over all the rain times and through the cold ones. Maybe she had already smelt the spirit that had stolen into my body and she pitied me for the days to come. In any case, Healer was keen on the caves and swept his hand through the air when I worried about the forest before them.

'Nothing to Bud and I,' he scoffed happily. 'We will tear up the trees to make a new family ground and the wood will feed our cookfires for a thousand lifetimes.

I did not doubt that he would and that the family would move on from the flood and find peace and plenty in the new caves. But the dull words and petty chatter and face-saving of the others in the circle filled me with foreboding. Of course I could not gainsay Healer. Yet when I stole a look at Bud, it seemed she knew that in my mind, I already had. And that she agreed.

The rains poured on for days and it seemed to me the cooling torrents did less than I was accustomed to them doing, to ease the heat. Though everyone urged the young cousins to come to me at night and get some of Elder Bad Luck's good luck, I could not always help them. Instead, I sweated in the dripping forest and took less and less pleasure in food or the flesh of others.

It took long before the thickest of elders had finally saved enough face to agree that we would go through the forest and shelter in the new caves under the new cliff. It was less good sense and more that the water had come fully halfway up the cliff to meet us that finally made them all agree.

What Old Young Bud might or might not have smelt became plain enough by the time we were moving through the trees. I burned with inner fire no matter how cool the shade.

Some forest spirit had wormed in through the cut in my foot and it swelled purple and yellow like a ripe and rotting fruit.

Bud or Healer could have fixed me in a heartbeat but I dared not presume to ask. Snakebites and cuts and broken bones were plentiful enough in the youngsters who ranged through the trees to feed us and it would not be the first time I had cast out one of these impertinent intruders. I needed only to wait.

But not all such spirits are alike. As I limped on in the green shade with the family around me and their love suffusing my being as it never had before, I thought on how my journey this way in times past had not seemed so long and that I did not remember the upward tilt of the ground punishing me so much as now. As my mind wandered, I did not think to look in on my foot and anyway it was beginning to hurt less so perhaps my body would soon oust the meddling spirit in a burst of cold sweat.

Even in the green shadows of the trees with the scents of birds and animals and the smell of dead leaves and dirt all around, I might have seen or smelled the black rot of death creeping up my legs and begged for Healer or Bud to come. But it was others who took up that cry in the end. I heard them as if from far away, 'Someone get Healer! Bad Luck has fallen. He cannot rise!'

The heat rose up in my body and coursed through my blood and I knew I had left it too long and I was lost to the spirit assailing me. There was no pain and I wondered, *will I see its face in the place between, before it devours my soul? Will I join the ancestors or be forever lost?* Both would have been more to my liking than the damnation that came instead.

For instead of being devoured or ceasing to be altogether, gorged down by a nameless spirit of the earth and the roots and trees, the dream I had fled all my sleepless life rose up and dragged me away. Its poison violet tongue like spider-silk on the breeze through my life, now strong as a snake made of living stone in death, coiled about me and pulled me through the air.

Though it was only a glimpse, it seemed to me that I lost all the ground we had trodden, flying like a shooting star back through the trees in the night as my family wailed and keened after me. At the clifftop, I saw that the water in the valley had sunk and the river though swollen, moved sluggishly in its new resting place.

Water covered our old home and faint orange light shone up through the swirling surface. Into that light I plunged like a moth into flames. A cavemouth, a tunnel beneath the water, orange light, brighter and brighter and then the shrieking mad woman was before me and I was trapped in the glittering caves of her domain of blue hues and I could find no way to leave.

And then we spun apart and I tumbled away into the midnight depths.

For an instant I looked in through layers of lattices, gleaming channels and honeycombed spaces. A topaz mist swirled everywhere, in every space and I could feel its potence. Movement flitted, a figure danced far off, beckoning and I tried to follow it but… She was there again.

I've got to get back… Back where? Something hurts, something's wrong…

But I was gone again too soon, someone else in my place; stuffed impossibly into my time and my space.

Susan – Jan 2098, Cornwall Hill, Akarana Island, Aotearoa Archipelago

When I was kid, we used to make huts in the junk room upstairs. Dad kept the same layout when he bought the apartments and Aunty Anna did them up, so the junk room was still there; more or less empty after the move except for a few bioboxes of random and not so random crap.

Cleaning nanites'd gone on the market in the mid twennyfifties when I was maybe eight. By the time I was fifteen, I could barely remember what house dust looked like and my dad was a god unto the masses – yet again – and internationally reviled by manufacturers of household cleaning implements and reagents, toxic and eco, one and all. Didn't stop the government giving him some poxy national award, though. Back when the government mattered albeit by the skin of its teeth.

But we didn't get any till nearly a decade after it'd come out; they creeped Mummy out too much. But if we'd got them sooner, I may never have known Daddy had lied to me.

I was thirteen and my cousin-like friend Aaron and I were getting stoned and trying to sneeze quietly in the still-dusty junk room with the light off. We heard footsteps on the stairs, probably someone coming up to use the upstairs toilet but we scrambled to the back behind stacks of boxes and tried to hide anyway.

I sat in a pile of junk and something cold and sharp poked me in the bum-cheek. I made Aaron help me dig it out of the pile to see what it was. Then, a few days later, I lugged the mainframe downstairs to my room. A few days after that, I presented it to Daddy.

He said it was an old piece of junk he kept for sentimental reasons but that didn't explain why it was the only thing in the junk room crawling with cleaning nanites when we didn't yet have a set for the house. Or why it had a custom adaptor for modern tech allowing access to it from anywhere. Or indeed, why it was mysteriously fully charged despite sitting around disused for twenty-odd years. I nodded at him and marvelled that I – I, a mere teenager – had caught the old weasel in a lie.

I never told him I'd blown a month's allowance and rented cloud-power to crack the encryption on its antiquated internal storage mechanism. He never found out that I'd seen everything, everything he was hiding there. The hours of footage can't have been real since people didn't fade in and out of existence like CGI. But the notes and calculations and screeds of dead-end speculation Daddy had made about the 'ghost' made it seem like he did think it was real.

There were actual digitised photographs of a yellowy paper – paper! – notebook with entries from Daddy's settler ancestors on the European side dating all the way back to the settlement days, too. As if he was a member of some secret family cult or something.

It was some whacky superstitious shit for such a militantly scientific guy like my father, whose life and livelihood were science. I was raised on science and finding out he was sitting on a pile of woo-woo that might've started wars in the wrong hands let alone made a lot of news curators gleeful millions of hits, was quite the mindfuck.

I would've been angry with him if I didn't find a whole chapter of notes on my own secret buried in a subdirectory. Not precisely my secret so much as the fact my father and I apparently both had the same one. In case his notes weren't enough, he'd mocked up pictures with disturbing accuracy right down to the strange blue haze.

I was sixteen when I finally tried to tell him about my dreams, thinking maybe he of all people would understand. Maybe he'd let me at the mainframe legitimately. But he'd shaken his head and lied. Again. 'Only dreams, Susie. You've got a lot of hormones racing 'round in your body right now. I had vivid dreams at your age, too.'

I tried to stop being mad at him in my twennies but I couldn't. The face never went away, no matter how many bull-shit growing pains I stopped having. And whenever I spoke with him, it came bubbling back out. I couldn't stop wonder-ing, had he had the dream last night? Was it something our family did to make it happen, collectively? Unconsciously? There must be some explanation. Dad— Bloody Tristian, had obviously struggled with it all his life. Why wouldn't he want a second pair of eyes? Stubborn lying arsehole.

Now, like Mummy, the old house was gone. On the night we'd watched it get torn down, the face flashed up like it was right in front of me. The next thing I knew, I was doubled over gasping and Dad— Tristian, was unconscious on the floor.

That'd been back in November. Now it was January and I didn't know if I could see another crappy moon picture or dumpling ad without crying. It had been the shittiest Christ-mas of all time with Mum gone, Tristian in a coma getting worse by the day and the face haunting me like never before in my dreams every night.

Tristian was dreaming non-stop, too and it was driving his body downhill faster and faster. The super-geeks at Spume themselves couldn't tell us what the hell was going on. They'd never seen anything like it.

It was around three AM and I'd been yanked out of bed by a blood-pressure alert. I could've checked his life support from my room but I wasn't like Davey. I couldn't be so bloody practical about it.

I stared down at him and shivered.

Jesus! Mum died in the same bed!

He was thin and maybe it was the soft bedside lighting that'd faded on when I came in but he seemed paler and more wrinkled than the day before. He looked way too old for his eighty-five, nearly eighty-six years. But for his shallow breathing, he might've been dead already. His blood pressure had dropped but it was nothing serious. It looked like his brain was slightly quieter than usual, too but the patterns hadn't changed.

Keep dreaming, Daddy.

It was the only thing stopping Davey from pulling the plug.

Ado – 4500 BCE, Taiwan island (Kozan)

Sea, cliffs, huts, an island? Subsumed.

'…f he leaves, it won't be long before the mainland peasants are all over us, you know,' I found myself saying.

'He won't leave, Ado,' Mayaw answered, and then, 'Ach! Now look what you made me do you stupid weird-child!' I watched as blood welled from his palm when he pulled out the fishbone. It was strangely peaceful to see, in my exhausted state. I was feeling peaceful except the niggle in my head that never left, the one that never let me stop picking fights with people…

I never meant to, it always happened. I tossed my head, indifferent. It was mean of me. But still, it was only a cut from a fish bone. 'He will go, he has to go, he's said as much. The mainlanders are being slaughtered by the wasted, or whatever they are, and it's making us look bad. He has to join with the others like him and fight; if there are such others.'

'He doesn't have to go. What do we care about mainlander gripes?' Mayaw tried to fob me off, impatiently sucking at his palm while trying to wave flies off the fish. 'Can't you give me a hand with this anyway? You were meant to.'

'We can't sit around gutting fish and pretending nothing's going to happen. He will go and then the mainlanders will be at us. Maybe one of their ancients will find us and bring their family here? And what if these… wasted, kill him off? If he can be killed off?' I was meant to help him but I refused to feel guilty if he was going to be all… not agreeing with me like this.

'How will they be at us, Ado? Why would an ancient cross the rocks and the sea to bother finding us? What do you think they're going to do? They can't see us from the coast.'

'We go to them.' I let my hair fall over my face and shoulders, and conveniently perused his sturdy black legs. He slit and scraped at scales and the smell of fish rose in the room. Under my hair I flushed, thinking it reminded me a little of my own smell and if he could smell it and maybe I wanted him to… Exhaustion was fun sometimes.

He sighed. 'Our ancient goes to them, flies across the water to them dragging us and our trade boats with him, the same boats he makes us in a hair's-worth of the time it would take us to dig them out. We're gods from across the sea to those stupid dogs on the coast, Ado, they have no idea where we come from.'

'We should go.'

'Go? Go where? Why? How even?'

'I told you why. I don't know where. I think we should go… somewhere else.'

'Who's we?'

'All of us. At least you and me.'

He sighed and paused his work. 'Have you been dreaming again?'

I didn't answer though all traces of fantasy dissipated and the fish smelled like stupid fish again. He didn't get it. I hadn't been dreaming. I couldn't stop dreaming. It hurt my head. It hurt my stomach some days. I had to get away.

'So yes, then. You've been dreaming and that means we should leave our beautiful island that gives us meat and fish from the sea and plants, endlessly, keeps us warm and safe from mainland peasant dogs; and their stinky dogs for that matter. You want us to up-sticks and go nowhere you can think by no directions you know, is that it?'

Misery stole over me, then. When he said it like that, plain as day, I couldn't deny there was a certain madness to it. But the dreams, I knew what they were telling me. I knew the woman that came, the face, was warning me or wanted me to find something, or well, it was always hard to tell, exactly, but something.

Her language was some drivel, mainlander maybe. I could only guess the odd word. I had lived on Kozan all my life, how would I know to dream such a thing unless it was a demon visiting? Or a goddess? But I could never understand her meaning. There was only her face and her voice, screaming from her strange blue and violet spirit place.

The ancient and the elders told me she was a weak spirit, perhaps of the sea or a dried-up river, and to ignore her but it was as if she was pulling at me. It had started making me wake up vomiting, some mornings lately.

Mayaw was looking at me, studying me, I could see him from inside my hair. 'You need to eat more,' he said. He held out a fillet.

That's not going to work this time.

It did though. My hand took it before I could sulkily refuse, and I practically swallowed it whole. Hunger engulfed me so fast I almost passed out and I hopped to the work with him instead of getting up and stomping off like I'd planned. I scarfed a third of the fillets raw before we were done.

Where did that come from?

It became apparent where it'd come from when I realised my bleeding had stopped a few sunsets later. That ended my leaving plans, such as they were. Or held them up anyway. It was only a baby. I could take it with me. Or I could give it away. There was no question of my leaving before I had it though. I might need the ancient for the birth.

And I did. The baby came, a boy, I dimly heard everyone remarking; along with, 'she's bleeding, get the ancient!' But he didn't come. I was right. He had scarpered for the mainland to find the wasted. Pain deepened in my body and crimson closed over my eyes, chased by deeper red and hovering blackness.

It was the old thing you heard people say from hunting accidents and so forth, I didn't know it was me doing the screaming and all that. The face was there, the whole woman now, bathed in blue light and screaming in glee and I knew the elders and the ancient were wrong; she was not some feeble Shade. She was something else, something strange yet strangely familiar.

She reached for me and her hands were real as sharks' teeth but before she tore me away, the red and black unfurled and a mix of my baby's screams and my own filled the afternoon air.

'Let through! Let through! Come on, hurry chickens! Out of way. I save.' I heard an unfamiliar voice as if from far away.

Then a young black face with pools of ancient darkness for eyes replaced the screaming blue in my vision.

The hermit from the mountains?

I had never seen her but I knew who she was; who else could look so… different to the rest of us. She was a goddess, some said. She lived in the mountains beyond the end of our huts and sometimes came to us, slipping like darkness through the rings of heads rotting on their stakes around the guard-circle to appear amongst us, ageless. Nobody knew why or when she would return. Lucky for me she chose that day.

'There we are,' she said. 'You'll stay alive today anyway.'

She could channel like an ancient! Who knew? She stayed in the huts after my boy was born and we spoke often. 'Tell,' she said to me one day, in her child's Kozan. 'You have dream? Face? Woman? Like me, a little bit?'

'Yes! I do! But… How do you know?'

'I watch you. I remember you, your mother, her mother, some man, some man before him, always a few, every new brood since…'

'Since wh——?'

'What she say?'

'I don't know. She has strange words. Something about a rock, maybe?'

'Toakoaruahuikhuk,' she said. 'Bit like that?'

'Yes!'

This was the first time in my life that she has come. She plays elder to me yet she looks younger than me. How could she have been watching me?

'You not happy,' she remarked, peering in to my soul with dark eyes.

It wasn't true right then but I knew what she meant. Still, the argument sprang out as if a spirit stole my voice. 'I am! My child is strong and he feeds well, see how he finishes the whole breast and grasps for the other. Who could ask for more?'

She smiled. 'You could. All same, everyone, all same. Dreams and angry words, someone say sky is big, you say sky is small, like now. Always the same. This forest is bad we should be closer river. This river is bad we go in, up. This land is bad we should move… someplace. Look! Land over sea! We go, why we not go? I go, you come or not! Always, always, always, angry, moving, moving, moving. Your boy will be the same. Some child after him, who knows? Me! I know. I have watched. You want to go, girl, I will help you. This place, many people soon, anyway now your… ancient all gone. Men come, maybe other kozan family, maybe mainland, take heads anyway, have you and your sisters for after, mmm, mmm, mmmmm! Like your ancestors before. Always happens. One moon, ten moons, doesn't matter. Best go sooner, I will help. There are new places, across the sea, I have been… I have seen…'

How could you have?

'But the ancient will come back.'

'Fff.' She shook her head. 'He already not coming back.' She reached behind her and brought something before my face. I did not know what it was but I shrank back, clutching my boy closer. 'He sleeps now,' she said but I only half eased my grip.

In her hands was an object of fell design. Dark fire-rock hewn to impossible shiny smoothness, flat bottom, three sides rising to its glittering tip, sharp as a bone needle and seamless as a river stone. She tossed it from one hand to the other, careless of its smooth surface and evil points, defying the normal Way of Things. Though I could not fathom its purpose, I knew it was evil and tried not to look at it.

'But if he went away—'

'I brought back, stupid.'

'You went with him?'

'What you think, thicky? How else I bring it back?'

I'd asked for that. And I did not want to talk about the strange pointed stone.

'Who—?'

'Other one like me, Healer. My thicky man, lived over there, edge of guard ring.'

He did look like her! And different from us; like her. How did I not notice?

Because he's always been there.

The rain had come outside and I could see a puddle growing outside our hut through a gap in the skin hanging over the doorway. My boy was sleeping now and I imagined shouts through the rain, the sounds of fighting and dying. The daydream rose up, men bursting in, wet with rain and blood to tear my boy from my arms and cave in his skull before sharing me. I shivered in the wet heat.

'Good dreamer, you,' remarked the hermit.

I jumped. But she said, 'tzaakh! No need girl. I old, no devilment, you're like a child to me.'

Some days after, she took me into the forest and showed me things she had made. Dugouts, far enough away from the sea and big enough to make me laugh.

'I know, I know.' She held up her hands. 'You don't carry. I carry.'

'But nobody will come with me.'

'They will,' she said.

And she was right. One night everyone awoke and scrambled from their huts into the moonlight. Up the island came screams, the clatter of spears and the smell of smoke. It would be long before the mainlanders reached us, but reach us they would.

'Everyone!' I shouted, above myself and not caring since the ancient was made wasted and the eldest amongst us were stupid. 'Come with me. We need to go, get away!'

'Go where?' Mayaw shouted back from somewhere in the dark. 'Besides, Ado, that's your solution for splinter in the finger, leave the island. I say we stay and fight!'

Murmurs of agreement. Maybe more would have come if I was an elder, if I couldn't help but disagree with everyone and everything, right or wrong. But instead, I was me. 'Well go or stay. They will come, maybe now, maybe tomorrow and there aren't enough of us to hold them off; can't you hear all those voices? Up here in the hills though we are? I have a plan and any who want in are welcome.'

Rainclouds ate up the stars and reached for the moon as those who had not sloped back off to sleep gathered up children, babies and little else but the pots of ashes of the dead. I didn't give them long. The shouts and burning went on as the storm came in. In the deeper dark I could see the flames all the way down to the coast where flames reached up to the clouds.

A funny group of all ages began to gather around me and feeling the first drops spatter was enough to send me off. I lead away with my baby boy, grizzling through the forest and what turned out to be enough others to fill the hermit's four dugouts.

'Now what?' I shouted into the undergrowth.

'I nearby girl. No need noisy.' She appeared like a Shade before us and hopped into my dugout. 'You got food? Water?' she called out.

A few shouts answered. I had fruit and dried fish, enough for a few days. 'Why can't you fight them off for us?'

'Too dangerous. They have one like me. One of us get made wasted and big round-head from over the mountains not here to catch it, no more island, maybe.'

Nobody said anything, we all knew it was true.

As the rain wet our hair and soaked through our clothes, we cowered in the dugouts as they rose into the air. They tore the forest and earth beneath us as we sailed neither duskward nor dawnward, over the island and into the dark ocean, foaming in our wake as if we were on it and not over it. She set us down beyond the storm in a shush and hiss of tired foam and told us to get heaving at the oars.

One oldster, Tuwna, knew how to find ways but as he put it, 'The way to where, Mother?'

'That way. That star, those stars, you keep it there and them here, you see? And the moon, this way and you know it wrong if sun comes up not that way.'

He didn't see, not really but she stayed with us and kept us pointing in the right direction. Not that it stopped us nearly thirsting to death on the deep ocean where the sky stretched to the edges of the water and no rain came for days, starving to death, sickening to death, dying to death. I used everything I had spare to feed my baby and my breasts sagged down and stretched taut over my ribs.

Many lives and many days later a voice said in my ear, 'we come.' A hand held my head and put a pot of cooled piss to my lips. 'Drink,' the hermit said.

Barely a dugout-ful of us was left by the time we came up the beach like turtles to rut. We were greeted with painted faces and spears but the strange men lying in wait beyond the trees had no ancient and so we became the mainland dogs we'd fled and our new life began with the fire and screams we'd left behind on Kozan. It was only me that got caught in the chest by a lucky throw.

'No!' The hermit goggled at me, trying to heal me, probably but she'd got to me too late and I got out one last gurgle and a thick warm spurt of blood before my world went from red to black to sea and sky and earth then blue and violet and full of a demon woman's screams as the face from my dreams rose up before me to gloat. I hadn't gone far enough away after all.

I spun away into the blue and panic crashed in.

I have to get back.

The figure flitted, far away and inward and this time…

This time?

…I chased it. Through blue and purple lattices and honeycombed crystalline caves and somehow… up. We burst out…

From where?

…into a… *special place?* The figure, a woman, her, the face, no, like the face, gesticulated and spoke in the same language as the face. Her expression was urgent, pleading.

And then I saw the knot, lumpen, roiling and huge before us, blue flowing coils locked in the crystal, tangled with a deadly thin swirl of deep violet. From the coiled mass, stretched cords, misty yet somehow solid. They flowed up and… *out?* And, she pointed to the swirling tangle and took hold of me, gripped my soul. And for an instant, I was lost and…

'Oh Flower.' I gloated softly.

A geyser of blood, a… Shade? A… *bond forming?*

But something pulled us apart. The face.

She found us…

Had we hidden?

Feelings tickled, needled, on the horizon of my awareness: aches, pains, numbness, tiredness and memories of the hospital decades ago. I didn't know why but I wanted to be nearer those feelings, not here in this blue pit of madness, back, back in my… my what?

Something's wrong…

But I didn't know what it meant; that place in my soul was too far away to reach. It was like this place was growing more real and there was…

…pain?

But it was too late. I was gone again; the branches and trunk of my soul pushed back into a seed of myself in a… *heartbeat?* I had no time to think more, work out more.

Again and again, I spun away and fled into the blue and the figure showed me the knot and deadly coil tangled up in it, the flowing lines stretching up and out. She gesticulated in anguished urgency; showed me her memories of… *channelling the Flow? Murder?*

But She always found us. Again, and again and every time I… *weakened more. I'm weakening! I have to get back!*

Seas and impossible storms, resin-scented canoes full of plants and animals and lice and sickly infection, elation at the sound of waves on a distant reef, seabirds in the sunrise signifying land ahead after weeks of parched rowing and dried fish, exhausted arrivals, battles and blood and blending and marriages and breeding. Sharp black faces growing round and brown, thin lips filling out and straight, dark hair curling up in the island sun. A thousand shards of a thousand lives, pulled from one dream and thrown into the next, death after death after death. Spinning apart, fleeing into the crystal blue depths only to be found yet again.

She gibbered and raged and grew angrier and angrier each time, as if something… unexpected was happening. If I'd been anyone else, I might have given up, never tried to surface, to come back to myself, never wondered what was happening to me, slipped beneath the surface and flowed with the dreams to…

Where? From where?

But the where was me. The what, when, where, how and why? Why? Why? Why? Questions! I was made of questions. Before now, I might have said it was when my grandmother had interfered with me and been frightened away by a noise.

She'd died the next morning and come back to me, deranged, probably not realising she was dead, the next night. Then for many nights till my uncle stopped her. I would have said it was that which made me start asking, how does it work? How are things made? How is the universe put together? What's possible? Her presence haunted my first waking years.

But now I knew it hadn't started then. It had started before I could remember when the face first entered my dreams. When I first started having dreams.

Was it her presence inside me since there'd been enough braincells clustered together to pass for me, the proto-Tristian? Or would I have always been someone who needed to know? Who couldn't let things go?

But whatever it was, needing to understand was what kept me refusing to give up now – whatever giving up meant – and to keep asking whenever I was allowed a sliver of consciousness.

How long have I been here? Where is here? What does she want? Why is she doing this?

At the edge of my awareness hovered something, something comfortable, a bedroom that no longer seemed real, with sheets and wallpaper and furniture and tech and clothes and a body that surely needed to eat, drink and get clean… A heart that had to pump blood to my organs and my brain. That had to… *keep beating.*

Then there was a flash, a tug whose urgency seemed weaker and more alien than the dugout canoes, grass skirts, shell necklaces, leaf mats, clay pots, adzes, jade trinkets, casual hours spent hewing, weaving, threading, hunting, fishing, slaughtering, bartering, gutting, fucking, eating, sparking embers, telling stories, sleeping in stone and thatch huts, fighting and beheadings, grizzly trophy jewellery, and skeletal mementos of the dead and gone, the island worlds I was being shown in a relentless procession, each ending back here, with her, wherever here was, whoever she was.

But small as it was, I felt it. A tug on the arm of my ailing ghost. And looking… *down,* I saw a face I recognised.

'Tristian!'

'Dad?'

'Yes.'

'Dad! What is this place? Who are all the… people?'

'Hell, Tris. I'm sorry son, the church, the prayer, it didn't help, it didn't make the face— We're in hell, son. I'm sorry. I made us go to hell, all of us. The devil, Tris, watch out! The devil!' His scream rose up shrill as he fled away into the glittering blue depths. A shiver went through me because though I could understand his words, they made no more sense than the gibbering face of my dreams.

My father is here! He died and now he's here!

His madness didn't matter and nor did my surprise. Where and what this place was didn't matter either. All that mattered now was that I had to get back. And as my father had fled, I'd seen it. Deadly thin and dark as rot, the deep violet thread coiling out of the shining lattices, through him, into me, onwards and away.

And as I was crushed to a guttering spark of myself, yet again, it gave me an idea.

Sarah – early Nov 2098, Cornwall Hill, Akarana Island, Aotearoa Archipelago

'Fuck, Cousin, should you be out of your coffin looking like that?' Louisa gasped when she opened the door. I guessed our virtuals hadn't impressed on either of them how sick I'd been.

It was only a couple of blocks to the top of the hill where they lived in the same block Grandad had moved to after the funeral and it was a dry blustery day but in hindsight I should've Ubered it anyway. I was sweating and dizzy by the time I got to their door, even after the breather in the lift. Maybe that was why I looked worse than when I'd pinged them to see if they were up for a visit.

In the end, I couldn't get better without buying meds but after that the bug had run its course okay. I remained sick enough to smugly send my vitals in to work and get authorised for a few more sick-leave extensions, and well enough to go to Louisa and Gilly's and whine at them about the Neil situation for the millionth time. I worried they'd get as sick of hearing about it as I was of talking about it. But I couldn't stop.

Louisa didn't say much but I could tell she agreed with Gilly. 'For fuck's sake Sarah. You need to fucking take this to your HR. It's so wrong on so many levels. It's fucking harassment, cut and dried. I mean, at best, it's fucking breach of copyright or something, surely?'

'But he'll only say—'

'It doesn't bloody matter what he says! The minute he bloody streamed you having sex, he was breaking the law— And all those other deadbeats saving it in work systems, surely that's illegal? Or… against company policy at least?'

'But I told him he could!'

'What? That he could broadcast your fuck-face to all his— uh, your colleagues? Do you know if that's all he did? Jesus, Sarah, who else has seen that footage?'

'No! No! I didn't say he could show it to anyone.'

'Well, what then?'

'I told him he could…' I sighed and felt my cheeks getting hot.

'What? He could what?'

Louisa got up and went to the kitchen island to make coffees but there'd been no eye contact with either of us. Gilly was right to be frustrated. I was getting bored with myself! Like she'd already said a million times, what would I have told me if I'd come snivelling to myself with this?

But grow a pair didn't help. It wasn't that simple when it was me going through it. Gilly was looking at me with the special Gilly™ relentless exasperated expression I knew I'd love her for all over again later though her eyes were burning inconveniently through my denial right then.

'I told him he could record us. He said it turned him on so I didn't… think it mattered.'

'Oh.' She partially deflated. 'You didn't say he could share it though, did you?'

'Well no. But I didn't say he couldn't.'

She looked pained. 'Well, I don't reckon it matters. I'm sure if you took it to HR, there'd be something illegal about it. Leaving porn on company storage, no? It's wrong Sarah! And every minute you don't, every day you keep sleeping with him, he's going to keep on using you and he and his creep cronies are going keep laughing at you behind your back. Come on Sarah! This isn't you! This is not fucking you!'

'I'm not sleeping with him any more!' I said. But a tickle started in my stomach at her expert compli-goad. My tone was lamely defensive at best.

'Oh Christ! Details! You haven't stopped getting him off and he probably hasn't stopped filming you doing it! Is that fun for you Sarah? Do you feel like you can refuse him? Jesus, that sounds like workplace harassment to me. Or bloody something.' But her crossness had a playful softness now.

'What… can I do though?' I looked down at my hands.

'Well at least you know you need to do something now.' Louisa's voice floated over to us from the breakfast bar. 'Finally,' she added with an exaggerated sigh that made us all laugh.

Two coffees sat on top of the machine keeping warm and she was lifting the third off the tray. The bulldozer had done its work and now the roller was smoothing over. They'd made their point and I was comprehensively galvanized.

I didn't know what to do. I could go running to Grandad and beg to use his lawyer-power or something; if I could stomach the embarrassment of telling him what had happened. But Tristian had taken Nana-Joanna's death badly – well, who hadn't but she hadn't been my partner for nearly sixty years.

In any case, I didn't want to add to his grief with my stupid problems. Plus that might've ended up being a case of killing the roach by knocking over the building; I was sure not everyone at the station had been in on Neil's shitty little game; they didn't deserve to lose their jobs over it. No, I was an adult now. I could wallow forever and get stepped on in the process or I could get the fuck up and stand on my own two feet.

Nathan – late Nov 2098, Spume Prison Stasis, Cornwall Hill Estate, Akarana Island, Aotearoa Archipelago

I must have stared at the wall under my plaque a thousand times and not seen it, a smooth square with no angel designs on it. Bad bloody UI design was all there had been between me and my peaceful check-out. I touched the panel and it opened on a twentieth-century wiring box or some dumb shit like that.

There was no smart-arse retro way of showing the next bit. When I dug into the cable bundle, I was virtualled into a plain old system schematics holo.

At last!

My new super-brain soaked up the system as I walked through the plans, zooming in for more detail in the likeliest looking bits. There was nothing that would alert them to my plan till it was too late.

They must've thought their system was so shit hot it wouldn't fail and kill anyone. Or more likely they didn't give a shit if a wet-foot carked in the joint. It didn't matter anyway, I had what I needed. It was time to go.

Yeah but… No rush is there? I'll be dead for a long time so…

I kept poking around, the ghost of my old curiosity refusing to die. And I stumbled on a juncture sprouting comms streams. I followed one and ended up in a red building with slots on the wall outside. There were cupboards on the other side of the wall and they opened into...

Ah, yeah, okay, shame I couldn't've got a job with these people. I could've showed them a thing or two about set design.

It was the lazy thought of a Nate of another time. My lips barely twitched let alone smiled.

The place was meant to be tricked out like a twentieth-century post office except the loser graddy didn't know their history and hadn't worked on a shitload of vintage movies like I had. It looked wrong.

Yeah, yeah, okay but who cares.

Apparently I did because I kept fiddling. The message in-boxes behind the cupboards were easy enough to figure out. I found mine and saw some peeps— people had tried to book visits, again and again and again. Mum, Dad, Chen, Cherie and Shane. One from Teens. And all of them had been fobbed off or declined.

For the early ones there was a bullshit history of made-up medical issues, stasis chamber instability, another visit application in progress. Shit, shit, and more shit! But the later ones were what made my dream-blood boil and I had nobody to blame but my idiot self.

Too late this time, Mister Richards-Mann. But all subsequent visitation request will be declined. As you have requested.

'Fuckin' cunts!' I screamed at the screen. 'You're a bunch of fuckin' wankers!'

The system ignored me.

Fair enough. My fault for making 'em do it, I s'pose.

I cleared my inbox; cleared all the inboxes; in the world. I found a setting to ALLOW ALL VISITATIONS. It would probably flag shit up everywhere on the planet but I didn't care. I wouldn't be around to get busted for it and maybe a few people would get to see their friends and folks one last time before they died or their minds were too cooked to recognise them.

There was plenty more of the system I could have played with now I'd found the schematics. I could have worked out how their top-secret dream-tech worked and in times gone by I wouldn't have been able to hold myself back. But I was down to zero-fucks left to give. Or maybe zero-point-one because instead of heading back to the lab to switch my profile into goodnight-Nate mode, I found myself idly trailing another one of the external comms streams.

And then.

O… Kay?

A cage as tall as high-rise overlooked an apparently endless ocean. The Google-tower rose in the distance behind it and between here and there was a tree-lined highway. You were meant to feel remote and exposed at the same time, I guessed. I felt nothing but calm.

I'd never seen a pigeon in real life but the ones crowding out the cage looked realistic enough to me. Their cooing was peaceful. A kind of…

…fitting last stop.

I stood and watched them a while. Sometimes one would take off through a round hole in the netting. It would fly out over the water with a note in its claws and disappear into the blue. It seemed… appropriate, uh… imagery for my final moments.

Only sometimes they came back. Checking the system, I saw data-packets flow between the cage – the… loft – and the graveyard each time a pigeon came or went. There was no way over the water. I tried putting a foot over the edge and froze; it was how the place was coded. I paused a bird to read its note and might've smiled if I wasn't past caring.

The *jǐngchás* outsourced nearly everything penal to Spume. But they weren't taking any chances with criminal records. Spume fed the cops everything about prisoner visits, visit requests, so-called medical events (wankers) and – looking at the logs – a note-format that was hardly used; a recommendation for sentence adjustment.

I guessed the cops acceptance of that seldom-used advisory, would mean a pigeon coming back over the water with their authorisation. And if it did? Who knew? Maybe just bam! Somewhere in the world, a lucky only-half-lobotomised wetfoot wakes up. However it worked though, without the cops' say-so, the system had no power to change someone's sentence. The cops had the final say and the water's edge was their firewall.

I could send the advisory myself…

And I could've too. Without realising it, I'd found the interface to manually generate a message.

But did a real-life cop look at it? Did they ask questions to real life Spume people? They must.

It wouldn't be that easy and you know it. Come on Nate, dickhead. Stick to the plan.

And I did. I glimmered from the pigeon cage to the schematic and back into my mausoleum. I took one last long look at my coffin and couldn't make myself open it any more than I could before. I went into the storeroom, switched my profile, snapped down the link and hung in the rain as a chill flowed into my veins and red and black gathered like a storm at the edges of my vision and rushed in to take me under.

Sorry Teens. Bye. Sorry, Mum, Dad. And Chen, you were…. the best, too good for me, sorry for everything, I wish I'd been better. Jesus, let it be quick, let it not hurt. Fuck I'm a wimp—

Fetu – 2000 BCE, Samoa

This time there was a blurring of the minds, a tight wriggle of space between my thoughts and his as if I saw the world through two pairs of eyes.

He's dying, no, I'm dying, that's why…

Fever warmed my body though my skin shivered in the rain. The sail was down, safe from the tearing claws of the storm. The sky seemed brighter and smaller than it should have been. The sea surrounded us like angry mountains and some part of me knew we had come to the heart of the storm and it would not be long before the sea tossed, tumbled and tested us again and this time we would not live.

Land, the land I had promised them all, the land she had promised me, where I would be safe from the dreams, was nowhere in sight. The dugout had taken on water and who knew how many chickens and pigs – and babies – had drowned.

…safe from the… dreams?

Gone again.

'Fetu!' The shout came from a distance, as other voices joined it.

'Fetu! No!'

Red rose up in my eyes and I could no longer feel the rain. Warmth spread through me though the sun was nowhere in sight and I sighed and would have dropped my oar and slept if a strong hand had not grasped my shoulder and shaken the warmth away, shaken the red from my eyes, shaken the teeth of pain from the driving rain back in, shaken a grain of strength back into me.

Awake again, I heaved at my oar as we passed back into the black of Tangaroa the sea god's fury. Up one sea and down another, heave! Up the next and down to the moving valley between with a crash of foam. My strength ebbed away again and the warmth began to mount no matter how I tried to stay awake.

The red grew over my eyes though I tried to blink it away and a darkness I knew was the final darkness I would go through to the ancestors, hovered beyond the red.

'Fetu! No!' Her voice this time. Was she Tangaroa after all? Had he taken her form and lured us into his kingdom to claim us?

'Fetu! I'm here! Keep going! I'll heal you when we get there!'

Far away my arms worked the oar and it was no doubt some trick of the fever that made it seem as if sunlight shone from the edge of the storm and a strange path through the seas opened. Through it I saw the distant rocks of a reef and the blue of a lagoon beyond. And as the darkness came for me, the green and grey cliffs thrusting skyward from the shore, came clear as the curtain of rain parted for the sun.

The light was a faraway speck in my eyes as we neared the lagoon entrance but I saw her clearly anyway, standing on a rock, waving us to safety through the reef, the dark woman with the strange face and the odd way of talking who had sent me on this journey and now waited for me at its end.

But she was here only now! How did she get there?

Unsure of who I was now, me or this other… *Fetu?* I flashed across empty miles of sea, over the endless coast, through burgeoning stone cities and into the ground before the face was there again and yet another soul that could not understand me spun away into the maze of blue lattices.

Samoans!

I held on to the thought as the memory of sea and fevered strain at the oars faded and I grew to fit myself again and my idea, my hunch, remained. I looked for my father, gibbering in the depths but I couldn't find him and this time when I was forced down into the dream, it was different.

I felt as if something was finally tearing, a placenta from its womb before its time. I felt pain, bleeding in my soul and for an instant I was somewhere else, a dark room, a canopy of instruments and a web of tubes in and out of my body, stabbing pain in my chest.

My heart!

Then the blue and violet place, my room and the oncoming dream blurred together and under I went again and the dream stretched my final moments into days, weeks and years.

Chen – late Nov 2098, from Cornwall Estate to Beachlands Hill, Akarana Island, Aotearoa Archipelago

I never expected it to happen to anyone I knew, least of all… Tina. But in the end, it was your typical influencer story and I reckoned, like I always did and like Nate would've too if he'd been around to see it, that the humiliation wasn't worth the fame. Maybe not all the ding, either.

TrueLife™ didn't lie but the things Yang's space showed! It had to be tech she'd got hold of somehow. Maybe she'd caved on the bullshit identity thing and used family connections. Whatever it was, I probably wasn't the only one blown away – not to mention grossed out – by it.

Fixing up those peoples' apartments, that was thanks to the little present I'd given her, not whatever crap all those desperate single parents spouted; not that I'd've blown either of her secrets. It probably explained where she'd gone, too. Down south to be with 'her people', never mind that she'd misfired by a suburb or two and landed in one of the ponciest blocks on the island.

Yeah, so, near 'her people' but not of them, apparently.

And Jeez! Didn't she watch the bloody news spaces! Didn't she know about the quakes? Why did she think all those places were such a steal at the moment?

Well. Comparatively.

Still, how long had that medical tech been around? Had the rich been using it for years? Unlikely, it would've got out sooner. Or maybe it'd only recently been released and this was it getting out. Maybe Tina was doing us all a favour and after her woo-woo died down, Yang or someone'd sniff out whoever had made it. He was probably on the case right now.

It didn't explain what was with the big black guy she had with her who grew out of the baby; Mister Sky god. Fuck, shouldn't he've been blue and grey with lightning shooting out of his bum or something, instead of black? Jeez, I mean, if you're gonna spout shit at least go all out!

He was some kind of throwback like me, obvs, or maybe foreign and dumped here at the arse-end of the Earth somehow – a big somehow, that, given how tight security was on the MagLevs – when they thought the experiment'd failed… Except it hadn't and the most unlikely crazy in the world had come across it.

Yeah, nah. Unlikely.

Well, I didn't know, did I? Who the hell could explain the way that thing, he, grew like that? And the stuff he did! Or maybe he wasn't really doing it. It wasn't like you could see rays of healing woo-woo coming out of his eyes or anything. But he must've had something to do with it else why would he've been with her in every single bit of footage? What kind of hold did the crazy-woman Nate left me for…

…okay, enough!…

…have over him?

Or him, over her?

I had to hand it to Yang. He showed her what was what in the first interview. He acted all interested and like he was taking her seriously; let her spout her mental *haurangi* woo-woo then – as Nate would've said – Bam! In with the footage of the flash under the construction tarp and the weird tech floating up the side of the foundation pit and out over the wasteland. And the spooky fading glow in the hole, after. Anyone could see it was connected to God-Dude; Yang hadn't needed to wink at the viewers.

And if that wasn't enough, there was the porn. Fuckin' classic! The dumb woman'd got sloppy with her editing. The standard lame soundtrack and fake digs would've masked her as well as anyone if she hadn't missed a few frames.

Of course someone'd gone through all the millions of seconds of her skinny pimply botty waving in the air while God-guy jack-hammered away. They'd combed and combed it and struck pallid spotty gold. There was an instant of footage where the fake stuff hadn't been applied and you could see her overs on the floor, hear a snippet of his grunting, smell the real smells of the apartment around them, everything.

It'd got run through all the usual algos. Who knew, you could get a decent match on someone from shots of their naked bum-hole? But it turned out they didn't need to anyway because the idiot had uploaded one of her, uh, movies, and forgotten to strip out the ID tags; Oh, Teens, Teens, Teens. Rookie mistake!

But after all that it was one of those, oh fuck-humans-are-morons moments anyway. It didn't matter about Yang's footage. It didn't matter that she'd been outed as a liar and a cheap and nasty porn-star. Like all the crazies with nothing left to lose, she'd leaned into it. Her surreal *fēng kuáng-de* second interview with Yang sent her fucking… Movement space to the bloody stars! Okay she had a point about the old-school sexism. But it beggared belief how dumb people were! Man! What century did she get all the stuff about men and women from? Did she know I'd been at Nate's op when we were teenagers?

No wonder the Pete creep was slurping up recruits nearly as fast as her! Maybe if she hadn't just helped out single parents with vaginas, she would've got more followers than she already had.

And as if that-all wasn't enough, the completely unerotic, cheap, badly shot pictures of her getting… penetrated by the – oh for fuck's sake! – god-rod were suddenly an international fucking MotherEarthCreampiedByTheSky meme and she'd wasted no time making her vids NF. I didn't want to ruin the makeup I never wore by finding out how much they were trading on the exchanges for.

Well, whatever, so she was rich now. For the second time in her life. Fuck it, it had nothing to do with me. People were dumb and that's how it was. And anyway, I'd started seeing more of Cathy and Doug and I was feeling a lot more kind of… balanced.

I started going into dating spaces and they were crap but at least we had a few good laughs eviscerating all-like, two of my weekly 'suitors' the eves before our off-days on each off-chance we were in sync.

At some point, I decided I'd make myself stop thinking about stupid Tina. She was out of my life and not my problem any more. But that was the trouble with me. I cared too much.

If Nate hadn't bloody well told me about all the awful stuff he'd dug up on her. If I didn't already have first-hand knowledge of what a *makutu*-touched *fēng kuáng* unit she was, probably because of said awful stuff. If I hadn't've taken the bait like every other wet-foot pleb online and checked out those few seconds of gross and fateful vid. Yep, if I'd been able to see the future, well then, I probably mightn't've ended up choking out my last breaths on the plushest carpets puke could be cleaned up off, later that first off-day after twenty-one days of work in a row.

But for all her vomitus 'success', I'd heard her voice in that disgusting instant and I'd known straight away that it was definitely not the voice of someone having a fun time. There was no sacred love in those frightened gasps.

Then my nuisance bloody mind'd started ticking and before I was out of bed in the morning, I'd imagined a whole parallel universe for… Tina behind her grotesque new fame.

Given how unlikely the whole coincidence was with the woo-woo stuff, I got it into my stupid trusting brain that the more or probably most likely scenario was different from what it looked like on the tin; whatever a tin was. No, I reckoned more likely, her past or family connections or whatever, had caught up with her. And now she'd got herself mixed up in something she couldn't get out of. The guy raping her – whatever delusional name she gave it – was some piece of her history come back to haunt her, I knew.

I'd never've dreamed she'd've gone and done what she'd done with the, uh… maintenance ingot I'd dumped on her. It'd kind of been out of sympathy for her if I was completely honest with myself. That and to keep the heat off me.

But no matter any of that, I should've got a backbone on and gone to her sooner. If whatever corporate gods above the rainclouds'd wanted to find out, or if they ever did anytime anyway, they would have better hackers than me on the case. I'd go down in flames no matter how well I reckoned I'd channelled Nate, purged myself outta the block system and covered my tracks. Waiting it out to see if Tina got busted was futile and pointless.

But how could I have known the weird guy would appear out of nowhere and all the freaky *makutu* stuff would start happening? How could I have known people would get behind her *fēng kuáng-de* shit?

But she couldn't've moved where she did if I hadn't made it possible. She would still've been safely chained to her nine-til-nine in a BudLike™ stupor along with most of the rest of the wet-foot world which she for some reason desperately wanted to be a part of. So, I couldn't deny, I was partly to blame for everything and I had to at least try to get to her. It's what Nate would've done.

I ordered in a massive breakfast, the healthiest I could afford: broccoli, three types of beans, a chub of the high-grade nutrient supplement Nate'd put me on to for an extra pick-me-up – RibEyeReminiscent™ – and some plain pancakes washed down with a giant steaming mug of premium Instant™. I did the maths and worked out I could've afforded an Uber both ways that'd've left me skint so I decided to only blow ding on a few strategic stages of the journey instead.

I spliced my overs into pouches for food and an Instant™ bladder and tried to talk myself out of it for the first two hours of the journey. Then I got too tired to think and the journey became an exhausted blur of one foot in front of another on aching legs until I reached the blessed relief of each 'permitted' Uber stage.

Five hours later, my maps finally told me I was about four kays out but I couldn't walk any more. It was around two in the afternoon and the rain was whipping me like a bitch. The wind had almost blown me over the crumbling seawall a couple of times as I'd schlepped through Beachlands and around the headland.

The rising ground was nearly too much for my legs to handle and millennia of human invention and innovation could do nothing to ease the sting of blisters on my toes. My legs were shaking with fatigue and though I'd squatted like a wasted student on the roadside to pee about three times already, my bladder was threatening to burst yet again.

My legs lasted another hour before I caved and got an Uber the last few hundred metres around the bend and up the hill to, apparently, Tina's block.

I tried to ignore the quiet. I'd seen the weird foaming water in the news spaces. I'd seen the coverage of how the rich were all scuttling inland like rats, sending the prices of the highest penthouses on the highest inland hills past the moon to Mars. But being out here where rich had pissed down the hills on the poor by the seawalls for decades and seeing the deadness of the place was a whole different level of shiver.

We really do live on a fuckin' island in the rising sea!

As the Uber chuntered upwards, I glanced over my shoulder at the sea. It was a smooth shiny sheet of grey with a storm rolling in to cover it up.

I grew up by a wall and I'd learned to keep an eye on the sea but that didn't mean I liked looking at it. I turned around and got out of the Uber, trying not to spare it a second thought.

Tavita – 1959, Samoa to New Zealand

'Plenty for you here boy! Coconuts, bananas, fishing, building. Big as you're getting, there might be an opening at the docks, what about that eh? What you want to go off to Auckland for?'

'That's it? After all my school, all my maths, my English, the science, all that? Only bananas, coconuts, fishing and working in the heat all day? What's the point of all my schooling?'

'Well that's what I always said to your mother; oy, don't you eyeball me boy!' His meaty brown palm caught me across the side of the face but his heart wasn't in it so it was only numb and tingling for a minute. I looked back down at the mat and watched a rat out of the corner of my eye, nibbling on something white, probably breadfruit from this morning. Maybe a bit of dirt from my sister Talia's foot mixed in but it didn't care.

My father went on. 'That white man school fill you young fellas up with ideas, make you get too big for your boots. And make you lazy, too. That what's wrong with you now boy? This place not good enough for you now? That school make you think you better than your elders?' He shoved me in the shoulder.

I am better than you! You don't know anything!

I thought it in English so he wouldn't know what I was thinking if he caught me thinking it. No way was I going climbing for coconuts today, there was a storm coming. By the time I got to the palms, it would be time to run for shelter. Everyone else had gone anyway but only because they were stupid.

Talia would be dry enough at the school, my mother would only feel the rain hammering on the dirt above her grave near the church on Apia. I'd have to get soaked running back here. Anyway, I didn't see him getting off to the docks to load up pellets; the slave-labour he'd threatened me with. He wasn't going to waste time leaving with the storm coming in. That's how it'd all started; with me not getting out of bed.

Tangaroa's first warning breath hissed through the thatch and heavy drops thudded in the dirt outside and I got myself a proper thick ear with the smug grin I couldn't help growing as I turned away.

'Yeah real funny aren't you boy? How about I tie you to a palm trunk before the storm comes properly in, eh? How about that? See if you're smiling then, eh? What's that? You gonna fight me now? You think you're a man now?'

He'd spotted my look too fast, my anger. A second of my eyes up to his and boy was he annoyed – scared, I'd realise, years too late. At the time I was too scared of the beating I'd get if I didn't take the one I was being given with enough re-spect. He cuffed and shoved me and I lurched and stumbled around the *fale* without fighting back though I'd grown tall enough to look down at him.

Feeling the power of those dock-worker arms, wrapped in muscle hard as the ringed bark on a palm, I got less and less angry and more and more scared by the minute. He stopped when Talia skipped in early from school, all hello there little girl, what did they teach you at school today? You come home by yourself or that pretty little Lilly's sister bring you, eh?

Discussion over.

Still, I'd been sent a sign. Nobody would believe me so that's who I'd told. Some days before, Talia had gone and lost herself somewhere with her friends after school. The little beach where Ethel, the black skinned district nurse who spoke bad Samoan and bad English but could fix you up better than a doctor, normally rowed into on her visits, was empty. I looked up and down it for Talia then stood staring across the lagoon for a while, enjoying the peace and quiet.

That's when I felt the pull, the sand stirring up along the beach. And a soft wind wrapping me and nudging, tugging, blowing up white on the water, pushing the wavelets out and away towards the port of Apia. And I knew that meant Auckland for me.

The breeze nudged and pulled at me and dragged the water out and back in suddenly, till I was standing in the lagoon up to my knees though I hadn't moved; go, boy, or else; I knew it meant. I turned to go look somewhere else for Talia. The water tugged at my ankles as I waded back in with fish darting away under the surface and clouds of sand bursting up from the bottom when shellfish hid from the shadows of my feet.

Auckland was where the bananas my father stacked and loaded went. The people there were the ones with the boats and cranes that came out to get everything we grew and tended and picked and readied. They were making big money out of our sweat, why couldn't he see?

I didn't see why my father was so against my going anyway. My cousin Siole had gone to work in the factories and his brother Sione, to train to be a priest. I wouldn't be the first to leave and it wasn't as if I wouldn't come back. Besides, I'd be so rich he wouldn't complain when I built us a house in Apia with a 'lectric light and big soft beds.

I decided then and there I'd go with or without his permission. I met Talia on the way back up from the shore and grabbed her by the ear to drag her home and pretend I'd found her.

I hadn't dreamed the dream for a long time but that night as rain drummed on the thatch and stirred up the earth between the *fale's* stilts, I saw the face between waking and sleeping. It was faint like always, more of a thought than a picture. It hung in its blue-purple place. Its lips moved without sound and its face looked angry and sad.

It was telling me to go, I was sure; and asking me why hadn't I already gone? The foam on the sea and the strange wind. It can't have been a... coincidence; I used the English word in my head, easily now. I had to go. I had to make my father understand, or if I couldn't, I had to go anyway.

Time to change... tactics. Next morning, I was up... without complaint, played with Talia and helped her eat her breadfruit and followed respectfully behind my father. He'd stayed angry and didn't speak to me but I knew he'd get over it; couple of days maybe. When the path split, I walked off to climb coconut palms without a word or an... insolent look backwards. Then I doubled back and went to the docks. He wouldn't've known I'd gone till he got home that night.

Betty worked next to me at the Watties factory and though she was a white lady, one thing lead to another. I raised Rodney alone in the end, though. I wished I could have hated the factory or at least my cousin for getting me the job there but I knew it wasn't the factory or my cousin's fault that Betty died in the hospital. Her family reckoned it was my fault because brown babies weren't meant to come out of white ladies. But I knew it was God's way of punishing me for parting ways with my dad, silent and angry, on the day he died at the docks.

I felt pinched pain as images of a New Zealand of decades before I was born but which I recognised nonetheless, faded. The last bindings of my soul strained to pull free from my body, bleeding whatever it was souls bled. A melee of sensations whirled through me.

I felt my room with its modern walls and bedsheets and tubes and bags of liquid; and the pain that lived there, fading away. I tasted the blue place with the face, grimacing, gloating and gibbering, excited now, and I knew why. And memories from another time threaded through everywhere, smells, sounds, feelings and thoughts. And then I spun away again. But I remembered my hunch and called after the fleeing other, Tavita, who I knew now could speak my language.

'Hey! Wait!'

But he was gone, fled into the blue. I half fled from the face, half chased Tavita into the lattices and shining layers and found my father instead, hiding, cowering.

'Dad! Help me! I need you to help me!' It was him, I knew, without knowing how I knew. The impression of him, whimpering, terrified.

'The devil, Tris. Watch out! We're in hell Tris. Sorry, son, I sorry...'

'Dad! I need you to pass on a message. I can't speak with her, there are too many... languages. I need you to ask the woman, the one at the... top, what she's trying to tell me. It's important, Dad!'

'...devil, Tris. Watch out, I'm sorry, we're in hell, I've brought you to hell, the whole family, sorry, son—'

I tried to hold on to him knowing who I was, the grain of presence left in him. I took his shoulders or some sense of them and shook him or some idea of it. I called his name, my dad and his full name, Peter Robert Laufala, but he cowered and gibbered and though he knew who I was, it was as if he didn't see me, as if he was elsewhere.

With a tearing pain and sinking heart, I realised I'd never get through to him and it wouldn't be long before She found me again and then I'd be lost. One last time, I tried, 'Well fucking help me get out of hell then, Father! Fix what you fucking broke!' My roar echoed through the lattices and he looked up and I felt his comprehension.

Though he didn't break anything, it's not his fault, not really.

'Dad! Do you understand me? I need you to take a message... up the... line? Look! See it?'

'I'll try, Tris.' His words startled me. They were clear, lucid, strong, not a shadow of his former quailing. 'But they're all mad, Tris. The lot of them. Everyone goes crazy here,' he said.

'Try, Dad. Please! I can escape, I know I can!'

It was a lie. I was more and more sure I couldn't. Warm drowsiness washed through my soul, edged with searing pain as I gave him the message to pass along and up.

I half – more than half – expected him to stay where he was, cowering behind a glittering formation in the blue, returning to his gibbering stupor. But he flitted away, somehow now with purpose. And so did I.

She would always find me and though I didn't know why, at least now, I knew how. The violet coil wound through the blue, studded with souls like beads on a tangled necklace. It began with Her then came the other one, the one trying to help me; there was a mystery there, I knew; but I didn't have time to solve it.

The others came scores, maybe hundreds of them. And I was the last, the last in this place anyway. When I followed the dark violet passing through me, it went only to a place in the blue that somehow made it hard for me to move through, like wading in purple oil.

There was no question of getting away from Her; she could always find any of us. But the thread was long and she had long since lost her mind. She knew I was here. She must have been somehow drawn to me; maybe because I was the... *last? Latest?*

Because I'm still alive!

If I kept moving, all she could do was trace the endless coils through the layered crystal depths to find me. That was how I bought myself some time, a bit of time, one instant then another then another; which was what we all did, all the time. Only we preferred not to know it.

Berry – Nov 2098, inside The Stone

I did not suffer as much as Flower would have liked. Though I was trapped in the Stone, I was not bound to it as she was bound. I left no bond behind me and so nothing was broken against Earth and Sky and no agony was mine to bear. And seeing this, she shrieked and raged and I fled from her, seeking to hide in the glittering lattices.

She chased me and chased me through the violet-black depths and sometimes she caught me and her touch made me live the worst parts of my life over and over until I could pull free of her and hide again.

Had I not been smug maybe it would have ended there. Maybe in dragging my soul to her and knowing my life was over, her business with the world would have been done and she would have let herself go, to unbind our souls, come apart and drift through the glittering blue halls as the lifeless essence of Shades. But when I fled from her and hid from her and mocked her every time, her rage and pain flared anew. 'I am not done with you! You will suffer yet! You and yours will never know peace!'

And I knew that it was true for as the deep violet coil of our bond stretched between us, so too did it suddenly lengthen as I watched. It grew on and out through the crystal surface where we could never again go. I knew then, that though I had given myself over to her, my living baby was not safe and I wept and could do nothing more than haunt the crystal halls of my eternal prison and listen to Flower's fey and hateful cries.

And then the others began to come.

I knew they were my scions – *I must have birthed a daughter.* I knew them all for family though their faces changed colour and shape and that which bound us together stretched longer through the ages.

As more came, their suffering grew within me. One after another, Flower brought them, dragging them on the poisonous purple thread of the bond entwining us. And as their numbers grew, their torment became an ever-sharpening pull on the stuff of my soul.

Her pain and rage drove her mad and madder yet and I did not believe she could have planned it. Nonetheless, she somehow learned, whether by accident or by design, to torment me though she could not hurt me.

Without a body to check the roiling assaults of memories, a Shade was a pointless vessel, I learned in time, trapped in the Stone with nothing to do but muse. We should never have been allowed to linger after the shelter of our flesh was gone. A Shade was a thing of a moment or a night and our enduring here was against Earth and Sky.

What the others had to suffer was the seed of my anguish that grew and branched as my family spread down over the world. That their unbridled laughter rolled on into endless pain, their loves that could know no touch angered themselves into hate. That their rage which could know no vengeance screamed into the blue until it was spent down into exhaustion with no eyelids to droop or head to sag in sleep. It was all my fault.

'I'm sorry, Flower! I'm sorry! I did not mean for this to happen! Please, hear that I am sorry! Let it go, Flower! We are breaking the rules of Earth and Sky, Flower! Please! Let us go!' I begged and raged at her as she dragged in Shade after hapless Shade. I pleaded with her for moments, nights, summers, I could not tell. But she could not hear me or would not listen and the weight of their suffering grew heavy and sharp until I wept inside the Stone and my tears filled and filled my soul with no eyes to let them out.

I was a channeller of the Flow and whatever the mysterious workings of Earth and Sky that allowed it, it gave me some comfort. The Stone was full of Flow. It eddied and drifted through the layers and lattices like blue and violet morning mist. When I pulled it to me, it staunched the raging torrent of memories and brought me back to myself, for a moment, an instant till the Flow leaked away into the blue and the evil bond sang with the others' anguish again.

They were not so lucky and in time, such as a Shade with no body to mark its aging can perceive, their memories rang along the bond and their suffering became mine. After a time, I forgot what a lifetime was beyond distant memories of children, seasons, summers and warm flesh. I was of the living but no longer one of them. But when he came, a bright glittering Shade, anchored to his flesh, taken too greedily and too soon, I remembered.

I remembered the times I had slept nestled between the warm bodies of my family. I had lain awake and pulled in a breath of the Flow so I could watch those rare and strange ones amongst my cousins whose souls sleep-walked from their bodies in their dreams.

And I knew he was like them.

And I remembered the day, though the steaming heat had almost fought it away before I came properly back to myself, I had not missed it; the ghost of a sinister chill like you'd never get that time of year, leaving my body as I ran, after I had nearly trapped my soul in the Stone while my flesh was whole and alive.

And too, I remembered how I had escaped and I tried to tell him for, as well as clinging to life, I could see as clear as day that he was the first channeller of the Flow I had seen, in a line of souls longer than I could count. It should have been easy for him to free himself and yet he did not.

I showed him the place where all the souls of those channelling at the time I had made my mistake had been snarled up in the violet evil thread of Flower's rage and hate. I tried to tell him that though I could see he clung to life only weakly, he need only fill himself with the mighty rush of Flow that swirled about the lumpen tangle and he would have the strength to pull himself free.

But he did not understand and Flower went at him and at him and at him. She forced upon him, the memories of those others not fast enough to evade her clutching grip and slowly his strength ebbed away and I saw he would soon be spent.

And I could do nothing.

At least, till I felt Flower's haunting change. The tugging torment of memories began to quiet and a new whisper rose. Up from his white-skinned gabbling soul, through the sing-song brown round-faced and large-lipped, louder the clamour rose.

Words that had no meaning and yet I could somehow sense all meant the same roared through the violet cord of Flower's hate. And finally, I sensed though I knew not how, it came nearer. From the shiny black, straight-haired fine sharp faces near me in the blue, clear and smooth words coalesced from the formless noise.

Ways of speaking have changed and the world is not the same. The islands, the coast, the yellow river, the red soil, the green forests and the cliff are gone, so the others have said. The one who sends the message is from your line of daughters, numbering more than the family in the forest by the river and as many times more of that number and as many times that many again, and yet again. He cannot understand you and he needs to leave this place and he wants your help.

And though the words were nonsense since there could not have been that many daughters in a line and so there could be no bloodline of mine, I felt their meaning nonetheless. It grew in every soul, filling them with understanding passed up through Flower's haunting in a way that made her scream and rage. She pulled the violet coil and drew us tightly to her, grasping at the new one as he weakened, refusing to let him go.

But that only made it quicker for me to find the one I needed and send my answer back.

471

Tristian – Nov 2098, dreaming, Cornwall Hill,

Akarana Island, Aotearoa Archipelago

I felt her reply come down. Down from some place lost to history and covered in centuries of city-ruins, dust and the movement of the land. Down through generations spanning continents and oceans. Down over the planet to the islands of Samoa and across the short stretch of sea from the Laufalas on the islands to me.

I'd always thought I was a Laufala in name only. We'd considered me taking Jo's name, for the laugh! I was the fourth in a line of coincidental sons since my great-great grandfather Tavita Laufala had come to Auckland from the islands; that was the only daft reason the name hung on. And that had been when the country was three islands and not three hundred and three.

Maybe I had the height and the build of our islander ancestors but I was a mongrel really; settler stock: Irish, German, Dutch, English, who knew what else. But now it seemed, Laufala was more than only my name.

I couldn't say how long I'd lain locked in dreams though I knew now I was hovering in the instant before falling through sleep into death. The sharp pain was softening and far away in my body, I felt a dark cold stealing up behind the warm drowse as my soul forsook its home for the last time.

But my message had reached her, the one trying to help and I went to her and she showed me, though by then it was too late because the other had seen us and knew what I planned to try. And she pulled on her violet cord of pain and rage.

She pulled and though I knew, could feel what… Berry, had given me to know, it was all I could do to stand against a desperate collision of memories as… Flower pulled us into herself and we collided with each other… *against Earth and Sky*.

I drifted and sank beneath a thousand swirling minds, each brimming with madness and roiling memories. A part of me knew I should be more afraid than I was but a deadly peace stole over me and as it came down like warm wool over my cold naked soul, I yearned for it more and more. But my need to live whirred on like an angry wasp trapped in a bottle.

I pulled the blue into myself as Berry had showed me and I felt somehow stronger as she had said I would. I turned to Flower as her face neared mine through the tightening thicket of my ancestors' tormented… Shades.

'Why?' I said. 'Why are you doing this?

But she only grimaced and pulled and I got angry and did as Berry had said I would need to. I drew in more of the swirling blue light – as much as my soul could hold – and dived into the lumpen knot and roared and yelled and fought my way up, out and away with Flower's final entreaty echoing through my being: *Free us*.

Homing in on the pain anchoring me to my body, I tore myself free of the screaming ghost, bursting up through blue-violet depths and away across a vast burning broken land shrouded in night, yet flickering with city lights near its coast, through a crimson ocean dawn, over the planet's curve and down through the equator where grey spheres the size of cities bobbed in the ocean. I settled back into my body in my dim bedroom on a grey rainy morning at home.

But as I flashed over the earth, I knew something wasn't right. Something dragged at me, a jangling… *Flow* that burned cold in my soul and something rotten and rageful, anchored in the place of the blue and violet dream.

Still, who'd rather die than live? I catapulted myself into wakefulness anyway. I turned my last gasping breath into a hopeful next one. I lay on my bed, my heart restarting, my panting breath beginning to slow. I opened my eyes and blinked and knew I'd made it out and I was alive.

I came awake properly and my vision cleared and I started to wonder:

made it out from what?

Why wouldn't I be alive, anyway? But ah yes, that was it. Memories of blue, an angry woman and a sad one, a whimpering man and the ancient tortured bloodline of my ancestors' hung in my awareness like a firework in the shape of a phantom face, hanging in the air over the Auckland domain at opera-in-the-park, in my distant youth.

Free us…

It echoed through my mind.

It was all clear, laid out before me, a dazzling brilliance of understanding. For an instant I saw the oldest secret of my existence, rooted in a septic vendetta spanning millennia – *a living breathing family curse!* – laid out in flaming topaz-white clarity. Then slowly, floating ember by floating ember, its light cooled to blue then purple then black, fading into the violet dream which I became surer and surer, it had been.

Finally, all that remained was the tingling of returning life to my limbs and some out of place sense that I had not completely returned from… somewhere. That I was yet tethered to something far away, ancient and fey. I balled up my fists in frustration knowing I was forgetting as I forgot. But it all slipped away anyway and there was nothing for it but to sit up.

'Fuck!' I growled.

'Tristian? Jesus! Dad! You're awake! Oh my god! Davey! Get over to Tristian's place! He's up!'

Susan exploded into the room and grabbed my shoulders.

Tina – late Nov 2098, Beachlands Hill,

Akarana Island, Aotearoa Archipelago

Pete and his idiots were beginning to seriously anger me. I had more followers than him, now. Millions more. But still, they wouldn't stop. They were threatening me and some of them had turned up downstairs.

They couldn't get in but I was so startled to see them, the walls had closed in. I thought of calling the *jǐngchás* but the idea clenched my stomach with anger as well as sending a shiver down my spine. I didn't want them looking into me. Not that I needed it any more but the sacred nanite ingot had hardly shrunk and if they found it… Well, it wasn't worth the risk.

Another herd of the little fuckers had taunted me from the door downstairs this morning and made me feel yucky and anxious all day. No amount of weed, Total™ or coffee helped, not that it stopped me persevering with all three. Morning agitated into afternoon and I sat at my desk halfway through yet another coffee I couldn't remember making, J™ at the ready.

Rangi was staring out the window as usual which was fine because it meant I didn't have to teach him or... anything. Then as if it had read my thoughts, the building pinged me and I jumped. Fully expecting to see a bunch of Pete's dirty looking wet-foots at the block entrance, it was out of relief at it being anyone other than them that I let Chen – fucking Chen! – in before I had time to think.

What the fuck?

I was having second thoughts by the time she was at the door but I couldn't leave her loose in the hallway. I pinged the coffee machine for another cup as I opened the door. It was like, after, like, everything, we were going to sit down and chatter crap together as if we were old friends. Her showing up was so surreal, I couldn't think of anything else to do; it was as if my body was on autopilot.

'Uh, Hi Teen… Tina.' She said standing in the doorway gawking past me at Rangi by his window. I hadn't seen her in months and after… everything, suddenly here she was.

I said nothing.

'Tina. Um, I—'

She was obviously on some mission coming all the way out here. I didn't bother to ask how she'd found me. Half the actual world knew where I lived by then; I didn't care. The way she looked seeped slowly into my mind. Her face was tired and disgustingly sweaty when her hood peeled back. It was hard to tell through her overs but I thought I could see her legs shaking. She'd probably walked all the way out here like the wetfoot she was.

Her coffee was done and I took it off the machine. I think she was as surprised to receive it as I was that I handed it to her.

'N— Nice view.' She said lamely, her eyes on the coffee in her hand.

'Is that why you came here? To tell me you liked my view?' The tense anger in my voice blew up from nowhere inside me. I didn't put my hands on my hips but I channelled it.

Just at the edges of my vision, the walls started closing in. I was glad I could afford to pay away ads because I was struggling to keep a calm face without their annoying pink flashes.

Nate…

I hadn't thought of him in months, months! I would never have thought of him again if she hadn't showed her skinny little face at my door.

'What do you want, Chen?' I asked. I think a part of me was genuinely curious.

'Tina,' she blurted like a frightened child, 'You've got to stop! You're going to get yourself in trouble!'

'Really, Chen?' My voice was a droning drawl. 'You came all the way out here because you're worried about me?'

I pinged the machine to make more coffee for me and my hands were shaking with anger as I picked it up.

We both knew she didn't give a shit about me. The memories Chen brought up for me, the weed, the caffeine and the anger mixed into poison in my mind.

Cornwall, Nate, Grandad…. Grandad… Sarah… No!

'Did you come here by yourself, Chen?'

'Why?' she asked and I could see the fear in her eyes and it kind of excited me, in a sluggish sort of way.

'Ah, so you did. You came out here all by yourself, to what? Stop me or something? Are you actually in with that Pete freak, Chen? Honestly, I would've expected more from you! I always thought you were smart, well, considering your, uh, background, anyway. Haven't you seen what I've been doing, Chen? I'm trying to do something good for us, Chen. I would've thought given where you grew up—'

Then the little shit's voice unstuck. 'In case you didn't know, Tina, where I grew up is falling into the sea and you're sitting up here in your massive posh tower making out like you're going to make it all better with your freakshow experiment and your bloody DIY porn. Yeah, well, nice thought, Tina – or should I say, Elayne – but you're full of shit. All you are is a fuckin' stoner *makutu'd* rich-fuck in the end. Whatever dodgy experimental shit this' – she stabbed a finger at Rangi – 'is, doesn't matter. You're using it all to get rich and famous like every loser bloody influencer since the beginning of time! You don't want to do any good in the world! You're only a spoilt fuckin' brat looking for fuckin' attention! Jeez, what are you gonna do when whoever made his tech finds you, Elayne, have you thought about that?'

My stomach heaved and I struggled to keep the ground from tilting under my feet. My mouth opened and closed but no words came. I could have sworn the little roach looked satisfied. Too bad for her she mistook my anger for confusion. Rangi was fucking not tech!

'So it's true,' I croaked. 'You two were fucking cheating on me the whole time.'

'Eh?' She had the decency to look genuinely flummoxed. 'This *fēng kuáng-de* shit again? Oh, you know what, Elayne, it doesn't matter!' She said as I quietly fired up the latest bit of code I'd been working on. 'In fact, fuck it. Yes, Elayne, I did come out here to try to stop you but, for your fuckin' information, no, I've got nothing to do with that infected roach-rat arsehole, Pete!

'But okay, no, you're right. I wasn't worried about you. I actually give negative fucks about you. I did it because it's what Nate would've wanted. Remember Nate, Elayne, your boyfriend? Oh, and by the way, no Elayne, Nate and I weren't going behind your back – for fuck's sake, give us both some credit! – but yeah, I'm still in love with him, if you fuckin' must know. Happy now? Does that make you feel better, Elayne?

'Jesus, when Nate told me he'd found out about you, I didn't know which one of you I wanted to strangle harder! I couldn't believe he was considering not telling you and staying with you because he felt sorry for you! Argh! Thinking about it makes me sick, Elayne! But you know what? Nate's gone now and none of that matters any more. All that matters is that I know. You aren't one of us, Elayne. I mean, sorry for all the stuff that happened to you an' that; nobody deserves that, I get it. I get why you ran.

'But you could at least have been honest with Nate, if not all of us. And anyway, I could tell before I found out, something about you was off; you would've been better off telling us, telling me! All Nate's friends said the same thing when you guys got together. We all knew, Elayne. I mean, not knew-

knew. But you were a fuckin' idiot trying to pretend to be like us with your stupid lame street-talk and your pathetic 'toos and your useless fake accent. You'll never be one of us. You'll never know what it was like to have grown up with no— Whaaa—'

Her voice choked off as I opened a call to her and rammed my code hard down her messaging port.

She was going to regret being oh so fucking right, now, the little fuck! I was a Laufala and tech was in my blood. For a split second I wished they could see what I'd made. I wanted to see the pride on Mum and Grandad's faces, the admiration on Sarah's. It was a variation on something she and I had worked on as children after all. What child other than a Laufala got to play with the tech we had as kids?

I smirked at the shock on Chen's face when my hack took hold of her tech. It shouldn't've been possible but it was: her body locked up as if she'd been arrested. She started shaking and a thrill of fear – and, was it excitement? – shivered up from my diaphragm and tingled over my temples.

I'd done it! Me, without so much as a basic PhD! I'd figured it out on my own, how to hack into the literal heart of the nanotech my grandfather had invented and which practically everyone depended on, to do... everything. The rich were fucked now!

I knew it was a bit of a pissy prototype and I couldn't help worrying slightly about side-effects. Chen fell over backwards and started spasming and I wondered how much damage it was doing her.

'Sorry Chen. Nate shouldn't've told you about me. You can blame him if you want but I can't let you leave here now. Whatever you think of me, I'm trying to do something good here, Chen, and I can't have you fucking it up for me! That Pete creep and all his thugs are making my life hard enough without you helping them. You get that, right? Ah, I see... No-you-don't! None of that!'

I was talking to buy myself time to think more than anything but then I noticed her shifty little eyes were off in her tech and her filthy little lips were moving in that messaging way everyone knew. I'd been sloppy with her access but since she'd been dumb enough to telegraph the fact, I cut her off before she could send any more. Not that anyone would be able to find her here anyway.

But I wasn't sure what to do next. I kept talking, kept thinking.

'Not as dumb as you thought I was, Chen?' I asked. Her jaw worked and I shook my head. 'No, no, don't bother answering, I know you can't talk.' Her eyes widened at that, silly bloody child, she hadn't known it was me! I kept talking. 'And I'm afraid that's how it's going to have to stay. You shouldn't've come here, Chen. It's your own stupid fault you nosey little wet-foot piece of fluff.'

I was only trying to freak her out. I wasn't going to do anything, I decided. How could I do anything to Chen? We'd had our differences but to – what? – beat her brains out or something? When it came down to it, I wasn't sure how I'd start with her lying there like, defenceless.

But I didn't know what to do. My head was spinning with caffeine and weed. She was sprawled on the floor practically frothing at the mouth and it made me feel sick.

'Rangi!' I said trying to keep the fright out of my voice. He'd come over, probably attracted by the argument or something. 'Take her to the bedroom!'

For once he didn't ask stupid questions. He picked her up like a newborn and once she was on the bed, I locked the door behind us. Rangi went back into the lounge and necked a Total™ and it inspired me to do the same; better trying to think on a full stomach.

He'd started getting the stupid baby look he got when he was about to overflow with questions and I couldn't deal with them right then so I locked myself in my room with another coffee and a couple of Total™s, for... in case.

What the fuck am I'm going to do with Chen?

Then another troll from Pete in the holy Movement space made me clench up in rage and I forgot about her temporarily.

'Rangi!' I said. 'Come on, we're going to sort this arsehole out, once and for all.'

Rangi – late Nov 2098, Te Puru, Maraitai,

Omana and Beachlands Hill, Akarana Island,

Aotearoa Archipelago

It was like no other battle I have seen. There was nothing to take from the enemy and at first, nothing to defend. It was a senseless waste of life and strength but the orange slurry had my soul in its grip and so I did as my demon Mother… *Papa* bid lest she choke off its beautiful evil flow.

And then what would become of me? Would the pain of its loss make me… wasted?

Leaving the inexplicable prisoner in our… apartment, I strove against the whispers of madness as I flew us to the battleground which my demon mother said she had arranged – arranged! She told me our enemies would be there though not how she knew. I could not understand why she did not want us to travel in the Uber-beast or over the ocean to preserve the ground, but I knew from the set of her jaw that she would hear no argument.

Cracks and disturbances in the strange flat substances of the demon-world earth followed us as we drifted up and over the hill by the sea and down to the place she directed me, some distance back from a rubble-strewn shore. We alighted at last, on a great flat place of black rock with an evil sheen to it not unlike the fell substance that oozed on the ocean's surface. It was pitted and cracked and marked with great fading yellow and white stripes like the bodies of wasps.

When my feet touched the earth, I looked to the grey sky and breathed hard in an effort to staunch the whispers and perilous memories aggravated by the Flow I had channelled to fly. I strove to drink in the sight of the clouds, strange though they were, and fought to fill my mind with the hiss of air in my lungs. It was some time before I came back to myself, nagged by Mother, tugging at my... sleeve. It helped me also, to think in the new demon language for the effort took me away from the whispers welling up.

Blinking, I saw that the enemy had indeed come as she had said they would. They were unarmed and did not try to conceal themselves. They stood in idle knots on the great flat battleground, goggling and gawping at us and slowly beginning to approach.

But as they neared us, they took no angry stances and shouted no challenges. Perhaps they hoped to overwhelm us with their numbers alone? To sit on us in a great pile, perhaps and crush the breath from our lungs, grinding us down with the sharp bones of their bottoms.

Mother stood near me and lifted her voice above their chatter. 'So did Pete the pervert creep have the guts to turn up or what?'

By now I understood many of the words she spoke but I could scarcely make sense of what she had said. Some sort of challenge, I supposed. Those nearest backed away while others drew in behind them until we stood surrounded by harmless-looking dark-clad foes. Only a pair against so many and yet they hesitated!

But then from amongst them, emerged a single figure, almost my equal in stature though his condition was impossible to tell through his... overs. His... hood peeled back and while Mother was fish-like and ever on the edge of anger, this one was pig-like, motley, putrid, ill and if I was not mistaken, terrified.

A contest of the greatest of each foe then. I see.

It was not the old way, the good way. But I remembered, it had begun to grow popular in… the newer battles. It made more sense, a grain of sense I could cling to in this world of madness. I was glad of it for the little comfort it brought for the strangeness of the place ever worried at my mind.

I made ready, knowing never to underestimate an attacker. Fear itself after all, was a powerful enough weapon and I smelled his fear strongly as he approached. Still, I wondered how this battle might be joined, so slowly did he walk. How might our blood stir, in the absurdity of this arranged meeting, to the hot fury we needed to slaughter one another?

Sweat began on his face as he neared us and I heard Mother's breathing change as her thin lips stretched into a smile.

'Hello Pete,' she said. 'Still feeling like the big brave boy today, are we?'

Ah. She will goad him. The demons are not so different after all.

I readied my limbs to leap, to dodge, to strike, to lash out with the Flow and feel the burning response as he did the same. To give him his due, he summoned a brave sneer to his face.

'I don't need to be fuckin' brave to take down you and your freak, you dumb slut. Looks like it's half dead already with all that choking. What's wrong with it? Hard night on the breath-play or something?' His bluff was as pitiful as it was nonsensical and yet I stood ready, for who knew the ways a demon might attack.

'No? Go on then. Take us down Pete,' Mother sneered back. 'Show us what a man you are.'

Even through the strange overs he gave himself away. He moved like an infant recently learned to walk. I knew which way his quivering body would twist a slow instant before he moved. His lunge was ponderous as a tottering elder making a final stand for his family in a bid for a quick and honourable end.

It was all I could do not to smile, almost fondly for demon-kind or man, it seemed an untrained boy was an untrained boy nonetheless. Certainly, I could not bring myself to channel the Flow against such a feeble assault. Indeed, as he wobbled towards me and I deliberated on whether to simply step out of his path and let him fall on his face or cuff him senseless and let him rise for a second try, Mother herself surprised me.

She darted jerkily in front of me and lashed out with an unpractised foot to his groin. It was a way of fighting such as I had never seen and I supposed it must be taught to demon-spawn as they grew. Clumsy though it was, it was more than I expected from her. Perhaps this was why our gathered enemies were so fearless, for if they could all fight thus, well, it might have been an amusing battle but a battle nonetheless.

To my surprise, her toes struck true and instead of re-joining with a mighty blur of limbs, our adversary sprawled, squealing, on the ground and clutched himself comically. Now his head would roll from his shoulders in a spatter of blood, severed with the weapon Mother had surely brought with her.

But no! Instead of ending the fight honourably, Mother drew back and waited as he moaned and blustered and got shakily to his feet. I stood stunned by my confusion alone.

'Your rich-fuck parents teach you that?' he bawled. 'That's prob'ly what all them rich kids get taught! She's nothin' but a spoilt brat in the end!'

He reached within his overs, their substance parting as he channelled the strange demon Flow. The next instant he had produced a thing not unlike the pots of orange slurry though it was only filled with water. He did not open it as the orange slurry pots were opened, he pointed it at us with panic and hatred in his eyes and this time I could not but open my mouth to mock him. For what harm could water do?

But before I could utter a word, the liquid sprayed forth and I heard Mother scream. I turned to see what ailed her then I too felt its devil burn in my eyes. For an instant I lost my sight. Mother's screams rose as he waved the spraying pot back and forth, dousing us in the strange burning water and roaring words I could not understand. I grunted despite myself for though my sight returned quickly enough as the fusing healed me, the stuff surely made a powerful sting.

I did not look around to Mother but channelled Flow to heal her since she'd never learnt. Her screams waned into sobs then gasps as the enemy's pot ran dry. His rage faltered and his voice grew ragged when he saw he had done no lasting harm.

'Impossible! That's fuckin' impossible!' he growled, over and over.

Stealing a glance at Mother, I saw the last of the marring disappear from her overs as they healed themselves. By then she was unblemished and as always with the healing of the Flow, she appeared less sickly than before she was injured though some of her strange yellow hair would take time to regrow.

I could not help wishing I had seen what the strange fluid had done before I healed her. But no matter, its sting had been strong enough to stir my blood and though I had not seen it, I did not doubt from her screams that Mother would have been sorely injured indeed and perhaps perished had I not healed her in time. And then I would have been alone in the demon world aching for the orange ooze with no means to get my hands on any. And the whispers rose in my soul at the mere thought and so now there was indeed something to defend.

The enemy was backing away, chittering, 'Impossible! It's fuckin' impossible!'

The others were murmuring, angrily, I thought, though it may have been fearfully. I was already gathering myself when Mother said, 'do it Rangi!'

Though I was coming to know the shape of this strange battle and my blood was at last rising, it was with some restraint that I reached out with the Flow and crushed his bones. His face was more confused and dismayed than anything as he crumpled with a stilted childish whimper, shapeless, bloodied and lifeless to the ground. When I nodded to Mother to take his head, I saw that she had paled and at first, she made no move towards him.

For a time, she shivered and looked ill and I thought she would vomit as she often did; some sort of demon malady no doubt and who was I to say it was not simply the way of these creatures; perhaps it was no malady at all. Her shaking abated as I knew it would and she nodded and smiled – grimaced – at me and went to the body. Now, surely, the weapon would appear. She would take his head and hold it aloft and our new vanquished would hail our victory loudly. Then this would all be at least a little less strange.

And I am so tired of the strangeness; so tired.

But it did not go the normal way. Mother squatted down and instead of doing the foe his honour, such as the snivelling fool deserved, she prodded the ruined pile of flesh as if searching for signs of life! As if that were not baffling enough, the enemies about us had taken to gasping in disgust – if I was not mistaken – and milled about and soon began to flee though the fighting was done! A few at a time at first then more and more, hastened to a far-off corner of the great flat rock, streaming into some cavemouth I had not known was there.

Their departing numbers brought Mother back to herself. 'No!' she hissed, rising. 'Rangi! They can't get away! Get them all! Get them! Rangi! Fucking obliterate them or something or I'll rip your dumbarse gormless fucking nuts off! Rangi! Now, you idiot, now! Before they get away or we're fucked!'

Never had I seen such fire in her eyes. Never had she taken me by the neck in her bony powerful fingers and shaken me so. I feared the time of feeling the burn of her demon Flow was nigh. But though I knew I needed sorely, to obey, I could not be sure of what she asked, such a spattering of words had she issued in a tone and timbre I was unfamiliar with.

'But *Papa*, I do not understand,' I begged.

'Argh, for fuck's sake! Break them all you idiot. Destroy them! Kill them! Now, Rangi!' And I shrank back at the snarl in her throat.

There were yet some meanings I could not piece together but… break was clear enough. So, I did as she asked for now as if to remind me how much I needed her, my body and soul had begun to itch for the orange slurry.

As ever, the Flow was a blind and blunt but deadly weapon to wield. I made a globe of power with Mother and I at its centre and pushed it outward like an unseen bubble of crushing strength, out and out and out. Our foes were crushed in a heartbeat, crumpling shapeless and bloody as their squealing little champion had moments before.

To my surprise, the ground on which we stood crumbled beneath us shining grey daylight on a ground much like it some distance below. And the same again and again and again as if this part of the earth were covered in layers of black and white-marked shell.

Soon we hung in the centre of a great sphere of my strength with a mighty pit full of drifting vile dust where flat black rock and hapless foes had been an instant before. Were there any channellers of the sort of Flow those here often channelled like Mother, their wits had certainly not been about them. Not a single one had fought back and now all were torn to dust and less than dust, joined with the broken demon earth stretching down to the sea and far up the hills around us.

I looked about me at the ruin, thinking on our unworthy enemies snuffed out as they had fled. It could hardly be called a victory. As if in reproach for my cowardice, the wind howled suddenly up from the sea, filling the silence our sickly enemies' voices had previously occupied. Large drops of rain began to fall and Mother channelled into our… overs to bring our… hoods between us and the world though it was only wind and warm water caressing our flesh.

A sharp and unfamiliar stench drifted up and I feared what harm it might wreak on my soul. There were things in this world the fusing could not shield me from, the orange slurry and its dread hold over me was proof enough of that. As if the thought had summoned it, my yearning for it flared within me and I became impatient to leave.

Though the memories spun and the whispers rose to a roar, I took us far out over the water, ignoring Mother's fingers digging into me as she hid her head and whimpered. Though any fool could see the ocean was poisoned, I could not understand her terror of it. Surely it was harmless enough to fly above. But then for the first time I marked the lifeless sky, filled only with clouds and rain and sometimes a lone nightmare mosquito on its strange bloodless hunt.

No gull cried nor did any fish splash or flash in the shallows and with this observation came chill terror. I knew then that I knew nothing of this world, less than I thought I had known. Poison and death took forms I could not begin to imagine. And all that kept me from letting myself and Mother fall into the deadly waters to do with us as they would was the fell yet familiar pull on my soul, weak but steady, from beyond the horizon.

The Stone is somewhere. There is a way back, a way home… somewhere.

Mother made only the weakest of objections when I took us into her cave the fast way, through the… glass high up on the… building side. I paid her no mind as she set off to the… toilet where I heard her vomiting as was her wont. Perhaps it was how they spawned. Of her prisoner in the… bedroom, she said not a word.

Provoked by my channelling that day, the memories whirled within me and the whispers had grown to a roar. A pain had stolen over me as we flew, throbbing in my soul like a deep and formless fear.

As we entered the cave, it crossed from spirit to mind and at last to sharp needles of pain skittering up my spine to burst within my skull. The fusing did not answer with healing as it should have and strange though it was, a chill of recognition stole over me.

I must not remember…

I glutted myself, drinking bottle after bottle of the wonderful terrible ooze, hoping it was merely being too long without it that ailed me. And indeed, as I gulped and… guzzled,

the abatement of the itch and perilously beautiful flavour filling my mouth went some way towards staving off the whispers and the pain did indeed shrink back from body to mind,
mind to soul. By the time Mother returned, it was almost gone.

Almost.

Elayne – late Nov 2098, Beachlands Hill,

Akarana Island, Aotearoa Archipelago

I came to and nearly jumped out of my skin. We were leaving the coast, flying out over the water. I discovered my arms were wrapped around Rangi and from the way my neck was straining, my face must have been buried in his shoulder. I put it back there so I didn't have to see. Anything.

It had got out of hand. On our way there, I'd started thinking it was a bad idea. I wouldn't have done it if Chen hadn't wound me up so much! I was going to tell Rangi to take us back but there had been so many people there.

So many! Shit! So, so many!

I had to go through with it. I was only going to have Rangi scare the guy a bit, levitate him, singe his hair, make a fool of him. Something.

But then he'd called me a rich-fuck… *like Chen*, as if she'd already outed me. He'd sprayed the acid on us and after that all I could remember was pain. I probably would have died if Rangi hadn't healed me. I thought I was dying. I remembered blindness and the feeling of air blowing over my actual skull as the acid burned away my flesh. I'd heard my eyes boil and smoke in their sockets, I'd heard it!

Then Rangi's power had come. My skin had grown back, my sight had returned. It was nearly more painful than the acid and somehow, exhilarating, too. It'd left some of my hair missing but I guessed lost hair wasn't an actual injury; I was due a nano-shave anyway.

I'm used to it! I'm used to his freaky healing, like it's normal!

That much acid would have burned through to my brain. I could tell from my pathetic whimpers that my voice was hoarse as I clung to Rangi so he didn't drop me in the water. I'd felt like that enough times to know I'd been screaming.

I was angry.

But I wasn't sure what had happened. My mind had gone blank in the way that it did sometimes. There was red rage, hatred and then, maybe I'd bolted, or… fainted? We were here now, flying. Like that was normal too.

I saw that Rangi was going to take us through the window and I was too wrecked to do much more than whisper, 'no.'

Once we were inside and the glass had repaired itself and my account had debited some piffling amount, my stomach suddenly heaved. I made the toilet in time to lose everything I'd ever eaten in my-like, life.

Vomiting helped as it always did. I was calmer after spewing but that wasn't necessarily a good thing. It freed my thoughts up more and then the picture of…

…a crumpling body… …the ground disappearing, dozens of people.

I retched again and this time I tried desperately not to start thinking afterwards. Rangi had guzzled half our Total™ and gone to do his dormant squatting thing by the window. I left it transparent as a reward for… handling us when I'd… whatever I'd done, wherever my brain had gone. That, and I was too sick to do anything, anyway.

I necked a bottle of Total™ and the itch I hadn't realised I had, eased. I ordered more bottles, barely thinking about it. I had to get out in front of this, I knew. There would have been at least one of those wet-foots livestreaming. They were all gone now so I had the upper hand. None of them were around to answer any questions.

No regrets, fuck it, none!

I did a quick edit on my footage. They didn't need to see Rangi swiping the idiot down as if he was no more than a baby roach. The acid on the other hand and what he got for trying to fuck with gods, that all went up complete with the spinning holo of authenticity.

I recorded a quick voiceover to explain what had happened and why it had unfortunately been necessary to take out the threat to the Movement. I managed to get it posted in the space before a round of shaking overcame me. I clung to the bench and as soon I could move again, I got the coffee machine turned on. I needed something to calm my nerves.

I should have gone on to the space and talked with my followers live but I just... couldn't. I'd done nothing wrong but I couldn't face anyone right then. Because... Because Rangi'd flown us and that... always discombobulated me. That was the only reason.

I watched the messages pile in and spent the afternoon replying from offline. I ordered food but ended up slugging Total™ with the bioboxes unopened on the bench. Rangi wouldn't leave the window, even after dark, so I left him to it and shifted to my bedroom with an extra few Totals™ to keep me going through the night.

I must have slept, scientifically speaking. But I hardly remembered it. I replied to message after message trying to ignore the visions that wouldn't stop. Whenever I lost whatever distraction, I saw bodies screwing up and blood bursting from their orifices like a giant invisible hand had taken hold of them and squeezed. I saw the tarmac on the top of the old parking building we'd met on crumble to dust, less than dust. And the level below and the one below that...

No matter what I did, I couldn't shut the memories out. I was sick and exhausted by morning and awake or asleep I couldn't stop seeing what we'd done. I made coffee after coffee. I hardly noticed when the meal from the night before expired and melted down as I inhaled yet another bottle of Total™. I did notice how much Rangi was drinking and how agitated he seemed, but I was too busy to care.

I buried myself in fan messages until my bladder was ready to burst but nothing worked. I felt my mind going where it was too sore to go anyway.

Then suddenly I remembered Chen.

Fuck!

She was lying on her side on the bed and the room reeked of disgusting things I didn't want to think about. I called in a clean. Then I heard a noise like wind through an alleyway in the distance and it nearly made me vomit.

She was breathing but her face had gone an awful greenish colour and that was when I remembered the tech.

'Chen,' I said. She didn't answer but her body started shaking and jerking.

Holy fuck! She's dying!

Then I flashed on what the disgusting acid guy had said before he'd… My stomach heaved.

No! He got what was coming to him!

And maybe she had outed me already. He had sounded like he'd known; like everyone knew! Who else could it have been but her? No, fuck her. I didn't owe her anything.

No matter that I'd got my face and hair done, that I'd replaced my normal on-board nanites with the government issue grey ones that you couldn't tune clear. No matter that I'd copied all their stupid trashy webbing patterns all over my face and wore the same shitty standard-issue hemps they wore. No matter that I was fucking helping them! All they could do was fucking suspect me and attack me and abuse me. And she'd helped them!

Fuck that!

Now the mattress was clean, I noticed the grubby little fuck was dribbling. I needed to get rid of her to stop her making me bloody ill as much as to make sure she didn't fucking squeal on me more than she already had. There was too much at stake to let her go. Everything I'd achieved would have been for nothing if she went and ruined it all, if people left the Movement, cancelled their subs to my space.

We had momentum now. I only had a vague plan in my mind but I'd get to the details when I needed to, no matter what it took. What was one pissy life compared to a whole revolution? Nothing! And anyway, she was right, people had already died. Some of them were the ones who needed saving.

Saving one little shit who'd betrayed her own and left them behind would have been an insult to all the good honest people who'd accidentally lost their lives to the Movement that morning. No, the more I thought about it, the more I realised I had to do… what needed to be done.

'Rangi!' I called.

But he didn't come.

Chen lay quietly dribbling all over the mattress which I suddenly realised I couldn't see as clearly any more.

It's not that late. Why's it so dark?

I went into the lounge to see what wrong with Rangi but he was doing his normal thing, squatting by the window. Then I saw it. Coming in through the grey, a wall of blackness that was oh so wrong.

No! Holy fuck! No!

Red closed in on my vision and everything went jumbled, sights and sounds coming to me at random, my own voice sounding like someone else's.

…Rangi! You've got to stop it…   …Rangi!... …something!...

Was it me screaming? Or only thinking the words?

Did he turn? Look around at me in confusion? More screaming?

Then calmly, far too calmly, 'I will try.' I was sure that was him.

There might have been the tearing shatter of glass, the salty rotten smells of exposed seabed. But I was sprinting for the door by then. Racing for the lift. Fleeing. Up. Up was my only hope.

It wasn't until much later that I'd remember Chen lying dying in Rangi's room and the sacred nanite ingot with its glistening corner peeking from beneath the valance around his bed.

Nathan – late Nov 2098, Spume Prison Stasis, Cornwall Estate, Akarana Island, Aotearoa Archipelago

Dying was lights out. There weren't any ghosts or whatever hokey things people used to believe in. You fizzled out and your body got sent to the recycler.

And if you were a wet-foot like me, your company reassigned your apartment to some other employee and all that was left of you if you were lucky were a few sad people and maybe some hungry kids.

Nate, you're a FUCKIN' loser!

I thought, appropriately, as my eyes pinged open in the blue.

I blazed up the link like a cockroach under a dishwasher. All quiet in the mausoleum. Checked the storeroom and there was my death profile plugged in where I left it. Opened the panel and went inside the schematics. All systems humming except some weirdness at the… delivery plant.

Shit!

Drilled into it and bam! I was right in the middle of a swarm of cops!

They were everywhere, checking shit, checking all the shit in the whole city. I don't know why I cared considering I'd been busy offing myself. I think it was some kind of deeply ingrained fight-or-flight response to *jǐngchás* which made me pull up the cloak I'd rigged for snooping around the system back when I cared if I got caught.

I started following them, trying to work out what they were after. But they either weren't talking or I was only getting half the story because they were talking to people outside the system. They were mostly infesting the city, hanging around the virtual tricked out like a water treatment plant where the fine-tuning for all the stasis-pod feeds lived.

I went back to the graveyard to think because all the cops were freaking me out though they couldn't see me. There was one there too, now, like a loan reconnaissance roach. But a lifetime of experience pissing around on the job meant I could smell my own pretty well. He was trying to look busy on the clock. Nothing for it but to go back to the plant and keep an eye on the main swarm.

I definitely wasn't into all the weird stuff Teens'd latched on to. I didn't believe stuff was meant to be or anything like that. But, fuuuck, if I didn't appear right behind one of them as he muttered to himself sounding pissed, 'this stuff is all working fine. Fuck, if this is what I think it is, I'm fucked.'

Fuck! Neil? Neil Maclaren-Pukeroa? You? You're a jǐngchá now?

I'd've recognised his voice anywhere. We grew up together since he and his booze-maggot folks lived next door. He was one seriously cold slippery motherfucker as a *háizi*. No surprise given how his folks were to him. But man! I mean, okay, we all hated roaches from the year dot. But I remembered feeling sorry for them when I watched him pulling them to pieces to see how many bits missing they could have and stay alive. We were about four, then. Chen told me he'd moved on to rats when he got older and I believed her.

And not only that but he'd been about the only hacker in the neighbourhood who was as good as me, if not better. Plus, rumour had it he'd actually got his PhDs. Looked like the rumours were true because here he was, a cop. The smartest baddest wrongest fucker on the southeast coast, an actual cop!

Yeah, okay, so that thought was useful right when I only had a second to be horrified. Then off he popped with me slip-streaming packets and shitting bricks behind him till we popped out of the air in the storeroom. I hadn't gone straight there from anywhere besides my mausoleum before but I s'posed it made sense that you could.

And anyway, he's trained in the system. I had to work it out for myself. I would've got there...

He started tinkering, figuring out how it all worked. I was surprised he didn't already know but guessed it wasn't part of his job. I went to a random profile pack to see how you found the prisoners it was hooked up to from this end and that was when I saw what I'd done wrong. Not that it mattered because it looked like all the meds in all the profiles had been changed to some kind of baseline package.

My death pack was there, set up like before but it too just had the baseline ingredients and settings.

Okay, so it wasn't my fault I didn't die after all.

Or maybe it was. Was there an alert I hadn't spotted after all?

So much super-brain and I'm losing my touch anyway!

Or was it a coincidence? I didn't have time to work it out. I ripped the poison profile out of its connection to me, hopefully before Neil saw anything happening.

I threw it right past his bum to the bin under the lab bench, deleting it from the system. He looked up but didn't turn so I guessed my cloak was holding up. Or maybe it was just the way this part of the virtual was set up.

The way Neil moved, gave me a bad feeling though. Whether he'd worked on this part of the system before, or not didn't slow the bastard down much. He had it sussed in half a minute, like I had all those months ago. Then he went straight to my fake PRISONER profile and opened it up.

I watched over his shoulder and a chill went down my spine when I saw how wrong I'd got it. Neil was seriously pissed now. 'Shit, Sarah! Why didn't you find this you fucking stupid little cunt?' And I heard how his accent'd changed over the years to be like the dry-foots. And if anything it sounded colder and nastier than it ever had.

Then he spoke to someone outside the system and that froze me up worse because suddenly he sounded human. 'Okay, call off the airstrike, I think I've found it… Yeah there's nothing wrong with the stasis pods. Someone's arsed about with an actual master profile. I'm resetting it now. I reckon you'll see the spend drop-off in a few minutes.' I could nearly hear how sharp his brain was, in his don't-fuck-with-me voice with a watered-down drop of our old seawall accent.

What would I sound like, now?

Then, like his words were magic, I felt the change. It was subtle. I felt slower, like an Uber burning downhill when its battery ran out. I was thinking as fast as always but I knew I'd slow down if I didn't juice up again before I hit the flat.

Even if they didn't trace my meddling back to me, it wouldn't've killed me to go back on the old profile; back to the blue and the rain and the brands and the waves of chill. But now with all the stuff I'd speed-learned, I fully understood how their data mining messed brains up and made people come out vegetative.

It didn't seem fair, though nobody could ever expect fair out of life, I couldn't help feeling the… injustice of it. The idea of going back there seemed ten times worse now. I was safe from the chill-drug but it wouldn't be long before they switched everyone back from the baseline to their usual pro-files. Then it would only be a matter of moments before they found my monitoring hacks.

Well, my fun in the super-brain-school sun was all borrowed time anyway.

My whole life was if I really thought about it. Everyone was going to die, it was only a question of when. So why did it matter a shit? Why did anything matter? The rainbow face would disappear along with its voice that was somehow never there.

The chill would crash over me and wash away my worries in the warm wet blue calm. I'd make faces in the rain and say the names of *dōngxīs* and their brands out loud and forget each one as I said it till my time was up, one way or the other. I'd been about to check out anyway. What did I care?

And anyway, though my *nǎozǐ* wasn't getting its special smart-juice, maybe it'd given me enough of a boost to not come out so bad.

Three more years, Nate. You're kidding yourself.

I knew it. But still, it didn't mean I'd forget I was dreaming. The fuckers couldn't take that away from me. Maybe once they'd all left the system and put me back in my drugged-out stupor, I could sneak back in and do the job of checking out properly.

I'd seen from what Neil'd done how to do it right the next time so it didn't bring the whole system down. Yeah, whatever. This shit didn't matter. Neil could do what the fuck he liked. Why was I hanging around watching him?

Just as well I was though. It turned out he wasn't finished. 'Yeah, course.' He said to whoever it was outside the system. 'I'll look into it now... Nah, definitely not a glitch. Someone's been tampering with it, it looks, I dunno, weird... Yeah, give me time. I'll get back to you, okay?'

Whoa! Too creepy! He sounds so normal, like he can switch on humanity!

Then the crafty bastard... simultaneously virtualled into a bit of the system I hadn't seen before and stayed in the storeroom. That was the problem with tech, you could jack up online spaces to do things that were physically impossible. Stuff like that always hurt my eyes but I watched him as well as I could.

I shivered under my cloak when I saw the speed he was figuring stuff out! Jeez! It wasn't anything I couldn't understand. But he was putting it together fast all right.

Packet logs, I knew all about them. Piece of piss. Then…
Yeah, okay some kind of accounting. I couldn't get a handle
on it looking over his shoulder but that was because I hadn't
learned it before. It would've taken me a bit of time to suss
out, that's all.

Anyway, it was easy enough to see he was matching network traffic to the accounting numbers by date. Nothing I
couldn't've handled. He paused on one of the accounting
pages and the names of some chemicals jumped out at me and
then I knew what he was up to.

Uh-oh.

The next thing he got into didn't do much for my state of
mind either, because it was some kind of change audit trail. He
stopped scrolling right on the lines:

[2098051822:03:14.34] PACKAGE DEACTIVATED by
user [] [] [] [] [] [] []: PRISONER

[2098051822:18:43.09] PACKAGE RENAMED by user
[] [] [] [] [] [] []: ENHANCED INTELLECT (EXPERI-
MENTAL) -> REHABILITATION

I reckoned with the null fields, he'd be stuffed. But no! Up
came the date-matched packet logs and bam! On to the schematic they mapped.

Jeez!

It was kind of a buzz watching him work. Okay a cold
creeping-the-shit-out-of-me type of buzz but pretty…. Admirable, yeah that was it. Admirable.

De— De— Despite, his smart-arse date range which he'd
got from the accounting system he had about twenty shitloads
of packets to sift through anyway. Not that it held him up
much. He was chewing through them way too fast for comfort!
As I watched… mesmerised, he'd whacked a filter on his
search so there was about only a tenth as many packets to go
through. There was no doubt about it, he was coming for me.

I probably had minutes left. Or make that seconds, since
I saw another filter pile on and the packet log thin out another
few fuck-tons. Given I'd spent the last few weeks and all the
grit I had, trying to rub myself out, you would've thought I

wouldn't have given a shit about being busted. But that was the thing about my death-wish frame of mind. Anything was worse than dying.

Once he nailed me, they'd have a perfect excuse to up my sentence to, aw, say, I dunno, how 'bout for-bloody-ever. I'd probably get experimented on and all sorts of shit and nobody would ever know. When I thought of it like that, the best thing that might happen was that they'd put me back to how I started here, having my data harvested and my *nǎozǐ* gradually turned to mush.

Maybe I wouldn't make it through my sentence and my body would wind down and eventually get quietly unplugged and recycled. I couldn't handle that they'd won.

Yeah, fuck it, I'd rather be dead.

And a guy who'd rather be dead is one dangerous motherfucker to have root access to your systems. Maybe it was the last of the magic juice from my pirate profile still working. Whatever it was, I suddenly fired up and I blazed!

I flew up the trail of Neil's packets to cut his connection. I hauled arse through the schematic to the user registry and trashed his user profile so it would take them ages to get him back on. That bought me a bit of time but I knew it wouldn't be much.

I burned over to the pigeon loft. I was only going to do mine but fuck that. If I was going down, I'd go down in fuckin' flames! I dusted off the sentence-adjustment format and pulled all the profiles I could find. In the virtual it was like grabbing a pack of twentieth century post-it notes or something except then they all merged and what should've been a gazillion birds was only one as I rolled up the note and clipped it onto its leg.

I had the place for system logon connections – a weird room full of booths built into a clear barrier down the middle and old school telephones on each side – and the storeroom opened, too. Seeing them all at once was giving me a headache. If they caught me, I was more toasted now than I would've been if I hadn't been trying this shit. I would have to work fast if my idea had half a chance of working at all.

It was one thing for Neil to dick around and show his bosses, what a clever – okay, brilliant – shit he was. It was another for one of their employees to get maliciously booted off the system by what was basically an anal intruder. I could see they were fixing up his user, trying to repair the profile from a backup and get him back on to the system. It wouldn't be long, now.

But still, however I was about to get fucked up was worth it for the sight of what I'd stirred up in the pigeon loft. When I let go of the one bird it cloned. And cloned and cloned and cloned and cloned. There were millions of them by the time it was done.

They swarmed from the loft, impossible for that many to fit through slots that small in real life but hey… The whole fake sky was dark with them like a storm blowing out to sea. I could nearly forget I was about to be drugged into oblivion for the rest of my short life watching that. It didn't matter that it was a virtual inside a dream. I'd never forget the sight.

They'd all disappeared into the blue in a minute or two. Then I had about three seconds of quiet before Neil poofed back into the storeroom and was hot on my trail again fast as a roach up a dirty leg.

I was out of moves then. That was my plan, done, for better or worse. The cops'd have a system-full of requests to look through. They'd get in touch with Spume and the lot of them'd be purged or auto-rejected or whatever. Gosh, darn it, wonder what happened there? No hard feelings for the wee fuckup eh people? Let's all have some premium weed and a bowl of real vegetables what-what?

But at least I'd tried.

I stood by the loft looking out to sea with half an eye on Neil. He'd nailed it down to a few familiar looking packets now. He didn't have any user info but with those packets, he didn't need any. I might as well've done a dream-poo on the virtual pavement every metre or so, to show him the way.

All my traipsing through the system over the months was holding him up a tiny bit. He followed the flow around the city streets, to the Google pit, to the post office, to the logon booths. He'd have to hit the graveyard soon then it'd be seconds before he got up to his evil psycho neck in my arse.

I watched the sea and the sky and I was weirdly excited to see what happened when he busted me at last. I shut down the other spaces so I could chill looking at the water and the blue for my final moments.

Except it wasn't blue any more. Coming over the horizon was a big black cloud. I squeezed my eyes tight to see better. Neil must have done the deed already and this was how it'd look with them dragging me back down to calm blue watery hell.

The storm came on, darkening the sea. I remembered the storms at home and smiled sadly. I'd never see real rain and feel real wind blowing at my overs again.

The sky got darker and the first thunder started in my ears as the cloud got nearer. But I couldn't understand what they'd done to me. It didn't feel like the storm was coming at me or closing in around me or a hole of darkness was sucking me in or anything.

There was only a normal shadow on the water with lighter blue bits where the cloud split to let through the sun. It was nearly right over me and its roar was deafening by the time I realised it wasn't thunder but millions of flapping wings. Then the first birds piled in to land.

They blasted in through the slots so fast there was a blur where the flock bottlenecked into physical impossibility.

Ah, okay. Well, at least I tried, eh?

These would be all the reject messages. The cop systems probably kicked them back automatically because of the suspicious level of activity. I couldn't help feeling a bit disappointed that it had happened so… fast; that it couldn't have at least messed up the system for a while; made life hard for them for a few hours while they figured it out.

Mine would be in there somewhere but there were so many coming in so fast I bounced off the interface when I tried to stop one and read it to check what was happening. It must have locked up trying to process so many updates. You'd only see that kind of freeze in the cheapest of tech, nowadays.

It was such a freaky sight watching all the birds blaze in that I nearly forgot about Neil.

What am I still doing here?

I opened the storeroom and he was standing there looking pissed. 'Hey! Can anyone hear me? Fuck!' He shook his fists then flipped off all the screens he was looking into. I opened a few more spaces and noticed the few cops left in the system were as pissed as Neil and I saw why when I opened the schematic.

The system processor was fuckin' maxed! FUCKIN'-A! I'd basically staged probably the first denial of service attack on a system in about sixty years! All the system interfaces were locked up handling the inbound messages.

It wouldn't last long, I knew. I could already see the processor loads dropping. It would be back to business as usual pretty soon, I reckoned. Somewhere in some mountain fortress, fans were cycling up, auto-buys were transferring and QBITS and cloud CPU were getting dynamically allocated. No doubt about it, I'd put on a decent show. I'd got myself a bit longer. But that would definitely be it for me, any minute now.

But I couldn't let go. A few more minutes and another few minutes. That was how people all lived life anyway wasn't it? Only they didn't know it.

I burned across town to the booths and I could see Neil's connection. I was as *stonkered* as the cops with the controls all being locked so I waited at his booth for the load to die down. As soon as it did, I'd axe his connection and fuck his user profile up again, at least give myself a few laughs watching them trip over themselves getting him jacked back in.

It didn't take long for the system to resume normal activity. I could see cops getting back to work around the town. Or fizzling out of the space. I pulled Neil's plug out and…

'Gotcha!' said a cold hard voice behind me. I jumped and turned and there was Neil him-bloody-self. I tried to bail back down the link and that's when I realised he'd frozen me up. The crafty bastard must've set a traffic alert on his own connection.

Then I realised we weren't in the booths any more. We were inside some kind of vault and he was standing in front of the door which I had a feeling was locked from the outside.

See, the thing about being a hacker is that you've got to be flexible and you can't go getting too up-yourself about the latest and greatest. Old stuff doesn't always mean bad stuff. I had to hand it to Neil, he might've been an evil psycho fuck but he wasn't a dumb-fuck. The sneaky sod had trapped me with adapted fuckin' anti-virus software.

I turned around to face him.

Whoa!

I remembered those cold eyes like windows into hell and that… attitude he had. Yeah, I was ready for the worst but I couldn't help shivering seeing the look in his eyes like he wanted to treat me like his roach pets from all those years ago.

If anything, he looked scarier with his big strong jawline, blonde bun nearly ripping his scalp off. He had big wide shoulders and he'd grown up a good few centimetres taller than me in the end. Unlikely he'd recognise me given I was Natalie back then and it wasn't like I'd tried to stay in touch with him!

I stood up, tall as I could like a twentieth century military man. I saluted with a grin on my face though back in the flat in the real world, my wasted half-dead body was probably shitting the bed. 'Hi Neil,' I said. 'How ya been?'

He looked at me all confused. 'Hey! What the fu—?'

Sarah – late Nov 2098, Cornwall Hill Station, Akarana Island, Aotearoa Archipelago

No cop ever expected as much excitement as we had that night. Layers of *brass*, as Neil called them, that we didn't know existed, triggered alerts he himself with all his high and mighty rank and extra training probably hadn't seen. We all had to wake up and log on to work with bottoms puckered ready for action.

As for going into the station at stupid o'clock, well, I could see in the system as I ubered the few blocks down the hill through the drone-lit rain, that was Neil's idea. I wondered if anybody else would question the sense in it. Doubtful given how chummy they all apparently were.

Nearly every officer on the force started showing up after I'd arrived. I could hear their grumbles as they shucked their overs and the smell of damp station floor filled the air. They were all as confused as each other as to why we had to be in. Neil himself of course didn't deign to appear.

If any of them were smirking about how wrecked I looked or anything else, I didn't see. But I could tell as much from what they didn't say and do as what they did. There wasn't a single, oh hey, you're back, how are you feeling? Nothing. It confirmed what I already knew. The weight of knowing bore down freshly, as the desks filled up. It felt worse after weeks of not having to face them all.

As my overs peeled off, I felt like I was stripping despite my uniform and I couldn't get my legs under my desk fast enough. Trying to pretend nothing was wrong, I found Neil inside Spume when I logged on like he'd told me to. He clocked me but he was preoccupied with something and waved me away so I dimmed down the virtual and did as he asked, nothing. Nothing in Spume anyway.

I had no idea what had happened but I knew it must have been big. Spume was crawling with people I'd never seen before, doing I had no idea what. Still, I didn't know how long I had before the show would be over. And no matter how many virtuals I opened, how brightly I turned them up, completely obscuring the station around me, I couldn't shake the feeling of being stared at and leered at by the people who were meant to be my colleagues and might otherwise have one day become my friends.

Enough is enough.

I'd known it after my visit to Louisa and Gilly's but I learned right then in those stretched-out moments, the difference between knowing and finally understanding. Then I couldn't wait any longer to act. It didn't matter what I did, I needed something to happen, something to change, whatever it was. I couldn't go back to being miserable every day the way I'd been before I got sick.

On any other day, in my usual calm and rational state, I might not have done what I did. But the disgusting hour and my barely-recovered immune system made me reckless. And therefore dangerous, to myself for sure but hopefully others, too.

I got to work collating, annotating and padding out with as much formal cop crap as I could muster. I didn't take a breath before sending it all to Jimmie for the morning and that was good because as soon as the delivery confirmed, my reckless-dangerousness guttered and I started hyperventilating.

'Steady on Sarah!' The trashily-tech-decorated little dick-weed next to me said. 'Neil's not in the office!'

I heard a laughing 'oop!' Then everyone went quiet.

What's that supposed to mean, Kevin? Say it! For fuck's sake, say it! Loom over the little wet-f… uh, shit and say it! Make someone admit it!

But it was four in the morning and I'd only that second put what felt like my life on the line. And while looks and leers were one thing, to get practically slapped in the face with it was another. My mouth opened and closed and my voice wouldn't come. Playing it back, I probably looked a bit confused rather than like my world had turned upside down. The fucking little shit constable had come out and unashamedly said it.

I looked around, wild-eyed And red-faced. a dozen-odd straight faces stared back and I could see that all those slimeball shits in the know, now knew that I knew. I might've been shocked all over again to notice how fucking… many of them had been in on it! Well under half the station at least but…

Jesus! Twelve of them have seen me… Ugh!

Others were starting to notice and a few heads were turning to look at me in mild confusion.

I might've crumbled, folded up in my chair and cried in humiliation. It might have been a good idea, might've made the lot of them see the hurt they'd caused me. Of the twenty, they couldn't all have been un-empathic fucking psychos like Neil, could they? But before I could react, my peripheral vision filled up with a thousand improbable messages.

Eh? Oh… Okay.

Neil had always said he would get around to taking the grunt admin credentials off my profile and for the first time, though my cheeks were hot, my mind worked clearly and coldly. I hadn't badgered him like I had with the footage thing, it hadn't seemed that important. All I had to do was ignore the admin messages and clear them down now and again. They never bothered me; Spume authorisations only trickled in at a couple every few months or something anyway.

But now it was as if the blindfold had fallen off my eyes. Demoted as I was, how easy would it have been for him to take away everything he'd given me and leave me with only a bunch of lame professional development verifications and an HR file full of rot? He could strip my role back down to the drudgery it had been and use the dirt in my file at appraisal time to keep me there forever. There was probably a way to make the 'cautionary demotion' permanent too, if he wanted to.

As to why he'd bothered with such an elaborate bloody plot in the first place, well, it'd got me to sleep with him hadn't it? It was the only reason I could think of but if I was right, well, how pathetic! The sheer sadness and infantile insecurity of a person who needed to, what, pay people with promotions to date them. And well… shit-eh? What did that make me? A massive gullible fool in the best possible light. The light no-body ever saw anybody in, including themselves.

Fuck. I mean… Fuck.

I shook my head slowly at the simple disgusting enormity of my naivety.

If the case file I'd sent to Jimmie didn't make the old coot follow her protocols and do something, which given what I'd seen of her it probably wouldn't, well, I knew I'd be at Neil's mercy a few hours from now. Then there was no telling what he'd do when he found out what I'd been up to.

With that, another chilling realisation washed over me; I hardly knew him, for all the time we'd spent together. I couldn't so much as guess what he'd do. Jesus, was there no end to what a child I'd been? I'd told him everything about myself. I'd told him about Elayne and… everything.

I might have been a lot of things – more things than I thought, apparently – but thoughtless wasn't one of them. Not usually anyway. But nor did I usually get a flu so bad I had to literally take antiviral meds to kick it. And I didn't usually real-ise I'd been played for a fool on so many levels and lost years of my career after being called physically into work at four in the morning while still weak from said yuck flu. My sputtering recklessness flared a-fucking-new and since Kevin the dweeb constable serendipitously had my old job, I decided in-for-a-satoshi, in for the whole bloody bitcoin.

For a few glorious minutes – and I was sure they'd be my last before Neil came down on me like a falling fucking building – I became Elayne. Elayne the way I remembered her: impulsive, silly, unstable, hilarious, completely reckless and dangerously inventive.

Next to me, I could see Kevin's eyes widen crinkling up the glittering web-pattern they'd configured their tech with. I knew the swathe of Spume authorisations were now filling their work virtual from horizon to horizon. I knew they didn't have any idea why they'd been called in or that something was up with Spume; only Neil and I from this station did and I'd begun to suspect that was a major slip-up on his lordship's part. And if it wasn't, I was bloody going to make it be.

The authorisation requests must have been something to do with what was happening in the system. I knew Kevin wouldn't be dumb enough not to query that many turning up all at once like that. Indeed, their gormless barely-post-teen face with all its dreadful trashy grey webbing was already turning this way and that looking for someone to mewl to.

Hoping Kevin wasn't one of those people who recorded everything and uncaring of how suspicious my hand half covering my mouth for the benefit of the station was, I bent close to their ear and muttered, 'Just bulk 'em up, authorise 'em and put 'em through.' No exact mention of what but I imagined that'd be a flimsy defence if it came down to it.

But fuck it.

'But, Neil——' they stammered.

And – oh Jesus! – the way they said his name! The same vomit-inducing lovesick way I'd said his name! Jesus, my eyes were getting well and truly opened this shitty morning weren't they!

'Neil's not here, Kevin. I'm the ranking officer on the station, how do you think I knew you were seeing them?'

'O—— Oh, but, Neil——'

'It's an order, Constable!' I tried for menacing calm but given I didn't want anyone else to hear I may have succeeded in creepy schizophrenic whisper instead. But whatever.

I didn't know if it could be an order anyway. Jimmie had said I could keep doing the role but would the system have let me log it if I'd tried? Luckily, I never had to find out. I let the virtual come up around me and saw all the – what? Paper bag things? Were they called envelopes? – defy physical laws and bunch up in Kevin's pasty virtual little tech-tooed hand before they swiped them green to authorise and fed them all as one into a slot on an antique-brick-styled wall.

The system froze with the paper partially in the slot and for a second, I was worried something had broken. But it came back seconds later and the messages were all cleared like when I used to process them. Our systems were quiet and empty apart from all the usual job-creation crap that kept us bored at our desks day in, day out. Back to business as usual, move along, nothing to see here.

I left Kevin to it, hoping I'd got them in trouble in some way I'd be able to plausibly deny and snigger about as I went down in flames at dawn. Next, I pulled up the same virtual I had on the fateful Richards-Mann day when Neil had fucked me over with his faux-compassionate afternoon off.

That's when I saw he was untouchable at the moment. It wasn't only him. There was some weird suspension over the system because of the Spume fracas currently in progress. I could ask it to do stuff, locators, identity checks, all the usual things. But none of it would happen until the suspension came off which I guessed would be when Spume was… fixed, or whatever.

Well, fucking better yet!

Then I was out of the system and done but for one last thing. My energy was failing and my courage with it but I pressed on anyway. I went into Neil's office and there in sound-proofed solitude, I recorded a tearful Elayne-esque addendum to the case file I'd sent Jimmie.

'Hi Jimmie, in light of my findings – which you will by now have perused – and as you'll no doubt appreciate, I find myself unable to bear proximity to the persons aforenamed, given the issues of harassment and subsequent mental health such proximity presents. I am of course available to work and indeed, as acting ranking officer on the station, I will endeavour to fulfil my obligations to the absolute best of my ability. But I regret to inform you that I will not be able to attend the station in person for said personal health and safety reasons and will only be available virtually. In any case, I do not foresee this impeding my ability to work in any way. I trust you'll keep my case against the aforementioned staff members confidential in accordance with protocol.'

Then, staying logged on to Spume as instructed, I amazed myself by successfully bullying a lot of confused officers back home to bed and went the same way myself. Nobody had told me I couldn't. I should have tossed and turned, dreading the next morning when Neil finally caught up with me. But instead, I drifted off to sleep with a smile on my face as I pictured the look on his, when the delayed arrest slammed down on him as soon as whoever was in control released our systems.

Neil – late Nov 2098, Cornwall Hill, Akarana Island, Aotearoa Archipelago

Why hadn't bloody Sarah nipped the problem in the bud in her first shot at the system, completely untrained? Yeah, well, okay, when I thought about it like that... If only she'd been a bit bloody cleverer and seen this when I'd sent her in to check on that wet-foot loser we'd arrested months ago, I wouldn't've been jangled awake by a work alert at shit-o'clock in the morning for the first ever time since I was in bloody training.

I couldn't imagine being awake at that hour let alone what could be so bloody urgent the duty sergeant couldn't handle it. I mean, Spume but… well, that was Spume; what the fuck could I do if anything went wrong with that? I had the training but… Ah. Okay, it was Spume.

Well, shit-eh?

The realisation that something pretty hardcore had happened should've given me a sinking feeling but instead – oh god, how stupidly! – I was kind of excited. Especially since I reckoned I'd have to show the flag as the regional custodian and leave it to their experts to sort out.

I sat in bed and bleared into the alert details. Of all the ridiculous things, it was some kind of corporate problem. What the hell did that have to bloody do with me? Or the

jĭngchá'marie for that matter. I was contemplating a piss followed by a coffee when I was suddenly dragged unceremoni-
ously into a weird auditorium virtual; just a still image – a still
image! – of the guy speaking and his voice.

'…how this happened? What caused it? We find this out
in time, *ja*? We need only stop it right now or this whole setup
goes kaput, *ja*? And then I eat you arseholes for breakfast, see?
All the blaming and bitching, later, *ja*? I want anybody, anybody with system access getting on this case. You get them out
of the bed and you get them logged on and looking.'

He was speaking old English and had a line-up of human
translators in booths either side of the massive still; I was getting one of the translation feeds but I swiped it off; I could
speak the old gabble as well as any bloody rich-fuck because
unlike some layabouts, I'd taken the trouble to teach myself.

He had a weird accent though, to be fair but you're gonna
get that from foreigners I s'pose. Together with the massive
dark brown neander-skull in the picture, which was probably
there because of his legendary e-squibness now I thought
about it, it could only be Paresh Steel, the Spume CEO-and-
founder his royal poncy self, virtualled in with some special-
tech-for-e-squib-retards.

Whatever this was, it was serious else nobody would've
gone and got him off his rooftop golf-course or wherever a
rich dickwad like him hung out; and whatever a golf-course
was. Still, I doubted it would have anything to do with me.
Until I started listening, anyway.

Fucking Sarah!

And not in the good way either.

The meeting must've started before I got alerted because
aside from the briefest of summing-ups, that was basically it. I
listened to the orders, such as they were, waited till the auditorium booted me off then went into my Spume account.
There were a few dozen other cops in the archipelago with
access under me. And of course, bloody Sarah because I'd forgotten to revoke her.

Shit!

The last bloody thing I needed was her getting underfoot. I split my vision and abused my position to force her personal tech to wake her up. Through all my exhaustion, I managed to get a sneaky perv at her boobs when she started out of slumber with a *háizi* squeal and quickly pulled the sheets up to her chin.

'Get your arse into the station. Get logged on to Spume and do nothing, okay,' I said. I was tickled by the idea of her dragging herself out of bed unnecessarily and schlepping into work.

'But…'

'But nothing. Fucking log on and do nothing. Is that understood Inspect— oh I'm sorry, Senior Sergeant?'

'Y… Yes. Okay.'

'Okay fucking what?' I roared.

'Okay Sir,' she squeaked and shiver me timbers if me timbers didn't quiver at her amusing shock.

I cut the call and got all the other no-hopers with system access out of bed, logged on and milling around pointlessly in the massive Spume system virtual. I had time to snigger a little bit about the idea of Sarah arriving at the station to discover nobody but the lard-arse duty sergeant.

Then I changed my mind. If there was one thing I hated besides most of the human race, it was sleep deprivation so I woke all the other tossers at my station up too. If I had to be up in the middle of the night then piss on the lot of 'em.

'All of you, get into the station and wait for my orders… No, don't give me any shit. Do as you're told and make a fuckin' shape, the lot of you, okay? Or I'll write the bloody lot of you up.'

Is that a thing? Oh well…

For all the urgency and much as the Spume virtual was always a bit awe-inspiring to me though awe wasn't exactly my schtick, things suddenly went quiet. Nobody knew what they were doing. But the absurdity of the situation and the novelty of seeing cops from all round the world milling around in the system like drugged roaches weren't enough to distract me from my unease.

I wished I could've said I had as little clue where to start as the rest of them but sadly, with a certain sinking in my gut I'd learned to trust, I was more and more sure my hunch was right. And if it was, I didn't reckon anyone in all the heaving mass of gormless *jǐngchá'*marie and other assorted personnel would notice me dimming out for a few minutes to make a coffee so I could think properly. Jesus, if I'd known it would be basically my last supper, I'd've gone all out and cooked a full brekky along with it.

High lord rich Neander-ponce had briefed us before fire-and-forgetting us at the job; which I admired. If I hadn't been crapping myself, I would've liked that the mighty Spume with all its failsafe alerting and secret proprietary mind-fucking tech and everything, was imploding.

But the PR disaster I'd get dragged into let alone the blame I'd have to slide off on to Sarah, if all the wet-foots in stasis croaked at once put a massive damper on the night's entertainment. I could've sworn I saw my job flashing before my eyes. It was pretty motivational.

Spume had basically scrambled anyone with any system knowledge they could get their hands on. Our job was to help figure out what'd baffled the bigshot Spume geeks themselves. It should've been a piece of proverbial for them except that the system – the most advanced fucking system on Earth – apparently thought it was healthy; not a single alert pinging anywhere.

All we knew was that the corporate bloody gas-giant's cash reserves could cover the losses but their manufacture and supply couldn't keep up with demand across all regions. All the wet-foots were going to croak in stasis – which was fine in my book – or worse, wake up from the critical pharmaceutical drain. Once the coffee had got me alert enough to process the information, the coldness really started in the pit of my guts and slowly iced up my spine.

I'd kept an eye on the system since the first weirdness with Richards-Mann. Bloody Sarah had complete faith in the system and I wished I hadn't been the same. I should've checked into this myself months ago when I saw that little pleb's neural activity being weird. But it was Spume. How the fuck could they not know what was going on!

We were being coordinated by the time I was dumping my mug in the dishwasher and brushing at a couple of annoying drips on the bench. And I'd started to freak out more comprehensively which I really wasn't well suited to. Some big boss had flown into the virtual squawking and shitting on everyone with position-justifying incomprehensible instructions; I could smell my own fifty kays away. I nodded and yes sir'd, ignored her and skulked off to the stasis pod interface – which I found simultaneously calming and amusing – desperately hoping my hunch was wrong.

But it bloody wasn't.

Well, fix it first, figure out a way to shift the blame later.

I got out in front of it and kept reporting in to the pissy coordinator like I was figuring it all out for the first time.

Fixing it was easy enough and if that'd been all there was to it, it mightn't've been necessary to shift the blame; it could all be put down to a system glitch. But the logging anomalies behind the little bastard's pharma profile were too weird for anyone to miss and I had to make sure I was the one to not miss them rather than some goody-good wanker with career ambition burning out their arse. If bloody Sarah had been a bit smarter and worked this out, I wouldn't've been here now. Useless!

I got tracking and the more I tracked, the weirder it got and the harder I saw it was gonna be to pin this on Sarah considering the logging showed it'd been after I let her at the system. I might've enjoyed getting the old hands dirty with code for the first time in ages if my arse wasn't so comprehensively on the line. It wasn't all our fault but it was our fault enough for a sacrificial firing or ten.

I caught the little sod though.

That must count for something.

Except I wasn't sure what the bloody hell it was. It all pointed to the Richards-Mann profile, timing-wise, and that was impossible enough given he was drugged-up and probably half lobotomised by now.

But the avatar had no system user handle – which was more impossible; like a non-player-fuckin'-character coming alive – and it looked like a sort of… person wearing a grey sheet like something from a frickin' *háizi* movie.

And then it talked! It fucking talked! 'Hi Neil. How ya been?'

The next thing I knew, my joints locked up. 'Hey! What the fu——?'

But the thing in the sheet and the whole Spume virtual disappeared and I was suddenly back in my kitchen, right on the edge of losing my lunch. I was under arrest! Me! Under fucking arrest!

This is you isn't it, Sarah? You little shit. Now you're fuckin' in for it.

Rock – Nov 2098, Rock's Tower, Germany

'*Ja*, November again and still no results?'

'No sir. Nothing. Well, not nothing, there've been millions of views a bunch of speculative conspiracies but—' It was *mein* top tech boy; one of *mein* numerous sons. Blind with crippled legs but an acceptable brain. I had of course known the news would be bad again when he had come himself instead of sending one of the non-family staff members. Less risk of injury, *ja*?

'*Ja*, but nothing useful *nein*?'

Ja because I could imagine Bud being technically incompetent. It was likely she was living on an island somewhere, *ja*, maybe like an animal or a primitive ape creature after the world left her behind. *Mein* mood was becoming angry as the strategy of using the cloud to attract her continued not to work.

And also, it appeared her thoughts did not stand out among the others as usually happened when one of *mein* inferior colleagues tried to access our mysterious shared memories.

For me this was a nuisance because of course, attempting to stimulate an individual response in our strange unstable spirit network of dreams and memories in this way made risks of instability in the weak minds of the colleagues distributed over the planet; super risky! *Ja*, I was beginning to wonder if it was time to put them all on *mein* shelf; such was the extent of *mein* annoyance.

Pointless to kick the technical-cat though, *ja*?

'Ah, *ja*, that will be all, uh…'

'I'm—'

'*Ja-ja*, off you go now.'

So it had been a year and I had felt concerning changes in the fusing. I needed to find her quickly or *mein* fun and *mein* very existence would be inconvenienced. *Ja*, it was time to make the risk and get her remembering where she dropped her toy for me, so I reached expertly into *mein* own memories and down deeper in the strange and fascinating way of the fusing. Focusing on Bud, focusing on images of her holding the prism containing the essence of her tribesman or whatever it was.

Ethel – Nov 2098, Cornwall Hill, Akarana Island, Aotearoa Archipelago

Darrin had something for me; the searches on the… cloud and suchlike. He had sent it through the machines but I had not opened it though he had seemed excited. A year on from the excavation and the great flash, malaise gripped me. Healer was free, I knew and I could not find him. Some days his memories whirled across the fusing. And the fusing itself had changed.

Ancient memories fountained forth in my mind at random, as if a rock had been lifted from a hidden spring. They taunted me with familiarity but hung tantalisingly at the edge of my understanding.

A life lived atop a cliff with a kind woman who rose up from below with food and loving hands.

I know her.

But I could not place her.

A girl with a baby on an island, full of angst and the woman who lured her across the sea and got her killed.

I remember.

Or I thought I did but try as I might, in the end I could not.

Too long ago…

The dratted little John lingered and I could not see my way clear to… do something about him, so confused was my mind. I leaned heavily on Darrin and the others to keep everything going though it pained me to leave the organisation rudderless as I felt I was doing.

Waves of strange anger and pain washed over me through the months, sending me to my bed with knots in my stomach and an aching head and waking me in the night covered in cold sweat. Now and again, I was given some reprieve and I knew I should use such peaceful times to think on what could be done to further understand the change in the fusing; perhaps fly at last from these shores and go to the ancient resting place of the Stone itself. Instead I dozed the days away and during that grey rainy November, with rumours flying that old Laufala was at death's door, I made a mistake.

I drifted off to nap in the afternoon but sleep was hungrier than I had anticipated and it swallowed me whole and deeply and I dreamed past the barriers of my own mind and out to those of the others.

I walked in dreams with my ancient colleague, to a time when these islands were shrouded in warm misty rain and cloaked in trees and ferns. I did not have names for the plants and animals I found when I came here. It would be long years before my ancient family landed on these dreaming islands and assigned them.

But I had watched their meandering journey down over the world for enough generations to know they would be here someday so I had gone ahead to learn the lay of the land for them. And to get some peace and quiet for they could be a quarrelsome handful sometimes.

Wetas, they would call the things scuttling over sharp rocks in damp mossy caves and the forest floors. Tasty, I called them. Same with the furtive kiwi I caught creeping about at dusk.

From high aloft I surveyed briefly the terrain and the coasts and rivers. I ghosted amongst the trees and noted with pleasure how the creeks wriggled with kōura and great slithering black tuna in the night; also edible, I was sure. I could not be bothered to find the creatures booming in the night-shrouded undergrowth but it was no inconvenience for me to bring down and sample the charred meat of a thundering brown-feathered giant one daybreak, testing its flavour for my people when they eventually came to these shores. Moa, they would call it and hunt it to extinction for its feathers and its meat.

More morsels whirred, tolled and flashed kaka-red in the dark green of the canopy but my sleep was thinning by then and my mind had something it wanted shown; *that someone wants...* So, tittered at by the ancient memory of pīwakawakas flitting through undergrowth, I found a spot and stood listening to the peaceful chime and squawk of tuis drifting from everywhere and nowhere in the green afternoon shade.

And in that damp gloaming peace, where mine were the first human footprints on the bark-strewn forest floor, I gently raised a monstrous wedge of rock, earth, roots and trees from the side of the sleeping giant that would one day be called Maungakiekie and later One Tree Hill. And I cast the shiny black prism containing the old oaf Healer's wasted spirit, at last into the darkness.

Before the roots could begin to dry in the sunlight or the kōroke knew to squirm in the sudden heat and brightness, I settled the great mound quietly back in place, burying what I had thrown down deep beneath the rock and clay before people came to this place. This place where the late Joanna and the extant Tristian's old gaff had until a year ago stood alone at the edge of the wasteland.

Forward down the years to the birth and life of the city and in that house as it then was, my sleeping mind tarried for a short while, drifting through the rooms I had seen through their cameras, nudging thoughts of unprecedented sprits and odd liftings of the soil. Then as a grey and rainy dawn grudgingly paled the sky outside my block, my dreaming thoughts sped over the land, off the coast and deep under the ocean where cracks running counter to the usual warp and weft of

the planet's mighty mantle had begun to appear against Earth
and Sky.

I awoke with puffy eyes darting about in the half-light; annoyed at myself for having slept so long. I felt as if someone
was watching me though my room was empty. And I knew
then that I had dreamed too freely and too much.

Tristian – late Nov 2098, Cornwall Hill,

Akarana Island, Aotearoa Archipelago

It was as if I'd drunk something, cool water from a mountain stream I'd never visited. An eerie freshness flushed through my soul and churned through my veins carrying with it a dark infusion of… What?

Some kind of burned-out rage? Jesus! What made me come up with that?

The feeling persisted, tingling through my body. Susie hovered over me as my vision cleared. She was speaking, I could tell, into her tech. She stopped when I looked at her, finally fully awake.

'Daddy,' she said.

Daddy? Wow!

For the first time in – what? – decades, there were emotions in her dark eyes I thought I'd never see again. With her big shoulders and dark bun pulled back from her pale forehead, she looked more like Jo than ever. But mainly, she looked like she cared.

'What happened?' I asked.

'You— you've been in a coma!'

I got it straight away, her incredulity. How could I not know, right? So, someone must've been worried about me. I felt fine now but, dear-oh-dear, I could already feel it, how much of a terrible person I was about to be. I couldn't resist! To see that look in her eyes again after so many years and realise how thirsty I'd been for it! I had to milk it. I had to.

'Oh— Oh, a coma? Bloody hell! What was it? What happened?'

It was only half an act. I was confused. And I did remember somehow… *being pulled, flashing… outward, away?* I guessed they'd had a rough few hours of it, or whatever time. But I was awake again now and I'd let on how fine I felt in a few minutes. Just a few more naughty minutes.

Davey burst in the door, then.

'Oh my god! Tristian! Jesus Christ, you're awake! Da— Tristian! Do you know who I am?'

'I, uh, course. Su— Jo— Davey. Course I do.'

'Well, the sleep hasn't done his memory any good, I see.' Sue said drily though tears stood in her eyes.

Davey goggled at me. 'But I don't understand, how can you be— awake like that? I mean, we had— everyone trying to work out what was wrong, Da— Tristian. Nobody had seen anything like it before! It was a wonder you…' Her face fell and I understood why when she finished, 'kept going.'

Ah, you'd given up. Okay, Okay. Better be nice now.

'It's okay Davey. I'm okay. I feel fine, it's all fine. I'm, uh, famished. That's got to be a good sign, doesn't it? Come on, let's get some coffee on.'

I saw their arms, twitching, wanting to open, unsure. We'd never been a huggy family, not after they decided they were too big. I held out my arms and they… well, didn't exactly jump on me but hey, I was in the desert and I wasn't gonna turn down a drop of drizzle.

I pinged the coffee machine, or tried to.

Eh?

I tried again and realised something was wrong. I tried checking the time, checking my schedule, looking for messages, bringing up a delivery menu but there was nothing.

'My tech! Jesus, what's happened to my—?'

Both of them jumped back from my bed, then. 'Fuck!' They yelped as one.

'Dad! Your face! Your skin!'

'Eh?'

'It's— It's—'

My face felt fine then I felt a feather touch on my neck, another on my bare arms and more on my chest and back. I looked down and saw my skin bulging alien-esque, bubbling, peeling back and flaking away.

Jesus!

But I felt fine, better than fine. It didn't hurt. My skin, my body tingled with the burning cold. A drift of dandruff formed around me as Susie and Davey twitched away into their tech and gasped and goggled at me, hanging back as if I was contagious.

'Dad? This is Paulene Jónsson. He's the biotech guru; well, I mean, another one, anyway. He was helping us while you were, uh, asleep. Paulene, can you see him? Dad, Dad! Listen! Open up your biotech port.'

'It's okay, Davey. I'm fine. Of course I remember Paulene from when your uh, mum was… Anyway, there's no need to shout, I'm right here. But I can't see Paulene, like I said. My tech stopped working.'

And my skin'd stopped falling off me, too by then. And the tingling abated though now I could hear a strange rushing hiss that somehow didn't impact the sound in the room; like the roar of a distant crowd.

'What do you mean your tech's not working?' asked Susie.

'See for yourself.'

'Okay… He's right. It's not pinging. His handle is just, vacant, idle. It's like. Oh wow, weird! It's somehow, disused.'

No matter what we tried, I was showing up tech-less as the day I was born. Davey and Susie talked with the doctor, invisible to me, and he did his best. But through them, he admitted, this was all completely new to him and there wasn't much he could do without a connection to my biotech. He asked them to collect some samples, skin, spit, urine, blood etc and get them on a MagLev to him. We'd look into it more once I was back online.

After half an hour or so, I said, 'Alright, look, out you go, I'm going to get up and get dressed, I'm starved.'

'Dad, no!' Davey said. 'You can't just get up. Paulene said you probably wouldn't be able to walk for weeks! We had to put you on those exercise meds and install a software patch in your biotech to keep you from bloody atrophying!'

'Well, I feel fine. Go on, clear off, I'll shout if I've atrophied, all right?'

The door grew closed behind them but I suspected they didn't get any further than just behind it. I couldn't understand the fuss they were making. I felt on top of the world and though it'd been, like, a month or something, my body wouldn't't've gone that far downhill.

Then again, I am eighty-five, I s'pose.

Without my tech, I felt vulnerable. I could neither check whether they were peeking in nor boot the pair of them out. Failing to trust them and partly fooled into the conceit of privacy by my unenhanced base-model senses, I prepared for the worst outcome. Gingerly sliding my legs over the edge of the mattress, carefully planting my hand on the dandruff-coated sheet beside me and tentatively… bouncing out of bed!

Whoa! That was… too easy?

I got up and got some clothes ready. I tried and failed to trigger a nano-wash and hit the same brick wall opening up a view to take a look at myself.

A crude manual check revealed disturbingly smooth skin, as if my wrinkles had all rotted and peeled off. But if I'd been flayed or necrotised by some mysterious bacteria, I would have expected it to hurt like billy-o! And I would have expected the skin under my epidermis to be red and raw instead of pale, soft and smooth.

Healthy.

I gave up on all personal grooming and vanity; it'd have to wait till I was back online. But once I was in the kitchen with Susie and Davey, the more we tried, the colder I grew inside. We decided to order in an advanced diagnostic but I knew what it'd tell us when it came. My tech was gone and that could only mean one thing; one perfectly possible but shittily, creepily, crappily, improbable thing.

Jesus! My body's started rejecting my own invention! This can't get out.

The 'kids' made me coffee and food and watched as I ate, looking at me as if I was going to explode. I lost it with them, a tiny bit.

'Christ, you two! I'm not going to melt, you know! Jesus. So, I had a bit of a spell for a while, I'm all right, now, look!' I clapped my hands and snapped my fingers. 'All tickety-boo, see? We'll get my tech sorted out. We'll keep an eye on me and—'

'Dad—' Susie tried.

'No, listen! Stop tiptoeing around me, will you? We'll just— We'll get in the hardware diagnostic, we'll keep an eye on me, try to figure out what happened but I'm fine now, okay? I'm absolutely—'

'Dad!' Davey roared. 'You've been in a fuckin' coma for a year! We were going to switch you off! I've been doing your job! For a year!'

Oh.

'Oh.'

'Yes. Oh!' Davey snapped.

'Okay, okay. I didn't know. Sorry. I— It's only that I feel so g—'

'Oh my god!' Davey's shriek made us jump.

Susie was the first to unfreeze. 'Jesus Davey! Don't shout like that, you just about gave me a heart attack. What's wrong— Oh shit! What is that?'

I turned to find them looking towards the window and it was then I noticed the light had changed. I followed their gaze and saw and the sky had… shrunk?

'That's, uh, different.' I said.

We rushed to the window and I wished we hadn't.

'We're fucked.' Davey said, her voice oddly calm, her shock of a moment ago somehow gone.

Nathan – late Nov 2098, from Cornwall Estate to Omana and places in between, Akarana Island, Aotearoa Archipelago

The sheets felt good on my skin, clean and soft. I moved to feel 'em— them rubbing me. I was warm an'— and dry and nice and drowsy. I was pretty much ready to roll over and go back to sleep but a feeling started behind my eyes. I tried to screw them shut to get rid of it but it got worse.

Finally I couldn't take it any more.

'Fuck it,' I moaned and brought my hands up to my eyes to give them a rub.

The itch turned into a burn and I had to rub harder to ease it. I was well awake by then so decided I might as well open my eyes.

The light blasted in and I snapped them shut again. I put a hand over them and eased them open. Everything was blurry and the light was uncomfortably bright but it started coming right so I kept them open. The bright faded to grey as my eyes got a handle on themselves. The drowse started lifting, faster and faster till I was actually keen to get up.

Man. What happened?

I turned over in the blue and white sheets in time to see what looked like medical machinery and a stool the same colours as my bedding melting away on the floor. I could see the nanites cycling in to break it all down then flow out under the door crack.

The door itself was moving, like the outside of it had turned into some kinda— kind of thick liquid, like paint running down and out under the crack instead of spreading in a puddle on the floor like it should.

The active alloy… Shit! What…?

Then a message pinged up. I opened it and a virtual ambushed me. It was a woman in a white room with rich-person sea views, high up and as far away from the sea as possible. She looked familiar.

Congratulations on completing your therapy Mister Nathan Richards-Mann. We at Spume hope you have grown through your therapeutic journey and we're overjoyed the Akarana Island police department agrees with our assessment that you're ready to re-engage with your friends, family and greater society early! Because your therapeutic stasis was longer than ten months, we're delighted to inform you that you qualify for a range of our complimentary re-integration services including basic vocational courses, peer support groups, listings for paid medical research participation positions and COASTAL DIGS, our special accommodation assistance space for those of our clients ready for a fresh start. Why not connect to the handle shown after this message, to browse the list of available services? We'll have you up and running and contributing to the community again in no time! We can't wait to help you out again soon and hope you'll return to Spume again and again whenever you need help with your mental health and wellbeing! Don't forget to keep this message so you can find us again at any time. Congratulations again, Mister Richards-Mann and we wish you a safe and happy life. Please do take a few moments to complete our automated feedback interview at the end of this message and have yourself a very merry Christmas! Only six weeks to go, don't forget to get in those last-minute purchases!

And then my thoughts went spinning. I was arrested… Peaches… Crazy ol'— old Zhang… And… Faces? Faces in the… rain? Faces in the rain… Profiles? Food?

Only as I lay there and tried to remember, some stayed but more slipped away. There'd been a lot, I knew. A lot I should remember; that I needed to remember. But the harder I tried to hold on to the memories, the more they leaked away like the rain in the alleyway outside was washing them all down the drain and into the grey.

I lay in my bed and couldn't shake the feeling something bad was coming for me, either. I felt like an arrest was gonna...

…go-ing to, Nate, come on, say it with me go-ing…

…Oh yeah. Yeah-what? Yeah, but okay, go-ing to jam me up any minute and then I'd be… What? What would I be? I'd wasn't a complete dope. Obviously from the Spume gear, I'd been in the joint. So I must've been…

Ah, yeah, arrested.

But it's only been the night before. No…

…more than ten months…

I couldn't get my head around it. I did remember being arrested. And Teens sitting with me a couple or few times. They were sketchy, like I'd been wasted or something but I knew they'd been real. Other than that, nothing came.

…more than ten months…

But I hadn't been anywhere or done anything since… the arrest? I tried to think back and a few… fragments came: the arrest, crazy old Zhang, yeah, yeah, it was all there. But the memories were cooled off or far away or quieter or…

Older?

Well, older than ten months, apparently but there was the big black nothing in-between that worried me most; some weird shit'd… had gone down.

I got online, as if the answers would all be there. Then like they'd been waiting for me to access my tech, my ads fired up with a vengeance and though I hated them like everyone hated ads, I suddenly burst into tears, fuckin' tears! It was like my tears knew something I didn't.

Tech was so normal it took my mind a second to go back and clock that I had full access… *again?* I could message, watch movies, buy stuff – well, if I had money anyway. I could do whatever. And it felt like a massive, I didn't know, relief maybe?

I sat up and swung my legs slowly over the bedside thinking I'd feel all crappy and tired like I always did in the mornings before work. But my body felt light and full of go.

Ah, why is that wrong?

But I was sure as shit it was. The drawers on the bed were full of all my old gear but it had been cleaned and folded up and there were a bunch of standard issue new hemps in them. Course, the idiots had printed them way too big, or so I thought till I got them on and they fitted perfectly.

Okay. I, uh, got fat?

Who knew how the Spume stasis worked anyway? Maybe I was still in it. Maybe it only felt like I was waking up and that was why I didn't feel like I was getting up after a hard night on the BudLike™. But then why the message? No telling, really. They were Spume, the wankers themselves. It could be some freaky trick to psyche me out or whatever. But then again, whoever came out of Spume with their brain in working order?

…experimental… hallucinations.

Yeah okay, I had no idea where that thought came from but I had a feeling it might've been important. Still no matter how hard I tried to grab hold of it, nothing came. And anyway, my tum-tum… *stomach, Nate…* Oooh-kay? My stomach then. My stomach growled at me and without thinking I was on to the PrimeFlixK-BellPharm virtual piling into their food menu.

Whoa! Fuck!

My balance showed in the top corner as usual but I was rich, fuckin' rich! For a second, I couldn't think how it was possible but the last entry on my statement gave me a clue, not

only to where the ding— money, had come from but also today's date.

I'd been under for two years.

No!

And three days, fourteen hours, nineteen minutes and
four seconds. A little voice in the back of my head said it was
weird I'd worked that last bit out that fast but mostly I was
blown away that I'd missed my own thirdieth …*thir-t-ieth Nate,
come on…* Yeah, thir-t-ieth…

Eh? Where am I getting that?

But I'd missed it anyway. I was bloody thirty all of a sudden. And rich. Yeah, missed my thirtieth birthday and got rich
which reminded me again…

Shit! My hacks!

I did a manual system scan which was freaky because there
was no such thing as a manual system scan till I coded it right
then, on the spot. Maybe I was an all right hacker but…

Shit-eh, I'm a better one now.

There was no special monitoring, no hidden honey-traps,
nothing. I'd gone in and checked whether anyone'd been sniffing around my code without stopping to wonder how I knew
to check half the stuff I did.

Even then it was only half a thought because I'd suddenly
gone like a blackbird and seen something shiny.

Yeah, I, uh, know what a blackbird is…?

Apparently, I did. The… Ah, yeah, turned out I'd guessed
right. The place all the ding— money had come from, my
points hack which I'd seeded a couple years before I got arrested had been quietly ticking up my balance. I wouldn't have
noticed before I went inside because I would've been, well,
eating. But without using it, well, one two's two, two twos are
four, four twos are eight and all that, and – hehe – more.

Premo!

My other stuff was all there too, so apparently the cops
had locked me up and left me alone to… what? Come back
out and that's it? The library handle and all the dead-end dy-
namic aliases that kept it hidden. I mean, it was okay, pretty

good for a…. What? A kid? Well, I was older now. But did the years count if you'd been out like a… *lizard?*

My code all did the job but… I could think of, I dunno, optimisations or some shit like that. All my illicit – *whoa! Mister big-words now aren't I! So I… wasn't always? What happened?* – stuff was all there, all in pretty good nick. Except now it looked, uh… cute. Like little virtuals we all used to make in basic school and save down to our logs to show our mums and dads. How had such obvious stuff taken me so long to come up with?

It started to dawn on me that I was kind of on fire. Maybe the rest had done me some good after all! The delivery drone pinged me from the poor-door and I walked to my door to go down the hall. It peeled open and I froze.

Shit!

The air blowing through the door ponged like dirty socks and piss. The lights flickered, suddenly too bright and my stomach clenched up. I started looping that I wouldn't know how to get back once I went out there.

Diagnosis: Agoraphobia…, breathe deeply… Eh?

Whatever it was, it worked. I had myself chilled out in an… instant, and stood there wondering, since when did I know a word with that many syllables.

And how do I know what a syllable is?

But the panic cooled and my stomach rumbled and panged again so I made myself walk and wonder at the same time. I had another little freakout at the poor-door. The sky looked massive and angry but then a gust of wind pulled at me and those same ads-tears came back.

That's right, weather! Fuckin' weather!

I took my box of super posh veggie curry off the drone and walked out under the sky to stand in the daylight. Without overs on, the cold started eating into me and my stomach re-minded me it was there and I didn't give a shit. The clouds were racing overhead and I knew there was gonna be a… *uh, what's a stonker again?* Whatever it was, there would be one blowing in any minute but I stood there and stood there and stood there anyway. My tears rolled faster and faster and I shivered and smiled and cried all at the same time with the wind blowing hard in my face.

I would have stood there for longer, but a weird part of my brain fired up and I knew I was heading for some kind of blood sugar crash… *nutrients fully drained…* Whatever it was, I knew I was more than hungry and getting cold and wet would make me sicker than it might've normally done.

Yeah, okay, okay, who am I? My fuckin' mother?

There was no sign of the freakouts on the way back down the hall. Back in the flat, I scoffed like I'd never eaten before and nearly ordered something else though posh veggie curry was a meal for two. Then suddenly I forgot everything about me and food and anything else.

Mum and Dad!

I pinged them and that was only the start of how wrong the day was about to go. Their handles had disappeared. And handles didn't disappear! They would've been greyed if they'd died; archived after a while, months, maybe years. But not gone like that.

Chen.

Just before I pinged her my tech lit up a recent message from her. But she would have known I'd never get it. Unless she knew I was coming out soon? But how? Unless she had something to do with me getting out? How long was I meant to have been in stasis anyway?

…five years unless… something about therapeutic outcomes?

Had I got out on good behaviour? I didn't bother… dwelling on it. I didn't open Chen's message. I went straight to pinging her a call and got her messaging. Her handle was weird, like she was online and taking calls but pings went to her messaging anyway. I started getting a bad feeling. I couldn't have said if it was the way nobody picked up my calls, the quiet in the building or what. Something was off.

'Hey Chen, I'm, uh… out! I'm out! I can't reach my mum and dad. Their handles are gone, they're gone!' I felt like a dork, burbling away but I'd started panicking about Mum and Dad.

Shit! Teens!

Now I'd gone and got in touch with Chen before my girl-friend! I kept telling myself, *two years, it's been two years for everyone else.* But I couldn't believe it though I knew it was true. I couldn't see any reason why Teens would've moved.

Even if it really had been two years, it wasn't like she would have saved up to buy a house or anything. Then I froze up like a frightened *háizi* trying to work out if I should go straight over or ping her first.

...Too late this time, Mister Richards-Mann. But all subsequent visitation request will be declined. As you have requested...

The memory came up from somewhere and it was like the others I'd been having. I knew it was important. I couldn't work out what it was about. Two years suddenly didn't seem short. Anything might've happened in two years. Maybe she'd moved on after...

After what?

I didn't like that I kind of felt... relieved about that thought though I couldn't work out where it had popped up from. I pinged her and got her messaging as well. Then I froze again.

I imagined what she'd see when she opened the message. Me, looking all sick and messed-up from being in stasis for so long. She'd probably find me gross. I'd probably find me gross! I was scared to fire up my cameras to check myself out.

'Uh, Teens,' I said. 'It's me.'

Then I felt too stupid to say anything else so I hung up.

Fuck it.

I clenched my teeth, blazed through the door and up the hall to her place. I wasn't going to burst in. I kept having to tell myself, *two years, two years, it will be weird for her; easy does it Nate!*

I pinged her door and a second later it peeled open and a stranger stood there staring at me.

'Uh, can I help you?' she asked after I'd gawked long enough for it to get weird.

'I... Uh, is this, Tina's place?'

'Nope. It's my place.'

'Oh. Uh, sorry.'

I would've turned around and bolted if she hadn't asked, 'Are you from next door?'

I didn't know how long she'd been there or why Teens had moved out. She might've got nosy and pinged my door and known I was in the joint. I went all red and my cheeks got that hot feeling like when my mum and I both knew she'd busted me cranking one out but she didn't say anything so I wouldn't be embarrassed.

But I'm innocent! Aren't I?

I couldn't remember why they'd put me away. But I also couldn't handle a stranger knowing I was an ex-con. My cheeks burned thinking about it.

'I, uh, I live down that way a bit.' It wasn't a lie.

'Oh well, okay, I'm Andy. Nice to meet you…?'

'Nathan— Nate.'

'Nice to meet you Nathan-Nate. No offence but I'm gonna have to go back in now, okay? I'm all for friendly neighbours and that but I don't want to lose my job, okay? So I'll see you round.' She had that voice on, like you get when you're talking to an old sick person or something; that way you kind of feel sick knowing they're gonna die soon or whatever.

I must look like shit!

'Yeah, sorry, yeah, all good. Yeah.'

The door was closing and I was racing like a frightened roach back to my place before realising I'd clocked her posh voice and cute face. And then I felt extra bad for noticing when I should have been concentrating on wondering where Teens was.

There wasn't much more I could do now I'd left Chen and her messages. I could ping all my buds but I wasn't, kind of, ready. Instead, I decided to walk down south to find my folks. I'd spotted my old overs in the drawer with all the free gear from Spume. They fitted all right but pinged me a warning about having to… redistribute or something, as I pulled them on.

Weird.

It was light outside and I reckoned it'd take me about eight hours so they'd probably be awake when I arrived.

I could get some posh grub to munch on the way there. Then again, though I struggled to believe it, I'd been in stasis for two years and from everything I'd heard I shouldn't be able to think straight let alone walk like, forty kays or something. Then bam! I knew it would be fine, as long as I had enough to eat. I didn't know how I knew but somehow I did.

Is it really a good idea though? To go all that way from a lying start? Ah! You're being a lazy arse, Nate.

Maybe all the stories weren't true and Spume didn't mess people up after all and maybe my brain would be all right. Then wouldn't I feel like a dork for spouting all the conspiracy crap about them that I had!

You were right. You got lucky is all.

Whoa, okay. It was my memory but it was like someone else was talking in my head. Someone who knew stuff I didn't or maybe someone who remembered stuff. But anyway, I needed to find my folks and the posh grub idea had given me a better one.

The money wouldn't last forever but given the weirdness with their handles, I reckoned the problem was worth… investing in. Half an hour later, I was in an Uber heading over the Mount Wellington bridge. I couldn't help feeling a bit bad as the fare ticked up. If Mum and Dad had found out I'd blown that amount on so much as half a trip when I could've walked for free, they'd have had a meltdown.

Having so much sea all around me gave me the *xiǎo*-shits but going over the Mount Wellington bridge kind of felt cool, too, like flying. The water was moving and I knew it was something to do with tides. Except what was the point of knowing stuff about the ocean?

Where all life began and is now busy ending…

Yeah, okay. True. Whatever way I'd learned about tides was probably the same way I knew there was something a bit off about this one. The water was moving faster and faster under the bridge and out…

East.

Yeah, east. Or whatever. Watching it creeped me out a bit so I looked straight ahead instead and watched the Manukau seawall getting closer as I cruised down the south side of the bridge. I tried hard not to notice I was in the only car on the road and there were zero… pedestrians. Then my spine really started tingling and it wasn't easy to keep telling myself something was only a bit off.

As I turned off for Beachlands, I was nearly too scared to go into the public broadcasts space. And when I finally did, dis-cov-er-ing – *uh, eh?* – there wasn't anything there, should've made me feel better. But it didn't.

The road was quiet and all the rich-fuck blocks up the hillsides looked empty and dead. I kept my eyes off the water as we turned in and up to get up over Omana and down to the…

Whoa!

Everything stopped halfway down Omana. The Uber pulled up with a gut-splurging yank on my seatbelt and the Uber virtual blew up red with alerts I'd never seen before. It should have known what was up ahead, well, or wasn't up ahead any more. But it hadn't. Its maps were out of date. Which was impossible.

Whatever'd happened to the hills was like nothing I'd ever seen. There was a brown and grey curve all the way down to the Maraetai basin. Blocks, roads, seawalls, all gone. Flattened like a giant heel had stomped it all to dust. The rain was coming down in sheets now so I couldn't see how far the mega-squash went.

I started shaking. I tried to think where Mum and Dad's place would've been. But I couldn't map it out in my brain. Not at first anyway but then something messed-up happened. I looked out at the… wasteland and got little glimpses of its… sheer expanse through the… squalls. Then I could see all the angles like it was a virtual.

Except it wasn't. I'd grown up around there so I knew the buildings, the streets, which bits of seawall were in the best and worst nick and where the walking paths on top of them were safe to use. It was like those memories were an overlay on the big bare bit of ground stretching out about fifty-odd kays in front of me. Then a number pinged into my brain and I stamped my feet on the Uber floor and screamed at the wind-screen.

'No! Fuckin' No! It fuckin' can't be! You fuckin' fuckers! No!'

Five-point-three-four kilometres inside the area destroyed by anomalous blast radius…

'No! No! No! Fuckin'… No!' My belt released and I bent over with my head in my hands rocking and crying into my palms. Then the smell of piss and sick burst into the Uber and I looked up, shaking and saw I was suddenly not alone any more.

'Ch— Chen?'

'Nate!' The veins in her neck were bulging and her eyes were red and swollen. 'Nate!' She sounded like she couldn't breathe. 'Nate! HELP!' It was like she was being strangled and I could hardly understand what she said. Then she… flickered and the connection died.

'Chen! Where—?'

But she was gone. It happened so fast I wondered if I was… hallucinating. Then she connected again. Only this time the call dropped before she could say anything. She flashed up for an instant and vanished again; I'd never seen anything like it. Again.

It doesn't matter.

It was the weird part of my brain talking again.

As long as I'm fast enough, I can trace the connection's after-image through the cloud… I… can?

Apparently, I could. And I did. As I did, I could see how it had always been possible, not that hard, just… I wouldn't have thought of doing it that way or something. As I followed the fading circuit through the public tech between me and wherever she was, I found myself mapping out the cloud and where it'd been… what? Ripped? Ripped out of existence in the strange… blast radius.

By the time I found the apartment Chen had called from, I'd also figured out why my parents' handles'd vanished. They'd be back online once the system had caught up with itself. So much cloud had been destroyed so fast, any active handles in the area would show up missing until wherever they were backed up to restored them to circulation – once the public nanotech colonised the… affected area again.

Only I knew what colour they'd be when they came back and I shivered thinking about it.

Deal with it later!

'Come on you shit-bucket! Turn around!'

Not that the Uber understood me but I was setting up the new destination while I was shouting at the piece of junk anyway. Minutes later, I was rounding the headland and about to turn up towards the block Chen had called from. Her being all the way out here didn't make any sense but I knew with my weird new knowing, that my trace was right though it had been touch and go with the after-image fading so fast.

But as the Uber turned, I couldn't help looking out to sea and that's when I saw the loon standing on the seawall between two broken-down buildings with his arms open like he was fuckin' worshipping or something.

'Stop!'

It did and I got out and ran towards the guy and that's when I noticed all the water was gone and every basic school-aged *háizi* knew what that meant.

Holy-fuck-I'm-dead!

The guy was further away than I'd thought. There was rubble between two buildings and he was standing on the last section of… intact wall before the heap. The mud past the wall stank of poison and rot and my instincts screamed at me to run the other way. I couldn't see how he'd got up there unless he was a fuckin' good climber, anyway.

A climber…

Well, yeah?

A climber… Oh yeah!

And I suddenly knew, what I must do. It wasn't like a route-map lighting up in my tech but not far off. The rubble was suddenly easy to get across. Stable foot-hold here, hand holds there… and there. And there, a way up, almost to the top of a half-collapsed bit of wall but… Yeah, I hadn't noticed before but there were no blue nanites so it would hold me and then, yep, *ten-cm rise, eighty-one-point-two-cm gap,* easy to jump up and across to the dude. Simples!

I was on the case and halfway up before I realised it. The guy was standing there, overs hood fully open and arms out like a mental bloody teapot or something.

Whatever the f—

Nope, okay, apparently I did know what a teapot was, well… Great. The closer I got the more I started hoping he'd come down willingly because an oik like that was going to take some carrying! And I had minutes! It was as if there was another thread running in my brain counting down the time. Nah, it wasn't like it at all, there actually was.

I reached the guy. He was facing out to sea and didn't notice me but that was no surprise given the noise. I was about to reach out and tap him on the shoulder when I couldn't help but look at the water. And there she was. The fuckin' apocalypse!

We're fucked.

It was a wall of black coming out of the grey rain over the sea. It was demonically tall like a moving wall of water rolling in to smash us into… oblivion.

Nine-hundred-and-fifty-seven-point-nine-one metres, likely total shockwave amplitude… probably extinction level…

'Fuck the fuck off!' I shouted at my burbling mind. Then, 'Dude! Hey, Bud. You can't stay up here man.'

I nearly laughed at how *fēng kuáng* I sounded. Sure he couldn't stay up here but we were out of time. It'd taken me, what…

Two minutes and nineteen seconds…

'Shut it!' I shouted at my mind.

But however long it'd taken me to… parkour – yeah that was it, up the wall, we didn't have half that long again to get back down. And anyway, the nutjob wasn't listening. He stood with his arms open, gormless, as death came in from the ocean.

I relaxed then. I went limp and squatted on the wall. The… tsunami was so high I could barely understand what I was seeing. That much water, that upright. It was as if it… defied the laws of physics.

In fact it does not— Shut up!

It felt like it was nearly on top of us though I could see a long stretch of bare mud and open foaming ocean in its way. But I knew it wouldn't be long. The top of it was curling over ready to scrape the buildings off the land.

And probably the land into the sea!

If Chen really was up the hill somewhere, I doubted she was going to be any less fucked than me and whoever this guy was.

Maybe we'll get our heads knocked together on the way to the bottom of the sea and we can say hi before we die.

I laughed to myself, giggled like the loon next to me might've done if he'd grown a voice. The roar of the water was deafening. Much as I didn't want to, I made myself look up into the angry black face of death itself. It towered over us and blotted out the rainy sky. Though it hadn't yet reached the land, evil salt-smelling spray was already raining down over the buildings and rubble.

I couldn't help but think what a joke the seawall would've been if it'd been in halfway decent nick let alone the wreck it was now. This was the death of the island, maybe the whole archipelago or life on fuckin' earth itself. My weird new brain kept feeding me the calculations and I couldn't shut them off though it was my final bloody minute of life.

Forty-two seconds to be precise, forty-one, forty… Fuck off!

Then the face of the wave went white, like it was exploding with foam all at once. It wasn't as if I'd seen a tsunami breaking before. Anyone with half a braincell spent their life keeping as far away from the sea and its creepy noises and disgusting smells and all its types of waves.

And I had more than half a braincell never mind my being a show-off thinking it. So I wondered, like I had nothing better to think about in my last few seconds of life, if maybe there was something strange about the way the wave was breaking before it hit the land.

And I knew I was right.

The cracking sound like a zillion lightning strikes nearly burst my eardrums a second later.

But why? It didn't hit anything…

And then the white water stayed in the air. It bubbled and boiled and shot foam and spray high into the sky like it was hot though I knew it wasn't. And it stayed there. And no matter how much it boiled and broke into spray, I suddenly realised none of it was landing on us any more.

I looked along the coast and as far as I could see there was a wall of white water standing up in a way that wasn't possible.

…experimental…

Ah. Yeah, okay. You faar-haaa-haaa-kaar! It was a… fragment of memory. But a bigger one than before. The profile, the fuckin' profile!

I laughed out loud over the roar I knew I wasn't really hearing and did the finger to the impossible foaming wall of water I knew I wasn't really seeing. And as if on… cue, it settled down and slid bit by bit back into to the sea, hissing and spitting as if telling me it would be back for me another day.

The white water creamed back over the mud and slowly but surely, the roar died down leaving the sound of the ordinary rain which I knew was all there'd been all-a-bloody-long. I had to give the chemicals I'd buggered my brain with some credit, they made pretty realistic trips!

Next to me the dude — some kind of… differently-abled guy, maybe an ex-con like me — had crouched down and hidden his hands in his face. He was shaking and I got up and patted his shoulder. 'Come on Bud. You don't want to stay out here. Where do you live? Come on, let's get you home.'

I sound like a ponce.

I thought the hallucinations were done but I kept my eyes inland anyway; I'd take land-based hallucinations over water-coloured ones any day! It was all very well knowing I'd been seeing things but when it'd happened it was a bit too real not to shit me up anyway. For a minute I'd thought I was going to die.

But it turned out the chemicals had more surprises in store for me. Beside me, the guy said nothing, didn't so much as look at me. I tried shaking him and jumped a tiny bit at how big his muscles were. And how tight! He was wound up like a spring and shaking like a crane in a, heh, a *stonker.*

'Come on Bud,' I tried again, and this time he looked up at me. That was when I saw his face was black as storm clouds. He had super-white teeth and red rimmed eyes.

Unknown origin: likely Austronesian, unusual throwback.

Interesting. But I didn't have time for all that weirdness now. I had to get to Chen. I had no idea what was up with her but I knew she was in trouble.

'Bud, come on!' I said, shaking him. But he only stared at me then suddenly levitated off the wall, floated up the hill and disappeared into the rain before I had a chance to say no fuuuuuckin' way! Then I was alone like a loon in the rain on a breaking-down seawall.

Of course, this was how it happened wasn't it? Nobody came out of Spume with their mind intact. I replayed the last half hour in my mind and my shoulders dropped like a *háizi* getting a dud-root crimbo present. I could see it in my mind's eye: dude screeches to a halt in the middle of nowhere, blazes across a massive pile of dangerous rubble and up the seawall like a roach with a death-wish, gabbles away at the rain for a while then looks around like he's suddenly woken up there.

They got me in the end, after all that… All what? I dunno, there was a lot of something wasn't there? Wasn't there?

The rain started easing off and I peeled my hood back to feel it on my face and let it wash away my tears. I went back down the wall the same way I'd come up. Jumped over and down the gap, climbed down the most stable rubble, over the safer bits and back to the road. My Uber'd gone to sleep to charge and I stood looking back out to sea for a while before I got in.

I got it. My brain was fried. It would be like that forever, for me. I'd have to figure out a technique for… recognising the hallucinations and maybe finding what… triggered them; maybe it was the rain, for all I knew, given I'd been inside Spume. But I had to get to Chen first.

Or do I?

If I'd seen an impossible tsunami and a flying… Austronesian, why couldn't it all have been a cooked daydream? The call-trace was pretty far-fetched. And, how could Chen's call have got cut like that, anyway? Stuff like that never happened. The tech was too good, too much redundancy, too much bandwidth.

I slowly realised I was right. She hadn't called me. She wasn't here. What the bloody hell would she be doing all the way out here anyway?

But then a good thought pinged up. What if all the other stuff wasn't real either? I tried Mum and Dad's handles again and they were there! They were… dead.

But I didn't believe it. I couldn't trust anything any more. Which itself was cooked. Maybe that was part of the *haurangi*-ness; that you didn't know what was true any more.

I took one last look back at the seawall and the rubble in front of it before getting back into my Uber. It was a hardcore pile of rubble. Hallucinations or not, it would've taken a cray-cray fucker with a hardcore body to get up there, all right. Or, well, maybe it wasn't really there and I hadn't been up it. I'd been in prison stasis for two-years. How the fuck could I have a body-on like that? Maybe I'd been standing there beside the Uber all that time. I had no way of knowing any more.

I made the Uber turn around and take me back to the crater. I got out and kneeled down to feel the mud over the rise where the road ended and the destruction began. My overs came up covered in shiny smooth mud, no lumps, no rocks, only soft… silty mud. The place would a be dust-bowl if it ever dried out.

I couldn't stop my mind imagining it, the wind coming up, blowing the dust across the wasteland like… ghosts… Faces…

I tried telling myself it wasn't real, that I was hallucinating. I closed my eyes and opened them again but the mud and rain didn't go anywhere. I checked Mum and Dad's handles and they were dead and grey.

But how do I know it's real? How?

Real or not, the wasteland and my folks' handles weren't changing no matter how hard I tried to un-imagine them. Neither were the rain and my growing Uber fare and all I could think of to do was go home and go back to sleep. Then through all that, my stomach moaned like a… whale giving birth and suddenly felt like it was going to… implode.

Food delivery drones would've gone anywhere for a buck but I suddenly had to be at home. Though apparently, I hadn't been out for two years, the sky felt too big and though I was bone dry in my overs, it felt as if the rain was too heavy and wet and if I stood in it any longer it would drive me under the mud. The world was squeezing me and I couldn't breathe. I started gasping.

Easy, panicking, breathe slowly, deeply…

This time it took me longer to get a handle on myself, scary-longer. The quiet of the buildings and the sea made it worse when I would've thought they'd make me calmer quicker. Instead it was like the quiet was crushing me with poison loneliness.

But I got there in the end. My breathing slowed and the last of the mud melted off my overs' gloves as I belted into the Uber and pinged it to take me north and back over the bridge, away from hallucinations and ideas about ghosts in the dust.

I squished into the corner of the Uber as it came up to the bridge turnoff by Manukau. My stomach was grumbling and moaning so much it hurt. I felt dizzy and though my overs and the Uber's climate control were both… infallible, I felt cold.

I had my posh grub tucked away in a pocket but weirdly, it wasn't what I wanted. Any other time, I would've thought it was hilarious not feeling like posh food. It was the kind of thing poor old Teens would've come out with when her personality disguise slipped, not that I ever held that against her. I knew she had her reasons and she wasn't doing anyone any harm.

Oh, I'm not really in the mood for veggies tonight, Nate, can't we get a pizza?

In the mood for veggies. That was fuckin' priceless. Most of the world couldn't afford to lay eyes on a vegetable let alone eat one. If only she'd known how obvious she'd been, and not only to me, to all of us. To Chen, Shane, Mum, Dad, everyone. But none of us guessed the truth though it was staring us in the face.

Where are ya Teens?

For all her lame fake seawall-basement-talk, I was coming round to her way of thinking on the food front. I had enough satoshis to fork out for my own bloody wrack-space in a hydroponics joint and the seeds to go with. But what I really wanted was an honest-to-goodness fake pizza dripping with the nastiest yellow Notzzerella™ that left the special puke aftertaste of home and a giant slug of glow-in-the-dark orange-ish flavour Beyond-Juice™ to smooth out the sandpaper vape and disgusting taste of bargain basement budget BudLike™ sneaked in to build up your appetite for a super-sized bio-tub of toxically caffeinated Nocolate™ mousse.

Yeah baby! Those were the bright unnatural food-colours of making up after playfights with your school buds in the seawall rubble that nearly went a bit too far! Those were the tastes of windy nights skulking in half-flooded abandoned buildings with your friends and ordering food and weed on your mum's hacked account and hoping you'd stayed stoned enough not to feel the hiding when you got home. And those were the flavours of Friday nights in with the family watching an ad-free subscription movie your dad'd got for his annual work bonus and when the word weekend still meant something.

That was what I needed. A taste of home now that home was gone.

I tried calling Teens again but she went straight to messaging. I knew the longer I didn't ping Shane, the more explaining I'd have to do to the poor dude about why I hadn't got in touch. But the more people I thought about the more tired I got.

Later.

It would probably be quarter of an hour or so before I got home and the delivery stacks would be spiralling to the sky before long so I jumped online to order ahead and that's when the newsfeeds smashed into me, everyone one of them wall to wall images of a wall of white water standing metres off the coast before sliding back into the sea.

Well, fuuuuck me!

It had happened! Nobody knew any more than I did about what, exactly, the fuck had happened. But I hadn't imagined it!

It would've crushed the islands. What about the rest of the world?

I might've been seeing things with the flying dude and everything. But I wasn't so sure now. I remembered the feeling of his big hard muscles when I was trying to get him to snap out of his freak-out or whatever he had going on.

And why would I have imagined a face like that when I'd never seen anyone with that kind of skin in my whole life? The flying was, well, yeah, cooked. But so was the tsunami. There was some weird shit going down but it didn't matter, not if Chen really had tried to get through to me and she really was in trouble in some posh dive in the middle of nowhere.

By the time the Uber'd got all the way over the bridge, turned around and taken me back out south again, the fare was so big it was funny. I'd scoffed all my posh grub after all and my guts were already starting to rumble again but they weren't hurting like they had before.

I never used to get hungry like that. Did I?

Then again, I'd basically jumped up and run out of a two-year coma. Some weird shit was going to happen; surely it was. I was surprised I'd managed all the stuff I had.

It was dark when I reached the turning and as I cruised up the hill, my spine tingled at the sight of the… unlit buildings. The windows were black in the penthouse furthest up the slope where the richest of fucks without a care in the world about anything should've been.

They can't all be asleep! Can they? Do rich people go to bed early or what?

The rubble finished and the garden-style entrances started where the poor blocks finished. The Uber stopped by a gate near the hilltop and I piled out and stopped dead with leaves tickling my arm like they were taking the piss out of the idiot staring at a locked door. I pinged the flat Chen's call had come from and of course, there was no answer.

I went back out to my Uber. The ground had dried and the wind was revving up for another storm. I glanced down the hill at the sea to check it wasn't rising up to swallow the land again.

I looked up and my eyes… alit on one of the floors and I knew in my new weird way that I'd counted forty-two without realising it.

Or was it another hallucination?

I made myself go back and count them again and found myself looking up at the same angle as before. Maybe. It was hard to tell. But it didn't matter either. There was no way I could… scale those walls. There was nothing anything that wasn't a roach could get a hand-hold on.

Plans for kit did come to mind. Kit I'd never known existed but suddenly now knew did exist. Or could. Electronic suction cups, magnetic soles, it wasn't that complicated. I could get the blueprints online or… code them up myself? Yep, apparently that too. Then I'd need the raw nanites… Which was the problem, of course. I had a load of satoshis all right but not enough for that! I wondered if Chen had got any further with our theory. And how would I ever know if she had?

But I had to do something. If she was here, I couldn't leave her. Not Chen.

I went back inside to the locked fire exit and started work on the impossible: hacking the building. Only it wasn't impossible any more. Difficult maybe, but I could see how it could be done! It would take time which I didn't think I had because of how sick Chen had looked – and smelt – on the call.

Poking around the building's security got my coding brain going and I remembered some old routines I'd written before I'd gone inside. I broke out a dead-end alias and my heart kicked up. If I got busted packing code like this, I'd be back in stasis forever.

It took me a few minutes to soup it up a bit so it was less amateur and more cop-proof. Then I sent it into the cloud with fingers, toes and nose-hairs crossed that it was secure enough. It pinged back in a nano and plugged me into an antique SSD I'd got working and jacked into a hive interface made of reconditioned nanites I'd scavenged from the wasteland on Cornwall estate. And fuckin' amazingly, it hadn't stopped working and Chen had been on it since I'd been in the joint!

Chen – late Nov 2098, Beachlands Hill, Akarana Island, Aotearoa Archipelago

I'm an idiot!

It all came out. I'd tried to be the bigger person. I'd always tried to do what was right for everyone, Elayne, Nate, our friends, everyone. Everyone but me. So, when she'd crapped on the *fēng kuáng-de* stuff about me and Nate going behind her back, yet again, something in me snapped.

To be fair, I could never've known how far gone her mind was. She was fully *makutu'ed*; cooked as a motherfucker. From the look on her face, I thought we were both being arrested but then she'd started in with the whole world domination thing and though my stomach was clenched up and the muscles in my arms and legs were straining at the tendons so hard I was sure I could feel them tearing and snapping, a shiver ran down my spine. She was in way over her head with tech like this. I'd never heard of anything like it before. Only the cops could do this, it was the way tech was made. It shouldn't've been possible. Nate had explained it all to me.

I gasped and found I could breathe; barely. I tried to move and only ended up falling arse-first on to her plush carpet.

Elayne took a step towards me and I would've shrunk away if I'd been able to move. I would rather'd she'd've screamed at me than spoken in the calm cold voice she did, then. 'Sorry Chen. Nate shouldn't've told you about me. You can blame him if you want but I can't let you leave here now. Whatever you think of me, I'm trying to do something good here, Chen, and I can't have you fucking it up for me! That Pete creep and all his thugs are making my life hard enough without you helping them. You get that, right? Ah, I see… No-you-don't! None of that!'

Something about her voice made me think – hope? – she wasn't actually going to kill me. Or why wouldn't she just've done it straight away? Or was she psyching herself up to do it?

A part of me was hoping I had been randomly arrested. That had to be better than being trapped with this nutjob! Hadn't Nate been forced into a paddywagon and taken straight to the station though? Maybe it was taking a while to get all the way out here. I'd have believed anything over be-lieving anyone but the law had access to tech like this.

Man! Since when were the cops the least worst option!

But no paddywagon came. I stayed frozen on Elayne's car-pet. I desperately pinged my tech and discovered it wasn't fire-walled. If I'd only clocked that sooner, I would've been able to get help. I started sending SOS messages to everyone I knew as soon as I realised I could. But Elayne spotted me sub-vocalising and my tech access suddenly disappeared leaving a throbbing migraine behind it.

Jesus, it is her.

As if she'd read my mind, her lips curled up in a bone-chilling smile. 'Not as dumb as you thought I was, Chen? No, no, don't bother answering, I know you can't talk. And I'm afraid that's how it's going to have to stay. You shouldn't've come here, Chen. It's your own stupid fault you nosey little wet-foot piece of fluff.'

My stomach was cramping and my bladder started to leak. I could smell my own wee and fuck me if I didn't feel embar-rassed knowing Elayne could too. Never mind her big weird pet. I felt dribble on my chin and my face was going numb.

Elayne evil-geniused on but the pain got too much for me to understand her. After a while, I felt myself being carried and dumped somewhere in the dark, on a bed I realised after a while. A window undimmed and daylight shone on me but I was hurting too much to care. My muscles spasmed harder and my actual bones ached.

I don't want to die! Please! I don't want to die, Elayne! Let me go! How can she be doing this? How?

I would've pleaded it out loud if I'd been able to talk. Maybe it was better I couldn't, given how desperate and pathetic my thoughts were. I hadn't imagined when I'd got up that morning that I'd be murdered in the afternoon. It didn't... compute! I couldn't die. I couldn't!

It slowly filtered through my mind that everything'd gone quiet and I was alone. The lock on my muscles had got so strong, all I could do was shake and spasm in a terrified ball of flesh, bone, meat and juices on the mattress. Red spots raced at the edges of my vision.

I blacked out and came to, I didn't know how many times. I could hear Elayne in the room next door after dark and I spent the night fainting and coming round again. I could smell my sick, shit and piss through a red and black haze of agony and as the light got brighter I felt myself finally fading away. I was amazed I'd lasted as long as I had. I knew I was dying and it was a relief.

But somehow, I came around again and was disappointed, actually annoyed to find myself alive. My stomach suddenly spasmed and vomit spurted like it was being squeezed out of me. My head was luckily turned towards the mattress so I didn't choke on my sick.

I felt my underwear fill with fresh diarrhoea and wee as my bowels and bladder gave in one final time to whatever the strange code was doing to my biotech. Until this happened, I wouldn't've spared a thought to think cyberattack might be a danger! I would've expected Tin— Elayne to punch me or kick me or swear me to death before worrying she'd be able to do something like this. It must've been to do with her upbringing.

She was part of the Tech Family in the end, whoever else she tried to pretend to be. They must've had secrets nobody could dream of and if that was true then I was… *stonkered.* There was no way I could hack my way out of a trap with three generations of Laufala genius behind it.

Nate was the only person I could think of who might've managed it if he was lucky. But Nate'd been inside for over two years now. Nate was gone. Sometimes I felt like the world'd flowed over him and I was the only one who'd seen him drown.

What would you do Nate? How would you get out of this?

My stomach clenched again but there was nothing left to come out either end. I lay with every muscle unnaturally tensed, retching, cramping and moaning on the bed. My muscles strained and pulled then I felt myself start to fade again. Something had got too much. The tech was pushing my body further than it could go and my metabolism couldn't keep up.

A coldness that was familiar though I'd never felt it before stole over me and I knew if I couldn't break free of whatever Elayne had done to me soon, I'd be toast. I pinged my tech frantically but it was dead as an antique concrete block.

Think!

My vision was black and my head swam with nausea. Sharp pains jolted out from my ligaments and joints as my muscles strained and threatened to rip my bones apart. My shallow gasps amplified until the whole world was hissing whimpering air and red-flecked blackness.

Where the fuck is Elayne? Where's she gone? She can't have meant to kill me! Can she?

I gave my tech one last painful try and whether it was because my biotech had some failsafe I never knew about or I'd pinged it in some random way I would never've thought of before, I suddenly felt my muscles ease. Not completely. I still couldn't move. But the impossible tension in my joints died down enough to let me breathe easier.

My vision came slowly back and I realised I'd accessed some medical subsystem of my tech. It had counteracted whatever Elayne's shit was doing to me and though it wasn't up to much itself, it must have been able to interface outward.

I was cramping up and the smell of my own… waste filled the room and made me gag. I worked at the subsystem hoping whatever code Elayne had infected me with wasn't smart enough to detect hacking attacks. I had to work hard to breathe which meant I was literally hyperventilating the whole time and the dizziness slowed my thoughts something epic.

I saw the hole eventually. My tech had a hook into my endocrine system which was normal. I'd activated it with my desperate flurry of pings and it'd done the only thing it could without expensive medical tech helping. It'd forcibly activated my parasympathetic nervous system and confused the fuck out of whatever evil of Elayne's was pulling my strings from the other end, partly relaxing my muscles in the process.

I knew some stuff about biochem, nowhere near as much as Nate or a proper techie and in that moment, I would rather've known nothing than the little I did. I knew there'd probably be side-effects from whatever hack the tech had done to loosen me up but I had no idea what they might be and that made it scarier.

But I couldn't think about that now. Elayne could be back any minute – I couldn't understand why she'd been gone so long in the first place – and though I'd got myself a bit of breathing space, I didn't know how long it would last.

As luck would've fuckin' had it, the subsystem had no direct access to anything else other than to acknowledge requests and act on my biology. But it was at least a subsystem of my tech and Nate had once shown me how to jack up a downstream connection to piggyback information on harmless ACK messages.

I knew enough about tech to know what I needed to send and as the minutes went by, I managed to pull together a picture of what'd happened to my tech. It was like trying to spoon Total™ back off a table into its bottle, possible but *fēng kuáng-de* to've had it in your house in the first place let alone tipped it on your furniture.

Elayne's hack was like a giant virtual roach with a thousand legs'd smashed its carapace through my messaging space and put a sticky foot into every system I had on board. It wasn't exactly clever. It was more that it was everywhere in the most unlikely kinds of ways. I could see how to get rid of it but it was going to take time, maybe more time than I had. I started trying to unpick it, deleting its tiny handles out of all my sacrosanct fuckin' address spaces.

At the same time, I reached out through my address book as fast as I could which wasn't very fast given how I was accessing myself. I sent messages to everyone I knew. I tried calling but my access was so slow my system could barely make a connection let alone hold one.

Until it did.

It must've been because he was close that I'd managed to open the call. And I lost him so fast I doubted whether it'd been him; it couldn't be him, could it? Nate was in gaol.

Then I heard the door melt open and someone stood quietly in the doorway. I froze as the familiar slithering dust of a nano-clean flowed around me then I heard Elayne shout something and scurry away.

Maybe she's going to let me live after all!

But if she was, wouldn't she have let me at least breathe? Whatever vile plan Elayne had for me, after a while, I realised I was alone again and the light had gone strange. but I had no time to wonder about it; no telling how long before she came back. Or before I blacked out forever.

Call logs didn't lie but I had no time to check them. And no time to believe in miracles though a tiny desperate part of me had lit up with the stupid desperate hope of a high-school-*háizi* crush. Maybe if I hadn't been knocked in a dizzy hyperventilating daze trying to make sense of what'd happened, I might've seen the attack coming.

'Ah FUCK!' The words came out in a strangled gasp as I lost the little control I'd won back. My muscles seized up worse than before. I tried the medical subsystem again but this time it was as dead as everything else. I glimpsed what'd happened before my tech virtual disappeared.

Elayne's monster code had quietly burrowed in behind me and found the loophole I'd climbed through. As soon as I'd tried tampering with it, it'd flashed back along my access trail, found the subsystem I'd got in through, slammed me out and locked the door behind me.

I was lucky to've got out the call I did, not that it would do me any good if it hadn't been an actual hallucination anyway. This time there'd be no getting back into my tech. The very last door to myself had been closed and my body was shutting down.

Cleverer than I thought.

It would've been a sobbing whimper if my throat wasn't locked up so hard, I couldn't breathe. Red closed over my vision again and darkness followed it. I heaved in a few more breaths before my muscles ran out of steam and I couldn't pull air through my windpipe any more. My own body was suffocating me.

Did she know this was what her code would do? Did she do it on purpose?

I reflected a stretched moment of asphyxiating agony that I was dumb to give Elayne the benefit of the doubt and credit her with not actually meaning to kill me. Another thought whispered like a dying echo.

Nate is out. He's alive.

Cold spread through me.

Nate's out. At least he got out. And he's okay.

I decided to believe it. I decided to leave the world believing there was at least a tiny bit of justice for good people. Then I would've closed my eyes if they hadn't already've screwed themselves shut. But as much as I could anyway, if only to end the torture, I let myself go.

White heat exploded in my vision and I knew it was the end at last. I felt strong hands shaking me sending sparks of pain through my body. A tauntingly familiar voice was calling my name. All hallucinations, I knew. Only my brain chemistry doing back flips as my nervous system guttered and went out.

'Chen!' Clearer than it should've been.

It felt like I was breathing again, gasping fire into my lungs. Whoever said any shit like dying was some kind of painless letting go at the end was a massive liar. My lungs burned. My head throbbed and blinding light tore at my eyes like roaches were eating me alive.

'Chen!'

Make it stop. It hurts too much! Please, make it stop. I'll die, I don't care. I'll die now. Take me now!

'Chen! Come on! Wake up!'

Nate?

'Come on! We've got to get you out of here.'

'Nate?'

A head and shoulders solidified as the whiteness faded to the greys of an apartment.

'Nate. You're… You're… huge!' It was all I could get out before passing out. I felt him lifting me, carrying me some-where. The next time I opened my eyes, I found myself slumped against a massively muscled body in the back of an Uber heading north over the Mount Wellington bridge.

Rock – late Nov 2098, from Rock Tower, Germany to Akarana Island coast, Airborne

Jawohl! There it was in a flash, as if I had caught her sleeping.

Dense forests, a damp and warm scent beneath several species of fern, a certain sound of twittering and booming birdsongs, a particular appearance of volcanic terrain, all recognised and located instantly by *mein* exceptional recollection. A very big lump of earth lifting, a prism – Oh *ja!* – falling and I had it, *jawohl!* A collection also, of other details which confirmed she knew too much and so must be eliminated.

But first the prism. Perhaps she was no longer there but that was inconsequential. I would locate the dull savage easily through her connection to the Stone. Only her buried treasure, the naughty little treasure that seemed to have unburied itself, was important now.

Mein handy blue and white duffle bag was packed in a quick jiffy and off I went to *mein* tower roof for take-off. Designed for use at altitude, *mein* sophisticated tablet steered me far south towards the funny little islands where tech was invented; marvellous in *mein* remarkably informed opinion, though this pesky body would not accept it and I was stuck with only advanced external devices.

Peep-peep-peep-peep-peep! High over the planet's equator, the device complained with red alert messages and checking the details, I saw *mein* beautiful prison corporation was in some sort of financial panic. *Ja*, inconvenient.

High above the clouds, I opened a conference call and bossed around little office ants all over the world. The alerts turned green a short time later and so the bossing had worked beautifully. *Ja*, a little money trouble, a strange technical problem. Boring, from *mein* point of view or so I thought until later.

I advanced again, the device guiding me over the sea. I noticed the fascinating progress of Laufala and Rahui's cleansing project and considered bursting one of the super-enormous balls of floating toxic waste, for the purposes of amusement. *Ja*, because imagine them trying to understand how it happened! But also, I could float one up and place it on land in some improbable location and wait to see the fun when their satellites discovered it. This could be hilarious, *ja?*

But I was travelling at considerable velocity and nearer *mein* destination, with darkening of the skies because of *mein* movement through time zones. Also I was suddenly distracted by the dropping of *mein* device. For me this was not normal! Usually, I took such care I had lost the habitual procedure of securing its wrist-strap so gravity made its job and the object fell quickly away. *Ja* but it was because *mein* stomach felt ill, as if a hand was squeezing it.

Considering *mein* invulnerable condition, this should not have been possible and neither should the unpleasant sound originating somehow in *mein* brain like a beehive had been disturbed. The problem in the stomach stopped and the sound reduced in volume slowly but did not seem to terminate completely.

I knew it was not a real sound. It was a sound heard only by *mein* mind as the trails of *mein* colleagues over the water were seen only in *mein* mind. The appearance of hearing and seeing was *mein* human brain only making sense of the confusion, *ja?* Jamming the supernatural perception into the senses it had available.

But what has caused it? What has happened?

Angrily, I dived in pursuit of *mein* device and caught it before it was destroyed by a high velocity impact on the ocean surface. After that, I secured its comfortable wrist-strap and continued *mein* journey. *Ja*, because this was the second time I had felt such a disturbance in a year and now it was significantly greater in size. Very concerning, *ja?* I felt certain it was related to the naughty little escaping colleague. Or, the other way round, *ja*.

Once I was close, I became delighted to see two of *mein* beautiful blue trails terminating somewhere in the cluster of islands. I of course expected one. But two was an extra bonus. And with considerable additional happiness, I observed one of them was strange in a way I had never seen before; thicker than usual. Something new after so many centuries! Such novelty caused me inconceivable joy! *Ja*, but of course I knew it could also mean something in the Stone was changing and this could be a substantial concern – as if the strangeness of the fusing over the past year was not already sufficient concern!

I slowed to follow the trails over the sea and observed as the day progressed, that they led to one of the larger islands; *ja*, Akarana Island they called it now, according to the device. Fascinating to see how the rise of the sea levels had submerged the New Zealand islands. So many little Kiwis in their black and white jumpers drowning in the water must have been considerably entertaining, *ja?*

Ja, but the rain was unbelievable in that part of the world! As I approached there was substantial precipitation in progress. But it did not matter because the super-fun fantastic show began approximately beneath me, some distance out to sea.

The disturbance beneath the ocean surface was so large I had to rise to a higher altitude, nearly to the limit of safe usage of the handheld device and where the air was unpleasantly cold. I switched the device off to be safe. I knew I had come to the right place because the special trails of the colleagues confirmed it.

Though the cold and composition of the atmosphere at such altitude would have extinguished normal human life, I was delighted to be present at the precise moment of the water explosion. I watched as it burst up, high into the clouds and a powerful shock wave spread in the ocean around it.

A disturbance of such magnitude, would of course make far reaching consequences so I made a note in *mein* mind to inform *mein* organisation in key locations. Special emergency protocols would need to be implemented to ensure none of the beautiful work or a small number of the more useful staff were lost. Oh *ja*, but I had to watch the show first!

The wave was unbelievable in size, like the entire ocean had a wrinkle spreading across it. The poor little islands would be finished completely off now, no more Kiwis, all gone! In the considerable time I had been alive, I had not been able to observe the sudden inundation of such a substantial landmass; never lucky enough to be in the right place at the right time. *Ja*, so I watched with great anticipation as the disturbance approached the land.

But, as the expression is going, shit was getting weird! One of the colleagues on the island released a considerable amount of power and the wave exploded against it so that not just one island but the entire cluster was preserved. To the little Kiwis, it would have appeared as a lot of water coming to eat them up, boogie-boogie-boogie-woogie! *Ja*? So scary! But, to me, I could see the blue of the Flow shielding against the water, *ja*, beautiful!

For me, this activity would have caused no problem. But *mein* colleague's minds were less well designed and the use of such a volume of energy would probably lead to the collapse of the colleague. Then we would for certain have the bull getting into the China-shop problem.

I sped along the smaller of the two trails to find the compromised colleague, atomise them and get them into the handy blue and white duffle bag before they became the nuisance. After that, I would retrieve the old stupid friend, Bud and stop the mischief she was creating further inland.

By now it was afternoon and I had reached the coast. A short distance below the clouds, I hovered. The colleague's blue trail ended in a residential complex on a steep hill. But before I could descend like a sort of super-hero, more excitement came. The handheld device made a special notification I had never expected to hear. Well, perhaps a little part of me was hopeful, *ja?* Or I would not have set up the special notification in the first place.

I would have to address the issue of the dangerous colleague first of course. But *mein* smile now was almost hurting the face for such an unexpectedly fascinating novelty had occurred.

For so long, I had made the beautiful experimentations. The Nazis had presented me with a perfect situation to make the most fantastic science. So many thousands of years then boom! *Ja*, such brilliant ideas had come from those few short years of conflict.

But, as they say, the writing got on the wall for those ones and I hid while it was all settling back down. *Ja* but I was able to continue the research and when finally young Laufala came up with the nanotech, well, everything was brilliant and coming together. And now the adaptation of the human brain was progressing yet again! From nowhere, suddenly, an evolution took place! *Jawohl!* This was a beautiful day!

Mein *little tiny micro person Richards-Mann, you pulled it off,* ja? *Fascinating! Beautifully fascinating! And on the exact same island for convenient retrieval once I am finished with these other ones.* Jawohl! *Such a beautiful day!*

I descended carefully towards the window through which the blue trail passed.

Tristian – late Nov 2098-early Dec 2098, Cornwall Hill, Akarana Island, Aotearoa Archipelago

In the days after the tsunami, we floated around the house, all unsure what to do or how to be with each other or – at least in my case – ourselves. Annihilation had reared up and subsided in minutes; too fast to react to but demanding a reaction anyway. I felt frozen in terror, in a moment that had already passed me by.

I gleaned from the kids that a few of the new islands were inundated; a few lives lost though it hadn't touched us. They'd shared nothing of the rest of the world with me and I hadn't asked. I couldn't seem to ask.

My voice stuck in my throat whenever I thought to speak about it. The image of the wall of water smashing into an impossible blue forcefield, exploding into foam almost on top of the coast, looped in my head and joined with the blue face, fiercer than ever, to crowd my dreams at night. A part of me knew it didn't bear mentioning. The whole thing was unbelievable enough without adding the crazy hallucinations of an old man recently out of a year-long coma to the mix.

But though its impact was negligible, it had turned everything upside down anyway. If it happened once, it could happen again. Our time was running out. I was positive the kids felt the same, that all our tongues were frozen and our thoughts unable to move on from what had nearly happened.

Susie and Davey drifted through the house with tech-vacant eyes and I floated between them, wanting to want to find out what they knew; about the epi-centre; about the rest of the world. But ever unable to ask. All I got out of Davey was that the archipelago's seismology people were silent on the matter and that only made it worse.

My skin didn't flake again and when the kids exclaimed about my head one day, we fished out a mirror from upstairs whereupon I discovered my stubble was black. It was like I'd grown younger in the coma. And that lined up with how I felt too though the strange hissing in my mind wouldn't go away.

My tech didn't come back online either. I couldn't ping anything or access any systems and where my epidermal nanites had gone nobody knew; there wasn't a trace of them anywhere on my body. But I knew it wasn't completely gone because I heard the kids talking one morning.

'Susie, I know what you believe you saw but it's impossible—'

'Fuck you Davey! I saw it. You fucking saw it. You were there. Don't try and shut me down with your holier-than-thou atheist crap! You're just like him, you know? You think the world's one big happy fucking scientific family, that all that spiritual nonsense is a thing of the past, blah blah blah. Fuck, Davey! Have you been online lately? Have you seen that crazy woman's footage, the baby with the flaking skin – just like Dad's when he woke up! – that grew to adulthood in, like, two days, the fucking-like, tsunami, Davey, remember fuckin' that at least—?'

'Susie, Jesus, not all this again. Please!' She sighed. 'Look, okay, I admit it. Leaving aside the tsunami – they've already confirmed there was an earthquake anyway, yeah, a weird-ish one but whatever. I don't know what I saw, all right? He was standing behind me, I made us coffees. Next thing he was holding his mug. He could've reached—'

'Fucking bullshit and you know it! He was way too far—'

'Look, Sue, we don't know, okay? We just don't—'

'Christ, David, get with the program. Something's happened to him! Something's different! What about his hair for fuck's sake? And the explosion that made no sound but wiped out a whole suburb of poor— uh, people the day be-fucking-fore the tsunami hit! Get online and keep the fuck up, David. Something's happening in the world we don't understand!

'Search the Mother Earth woman and come back to me, okay? Or failing that, ask the man of the moment him fucking self about his past! Go on, Davey, I dare you! Ask Tristian if he believes in ghosts. Don't listen to his answer, Davey, watch his fucking face! I'm not talking to you about this any more until you can open a crack in your stuffy bloody atheist mind and let some fucking sense shine in. Until then, I don't want to hear a bloody word more of your condescending shit!'

It was a pretty standard Susie versus Davey barney. I hadn't a clue about half the nonsense they were on about, besides the Omana catastrophe – Jesus, that was a tragedy! But I was sure it would blow over between them, like it always did.

The point was, I'd been in my room with the door closed and discovered when I went out for a glass of water that they were upstairs and outside on the balcony. So my tech was definitely connected to the house somehow or there was no way I'd have been able to hear them.

I waited till the following day then went up to see if I could figure out why the random connection had happened; and why there. The roaring whisper followed me to the roof terrace, unchanging and no less audible out in the breeze as it was in the quiet of my room. Wind harried cumulous from horizon to horizon, morning sun burning through in patches.

It was a standard, mediocre grey Auck— Gah! Okay, okay, Akarana day. They'd told me it was November and the temperature was about right though I couldn't check exactly, myself.

But despite the cloud something seemed different. The sky seemed brighter though it was grey. The air seemed clearer though low cloud drifted between buildings threatening to become fog. It was as if I could see…

How everything… fits together? Waves, particles… Tripe!

It was impossible, I knew, my mind trying to join dots and make patterns out of chaos. I'd been in a coma for a year after all, my brain must have been in some kind of readjustment process.

I turned and looked out to a calm and glittering sea and it seemed to me I was looking through the blue band of a rainbow. It stole into my awareness and the more I looked, the clearer it got. My eyes followed it idly at first as if unpicking a trick of the light; then with increasing curiosity the more real it became.

It was somehow there but not there. It didn't obscure anything or change the hue of anything it fell on; almost as if it had been borrowed from another reality and superimposed on mine. I traced it slowly, above the city, out over the coast, across the sea and into the water at some indeterminably distant point.

I turned and looked back toward the door and it was gone, over to the other side of the terrace and it wasn't there either. Back westward and there was the edge of it, a bit to the north and it aligned with me again. A curling haze twisting gently away to a north-western point on the sea, a thin twisting coil of violet in its heart.

More and more curious, I traced its path back towards me, and noticed it divided, somewhere between the horizon and me – or no, there were two of them stretching away to the same point in the ocean – and that was when, with a quickening heart, I saw the other ended in a building a short way down the hill.

I somehow knew answers lay there. There was someone like me, in there.

Excited, I pinged my maps and – of course – they weren't there.

Fuck.

'Fuck!'

'Dad! What's wrong?' Susie materialised behind me. She must've been sitting just inside the door. Come to think of it, I'd known she was there. I'd… heard her breathing.

Wow. Okay. That's not weird. But actually… Good.

'Susie, I need to go to that building, there.'

So could you give us a hand chasing rainbows? Yeah, better not…

'Eh? So, uh, go then? Oh, you want me to come with you, just in case it's dangerous? Oh god Tristian, it's fine, serious—'

'Eh?'

Then it was her turn to look confused for a moment before realisation dawned. 'Oh!' She said. 'Wow! Yeah, I s'pose you wouldn't know would you? All the prisoners and everything.'

'The-what now?'

'Yeah, the police did some kind of blanket pardon thing. On the tsunami day coincidentally. They're being cagey about the details but it's some sort of new policy on rehabilitation or, I don't know; sounds like a circus to me. But anyway they were all loosed from stasis and now, theoretically, they're at large in the community; whoa eh? So I thought that's what you were scared— Oh yeah but the other thing you wouldn't't've heard, unless Davey's told you? No? Oh man, Tristian! You're gonna flip! No, I mean, in a good way, don't worry.'

'Um. Okay?'

'Sarah's been made commissioner! Your granddaughter! What is she? Twenny-eight? Twenny-nine? Not bad going, eh?'

I felt bad for not feeling that good. It was an achievement. It was. But I had… bigger things on my mind and I couldn't muster any excitement. Didn't stop me trying though.

'Oh. Wow. Commissioner!'

'Well, acting commissioner. Other chap got axed for some sort of misconduct, she's not allowed to say too much while it all… goes through or something. But possession is nine-tenths eh? If it's not made permanent, well, it's on her CV now innit. It's a step in the right direction, right?'

I nodded. I couldn't get over the change in Susie. And I couldn't get enough of her being nice to me. And a part of me couldn't help being amused at the irony of her enthusing about Sarah's promotion in the police who she probably hated on principle.

Then she paused as if remembering something. 'So, in that case, Da— Tristian. What are you afraid of then? That you'll have another spell or something?'

'I'm not scared, Susie. I'm fine. I, uh, don't know how to get there is all. I've got no maps. My, you know! My tech.'

The fucking parent of tech has turned into an e-squib. I've got to sort this out!

'Oh, wow. Right, yeah, wow. Of course. Okay, don't worry. I'll take you. I'll get an Uber. It's the big foster place, anyway. Everyone knows… Anyway, no problem. Let me just get my overs, it's nice-ish now but, you know how it can change.'

'Oh that's, that building! You know, the owner used to live next door to us?'

'Yeah, yeah, good, whatever, Dad, come on, let's go if you want to go. I've got to work.'

I followed her inside and didn't tell her I thought the city looked different now. There was no point, I couldn't put a finger on how; it was something to do with the buildings and streets; something slightly off; like small things had gone missing.

Nor did I tell her about the silk-fine coil of dark violet that curled through me, divided and snaked – more faintly – out to wind about my daughters then from Davey, it divided again, curling out, fainter again, through the wall and away. A chill stole over me, stirring up a whisper in my mind.

Free us.

And a bizarre thought.

So, Elayne is alive. I could find her with this!

Then:

How the hell do I know that?

I shook my head in confusion and the pair of them clocked it. I heard their questions load up and knew their mouths were taking aim. Then the Uber showed up and saved me.

I saw Susie stiffen as we stood at the building entrance.

'Uh, Tristian,' she said.

'What is it?'

'I'm not sure if we should go up—'

But the doors melted opened and I said, 'come on, let's go.'

'I—'

'Come on! You said you needed to get back to work, didn't you?'

It was my turn to freeze when we emerged from the lift moments later and stepped into their reception area; an apartment with a few walls knocked to create an open-plan seating area if I wasn't mistaken.

I had barely a second to take it in before I saw the guy behind the reception desk, his severe grey bun straining at his forehead above rat-like features.

Okay, maybe she had a point.

John at least had the decency to look simultaneously surprised and sheepish and it took me a minute to start wondering why my NDA wasn't flashing.

Oh yeah! Ha. Broken tech's good for some things, at least!

Having no such benefit, Susie briefly cringed beside me before her face relaxed, presumably after she'd dimmed the thing back down.

Not our fault, we can't have known he was here.

Technically, we could though. The NDA must have warned Susie at the building entrance. But I pushed the thoughts aside before I could get into the usual spin of trying to work out our liability in the situation. I needed to be here. I'd get my own bloody lawyers on the case if John's mad old father clocked the breach.

If it's a breach, it probably isn't, not really— Tristian, stop!

Back outside my head, nobody knew what to say. John looked this way and that, avoiding our eyes as much as we were avoiding his.

What the fuck is he doing in a foster home of all bloody places? Jesus! Don't these people do background checks?

But of course, thanks to Jase and his lawyers, they'd have found nothing if they did. Then the silence was broken by a voice too young and rich for its owner.

'Well, my goodness me! I know who you are Miss, but who's this lovely young thing? Gosh, he's the spitting image of your poor old mother's… er… boyfriend, in his younger days. I lived next door to your mother back before you were born, did you know, that?'

Ethel Bell hadn't aged a day. Which was fortunate considering she must've been a hundred if she was a day, back when we were neighbours nearly sixty years ago.

It can't be her!

But it was. It was as if she'd been frozen in wrinkled antiquity. Her face was pale and blotchy, grey-white hair hanging stringy, almost to her waist and her eyes were… avian black; somehow simultaneously clear, beady and fevered. She was as tall as me, maybe taller.

Must've looked older than she was back then.

It was the only explanation. And it was the least of my concerns. Mostly I was fixated on the blue mist that curled in through the wall and enveloped her.

I've come to the right place. Either that or it's bloody realistic hallucination!

I watched it, mesmerised as she motioned us over, sparing an apparently dismissive glance at John who remained awkwardly silent as we stepped, equally discomfited, past him to the back of the room. We followed Ethel into another open-plan lounge-come-office chamber with a kitchenette and a bank of screens; all powered down.

She offered us coffee and only I accepted; the others I'd had that day didn't seem to have done much. I watched as she operated the machine manually. The little server-drones parked either side of it stayed put and she handed me my mug the old-fashioned way.

Blue eddied around her like sluggish steam, clinging, never breaking away in dissipating clouds. Soft and hazy as it was, it looked sinister, somehow like a tether. And there was no violet centre to it as there was to mine. I kept having to remind myself Susie couldn't see it. And that it was rude to stare.

There was no good way of getting rid of Susie and no way at all I was going to bring up an ethereal haze of woo-woo in front of my child; especially this one! So it was as well she said she'd come back to get me in an hour and excused herself; probably spooked by the NDA; as I should have been. But this was too important.

Then suddenly I was alone with the woman whose strange son I'd gotten killed all those years ago. I had no idea where to start and her silent stare didn't help.

She'd plonked herself in a sofa and motioned me to take the one opposite. As I sat, I noticed what lay on the coffee table between us. It looked like a broken prism with shiny black sides and a centre that glinted azure when it caught the light.

I had no clue what it might be, some sort of souvenir, a bit of bizarre jewellery or something like that. Yet anodyne as it looked, its deep blue core exposed by the jagged surface along which it had apparently cracked asunder, sent a faint chill of recognition down my spine.

I saw Ethel clock me staring.

'He's gone. I might know how it happened. But it's empty all the same,' she said as if it explained… bloody anything at all. I waited but she didn't elaborate. After some time, she puffed out a sigh and said, 'So, what can I do for you young man?'

'I, uh, had this… um, dream. A blue face and then. I, uh saw——'

She waited.

Not helping!

'Something's happened to me. I got sick. I dreamed—There was a face. Then when I woke up – months, a year later – my tech was gone and I can't get it back. And I saw this… beam or something. A light. It led me here, to you, I thought you could maybe help…?' I realised I was babbling and trailed off.

Yeah, okay that-all doesn't sound crazy. Not at all! Come on Tristian, get it together! If she's got security, she's gonna be calling them any second!

But unexpectedly, Ethel cocked her head and narrowed her eyes at me, as if she'd suddenly noticed something.

'Who did you say you were again?'

'Tristian, uh, Laufala.'

I knew how I looked; how I sounded; too young. I expected to have to prove my identity to her. I hoped I'd be able to. I had no idea how I might without tech. And if I could I hoped she was too old to go weird in the presence of – vomit! – celebrity. But again to my surprise, Ethel was unruffled.

'Interesting,' she said in a slow and deliberate voice. Then she went oracular on me again, musing gibberish with steepled fingers. 'My Healer does the impossible and escapes. A disturbance in the fusing nearly tears my soul from my body at daybreak and I throw up for the first time in, well, years would be an understatement. And a few hours later the earth moves and the seas rise up; and recede, not my doing either this time! So whose is it? And a few days later, Laufala comes to visit with tales of things he really oughtn't have heard of and looking younger than he has a right to.' She nodded to herself. 'Yes. Interesting.'

Christ. She's three sheets to the wind.

I hoped desperately that she wasn't though. Or where else would I go to figure out what'd happened to me? Maybe she was having a bit of a senior spell – no shame in that! – and she'd get lucid again. She seemed present despite the babble. But she was elderly.

Look at Jase. Look at a lot of our friends, doesn't matter what you do with your life, time gets us all in the end… Yeah, okay, mind on your job Tristian!

As if she'd heard my thoughts, Ethel seemed to snap back to herself. Her eyes focused on me and she smoothed her hemps with wrinkled hands and rested them on her thighs. Then with an urgency that made me sit up straight she said, 'I'm very glad you came to me. Very glad indeed! Quickly now child. Collect your thoughts – I know you're capable! Then out with it all in a manner befitting your, uh, age. And then we'll see what we can do, yes?'

ACKNOWLEDGEMENTS

It takes a village to write a book and that's saying something coming from me! I err on the introverted side and am generally content to work away with food dropping in through the mail slot or sliding under the door now and again. But this book could never have been what it is – whatever it is! – without the support of a lot – a lot! – of friends and family.

Special thanks to my partner Tricia for all her support and staying interested over the twenty-six months it's taken to, uh, nearly be finished. And also to my sister Claire for her useful and detailed feedback and not the least for creating the amazing character map.

Up there with those two are Jana Keir, fellow New Zealand author and beta reader without whose excellent feedback the book would never have been polished as much as it has been. And of course, my editors Donna Blaber and Natalya Newman for their attention to detail – good quality for editors to possess, that! – and also a raft of useful and detailed feedback.

Thanks also to Mal and Noreen, two other friends who have kindly agreed to further beta reads and are squinting away at the time of writing these acknowledgements.

It's been a journey and now it continues!

Dan Williams, Author
Instagram: @danstofer
TikTok: @danwilliamsbookperson

Twitter: DanielW48099544
WWW: https://danwilliamsbooks.com
Facebook: facebook.com/danwilliamsbooks

ALSO BY DAN WILLIAMS

Aroha

It's the early 2040s and Joanna's fine with her random urges. She's confident in her ability to paint masterpieces that fetch millions in a world of shrinking coasts, violent storms and all but outlawed paper. She's clueless about everything else and the discovery that although dead, her mother Aroha is far from gone and is largely disapproving of her choices is just another thing to worry about. Aroha is an anomaly with shaky mental health, a soul without a body who can still touch the world but probably shouldn't. She has awaited her daughter's return home for twenty-four years and is none too happy with the lazy, messy, pot-smoking result. As if things weren't hard enough, without a mortal body to help manage her phantom physical urges, Joanna's new boyfriend Tristian, with his loose wandering soul and tight morals, presents an awkwardly arousing distraction. A distraction from the secret Aroha desperately wants to hide from Joanna.

Available in Paperback and eBook on Amazon ISBN-13 979-8680088050, ASIN B08GYHNVHK

* 9 7 8 1 9 1 0 2 7 6 0 5 1 *